SOVIET NAVY WIDENS
INDIAN OCEAN POWER

osses Seen Heavier Than Soviet in Atomic War

ce

issile

**Chinese Delegates in
Moscow for New Talks**

isco Chronicle, New York
eader's Digest, Fortune,
o Examiner, 1978-1980.

OUR ICBM'S
ARE IN D___GER

D1017344

viet 'Germ War'
cident Reported

ew Soviet Troops
n Afghanistan'

Russians Build 2nd
Naval Pier in Cuba

The Hill of Summer

ALSO BY ALLEN DRURY

The Advise and Consent Series
ADVISE AND CONSENT
A SHADE OF DIFFERENCE
CAPABLE OF HONOR
PRESERVE AND PROTECT
COME NINEVEH, COME TYRE
THE PROMISE OF JOY

Other Washington Novels
ANNA HASTINGS
MARK COFFIN, U.S.S.

Novels of Ancient Egypt
A GOD AGAINST THE GODS
RETURN TO THEBES

Other Novels
THAT SUMMER, A California Novel
THE THRONE OF SATURN, A Novel of Space and Politics

Nonfiction
A SENATE JOURNAL
THREE KIDS IN A CART
"A VERY STRANGE SOCIETY"
COURAGE AND HESITATION (with Fred Maroon)
EGYPT: THE ETERNAL SMILE (with Alex Gotfryd)

ALLEN DRURY

The Hill of Summer

A NOVEL OF THE SOVIET CONQUEST

Doubleday & Company, Inc., Garden City, New York
1981

Library of Congress Cataloging in Publication Data

Drury, Allen.
   The hill of summer.

   (A Novel of the Soviet conquest)
   I. Title.   II. Series.
PS3554.R8H54   813'.54
ISBN: 0-385-00234-3
Library of Congress Catalog Card Number: 80–1849

The title, *The Hill of Summer,* is taken from "On the idle hill of summer"
from *A Shropshire Lad*—Authorized Edition—from *The Collected Poems of
A. E. Housman.* Copyright 1939, 1940 © 1965 by Holt, Rinehart and Winston.
Copyright © 1967, 1968 by Robert S. Symons. Reprinted by permission of
Holt, Rinehart and Winston, Publishers.

On the idle hill of summer,
Sleepy with the flow of streams,
Far I hear the steady drummer
Drumming like a noise in dreams . . .

—*A Shropshire Lad,* A. E. Housman

CHARACTERS IN THE NOVEL

In Washington
Hamilton Delbacher, President of the United States
Elinor, his wife
Chauncey Baron, Secretary of State
Roger Hackett, Secretary of Defense
Arthur Hampton, senior Senator from Nebraska, Majority Leader of the
   Senate
Herbert Esplin, senior Senator from Ohio, Minority Leader
James Rand Elrod, senior Senator from North Carolina
James Monroe Madison, senior Senator from California
Mark Coffin, junior Senator from California
Linda, his wife
Lydia Bates, a hostess
Clement Chisholm, junior Senator from Illinois
Rick Duclos, junior Senator from Vermont
Bob Templeton, junior Senator from Colorado
General Rutherford ("Smidge") Hallowell, U. S. Army, Chairman of the
   Joint Chiefs of Staff
General Martin ("Bump") Smith, Chief of Staff, U. S. Army
Admiral Harman ("Snooze") Rydecker, Chief of Naval Operations
General Bartram C. ("Bart") Jamison, Chief of Staff, U. S. Air Force
General Robert ("Gutsy") Twitchell, Commandant, U. S. Marine Corps
Major Ivan Ivanovich Valerian, a defector

In Moscow
Yuri Pavlovich Serapin, President of the Soviet Union
Ekaterina Vasarionova, his mistress
Marshal Vladimir Alexeivich Andreyev, Army
Marshal Andrei Andreivich Krelenko, Air Force
Marshal Gavril Petrovich Shelikov, Strategic Rocket Forces
Admiral Anastas Nikolaivich Valenko, Navy
The Foreign Minister
The Defense Minister

At NATO headquarters
The member nations

In Havana
The President of Cuba

At the United Nations
Prince Koahumahili ("Koa") of Tonga, President of the Security Council
Libya, President of the General Assembly
The Prime Minister of Britain
The Prime Minister of India
Ju Xing-dao, Vice Premier of the People's Republic of China
The Secretary-General
Ambrose Johnson, U. S. Ambassador to the UN
The media
Fabrizio Gulack, a friend to mankind

Dedicated to The United States of America
and the confounding of her enemies

SOVIET INTENTIONS . . .

"We have never, and will never, hide the basic fundamental provisions of our military doctrine."

—Marshal A. A. Grechko

"There has not been, there is not, and there cannot be, class peace between socialism and capitalism, or peaceful co-existence between the communist and bourgeois ideologies."

—Peaceful Co-existence and the
Security of the People,
Colonel I. Sidelnikov

"War between countries of the capitalist and socialist systems will have a violent and an acutely defined class nature of a fight to the death."

—Military Art in the Postwar Period,
Colonel A. A. Strokov

"A new world war . . . will be a struggle for the very existence of the two opposing world-wide systems, the socialist and the capitalist. This war will decide the fate of all mankind."

—The Great Soviet Encyclopedia

"The purpose of the Soviet state is the complete and final victory of communism on a world scale."

—Pravda

"There has never been on this entire planet and in all of history a regime more cruel, more bloody and at the same time more diabolically clever . . . Only force can soften or make yield the Soviet system. The entire regime rests on brutal force and thus it recognizes only brutal force."

—Aleksandr Solzhenitsyn

AND AN AMERICAN OBSERVATION . . .

"Denial is the earliest, most primitive, most inappropriate and ineffective of all psychological defenses used by man. When the event is potentially destructive, it is the most pernicious psychological defense, because it does not permit taking appropriate action which might safeguard against the real dangers. Denial therefore leaves the individual most vulnerable to the very perils against which he tried to defend himself. . . . It is easier to deny reality, when facing it would require taking unpleasant, difficult or expensive actions."

—Bruno Bettelheim

NOTE TO THE READER

The Soviet intention to destroy the United States and achieve the conquest of the world, which appears fictionally in these pages, is based upon official Soviet documents. All quotes used at heads of chapters or in the body of the text are taken verbatim from official Soviet sources.

The authenticity of these documents has never been challenged. Despite the hard-working efforts of Soviet apologists in the United States, and the frantic scorn of many American critics toward those who write or speak of Soviet intentions, the Soviets themselves have never made the slightest bones about what they plan to do.

The documentation covers a substantial period of time, from Lenin to the present day, during which they have followed the aims and objectives set forth without change or deviation in the slightest degree. From time to time, usually determined by the personality of the then occupant of the White House, tactics have changed.

Objectives never have.

It did not seem to me that it was necessary, in current Washington novels, to resort to such gimmicks as the highjacking of Air Force One, the kidnapping of the President, Presidential mistresses slipping in and out of the White House, threadbare reworkings of Watergate, and the like.

These are the gimmicks with which the reader is beguiled away from the reality that confronts us—opiates of the people, as it were, encouraging them to feel that the great danger of the world we live in is fictitious and can be comfortably shrugged off and forgotten.

Rather, in THE HILL OF SUMMER and its coming sequel, THE ROADS OF EARTH, I thought I would use the ultimate terror—the end of freedom and the death of the mind under the kindly auspices of the Soviet Union —which surrounds us everywhere, confronts us on every continent and every sea, and each day advances upon us a little more openly and a little more successfully than it did the day before.

This novel, like others from the same pen, is written in part to record some sense of the tensions of our times and how American leaders strive to handle them; and partly as a warning against trends which, having gone on for so many years unchecked, have now brought America to the greatest period of peril she has ever known. It is very late on history's clock for the free democratic experiment that has survived through all challenges for more than two hundred years. It may not yet be too late, providing we react and recoup in time.

Whether time belongs to the Soviet Union, as its leaders and ideologues sincerely believe and determinedly seek to achieve, day in and day out, by any and all means at their command, or whether it still belongs to us, the next few years alone can tell. This novel suggests one scenario—a grim one, but one that actuality, if we can act with sufficient decisiveness and speed, need not inevitably support.

The steady drummer whose message can be heard "on the idle hill of summer, sleepy with the flow of streams," need not necessarily be heralding final disaster for us. He may be heralding a new and happier day.

But only if we heed his warning and respond with courage and foresight worthy of the brave men and women who have gone before and at great cost to themselves have saved for us, up to now, this "last, best hope."

Allen Drury

BOOK ONE

1

The President died at 6:27 P.M. on Monday, the Fourth of July.

There were immediate comparisons, most of them farfetched, with Thomas Jefferson, John Adams and James Monroe. Jefferson and Adams died within hours of one another on July 4, 1826. Monroe died on July 4 five years later. This was the fourth President to pass away on the national anniversary.

Some of the two great Founding Fathers' fame was automatically conferred upon their controversial successor; and with it, some of their finer attributes as well, which many felt he did not deserve. Others, less knowledgeable, could be convinced he did.

The media could not be blamed for his inadvertent canonization: the coincidence was too neat to pass up. He had died at exactly the right moment.

He would have approved of his eulogies, because before his totally unexpected demise there had been time for him to convince himself that things were going reasonably well with his policies around the world, and to impart his satisfaction to enough of his countrymen to guarantee them a relatively relaxed and unworried holiday.

This was what they obviously wanted. He had not disappointed them.

He had, in fact, made one of his carefully homespun television addresses to the nation almost exactly seventy-two hours before, on Friday evening. This, in part, was what made his sudden departure so shocking; this and the fact that he had apparently been in excellent health and had, indeed, just extended his jogging time by ten minutes and reduced his pulse to fifty-five, which the White House physician said was fine, but don't overdo it.

His blind absorption in his pastime—as though all his troubles could be forgotten in regular frenzied trots around the Mansion grounds—was cause for worry on Capitol Hill and among such astute Cabinet members as Chauncey Baron, the Secretary of State: but there was nothing they could do about it.

"It seems to make him happy," Chauncey had confided to the Senate Majority Leader, Art Hampton of Nebraska; and Art had passed on the comment to Senator Jim Elrod of North Carolina and Jim's son-in-law,

Senator Mark Coffin of California, when he said good-by to them on the eve of the brief Congressional holiday recess.

"Got to keep him happy," Jim Elrod responded, about a man whose decisions, or lack of them, were worrying him increasingly. "Don't want him to be both mistaken and *un*happy. The combination might be too much for him."

"He's doing all right," Mark said defensively, being one of the few in Congress who still approved, in general, of the Chief Executive's policies. "I don't think he's making all that many mistakes."

"Enough," Jim Elrod observed crisply. "Quite enough."

But that, of course, was not how the President himself saw it; and when he went before his countrymen on Friday evening it was to reassure them, with his usual earnestness, that while the United States faced many problems foreign and domestic, still it could be of good cheer that on this most sentimental of all national weekends, "my Administration and I are following well-thought-out programs designed to solve these problems as swiftly and surely as we can. I know you will help me. We *will* succeed."

And he had clenched his fist, in the manner of one of his less effective predecessors, and it was almost as though a big bright light labeled "CONFIDENCE" had flashed on above his head.

Watching this performance with his son-in-law and his daughter Linda, his three grandchildren Linnie, Markie and little Jim sitting in his lap, Senator Elrod had shaken his head with a puzzled sigh.

"I swear I don't know what's happened to that man since he took office," he said. "He's as bad as that other little fellow. He started out so strong and then somehow it's all—fizzled out. He's just lettin' everythin' slide. Just everythin'. I don't understand him. I thought when we gave him that $10 billion emergency defense appropriation—"

"*You* gave him," Mark interrupted. "I voted against it."

"More fool you," his father-in-law said calmly. "Anyway, when the *Senate* and the *House* gave it to him, we thought he was goin' to use it to bargain with the Soviets. That's what he indicated clear enough to me and others on the Hill. But he went off to that summit meetin' and he didn't do anythin' with it. He didn't do a thing. He just let it sit there. It's still sittin' there. And they're continuin' to push us back everywhere around the world. He's yieldin', yieldin', yieldin', just like that other little fellow. I tell you frankly, I'm scared to death about it."

"*He* isn't," Linda said, gesturing at the screen, and they fell silent while the President made a brief tour of the globe to show his countrymen how right everything was.

"I know there are some of you," he said, face earnest and intent, "who are worried about what appear to be successful communist advances in some troubled areas of the world. Some of you are worried about what appear to be unfriendly, even actively pro-Soviet governments in some areas of South America, such as Nicaragua, El Salvador, Panama and Guatemala. Others express concern about the new government in Zimbabwe, the apparent triumph of Cuban-led guerrilla forces in Namibia after the United Nations' Security Council veto of the resolution to give aid to South Africa. Some of you are also upset about the radical movements that seem to be threatening take-overs in Kuwait, Qatar, Oman and perhaps even Saudi Arabia along the Persian Gulf. Still others fret about Soviet hegemony over Afghanistan, Iran and Pakistan and the recent incursions into Kasmir and Northwest India.

"I assure you"—and he looked even more earnest, full of sheer, simple goodness—"that your government is aware of the potentials in all of these situations, and that we are doing everything we can, consistent with our principles of tolerance, understanding and non-interference in the affairs of others, to encourage these new regimes and movements to pursue a democratic course and one friendly to us. We think we will succeed in this purpose."

"Some areas of Latin America!" Senator Elrod exploded. "Nicaragua, El Salvador, Panama, Guatemala—puttin' the Canal in pawn and guttin' the heart right out of Central America, as inevitable as day and night while we sit by wringin' our hands like a bunch of old maids—that's 'some areas'? And lettin' 'em get a clamp on all the Middle Eastern oil routes from Suez to the Persian Gulf? And virtually wet-nursin' 'em into Namibia in Southern Africa, where they'll be in position to close off the Cape of Good Hope route to us? And watchin' without a murmur while they start stirrin' up trouble now in Greenland and Norway, which is also goin' to give 'em control of the northern route pretty soon, unless they're stopped? And sayin' nothin' at all about Yugoslavia? We shouldn't be worried about all that?"

"He was going to send some cruisers," Mark pointed out with a wryness that conceded his argument lost before it began.

"But he didn't do it, did he?" Jim Elrod demanded. "First he said he would—and then he changed his mind and didn't. And what did that do to international respect for his word, and international perception of what kind of man he is? He's nothin' but a piddlin' coward, I sometimes think. Just a piddlin' coward with nothin' to piddle in. And I think the whole world thinks so too."

"Now, Daddy," Linda said, "calm down. I'm sure he's doing what he thinks is right. He's trying to use reason in all these situations and not use force. How could he use force without bringing on a war? And do you want these three"—indicating the children, now sprawled out on the floor, bored and playing with coloring books—"to be the victims of that?"

"If things don't change and change fast," her father said grimly, "there's goin' to be so many millions of victims everywhere that three more aren't goin' to matter much."

"How can you say that about your own grandchildren?" she demanded angrily. "They matter to me! And they should matter to you!"

"Of course they matter to me," Jim Elrod said, more mildly. "But they aren't goin' to be saved by pussyfootin'. They're goin' to be saved by bein' strong. And he just *isn't* strong."

"It seems to me," Mark said, while on the little screen the subject of their discussion went on with his determined optimistic accounting, "that he has been quite consistent in his policies. He doesn't believe in big-stick diplomacy and neither do I. I admire him for sticking to his principles."

"It's all very well for you to say you don't believe in big-stick diplomacy," Jim Elrod said, "but when the Soviet Union is usin' it everywhere in the world, either directly or through its miserable cat's-paws like Cuba, then we'd better be a lot tougher than we're bein' or we're goin' to get pushed right back to Fortress America—we're almost there now—without anythin' left to defend the Fortress. You've got to be strong in this world. Strong, strong, strong!" He sighed and concluded somberly, "And he's weak—weak—weak."

If this was true, however, it was not apparent as the President neared his peroration. A certain tension entered his manner: it was obvious he was coming finally to the real heart and purpose of his unexpected address (arranged with the television networks almost spur-of-the-moment by the White House press office). This was to allay as much as possible the general concern that had greeted the new and unexpected turn of events in Moscow just five days before. He approached it as always from his own unique and wide-eyed angle.

"There are many reasons for hope. One of these is the recent event you are all aware of, the coming to power of a new leader in the Soviet Union. He is young, he is vigorous, he is, as he assured me in a telephone conversation we had just yesterday, as dedicated to peace and good relations between our two countries as I am and you are.

"I know we all welcome the rise of Comrade Yuri Serapin to the offices of General Secretary of the Communist Party, Chairman of the Council of Ministers and President and Commander-in-Chief of the Soviet Union. I know you join me in congratulating him upon his new post. It augurs well for all of us."

"It does?" Senator Elrod inquired. "He's just as bad as the old lot and twenty years younger, with no really basic memories of World War II, no understanding of the need for restraint in world affairs, no maturity, no seasoning—commanding enormous power and confident he can push us around anywhere he pleases. *That* augurs well for all of us?"

"Jim," Mark said sharply, "for Christ's sake, give everybody a chance, will you? It could very well mean a very significant change."

"That's what I'm afraid of."

"You're impossible, Daddy," Linda said. "Suppose we just stop the debate and let the President finish, shall we?"

"Chauncey and the Vice President and the Joint Chiefs of Staff aren't all that happy, either," Senator Elrod observed as a parting shot. "They're goin' along because they have to, but they're worried as hell."

"And so I say to you, my countrymen," the President concluded, "that you should go forth to celebrate this historic Fourth of July weekend—one more in the long, wonderful story of our nation—with good hearts and in good spirits. Our problems are many, but we are aware of them and we are doing our best to solve them. The desire for permanent peace is universal. We will do everything we can to co-operate in achieving it. On that I give you my solemn pledge.

"Have a good holiday. Elizabeth and I intend to."

And he smiled and waved and in seventy-two hours was dead.

And the world, already changed in Moscow, changed in Washington too.

Yet up to that point it was, as many agreed, a good holiday. There were some in fact who said that particular Fourth of July was "the best in years—the quietest and most peaceful—the most relaxed and happiest." Others said it was "a real relief, after all we've been through lately!" Still others agreed, "We certainly deserve it!" Some few others, rewarded with skepticism and disbelief, ventured to suggest uneasily that it was "too peaceful . . . too calm . . . too good to be true."

Looking back, these last were the ones who proved to be right.

Nonetheless, when the long weekend began, it did appear (aided by the President's reassurances) that it would be one of the least troubled and most serene holidays in quite some time.

Domestically, things were about as always: not ecstatically good, not agonizingly bad: wobbling along in their usual course. As America moved on toward the later Eighties, the chronic shortages of fuel and energy were exacting their toll in reduced travel, reduced comfort, reduced services, a generally slowed-down and increasingly threadbare society. It was finally beginning to be accepted that the great days of the lavishly careless post-World War II era were gone, probably forever: but people managed. Even the American human animal, accustomed as it was to its habits of waste and squandering, could adapt when it had to: nobody really enjoyed it much but everybody had grown used to it.

Inflation was a constant worry, rarely checked and then, it seemed, only momentarily: but people managed, nobody quite knew how. Unemployment was rising at a frightening rate as industry declined and jobs were phased out: but somehow government aid and resources could still take up enough of the slack to ward off serious social disturbance. How long this would last, nobody knew: but somehow people managed. The crime rate also never stopped rising: citizens were mugged in the streets and murdered in their homes. Civil chaos grew. City governments were increasingly helpless in the face of this: but somehow all who were fortunate enough to escape being victims were able to sigh and shrug and scuttle safely home, thanking God for their luck.

Abroad, as the President had admitted, there were some things giving cause for worry, but not if one had faith such as his. It was true that the situation in Central America had deteriorated rapidly, exactly as the realistic had predicted after the revolution in Nicaragua: dominoes were falling as fast in that region as they had fallen in Indo-China after the triumph of North Viet Nam. El Salvador had gone next, followed by Panama and Honduras. Guatemala was teetering on the edge. The wave was sweeping upward toward Mexico even as its vibrations were beginning to make themselves felt in the northern tier of South America from Venezuela on down into Brazil, where Cuban-inspired revolutionaries were day by day more active.

In Africa, the smaller political entities were reverting faster every day to the ancient patterns of mutual tribal slaughter; the continent was in chaos and the Cuban-led guerrillas who had finally seized control of Zimbabwe and Namibia had an easy task of it despite the efforts of South Africa, blocked by the United States as the President sought to hold his black constituency for next year's election.

Farther north, the Israelis and Egyptians were still holding on, but only because Soviet-backed revolutionaries were distracting many of the Arab oil states with their growing threats to governments too weak to defend themselves. The countries the President had mentioned were the most severely challenged at the moment, but the disease was everywhere. It was only a matter of time, and time did not seem to belong to the few remaining friends of the West.

In Europe, NATO struggled on with increasingly aged weapons that the United States, its munitions industries hampered by lack of oil and materials even as its President unilaterally cut back and cancelled many of his country's weapons and commitments, could not replace. So far only Italy had openly gone communist; given the cheerfully ungovernable nature of Italians, this was not all that much help to the Soviet Union. But the example was there, however imperfect, and its effect was being felt in all the countries of Western Europe. "Who will be next?" *Time* magazine had asked in a recent cover story; and the informed guesses sent shivers through the little huddle of remaining democratic countries.

In Asia, which the President had carefully refrained from mentioning, China, though appearing to be in sheer size and manpower an effective counter-balance to Soviet imperialist expansion, was not yet a major industrial or military power in terms of what it could put in the field, in the air and on the seas. Dominoes were continuing to fall there, too, pushed by Soviet-supported surrogates. South Korea and the Philippines were the latest. International fears and outrage over Afghanistan had been successfully ignored. Iran, Pakistan and the Indian invasion had followed inevitably while the United States, making threats only to find itself unable to support them, groaned feebly in the West.

The Soviet Navy was in all the seas and off all the continents, its control of the oceans now complete and, as the United States Navy continued to decline as a result of cutbacks in the late Seventies, not only unchallenged but virtually unchallengeable.

The careful plantings of seven patient decades were one by one being harvested by the Kremlin, and out of Washington in these later Eighties there came empty protests, futile warnings and pleas for peaceful co-operation that fell on cynical ears and brought only amusement to minds that had never intended anything but the final destruction of the capitalist system and of America as its last remaining defender that could be said to have any capability at all. This capability was now in such difficult disarray that it was being treated with virtually open contempt by the Soviet Union.

But this President said all of this was not so. He said his countrymen should ignore the ominous signs everywhere apparent around them. He said all was for the best in this best of all possible worlds for America's mortal enemy, and not to worry.

And such was his countrymen's desperate need for reassurance as they stared at the growing abyss beneath their feet, that with a deliberate submergence of mind and will they were able to put it aside, as he had suggested, and enjoy their holiday. A few such as Chauncey Baron and Jim Elrod, Vice President Hamilton Delbacher, the Joint Chiefs of Staff and some few other muffled and frequently censored voices in the media were desperately worried and unhappy. But for the majority it was a time to forget, to relax, to have fun.

Time in its standard holiday mood-piece summed it up for them in much the same spirit as the President:

"Americans were beset on many sides this week, but as the nation prepared to celebrate its anniversary there was a noticeable optimism abroad in the land. As families checked their gas gauges and gathered their gear, prepared to go to the beach, swim, picnic, be with friends, a happy relaxation seemed to send up a pleasant murmur from Cape Cod to the Golden Gate. Obviously, most agreed, it was a time for reaffirmation of faith and confidence, for recapturing the certainty that, whatever their troubles, Americans would, as always, win through. A spirit of renewed hope, of optimistic rededication, of—"

And so on, for five hundred glowing well-chosen words.

On the idle hill of summer, America dreamed.

Elsewhere, others were not so idle. When the startling news of the President's death of a heart attack flashed around the globe on the holiday's last evening, they wondered, with the ponderous and undeflectable single-mindedness that had brought them to the pinnacle of power they now occupied, whether the time had not come to put into operation plans, long since perfected, which would bring once and for all the final defeat of capitalism and the conquest of the world.

2

"A new world war . . . will be a struggle for the very existence of the two opposing world-wide systems, the socialist and the capitalist. This war will decide the fate of all mankind."

—*The Great Soviet Encyclopedia*

To this goal the man of fifty who sat in the vast office in the Kremlin once occupied by the modern czars Stalin, Malenkov, Khrushchev, Brezhnev and Brezhnev's successor, had been dedicated all his life.

He could scarcely remember now a time when he had not believed this; he could barely conceive now of the few moments of doubt when he had dared wonder about it.

He could not, in fact, conceive of having challenged it, ever, for it had been a part of him for so long that he had never really known, or thought, of the world in any other way. The system which had educated him, trained him, brought him to manhood and ultimately to what was now the world's most powerful office (still claimed for the President of the United States, but in a tone ever more desperate and more defiant as what he believed to be the inexorable facts of socialist triumph were at last beginning to penetrate even the most obtuse skulls of the West) had given him no other option.

He was literally unable to imagine that socialism, and above all the Soviet Union as its leading embodiment and the world's most powerful nation, was not going to win the final battle for control of the globe. In recent years the words "decisive" and "decision" had increasingly become a part of Soviet education and official Soviet military and political thought. Ahead lay the "decisive" battle in the war that would "decide the fate of all mankind." Indeed, the war was already raging, and it had been for many decades, whether it had been known to the West as "local wars," "wars of liberation," "peaceful co-existence," "détente" or just simply "peace."

"Peace," Vladimir Ilich Lenin had said, "is a means of gathering together one's forces."

If the West, and particularly the United States, persisted in regarding "peace" as some state of euphoric relaxation entirely separated from the constant war of communism to conquer capitalism, then that was the West's hard luck. Nothing could have played more directly into the hands of Vladimir Ilich's heirs and true believers.

And no more legitimate heir or truer believer existed than Yuri Serapin, now elevated by fate, his own strength, determination and what he believed to be the inevitable tides of history, to the joint offices of General Secretary of the Communist Party of the Soviet Union, Chairman of the Council of Ministers, President and Commander-in-Chief of the Union of Soviet Socialist Republics.

He was sorry, in some secret area of his mind, which was the only place where he dared express it—so all-pervasive was the unrelenting spying of the state, even upon its leaders—that Joseph Dzhugashvili had chosen to take for himself the name "Stalin," meaning "steel." Because he, Yuri Serapin, felt that he had even more steel than that old man; and he had the advantages that he was much younger and much more resilient, and that the armed forces he controlled on all the continents and all the seas were infinitely greater than any Stalin had commanded in his day.

Of those armed forces he was both parent and child, because from his earliest school days he had known that he would find his way to power through their steadily growing ranks. Like all Soviet children, from almost literally the moment he entered the log-cabin schoolhouse in his native Bratsk, far to the east in Siberia, he had been taught to revere the armed forces, whose task was the defense and triumph of socialism in the coming onslaught of the imperialist capitalist forces of the West.

He and his classmates, then aged five, were told this within an hour after they had taken their seats at the long wooden benches; and by the time he had moved on into the higher grades the armed forces had become even more holy; because now, in the aftermath of the Great Patriotic War of 1941–45, they had one enemy above all others upon whom to concentrate their planning and their hatred. He had come to maturity believing with the blind, unquestioning faith inculcated in all but the most skeptical Soviet children by their education that the United States of America was history's most evil power, bent upon the conquest of the world in the name of a capitalist system that Vladimir Ilich, Karl Marx and Friedrich Engels had proved beyond a doubt to be inimical to every decent instinct of the human heart and every program for the betterment of the human race.

There was simply no question of this in his mind. The Soviet system permitted no doubt about it. Everything else was shut out. No other view of the world existed because the state did not allow it to exist. Fearful punishment or death or both awaited anyone who dared deviate.

No slightest good was conceded to the enemy. If the enemy had given invaluable and indispensable assistance to the Soviet Union in the Great Patriotic War, a fact which for a brief period had to be publicly if grudgingly admitted, that was solely because the enemy at that moment was interested in defeating Hitler. With Hitler gone the enemy was now free to concentrate once more—as it had tried to do in the early days of the Revolution when American forces joined other Allied states in attempting to invade Russia and overturn the Bolsheviks—upon the destruction of socialism and socialism's chief leader and defender.

This imposed upon socialism's chief leader and defender, of course, the obligation to destroy capitalism's chief leader and defender before it destroyed socialism's chief leader and defender. And this justified all things, every type of force, blackmail, subterfuge, subversion, deceit, betrayal— all the things that were lumped, in Vladimir Ilich's all-embracing definition, under the heading "peace"—"a means of gathering one's forces." Eventually, if the enemy forced the issue, as it constantly threatened to, a world war would be justified. This could never be an "unjust" war, of course: always a "just" war. Because a war fought by the Soviet Union, so its citizens were told, could never be anything else.

These were conclusions, however, which it took Yuri Serapin a while to formulate satisfactorily in his own mind, even though they were drummed into him virtually every hour of every day by his education and by official propaganda.

It had early become apparent to his teachers, all of them of course members of the party and under tight party control as they were throughout the Soviet Union, that in their sturdy, dark-headed charge, with his broad half-Asiatic face and his stolid Asiatic expression, they had a mind and character that held great promise for the state. They molded it as rigidly into the pattern as they could and then sent it forward, a human missile already well set on a course of undeflectable hatred and contempt for the capitalist enemy, to the higher echelons where it would get its final honing and be placed in the arsenal of those who would eventually guide the destinies of the state on the path to inevitable victory.

His parents were essentially simple folk, his father a Great Russian from Moscow who had been sent to Siberia, not as punishment, but because he had a good brain and was a good and loyal teacher. His mother was the placid, imperturbable daughter of a trader from Mongolia who had been invited to enter Russia for a time and then been returned, properly redirected, against the day when his help would be needed to bring his native land finally and securely under Soviet hegemony.

They had been at first overwhelmed, then immensely proud, when they were told that their only child had been chosen by the party and the state to become one of those who might someday lead the nation. He had not seen them much in recent years, since he had been absorbed into the central workings of the party machine, but from time to time he would receive a short letter—always, naturally, passed through the state censorship before it reached him—in which they reiterated their love and pride. He always tried to answer, though his education had conditioned him long since to understand that if it ever became necessary to sacrifice them in the interests of the state, he would not hesitate to do so. Fortunately this could never happen, for they were as loyal as he; but it did serve to place a noticeable distance, not only geographic, between them. He knew the party considered this good, and he did too: it did not pay to have emotional ties too close. They were a human failing that could lead to human weakness; and this the state could not tolerate in its leaders if it was to win the ultimate victory.

Between his fifteenth and eighteenth years, now transferred to the special leadership school in Moscow, he completed the full 140 hours of basic military training expected of all Soviet youths save those in such inferior physical or mental condition that it was out of the question. There were not many, nor did the party waste even these if it could possibly be avoided. Some were assigned to administrative educations, some to more menial tasks; nearly all were blended ruthlessly and efficiently into the armed forces of the state—those armed forces which are intended not only to give communism its ultimate triumph in the world but which also, of course, make it impossible for any revolution against communism to break out at home.

Because this other function of the armed forces had been recognized very early by Vladimir Ilich, the party had always made very sure that its control of the armed forces was absolute. Therefore, as soon as his abilities were realized, there was no question where Yuri would go. Conscripted at eighteen, as are all Soviet youths, he served two years in the Army, then was given the unusual privilege and duty of serving another two years in the Air Force and then still another two in the Navy. He was then assigned as a junior officer, to GLAVPUR, the main political directorate of the Soviet Army and Navy, and began that dual career of political agent and military man that has been characteristic of most of the Soviet Union's top leaders ever since the Revolution.

That he would eventually move into the top echelons had never been doubted by the party nor, when he saw the direction in which it was ordering his life, by himself. He knew he was very intelligent, very quick and very adaptive: his grades and honors proved that. He also discovered in himself a vein of hidden ruthlessness that was all the more effective for being silent and unnoticed by his contemporaries. Instinct told his superiors that it was there. They knew he was one of them, these aging men who had intrigued, betrayed and murdered their way to their positions of influence and power in the party and the state.

He was the new generation of incorruptibles, so dedicated to communism that there could never be any question of his loyalty or usefulness.

It was decided, however, that this had to be proven beyond the last possible doubt before he could finally be accepted. At twenty-four, soon after he was assigned to GLAVPUR, the opportunity arose when he fell in love with a girl from Gorki named Irina Kasovera.

Irina was assigned as political officer with a women's civil defense regiment. Civil defense, too, was part of Vladimir Ilich's "peace." Enormous subterranean fortifications were being built all around Moscow and other major cities to house the Politburo, the military general staff and the highest-ranking members of the bureaucracy when "peace" inevitably was succeeded by war. This aspect of "gathering one's forces" was also being attended to with great thoroughness.

He had only to touch a button on his desk today and instantly the secret passageways would open, the automatic shuttle cars would appear, he and other members of the Politburo and Central Committee would be whisked away in less than a minute six hundred feet underground into the mightiest steel and concrete bunker history had ever known.

Irina's regiment was assigned to help build one of the seventy-five such installations along the beltway around Moscow. Inevitably she and Yuri met in the constant classes at GLAVPUR. Perhaps not so inevitably, because he had consciously steeled himself against just such a weakening possibility, they fell in love.

Very soon this was noted in higher circles. With patient calculation a decision was reached to let the romance proceed to the point where its termination would be a terrible testing for him. To make it even more terrible, it was decided to make it a political as well as emotional testing. It was determined that if he survived that, he would be ready with no further question to become one of the rulers.

With a terrifying abruptness, after they had known one another six months and were beginning to think seriously about petitioning for permission to marry, he arrived at GLAVPUR one morning to find his fellow students buzzing with "what happened to Irina Kasovera."

"What?" he demanded, in sudden frantic alarm. "What happened to Irina Kasovera?"

"She has been charged with treason to the state," he was told, a certain jealous triumph in the voice (female) which enlightened him.

"It is absurd!" he cried.

"Tell that to Nikita Sergeyevich!" his tormentor advised him with a happy relish as she flounced away.

He did not tell Khrushchev, though at first in his near-insane pain and bewilderment, he almost thought it would be worth a try. Instead he hurried into the office of the commander of his section, and there met a stone wall.

"Irina Kasovera?" was the bland-faced, opening question. "Who is Irina Kasovera?"

"She is—" he began shrilly; then with a great effort made himself stop and speak more calmly, though his voice still trembled. "Irina Kasovera —Student Kasovera—Squadron Adviser Kasovera—Troop Political Officer Kasovera—"

"Please," his commander said with lifted hand. "Must we have all her titles? I do not know this Irina Kasovera. Tell me about her."

"You do know!" he burst out. "She was in your class just yesterday!"

"Oh? Then where is she today?"

"I don't know," he cried, "I don't know! I know only that—"

"Yes?" his commander asked, a dangerous little edge coming into his voice. "What do you know?"

"I know that—" he began, then faltered and rephrased it. "I know only that someone must have made a terrible mistake about Irina Kasovera."

"There is no mistake about Irina Kasovera," his commander said with a sudden harshness of his own. "She is a traitor to the state and a lackey of the capitalist forces that are determined to destroy the socialist Motherland."

"How can she be?" he cried in angry protest. "It is impossible! She is as loyal as I am!"

"If you are loyal there can be no question of your decision, then," the commander said calmly. "Come. Let us pay a visit to the traitor Irina Kasovera."

"She is *not*—" he began.

"Come!" his commander said sharply. "No more talk! Come at once!"

Even now, having risen to the pinnacle of power, he could still awake sweating in the night when he dreamed of that short walk down the dingy, gray, paint-flaked corridors to the room where they held her prisoner. His whole being cried out in agony at every step. He could not believe it. He did not believe it. He never believed it. He did not believe it now, as the commander had only two days ago, so many years after, found out.

But the charade, for charade he knew it must be, proceeded according to plan. The door was flung open by an armed guard and he was thrust into the room by a strong hand between his shoulder blades. Before him sat Irina, trembling in a chair, the blond hair that he had loved to run his fingers through sweaty and disheveled, the smooth body he had loved to hold in his arms shaking as if with a frightful fever. He saw in her eyes that the fever was death—a death ordained by the god he worshipped. He hardly knew what he was doing, so violent was the turmoil in his mind and heart.

"Ask her!" the commander ordered harshly. "Ask the traitor Irina Kasovera if she is not the traitor Irina Kasovera!"

"I—I—" he said, and only a strangled clicking sound came out.

"Yes?"

"I—cannot."

"Very well," the commander said. "I will." And without warning he reached down and slapped Irina twice across the face.

She screamed, her head yanked back, tears burst forth as the ugly red welts appeared.

"Are you not the traitor Irina Kasovera?" the commander asked softly. She shook her head. Again his hand snaked out, twice came the thud of flesh on flesh, again she screamed and clutched her neck, as though this time something had been broken.

"Stop!" Yuri cried. "Oh, *stop!*"

"Are you not the traitor Irina Kasovera?" the commander repeated, still in the same soft voice: and waited.

After what seemed to Yuri a very long silence her voice finally came, in a whisper:

"No."

"Ah, ha!" the commander said, and once again, harder still, the slaps, the screams, barely audible now, the sound of something definitely cracking; and this time the gently swaying blond head did not come up again, and there was a silence broken only by the heavy breathing of the commander. Yuri could not hear Irina breathing any more, though he knew she must be. *She must be.*

"Very well," the commander said. "Since the traitor Irina Kasovera will not speak for herself, then you must speak for her. Guard!"

And the guard came in, and through the strange red fog of horror, revulsion and protest that seemed to envelope him like a living thing Yuri heard the commander say,

"Guard, you will write down the statements of Comrade Serapin. Student Serapin, do you see before you the body of the traitor Irina Kasovera?"

"I—I hope it is not her body," he said stupidly. "I—I hope she is alive."

"Does it matter?" the commander asked indifferently. "She is—or was —a traitor. If she lives, the state must punish her. If she is already dead, it is saved that trouble. I repeat my question: Student Serapin, do you see before you the traitor Irina Kasovera? Open your eyes!" he added sharply. "You cannot see anything, like that."

"I—" Yuri said. "I—"

"Yes? Well?"

But, looking anywhere in the room except at the crumpled figure in the chair, he could not, at the moment, say more. So the commander spoke for him.

"Comrade Student Serapin," he said in a detached, almost thoughtful tone, "who values his future with the party and the state, and is regarded by the party and state as one of their most promising sons, is aware that at this moment he must decide his entire fate. Therefore, with that in mind, he declares that he totally rejects, condemns and abhors the traitor Irina Kasovera and abandons her to the fate she deserves. *Is that not right,* Comrade Student Serapin?"

"I—" he began again. "I—"

"Enough 'I, I, I,'" the commander said impatiently. "The proposal being made to you by the party and state is clear to you, is it not? Is it not?"

He hesitated for what seemed to him, again, a very long time; and at last, because he accepted now the fact that she was dead, that it was all over, that something had died in him too that could never be reborn, and that he must now go on as they wanted him to and do their bidding forever after, he whispered, very low:

"Yes."

"Good," the commander said. "That is a wise decision, Comrade Serapin. Now repeat after me: 'I, Comrade Student Serapin, declare that I totally reject, condemn and abhor—'"

And dully he had repeated it; and then had managed to scribble something at the bottom that remotely resembled his signature; and then, after one last look through almost-closed lids at the silent figure in the chair, he had felt himself propelled back into the corridor, where he promptly threw up and fainted.

Some time later—they told him it was three days—he came out of his coma in a fine hospital in a Moscow suburb, one of the superior-grade institutions maintained for the exclusive use of the party elite and their families. He had an excellent doctor, caring nurses, a week of the best possible treatment. Then he was subjected to an examination by two psychiatrists and was enough himself again to know that he must say only— and repeat it many times in a tone of great relief—that he was infinitely grateful that he had been rescued from the anti-revolutionary, pro-capitalist wiles of the traitor Irina Kasovera; and presently was discharged and back at his duties again. Six months later he married the red-haired bitch who had taunted him about Irina—she was the daughter of one of the top officials of the KGB, and an excellent party match— subsequently bred her, without passion, to create three more little party members whom he barely tolerated and did not see much any more; and in due course did the expected and took himself the mistress, Ekaterina Vasarionova, whom he still had.

But he did not forget Irina: and one of the very first things he had done five days ago following his election by the Central Committee to be head of the state was to direct that the commander, now a retired colonel living with his wife in a dacha near Yalta, be brought before him. And when the white-haired old man, now in his seventies, had been brought shaking and crying to this very room, he had taken great pleasure in beating him back and forth across the face until in him, too, something cracked and the head hung down and the breathing stopped and nothing more was there.

This had come easy, now, though it might not have for a while after Irina died. But he was on his way up in a cold and brutal world, the bleak, unloving jungle of the top communist echelons, and one learned— fast, or one did not survive.

It had not been so very long after her death that he had been able to tell himself with pride that Joseph Dzhugashvili was not the only one to whom the pseudonymous "Stalin" might apply. He, Yuri Serapin, was worthy of it too.

After his return to his duties, he was given a year of further special training at the Frunze Military Academy which produced all the top officers of the armed forces, and then was assigned to the Zampolit, or Deputy Regimental Commander for Political Affairs, of the Moscow district.

There he served for two years with distinction, supervising the political instruction of the ordinary soldiers of the Soviet Army—two two-hour courses weekly in Marxist-Leninist theory, one hour of instruction in the Marxist interpretation of current events and special talks in the field lasting up to three hours at a time. He particularly distinguished himself in these, giving them with a dramatic flair and imparting a sense of scowling, implacable dedication to communism that his more impressionable troops admired and tried to imitate. He also was in charge of the permanent propaganda displays that hung in every barracks, mess hall and club, and of the amateur dramatics, special shows and rallies in which all troops were required to participate, thus demonstrating their loyalty to the party and to the great men, who, far away and high above in their special world, guided the destinies of the state in the holy heritage of K. Marx and V. I. Lenin.

Beginning soon after the ending of the Great Patriotic War and continuing unchanged to this very day, the constant theme throughout all this was the perfidy of America, the deceit of America and the need to hate America, which was, as the leaders taught, determined to launch world war and destroy the communist world despite any pratings of "détente" or "peace" or other deliberately confusing smoke-screens the capitalists might try to create. America was evil, never to be trusted, always to be deceived and betrayed. To work for the final destruction of America and the capitalist world it represented and led was the highest duty of the Soviet citizen. Through all political seasons and all fluctuating political weathers, this basic purpose never changed and never wavered.

From Zampolit Moscow he was assigned for four years to the state security agency, the KGB, and soon found that its mission was to conduct an unending war upon all Soviet citizens, America, other democracies, and everyone and everything that the great men in the Kremlin thought might somehow threaten the safety of communism and, more particularly, their own powers and privileges.

In the grim gray building at 2, Dzerzhinsky Square, next to Lubyanka Prison two blocks from the Kremlin, he learned that while America was the first priority foreign enemy, of no one and no thing was the KGB a greater enemy than it was of the freedom of the Russian people. He was taught and became a participant in the techniques by which a tiny oligarchy keeps 250,000,000 enslaved; and came to understand how it is that the masters of the Kremlin are convinced that their final battle against the capitalist world will indeed "decide the fate of all mankind"— permanently.

As a favored child of the state he had been spared some of the more onerous restrictions imposed upon nearly all Soviet citizens and had taken the rest for granted. Now he perceived them for what they were: the most thorough means ever devised for keeping a population in such subjugation that it could never again rise up against its conquerors. Defeat at the hands of the communists meant final and absolute defeat, *forever,* with no mercy, no appeal, no hope, no possible chance, *ever,* of rebellion or recapture of lost freedom. No conquered people on earth gave more certain proof of this than the Soviet people themselves.

He had sensed, but until now had not had the opportunity to understand in all its ramifications, that all those conquered by the communists are under the absolute control of the state literally from birth to death. In every apartment building and village complex an *"upravdom,"* or "master of the house," keeps a daily logbook of all births, all deaths, all comings, goings, activities, illnesses, any suspected "thoughts disloyal to the state," virtually every single act of every individual within the area. Through the *upravdom* every Soviet citizen is on file, not only in the place where he lives but in Moscow, where highly sophisticated computers kindly and naïvely granted by the American President, J. Carter, make even more absolute the control of the state.

Combined with the *upravdom,* Yuri's instructor informed him with a smile smug with satisfaction at the cleverness of the system, is the second means of absolute control, the "internal passport" given to favored Soviet citizens when they reach sixteen. This passport contains the bearer's vital statistics, those of his close relatives, his ethnic origin, social class, draft status, the location of his birth certificate. Internal "visas" stamped in the book list every place a citizen has visited in his entire life for a period of more than three days. If the citizen stays more than three days in any area, he must present his passport for registry with the militia which forms the enforcement arm of the KGB. The KGB may put in the passport restrictions that bar the citizen from some areas, confine him to others. Immigration into Moscow, for instance, is rigidly controlled and few citizens other than party members and those needed to provide food, domestic help and other necessary services to the elite are allowed to enter and reside in the city.

Farmers living on collective farms are generally permitted no more than one-day passes, and those only to nearby villages. In cold reality, they are serfs, bound to the soil as surely as their ancestors ever were under the czars.

An employment record forms the third clamp upon the citizen, starting with his first job and staying with him through his working life, containing every detail of type of work, pay, hours, efficiency ratings. If a worker dares show signs of rebellion or dissent, his work record can be lifted by the KGB and after thirty days' unemployment he can be declared a "parasite" and banished to Siberia or a prison work camp.

In this system, effectively imposed by a tiny handful upon 250,000,000, the only possible chance of rebellion or protest must come from the ranks of the artists, writers and journalists favored by the state for their contribution to the Soviet cultural image in the eyes of the world; and those among these favored ones who dare to rebel are denounced, harassed and —if they remain obdurate and cannot somehow manage to defect to the West—are imprisoned or ordered to "internal exile" in some remote area or sent to psychiatric clinics for "special treatment" where drugs and surgery reduce them to vegetables unable ever again to use their talents, let alone threaten the state.

There was a brief period, learning all this, when Yuri felt an instinctive horror and protest; but he knew even as he felt it that it could come to nothing. The decision about his life had been made for him by the state when he was a child. It had been confirmed by Irina's murder. He had reconfirmed it himself by his willing acceptance of all he had been taught, and his growing and by now absolute faith in the teachings of Marx, Lenin and their ruthless inheritors. He was one of those for whom Milovan Djilas, the dissident Yugoslav, had coined the term "the New Class"—the rulers, the elite, the favored who exercise the dark machinery of the Soviet state and receive in return their private apartments, their motorcars, their dachas, their Western luxuries and television sets, all the appurtenances of their tight little world that exists so snugly in the heart of Moscow, above, and fiercely protected from, the great gray mass of the Soviet millions who will never, ever, be able to overthrow them now.

Unless, of course, there is outside pressure of sufficient strength to crack the system. And that could come from only one conceivable source. And therefore, once again, it all came back to building up Soviet defenses to an impregnable level while simultaneously subverting and eventually destroying the only power on earth that could possibly pose such a threat, the United States of America.

Against the enemy, he found, the KGB had many weapons and employed them daily on a worldwide scale. Infiltration of other nations, particularly America itself, by "illegals," some of whom have been in place for many years awaiting the day when they will be called upon to serve an invading Soviet force . . . infiltration of many other nations' intelligence services . . . recruitment of willing dupes, particularly American, often in the American armed services, who can be persuaded with money and flattery to steal secret documents and transmit them to Moscow . . . cultivation of those naïve souls, particularly American, many of them prominent in literature, motion pictures, the arts, who need only a slight flattering push to persuade them to oppose their own country and defend and rationalize Soviet behavior, no matter how vicious and anti-human . . . the dispatch of "scientific"—"artistic"—"cultural" groups to the United States (each including, and accompanied by, disguised KGB agents) some of whom occasionally slip away into the populace to remain as agents in place, others of whom occasionally defect with great fanfare and are allowed to go instead of being killed, as they easily could be, because they too may be of use later . . . the "disinformation" directorate, devoted to planting with some members of the American media who are only too willing to believe and publish the worst about their own country false rumors, false reports, false "news items" derogatory and destructive to the United States . . . the Executive Action Department, responsible for kidnappings, sabotage, murders—in KGB parlance called *mokrie dela,* or "wet affairs," because blood, of course, is wet . . . the constant surveillance and deliberate hoodwinking of American tourists, diplomats and journalists in Russia, in the hope and intention of trapping them in compromising situations, preferably sexual, which can be used to force them to become spies or willing propagandists for the Soviet Union . . . the constant attempt, in the United States, to suborn businessmen, students, government employees, professors, artists, journalists, anyone who in any way can contribute to the weakening of America and the ultimate victory of the communist state . . . constant attempts to stir up revolutions, rebellions, "people's struggles for liberation" in Africa, the Middle East, South America, Asia—every spot of land or tiniest political entity that can be used in any way at all, no matter how minute, to alienate America's friends and supporters and weaken America's position in the world . . .

A constant, unending, 'round-the-clock, worldwide pressure, never ceasing for a moment, to destroy and tear down the hated enemy and remove it—forever—from the pages of history. Anything and everything, everywhere and always: a ceaseless gnawing-away on every continent, in every sea, a million little mice, while Gulliver, supine and enchained by naïveté, good will and earnest hopes for "peace" responds halfheartedly, feebly, emptily, if at all—because he *simply cannot believe* that any system of government can be so consistently hostile, implacable and unremittingly evil . . .

All of this Yuri studied, learned, absorbed. His heart died some more. His human instincts, by now close to total obliteration, withered further; he was becoming the man of steel, the perfect Soviet robot. And he believed. It was not a pose, not a pretense, it had long since passed beyond conscious effort. He *believed*.

All around him were his fellow members of the New Class, equally fanatic, equally dead inside. There was simply nothing there for the West to talk to. The words both sides used might occasionally have some similarities, but the meanings were as far apart as the poles. Yuri and the generation that was rising with him toward eventual control of the Soviet state could not be touched by the arguments, the appeals, the naïve and simplistic attempts at friendship, of the West. They scoffed at the arguments, scorned the appeals, simply were unable to conceive that there could be any friendship. It was all a capitalist imperialist plot. The truth had been vouchsafed to them, and they *knew*. And like the robots they had become, they proceeded undeviating and undeflectable toward the goal their gods had told them was theirs, the final defeat of capitalism and the triumph of communism which would indeed "decide the fate of all mankind"—forever.

Through all the years of his education and training ran the one unchanging, implacable theme: the monstrosity and evil of the United States.

Very briefly, at one point that now seemed long ago, Yuri had questioned this: never openly, for those who raised such questions openly did not remain around to repeat them. But for a little while, harking back perhaps to Irina's murder for no other purpose than to test and strengthen his own loyalty and dedication, he had wondered if America could possibly be as sinister as she was always portrayed in official thought—as sinister, in fact, as he now knew his own country to be. The sheer insistence and weight of the anti-American campaign overreached itself for a brief time in his mind: he just could not believe it. It was too irrational and too much. But he never, ever expressed this to anyone; and in due course it was proven to him by the things he experienced and saw for himself that his doubts were foolish. America was everything his mentors said it was.

After his service with the armed forces, Zampolit and the KGB, when he had finally become the dedicated and unhesitating killer his superiors desired, he was given the chance to see for himself. He was considered totally safe now: he could be sent to Washington under the most standard of all KGB covers, that of a "diplomat" attached to the Soviet Embassy. Second secretary was usually the favored title, although in any given Soviet embassy anywhere in the world, at least two thirds of all officials and employees, whatever they might be called, are KGB members.

So Second Secretary Yuri Serapin went off to Washington, where he remained for four years, one of the key men in the KGB network that covers the United States in all major cities and in many other vital areas such as power grids, industrial concentrations, military bases and the like. Behind the barred and shuttered windows of the Soviet Embassy, behind the iron gates and iron fences that keep in the happy fortunate children of the Revolution and keep out the miserable downtrodden unfortunates of the decadent capitalist monster, he received and transmitted each day the unending stream of information that funnelled in from all over the American continent. Almost daily he put on his best smile and his most charming manner (both very effective) and sallied forth to lunch, where he could be found eating at the Metropolitan Club in chummy intimacy with the impressed columnists of the New York *Times,* at the Cosmos Club with the sage pundits of the Washington *Post,* or at some other see-and-be-seen place such as the Sans Souci restaurant with other bedazzled journalists of the lesser breeds who were convinced they were being told the intimate secrets of the Soviet Union on a delightfully flattering one-on-one basis.

From these conversations Yuri returned to file his reports to Moscow. Never, as he remarked contemptuously in one of them, had he met so many egotistical fools begging to be misled. With great gusto, he misled them in every way he possibly could.

Three or four evenings a week he donned tuxedo and, accompanied usually by his lumpy, spiteful wife, with whom he maintained the most tenuous of relations and those strictly because he and the party both felt that he needed a partner on his forays into society, he went forth into the diplomatic and social worlds of Washington. These affairs ranged from the White House on down through the diplomatic corps and from there to the society-page ranks of the risers, the fallers and the precariously balanced in-betweens. He forewent his healthy taste for vodka and restricted himself to mineral water or wine. His job was to stay alert and keep his eyes and ears open; and this he did with a shrewdness—and sometimes a faked drunkenness—that brought him still more information about the strange land in which he found himself.

By the time he was recalled to Moscow to join the American and Canadian section of the Politburo he had reached for himself the unshakable conclusion that was to govern his life and thoughts absolutely thereafter and control his view of every situation everywhere in the world:

The Americans might not be the world's most sinister people but they were certainly the most self-destructive; and therefore it was really very easy to assist them to their end and thereby give the world to communism, just as Marx and Lenin had predicted, while at the same time guaranteeing his own position and the future power he was now certain he would achieve.

"The United States," he told one of his very few trusted friends when he returned to the Kremlin—there were not more than three, and this was a large number for a rising Soviet leader to have—"is a dying plum waiting to fall off the tree. We must continue to shake the tree."

And this they did with a grim glee, for they were now entering upon the great years of risk and challenge—exciting, because each time the Politburo could not quite be sure but what the moribund animal might yet revive to thrash out at them. At first cautiously, always cautiously— but then with increasing boldness as in Afghanistan—the probes had begun.

In America, he had found, it was the received faith to declare that the "defeat" of Nikita Sergeyevich's gamble in launching the Cuban missile adventure had resulted in a drastic change and speed-up in Soviet rearmament. In actual fact it was known in the Kremlin, and to all foreign observers who ignored glib journalism and carefully analyzed the Soviet record, that there had been no increase, no "spurt," no change or slightest deviation from the steady build-up that had been under way ever since World War II and had continued without hitch or tremor straight through the Cuban crisis to the present day. The then leader of the corrupt capitalist state, J. Kennedy, had himself backed down as fatefully as Nikita Sergeyevich by not insisting upon on-the-spot inspection of the missile sites. (The fact was buried by himself and his relieved countrymen in a retreating squid's-cloud of self-congratulatory rhetoric.)

This permitted the retention of some of the missiles already in place in Cuba. In due course it permitted the addition of more. In due course it permitted the enlargement of the Soviet submarine base at Cienfuegos. In due course it permitted the introduction of many much more sophisticated Soviet weapons ninety miles off the American coast. In due course it permitted the introduction of the Soviet brigade that was first declared "unacceptable," then humbly bowed down to by the later leader of the dying capitalist state, J. Carter. And in due course it paved the way, with virtually direct American aid, for the series of Soviet-Cuban revolutionary moves that first toppled the pro-Western government of Nicaragua and then, with inevitable and inexorable momentum, moved on into El Salvador, Honduras, Guatemala, Panama and now was at the door of an increasingly nervous and wobbly Mexico.

Along with this went the Soviet-Cuban adventures in Africa, the capture of Ethiopia, Angola and more recently Zimbabwe and Nimibia; the constant probing and challenges in Europe and the northern Atlantic; the virtually unchallenged—save by nervously wringing hands and official tut-tuts and oh-dears in Washington—use of surrogates to topple the few remaining pro-Western states in Asia; and the Afghan adventure, the

Iranian and Pakistan demarches, the invasion of India, the subversion of the Arab states and the now almost-completed capture of the principal oil sources and oil routes of the Middle East.

And even more important was a military budget far greater each year than that of the United States, resulting in the creation of what was now indisputably the greatest military machine in all history—a monstrous giant, glaring out from behind a mask of pseudo-humanitarian propaganda and pseudo-sincere good will, which successfully bedazzled and enslaved the gullible, the hopeful and the timorously naïve around the globe.

It had come as perhaps the greatest and most astounding revelation of their lives to Yuri Serapin and his colleagues that the most gullible, the most hopeful and the most timorously naïve of all were actually in the very country they were determined to destroy; and that most of those who exercised the power and molded the public opinion of the United States could be counted upon to nervously rationalize, explain away and generally sweep under the rug every single Soviet challenge whose acknowledgment might impose upon them the necessity for answer.

"If you pretend that the avalanche is not there," he remarked dryly to Ekaterina Vasarionova at the time of the Soviet brigade incident in Cuba in 1979, "then you may die happily convinced that the boulders that bury you are only little pebbles dropped by passing birds."

"This makes it easy for the passing birds," she had agreed, turning her arm luxuriously to admire the extremely expensive emerald bracelet (costing more than a thousand farmers in a collective could earn in all their lives) that he had ordered the chief KGB agent in New York to purchase for him at Tiffany's.

"It is becoming child's play," he had said with an impatient frown. "I cannot help wondering if they will not yet turn upon us."

"Never," she said scornfully. "They have lost their will to live."

And by now, when supreme power was his at last, and when it seemed that history might indeed have chosen him to lead the final decisive battle that would decide the fate of all mankind forever, he was as convinced of this as she.

Yet this conviction had taken a long time to reach final acceptance in the Kremlin. The habit of caution was so ingrained that even in the midst of the most dazzlingly successful adventures, the most astoundingly unbelievable defeats for a desperately blind, hopeful and peace-pretending American Government, the doubt still lingered, uneasy and obsessive: could it actually be true? Were the Americans really so naïve? *Were their leaders and opinion-makers really so weak and so afraid?*

Finally—finally—soon after the brigade incident, which was followed so swiftly by further advances in Central America and the completion at last of enough missile installations in Cuba to obliterate totally the

United States as a functioning society—it was accepted that this must indeed be so.

The unilateral cancelling by the recent Presidents and Congresses of certain conventional but necessary weapons, the voluntary abandonment by R. Nixon of much of America's chemical warfare capacity, the unilateral cancelling by President Carter, under pressure of a carefully communist-orchestrated outcry, of the neutron bomb—things that the Soviet Union had developed, and was continuing to develop, just as fast as it possibly could, to the outermost limits of capability and horror—the outstripping of America, almost impossible to catch up with now, in all conventional categories on land, sea and in the air—the refusal of some recent Presidents, partly from lack of power, more from lack of will, to take a firm stand on so many challenges—added up to only one thing in the minds of Yuri and his colleagues:

The United States was leaving the field of history. It was no longer an active contender. Marx, Engels and V. I. Lenin had been right. Nothing could possibly save the doomed capitalist enemy now. The corpse was turning putrescent. It awaited only the burial Nikita Sergeyevich had promised. (And even that grim promise had been nervously laughed and rationalized away by the incredible Americans!)

Who would have the great, the supreme, the honor-above-all-honors of presiding over this process—who would win the niche in history that might even outrank Vladimir Ilich Lenin himself? It was the great internal question during the four years Yuri served in the Secretariat of the Politburo and the succeeding six years in which he was a full-fledged member.

It was a time of enormous unopposed successes abroad as the power and the will of the United States rotted away, and of intensely murderous rivalries at home as a little group of eleven men fought viciously for the greatest honor history would ever bestow.

For seven of the ten years it took for him to achieve the goal, Yuri was obsequious, deferential, bland and colorless. The old men of the Politburo might be on their way to the grave but their murderous ambitions were as savage as ever. It was literally all one's life was worth to get in their way. How many times, despising Leonid Brezhnev as he stumbled and maundered his way to oblivion, had Yuri fawned and flattered and heaped vacuous praise upon the old murderer. How many times had he quietly, slyly, ruthlessly in the depths of the Kremlin, whispered the word or murmured the "confidence" that had resulted in some murder of his own. How many times, suavely and calmly and without a moment's compunction or human sentiment of any kind, had he joined and then skillfully extricated himself from the constantly spinning plots that presently resulted in the announcement that Minister So-and-So had "died of a heart attack while vacationing outside Moscow," or Minister Such-and-Such had "died of complications while undergoing an operation." How many times had he, Yuri Serapin, escaped by the slimmest of margins, the slightest of terrifying chances, from the all-devouring jealousies that riddled the hierarchy even as its imperial conquests went forward virtually unimpeded on all the continents and in all the seas.

How shrewdly and with what supreme but oh-so-cleverly-hidden confidence had he proved himself the best survivor of them all.

Because, one by one and method by method, the old men died: some by murder, some few by nature's impersonal hand, but all, all, succumbing at last. Many were succeeded by party favorites only slightly younger than themselves; five or six were succeeded by much younger men, drawn from Yuri's own generation. It was still the assumption that when Brezhnev's aged successor too tottered off to join the innocent and defenseless millions he had helped to send before him, one of "the next layer," as they jovially referred to themselves, would succeed to the seat of power.

But Yuri knew better; and the moment Leonid Ilich staggered his way into the pantheon of czars, he made his decision and began his campaign.

Of "the young assistants," only two were real threats to him. One was Minister of Justice, the other Minister of Foreign Affairs. The rest were weak-willed party hacks chosen because they were exactly that. Intimidations and promises, skillfully combined, brought them to his side. Two years ago he had been appointed Minister of Defense with the military rank of Colonel-General of the Strategic Rocket Forces, the most prestigious, because the most vital, of all the armed forces. The moment this happened there began a struggle in the Kremlin that almost cost him his life on three occasions. But he survived.

Two of these escapes were from actual attempts to murder him. Once he was almost run down by a speeding car as he and his two bodyguards crossed Red Square in a blinding snowstorm. It was shortly before 2 A.M. and he was on his way home from his Kremlin office. One of the guards was killed, the other crippled for life; only their heroic defense of himself, their instinctive action in shoving him headlong out of the way, saved his life. The survivor was now his personal secretary, perhaps the only living being he trusted implicitly. The would-be murder car raced on into the swirling mists and was never found.

The second occasion came at a lavish cocktail party for some one of the visiting American Presidents who seemed to come with increasing frequency to Moscow as they felt their powers slipping away. (Or so their visits were always presented on Soviet television and radio. They might be "summits" of friendship, co-operation and the earnest seeking of solutions to American commentators and viewers; but on the state radio and television of Moscow they were always represented as the visits of supplicants come humbly to beg the favor and forebearance of their masters.)

At one of these—he forgot which President it was in "honor" of (all desperately smiling and hopeful, in these recent years)—his principal rival, the Minister of Justice (under whose jurisdiction were the KGB and allied instruments of the people's justice) had brushed his hand, quite accidentally of course, while flourishing a pen to sign his autograph for some American State Department official. Yuri felt the smallest of stings, the greatest of alarm: he had not served in the KGB himself for four years without learning all the tricks. He had excused himself and left the glittering gathering so fast that he had not even had time to speak to his wife (whom he always suspected of being in the plot anyway).

He just made it to the hospital inside the walls, just had time to gasp out the name of the particular poison, before he fainted into the coma from which he did not emerge for a week.

Very fortunately the Minister of Justice had not thought to bribe the doctors; or if he had, their fear of the Minister of Defense tipped the balance in Yuri's favor. He was saved; demanded an investigation; a solemn secret conclave of the Politburo was held, electric with tension. The doctors testified on Yuri's behalf. Two weeks later the Minister of Justice resigned "for reasons of health," and two weeks after that, proving that his health was indeed poor, it was announced that he had "died of a respiratory ailment following a cold." The respiratory ailment was in the form of a rope, which Yuri had the satisfaction of himself drawing around the neck of his bound and helpless rival as the head of the KGB and the Chairman of the Council of Ministers looked on impassively in the underground depths of the Lubyanka. They had been present when Lavrenti Beria had been murdered, and they understood the necessity for such events.

That left the Minister of Foreign Affairs.

This was a tougher problem, for neither he nor Yuri was so foolish and unsophisticated as to resort to the crude methods of the late Minister of Justice. Both had used them, or ordered them used on lesser rivals, many times over the years; but now the situation had developed to a stage in which the final struggle for power lay so obviously between the two of them that neither could afford to be crude. It had to be done with the ultimate weapon within the party—dialectic. How true was each to Marx, Lenin and the inevitable worldwide triumph of the communist cause? How skillfully—or ineptly—had they advanced it?

Sooner or later there would have to be a full-scale showdown, and for several months Yuri sought desperately for an excuse to provoke one. It was not easy. The Minister of Foreign Affairs was a very shrewd man, almost as tough as Yuri, equally aware that one slip in their struggle would mean instant elimination and death. He too knew the moment must be exactly right; and presently he thought he saw it.

Following the Soviet brigade incident in Cuba, which had resulted in blatant and open humiliation of the United States as its President scrambled desperately to avoid having to face up to the fact of the brigade's presence and its hostile intent, there had begun an increasingly open flaunting of the United States in the Caribbean. The heretofore disguised shipments of "freight" that were actually missile parts, chemical warfare supplies and the latest and most sophisticated weaponry—the visits of Soviet submarines to "refuel" at Cienfuegos and the second base they were building while they actually delivered atomic and neutron warheads—became suddenly and deliberately more open. It had been obvious, from the extreme desperation with which the American Administration sought to evade the implications of the brigade's presence, that enormous propaganda could be made throughout Latin America and the world by emphasizing what the Kremlin regarded as the abject cowardice and failure of will on the part of the Americans.

Yuri led the Kremlin faction that successfully insisted on the newly blatant and more aggressive policy. It had worked very well until the day when two young American Navy pilots, catching the Russians, their own government and everyone else completely by surprise, had taken off in their fighter planes from Pensacola, Florida, to commit suicide—and achieve their objective—by ramming and sinking a missile-laden Soviet "freighter" eighty miles off the eastern end of Cuba.

The leaders in the Kremlin held their collective breaths. Had the attack been secretly ordered by the American Government, aroused at last, to test them? Did it indicate the start of a new and more aggressive policy that might, even at this very late date in the American slide toward inferior status in the world, somehow reverse the trend—or, at the least, result in a final lunge of desperation in which the Americans might in fear and frustration start the world war against which Soviet military doctrine had always warned? Had Yuri Serapin and what his rival immediately dubbed "the adventurists" gone, at last, too far?

This was the time to strike, and even as the world seemed to hang in the balance, the Foreign Minister did so. Again the Politburo convened in response to a demand from a member for the examination, criticism, "education" and expulsion of another. The American Government, though in an obvious internal uproar officially, had taken no stand despite the frantic clamorings of the media and the Washington press corps that it do so. Now, if ever, was the time to eliminate Yuri.

And for perhaps forty-seven of the fifty-nine minutes in which the Committee met, scarcely two hours after the attack, it seemed that this might happen. "Adventurism . . . voluntarism . . . self-aggrandizement, hair-brained scheming, subjectivism and arbitrariness . . . placing himself above the teachings of K. Marx and V. I. Lenin . . . attempting to hasten dangerously the inevitable course of history . . . unnecessarily gambling with the welfare of the state . . . placing his personal judgment above that of the Presidium . . ." and so on, while the Minister of Foreign Affairs roared in red-faced accusation before the grim-faced, silent Politburo and Yuri sat motionless with ice in his heart, wondering whether his responses would be sufficient to save him from dismissal and death.

Triumphantly at last his rival concluded; and he was in the very process of rising slowly to his feet, knuckles white as they clenched the arms of his chair, when the door was flung open and the undersecretary of his rival's own ministry ran into the room waving a piece of paper and shouting, "God be praised! God be praised!"—an incongruity that passed unnoticed in the turmoil that immediately ensued. He was a big man with a big voice, and after his instinctive tribute to the deity his government did not officially recognize, he made himself heard above the uproar:

"They are retreating!" he cried, his voice filled with a happy disbelief. "They are retreating! They have *apologized* to us! The fools, the fools, *they* have apologized to *us!* The fools, the fools!"

And so they had; and suddenly the President of the Council of Ministers himself was shouting, "It is Yuri Pavlovich who has done it! All hail Yuri Pavlovich!" And suddenly they were all, save the scowling and suddenly frightened Minister of Foreign Affairs, crowding around him, slapping his back, pumping his hand, embracing him in bear hugs, dancing and shouting and laughing hysterically in their glee and relief. And Yuri knew, with an inner triumph so great that he could barely contain it, that history had given him the final victory and that from now on nothing in all the world could stop his ascendancy to supreme power and the command of the final decisive battle that would decide the fate of all mankind.

"Here!" he shouted finally, snatching the paper from the undersecretary of foreign affairs, who thrust it eagerly and happily into his hand. "Let us hear what our brave friends in Washington have to say!"

There was a roar of scornful, boisterous laughter and when it died he read the message in a loud, sarcastic voice:

" 'To the honorable the President of the Council of Ministers:

" 'It is with profound regret and sincerest apologies that the Government of the United States of America takes note of the unfortunate incident in which two apparently unbalanced and deranged American pilots sank, without warning or provocation, an innocent ship of the Soviet Union during its peaceful passage on the high seas. That this incident should have occurred in waters near the shores of the United States makes this a matter of even deeper regret and shame for the United States.

" 'A preliminary investigation has disclosed that both the deceased

American naval pilots had been undergoing psychiatric treatment. It is a matter of the gravest concern, and will be a matter of the most severe and intensive investigation by the American Government, how they were able to secure the aircraft used in their inexplicable and inexcusable attack upon the peaceful ship of the Soviet Union. Suitable punishment will be meted out in due course to those whose laxity of command permitted this.

" 'The Government of the United States of America is prepared to make full reparations, in whatever amount is deemed fair by the Government of the Soviet Union, for the loss of this vessel, and to the bereaved families of all officers and crew members who lost their lives in this inexcusable attack.

" 'We will make sure its like does not happen again.' "

It was signed by the President of the United States himself, whose name Yuri read with a sudden viciously contemptuous emphasis that again brought a roar of sardonic, scornful laughter from them all.

The Soviet response was drafted by Yuri on the spot. It was signed with a trembling hand by a white-faced Minister of Foreign Affairs, who knew, as they all did, that he would not be around much longer. The message was stern, terse and unforgiving.

"To the President of the U.S.:

"The President and Council of Ministers of the U.S.S.R., taking note of the message received from you concerning the inexcusable attack upon an innocent Soviet ship by two agents of the American Government, accept the offer of reparations. We will transmit our requirements in due course.

"The Soviet Government warns that any repetition of such an incident or any attempt to interfere with the free and innocent commerce of Soviet vessels in the Caribbean or anywhere in the world will hereafter bring the most immediate, severe and decisive retaliation from the Soviet Government. It is hoped you and your government will bear this in mind, lest the most dreadful consequences fall upon you and all others in the imperialist capitalist camp."

Next morning the translations of American broadcasts and American papers were brought in and spread on the tables and they all crowded around, chortling and gleeful, to see. With almost no exceptions the tone of the popular American response was as apologetic as the official one; and nowhere in any account did there appear certain facts both the Kremlin and the White House knew about the incident:

The fact that amateur photographers on two American fishing yachts in the near vicinity had taken pictures of missiles, clearly defined, hurtling into the air from the Soviet "freighter" in the wake of the explosion, and then disintegrating; the fact that the "freighter's" frantic May Day signals to Soviet command headquarters in Cuba, clearly describing the cargo, had been intercepted, the code broken and reported immediately to the

White House; the fact that the "freighter" had also been carrying a number of containers filled with botulism virus and some of the deadliest nerve gases ever developed, which had fortunately sunk unopened with the hull to the bottom of the sea; the fact that two atomic warheads and a dozen neutron bombs had gone to a similar fate.

"Why do they not use these facts against us?" the aging President of the U.S.S.R. had asked Yuri in bewilderment. Yuri had shaken his head with an expression of contempt.

"They do not wish to upset the friendly Soviet Union. They do not wish to interfere with our delicate ongoing negotiations for another arms limitation treaty. They do not wish to endanger the chances for peace. And, of course"—the contempt became complete—"they are afraid of us."

Whether this was indeed the fact would never be known with absolute certainty in the Kremlin; but enough of the leadership was convinced of it so that from that point forward nearly all of them believed, with a heightened excitement and a deliciously dangerous tension, that it was true. "Adventurism" suddenly became a highly popular word, since the Americans appeared both unable and unwilling to respond to provocations.

The contrast between the policies and actions of the two powers was now complete in the eyes of the rulers of the Kremlin. Even more satisfactorily for them, it now seemed complete in the eyes of many of the world's peoples.

It was, in any event, so complete in the eyes of the Central Committee and the Politburo then when Yuri Serapin finally was voted into supreme command of the Soviet world by the ruthless little clique who ran it, it came as an almost routine endorsement of something that history by now had seemed to make utterly inevitable.

In all the essential ways that give people the chance to be kind, compassionate and decent, he was one of the most sterile, empty and pathetic beings on the face of the earth. He was also, as the man in charge of the most fearsome military force history has ever known, the most dangerous.

How to deal with him—if it was possible to deal with him and his equally inhuman colleagues—was now the task of the amiable, goodhearted, rather ponderous and essentially very human being who had just come to power in Washington.

Each, as Yuri Serapin had been convinced all his life, was the product of his history. The time was here at last to test which of their two histories was correct. Yuri entered the final climactic battle with absolutely no doubt of the outcome.

3

"The Soviet Union firmly and consistently follows a peace-loving foreign policy which flows from the very nature of our structure, persistently fights for preventing new world war, for decreasing international tension, for creating conditions under which each nation can freely develop."

—*The Military Threat,* General V. D. Ivanov

"There has not been, there is not, and there cannot be, class peace between socialism and capitalism, or peaceful co-existence between the communist and bourgeois ideologies."

—*Peaceful Co-existence and the Security of the People,*
Colonel I. Sidelnikov

"War between countries of the capitalist and socialist systems will have a violent and an acutely defined class nature of a fight to the death."

—*Military Art in the Postwar Period,* Colonel A. A. Strokov

Unlike the ruthless ideologue who now confronted him in the Kremlin, it was quite likely that the pleasant-faced, gray-haired grandfather who now sat behind the enormous desk in the Oval Office of the White House had enjoyed only a passing acquaintance with such official Soviet sentiments.

He was not an ideologue himself; and while past Senate hearings and the briefings he had received so far from his military advisers had contained general references to "the hostility we face in Moscow," there had not yet been time for many specifics.

He had not yet had the opportunity, as had some of the professional Sovietologists in the Pentagon and the State Department, to read the official Soviet literature in depth and discover the fact that there existed therein not one single word of friendship, co-operation, tolerance or good will toward the United States of America. He had not had the time, nor might he ever in the swift onrush of events that would now consume his

THE HILL OF SUMMER

every waking hour during the remainder of summer, to discover that the only attitude toward his country expressed in all official Soviet publications and all official Soviet pronouncements was one of hostility, contempt and sheer unrelieved, unrelenting, unmitigated hate.

Even if he had, he probably would not have believed it: for in his country, people simply weren't brought up that way. They were an entirely different breed of animal; and that was why not only he, but millions of his countrymen, were unable to grasp that there were absolutely no points of reasonable contact between themselves and their antagonists— that there was an enormously powerful military machine on the prowl out there whose commanders virulently, literally hated them *for no other reason than that they existed.*

Many Americans might be alarmed about the Soviet Union and concerned about its policies, but hardly a one spent every hour of every day actively hating the Soviet Union and actively plotting its downfall. This fact was of course not believed in the Soviet Union; and thereon rested the tragedy of what might well be the final years of humanity's life on Earth— for that matter, the final years of Earth itself.

Anyway—how could anyone named Hamilton Delbacher hate anybody? Vice President Ham Delbacher (pronounced Dell-bocker) the jovial Pennsylvania Dutchman who had succeeded to the Presidency when his predecessor had so unexpectedly collapsed? Ham Delbacher hate anyone? He couldn't remember that he had ever wanted to. His public image was jovial, comfortable, easygoing, smiling—a modest latter-day combination, somewhat less hefty, of Grover Cleveland and William Howard Taft, perhaps. And that was essentially what he was, though in recent months he had also become, beneath the public façade, something else.

He had become a deeply worried man, profoundly concerned about the policies which seemed to him, as to millions of his countrymen, to be taking the United States ever further down a road from which, if continued, there could be no possible return.

For this he had recently begun to come under the skeptical and increasingly hostile surveillance of those sections of the media that preferred to believe, with the late President, that if one pretended hard enough that there was no Soviet threat, it would go away miraculously of its own accord and there would *be* no Soviet threat.

The usual publications had begun to float their usual undercutting editorials; the usual columns had begun their usual snide intimations that "the White House is reportedly displeased with Vice President Hamilton Delbacher's foreign policy views . . . the President reportedly is considering dumping Vice President Ham Delbacher from the ticket next year . . . the White House staff reportedly categorizes Vice President Hamilton Delbacher these days as a 'war-monger' whose renomination would drastically injure the President's 'man of peace' image . . . Ham Delbacher is on the skids, according to some highly placed White House sources. They refer to the Vice President as 'Ham-handed Ham,' whose anti-Russian views are endangering delicate negotiations for a new arms limitation treaty . . ."

And so on. That was how it was done in *his* country. The Politburo didn't degrade and dismiss you and you didn't get murdered in the depths of the Lubyanka. The thousand little knives of Washington went to work instead, and presently you were stripped to the bone and glistened, whitely, in the sun.

He recognized this for what it was, a campaign begun at the instigation of the White House staff, and therefore in all probability originating in the Oval Office itself. He had confided his suspicions about this to his wife, and Elinor, with the tartness of her New England ancestry, had told him to "go in there to that two-faced weakling and have it out with him." This had been the Vice President's own inclination and, fortified by her advice, he had phoned and requested an appointment.

"How about a week from Thursday?" the White House chief of staff had asked in his lazily insolent way. The Vice President had not replied in the amiable manner to which he had (foolishly, he knew now) permitted the staff to become accustomed.

"How about tomorrow morning?" he had responded sharply. The chief of staff had bristled at once.

"He has a delegation of tomato growers from Imperial Valley coming in at eleven—" he began.

"He has the Vice President of the United States coming in at ten," Ham Delbacher said. "Or do I have to come over there and tell the press corps I'm being prevented from seeing him?"

There was a moment's dead silence, then a tone of ill-concealed hostility:

"Very well. Be here at ten."

"You may rest assured," Ham Delbacher said with equal coldness. (Today the chief of staff was dancing nervously around him, fawning obsequiously on his every word, but it had been different three months ago. And, the new President promised himself grimly now, it would be different tomorrow morning when he reorganized the staff. That, too, was how they did it in his country. The chief of staff would be perfectly safe in his person, but he wouldn't work at 1600 Pennsylvania Avenue any more.)

On the morning of the Vice President's heart-to-heart talk with his predecessor, however, the chief of staff had sent his third assistant secretary to take him in to see the President. The young lady had been very embarrassed but Hamilton Delbacher had put her at ease at once in his fatherly way. They had enjoyed a pleasant little chat, in fact, on their way to the Oval Office—so much so that she had returned to announce defiantly to her boss, "I don't think he's bad at all! I think he's nice!"

"He's the pits," the chief of staff had snapped, "and we're going to get him off that ticket if it's the last thing we do."

That had not, however, been the impression conveyed by the President, whom Hamilton Delbacher had decided quite some time ago to be a tricky and deceitful individual very far from his public image of moral uprightness, harried decency and honor. On this occasion he had been all welcoming smiles and sincere greetings.

"Ham!" he exclaimed, rising from his chair, hand extended with the greatest cordiality. "How nice of you to want to come by for a talk! I've been meaning to call you for the past month, but you know how things pile up."

"Oh well," the Vice President said. "At least we see each other every Monday at the National Security Council meeting."

"Yes," the President agreed, cordiality a trifle diminished. "That's one of the things I've been wanting to talk to you about, one-on-one."

"A silly phrase," Ham Delbacher observed, quite startling his host. "I prefer 'man-to-man,' myself."

"So do I," the President said hastily. "So do I. Sit down, Ham, and tell me what's on *your* mind, first. Then we'll talk about the issues you raise in the National Security Council with such regularity."

"And you probably prefer '*monotonous* regularity' for that one," the Vice President observed with a smile which for him was unusually wry, as he eased his ample bulk into the chair across the desk. "What I want to know first of all, is: am I or am I not going to be on the ticket with you next year? And secondly, will my monotonously regular views in the NSC have anything to do with your decision?"

"Well," the President said. "Well, Ham. You sound as though I've already made my decision."

"Haven't you?" the Vice President inquired with a calmness he did not altogether feel. It was, after all, a job with some influence and with a great potential for advancement, given the right, unfortunate circumstance.

"Certainly not," the President said promptly. "It's much too early for that."

"That's not what I read in Jack Anderson's column, the New York *Times,* the Washington *Post,* the Washington *Inquirer,* the L.A. *Times*—"

"Oh, now, Ham!" the President interrupted with an uplifted hand and a just-between-us smile. "You know how the media rattle on. Nothing gives them more pleasure than a good rumor, especially if they're the ones who started it."

"You didn't?"

"No, no, no. Why should I?"

"And your staff didn't?"

"Not if I know anything about it," the President assured him stoutly. Ham Delbacher looked unimpressed.

"Somebody did," he pointed out. "And it sure as hell wasn't me."

"You *mustn't* let it bother you," the President told him earnestly. "It's all fluff. So much of Washington reporting is, as we've both found out. Don't let 'em get you down, Ham! It isn't like you to panic."

"I'm not panicking," Hamilton Delbacher said. "But I do want to know where I stand. I take it I *will* be your running-mate again next year, then?"

"Well," the President said. "Well, now, Ham. It *is* much too early for that, isn't it?"

"Hmph," the Vice President said. "I thought so."

"No, no!" the President protested. His expression became thoughtful. "Not, that is, if you can moderate your views sufficiently so that you can't be portrayed as being absolutely and adamantly opposed to mine. It's good to have a contrast on the ticket, it helps strengthen it. That way, some people can feel that if I drop dead, you'll give them what they want. So they can vote for me with a clear conscience. Some degree of disagreement is fine with me. But I don't like it when it becomes a public issue."

The Vice President looked surprised.

"Has it? Not from me."

"And not from me," the President replied. A cold little glint came into his eyes. "Unless you're telling me I'm a liar when I say that."

"I'm not telling you you're anything other than what you know you are," Ham Delbacher said calmly, and was pleased to note that this shot had truly gone home. For a moment the President looked genuinely angry. Then the characteristic determined look of universal forgiveness and brotherhood took over again. He actually laughed.

"Hamilton Delbacher," he said, "you're a character. And one I respect, I want you to know. I do just wish, however, that you weren't so bitterly opposed to what I'm doing with the Soviets."

"It's what the Soviets are doing with us that gives me the creeps," the Vice President said. "If anything, in my estimation, you aren't doing enough in return."

"Yes, I know you feel that way."

"So do the Secretary of State, the Secretary of Defense, the Joint Chiefs and about six other Cabinet members," Ham Delbacher pointed out. "You have something of a split Cabinet at the moment. As you know."

"I do know," the President said, "and I take all that into consideration.

But these aren't easy times. Opinions differ, approaches differ. Arguments can be made with equal validity on either side—"

"Oh, I don't think so," the Vice President interrupted. "I really don't think so. It seems to me the preponderant evidence is on the side of those who feel the Soviet build-up and actions go far beyond any legitimate defense needs of theirs. It seems to me increasingly obvious that they are out-and-out aggressors in the worst of the old imperial style, and that they are pushing us right back to the wall everywhere around the globe. Somehow you don't seem to see that. Your view baffles a lot of us, I think."

"But a lot support it," the President remarked, unperturbed. "And only one out of all our millions bears final responsibility, and that's me. I believe I'm doing the right thing. My predecessors and their Congresses in recent years haven't left me all that many cards to play with, after all. Our military power is far from what it has been. I've got to deal from diplomacy where I can't deal from strength. Isn't that a fair assessment?"

"True enough," the Vice President agreed. "But you can *act as though* you commanded the strength—and indeed, we still have a great deal, you know, far more than you act like. You don't have to *act* weak. Half the battle is in acting strong, and in calmly and firmly doing what you know is right, regardless of their threats and blusters. You shouldn't let them get away with all these subversions and defiances everywhere around the world. You ought to call them on it."

"I try," the President said. "And they simply defy me and stay where they are."

"Because they feel you won't do anything with the power you still have," Hamilton Delbacher said. "Because they feel you're weak."

"And what would you do?" the President flared. "Have an out and out confrontation? Create big dramatic crises? Bomb the hell out of them? Start World War III? You and some of my other critics are awfully free with advice, it seems to me, but you in particular wouldn't find it all that easy to simplify the situation if you were sitting where I am. . . . Furthermore," he said, more calmly, "I happen to believe that what I am doing *is* right. I happen to believe that the Soviet Union is as dedicated to peace as I am. I believe they *want* to get along with us. I believe they want to make détente work, and have genuine disarmament, and cooperate with us to build a genuinely peaceful world. I take them at their word."

"Well," said Hamilton Delbacher, who may not have read all the documents but relied, like millions of his countrymen, on gut instinct, observation and common sense, "I don't. And I'm sorry, Mr. President, but I'm afraid I consider you very naïve—dangerously so—in this regard. I think we're in the last minute of the last hour, and I think that unless we can reverse the trend very sharply and drastically within, say, the next year, it is all going to be quite academic. They will have won, and the world will be on its way, without recourse or recovery, to universal domination by the Soviet Union."

"Bugaboos!" the President said scornfully. "Bugaboos! If you feel that way, maybe you should make my decision for me about the ticket next year. Maybe you should just withdraw."

"Oh, I don't think so," Ham Delbacher said. "I think I'll force you to drop me, if you want to. Then at least my leaving will have some significance. At least it will dramatize the two points of view and bring about a real public debate about them. Because I wouldn't go quietly, I promise you that. The country will hear a lot about it, if you kick me out."

"Are you threatening me?" the President demanded, genuinely angry this time, more so than the Vice President had ever seen him. "Because if you are, you'll be in a hell of a fight, and you'll know it."

"Why don't you get as upset about the Soviets as you do about your own political future?" the Vice President inquired, heaving his substantial bulk out of the chair. "Then maybe we'd be able to retrieve a few things in this world."

"You won't be on the ticket," the President said coldly. "I promise you that. You really are a war-monger, and I'd no more take you for running-mate again than I'd take Yuri Serapin."

"You're a lot more friendly to him and his point of view than you are to me and mine, that's for sure," the Vice President retorted, heading for the door. He stopped and turned back. "From now on," he added with a coldness equalling the President's own, "I shall say what I please when I please. And it won't be too friendly to you or to your precious Yuri, either."

"You'll be destroyed politically," the President said in a vengeful tone very far from his public image. "You'll be all washed up."

"Who gives a damn?" Hamilton Delbacher inquired. "At the rate we're going, down the road you're taking us, we're all going to be washed up in very short order anyway."

"War-monger," the President said, turning to the papers on his desk, hands trembling with anger. "Damnable war-monger! That's all you are. Thank God you won't have the chance to sit in this chair."

But that was where the President, of course, had been wrong; that was where the Lord—and Hamilton Delbacher could only regard it as divine providence at work—had intervened. In a strange way, somewhere deep in his being, when Chauncey Baron telephoned him three days ago at his son-in-law's home on the Eastern Shore and interrupted the family Fourth of July weekend to tell him the news, he had been completely unsurprised. He had known all along that it would happen this way. There

had been some instinct, hunch, premonition, what have you, that had told
him so. There *must* be one last chance for his view to prevail, before the
Republic went irrevocably down. There simply had to be.

And now it had come; and his confidence that he could handle it was
no stronger, and his course no clearer or more certain, than his predecessor's had been.

He wished now, as he had many times in his life and political career,
that he did have some absolute certainties to rely upon: some basic tenets
of faith about the world and America's place in it, that would permit him
to act with the absolute certainty the times seemed to require. He supposed his new opposite number in Moscow must have some; weren't they
trained for it from birth?

He recognized that this put him at considerable disadvantage: he would
just have to do the best he could, in his bumbling, stumbling, unideologi-
cal American way; and from a relatively peaceable and unaggressive
background, too.

He suspected, rather more than Yuri Serapin gave him credit for, what
Yuri Serapin was like, and the sort of background *he* came from. Enough
was known in the West—by those who would accept, not frantically
deny, the facts—about the dark and bloody corridors that led to supreme
Soviet power, so that the new President of the United States did not have
very many illusions about the new President of the Soviet Union. If it had
to come down to a contest between their two personalities—as, in the last
essentials, it always did when there was any sort of confrontation between
Washington and Moscow—then Hamilton Delbacher felt that in some
ways he labored under considerable handicap. He was not cold-blooded,
he was not ruthless, he was not devious, he was not dishonest, he was not
a liar, a murderer or a brute. He was a relatively civilized human being,
product of a relatively civilized society, not an automaton whose every
belief, reaction and move was dictated and conditioned by the party ideology.

He possessed the flexibilities of freedom; and, he recognized with a sudden little sigh as he surveyed the reports and papers that covered the desk
which was now his life, the weakening and open-minded fairness of the
best of freedom, too. His state religion did not tell him automatically how
he must react in every situation, for there was no state religion; nor did
his education and upbringing train him to respond automatically to every
stimulus without analyzing or trying to understand it. He was a man, not
a machine; and a typical American man, at that, which used to be
sufficient for the office he now held, but perhaps no longer was.

He had come into the world ten years before his antagonist, number
five in a family of nine children. His father had been a well-to-do dairy
farmer owning some eight hundred acres of beautiful land near York,
Pennsylvania, a patrimony built up gradually and thriftily by preceding

generations going back to Johannes Delbacher, who had settled there after the Revolution in 1783. The Delbachers had been good stock ever since; and now, today, when the family corporation, Delbacher Farms, owned almost three times as many acres as Hamilton's father had owned, they were good stock still. His two sisters and two of his brothers were still living; there were twenty-one children in the next generation; the farms did consistently well every year; and at the annual family reunion, held each Labor Day weekend, a review of the corporation business, delivered by his elder brother to an attentive audience of healthy, rosy-cheeked, well-pleased Delbachers, produced among them all a feeling of satisfaction and well-being that was rare in the troubled times their country was passing through.

Hamilton had never forgotten being seated one night at a banquet when he was Governor of Pennsylvania, just before his successful campaign for the Senate, next to the plump, beautifully dressed and beautifully bejeweled wife of the county chairman.

"I think," she told him with great satisfaction, "that we have all the best of what makes life worth living, right here in York County. I don't have any desire to go anywhere else." Ham, who had a desire to go to Washington, and did, nevertheless had to agree with her that the land of his patrimony was indeed unusually blessed in almost all things. It gave him a solid anchor from which to pursue the career that had brought him finally to the high and uneasy eminence he now occupied.

There was a long trail to cover before that, however; and its formative stages were all in York County. As the son of Joe (Johannes IV) Delbacher, he had a recognized place in the social hierarchy, and found that he had little trouble filling it. Four brothers were ahead of him, two brothers and two sisters followed; the way was well paved by the time he entered school and began to follow the family route that presumably would bring some of them back to help run the family operation. It was not until he entered high school that he realized that, much as he loved the farm, there was no real place in it for him; and realized also that he did not want it anyway, because he wanted to be a lawyer instead.

He broached the subject to his father with considerable apprehension; but Joe Delbacher was not in the least upset.

"That's great," he said, "as long as you realize one thing."

"What's that?" Ham asked, afraid that it might be a threat of some permanent break with the family.

"I'm sick and tired of paying out good money to an outside lawyer," his father said with a chuckle. "I don't care how many other clients you take on, just remember that your first and most important one is Delbacher Farms."

"Oh, I will, Dad," he promised fervently, quite overcome. "You bet I sure will!"

"Good," his father said, running a fond hand over Ham's tousled blond head. "Now, where do you want to go, University of Pennsylvania?"

"I think maybe," Ham said hesitantly, "if it's all right—I'd like to go to Harvard. And then maybe a year or two at Georgetown, in Wasington."

"Want to be a politician, eh?" his father said with a shrewdness that abruptly crystallized an ambition Ham hadn't even known he had. "Well, why not?"

"I don't think so," he said. "At least—I haven't thought about it."

"Sure you have," Joe Delbacher said comfortably. "Consciously or unconsciously. And why not? There was a Delbacher in the state legislature a couple of generations back—probably got hung, for all I know. No reason why you shouldn't follow in his footsteps—at least as far as the foot of the scaffold. I wouldn't want you going any further. In the meantime—Congressman Delbacher—Governor Delbacher—Senator Delbacher—*President* Delbacher? Why not?"

"You're making fun of me," Ham protested happily.

"Not entirely," his father said. "Not entirely. Stranger things have happened. Although maybe not to Delbachers."

But the old man—and now he was an old man, ninety-two but still as shrewd and sharp as ever—had lived to see it all, and had stood, tired and trembling with age but straight and upright as a ramrod, alongside Elinor two days ago at the hastily organized swearing-in in the East Room.

"Didn't get hung after all, did you?" he had murmured when Ham bent down to kiss him. "But watch it from now on. The odds have gone up about a millionfold."

"Yes," Ham had whispered back, eyes for a second grim. "I know damned well they have, Dad."

And he did know this; particularly when he began to truly understand the legacy left him by his predecessor.

Before that time of understanding, however, there had been a career typical of many that culminate in Washington.

There had been the early school years during which Ham was just one more of what their teachers referred to as "the interminable Delbachers," all blond, all bright-eyed, all intelligent, all rambunctious with a tendency at times to be downright unruly. Then had come high school, in which he was again preceded and followed by assorted siblings, so that it often seemed that they had never left the farm in the mornings, school was just an extension of their close-knit family life. This aroused some hostility and resentment from other less numerous family aggregations, but it did give them a substantial advantage in school activities and particularly in the class elections into which Ham plunged with increasing frequency. "Ham's going to be President someday," his brothers and sisters would announce proudly to their jeering classmates. "President of the class, maybe," the classmates would concede, "but that's *all*." "I'll settle for that," he always responded cheerfully, and in his sophomore, junior and senior years, aided by the diligent campaigning of his family, won every race he entered.

At Harvard, shorn of his family base and on his own, he did not do so well. By then, however, he had acquired the habit of campaigning, along with a real zest for politics, and before he left the university in his junior year to enlist for the closing months of World War II, he had pretty well determined that when he came home again he would actively pursue a political career.

He did come home again, safely enough, after service in the Battle of the Bulge and a two-year stint in the occupation forces in Germany. He returned to Harvard, finished his schooling, got his law degree in the upper third of his class and went on to Washington for two years—not to Georgetown, which no longer seemed necessary, but to the office of Pennsylvania's senior senator. There he spent two years of ever-growing fascination with the workings of Capitol Hill. His principal job was handling constituents' requests; every moment he had off from this he spent in the Chamber or at committee hearings, absorbing the routine and the business of the Hill. He also did something no one was aware of: he carefully noted the name and address of every constituent who wrote or telephoned. At the end of two years he had a basic file of some five thousand names, many of them in his own Congressional district. By then he had also met Elinor Seely, a cheerfully businesslike young lady from New London, Connecticut, who was working as a clerk in the office of her own senator.

He decided it was time to conclude temporarily his Washington experience and head back to York County. He suddenly realized that this could not be done without Elinor; and was delighted and overwhelmed to find that she had already reached the same conclusion. They were married at the farm two weeks after leaving Washington. He joined a law firm headed by an old friend of his father's, in the state capital, Harrisburg; and settled in for what he planned to be about five years of routine law work preparatory to returning to York County and entering politics.

True to his word, his father brought him the family business. His other duties revolved principally, as they had in Washington, around constituents' business with the legislature. He acquired further experience in the way in which his country's government works. It was not a very efficient system: no one was murdered to impress him with its virtues, nor was he called upon to murder anyone to achieve his ambitions. He emerged with a lifelong devotion to the often inept but basically goodhearted and well-meaning ways of democracy. He realized now that this had probably not equipped him very well to deal with Yuri Serapin, but he did not regret it. That was how it was: he would have to make do with what he had.

A year before his planned entry into politics the local Congressman was indicted for misappropriation of campaign funds and announced his unexpectedly early retirement. Ham convened a hasty family council. Elinor's approving vote was joined unanimously by his parents and all but two of his brothers and sisters; he felt confirmed and supported in what he fully intended to do anyway. He announced his candidacy, conducted a whirlwind campaign against six other contenders, emerged with his party's nomination, swept on to win election comfortably in November. Back he and Elinor went to Washington, accompanied this time by Hamilton, Jr., three, and Elinor Beth, one. He was given assignments on the House Judiciary and Armed Services Committees and settled in for what he again foresaw as a relatively lengthy time, perhaps twelve years, before he moved on to the next stage of what he had now decided would be a lifelong political career.

He was an attractive and confident figure, who appealed to the media; and very soon, to the annoyance of some of his older colleagues in the state's delegation to Congress, Ham Delbacher's name began to appear in almost every story of any concern to Pennsylvania. He did not deliberately seek this but he certainly made the most of it when he realized it was coming his way. He was a handsome man, six feet three, blond, blue-eyed, a steady set to his open and candid glance, an even steadier set to his chin, which had a way of lifting with a sudden sharp challenge when he found himself confronted with something he didn't like. But although he soon acquired a reputation as one who could not be pushed around or diverted from the course he believed to be right, he was never considered abrasive or cantankerous. He had too much easygoing natural charm, which had also been run through the mill of eight brothers and sisters. Large families seldom create prima donnas, though they sometimes hone natural leaders. His had done this for him and for it he would always be grateful.

A little sooner than he had anticipated he was given the chance to use his abilities on a broader scale.

The state party organization, faced with a tough contest for the governorship against a popular incumbent, turned in some desperation to Ham and asked him to run. The persuasion was not easy: he was just beginning to get well entrenched in the House, his ambitions centered increasingly upon Washington. He really had no desire or interest in returning to Harrisburg and there was no certainty he would win. The thing that finally decided him was not the arguments of party leaders but his own pragmatic reasoning that if he should ever want to try for the Presidency it might be a good thing to have administrative experience to point to. With considerable reluctance he finally agreed; ran; won by the skin of his teeth; spent four years in Harrisburg where he succeeded in reforming a good many antiquated procedures and came close to balancing the state budget; and thought constantly of how he might return to Washington. As it turned out, it was easier than he thought.

The state's senior senator, the same for whom he had worked as a clerk when he first came to Washington, reached eighty and decided, as had many of his constituents already, that it was time for him to retire. Two weeks before he announced his decision he invited Ham to come down to the Senate for lunch and told him about it.

"I'm not urging you," he said with a smile, "I'm just telling you. A word to the wise, et cetera."

"I'm not ready for the Senate," Ham objected, secretly delighted. His mentor saw through that.

"Nonsense," he said. "Don't give me this shy modesty crap. You're as qualified as anybody in Pennsylvania. More so. You want it, don't you?"

"Sure I want it," Ham admitted with a grin. "Who wouldn't?"

"Then go after it," the Senator said. "It'll meet you halfway. Maybe more."

And so it had. The campaign had been long and strenuous—two of his fellow Congressmen ran against him for the nomination, and his opponent in the final election was a former governor—but when it was over, Hamilton Delbacher was the new junior Senator from Pennsylvania. It had not been quite as easy as the old Senator had prophesied, but looking back Ham could see that there had never really been much doubt about the outcome.

Nor had there ever been much doubt that he would be a diligent and outstanding Senator. He was assigned to the Appropriations and Foreign Relations committees, where he was among those who watched with growing and vocal dismay as Soviet power spread steadily around the globe. He made many speeches, uttered many protests; as was customary in those days, his fears and those of the colleagues who agreed with him were greeted with scorn by the media and rejection by the White House. It was not until the closing years of his Senate career that it suddenly became fashionable to be frightened of the Soviets, and by then it was very, very late in the day. They were entrenched around the globe while America's power, despite the desperately wishful boasts of its Presidents that the country was "still the strongest nation in the world," had in reality dwindled to a weak and in many important ways ineffectual shadow of its former strength.

The result, as everyone in Washington was aware, became a general conspiracy of pretense that this was not the case. "The strongest nation in the world" remained so on paper and in the speeches of its Chief Executives and their Cabinet members, but the Soviets, unchallenged, daily roamed further across the seas and penetrated ever deeper into the continents. Flash-points occurred here and there, such as the Soviet brigade in Cuba, followed by Afghanistan: the United States President always backed away from anything that might lead to force, so no one needed to worry that anything unpleasant would occur. It was almost too late for that anyway. In the Kremlin, Yuri Serapin and his colleagues became ever more confident. In Washington, those who thought they saw the end of freedom and the death of the mind coming ever closer became more and more concerned. Their argument was essentially a call for prevention, which became steadily less possible as Soviet strength increased.

"There have been a dozen occasions in recent years," Ham said in one of his many Senate speeches on the subject, "in which the United States, with only a small show of force and a clear and emphatic show of will, could have turned back the Soviet advance with very little risk of war. Many times our Presidents have let the moment pass. They have equivocated, they have evaded—God help us, *they* have rationalized and excused the Soviets. So the Soviets have gone right ahead. Why shouldn't they, Senators? We have virtually invited them to. Each time we have done so, the next time it has been harder to stop them. And we have not stopped them. And now we have become so weak in relation to them that we may not be able to stop them. Our ability is going but our will, it seems to me, has already gone. And they know it."

This had provoked a sharp and angry debate, in which loyal Administration supporters such as James Monroe Madison of California and Majority Leader Art Hampton had argued heatedly that the United States was still far stronger than he portrayed it. His rebuttal, in which he had been joined by equally vehement colleagues such as Jim Elrod of North Carolina and Janet Hardesty of Michigan, had been to reiterate that the United States might still have some strength but it no longer had the will to use even what it had; and that the will was what counted.

How he had emerged, considering his reputation in the media as a hard-liner, as Vice Presidential nominee on the winning ticket three years ago he could never quite understand; except that there was a very real division within the party on the issue of foreign policy.

The candidate who was finally chosen to succeed the incumbent had advocated a tougher line himself; he probably could not have won the nomination without it. But, as he explained to Ham when he called him to his campaign headquarters at three in the morning and asked him to be his running-mate, he could not afford to go too far or he would lose much important support in the media and among the liberals. It would be up to Ham to do exactly what the President had described in their last, heated exchange a week ago: wave the flag, shake the big stick, provide a tough alternative many worried voters could look to as a balance to the President's own milder policies.

Neither Ham nor anyone else had imagined how much milder they would be.

In the opening weeks of his term, during the Senate fight over Jim

Elrod's $10 billion emergency defense bill, the President had given some indication he wished to be a tough, cold-blooded bargainer with the Soviets, a position the new Vice President thoroughly approved. But in the actual event he had proved to be as weak and naïvely obliging, as humble and subservient toward the Soviets, as "that other little fellow," as Jim Elrod called him with consistent contempt, never dignifying him by name. From the Kremlin point of view—and in fairness it had to be said, from the point of view of much of the major media and a small but highly vocal segment of the American electorate—he was an ideal President. "I wish he would be *firm*," Ham Delbacher had confided to Jim Elrod at the time the Soviets openly assigned six atomic submarines to duty out of Cienfuegos and the President had responded by ordering ten more helicopters to Guantánamo.

"He isn't firm," Jim Elrod said with a snort. *"They* know that. Why do so many here keep pretending that he is?"

More and more openly in recent National Security Council meetings the Vice President had begun to voice his misgivings. With caution but also with increasing candor, the Secretary of State, the Secretary of Defense, the Joint Chiefs, had begun to echo concurrence. The President's National Security Adviser, that anomalous figure whose position in recent Administrations had grown into one of virtual dominance over the entire Cabinet, sided with the President. They were a well-matched pair, the Vice President thought with a frustrated annoyance: they could be counted upon to rationalize, turn away from, apologize for, and accept anything the Soviets did. It sometimes seemed, he confided privately to the Secretary of State, that more time and attention were devoted by the White House to soothing the American people than were ever devoted to thwarting the Soviet Union. (The National Security Adviser, too, was being replaced.)

"I'm beginning to wonder," Chauncey Baron had said darkly only a couple of months ago, "whether they *want* to thwart the Soviet Union. If the thought weren't unthinkable, I'd begin to believe they were dedicated to helping the Soviet Union achieve every anti-American goal it has."

"Certainly it must seem so in Moscow," Ham Delbacher agreed glumly. "Certainly it seems to be the end result, every time there's the slightest hint of crisis."

But these were thoughts they kept to themselves, knowing there was in the President and his adviser no treason, only, as the Vice President and the Secretary saw it, an incomprehension approaching idiocy and a lack of will approaching cowardice. And there was no way, aside from their increasingly outspoken remarks in the National Security Council, to change the trend—although in recent weeks the Vice President on two public occasions had indicated sufficient concern so that his remarks were widely interpreted as an open challenge to the President. The upshot of that had been their angry interview just before the President's death. Now the Lord had given him the final word in their argument, and with it the commanding power. And what did he intend to do with it?

Chauncey and Jim Elrod had no hesitation or uncertainty in their advice. "Be strong," Chauncey had concluded the telephone call giving him the news of his accession. "Stand firm," Jim Elrod had urged in an encouraging conversation an hour later. Many others in the last two days had been equally supportive. But then, again, a number had not. That number included some of the strongest voices in the Congress and the country. Their cautionary comments indicated a deep-seated nervousness that he might plunge the world into war tomorrow morning. The only way he could do that, as he saw it, was to say no to the Soviets, who might then fight to achieve what they sought. Ergo, he was about where he had been, faced with the argument that to keep the peace he must surrender without a struggle what he believed to be the fundamental interests and necessities of freedom.

This did not strike him as the purpose for which he had been given the unexpected opportunity to be President of the United States. There must be a better way.

As to what it might be, everybody had an opinion. A great confusion of voices rose in the land.

"We would hate to think," said the Washington *Post,* "that just because a mysterious Providence has suddenly thrust Hamilton Delbacher into the office of President of the United States, the Lord has thereby given blanket endorsement to Mr. Delbacher's bloodthirsty ideas about the Soviet Union. Caution—caution—and more caution, is what we would suggest to the new President. Ham Delbacher has always been something of a saber rattler, but now his responsibilities are so great that neither he nor the country can afford the luxury. His sole aim, like that of his predecessor, must be peace. In the pursuit of it we urge upon him most earnestly something of that same tolerance, broad-mindedness, patience and understanding with which the late President approached the difficult task of dealing with the Soviet Union.

"It can be done, even by Hamilton Delbacher. Not only can, but must."

"It would be easy for the new President," the New York *Times* agreed, "to change course sharply and embark upon a more hostile and arbitrary approach to the Communists. To do so would, in our estimation, be fatal —perhaps literally fatal for the United States. The accession of Yuri Serapin in Moscow, coinciding as it does with the accession of Hamilton Delbacher in Washington, provides an opportunity that may not come again. It is an opportunity for a new beginning: a new beginning of peace.

"The new President was discreetly but clearly critical of the old for what Mr. Delbacher obviously felt was a too pliant and too yielding approach to Moscow's advances around the world. There is no doubt those advances exist in many areas, and that if a sinister purpose is attributed to them, they can be made to appear ominous indeed. Yet perhaps the purpose is not sinister—perhaps to this day the leaders of the Soviet Union feel uneasily that they are still being 'surrounded' and 'threatened' by the West. It should be President Delbacher's charge to ascertain whether this is truly the Russian attitude and, if it is, how it can best be eradicated. We feel a show of consistent good faith and willingness to negotiate in all things is the best and surest way to do this. We hope the new President agrees."

"The mood in this capital," Walter Dobius wrote with customary solemn pomposity in his column, "is divided between personal liking for Hamilton Delbacher and serious doubts as to his policies now that he has succeeded to office. Washington has watched Ham Delbacher develop over the years from a tall young giant from Pennsylvania, well meaning and idealistic, into the portly, paternal Grover Cleveland-like figure of his later years, outwardly amiable and easygoing but at heart a determined and unyielding hard-liner where the Soviet Union is concerned.

"Such policies now, we suggest, become him neither as man nor as President. If he is to lead us safely in a world that in many areas seems dominated by an excessive Soviet military and political presence, then he must exercise a restraint and vision he has not so far conspicuously shown. The nation must pray that he will find in his heart the strength to show such restraint and forebearance. We cannot afford tough-guy diplomacy now. The stakes are too high and the game too risky."

"Hamilton Delbacher," Anna Hastings wrote in a front-page editorial in the Washington *Inquirer,* "now has the greatest opportunity of his life to become the statesman he has always somehow just missed being in all his long years of public service. He is confronted, as are we all, by a Soviet Union pressing aggressively outward almost everywhere around the world. To understand that drive, to sympathize with the deep-seated psychological fears that cause it, yet to successfully contain its harsher expansionist aspects and keep them within the bounds of a safe and stable world community, is a task to challenge the greatest minds in America. The new President may not be one of them, but he is at least a decent and basically tolerant individual, equipped with a firm character and a deep devotion to his country. Now all he needs is restraint and caution. This is no time for aggressive adventures. We must pray he will refrain from an ill-advised machismo that could only make a serious situation desperate."

The sum total of all this, as he remarked to Chauncey Baron, was that *he* must exercise restraint, *he* must show caution, *he* must not do anything decisive or forceful.

"Why in the hell," he demanded with some exasperation, "doesn't anybody ever suggest that the *communists* exercise restraint, that the *communists* exercise caution, that the *communists* pull back and stop endangering world peace? Why is it always America who gets lectured, even by her own people? Why don't they ever lecture the other side?"

"It may be," Chauncey suggested, "that they can get at America where they know they'll be ignored by Moscow. The implications of this always escape them. America might respond: they know they can't influence the communists. Plus the fact that some of them, of course, would not be entirely averse to seeing the communists win. Not that this applies to the ones you mention, but here and there such do exist."

"Too many for my taste," the new President said tartly. "And I don't relish being lectured by Walter and Anna and the rest of them, either, even if their motives are pure as the driven snow. I'd like a few suggested solutions, not more home-grown Sermons on the Mount from the Washington press corps."

"Get used to it," Chauncey advised. "This is only the beginning."

This he knew, aggravated though it made him. He had lived with what he sometimes could not avoid considering that smug, self-righteous crew all his public life. This was not the first time they had told him what to do. Or the first time he might ignore it, either . . . except, essentially, that their advice now was sound. He must exercise caution. He must proceed slowly. He must not be rash or impulsive or hasty, too emphatic or too dogmatic or too antagonistic in stating America's views and seeking to strengthen America's position.

Because, quite frankly, he no longer commanded the power his predecessors had commanded. One by one, each in his time in the decades since the end of World War II, most had whittled, reduced, yielded, given, thrown it away, sometimes voluntarily, sometimes egged on by the press, sometimes forced by a Congress that on occasion seemed as hell-bent as the Soviets on reducing America to a minor has-been. He was the inheritor of all those misjudgments, springing from misapprehension, misunderstanding, fear, naïveté, lack of historical perception, lack of will.

No one had to advise him to proceed with caution, he thought grimly. He wasn't capable of doing anything else.

Yet now as he sat in the Oval Office, newly a President but already feeling that he had been there for years, so heavy were the problems that confronted him everywhere, he decided that he perhaps was not so badly off, at that. He might not have Yuri Serapin's automatic ingrained reflexes to assist him—the rigid dialectical approach to events, the conviction of history's inevitability and communism's inevitable triumph. But he did have things that to him were equally valid and, he felt, equally strengthening.

He had a lifetime's knowledge of the workings of democracy; a lifetime of knowing what it meant to live a free man; a lifetime of the American experience, which—for all its weaknesses, which were many—also possessed great strengths unknown to the dictators and peoples of the communist world. At least in his land people were allowed to be human; and while this reduced efficiency and absolute dedication to a cause by probably one-half, it also gave them a great stake in remaining free.

It was up to him to rally them to this if it were still possible. It would require great toughness and great sacrifice from a nation that in recent decades had not been notable for either. It would require a rededication to freedom and a determination to save it that would run head-on into the hedonistic desire of millions of his countrymen to go unconcerned and unbothered to whatever fate the Soviets, if left unchecked, might have in mind for them.

He had been warning for years, always evoking skepticism and scorn from America's major opinion-makers, what that fate might be. Now at last he had the chance to help prevent it, if it could still be prevented. The fact was not frightening, exactly, because beneath his fatherly aspects Hamilton Delbacher was, as the then Speaker of the House had remarked many years ago, one tough cookie; but it gave a man grounds for pause, there was no doubt of that. It also gave him grounds to be challenged, excited, inspired—almost, one might say, exhilarated.

"I intend to be strong," he announced aloud to the empty office, looking Abraham Lincoln, whose portrait happened to be hanging across the room, squarely in the eye. "I *will* be strong."

But it was not Abe who gave him answer. It was Chauncey Baron who hurried in, hardly waiting to be announced, with the latest news from Moscow.

It was as though *they* had heard him and wanted to find out things for themselves.

Well, so be it.

So did he.

Around the anxious globe the news was already flashing:

SERAPIN ASKS DELBACHER FOR IMMEDIATE SUMMIT TO DISCUSS "URGENT MUTUAL PROBLEMS." NEW PRESIDENT SEEN LIKELY TO ACCEPT.

And half an hour later:

DELBACHER "CORDIALLY WELCOMES" SUMMIT. LEADERS TO MEET AT UN ONE WEEK FROM TODAY.

4

"Recently, several generals, and even responsible government figures in the U.S.A., very thoughtlessly and imprudently extolled the military might of the U.S.A. However, the real state of affairs is such that our superiority in the latest kinds of military equipment has become a reality."

—*Methodological Problems of Military Theory and Practice,*
Colonel V. M. Bondarenko

And now, the new President of the Soviet Union thought as he worked late into the night reading and rereading the massive file the KGB had sent him on the new President of the United States, he had him. This man Delbacher would come to New York as his predecessors had come to other summits, full of boastfulness, no doubt, but holding in his hands no real superiority; and this time the leader of the communist world would set him in order. He would not do it as bluntly as he would like to do—the initial stages of the final confrontation should still be conducted, Yuri Serapin thought, with the necessary degree of deception to guarantee the success of the decisive strike—but the message would be clear. If the apparently rather limited individual who now occupied the White House knew what was best for himself and his country, he wouldn't press it. Instead he would accept deliberate Soviet duplicity at face value and be further confused. An innocuous communiqué would be issued, nothing would be changed. History would roll inexorably on.

Even so, there was much to do to prepare for this; and in Moscow, as in Washington, the intervening week was full of studies, reports, official comings and goings, the selection of members of the delegation, the preparation of public opinion. *Pravda, Izvestia,* state radio and television, local party organs throughout the country, were all ordered to present the same item, which appeared in *Pravda* on Page 3 at the bottom, almost lost alongside a review of agricultural production:

"The new President of the U.S., H. Delbacher, has agreed to come to New York in answer to the request of President of the U.S.S.R. and Chairman of the Council of Ministers, Y. P. Serapin. They will discuss changes in United States policy to further accommodate the peace-loving desires of Y. P. Serapin and the peoples of the socialist coalition whom he leads."

Other than that, news of the event did not appear directly in the Soviet Union, though several full-page articles did appear stressing the military might of the communist world and the state of readiness of the Soviet Union in particular. Two articles received special prominence: "Peace Principles of V. I. Lenin" and "Interview with Y. P. Serapin."

The latter contained statements of such emphatic challenge to the United States that the American Ambassador in Moscow took his career in his hands and cabled the President direct: "Must advise extreme caution summit. Serapin views published here today strongly anti-U.S. despite quote peace-loving unquote gloss. Would suggest consideration military alert duration summit."

This caused great consternation and controversy in the State Department and among the National Security Council staff when it was decoded and laid before them. It was not leaked to the media, which Ham Delbacher considered something of a miracle; and after giving it twenty-four hours' thought he did not sack the Ambassador, as one faction at State wanted him to do, nor did he do anything about a military alert, as the Joint Chiefs of Staff wanted him to do. Instead he decided to proceed, quietly and in order, to get everything ready for the summit, conducting himself publicly as though he fully believed in the good faith and integrity of those he would face there. However, he sent to Yuri Serapin, through the Ambassador, a private message he hoped might have some effect:

"Dear Mr. President:

"I understand that you have given an interview to your newspapers in which you are quite openly critical of the United States. This can only affect adversely the mood of your people on the eve of our meeting.

"I consider it unfortunate that you have chosen this particular time to express yourself in this fashion concerning my country, and I hope sincerely that your statements were not accurately quoted and do not accurately reflect your basic and continuing views. I am coming to New York with some genuine hope that we may be able to settle, or at least ease, some of the major tensions between our two governments. I think it would be helpful if you did the same.

"I look forward to our meeting as an opportunity for real, constructive progress toward peace. I am confident you do likewise.

"Cordially,
"Hamilton Delbacher"

Which, he suspected would have about as much effect as a cube of ice on a hot stove; but he had his own record to make and did not regret it even when he was subsequently informed by the Ambassador that Serapin had received the message without change of expression, comment or response.

"I feel a little like I did as a kid when I had to chop wood on the farm," he confided to the only individual he told about this, his wife. "I've just got to hitch my pants a little tighter and hit a little harder. If he wants to play tough, I'll have to match him. It's not the way I'd like to do it, but I may not have a choice."

"You may not," Elinor agreed, her dark intelligent eyes troubled. "Do you think you should make some statement here to prepare people for the possibility that nothing much may come of this?"

"Maybe I will," he said with equal thoughtfulness. "It might not be such a bad idea."

But when he did so quite mildly—saying, through the press secretary, that, "While the President sincerely hopes much can be accomplished at the meeting with President Serapin, he realizes that the obstacles to quick solutions are many"—the reaction across the country and around the world was upset and severe.

His countrymen, in particular, preferred hope, no matter what the evidence to the contrary might be.

"Senators," Mark Coffin said that afternoon to a silent and attentive chamber, "it seems to me regrettable that the new President, our old friend from Pennsylvania, should set out for his first summit with the Soviets in a pessimistic mood that apparently presupposes a disastrous ending to the meeting before it has even begun. I don't really see that this helps matters much, or that it can possibly induce a mood of confidence in the Soviets, any more than it does in the rest of us. I would suggest that the cause of peace might better be served by a more positive and helpful approach. Otherwise he may be guilty of doing inadvertently what he apparently fears the Soviets may do."

The comment had received immediate endorsement from such younger members as Rick Duclos of Vermont and Bob Templeton of Colorado—the "young Turks" of Mark's first days in the Senate, still standing together. It had been picked up on all the evening television news shows, and next morning had been prominently featured in the national press. Its immediate and most important effect was to spur the President to a decision he had been contemplating for several days. He put in a call to the Majority Cloakroom in the Senate and in a couple of minutes had Mark on the wire.

"Yes, Ham—Mr. President," the junior Senator from California said, sounding friendly but guarded. "What can I do for you? Take a spanking for my views?"

"No, no spanking," the President said amicably. "How would you like to be on the delegation to New York? I want to take along about six of you."

"What for?" Mark inquired with equal amicability. "Window dressing?"

"Nope, no window dressing. Support. Suggestions. Advice. Your good ideas. And also, I hope, a little better understanding of what we're up against. And your assistance in convincing the country that whatever comes out of it is acceptable."

"I can't pledge myself to *that* until I know what it is, can I?"

"No, I'm not going to exact that promise. Mainly, I want the Senate represented. I'm also thinking about taking six from the House, for the same reasons. This is new for me, after all. It will help to be surrounded by my own."

"Well," Mark said, "I don't want to sound stiff-necked about it, but I really can't agree ahead of time to support a conclusion we don't yet know. With that proviso, though, I'd be honored to be included. And pleased. And excited. As, I suspect, will be the rest of us. After all, this really is a watershed meeting this time, I think—the two of you being brand-new, as it were."

"Only we aren't really," the President said. "We've both been around for a long time. I've been reading up on our friend Yuri in a report the CIA's given me. He's quite a boy, with a grim background. He's not the charming little soul we used to know around the party circuit years ago when he was stationed here in the Embassy. He's a tough son-of-a-bitch. You have to be, to get to the top in that Byzantine setup they have over there."

"You're fairly tough yourself, in my estimation," Mark said with a chuckle. "Yuri may meet his match."

"I'd like to think so," Hamilton Delbacher said, suddenly somber. "But for it to be a 'match,' you know, it has to be a meeting of equals. And militarily, I'm afraid we're not."

Senator Coffin snorted.

"You know, ever since I came to this place people have been trying to convince me of that and I'm still not convinced. I know we've dropped back a good bit, I know in some areas they're definitely ahead. But overall, in atomic capability, economic strength and potential, the capacity to take a punch and come back to win in the long haul—"

"Who said there's going to be a long haul?" the President interrupted. "I'm told they've been training their forces for a blitz for the past twenty years. We may not have any time for a 'long haul.' It may be one, two, over and out. And *we* may be out. Does anyone, I wonder, really grasp the reality of that?"

"I'm in favor of a reasonable build-up," Mark said thoughtfully. "I've changed some in the last couple of years. But I still don't think our situation is desperate. And I don't think we—you—should prejudge what's going to happen next week in New York. You may find Serapin as anxious to find an acceptable accommodation as you are."

"Maybe," the President said, "but I wouldn't place any bets. . . . So, then: you will come. That'll help."

"Sure. I'd love to. I won't place any bets, either, but at least let's give him a chance. After all, war would be utterly insane."

"It depends on how you definite insanity," the President said, "and who's doing the defining. Anyway, you'll get all the headlines tonight. I doubt that I will."

Mark laughed.

"I expect we both will, which is only fair. Share and share alike. Particularly when I suspect the country is pretty well divided, anyway."

"They don't like the Soviets," Ham Delbacher said. "They're scared to death of 'em. At the same time, nobody wants to fight for what they like to tell themselves they believe in. So there we are. It poses a problem."

"Understatement of the week, but I still like to think maybe he'll be ready to seek a genuine accommodation."

"Oh, I like to think that too," the President said. "But it takes more than wishing to make it so."

And later, after he had announced the other Congressional members of the delegation—which included Jim Elrod and Art Hampton in the Senate, the Speaker and five other senior members of the House—he called in the Joint Chiefs of Staff for a lengthy briefing which was far from encouraging.

The sum of it was that the United States was now in the midst of that Eighties "Soviet window of opportunity" that had been predicted on all sides during the aborted SALT II debate at the end of the last decade.

In virtually all major categories and all major areas of potential conflict, the Russians were now not only ahead but undeniably superior.

This had been very close to fact in 1979–80. Since not enough had been done by the United States to catch up, and since the momentum of the Soviet build-up had not been deflected for one second by any pious American hopes for SALT II, the end result had been exactly as predicted.

The fears of many had been genuine, and now they had all come true.

There was no way to evade the fact, avoid it or hide from it. Millions of his countrymen, he knew, dared not let themselves think about it, preferring instead to pretend that it was not so. But it was so. And on him fell the burden of somehow finding the way out of the dead end—literally dead, if he failed—prepared for him by some of his predecessors with their futile and fatuous attempts to appease, cajole and deflect the relentless worldwide drive of the communist empire.

Figures which in 1979–80 had been ominous were even worse today. It was amazing, he thought, how complacent the country had managed to be even then, when the Soviet fleet already had 250 major surface ships to 175 in the American Navy; when the Soviets had 234 attack submarines to 78 American; when the only U.S. superiority was in 13 sitting-duck, fixed-wing aircraft carriers to 1 Soviet.

Similarly on land, taking the figures of bickering, disorganized, disunited NATO against those of the Warsaw Pact forces trained, equipped and rigidly controlled by the Soviet Union, the Americans and their allies trailed far behind: armies of 945,000 Warsaw to 630,000 NATO; 20,500 Warsaw tanks to 7,000 NATO; 10,000 major artillery weapons for Warsaw to 2,700 NATO; 3,525 fixed-wing Warsaw planes to 2,050 NATO.

And as between the two superpowers themselves, figures equally grim: 1,400 Soviet land-based nuclear-armed intercontinental ballistic missiles to 1,054 U.S.; 950 Soviet submarine missile-launching tubes to 636 American; total military manpower of 2,022,000 U.S., 3,658,000 Soviet (including approximately 100,000 officers and men trained in the deadly chemical warfare largely abandoned by a United States Government bowing to the cries of its own idealistic citizens); 50,000 Soviet tanks to 10,500 U.S.; 4,350 Soviet tactical warplanes to 4,164 American; 40,700 Soviet artillery weapons to 18,000 American; 523 Soviet major warships to 260 American. The American lead in nuclear warheads then—9,200 to 5,000—was already long gone now.

And in addition, a Soviet military purpose and training program based upon treachery, deceit, surprise—blitzkrieg sweeping over Europe, simultaneous lightning assaults on other strategic points around the globe, the official adoption of the nuclear weapon as not the last, but the first, resort of the communist avalanche.

And the will and determination to use it.

The Soviet lead in all categories had changed only in degree in the short intervening years, and the degree was much worse now. There had been little catching-up, despite reviving pressure for an all-out attempt. The intention might have been there in some areas of government, but the lead-time required many more years than were available before Soviet superiority became absolute. And meantime the Soviets, of course, were not standing still. In leaps qualitative as well as quantitative, they continued to hold their lead.

This was what he had inherited. His predecessor in his final speech had referred almost absent-mindedly, it seemed, to "the United States, the most powerful nation on earth." *Newsweek* magazine in a casual reference had begun a paragraph this week, "It remained to be seen whether the world's mightiest nation would—" *Time* said: "The U.S. remains, over-all, far more powerful than the Soviet Union." Where did they get that stuff? Not from the documents, the somber statements or the gloomy faces of the JCS that confronted him in his office now. Some people must be eating a private stock of happy-pie. Nothing he was being told now in any way gave support to such blindly overstated optimism.

There was, however, no point in brooding about this. Indeed he did not dare. He was walking a tightrope over the abyss, carrying his willfully wishful countrymen on his back. If he was to get them all safely across he had to take a deep breath, face straight ahead and keep putting one foot before the other just as though he were absolutely certain he would reach the other side. But he would not do it, he promised himself grimly, by trying to fool his countrymen into thinking they faced anything easy. He would tell them the truth.

Prompted by this, he decided that he too would make a globe-spanning speech before he left for New York. It was to an attentive nation and an attentive world that he spoke the following evening: his first major address as President and one that he hoped would set the tone for a long and difficult time ahead.

"My countrymen," he said gravely, looking straight into the television cameras, solid and comforting in his calm demeanor, "in this, my first talk to you since the tragic and unexpected event that placed me in this office, I do not intend to take much of your time. But it seems to me that I owe you an accounting of my views at the outset; particularly since I will be leaving day after tomorrow for New York City, there to meet for the first time the President of the Soviet Union, who, like myself, has just assumed the leadership of his government. No doubt he, too, wishes to know where I stand.

"My position, if it must be categorized for our friends of the media, is somewhat stronger than that of my predecessor when it comes to the firmness with which I intend to act in international affairs. This does not mean blustering, breast-beating, flag-waving or bullying. It means a calm and steadfast adherence to the principles of decency, fairness, tolerance and co-operation America has always believed in, and to which she has always tried, if sometimes imperfectly, to adhere. And it means this in a world which, in all honesty, lies at this moment under the heavy shadow of a Soviet military machine expanded far beyond any excuse of domestic defense or justifiable need.

"This Soviet increase has been going on for the better part of three decades. The end result is a serious situation in which I will say to you quite candidly that the United States is not in the fortunate position of easy dominance that it once was. My fellow Americans"—his expression became momentarily somber—"I must tell you that we are not in a position of dominance at all. My late predecessor in his final speech to you was yet able to find some grounds for optimism and comfort in this—perhaps because he did not discuss it very fully. I do not—though I must hasten to add that I do not find in it grounds for dismay, either. It is simply a fact we must face and a condition we must seek to better.

"Much will depend on the attitude of President Serapin when we meet in New York. We are now in that period, predicted by our military experts some years ago, admitted at that time even by our most optimistic pundits, when the Soviet Union has a so-called 'window of opportunity' to use its military power in harsh and imperialistic ways. It is also called *our* 'window of vulnerability.' We must not let it become so."

("How?" demanded Yuri Serapin, watching the satellite transmission of the speech in his Kremlin office.

("Yes, Comrade," echoed the new Minister of Foreign Affairs. "How?"

("Indeed, Comrade," agreed the new Minister of Defense. "How?"

(Happily they joined him in laughter, harsh, skeptical, filled with a smug, unreachable assurance.)

"What I intend to do," the President said, as though he had heard them, "is to proceed on the basis of what has always been the American position, one of steadfast adherence to the basic principles that have always guided our international conduct. There are, admittedly, many issues that lie undecided between the Soviet Union and ourselves. I go to New York determined to bring to their solution as much good will, willingness to compromise and readiness to adjust as I can.

"But," he said, and his voice suddenly sounded more grim, his expression became more resolute, "I do not intend to go there simply to rubber-stamp Soviet demands or yield to Soviet pressures. I go there to talk constructively and reasonably with President Serapin, in the assumption that he is sincere in seeking peace. Anything our talks can contribute to that will be a great plus for our two countries and, I would hope, for all nations who live in the shadow of our differences. We must find solutions for them, and we must find them peaceably with full regard to the independence, integrity and reasonable self-interest of both the Soviet Union and the United States. And with full regard to the well-being of the world at large.

"This, then, is the spirit and the mood in which I depart for New York. I go in good faith. I expect to be received in good faith. I have no reason not to respect President Serapin and I am assuming he will respect me. If not," he said, quietly but with an unmistakable firmness, "there are other options open. But I do not think we will need them."

("That is a good thing, Mr. President," Yuri Serapin said, "because you really, you know, do not have them."

("No, Mr. President," said the Minister of Defense, "you really do not."

("Not at all," said the Minister of Foreign Affairs. "No."

(And they laughed pleasantly together, once again.)

"My countrymen," the President concluded, his face relaxing into a friendly smile, "the times are difficult and the problems many. But we have much to be grateful for, much to strengthen us. I shall report to you fully when I return from the summit. In the meantime, be of good cheer as I am.

"There are difficulties but we will surmount them. There are problems but they will be solved. Peace will be preserved and strengthened in the world, and its blessings will be secured for everyone.

"Good night."

An hour later a statement was issued from the Kremlin.

"The President of the Soviet Union and Chairman of the Central Committee, Y. P. Serapin, welcomes the assurances of the President of the United States, H. Delbacher, that his intention in coming to their meeting in New York is to achieve peace. Such is the intention also of Y. P. Serapin.

"Peace is the desire of all humanity. Y. P. Serapin and the peoples of the communist bloc are determined to achieve it. The sole purpose of the Soviet Union is lasting peace. Nothing will be allowed to stand in the way of this goal."

Which was hailed with universal approval and relief in the West, where few were sophisticated or knowledgeable enough to realize that "peace" in one vocabulary meant one thing, while in the other vocabulary it meant quite another.

5

"Surprise—One of the basic conditions for achieving success in battle . . . Surprise is achieved by the use of various ways . . . by leading the enemy into error concerning one's own intentions, by preserving in secret the plan of battle, by speed and decisiveness of action, by hidden artificial maneuvers, by the unexpected use of the nuclear weapon and other new combat means . . ."

—Soviet Dictionary of Basic Military Terms

It seemed to Yuri Serapin, as the huge Ilyushin jet made one of its customary racing touchdowns at Kennedy Airport, that nothing more could possibly be done to create the perfect climate for his meeting with the new President. The world's desperate hopes for a resolution of Soviet-American differences, the unanimous approval that had greeted his response to the President's speech, the apparent American willingness (still persistent after all these years of empty hopes) to accept at face value and without close study Soviet pronouncements of good intentions—all appeared to be creating a climate in which Hamilton Delbacher would have considerable difficulty openly opposing Soviet actions. Not that Yuri intended this to be a summit of actions—rather it was to be a summit of deceit, deception and preparation for later surprises. But it too needed its favoring climate if all was to proceed as he wished. Future great events would be born at this meeting; their delivery must be well prepared. He considered all signs auspicious—except perhaps one.

He had been prepared—and yet not quite prepared—for the strength of the President's remarks. He had known him for approximately fifteen years, since the days of his own assignment in Washington; and while he had not developed one of those "friendships" which he had been careful to cultivate with the more gullible members of Congress and the media—pragmatic and devoid of all human feeling on his part, flattered and typically easygoing American on theirs—he had taken occasion to study the Delbacher personality fairly closely. Particularly because the Delbacher personality was one of the strongest forces on the Hill in opposition to the Soviet conquest: not always open, sometimes working behind the scenes almost as shrewdly as Yuri did on the other side; but always to be taken into account.

This had been increasingly true in recent months. It had been apparent to Yuri and his colleagues when Senator Delbacher had been nominated and elected Vice President that no friend of theirs now stood on the edge of power. The late President they considered safely taken into camp: he was one of those who were always secretly a little thrilled that the dour, unknowable Soviets actually—or so they deluded themselves—considered them friends. He did not realize that the degree of friendship depended entirely upon the degree of pliability and gullibility. Like most Americans, he wanted to be loved—and loved for himself alone. He did not accept the fact that he was being used, in the most cold-blooded and cynical way, to advance the Soviet cause. This made him easy to persuade that the Politburo was a collection of earnest, well-meaning fellows, devoted in complete good faith to the cause of peace. This they were, but it was *peace as they saw it*. This he did not realize. So he found himself led often down the garden path of Soviet promises, even as Soviet actions cancelled the promises and betrayed his own earnest hopes for a peace that was truly a peace—not, as V. I. Lenin put it, "a time for gathering one's forces."

So he let America's forces continue the downward slide begun by some of his predecessors, and hoped, now and again quite nervously, for the best. Meanwhile Vice President Delbacher was making it increasingly clear that he did not regard what was happening as being for the best. The Kremlin had long since placed two very capable agents on the staff of the National Security Council, and from their regular reports it was obvious that a steadily deepening difference of opinion was separating the President and Vice President. Yuri had been apprised of this as it developed and was pleased when the spies reported that the Vice President would very likely be dropped from the ticket when the President ran for re-election. It had appeared that his own problem in leading the final assault on hated capitalism and its hated leader would be much simplified. The late President's last naïve and determinedly optimistic address to his countrymen had confirmed this belief. Then fate—God—history—whatever—had intervened, and his problem suddenly become more complicated; not much more, considering the overwhelming worldwide military machine he now commanded, but enough to cause some thought.

Yet, believing as he did that history predetermined all, he knew there must be some reason why he was now confronted by a much more determined opponent in Washington than he had expected to face. Such a one might be much easier to provoke into some rash and overt response to Soviet pressure than his yielding and naïve predecessor; and since Delbacher would not himself do any provoking, but rather would be deter-

mined to follow a peaceable course as long as possible, Yuri would automatically be given the exclusive option of determining the moment when
the final battle would begin. Trained as all Soviet leaders were in deception and deceit, taught from the beginning of their party careers that
surprise was the single greatest advantage in dealing with the capitalist
enemy, he knew this gave him an almost invincible weapon. President
Delbacher's firmness, coupled with his characteristically American belief
that peace was a tangible state of non-hostility that could actually be
achieved with the communists, could be turned about into the most powerful weapon that could possibly be used against him. Despite some
slight, transitory misgiving, Yuri was basically completely confident that
he was the man who could successfully bring it off. History, after all,
made it inevitable.

The plane was rolling to a stop. On the tarmac in the suffocating heat
of a New York July he could see the Secretary of State of the United
States, the Secretary-General of the United Nations, the Mayor of New
York and sundry other dignitaries. He noted with satisfaction that the
President was nowhere to be seen. Beyond the dignitaries, reporters, photographers and cameramen of the world pushed and shoved in noisy competition to record his arrival. Beyond them, he noted with a wry contempt
he could not show now, an honor guard of U. S. Marines and U. S. Army
stood at attention: empty symbols, he thought scornfully, of a dying
power. As he emerged and climbed slowly down the steps onto the red
carpet, the Army band struck up "The Internationale," followed by "The
Star-Spangled Banner." How pompous, futile and meaningless that tune is
becoming! he told himself, the contempt surging stronger in his heart.
What little tin soldiers, playing a little tin song! And thank God, or history,
that it would not be heard much longer in the world.

He stood at attention, impassive, at the foot of the steps, until the
anthems were concluded; then the Secretary of State stepped forward,
smiled, shook his hand, stepped to the lectern and the bank of microphones set up facing the welcoming crowd.

"Mr. President!" Chauncey Baron said, an apparently genuine cordiality in his voice—*Why are they so self-deluding?* Yuri asked himself
with the wonderment he always felt when confronted by Americans. *Why
are they so stupid?*—"It is with real pleasure and genuine anticipation
that I welcome you to America today on behalf of the President of the
United States. Mr. Delbacher regrets that his duties in Washington prevent his being here in person until tomorrow morning when your conference begins, but he wants me to tell you that he is pleased and honored,
as are we all, by your presence here. He hopes that much constructive
progress toward peace will develop from your visit. Certainly he is determined to achieve this, and he knows that you are too."

There was a hearty, also apparently genuine, burst of applause from the crowd. It increased when he bowed his head gravely. Fortunately nobody knew what was going on inside that head. Not that it would have made any real difference if anybody had. No one would have believed it: and the end was inevitable.

"He wants me to say to you, Mr. President," Chauncey went on, "that he knows, as you do, that the prayers of both our peoples, and indeed of the world, are with you on this mission. Through a tragic circumstance in our country, you both have come to power at the same moment. It may well be an omen and an auspice. It can be a time for a sweeping away of old mistrusts and mistakes, a time to start afresh. A new age can now begin. We, like you, hope earnestly that it will."

Again Yuri bowed, again the applause rolled out. Yes, he thought, a new age will indeed soon begin. He would tell them so, but they would not understand his meaning. He could almost—almost—tell them exactly what he meant, and still they would refuse to understand it. What fools!

"Mr. President," Chauncey said, "we greet you and welcome you. May your stay in our country be a happy one. May the results be happy for the Soviet Union and America, and for the world. May God and history attend your labors. Welcome!"

He smiled again, turned and shook hands once more, gesturing Yuri to the microphone. The Soviet President stepped forward, looked thoughtfully over the crowd. Then he smiled, shook his head in mock dismay at the heat, loosened his tie. It was the sort of gesture he had learned long ago that Americans love. Sure enough, warm laughter and applause enveloped him.

"Mr. Secretary of State," he said in his heavily accented English, "Mr. Secretary-General, ladies and gentlemen: I come to you determined that this will indeed, as Mr. Baron says, be the start of a new age of peace for all mankind. I can only regret that the President of the United States did not see fit to meet me here at this moment so that we could inaugurate it together."

There was scattered applause, weak and uncertain yet determined to be hopeful. He continued in Russian, pausing for his translator after each sentence or two.

"The Soviet peoples and the peoples of the other socialist states are tired of tension and uneasiness between us. We want peace, as you do. A lasting peace! A genuine peace! A peace that will permit mankind to live free from war for all time!"

Applause again, this time reassured, heartfelt, genuine. They were taking him at his word: they always did. And so they should, he thought wryly, for he meant it. He just had a different kind of peace in mind.

"I too look forward with eager anticipation to the meeting of myself and President Delbacher tomorrow, even though I regret that he has not seen fit to be here today. I know he is sincere and determined in his purposes. So am I. Together we may be able to sweep away many things. Together we may truly find peace.

"My friends of America," he concluded once more in English, "I have known your country since many years, when I was stationed in Washington in our embassy there. I know you truly love peace. We also truly love peace. We will not rest until we have achieved it. That is the pledge of the great Soviet people, and their allies, to you!"

And there was no lie in that, he thought, no lie at all. He *was* pledging them peace: the peace of the grave, perhaps, the peace of the end of all their freedom, all their power, all their hopes—but peace. How else could the world be guaranteed peace except by the removal of the one power in it that was constantly stirring up trouble, constantly engaging in imperialistic adventures, constantly attempting to subvert history with the enticements of a doomed and dying capitalism? They had a duty to stop obstructing the inevitable course of history. Communism would help them do their duty. Then peace would truly come at last and mankind's future would be decided for all time.

Of the audience greeting him at JFK, of all the millions of Americans who saw and heard his message of arrival, he knew that only a small handful would understand the terms in which he talked of peace. They simply would not believe that anyone could give it the interpretation he, his colleagues of the Politburo and the vast majority of his countrymen, did. Scoffs and skepticism would greet any Americans who warned that in the language of communism "peace" meant something vastly different from what it did in America—that it meant, in essence and in fact, the total destruction of a free America, the total subjugation of America to the Soviet Union, the total "Finlandization" and absorption of America into the communist world—the absolute end of human liberty as Americans had always known it.

But *he* knew these things; and this too was an enormous advantage. He saw before him the welcoming faces, a little uneasy, a little uncertain now, just as he had intended. He went down the line shaking hands again with Chauncey Baron, the stately, dignified black from Nigeria who was Secretary-General of the United Nations, the rather grim-faced Jew who was Mayor of New York, and the rest.

He thanked God the majority of the Jews had finally been driven from the Soviet Union. It had taken a lot of time to work it all out, to make the world pay the ransom the Politburo had in effect set by charging each Jew a heavy exit fee. It had cost the West a lot of money to get them out, and now the West was having a lot of difficulty getting them resettled. Any problem for the West was a plus for the Soviet Union. How well it had all been handled!

"Mr. Mayor," he said cordially, "it is always delightful to be in your great city and see the vital, vigorous people of New York."

"We welcome you, Mr. President," the Mayor said smoothly, eyes for a second filled with hate. He knows us, Yuri thought. Watch out, little Mayor! You and your people will not be safe even here, when we have won.

Then he was being whisked in a siren-screaming caravan along the busy freeways into the great dirty city, its evening lights beginning to come on and transform it into the magical vision that hid so much capitalist corruption, poverty and crime. It could not fool him, any more than it could fool its own people. He could remember its excitements when he had come visiting, fifteen years younger; but the evil at its heart would never change until it was purged and washed clean after the inevitable triumph of communism. They ought to be happy to have the communists come, these pathetic people, he told himself. They ought to welcome being saved from themselves.

But of course he knew they would not: they did not have the sense. They would balk and argue and oppose and might possibly find enough residue of courage and self-respect to try to fight. None of it would do them any good but enough of them to be bothersome would probably try stubbornly nonetheless. He suddenly felt a great impatience and anger. Why would they persist in making it so difficult for him! Communism was their savior, the savior of all mankind. Why did the Americans persist in wanting to live their sloppy, inefficient, human, free lives, when the communist way was so well ordered and well run once one submitted docilely to it? It was so completely the answer to all the uncertainties and complications of capitalist living. They did not know what they were missing.

But they would.

The caravan screamed to a halt in front of the headquarters of the Soviet delegation to the United Nations. More red carpet, more greetings, this time from his own people in his own language. Those who had come with him from Moscow mingled happily with those who were stationed here at the UN. Inside, they told him, a welcoming party was about to begin.

"But I am so tired," he protested, rubbing his hand across his eyes but giving them a smile that belied his words.

"Come, Yuri Pavlovich!" someone shouted gaily from inside the doors. "We must celebrate your visit and what it will mean for the Motherland! You are home, now!"

"Not yet," he murmured under his breath to the new Foreign Minister at his elbow. "Not yet, but we will be."

Laughing together they pushed in through the happily welcoming throng and were carried along on a wave of joyful excitement to the party. High on the walls above V. I. Lenin, K. Marx and F. Engels looked down upon him with a calm certainty that matched his own. It was to them that he raised his first glass of vodka. A great cheer went up.

"Now, then!" Lyddie Bates said, beaming happily around the room at the special group of guests she had invited to an early supper at her house on Foxhall Road. "His arrival speech sounded reasonable enough, didn't it? He didn't sound as though he were going to eat you up, Mr. President. He sounded quite civilized, I thought."

The President looked wry.

"He's already making points. And I'm afraid I played right into it. I talked to him yesterday; I told him I would defer my arrival until tomorrow so that he might have the full attention of the media and the country on his first visit here as President, without any competition from me; I told him I would leave the entire show to him, as a courtesy and a consideration—and look what I got in return. The snide implication that I was deliberately avoiding him, deliberately being discourteous, deliberately trying to cast a shadow over our meeting, deliberately being against peace. He made it pay off very well, too. You've just heard all the nasty criticisms I'm receiving from the networks."

"You have to meet him more than halfway, though, it seems to me," Lyddie said, shrewd eyes sparkling in her wise old face. *"You* can't be the international grump!"

"He can be the international skeptic, however," Jim Elrod suggested. "He can see what else the man does before he commits us to anythin'. Seems to me Serapin's already given us an indication."

"I'm not going to commit us to anything," the President said. "This is strictly get-acquainted, for me. Anything positive that comes out of it will be an incidental, and I might add, an entirely unexpected, dividend."

"You really *don't* expect much, do you?" Mark Coffin said thoughtfully. "I wonder why not?"

"Oh, Lord, Mark!" Elinor Delbacher said in an annoyed tone. "You really are still as naïve as the day you came here, aren't you?"

"I don't think I'm naïve," Mark said with some annoyance of his own. "But I don't want to be an hysterical war-monger, either. I think they want peace."

"Why shouldn't they?" Elinor sniffed. "It's given them almost everything they've gone after for the past forty years. Why shouldn't they?"

"It's also kept us out of war," Mark said sharply. "Maybe that isn't worth anything to you, but it is to me."

"That's it, shift the argument and get personal," Elinor said, New England tartness responding. "You argue just the way they do."

"Maybe he's one of them," Linda said dryly.

"Oh, tush!" Elinor said, but smiling to soften it. "Stop being the Perfect Protective Wife and let him speak for himself. He's capable of it."

"Now, girls," the President said firmly. "Mark is another of my problems. He's going along tomorrow morning because I put him on the delegation. I couldn't have everybody seeing everything the same way. There has to be some 'high source in the American delegation' who will confide his worries to the media so they can talk about a 'behind-the-scenes fight over policy.' Mark's the ideal choice, you see. Also, if for some reason the Soviets want to pass any special messages to me, what better channel than our famous young rebel Senator?"

Mark smiled.

"You have me all figured out, don't you, Mr. President? I'm glad I'm such a vital part of the exercise."

"You may be yet," the President said. "Don't laugh."

"I doubt it," Mark said. "But it will be interesting to be there, that's for sure."

"What's the schedule on the meetings?" Senate Majority Leader Art Hampton inquired.

"We start with a dinner at seven tomorrow night," the President said. "I suggested we give them the day to rest up, and he seemed grateful enough for that."

"Our place or theirs?" asked Art's irrepressible counterpart, Senate Minority Leader Herb Esplin.

"Actually neither. We're there under the kind auspices of the UN. It will be in the Secretary-General's private dining room. The next day we get down to business, first a general discussion and then some meetings between just the two of us."

"With interpreter," Senator Janet Hardesty of Michigan remarked.

"That smooth-faced character has been in on every conference, spyin' on everybody, for the past thirty years, far as I know," Senator Elrod said. "Why don't you insist he be left outside? Serapin doesn't need him. He speaks English almost as well as we do."

Ham Delbacher nodded.

"That might be a good first issue for me to raise. Start a little strategic rumpus, right off the bat."

"Hardly a peacemaking gesture," Mark observed.

"No," the President agreed. "But harmless. A little test of will. It won't hurt anything."

"Better see what they have in mind first," Art Hampton advised. "They aren't such slouches at creating issues themselves."

And that, the President reflected as he and Elinor returned to the White House and an early bed before their scheduled 8 A.M. departure for New York, was true enough. The early editions of both the Washington *Post* and the Washington *Inquirer* were waiting when he got back to the Mansion. In the latter Anna Hastings had turned again to her favorite forum, the front page editorial, and was generally giving him hell for "this shabby, deliberately rude greeting for a man who may very well have come here disposed to be genuinely friendly to the United States." The *Post* was in the same vein, and no doubt the New York papers would be too; certainly the editorial comment from the networks news shows had been virtually unanimous.

Yet they all knew—or did they?—that Yuri Serapin was not "disposed to be genuinely friendly to the United States." Possibly they didn't know that. Possibly they were deluding themselves once more, out of fear, desperation or hope. Many of his countrymen, he knew, did this, including his predecessor and a couple before that. They wanted peace so desperately, they were so afraid to open their eyes and admit they saw what they saw, that they simply escalated the rhetoric and kept on talking about "the greatest power on earth . . . I assure you America is still, by far, the strongest military power on the globe . . . The world's leading power . . . We take second place to no one in the quality and strength of our arms . . . I am determined to keep America the strongest nation on earth . . ." And so on: none of it true any longer, unless you were thinking in terms of a long, dragged-out war of strike and recovery—and even then, extremely problematical.

He was already beginning to perceive, as he studied official Soviet papers on military training, civil defense and actual preparations at home and abroad, that they were thinking in terms of a short, sharp, decisive blitzkrieg whose outcome might well be decided in the first forty-eight or even twenty-four hours—with victory, they assumed, going inevitably to them, and all the rest mop-up.

There began to dawn on him, as he lay quietly on his side of the bed in the beautiful historic old house, eyes open in the dark, staring at the ceiling, that Serapin's visit might well be the first step in this: and that what had seemed a display of apparently spontaneous and casual personal annoyance in his words on arrival might instead have been the first careful step in a cold and ruthlessly calculated plan.

If so, he told himself with a sigh and a prickling of hairs along the back of his neck, Hamilton Delbacher of Pennsylvania, playing from a frayed and unsure hand, must be very, very careful what cards he used and how he used them. If he was correct in this instinctive hunch, Yuri had already won the first round by aligning the most powerful organs of the American media on his side. It was not an advantage to be minimized, since some of the most powerful apparently failed to grasp that they and their President belonged to the same country, and that in his dealings with the Soviets, they and all their hard-won rights of freedom to publish, criticize and condemn would go down with him if he failed.

His own arrival in New York, shortly after 10 A.M., was as well covered as Serapin's had been; and he took the occasion to attempt to redress the propaganda balance.

He was greeted by Chauncey Baron, the Secretary-General and—a nicely calculated touch—the Soviet Foreign Minister, looking more than a little hung-over, which he was. The delegation party had gone on until after midnight, and that plus the flight from Moscow had been enough to exhaust them all, even Yuri Pavlovich. Fortunately they would not be required to face the Americans until 7 P.M., so the Foreign Minister intended to get right back to headquarters after this ceremony and rejoin the ranks of the sleeping. Meanwhile, here was the stupid and hostile new President of the United States. He gave an enormous yawn behind his hand and prepared to pay outward attention, though his mind was woozy and far away.

"Mr. Foreign Minister, Mr. Secretary-General, Mr. Secretary of State," the President said after the two anthems were concluded, "thank you for coming out to meet me. Like President Serapin, I too am here in the cause of that lasting peace for which our two countries and the whole world yearn.

"I do not think, my friends, that President Serapin set things off on a very good footing yesterday when he expressed some annoyance at my not being here to greet him."

(The Secretary-General jabbed the Foreign Minister in the side with his elbow, and the Foreign Minister, just on the verge of going to sleep, righted himself abruptly and forced his eyes open.)

"I had told President Serapin just two days ago that I would deliberately stay away so that he might receive the full attention of the media on this, his first visit to this country since assuming supreme power in the Soviet Union—so that you all might have a chance to see him and meet him, unimpeded by any distraction created by my being here.

"Apparently President Serapin chose to use my absence, intended as a courteous gesture to him, to fabricate an artificial mini-crisis revolving around my alleged discourtesy to him. This has been dutifully picked up by the American and foreign press. This is no help to me or to the success of our meeting."

There was a muted gasp from the crowd and the Foreign Minister came fully awake. Wait until Yuri Pavlovich heard about this! The minister began to examine the President with a suddenly increased attention and a careful calculation. Perhaps he was not so stupid, after all; though there was no doubt he was hostile.

"However," the President went on, tone less sharp and more conventional, "I would not want this momentary lapse in courtesy on the part of President Serapin to stand in the way of our discussions; and I am sure that upon mature reflection he will not, either. The stakes are too high and it is too important that we understand each other. We must find common ground on which to settle our differences, not inflame them; and I know he will join me in that most sincerely when we meet.

"Our discussions begin tonight, and will continue, I suspect, for most of this week. It does not seem probable that major decisions will come from this meeting; rather, I think, a getting-acquainted and a review of our major problems. As many of you know, President Serapin is no stranger to the United States, having served four years in the Soviet Embassy in Washington some fifteen years ago. But both he and I are now in much different positions than we were then. So are many of our senior advisers, who will participate in some of the discussions.

"The United States, also, wants peace. We too want a stable situation in the world, not based on the military strength or hegemony of any power. We want a peace of equals, a shield for the world that will permit all nations to live in harmony without the overriding fear of a Soviet-American clash that could only devastate the globe and very likely send humanity back into a Dark Ages from which it might not recover for a thousand years, if ever.

"That is the charge resting upon Comrade Serapin and myself. I believe we are ready to respond to it with sincerity and good faith. You, and history, will judge us by what we do. We must not fail."

And don't you forget it, Yuri buddy, he thought grimly as the ceremony ended and he and his delegation were also whisked in siren-screaming procession along the crowded freeways into the great dirty, exciting city. Just keep it in mind, and don't try any funny stuff. Because if you do, he told himself bitterly, I am not too sure what, if anything, I can do about it.

But the main concern, for the moment, was the dinner tonight. After he and his delegation had reviewed several position papers offered by State, Defense, the Joint Chiefs and the National Security Council, they lunched quietly at delegation headquarters and went off to bed, at his orders, for naps. This was a homespun way to approach a major international conference but he wanted everyone rested and alert. For this reason, too, he had Mark call the Secretary-General and request that only wine be served at dinner, instructing his colleagues to take it very lightly, if at all. Then he turned in and, to his surprise, fell almost instantly asleep and did not stir until he was awakened at six to get ready for the meal.

"Mr. Presidents," the Secretary-General said, his dignified old face crinkling into a pleasant smile, "and all our distinguished guests: welcome to the United Nations and my own humble quarters. You must consider this room your home, tonight and as many times as you may wish to use it in coming days. We hope its comforts will attract constructive thoughts and genuine progress. May peace guide your deliberations and may peace be your conclusion."

There were smiles and agreeing murmurs. Mark, seated near the foot as became his junior status in the Senate and on the delegation, smiled with the rest and exchanged gratified sounds with the two Russians between whom he was seated. At the S.-G.'s direction the delegations had been carefully mixed in the seating arrangements.

"They may never be so cordial again as at this first meeting," he had told his secretary with a wry chuckle, "but at least tonight they are going to sit with each other and like it."

And so most of them seemed to be doing, Mark observed as the soup course came around, the first wine was poured, the initial awkwardness of meeting began to fade in a rising babble of talk. A wistful thought struck him suddenly: if only the friendly atmosphere could continue—if only everyone meant it—if only—

"You are pensive," the Russian on his right remarked with a deep but unexpectedly gentle laugh, "Why?"

"No reason," Mark said, smiling and turning to look at him with real attention for the first time: a stocky man about his own age, about his own height, darkly handsome, something more than ordinary courtesy in his interested glance.

"Or at least none you will tell *me*," the Russian said, continuing to smile. He held out his hand. "I am Major Valerian—Ivan, believe it or not."

"Mark Coffin—Mark," Mark said, returning a firm handshake that held his hand a moment longer than ordinary custom. He was being contacted for something: what? There were many possibilities but the simplest was probably that he had been designated Ivan's special-American-to-keep-an-eye-on. Very well, he was willing to go along. The man seemed pleasant, and sometimes even the best-trained of them must let his hair down. Perhaps Mark could find out something from Ivan, too. He decided to concentrate on it.

"Tell me," he said as they started on the soup, "where do you fit in all this?"

"Fit?" Major Valerian echoed, and gave a charming smile. "My English is—quite adequate, but some colloquialisms escape me."

" 'Colloquialisms' is a pretty good word for someone who doesn't know the language too well," Mark said with a laugh. "And you have virtually no accent. Perhaps your knowledge is better than you tell me."

"Perhaps," Ivan said, smile increasing. "Who knows? You mean, I think, what is my part in the meetings. Is that not right?"

"Ivan," Mark said, "you are astute, perceptive and omniscient."

"Also smart," Ivan said with a grin, clinking his wineglass unexpectedly against Mark's. "I am a member of the junior staff of what corresponds to your Joint Chiefs of Staff. A very minor member, but someone has to shuffle the papers and bring the coffee."

Mark gave him a humorous glance.

"My role exactly."

"Ah, but you are a United States Senator, Mark. If *you* must shuffle papers and bring coffee for President Delbacher, then you must also have a lot of people who shuffle papers and bring coffee for you. I, alas, have no one!" And again the charming smile lit up the sturdily handsome face. Ivan, Mark thought, feeling as though they had already known one another for years, is working on me with great determination. I wonder why?

"Have you attended one of these affairs before?" he asked as waiters whisked away the empty soup plates and the fish appeared. "I'm frank to say I haven't. But of course you all have studied us very carefully, so you know that."

"You *do* consider me omniscient," Ivan said with a chuckle. "Yes, I have studied you, and yes I know you have not attended such affairs before. Nor have I. It was quite unexpected, I assure you. But I was pleased." His voice lowered suddenly to near-whisper as he reached casually for a bowl of butter, leaning against Mark's shoulder as he did so. "I wanted to see these dreadful Americans I have been taught so much about."

"And are we?" Mark murmured, surprising himself by suddenly sounding as conspiratorial as Ivan. He was thankful that the Russian on his left was deep in conversation with one of the Congressmen on the U.S. delegation.

"I am not sure." Ivan said, straightening up, tone normal and matter-of-fact as he began to butter a roll. "I wish to study the matter further. Perhaps you can help me."

"I doubt if there will be opportunities."

"We will find them," Ivan said confidently, voice low again. "That is, if you agree."

"Surely," Mark said, equally low, a little excitement stirring. He didn't know what this was all about, but it made the summit suddenly much more exciting and mysterious. "I think," he added casually, aware that one of the Russians across the table appeared to be intrigued by their talk, "there are other subjects to talk about."

"Yes," Ivan agreed, voice perfectly normal. "Are you married?"

The question was so abrupt that Mark gave him a startled look for just a second. Ivan burst out laughing.

"It is entirely legitimate to ask," he remarked. "I am, with three children."

"And you know I am, with three also. Now shall we discuss their ages, traits, education? I expect in both cases they're still young enough so that they are pretty much alike. I expect they would start playing with perfect friendship if we suddenly brought them together in this room." He sighed suddenly. "Not later, though."

"No," Ivan agreed, and for a second his eyes darkened and his expression, too, became sober. "Not later. That is why—"

"That is why," Mark said with sudden grimness, "it would be nice if once in a while these summits would really accomplish something."

"Yes," Ivan agreed soberly. "Yes . . . Tell me: I understand you are one in the Senate who does not agree entirely with your President's hard line toward us?"

"Ah, ha!" Mark said with exaggerated emphasis, as the main course came, the inevitable steak, peas, potatoes. "Now we embark upon the standard conversation trying to separate the dissenters from their leader, is that right? Surely you've studied me enough so that you know all my answers on that—including the one that goes, 'However, when it becomes a question of supporting the President in a genuine national crisis, then like all loyal Americans I put aside my reservations and do whatever I can to help.' Right? You know that one?"

"Oh yes," Ivan said cheerfully. "We say the same. Not that it is necessary. We do not dissent. At least"—again his voice became near whisper as he permitted his napkin to slide off his lap and reached behind Mark's chair to retrieve it—"not many of us."

"So I understand," Mark said in a normal tone, for the Russian on his left was preparing to turn toward him. "It makes life interesting."

"What is that?" the other asked brightly, leaning forward to peer across Mark to Ivan. "What is my colleague saying that is interesting to you, Senator?"

"He is saying that in the Soviet Union there is very little dissent because nearly everyone finds the communist system to be perfect," Mark said calmly.

"There is *no* dissent!" the Russian said flatly. "I am Major Shelikov and I tell you that there is *no* dissent! It is not 'nearly everyone' who finds the communist system perfect, it is *everyone!* Is that not so, Ivan Ivanovich?"

"It is so, Anatoly," Ivan said with equal flatness. "We have ways of discouraging dissenters, do we not?"

"We do!" Major Shelikov said with satisfaction. "We do!"

"Good," Ivan said, leaning back a little and giving Mark the flicker of a wink from his left eye. "I knew you would support me. We must educate our American friends so that they will understand us. It will make the future much easier for everyone."

"Right!" Anatoly agreed as he turned back to the Congressman. "That is right."

"What do you suppose our two Presidents are discussing?" Ivan wondered in a matter-of-fact tone.

"Probably whether President Serapin is going to defect," Mark said evenly. His new-found friend burst again into his hearty roar of laughter.

"Nobody ever does that," he said. His laughter took on the intimate note with which he had opened their conversation. "You know, Mark. Nobody *ever* does that."

"Yes," Mark agreed softly. "I know that and I shall remember it."

"Good!" Ivan said quietly.

I have been deliberately offered a very alluring prospect, Mark thought wryly: my very own defector, giving me all kinds of signals. But is he? And why me? And is it all a devious plot to involve and embarrass me and the delegation? And if not, what am I supposed to do about it?

"It *would* be interesting to know what they are talking about, wouldn't it?" he remarked in a conversational tone. And he turned to watch the two Presidents at the head table and talked very little more to Major Ivan Ivanovich Valerian, which suited Ivan well as he too turned to his other neighbor and fell into animated and innocuous conversation.

Which, in general, was what had been going on at the head table, though there had been a few moments, the President of the United States felt, when he had provoked his opponent into something a little more personal and revealing. It did not surprise him to find himself thinking of "my opponent," for that was how he regarded him. Yuri had issued the first challenge in his remarks at the airport. He had picked it up in his own rejoinder earlier today. There had been an underlying tension from the first in their table-talk tonight, which he regretted. But he had not started it. He was prepared to meet it, and did so.

"Mr. President," Yuri had said in English as they entered the room simultaneously through different doors—at Soviet insistence, of course: some other kind of point was being made—"I must thank you for your acceptance of my invitation. I thought it best we get to know each other immediately."

"I was preparing an invitation to you," the President said, shaking hands. "You beat me to it."

"Yes," President Serapin said with a slight smile. "It is unfortunate you waited so long. I am afraid it has given me a slight psychological advantage in the world, to have been the first to act."

"It will not matter who has the advantage if we fail," Hamilton Delbacher said as they took their seats flanking the Secretary-General. "I think the peoples of the world want results, not propaganda games. Certainly mine do."

"I am not here to play games," Yuri Serapin said sharply.

"Good," the President said blandly. "That will eliminate a lot of unnecessary nonsense."

For a second the Soviet President looked genuinely annoyed; but any rejoinder was stopped by the Secretary-General's graceful little opening statement; and after that his presence between them kept things on an impersonal level for some minutes. Then Yuri made some reference to "those world leaders who have earned their way to authority" and the President thought he should respond. By any adult standards, it was childish to take offense; but by the standards with which relations were conducted with the communists, it was necessary that no slightest innuendo go ignored.

"It all depends on how they earned it," he said. "Those of us who came to authority after being democratically elected—"

"I was elected!" Serapin exclaimed with an emphasis that hushed conversation near them for a startled moment. "I was elected!"

"In our country we might consider it somewhat preordained," Ham Delbacher said. "It had been decided already, had it not? The party selected you at an early age, as I understand it, in the thought you might someday sit where you are."

"But no one knew whether or not I would," Yuri said. "I had to be elected directly to the office of President. And," he added pointedly, "*I* was."

"True enough," the President agreed. "I can't deny that. Why are we discussing it, anyway?"

The Russian looked smug.

"Just to make note of the fact that I have a mandate from my people to rule, and you perhaps do not."

"No, perhaps not," Ham Delbacher acknowledged. "Not direct, anyway, though perhaps more so than 350 votes out of 250 millions. Americans are not 'ruled,' in any event. They are much too diverse and independent."

"We have diversity, too," Yuri said proudly, "but all our peoples are united in the single purpose of serving the Soviet state."

"Muslims, Georgians, Uzbekis and everybody?" the President asked. "That is an amazing fact."

"It *is* the fact," Serapin said flatly, and turned back to his food.

"Mr. Secretary-General," the President said heartily, "this is an excellent meal. You have good cooks at the UN."

"Sound talk comes from a full stomach," the S.-G. said with a smile. "Someone, I believe, said that."

"A Russian, I'm sure," the President said with a wink which the S.-G., though a quick smile came and went, thought it best to refrain from acknowledging.

Yuri, however, had not missed it. Yuri, the President was rapidly concluding, missed very little.

"And why should a Russian not say it, Mr. President?" he inquired, with what Ham already recognized as a characteristically sharp little edge in his voice. "It is not a bad thought."

"Not bad at all, Mr. President," Ham agreed. "I shall drink to it."

And lifting his wineglass, he did so. Yuri reciprocated, with an ironic little bow.

"These wines," he observed, "are not very good. Are they American?"

"They are," the President replied. "I think they are delicious."

"They *are* delicious," the Secretary-General agreed. "We are delighted to serve them."

"We must have a vote in the Security Council," President Serapin suggested. " 'Be it resolved that American wines are *not* good and should not be served at UN functions.' "

"You know," President Delbacher said, "I really wouldn't put it past you, Mr. President. No detail too small to embarrass poor old America, right?"

"Of course I am joking," Yuri said, sounding more amicable. "But I think we might win."

"I gather you think you can win on most everything," President Delbacher said. "We might not like that."

Yuri Serapin leaned forward and looked him straight in the eye.

"I think we might not care," he said evenly, "whether you like it or not."

"I think this fish is *excellent,*" the Secretary-General said hastily.

"Keep calm, Mr. Secretary-General," the President said with a smile. "Our friend and I are not declaring war this evening."

"I hope not," the S.-G. said, with a laugh that, in spite of his attempt to keep it normal, sounded for a second as though he had considered it a real possibility.

"No," Yuri Serapin said, "not this evening, and we hope never, Mr.

President. We hope we can live in peace with you for many, many years to come."

"I'll drink to that, too," Hamilton Delbacher said, and did so. This time Yuri joined him with a smile and without further comment on the wine. But, as the President realized, the Soviet leader had been deadly serious in their little exchange. The Secretary-General had been right to be perturbed.

The next few moments passed without conversation as the President turned to look thoughtfully down the long table. His twenty Americans were outnumbered by the thirty-five Russians, but where they had been intermingled with one another in the seating, everyone seemed to be getting along with a reasonable congeniality. He noted that Jim Elrod was exchanging somewhat guarded pleasantries with one of the Soviet generals, that Mark Coffin seemed to be engaged in a genuinely interested talk with the young Russian on his right, that John Halliburton, the Speaker of the House, was performing his usual conversational ploy of talking so heartily and at such length that neither of his attentive Russian seat-mates could get a word in. The atmosphere in general seemed to be fairly friendly and relaxed; except for himself and his counterpart, who walked the tightrope of mutual tensions in a way the others could not.

It was a marvel to him how so many mutually suspicious and hostile men could converse so animatedly about nothing. How much mileage opponents could get from the innocuous trivia of daily life, when events forced them to be socially pleasant to one another. Tomorrow, he suspected, would be a different day. He leaned forward.

What time do you think we should start the plenary session tomorrow, Mr. President? We had thought somewhere around 10 A.M. if that would be convenient for you."

"My delegation has not considered this yet," Yuri said.

"No, perhaps not," the President agreed, "but I want to know what *you* think. It is up to you, after all, is it not?"

"Under the Soviet system," Yuri said stiffly, "which is truly democratic, these things must be decided by vote of my senior colleagues and myself."

"Oh, come now. Really? You have no final authority to make the decision?"

"None," Yuri said firmly. "It must be by democratic agreement."

"We will need a decision on it fairly soon," the President pointed out. "Why don't you poll them informally right now? Mr. Foreign Minister, what time do you think—"

"That will not be necessary," President Serapin interrupted, voice rising. "We will confer after dinner and send word to your quarters."

"And you *will* have to confer with them?" Ham Delbacher repeated, aware that his opponent was laying the groundwork for later delays and obstructions. "You can't make decisions independently yourself?"

"You have heard my statement, Mr. President," Yuri said coldly.

"And you mine," Hamilton Delbacher said with equal coldness. "My delegation wishes to meet in plenary session at 10 A.M. tomorrow. This is our desire and our intention."

"I must consult my delegation."

"Suggest 10 A.M. to them. It will facilitate matters."

"We will let you know."

"You be sure to do that."

And because in his last retort he had allowed more annoyance in his voice than he wanted to display, the President turned quickly to the Secretary-General and began to discuss the old man's hobby of numismatics. Serapin stared straight down the table, completely impassive and expressionless as he awaited the next course. God damn it, Ham told himself in frustrated anger, here we go again, the same damned pattern they have used in every single international conference since World War II. Anything to obstruct, anything to annoy, everything, no matter how small, a battle. If they would *only once* behave like decent, co-operative human beings, what a wonder and boon to the world it would be. Now it would probably turn out to be just one more headline of a very familiar type: AMERICANS BOW TO SOVIET DEMAND AS SUMMIT OPENS. It would only be an hour in the day, but from the American concession the Russians would ring every possible propaganda advantage, all over the world. His estimate of what could be achieved in this meeting with Yuri Pavlovich, he thought dryly, had just dropped by 50, maybe even 80, per cent. So had the chance that he would agree to a change of time.

The dinner ended at 10 and he was not in the least surprised when Chauncey called him just before 11 to inform him that the Soviet delegation had just announced to the media that its members could not possibly meet with the United States until 3 P.M. tomorrow.

He told Chauncey to tell the media that the United States would be ready to start discussions at 10 A.M. and its delegation would be present and in place at that time.

And so they were, promptly at 10 A.M. in the full glare of the world's television cameras and photographers. The tables which last night had accommodated their uneasy dinner had been rearranged so that one long table now divided the room. One side was centered by a massive oaken armchair flanked by two American flags, the other by a similar chair flanked by two Soviet flags. Pads, pencils, water glasses were placed at every chair. Each delegation had its set of water carafes, placed exactly opposite one another; a similar distribution of microphones had been made. The Secretary-General's staff had done everything humanly possible to make the accommodations of each side exactly the same, but the President told himself dryly that no doubt Serapin would find something to complain about—when Serapin appeared.

He and his friends were definitely not there at 10 A.M. but the American delegation, under strict orders from the President, displayed not the slightest sign of annoyance, impatience or anger. Rather, it was obvious to the watching cameras that its members were, if anything, contemptuous and amused by what they clearly regarded as a childish and immature gesture. There was much joking among them, several sallies at the Soviets' expense which television picked up; and finally, when all were seated, there began to appear copies of the New York *Times,* the Washington *Post,* the Washington *Inquirer, Time, Newsweek.* One by one, following the President's lead, they fell to reading; until the media could stand it no longer and someone called out, "Mr. President, is the American delegation going to sit here until 3 P.M.?"

"As long as it takes," the President said, smiling comfortably into the cameras.

"Do you think it will take that long?" someone else inquired.

"It depends on how childish our Soviet friends wish to be. We are here and ready to talk. The world is watching and expects us to begin talking. Possibly President Serapin and his delegation think they can gain even further attention by delaying matters unnecessarily. Maybe they can, though I think the world would appreciate conduct becoming the seriousness of the issues between us. When President Serapin and his colleagues decide to grow up, I assume we will begin. Until that time, my delegation and I are quite happy this morning, thank you."

And he turned back to his copy of the *Times* and calmly resumed his reading.

At 10:30 the CBS UN Correspondent was called out of the room, returning a moment later to say:

"Mr. President, the Soviet delegation has announced that they will be here at 2 P.M."

"So?" the President said; shrugged and went on reading.

At 10:45, CBS went out again, returned to say:

"Mr. President, the Soviet delegation has announced it will not be able to attend at all today, but will be here at 3 P.M. tomorrow."

"So?" the President said again; again shrugged and again returned to *Time* magazine.

"Well, you have to do *something*—don't you, Mr. President, sir?" the AP inquired.

"No," he said calmly, "we don't have to do a single thing. We are here and ready to discuss world peace. If they wish to obstruct and endanger world peace even further by not being here as they promised, that is their

business. If their word is as worthless as that, it is good for the whole
world to witness it. It is quite immaterial what frivolous games they wish
to play. We are here and we are ready. I don't intend to say anything further."

And again he returned to his reading, as did they all; and time continued to creep by. He was quite prepared to stay there until noon, declare a
recess and come back at 1 P.M. But at 11:23, just as the members of the
media, by now becoming terribly fidgety, were obviously gathering themselves together for another attempt, there was a sudden excitement by the
door, a sudden rise of tension in the room, a rush of cameramen and reporters to position themselves as advantageously as possible.

"They're here!" one of the reporters shouted.

"Of course they are," the President said calmly, closing his magazine
and placing it neatly beside his note pad. But neither he nor any of his
delegation turned around to look as the Soviet delegation, led by the Foreign Minister, filed in grim-faced, in the full glare of the floodlights and
the excited babble of the media, to take their seats across the table.

When they were all seated there was a final surge of excitement, a
heightened frenzy of journalistic competition as pictures were taken,
questions—all ignored—were yelled, and the President of the Soviet
Union, his half-oriental face stolid and impassive, entered alone and took
his place. The President of the United States rose, smiled and extended
his hand.

"Mr. President," he said cordially, "welcome to the plenary session of
this historic meeting. We trust you had a good night's sleep after our
pleasant dinner last night?"

For a moment Yuri Serapin stared at him, still without expression.
Then he rose, swiftly extended his hand with no pressure whatsoever and
as swiftly withdrew it. Without a word he resumed his seat, folded his
arms and stared across at the enemy, whose expression by now was beginning to look amused. As the President well knew, no Russian could stand
being regarded with amusement for long. Very soon Yuri said in a level
tone,

"Shall we declare this meeting formally open, Mr. President?"

"Certainly," the President said cheerfully. "Let us begin. Perhaps the
logical thing for this plenary session to do is establish an informal agenda
that you and I might refer to in our private discussions that will follow. Is
that agreeable?"

The Soviet leader shrugged.

"What would you suggest?"

"We will defer to you on that. After all, it was your invitation. What
did you wish to discuss?"

The death of your damnable country, Yuri thought savagely; but his
expression remained impassive.

"My delegation and I believe," he said, "that the most important item now facing the world is continued United States aggressive imperialism in all quarters of the globe. Next—"

"Just a moment, Mr. President," Hamilton Delbacher said, his face also impassive. "I am writing this down. Number 1, 'Continued United States aggressive imperialism'—where?"

"In all quarters of the globe."

"Right," the President said, writing busily on his note pad. " 'In all quarters of the globe.' And next?"

"United States imperialist leadership of the arms race being conducted by NATO and the capitalist bloc," Serapin said, his voice, in spite of himself, just a little uncertain at the President's apparent speedy acquiescence in these condemnations.

" 'United States imperialist leadership—of the arms race—being conducted by NATO—and the capitalist bloc,' " the President repeated, continuing his careful notations. "Those seem quite exciting. What next?"

"They are not 'exciting!' " Yuri snapped with a sudden anger. "They are the truth!"

"That is one of the things we will also discuss," the President replied calmly. "Go on, Mr. President. You must have several more damnations for the United States. What's the next one—Number 3, isn't it?"

"Yes, Number 3! United States imperialist subversion of the freedom-loving peoples of the world."

"My, my," Ham Delbacher said. "I never dreamed we were *that* bad. Give it to me again, will you, Mr. President?"

And he continued to write carefully on his note pad as Yuri obliged, biting off each phrase with an anger that was finally beginning to escape his control a little. He was not used to being mocked, and he realized suddenly that this was what his enemy was doing. He did not like it.

"Number 4, United States imperialist threats to world peace."

"Number 4," the President said, writing each word with great care, "United States imperialist threats to world peace. Don't you want the word 'aggressive' in there? It could go just before the word 'threats,' don't you think?"

"If you like," President Serapin said coldly.

"Oh no," Hamilton Delbacher said cheerfully. "Only if *you* like. Do you?"

"Put it in," Yuri grated.

"Right! Is there a Number 5, 6, 7?"

"A Number 5, only," Yuri said, finally quite obviously furious. "The duty of the Soviet Union and all freedom-loving peoples of the socialist bloc to completely and finally defeat U.S. imperialist aggression wherever, and in whatever forms, it occurs."

"Now you *will* have to repeat that one for me," the President said in the same cheerful way. *"That's* a mouthful! How did it go, now, 'The duty of the Soviet Union—'?"

" 'And all freedom-loving peoples,' " Yuri said, his face a study.

"Not too fast now!" the President said, and made him repeat it word for word, twice. Then he read it back and inquired innocently:

"Is that all, now, Mr. President? You're sure there is nothing else?"

"There is nothing else," Yuri said coldly.

"Well, that *is* quite sufficient to lay us low," Ham Delbacher agreed. "We just have one item we wish included, and we might as well make that Number 6—or 1-A, if you'd rather. Or possibly even 1. 'The Soviet drive to achieve military and political control of the world and how the world's liberties and freedoms can be adequately saved from this ruthless and insatiable ambition.' We feel that one topic will be quite sufficient for us, if we can discuss it with you, Mr. President."

"You may discuss whatever you please, Mr. President," Serapin retorted while the cameras swung gleefully from face to face, "since none of what you say can possibly be true."

"Now, Mr. President!" Hamilton Delbacher said in a shocked, mocking tone as the cameras bore in upon him. "That is hardly courteous! We have not said that to you, even though your charges are manifestly and on the face of them false, unjustified and perhaps one might say, deliberately lying in nature. We have refrained from—"

"They are not lies!" Yuri exclaimed angrily, while the cameras hurried back to him and the reporters buzzed excitedly. "They are the truth, as the whole world knows! And we will stop your crimes against the world! We will defend world peace! This is my pledge to you, Mr. President!"

"And it is exactly mine to you, Mr. President," Ham said, his own tone suddenly as cold and emphatic as his opponent's. "Exactly. . . . So it appears," he added dryly, "that we do have a lot to discuss, after all. We feared earlier you had considered the conference pointless because so much of the truth is on our side, and had gone home. At least now we know we will have a few things to discuss."

"A few," Yuri agreed grimly.

"Quite a few," the President said. "Should we appoint some subcommittees, do you think, to exchange information on various specifics we both have in mind?"

"That is the obvious way to proceed," Yuri Serapin said, his tone more mild.

"Good. Perhaps if the press and television could now withdraw—"

There were a few murmurs of protest, and he added, "We will release a full list of all committees to you."

"And a final communiqué, Mr. President?" NBC inquired.

"That will depend on what progress we make," Yuri broke in.

"In that case," the New York *Times* said in a murmur loud enough to be clearly heard, "we might as well go home right now."

And amid laughter from their colleagues and the American delegation —the Soviets remaining, as they had throughout, grim-faced and unsmiling—they gathered their gear and trooped out.

Fifteen minutes later the subcommittees had been named, the plenary session declared over, and a definite meeting time of 10 A.M. the following morning set for the two principals to begin their private talks. Mark was not at all surprised to find that Ivan Valerian was assigned to the same subcommittee on the northern Pacific areas that he himself was.

The newspapers professed shock, the television commentaries bubbled with dismay; the headlines went all out.

SUMMIT BEGINS WITH DISAGREEMENT. PRESIDENT COLD TO SOVIET TACTICS. HIGH U.S. SOURCE SAYS PROSPECTS "NOT GOOD" FOR UNDERSTANDING. REDS CHARGE "DELIBERATE U.S. BLOW TO PEACE."

"Well!" Elinor said from the White House with mock severity when she reached him in his suite at the Waldorf-Astoria just before he, Chauncey Baron and Roger Hackett, the Secretary of Defense, sat down to dinner. "I hear you were a bad boy this morning. How dare you upset our peace-loving friends from Moscow?"

"Didn't want to," he said cheerfully, "but somehow it just happened. I seem to be running well ahead of Yuri in the media for the role of villain."

"Far ahead," she agreed. "How can they be so one-sided?"

"I suppose they think they have their reasons. Though they don't help me much."

"How serious is it, really?"

"Not all that bad. We played a little game, as you know. He decided to create the first issue, so I decided to bluff him out. How did it look to you on television?"

"It looked as though you were perfectly calm and he was acting like a spoiled two-year-old. The impression in the commentaries and editorials, though, is that you were very wrong to make an issue over 'such a trivial point. What difference does it make if the meeting begins at 10 A.M. or 3 P.M. or even midnight? The important thing is to get things moving. Hamilton Delbacher added very little to that objective with his petty performance today.' That's Anna in the early edition of tomorrow's *Inquirer*. The *Post* isn't far behind and the *Star* weighs in with 'deep concern and perturbation,' mostly directed at you."

"Things are similar here," he said with a chuckle. " 'The President is already displaying his immature and even dangerous lack of grasp of the realities of Soviet-American disagreement. For all the world knows—and for all he knows—there may have been perfectly valid reasons for the Soviet desire to start the summit at 3 P.M. yesterday afternoon.' This is the *Times*. 'It would have been better to decide the question in favor of Soviet integrity and good faith. Without American acceptance of that, the sum total of this so called "get-acquainted summit" between the two Presidents may well be exactly zero.' Don't you think the record of the past few decades fully justifies American acceptance of Soviet integrity and good faith?"

"Indubitably," she said. "When are we going to see some of it?"

"I think possibly tomorrow. We've had our little tussle now, and I think he perhaps respects me a little more as an adversary. This may lead to some genuine co-operation."

"It would lead to a lot more if you had the military power to back it up."

"I know," he agreed glumly. "There, of course, is the sticking point. I'm not in much position to be really tough, and he knows it. But neither is he going to find me any push-over. I simply can't afford to be, or it's really downhill all the way from here. So, keep your fingers crossed for me."

"I may even pray for you," she offered with a little laugh. "I really mean that."

"I hope everyone will," he said quietly. "I could use it. What have you been up to today?"

"Giving Anna an in-depth interview with a new White House wife, which she is actually going to write herself. I'm flattered."

"I hope you watched that famous New England tongue," he said with a chuckle.

"I got off a few tart ones," she said with an equal amusement. "Have to live up to the reputation, you know. . . . Well, my dear: try to get a good night's sleep, and may all go well for you tomorrow."

"I'm not worried, I think it will. Thanks for calling, and all my love."

"You too," she said quietly. "I wish I could help you carry the burden."

"My God, you think you don't? Now you're being disingenuous. You help me always, and you know it. Good night, sweetheart."

"Good night, love. Give him hell."

He laughed.

"That's my girl. Moonlight and roses in one hand and the knife in the other."

"You know it, kid," she said with a chuckle. "Good night."

"How does she feel things are going?" Chauncey asked when he returned to the table.

"About the way we do. Anna and the *Post* and the *Star* are all blasting me for my unkindness to our friends. Do you remember that sarcastic World War II song Noel Coward wrote—'Let's Don't Be Beastly to the Hun'? I've often thought of it in recent years, for some reason."

"Yes," Roger Hackett agreed. "What line do you want me to take with my opposite number tomorrow?"

"What we'll all take, I hope. Try to be pleasant, but in any event be firm. No detailed figures, of course, no secrets or even semi-secrets. Their sources in the Defense Department and on the Hill and elsewhere around town have told them everything they can find, I assume, but let's don't make it any easier for them."

"I suspect it's just as well that you only appointed me a week ago," Roger said with a smile. "I can tell you everything about TRW, but I don't know much about the Defense Department yet. So I can't even be trapped into anything inadvertently."

"You can't be trapped at all, my modest innocent," Chauncey Baron remarked. "That's why he appointed you Secretary of Defense—you're so dumb."

"Well," Roger said, "I try to be. Especially in a situation like this."

"Couldn't be better," the President said. "Come on, let's forget the treacherous bastards for a little while and concentrate on a good meal. I think we deserve it, after today."

And so thought Yuri Serapin, the Foreign Minister, the Minister of Defense, the Minister of Production, the senior marshal of the Strategic Rocket Forces and Major Ivan Valerian, all of whom had been invited to the privilege of a private meal with the President. It had been a tense day for them too, but Yuri Pavlovich's strategy had obviously been the right one: in their usual fashion, most of the American media seemed to be pinning the blame for tensions on their own President. As a result he was already emerging in the minds of his countrymen and the world as an obstructionist, a stubborn man and clearly the principal obstacle to peace. It was with a happy triumph in his voice that Yuri proposed:

"A toast to the American media! Without them, our task would be twice as difficult!"

Their hearty agreeing laughter filled the room and it was with loud exclamations of approval that they greeted Ivan Valerian's response:

"Though a junior, may I take the liberty of toasting the great wisdom, foresight and invincible devotion to the cause of socialist peace of our great leader, Comrade President Yuri Pavlovich!"

This time they outdid themselves with approval, crowding around, shaking his hand, clapping him on the back, one or two going so far as to give him bear hugs. And so they should, he thought complacently: he *was* their great leader, and his strategy was sound.

"Comrades," he said, "please be seated, have some vodka and caviar, enjoy yourselves, and I will tell you how I see the Americans. I am sure it does not differ from your own view, but it will help you understand the course I plan to follow with this new President who believes himself to be so astute in outsmarting us. He is not, comrades: that is his error. Perhaps he suspects it, perhaps he does not. In any event, it will get him nowhere."

At this they applauded excitedly, faces already flushed with the first gulps of vodka, the first bites of black bread and caviar. They were flattered that Yuri Pavlovich was taking them into his confidence, which he did not have to do unless he wanted to. As if understanding this and how they felt about it, he went on:

"It is because I need your understanding, your support and, yes, comrades, your ideas and your help, that I am telling you this. Without your strong socialist support and the knowledge that you and the Motherland are 100 per cent behind me, I could not do the task which is demanded of us by our belief in the ideas of V. I. Lenin, K. Marx and F. Engels. Your support makes it easier for me to follow the mandate of history."

There were pleased expressions, murmurs of gratification. Ivan Ivanovich, whom he had taken under his wing several years ago simply because he had noted him to be a very bright young man who would continue to rise in the hierarchy, perhaps someday even to his own position, seemed most pleased and gratified of all. For a somber second he thought suddenly of young Yuri and wondered if young Ivan had been required to undergo the toughening he had. In any event he was here, and Yuri, with a rare sentimentality, saw himself in him, and was glad to have him so.

"Comrades," he said, his voice becoming low and intent, "there is no doubt that we have nothing to fear, now or in the future, from the Americans. Because of the far-seeing decisions of our collective leadership in recent decades, decisions in which several of you, like myself, have participated, we are now superior to the United States in all categories of weapons and in all regions of the earth."

There was a burst of applause, congratulatory looks, satisfaction.

"For this reason, any aggression or threats of aggression which may be offered by the Americans can at once be crushed and destroyed by the invincible forces of the Motherland. We shall crush them like ants!"

Again their applause, their warm approving self-congratulatory glances, their acknowledgment of what wonders had been accomplished in so relatively short a time.

"Against this background," Yuri went on, "the pretensions of H. Delbacher are absurd. He is nothing but bluff. He has nothing to back him up. He is a pygmy as he faces us, who are now the giants. *And he knows it.* Although he has agitated for some months in the National Security Council about increased defense spending, our sources there tell us that he was making no progress under the late President, who was even more of a pygmy than he is. Now he is President but he is still a pygmy. We shall crush the ants' leader as we crush the ants!"

By this time much vodka had been consumed. The outburst of approval exceeded all that had gone before.

"However, comrades—however. It is not to our best interests that any of this be mentioned to any Americans you talk to, except possibly by me. It may become necessary, if he shows himself unwilling to bow to the inexorable tides of history, for me to explain all this to H. Delbacher in terms he cannot mistake. I may have to describe his plight to him in so many words. I would hope that I would not have to do this, comrades" —he smiled dryly, they laughed gleefully—"but if I do, you may rest assured that I shall not fail the Motherland or the peace-loving peoples of the socialist-communist bloc. H. Delbacher will get the truth from me, and no mistake!

"But—I say again, that is for me to decide. It must be your goal, as it essentially will be mine, to confuse the enemy and conceal from him our historic purposes. This you will do and I will do. Thus shall we prepare the final battle that will decide the fate of all mankind.

"Surprise, comrades! *Surprise, surprise, surprise!* That is what we must achieve if we are to win at least cost to ourselves. That is the single and overriding purpose for which I invited H. Delbacher to this conference. We are setting the stage for the final battle. We must never forget this for a single moment.

"In the pursuit of socialist victory, no stratagem is too harsh, no deceit too extreme, no concealment of purpose can be considered evil. Nothing we do in the attainment of our great goal is immoral, because, since our purpose is the most moral in all history, nothing that contributes to our victory can *be* immoral. Our purpose is history's purpose; our cause is just and everything necessary to attain the triumph of our cause is just. This, comrades, is the true morality of the age in which we live.

"Therefore our purpose, our goal, our plans and strategies for achieving it must all—all—be concealed from the ultimate enemy whom we now face once again—perhaps for the last time—across a conference table. This table is as much a battlefield as the fields, hills and rivers of Western Europe across which we may have to move before long in one great, decisive strike. Yet it is my intention that when we do so, either we will be so strong that the mere threat will be enough to bring the world to its knees —which is the peaceful method we would all prefer—or that if the enemy forces us to use our strength, he will be so confused and deceived, so open to destruction before he can achieve his evil purpose of destroying us, that we will be able to achieve total victory in as little as forty-eight hours or perhaps even twenty-four. Such has been the teaching of our military staff, and such the training of our troops, for at least two decades. Such infinite pains, such intensive training, such endless perfection of details and such devotion to duty as we have instilled cannot be overcome by the hasty, improvised—and, I might add, panic-stricken—stratagems of a deceived and totally surprised enemy. Therefore everything we do must be designed to lead to the final victory.

"Comrades, with your approval, this will be my approach in my private conversations with H. Delbacher. He is aware that he deals, as the Americans say, drawing an analogy from card games, from weakness. He will try to continue the bluff of recent American Presidents that the United States is still equal to—even, as they claim, superior to—the U.S.S.R. in military strength. I shall try to encourage him with pledges of Soviet desires for peace, yet at the same time I shall make very clear that we ourselves do not believe his claims and that if threatened too much we will not hesitate to use our overwhelming superiority to crush the United States and with it, the entire remaining capitalist bloc, which has no other shield than the weak and steadily diminishing shield of U.S. arms. This, I hope, will induce in him a state of mind that will make him completely unprepared for the swift and unexpected onslaught of our forces.

"Comrades"—and his voice turned even more solemn and determined —"we stand on the verge of the great climactic battle that will decide the fate of all mankind. History is with us; victory is inevitable. In the names of V. I. Lenin, K. Marx and F. Engels, this is my pledge to you: we will not fail because we cannot fail. We have been preparing for the final battle since the end of the Great Patriotic War in 1945. For more than forty years we have thought, dreamed, planned, worked, trained, organized, devoted the major portion of our national budget, the finest and most dedicated of our youth and the finest scientific and military brains of the Motherland, to this end. While we have raced ahead, America has fallen behind. While we have talked of peace and prepared for war, they have talked of peace and let many of their most vital preparations rot away. *They have not really wanted to do the things necessary to remain strong and so they have become weak. They have not been willing to make the sacrifices necessary to secure their kind of peace, so now they will have to accept ours.* Their capitalist society is corrupt and rotten to the core; never have they been so vulnerable. Now is our opportunity and now we will seize it. The result is inevitable.

"Comrades, one last toast and then we must eat and I must go to bed in preparation for tomorrow:

"To the final destruction of the United States of America and the entire capitalist bloc. To the final triumph of Soviet arms and the final world-wide victory of the people's peace . . ."

"Gentlemen," Ham Delbacher said, pushing away from the table with a smile, "there goes another three pounds to add to my elephantine bulk, I expect. But I have to be strong for tomorrow. I don't want to kick you out, but sleep is also required."

"Let me propose a toast," Chauncey Baron said, raising his liqueur glass:

"To the President of the United States, to his country, and to the cause of peace. May God be with us and guide us so that we may be worthy of His trust, and so that all the peoples of the world may soon know a just and lasting peace in which all can live together in harmony; and may fear, hatred and conquest be banished forever from the earth."

"Amen to that," the President said quietly in the hush that followed. He sighed and said softly again: "Amen to that."

They were swept to the UN next morning in their heavily guarded limousines through sweltering summer streets whose hurrying throngs scarcely broke stride to turn and look at their siren-screaming passage. The big boys were on their way to talk again: so what? It had never accomplished much in the past and it probably wouldn't now. Most of those who saw them were only remotely aware of the terrible tensions and possibilities underlying their meeting, anyway: and the rest did not want to think about it.

The man who intended to "decide the fate of all mankind"—his way— and the man who hoped to bring a genuine peace to the world if he could, might almost have existed in a vacuum insofar as their New York audience was concerned.

That New York was typical of his country as a whole, the President of the United States was only too uneasily and unhappily aware. Despite the portentous editorials and television commentaries that had begun the day, he knew, with a democratic politician's lifelong instinct, that very few among his countrymen really understood, or possessed a really informed grasp of, the fearsome potentials of this latest summit. They were worried about it, in a vague sort of way; they knew, in a vague sort of way, that it might mean something bad for them if it did not succeed. But most of them would really rather not think about it. So most of them did not, except as something vaguely menacing, off there on the horizon.

In some generalized but nonetheless profoundly weakening way, he knew that he faced not only Yuri Serapin and his threats. He also faced one of the Soviets' strongest allies: the willful blindness of the American people, who knew in their bones that they were in deadly peril yet strove with all their might to forget it, and seized upon every slightest excuse to look the other way and tell themselves that they could go right on living their comfortable, selfish lives.

Ah, the good life! he thought dryly. Another year or two, if we can't manage to bring a change in the thrust of things all over the world, and you can kiss the good life good-by, dear friends, Romans and countrymen.

He had intended to keep his aspect solemn and serious when he left his car to enter the canopied walkway to the Delegates Entrance to the UN Secretariat Building. He found he did not have to work at it. It was the way he felt and it was obvious to everyone who watched his arrival on television. Yuri's limousine swept up behind his a couple of seconds later and he too debarked grim-faced.

Not all his countrymen were lethargic, the President noted. A small group of demonstrators, held back by police, greeted his opponent: GO HOME, SOVIET MURDERER, a placard demanded. A fleeting expression of annoyance crossed Yuri's face, but both he and Hamilton Delbacher knew he need fear no later embarrassment. The demonstration would rate barely a line in the newspapers and would not appear at all on the evening news shows. It was too routine to bother with—the sort of thing the news director at CBS referred to as "ho-hum stuff." If it had been directed against the President of the United States he knew full well it would be featured in the news all over the world.

Inside the heavily guarded building, from which the public had been barred for the duration of the conference, New York City police had temporarily supplanted the multi-national guards of the UN security force. They lined the corridors and flanked the private elevator that ascended to the Secretary-General's thirty-eighth-floor offices. To this aerie first the President of the Soviet Union, then the President of the United States, were swiftly lifted. Far below in the first- and second-floor conference rooms of the UN's many specialized agencies, the joint subcommittees named yesterday from both delegations were presumably at work. The UN had recessed for a week to make way for the gathering. All its facilities, by resolution of the General Assembly, were at the disposal of the visitors—an indication that in this house of many tongues, at least, there was full recognition of the summit's importance.

The Secretary-General greeted them gravely, led them to his own small conference room, opened the door. Yuri, the President was surprised to see, had not brought the ubiquitous official interpreter, though he himself had decided to forego any argument and instead had brought his own, a bright young man from the State Department. Yuri gave him a blank and questioning look, but before he could raise the issue Ham murmured something quietly to his young man. The young man turned on his heel and left before the Secretary-General had even opened his mouth.

"Gentlemen," the S.-G. said simply, "this room is yours as long as you need it. It belongs to you, and in a broader sense it belongs to the world during the day or days you may occupy it. Speaking for the world in my own modest capacity, we hope you will put it to good use and that from it may emerge an easing of tensions and some realistic and genuine contributions to peace."

"That is my intention, Mr. Secretary-General," Hamilton Delbacher said quietly.

"And mine," Yuri Serapin echoed, almost indifferently. "I will need cooperation, of course—"

"You will have it from me," the President said, equally offhand. "Providing you are prepared to be serious."

"It is you who must be serious!" Yuri responded with an anger genuine or faked, it was impossible to tell—but loud. "It is not I who attempts to make a mockery of these proceedings. It is not I who tries to come to this meeting with a spy disguised as an interpreter—"

"And the Secretary-General," the President interrupted coldly, "is not the world press, in whose presence such propaganda stunts as you are now conducting might gain you many headlines. They will gain you nothing from the Secretary-General, whose capacity here is entirely confidential, is it not, Mr. Secretary?"

"Yes, Mr. President," the S.-G. said quietly, "and I think I can best serve you both, and serve the cause of world peace, by withdrawing at once. Gentlemen, I wish you well."

And he bowed low, face expressionless, and stepped out, drawing the door finally shut behind him—not a slam, but quite emphatic.

For several moments there was silence, broken only by the heavy breathing of the Soviet President. The American President found after a few seconds that he had enough of this.

"I will say, Mr. President," he said calmly, "that if this is the mood in which you begin these discussions, then I really see no point in continuing them. Shall we leave right now?"

"If you like," Yuri Serapin said, again indifferently; but when the President made as if to rise he lifted a cautionary hand at once. "You will, of course, miss information vital to your country's survival if you do."

"Very well," Ham Delbacher said, resuming his seat. "Then suppose we stop this childishness and get on with it. We are utterly alone and there is nothing to be gained by it. So I would suggest you stop it, if you will, please. It does not impress me."

"It should," Yuri said with a grim little smile. "Since you have no arms with which to stop our inevitable triumph."

"Nor does that kind of language help, either," the President observed. "I must point out again that we are not in a propaganda forum now. It is simply you and me. And truly, Mr. President, I am *not* impressed. Balancing armaments is such a futile game. Spirit and will enter into it also, and compensate for many things."

"And you think your country has spirit and will?" the Soviet President inquired scornfully. "It is not the impression you give."

"I have spirit and will, Mr. President," Ham Delbacher said quietly. "That is obviously what I must impress upon you in this meeting. *I* have spirit and will. And if *I* have them, that is half the battle."

"We have gained many things because some of your recent Presidents have not had them, true enough," Yuri said with a smug little smile.

"Very true," Ham Delbacher agreed. "But I'm different stuff. Remember it."

"Mr. President," his opponent said, tone deliberately and annoyingly full of heavy pity, "I will remember it. But it really cannot compensate for the fact that your country is no longer strong."

"I would not advise you to test that out," the President said crisply.

"I would not advise you to try to bluff us with it," Yuri said with equal crispness. "Do you think we have no intelligence service at all? Do you think we do not know, right down to the last bullet almost, exactly what you have and do not have? Do you take us for children? We know your strengths and weaknesses, Mr. President. The first are few and the latter innumerable. Is it your belief that we can be intimidated by *you?*" His eyes darkened, flashed with anger, he slapped his palm suddenly on the table.

"Listen to me, Mr. President! The days in which you could intimidate us are gone long, long ago. The days when we could be threatened or bullied by the arrogance of the capitalist camp have vanished forever. You will never bully us again, never! Moscow speaks, the world dances. Try to stop that from being true, Mr. President. You will never succeed! Never!"

"I am giving you warning," Hamilton Delbacher said evenly. "Don't try our patience too far."

"Starting with the days of J. Carter," Yuri snapped, "you have rarely had anything else. It is not enough, Mr. President. It is not enough!"

"This childish shouting match is not enough," the President said, with a deliberate dryness that was, and was meant to be, a slap in the face. "That's for sure. Do you think we might discuss the substance of the things that divide us, and put the threats and bombast aside for a while? We agreed upon an agenda yesterday. Shall we attempt to discuss it?"

"Very good," his opponent said promptly. "Number 1 was 'Continued United States aggressive imperialism in all quarters of the globe.' We must insist that it stop."

"The United States," its President remarked in the same dry tone, "has not been an imperialist aggressor since the Spanish-American War of 1898 when we liberated Cuba."

"We liberated Cuba!" Yuri said angrily.

"You returned Cuba to bondage under your bearded stooge," the President retorted calmly. He too leaned forward abruptly and pounded the table, so suddenly and so loudly that his opponent actually jumped. "Lis-

ten to *me!* I said we have had enough of propaganda statements. I said
we must discuss the substance of what concerns us. There is no audience
here, no gallery to play to, no reason at all to make propaganda speeches.
We want you to stop at once the conquest and aggression which is threatening the entire world and conduct yourselves like responsible members
of the international community. There can be no possibility of lasting
peace until you do."

"How will you stop us?" the President of the Soviet Union inquired
blandly. "While you scurried frantically like mice in a trap, for instance,
we took Afghanistan. You could not stop us then and you cannot stop us
now. We next entered Iran, and while there had been high and mighty
threats before we did so about the military action you might take, when it
became a fait accompli in four days' time your weakling President wrung
his hands as he had before and cried like a baby for the UN to help him.
The UN, that helpless talking machine! The minute he condoned the overthrow of the Shah he made the seizure of your embassy in Teheran inevitable—we planned it that way, as one final test of a man we knew already
to be weak. The minute we saw how hesitant and ineffectual he was in
that crisis—and how popular his waverings were with his countrymen—
that minute we knew we had him and the United States on the run. Now
we hold Iran, have Pakistan intimidated, are infiltrating much of
Rajasthan, and what have he and his successors done? Nothing! Nothing!
Statements and cancelled threats and wishful hoping that words will
deflect us. Words will never deflect us! Arms alone will deflect us, and
you have neither the arms nor the will to use them if you did. Is it not
time to co-operate with the inevitable instead of offering further useless
gestures that achieve nothing but your own humiliation, as the world sees
again and again how helpless and cowardly you are?"

"*I* am not helpless," Hamilton Delbacher said coldly, "and *I* am not a
coward. You must not forget that things have changed in my country,
Mr. President."

"As they have in mine, Mr. President," Yuri pointed out calmly. "But
the already overwhelming and constantly increasing military predomi-
nance of the U.S.S.R. has not changed. That goes steadily on, increasing
and becoming more invincible, day by day. . . . Mr. President!" he said,
and he leaned forward, again, voice earnest, manner reasonable. "Why
should we argue this paramount and obvious fact of our time? Why
should we argue the inevitabilities of history? You represent a dying capitalist system, without sufficient conventional arms to fight and without the
will to use the nuclear weapon, which in any event is itself outnumbered
and made futile by our superior missiles and other means of delivery. And
we used gas in Afghanistan, we gave it to our friends of Viet Nam to use
in Cambodia: what makes you think we would hesitate to use it on you?
It is hopeless for you, Mr. President, hopeless! Why not save the world

and both our peoples from the terrible agonies of an exchange that would inevitably become nuclear and chemical—might well extend, even, into space? It would be so simple for rational men to arrive at a peaceable accommodation."

"It would if you wanted what we understand as peace," Ham Delbacher said, keeping his voice steady at some cost in the face of these horrors. "But you don't. You want a peace with yourselves in control, with yourselves as rulers of the world, with yourselves using the rest of us as milk cows and worker bees to support your imperial society. That is what you mean by 'peace.'"

"Mr. President," inquired Yuri Serapin softly, "has it not ever been so?"

"No, it has not 'ever been so'! When *we* talk of peace we mean a universal agreement on certain standards of behavior and restraint that will work for the benefit of all. We do not want others' territory. We do not want to impose our ways on others. We want to live and let live. We want to be left alone—we want to leave others alone—we want *you* to leave others alone. Is that too much to ask?"

"Clearly so, Mr. President," Yuri said, still softly, "when it is obvious from our successes that we and we alone are riding the true tides of history. Otherwise, why would we succeed?"

"You have succeeded—so far—because of the accumulated mistakes of the West. We have made it easy for you. In a sense, I cannot blame you for taking advantage of our mistakes; it is the human thing to do, if you are in the grip of an imperialistic drive for conquest that appears to be succeeding everywhere. But that does not make it right, Mr. President. Nor does it make it the best condition for mankind. Nor does it even make it best for the Soviet Union, which is becoming so engorged with other lands and peoples that it must inevitably—you talk about 'inevitable' history—collapse of its own weight and engorgement."

"We do not collapse," Yuri pointed out, still in the same soft, reasonable voice. "We make sure that every conquest is thoroughly absorbed before we move on to the next."

"By murder," Ham Delbacher said with a scorn he hoped would crack the implacable smugness before him. "By rounding up and shooting all political leaders, all journalists, writers, artists, creative people who could possibly oppose you. By destroying everyone who stands in your way. *By murder.*"

"Certainly," the Soviet President agreed promptly. "There has never been a successful rebellion against us, once we have taken a country. Nor will there ever be."

"You are monsters!" the American President exclaimed with a vast and weary disgust. "Monsters!"

"If you wish to call us that," Yuri Serapin agreed with a calm indifference. "But we are successful monsters. And words, Mr. President, will neither hurt us nor disrupt the inevitable flow of history which carries us to the achievement of our goals. Indeed, the Soviet Union and history cannot be spoken of as two separate entities as do your commentators of the West. We *are* history, and as such, it is right that those who oppose us should have no choice but to surrender and be removed permanently from positions in which they could do us damage. Those who oppose the will of history must perish for their sin, Mr. President. There is no other ending possible for them."

"I would like to hear you proclaim that openly to the West," the President said.

"I could proclaim it at high noon on the front steps of St. Patrick's Cathedral," Yuri Serapin said, "and not one of your millions would believe it. Only your intellectuals who have helped us so much, your journalists, your authors, would finally, too late, realize that it was true; and them we will eradicate as our first order of business, because there is no place for independent thought in the world socialist state. So why should we doubt the future? Not only the mistakes of leaders but the disbelief of your people are on our side. It is no wonder we believe K. Marx and V. I. Lenin when they tell us our triumph over capitalism is inevitable. Capitalism assists us in every way it possibly can to make the prophecy come true. Faith and results both prove that we are right."

"But you are not right!" Ham Delbacher exclaimed angrily. Again Yuri Serapin shrugged.

"To quote one of your corrupt capitalist sayings," he remarked, quite seriously, "nothing succeeds like success. Ergo, we are right: we are successful. Have you any counter-argument to offer that is as strong as that?"

For a moment the President did not answer, rubbing his cheek thoughtfully while he studied his opponent with a quizzical and contemplative air.

"I have," he said finally. "The argument of liberty. The argument of man's desire to be *left alone,* as I said a moment ago, to lead his own life, and for his nation to lead its own life, untrampled and undisturbed by others as long as it abides by the rules of civilized behavior. The right of the human mind to express itself in any way it wishes, consistent with those same rules. The right to *be free,* to live as one pleases as long as it does not hurt others, to have one's family, home, life, work, to enjoy what we call the individual's 'life style' *as one wishes.* The right of free speech, free travel, private property—all these things, which you do not permit in your society or in the unhappy slave populations you have conquered, *which simply make life worth living.* There is nothing in your cold jail of a system that can match that, Mr. President. Every human wants to be free, none wants to be slave. That is the great fundamental weakness of your system. It is there we will undermine you."

"You cannot!" Yuri Serapin cried triumphantly. "It is too late! For many, many years the peoples of the West have been warned of this by some of your intellectuals, journalists, writers; but the peoples have not wanted to believe, because they are peaceable and to stop us would have meant taking a firm stand against us. And that, they feared—and we made sure they feared it—might mean war. No one in the West wanted war, Mr. President. And now it is too late for anyone to go to war, because the peoples of the West have permitted us to become too strong. Our victory is inevitable. It cannot be stopped. Why do you persist?"

"Because I cannot believe," Hamilton Delbacher said, and his voice shook a little with his emotion for his own all too human country and his great disdain for the individual and the system, both so coldly and arrogantly inhuman, that confronted him, "I cannot believe that a system so remote from all the well-springs of human kindness, compassion, decency and tolerance as yours can be given such a victory over mankind. If there is a God, which I believe there is, and a final justice in the world, which I believe does exist, then it is not to be permitted. You may succeed here and there temporarily, but you cannot succeed in the end because your system violates all the things that give man his uniqueness *as man*. It will inevitably go down."

"But at what a price, Mr. President," Yuri said, almost in a whisper. *"At what a price!* I do not believe it is one you and the West will wish to pay. But!" he said, and his tone changed, suddenly harsh and overbearing. "It is idle to talk of this, since it is a price you *cannot* pay. I keep returning to the fundamental fact: *you do not have the strength,* and it is much too late to hastily acquire it. Many, many years have been wasted by America and by the West—many, many years have been lost to us. It is simply impossible for you to recapture them. That is the only argument your God, or anyone else, will understand, the only one that is controlling. There is nothing else left now."

For several moments they stared at one another across the table. The conference, the "get-acquainted meeting," the peace "summit" the media had made so much of, for all practical purposes was over before it had really begun and they both knew it.

Yet, for a little while longer, the pretense went on. As though they had rid themselves of some festering canker that must be disposed of before they could talk, they turned more calmly to the various areas of conflicting interest, taking them up one by one in much the same way: a challenge from the President of the United States, a calm and much less belligerent response from the President of the Soviet Union. It was still obvious that there would be no change of course by the Soviets unless forced by superior power—it was still obvious that Yuri was convinced there was no superior power—yet he set himself quite deliberately on a path of conciliation and reasonable amicability. His purpose, as he had told his dinner guests, was to create a climate of deception in which the enemy might be persuaded to let down his guard so that the weapon of surprise might be used most effectively when it seemed advisable.

At first he did not think he was making any headway with President Delbacher; but presently Ham's tone, too, became more agreeable, he began to concede the logic of certain of Yuri's arguments, there appeared to be an increasing tendency to refer, as Yuri did, to "inevitabilities . . . necessary accommodations to the flow of history . . . feasible alternatives to confrontation . . ." and the like.

By noon, when the Secretary-General sent up a light but refreshing meal, the Soviet President could congratulate himself that he had managed to convince the American President that Yuri's earlier remarks were "somewhat heated in a moment of argument—not really representative of the long-range ambitions and purposes of the Soviet people." Hamilton Delbacher appeared to accept this. His tone was relieved, indeed almost effusive, as he congratulated the Soviet leader on his "desire to find sensible alternatives on a genuine middle ground where both powers can live amicably together."

The President of the United States knew he faced a genuine fanatic. The President of the Soviet Union did not know he faced a consummate actor trained in the school of democratic rough-and-tumble politics. They were even able to draw up a joint statement and send it down to the S.-G. to be typed and duplicated for release to the press:

"The Presidents of the Union of Soviet Socialist Republics and the United States of America, having met in private discussion of the areas of disagreement between their two countries, are pleased to state that substantial progress has been made in achieving their desire to get to know one another better.

"A free, frank and far-ranging survey has been made of the trouble areas of the globe. The interests and aims of both nations have been fully explored. ["In three hours?" the New York *Times* inquired quizzically in the press room.] The possibilities of conciliation and co-operation have been thoroughly discussed. We conclude this personal meeting ["Already?" CBS said blankly.] in the firm hope and confident assurance that it has substantially advanced the cause of universal peace for the benefit of all mankind. ["That's nice," the AP remarked, "but I still think we need a press conference to sort this out."]

"We intend to meet again from time to time as we move forward peaceably and constructively together on the path to permanent peace. ["Pardon my crude language," NBC remarked, "but that's so much hypocritical crap."]

"We pledge ourselves to the peaceable solution of any further problems that may arise between us. ["*Goody,*" UPI observed, "for you."]

"Y. P. Serapin, U.S.S.R.

"Hamilton Delbacher, U.S.A."

And despite the noisy clamor, sparked by the AP, that they hold a full-scale press conference, word came down from the Secretary-General that there would be none. Instead they were swept away, back to their respective headquarters, and the media were left to speculate on what had really happened.

"Comrades," Yuri Serapin told his delegation jubilantly in a brief report half an hour later, "I think I did what I said I wished to do. I convinced H. Delbacher, who is an easily misled fool, that our purposes are peaceful and conciliatory. At the same time I reminded him firmly that the power of the United States is virtually non-existent. I think he will think twice, now, before he dares challenge us. He expects no surprises from us. Therefore, we must continue to plan with ever greater vigor to achieve surprise and with it the final surrender of the United States."

"Gentlemen," Hamilton Delbacher said somberly, "I have just had three hours with a fanatic who is determined to stop at nothing to achieve the Soviet conquest of the globe. We must be alert against surprises. There are various delaying actions we can take to protect ourselves and I intend to get started the minute I get back to Washington. Which I estimate"—and he looked at the ornate watch Elinor had given him on their anniversary two years ago—"will be in about two hours."

PRESIDENT ANNOUNCES SUMMIT REPORT TO CONGRESS TOMORROW NIGHT, the headlines said. **AIDES HINT "GRAVE CONCERN" AT SOVIET ATTITUDE.**

"You see?" Yuri exclaimed angrily when this news reached him just as he was climbing aboard the Ilyushin to fly home. "They cannot be trusted for one moment!"

6

"The Soviet Government . . . and their armed forces must be ready primarily for a world war . . . The armed forces of the Soviet Union and the other socialist countries must be prepared above all to wage war under the conditions of the mass use of nuclear weapons by both belligerent parties . . . The preparation and waging of just such a war must be regarded as the main task of the theory of military strategy and strategic leadership."

—*Soviet Military Strategy,*
Marshal V. D. Sokolovskiy

So," the President concluded his detailed report of the meeting to the members of the delegation, as they faced him solemnly across his desk in the Oval Office later that afternoon, "you can see why I came away with no faith whatsoever in the Soviets' word and no hopes whatsoever that they will co-operate in trying to achieve peace. The media, I notice, are already making a lot of the brevity of the meeting and demanding to know why it was 'the shortest summit in history.' It was the shortest because I could see there was no point in prolonging it. We were getting nowhere. In fact, if anything, we were retrogressing. How did the rest of you do?"

"The same," Art Hampton said. "Jim Elrod and I"—he glanced at the senior Senator from North Carolina, who sat grim-faced on his left— "were told in so many words that, 'Nikita Sergeyevich was not joking when he said, "We will bury you." But if you co-operate with history, then there need be no war. We do not want war. We want peace.'"

"We were told," Jim Elrod confirmed, "that there would be no need to bury us if we would simply have sense enough to surrender right now and get it over with. It wasn't put quite that bluntly, but almost."

"My group got much the same," the Speaker said.

"And mine," Mark Coffin agreed. "We were left with the distinct impression that the choice was entirely ours, because they are so strong that it is immaterial to them what we decide. They seem to feel they have us so outnumbered, outgunned and outmissiled that 'history,' as one of them said, 'has already made your decision for you.'"

"And how do you feel about it yourself, Mark?" the President inquired with a smile. "That your elders are still all wet when they tell you we cannot deal with these people?"

"What do we do if we don't deal with them, Mr. President?" Mark asked, and a little silence fell as they all turned serious faces to the portly man behind the desk. He returned the look thoughtfully and slowly nodded his head.

"Exactly. Of course I don't mean we can break off all relations with them—we have to deal with them. Perhaps I should have said, 'We cannot deal with these people except from a position of strength.' Perhaps I should have said, 'Strength is the only language they understand. Ordinary diplomacy based on give-and-take will not work because they believe in all take, no give.' Would that state it more clearly?"

"Your position has always been clear to me, Mr. President," Mark said.

"And has yours changed any as a result of the firsthand knowledge you've acquired now?"

Mark nodded, a little ruefully.

"It's changed some. But I still think we're strong enough to deal with them if we are firm."

"I was firm with Serapin," the President said. "I deliberately left him feeling he had convinced me to some extent, but I made no specific commitments and certainly nothing indicating any retreat or surrender."

"So what will you do?" Herb Esplin, the Senate Minority Leader, pressed.

"I have already announced," the President said, "that I will come to the Hill tomorrow night. I don't expect to come up there to pass the time of day. I'll have some specifics for you."

"What are they?" Herb asked. "We don't want to be too surprised."

"I'll see you get an advance copy of my speech by 6 P.M. tomorrow. I'll speak at 9. Will that be sufficient?"

"It ought to be," Art Hampton said.

"Just make sure nobody leaks it, if you possibly can," the President requested. "I want to retain a little element of surprise."

"Fewer copies, fewer leaks," Jim Elrod observed.

"Will you forego yours, in the interests of secrecy?" the President asked with a smile that indicated he didn't think Jim would. But Senator Elrod fooled him.

"If you think it will help you in this situation, certainly."

There was a murmur of assent. The President looked pleased.

"Thank you, gentlemen, I appreciate that. As I will hope for and appreciate your support for what I have to say. If you have any ideas you think should be incorporated in the address, give me a call any time up to noon tomorrow. . . . Mark," he said, as he stood up and began to ease them along to the door, "stay with me for a minute will you? I'd like to get your views on something."

"Sure," Mark said, flattered.

"Thank you," Ham Delbacher said, and when he had shaken the last hand and said the last good-by, returned to his desk, took off his coat and tie and gave a grunt of relief as he sank back into his big chair. For a moment he studied the earnest young face across the desk. Then he smiled.

"It's been an interesting two days, hasn't it?"

"Fascinating," Mark agreed.

"You know a little more now about the nature of the beast."

"Not really," Mark said. He smiled quizzically. "Does anyone, ever?"

"I think probably the simplest interpretation is the wisest," the President said. "They're very elemental people, these Soviet leaders. Bullies . . . many of them, including Serapin, probably murderers, direct or indirect . . . power hungry . . . imperialistic to the point of insanity in their vision of the world . . . intensely self-conscious . . . possessed of terrible inferiority complexes toward the West and particularly toward us . . . devious . . . liars . . . impossible to trust for a second . . . impervious to civilized standards of dealing . . . dedicated communists, convinced history has singled them out to destroy us and rule the world . . . cold-blooded, cynical, absolutely ruthless, without qualms or conscience except for a thin veneer sufficient to hoodwink many in the West . . . completely unsophisticated . . . very limited in really broad-gauge or sophisticated intelligence, but far and away ahead of us in sheer animal shrewdness and craft . . . bad people, by all the standards of the civilized world and all the standards of man's achievements in his long climb up from the primeval slime . . . still down there, in many ways . . . which," he concluded with a heavy sigh, "makes them damned difficult for us to handle. By contrast we are, as Yuri told me in effect, weak, equivocal, paralyzed by education, training, and the naïve—in their eyes—view that human beings must at least *try* to be kind, decent, tolerant, compassionate, forebearing and forgiving toward one another. They don't even try. It's against their state religion." He sighed again, "It makes it difficult."

"I didn't see all those things," Mark said, "but I saw some. Enough to convince me that your policy of firmness may be the right one, after all."

"Well, I achieved something, then," the President said with a smile.

"But," Mark said, "I don't agree we need more of an arms race than we've already got. I think our arsenal is quite sufficient and more would simply be redundant. So if you're planning—"

"I'm planning nothing but an attempt to restore some balance in the world," the President interrupted. "We must have it, Mark, whether I have you on my side or not. I would like your support, but I can go ahead without it if necessary. And I will."

"I would hope not," Mark said, but the kindly face he had known for almost six years was temporarily closed off, stern and unyielding. Presently it relaxed and the President said:

"Tell me if you saw or sensed anything particularly unusual while you were with them in New York. Was there anything that particularly struck you, any one person, perhaps, who stood out in your mind—aside from Yuri, that is, who is a pretty fundamental force himself?"

"He's a powerhouse," Mark said. "A terrifically strong personality, I thought. I don't envy you, having to work with him."

Ham Delbacher snorted.

"We don't work together, we just inhabit the same planet. Successfully, I hope, though I'm not placing any bets at the moment. . . . No one else? How about that young fellow you were talking to at dinner?"

Mark looked startled for a second. Then he smiled.

"You see a lot more than a lot of people give you credit for," he observed. "Yes, Ivan and I struck up a rather puzzling little friendship, I thought. He was working very hard to give me the impression that he wanted to defect. Next day in the committee meeting he was all official line again, we were imperialists, war-mongers, traitors to mankind and all the rest of that crap. Then as we were leaving he brushed past me and murmured, 'You will hear from me.' "

"If you do," the President said, "you tell me about it at once, O.K.?"

"Oh, certainly. I keep going back and forth on it. One minute I think maybe he meant it and the next I think I'm being deliberately set up for something. He is one who has a lot of charm—a quality you left out of your listing, which some of them seem to have when they want to show it. I'd like to believe he is genuinely friendly to us—next minute I'm sure he isn't. So there you are."

"There *you* are," the President remarked. "Either way, it's an interesting position to be in. Meanwhile, what's his full name? I can have the CIA and the FBI run a check and see if they know anything about him. Has he ever been stationed in this country?"

"Not that I had time to find out, but he may have. His full name is Ivan Ivanovich Valerian. About my age, married, three kids, attached to their general staff. More than just animal-shrewd, I think—really intelligent. And, as I say, charming."

"We'll find out what we can," the President said, and stood up again, extending his hand. "Mark: don't be too hard on this poor old man when he speaks to Congress, O.K.? And keep us informed on your friend Ivan. In this game we're in, you never know where an advantage will come from. Maybe he's one."

"I hope so," Mark said. "I'll do my best."

"You do that," Ham Delbacher said. "It could be important."

It was not until Mark had passed through the busy corridors of the White House and was out on Pennsylvania Avenue hailing a cab to go back up to the Hill that the thought occurred to him that Ivan was undoubtedly the reason the President had wanted to talk to him, all the time.

TENSION MOUNTS AS CONGRESS AWAITS PRESIDENT'S SPEECH. MOSCOW WARNS "WAR-MONGERING" COULD BRING "SEVERE WORSENING" OF RELATIONS. KREMLIN PROMISES "PROMPT REPLY" FROM SERAPIN.

"Mistuh Speakuh!" bawled the Doorkeeper of the House as he had on so many solemn occasions in the past. "The Prezzdent of the Yewnine States!"

And once again, as on so many occasions, the members of the House, Senate, the Supreme Court, the Cabinet, the Joint Chiefs, the diplomatic corps, the media and all the guests who had managed to beg, borrow or wangle a ticket to the public galleries of the House chamber surged to their feet and applauded as the tall, heavy, grandfatherly figure came slowly down the aisle, smiling, nodding, waving, stopping to shake the occasional outthrust hand as he proceeded to the podium. It was the first time Hamilton Delbacher had addressed the Congress since becoming President, and a wave of warmth, hope and genuine friendliness greeted him. It was very touching to him and for a moment his eyes misted. *I will try to serve you well,* he promised them earnestly in his mind. *I'll need a lot of help but I* will *do my best.*

He reached the podium, climbed the steps, turned to face them: a hush fell. The Speaker made the formal introduction, again the heartfelt applause broke out, to be succeeded once more by hush—tense, tingling, expectant. In the area reserved for the diplomatic corps the Soviet Ambassador, Valerian Bukanin, hunched down in his seat, head propped on his hand, shrewd little eyes narrowed and speculative. The President looked out upon his audience for a moment; smiled up at Elinor in the Family Gallery; opened the black leather folder that held his speech, turned to address the Speaker and the President of the Senate, then turned back to the Congress and the waiting world.

"My friends of the Congress," he began in an even, unhurried voice; "my fellow countrymen everywhere:

"Eight days ago, on the Fourth of July, as a result of the unexpected national tragedy that befell us on that date, I became President of the United States. I would have preferred that it not happen in this fashion, but it did; and so there has fallen upon me a heavy burden in a most difficult time.

"History will assess my predecessor in due course, so I shall not attempt it here, except to say that we will all miss his wise leadership and commanding personality. He served his country well, as he saw it; and it is not for me now to argue with or dispute his record."

["Just turn it around 180 degrees," murmured Bill Adams of the AP in the Press Gallery above. "That's his privilege," murmured Bill's young colleague, Chuck Dangerfield. "But," he added with a slight shiver, "let's hope he knows what the hell he's doing."]

"However," the President continued, "inexorably, time moves on: and it is what has happened since his death that I wish to discuss with you today.

"Almost simultaneously with my becoming President, there was a similar change in the nation that unhappily considers itself to be our principal competition—even, I am sorry to say, our enemy. Following the equally unexpected death of the President of the Soviet Union, a younger and much more vigorous man, Yuri Serapin, was elected by the Central Committee of the Communist Party to take his place. Immediately upon my own accession to office, President Serapin issued an invitation to me to meet him at the United Nations summit. The idea was, as I conceived it, that we would become personally acquainted, have a frank exchange of views concerning the differences between our two countries, and lay the groundwork for later negotiations that would strive as much as possible to settle them. This was the aim—my aim.

"But the thing that emerged most emphatically from our talk was this: the problems do exist, they are urgent, and unless there is a fundamental change in the Soviet attitude, there is very little hope if any, that they can be solved short of armed conflict."

There was an audible gasp from his audience, exclamations of fear and dismay in front of 100 million American television sets. Ham Delbacher's reputation for blunt talk had been established ever since he entered public office, but nobody had expected anything like this. After waiting for a moment for the disturbance in the chamber to die down, he went on in the same calm, inflexible voice.

"There is an absolute conviction in Moscow that the Soviet Union is overwhelmingly stronger than we are in atomic rocketry, chemical and space weapons and conventional weapons. There is an absolute conviction that history is on their side. There is an absolute conviction that we and all other nations friendly to us will inevitably be conquered by the communist system, which means essentially by the Soviet Union. There is absolute conviction that, as the late Premier Khrushchev put it, 'We will

bury you.' In Moscow this is not considered to be, as it is by many nervous—or foolish—Soviet apologists in America, a joke. He meant it and
they mean it. And they do not mean it in any comfortable sense of economic competition or political competition: they intend burial to mean
burial—the end of this free Republic, and the end of all free governments
everywhere—forever.

"I found Mr. Serapin to be absolutely intransigent, absolutely unyielding, absolutely threatening on this point. He and his colleagues do not understand language as we do: it is designed only to assist them in achieving this goal. Détente, peaceful co-existence, negotiation, appear to exist
in their minds only as means to a single end; permanent destruction of
freedom everywhere, most particularly in the United States of America,
which is now the only obstacle standing in the way of their imperial military machine as it moves forward toward what they believe to be the final
conquest of Earth itself.

"The question that faces us now, and most particularly faces me as
your President, is this: what do we do about it? Change our policies?
Conform to their demands? Admit their claimed superiority—let ourselves be bluffed—surrender? Or strengthen ourselves as fast as we can
and seek to achieve a position in which, at the price of a great deal of
money and sacrifice, eternal vigilance and a constant show of firmness
and determination, we can finally convince them that we must live together in this world, and that mad ideas of world dominance must themselves be buried and allowed to trouble the nations no more?"

He paused to sip from a glass of water, noting as he did so that his audience was absolutely silent, absolutely intent. He had not received a single round of applause so far nor did he expect to until he concluded; and
that, now, would be respectful but shaken and cold. But for once, he told
himself grimly, somebody from this podium is telling them the exact
truth. It is about time they heard it from a President, and if it scares the
hell out of them, well and good: maybe they'll at last wake up and start
rebuilding before everything is lost.

"Mr. Speaker, Mr. President," he said, "I regret more than I can say
that I must speak thus bluntly and harshly to the Congress and to the nation. Yet I think I am not alone in this interpretation of Soviet intentions
that I bring back from New York; I know the conclusion is unanimous
among our entire delegation. There is not, I will concede, the same unanimity as to what we should do about it; but the fact of the Soviet desire
to conquer the world is, I think, one on which we all agree.

"For myself, faced as I am with the executive responsibility to seek
some way out of this dead-end labyrinth we have gradually drifted into in
recent years under succeeding Presidents and Congresses, I must make a
decision and I must act. The various methods used by some of my
predecessors—the futile attempts to appeal to a United Nations whose

desires and decisions are contemptuously dismissed in Moscow—the frantic campaigns to line up support for blockades, economic sanctions, 'quarantines,' 'boycotts'—the futile scurrying about the world of Secretaries of State who return home empty-handed of realities but garlanded about with falsely glowing, spuriously hopeful rhetoric—all of these are both pathetic and pointless. One thing and one thing only moves the Soviets: force. And the iron, inflexible determination to use it.

"There was passed, two Congresses ago, a measure which is still on the books. It was given to my predecessor as a weapon that might strengthen his hand in his dealings with the Russians. He chose not to use it, for reasons best known to himself which we may never know. But it is there, free of the necessity of further debate and discussion, free for me to use independently and at once. This I intend to do."

For the first time there was a burst of applause; not unanimous by any means, but sufficiently strong to be heartening. He acknowledged it with a quick, stern-faced nod and proceeded to his conclusion.

"The so-called Elrod bill, introduced by the senior Senator from North Carolina, chairman of the Senate Armed Services Committee, places in the hands of the President the sum of $10 billion, to be allocated as he sees fit, for the immediate expansion of the armed forces. Tomorrow morning the Secretary of Defense and I will sit down with the Joint Chiefs of Staff and determine where it is to be used and for what purposes. By tomorrow afternoon I hope to be able to issue the necessary executive orders to put our decisions into effect—immediately."

Again there was applause, a little stronger now; but many, he saw, were still withholding approval. So be it: he had not expected universal consent. He would have much educating to do: but that was his job, and he was not afraid of it.

"My fellow Americans," he concluded quietly, "much will be demanded of us all in these coming months. I do not undertake this response to Soviet intransigence lightly, because it is a very serious thing. It carries great risks to be strong: but to be weak means national suicide. And that is something I as your President—and, I believe, a majority of you—are not prepared to accept.

"God bless you all and God bless the United States of America."

And he left the podium to applause which was very mixed, as he had known it would be, between support and disapproval; and was driven, in the usual racing, screaming rush of motorcycle cops and limousines, back to the White House.

It looked, as always, gleaming and pure in the hot, humid night. The city was limp after a long, exhausting summer's day and so was he. Elinor put her arms around him, said firmly, "It was great. I'm proud of you," and kissed him. Half an hour after he left the Hill he was in bed, sleeping like a baby.

But if the brief address had left him relieved and relaxed, now that his decision had been made and announced, it could not be said to have had the same effect on the rest of the world. There were immediate assumptions, particularly in the Congress and the media, that there must be great dismay in Moscow, that an immediate increase in tensions would inevitably follow, that "the same old pattern of act and react," as Anna Hastings put it in her editorial, would be repeated once again. The reaction in the office of the President of the Soviet Union would have quite astounded the instant critics of the President of the United States.

Yuri Serapin's colleagues of the Politburo, having watched the speech live via satellite, were jubilant.

"Comrades," he told them with a satisfaction in his voice that, for his usually stolid person, was the equivalent of jumping up and down for joy, "we have him. He has done exactly—exactly—what I intended. He has taken the bait. Now we must close the trap."

"Comrade President," the Minister of Foreign Affairs said solemnly, "the peoples of the socialist bloc salute you. Your genius has been proven once again. It is superb."

"It is the greatest possible contribution to the inevitable victory," agreed the Minister of Defense, not to be outdone. "It is unbelievably great."

"Thank you," Yuri said gravely. Secretly he had been startled by the President's sharp response. This rapidly changed. The end result seemed to him, too, to warrant the adjective.

"What will you do, Comrade President?" the Foreign Minister inquired, "now that the stupid H. Delbacher has taken the bait?"

"And what was the bait?" inquired the Minister of Defense, who was not sure he understood exactly what constituted Y. Serapin's genius, though he approved of it mightily.

"The bait, Comrade Minister," Yuri replied in a tone that dared anyone to challenge him, "was to provoke him to take some aggressive action that would give us the excuse to respond in kind. You agree that he has done so?"

"Oh yes, Comrade President!" the Minister of Defense said hastily. "Yes, I see that! I see it clearly!"

"Very good," Yuri said coldly. "Now tell me what you think we should do to respond."

"Perhaps a move further into India?" the Minister of Defense asked tentatively. "Renewed threats and pressure out of Yugoslavia? New troop concentrations along the Mexican-El Salvador border? A feint in Alaskan waters?"

"You have the essentials," Yuri said, "but, as usual, you are mistaken in your geography. Mexico has no border with El Salvador."

"Yes, Comrade President," the Minister of Defense said humbly. "I await your genius to correct me."

"If you had not challenged it so ill-advisedly," the Minister of Foreign Affairs pointed out sternly, "you would not need correction. Comrade President understands what he is doing. Listen to him."

"There need be no arguments, Comrade Minister," Yuri reproved him in the same flat tone he had used on the Minister of Defense. "If I must think for you all, I am quite capable of it."

"Yes, Comrade President," the Minister of Foreign Affairs responded, suddenly crumpled into a humility as great as his colleague's. "Please do so."

"Very well," Yuri said. "Now pay attention. . . . There will be a response by us, but it will be far, far greater than small minds can imagine . . ."

His statement was released in time for the morning newscasts in America. It was unanimously approved by the excited members of the Politburo, whom he asked to add their signatures to his. He intended this to hit the world hard. It did:

"In view of the aggressive militaristic speech by the American President, H. Delbacher, which he made to the United States Congress last night, the Soviet Union has no choice but to respond in kind.

"The Soviet Union regards the H. Delbacher statement as a completely unfriendly act—an act almost of war.

"Therefore it is the decision of the President of the Soviet Union, taken in association with the members of the Politburo and endorsed and supported wholeheartedly by them, that there will be worldwide maneuvers of all Soviet forces wherever they are stationed, at home and abroad. These maneuvers will begin at the appropriate time.

"This will be the decisive course of events, until there is proper response from the American President, his associates and allies.

"Y. P. Serapin, Chairman of the Council
of Ministers and President of the Union
of Soviet Socialist Republics

"Endorsed unanimously by Politburo members:
[with their signatures]."

"Comrade President," the Minister of Defense had inquired when the final language was agreed upon, "what is 'proper response' from the Americans to consist of?"

"That is for them to worry about," Yuri Serapin said indifferently. "We have our own plans to consider now."

And proceeded to outline, again to their excited and unanimous approval, what he thought they should be; knowing of course that until Soviet plans were further clarified there would continue to be the sort of divisive national debate in America that began shortly after noon that same day on Capitol Hill.

Jim Elrod, as chairman of the Senate Armed Services Committee, rose to defend the Administration position and do what he could to alleviate the panic that seemed to be gripping large sections of the country, the media and a sizable number of his Congressional colleagues.

"Mr. President," he said, addressing Rick Duclos of Vermont, who happened to be occupying the presiding officer's chair at the moment, "if Senators will permit me, I should like to make a brief statement today relative to the military maneuvers that have been announced by the new Soviet President, Yuri Serapin.

"To say that these maneuvers, which are evidently planned to occur around the globe in many lands and in all the seas, are of concern to this country, is of course absolutely correct. But to let ourselves appear, as some of us seem to be doin', to be panicked or intimidated by them is to do poor service to our own country and to the other nations that depend on us for assistance and defense. We cannot, I suggest, do ourselves or anybody any good at all by runnin' around like chickens with our heads cut off. This is exactly the state of fear and confusion the Soviets intend to create. It is exactly what we cannot afford.

"Mr. Serapin, whom some of us had occasion to see and study firsthand in New York several days ago is not, in my estimation, a man who can be impressed at all by chest-beatin', panickin' or other carryin's-on of a similar nature. He is a cold-blooded gambler who is doin' his best, for obvious reasons, to scare the pants off us. He is probably the most irresponsible, most cold-blooded gambler who has ever held supreme power in the Kremlin. With him the old, cautious generation of Soviet leadership has finally passed from the scene. A new group, much less matured and seasoned, with no real understandin' of what an atomic world war could do to us all, feelin' much less restraint and obligation toward humanity, has taken over. Thus the forces he is settin' in motion now are twice as dangerous as any warlike Soviet gestures before, because they are in the hands of younger men who really don't know what they're doin', when you come right down to it."

"Mr. President," Mark Coffin said, "will the distinguished Senator yield?"

"I'll yield gladly to my son-in-law the distinguished junior Senator from California."

"And don't try to make a family affair of it," Mark said, with a smile that removed the sting. "The Senator knows I am diametrically opposed to him on this, and it's as an opponent of the new Administration's course that I engage him in debate. . . . Mr. President, is it the Senator's contention that we are to be completely calm and not show any concern at all for the Soviet maneuvers that apparently will soon be under way throughout the world?"

"Of course not," Jim Elrod said. "The Senator is just teasin' me, now. I'm sayin' that the cooler and calmer we can be, the better. In fact I'm sayin' we've *got* to be cool and calm, because if we're not, then we're playin' directly into Mr. Serapin's hands. I know the Senator agrees with me on that.

"Now, for instance, I'm sure many of you, like myself, have read the mornin's editorials in the major papers of Washington, New York and the northeastern seaboard. You've all seen the extensive television coverage of Soviet troops preparin' to move out, and you've noted the mood of near hysteria that seems to be fillin' the entire media today. I'm just sayin' I don't think it does any good—for us. It helps the Soviets plenty, because it weakens us substantially. I think we should be deeply concerned—and all of us are that, I think—but we shouldn't be hysterical about it. It isn't the end of the world and it won't be if we can manage to be as cold-blooded and calculatin' as they are. A lot of it is bluff and that can't hurt us unless we let it."

"Does the Senator feel," Mark inquired, "that the President of the United States was well advised to resurrect a bill we passed three years ago, when the whole connotation of that bill is, as Mr. Serapin and his colleagues said, militaristic and, as they see it, threatening to them? Didn't the President do a great deal to provoke what is now happening?"

"You fellows on that side of it always get the cart before the horse," Senator Elrod said with some impatience. "You were a member of the delegation to that so-called instant summit we had, and you saw Serapin just as the rest of us did. You also heard the President's confidential report to us on his private talk with Serapin. I believe he felt he must make some dramatic and effective gesture that wouldn't be just words, but really mean somethin'. But you know that he didn't go to New York with any such intention, and he wouldn't have done it if he didn't feel it was imperative for our own safety."

"So we're going right on with what Mrs. Hastings in her editorial this morning called, 'the apparently endless game of "Can You Top This?" that we play all the time with the Soviet Union.' Only this time they've been provoked into a response much harsher than the provocation. How does that help the peace we all want?"

"Assumin' they want it," Jim Elrod said, "which I do not, there was no need for them to react so violently. It will be a couple of years at least before the things the President wants to do with that money can come on-line, and mebbe a couple of years after that before they're really effective. Meantime I think his hope is that the Soviets can be persuaded to negotiate seriously for arms reduction—which they've never done, in my estimation."

"And now, never will," Mark observed.

"Possibly," his father-in-law conceded. "But there was no need, as you say, for their reaction to be so excessive. It's a definite move to scare us into retreatin' and makin' concessions we simply can't afford to make."

"I think,"Mark said, "that the President ought to withhold his executive order and rescind his intention to use that money."

"How can he do that now without appearin' to be knucklin' under completely?" Senator Elrod demanded. "It's completely impossible!"

"And so to save his pride," Mark said angrily, "we're to plunge ahead with one more arms race and they'll do God knows what with their forces when they get them up to peak performance with these maneuvers. It's insane!"

"They began *this* insanity," Jim Elrod said, "and you know from your own observation that Serapin is deliberately provokin' us to guarantee that it will continue. I don't know what he has in mind, but I assure you it isn't anythin' for the health and well-bein' of the United States of America."

In much the same tone on both sides of the Capitol the debate raged on into the afternoon, as it was raging in a thousand places in the media and throughout the country. It was not until around 3 P.M. that Mark was approached by a page who told him he was wanted on the phone in the Majority Cloakroom and left the floor with a sudden hunch that something unusual, perhaps ominous, was going to occur. But it was not the President with a tongue-lashing, as he half-expected, it was Linda, speaking in a puzzled and rather troubled voice from home.

"Hi," she said. "How's it going up there today?"

"Vigorously," he said, "to put it mildly. Jim and I had a go-around on the whole situation and since then a lot of others have joined in. The sentiment's about equally divided on the President's decision and about a hundred per cent upset over the Soviet response. What's new with you?"

"A rather peculiar phone call for you."

"Oh? How, 'peculiar'?"

"Well, to begin with, it was a foreign accent, probably Russian."

"Oh, really," he said. A startled surmise began to take shape in his mind. "Male?"

"Yes. He said to tell you 'Believe-it-or-not-Ivan' was calling."

"I knew it. My dinner companion at the banquet in New York. I thought he'd gone home. Did he say what he wanted?"

"To see you as soon as possible, I gathered. He said he had 'discovered the reason for the chess problem.' I didn't know you were such a chess fan."

"I'm not," Mark said. "If I get the code right, he knows something about the maneuvers. He was making sounds like a defector, in New York. I wonder if—did you give him my number up here?"

"Yes, but I wanted to alert you before he called."

"Good. I may tell him to come to the house tonight if we don't have anything lined up to do."

"Nothing tonight. Lyddie's dinner for the President tomorrow."

"Fine. I'll tell him around 9 P.M., if he can make it."

Fifteen minutes later he was again called to the phone to hear a murmured, "Mark?"

"Yes," he said, naming no names but putting sufficient cordiality into his voice to let Ivan know he was welcome. "What can I do for you?"

"If you wish to play the chess game successfully, it is imperative that I talk to you about it."

"There are some moves I would like to know more about. You know where I live?"

"Oh yes."

"Can you come there about nine o'clock tonight?"

"I will try."

"Good. I'll be waiting."

"Excellent."

He paused a moment after the line went dead and then dialed the White House. Much more easily than he expected, he was put through to the President.

"I hear you've been giving me hell on the floor," Ham Delbacher said with a chuckle. "Have you called up to give me some more in person?"

"No, sir," Mark said with an answering laugh. "It's nothing personal, you understand. But I am concerned."

"God!" the President exclaimed. "You think I'm not? What's on your mind?"

"You remember a certain individual at a certain dinner party," Mark said carefully.

"Yes," the President replied with a quickening interest.

"He wishes to discuss the chess game with me," Mark said, feeling rather foolish and as though he were in a low-budget movie thriller; but the President got it at once.

"The chess—oh yes. Good. Where?"

"Cleveland Park," Mark said, naming the older residential area of the city where Linda and he had bought a home three years ago soon after his election to the Senate.

"Perhaps he would be more comfortable on the second floor," the President suggested.

Mark considered this offer of the White House family quarters for a moment and then inquired, "Would there be some good recordings for him?"

"An excellent idea," the President agreed. "Would he accept the second floor, do you think?"

"It would be a test of sincerity, at least."

"A car could be sent."

"Better mine. Less conspicuous. A black Buick, D.C. plates."

"Good. You'll be expected in the East."

"Good."

Later, after dinner, Linda and the kids withdrew to the basement playroom to watch television. He read restlessly for a while in the library until the kitchen doorbell rang. He had not been at all convinced that his visitor would come; the reality made him jump. He hurried down the stairs, heart beating faster, peered through the safety-viewer. A dim figure stood in the darkness he had deliberately created by leaving the back porch light off. A tiny flashlight quickly illuminated the face and was as quickly doused. He opened the door and drew Ivan in.

The Russian gave him a bear hug and a kiss on the cheek, as though they were old friends, but his expression was somber and his general demeanor dead serious.

"Where can we talk?" he asked in a whisper. "Is it safe here?"

"Reasonably," Mark whispered back—the genius they had for making the whole world conspiratorial! "I have another suggestion, though. Is this really serious?"

"After tonight," Ivan said with a grim smile, "I do not expect to see my homeland again."

"Where we are going, I can assure you, you will be guaranteed complete safety if you really wish to defect."

"I do," Ivan said, apparently completely serious.

Mark studied him carefully for several moments. The Russian returned his gaze with an apparently unflinching innocence. Finally Mark nodded.

"Very well. I am taking you to the President."

Ivan looked genuinely startled for a second. Then he smiled.

"I am honored. It will not be a waste of his time."

"Good. How did you get here?"

"I was ordered to come to Washington to familiarize myself with the embassy, which I have been doing, in preparation to come here soon on the staff. Tonight the Ambassador was invited to a party at the Nigerian Embassy. I was invited to accompany him. I made a big joke of exclaiming over the hors d'oeuvres and followed one of the maids into the kitchen, pretending I wanted to know the recipe. I kept going straight through the kitchen and out the back door, so fast they could hardly see me. I expect"—his face relaxed into a satisfied smile—"they are still looking in the bushes. I dodged through an alley or two, doubled back a few times, came out onto the street just in time to catch a taxi, had *him* double about a bit, drove past here twice to fix it in my mind, left the taxi two blocks away, walked through some more alleys, doubled about some more, and here I am. I think we should leave the same way."

"We'll take my car. It's in the garage alongside the kitchen where nobody can see us get in. First, though—" He went to the basement stairs. "Linda!"

"No one else must know of this!" Ivan exclaimed sharply, his face alarmed.

"My wife," Mark said. "A very good judge of character. I want her to see you."

For just a second the Russian's tense expression did not change. Then he relaxed and smiled.

"I am doubly honored, then," he said as Linda came up the stairs.

"Honey," Mark said, "this is my friend from the summit, Major Ivan Valerian. We are going to the White House."

"How nice," Linda said, coming forward, hand extended, eyes on Ivan's face. "Give Ham my love. Major? I am pleased to meet you."

"And I you, Mrs. Coffin," Ivan said, smile now completely relaxed. "Your husband tells me you are a judge of character. Am I approved?"

"A very good judge, I said," Mark remarked with a smile. "Isn't that true, Linda?"

"I'm not infallible," she said, relaxing into a smile herself but keeping her eyes steadily on Ivan.

"Your report would be very interesting to me," the Russian said with a sudden charming grin.

"I will have it for you next time we meet," she said. She thought for a moment. "Perhaps when you finish at the White House you could come back here for a drink—?"

The grin faded. Ivan uttered a heavy sigh.

"I will be in hiding then. But perhaps someday—"

"Oh, I see." She looked troubled. "I didn't realize your situation. Mark, are you sure what you're doing is safe? If Major Valerian is about to defect, isn't it dangerous to be with him?"

"They have no idea right now where I am," Ivan said confidently. "We will be safe to the White House. After that, I must rely upon the President."

"Well—" she said doubtfully.

"Don't worry," Mark said. "I'm taking the car. Ivan will be on the floor in the back seat."

"Yes, I think so," Ivan agreed. "No more chances." He held out his hand. "Mrs. Coffin, it is my pleasure. Someday I hope we may meet under happier circumstances, and you will give me your report."

"It's a date," she agreed, giving his hand a firm shake. "Mark—" She gave him a kiss. "You do be careful, now. When can I expect you back?"

"I'll call you from the White House about ten-thirty and give you a progress report," he said, returning the kiss. "Don't worry."

"I can't help that," she said. "I'll be waiting. Good luck to you, Major. I hope you succeed in your plans."

"With Mark's good help," Ivan said with another charming grin, "I am sure I will."

Ten minutes later, Ivan lying comfortably on a rug on the floor in back, they arrived at the East Gate of the White House, which was open, and were passed through immediately. The lights were out in the East Portico and they were hurried swiftly into the family elevator and up to the second floor.

At the house, Linda called down the stairs to reassure the kids and then began going from room to room methodically checking the windows and doors. Over the hum of the air-conditioning she had thought she heard the sound of another car starting up nearby, seconds after theirs, then fading away into silence. She had stood a long moment in thought, the hairs prickling on the back of her neck, then had taken a deep breath and begun what she considered her necessary security rounds. It took her a long while to calm down again. Long after the kids were tucked in she sat in the library, tense and troubled, trying to read. Every few minutes she gave an involuntary shiver and felt the hairs, again, along her neck.

"They're here, Mr. President," the level voice of the guard on the East Gate informed him and he uttered an involuntary sigh of relief. Young Mark was engaged in a dangerous business, based on two days' brief impressions of Major Ivan Valerian in New York. The President had spent the last several hours regretting that he had not urged him to be more careful. These were *not* nice people they were dealing with, and everything from a phony defection by Valerian to a KGB kidnapping of the junior Senator from California had sufficient time to command his imagination before the guard's quiet call. He was greatly relieved to receive it, and resolved forthwith that he would not encourage anybody in such an adventure again.

But perhaps, he thought now as the world settled down again into a reliable configuration, it might prove to be worthwhile in this instance. Maybe Valerian had something of genuine value to offer. Perhaps he was one of the rare ones who genuinely wanted freedom enough to try for it actively. If so what he said could be interesting indeed.

Quite deliberately, the President had removed his jacket and shoes, put on a lounging robe and slippers, taken out his pipe, made himself appear as relaxed and down to earth as possible. To see the President of the United States thus informal was a privilege not accorded many. If Valerian was nothing but a double agent, he would be one who despised the United States and its leader, and contempt, fear, hatred would override all other feelings. If he were the genuine article, he would be suitably impressed and become relaxed himself.

There was a soft knock on the door of the Lincoln Study. He called, "Come!" and one of the young in-house guards called back, "Senator Coffin and a friend, Mr. President." He got up from his deep leather rocking chair and opened the door.

"Come in, Mark," he said cordially, extending his hand as the guard withdrew. Behind Mark he saw the stocky, attractive young Russian, dark-eyed, handsome, a tentative smile on his lips and in his eyes.

"I recognize your friend," the President said, turning his cordiality upon the visitor. "Major Valerian, isn't it? I believe we met in New York at the summit"—wryly—"such as it was."

"Yes, sir, Mr. President," Ivan Valerian said, smile growing less tentative, more firm. "I agree with you, it was not much of a summit. Yet you grew to understand Yuri Pavlovich, I am sure."

"It's more important that he understand me, I suspect," the President said, gesturing Mark to the sofa and Ivan to the other leather rocker in the room. "I feel he pretty much fits the usual stereotype of a Soviet leader, does he not? Very rigid, very much by the book—very anti-American and very hostile toward us."

"Yuri Pavlovich is different," Ivan said seriously, appearing very much at ease now—perhaps too rapidly? the President wondered, exchanging a glance with Mark that he knew did not escape their visitor.

"Tell the President about him," Mark suggested.

Ivan hesitated for a moment, seeming suddenly not quite so sure of himself. "First," he said, "I wonder if—that is, if I should tell you what I know—I wonder if—"

"Do you intend to defect tonight?" Ham Delbacher asked bluntly, and it was with an audible sigh of relief that Major Valerian replied quietly, "Yes, sir."

"And you wish safe asylum with us?"

"Yes, Mr. President."

"You have it."

"Thank you, Mr. President," Ivan said fervently. "Thank you! Thank you!"

"You leave a wife and three children in the Soviet Union?" the President asked. "How can you leave them so easily?"

"They are with me here," Ivan said, "and if all went well tonight, they are in the hands of friends by now. If not"—his eyes were bleak for a moment—"if not, I can only hope they will not be treated too harshly.

As for me"—he spread his hands in a curiously touching gesture—"I must do what I must do."

"If you need help to bring them to you again," the President offered, "we will provide that, too."

"Thank you," Ivan said; for a moment was silent, apparently in the grip of powerful emotion; then again became matter-of-fact. "Yuri Pavlovich, as I said, is different. For one thing, you know, he is much younger. He is our youngest leader since the Revolution. He does not look at things in quite the same way as the old ones. He is much more daring in his actions and more—emphatic—in his approaches. He is not afraid to gamble. I have worked very closely with him. He is also very impatient—and very confident of himself—and very ready to use force, violent force, against his enemies. He has done so against his enemies at home, and now it appears that he is ready to do so against his enemies abroad."

"Yes," the President agreed, somewhat dryly. "We perceive that. What will it take to stop him?"

"Nothing can stop him," Ivan said firmly. "Nothing. He will proceed as he believes best to do, regardless of the consequences."

"So will I, you know," the President said calmly. "Do you think he knows that? Perhaps you should return and tell him."

"I cannot return!" Ivan cried in sudden dismay which, the President thought, appeared to be quite genuine. "I cannot return, Mr. President! Surely you will not—"

"No," the President interrupted, "of course not. Certainly I will not. How, then, do we impress upon Yuri Pavlovich that he cannot abolish us from the face of the earth simply because he is impatient, confident, violent and determined to do so?"

"And also, Mr. President," Major Valerian said, more calmly, "very strong. We are very strong, you know—Russia is very strong, her allies are very strong. We are stronger than you, I am afraid. I do not quite know how you will stop Yuri Pavlovich. But at least if you know what Yuri Pavlovich intends to do, you will know better how to respond, is that not correct?"

"Forewarned is forearmed, as we say."

"Exactly," Ivan said. "That is why I have come to you."

"How do you happen to know these things?" the President inquired.

"I told you he was attached to their general staff," Mark began, but Ham Delbacher interrupted with an uplifted hand.

"I know that," he said quietly. "The CIA and the FBI know it. We know quite a bit about Major Ivan Ivanovich Valerian. But I want him to tell me himself."

"I am ready to," Ivan said with equal quietness. "I knew you would investigate me. It is only prudent."

"So?"

"Very well. I have known Yuri Pavlovich, now, for perhaps five years, more or less. I came to his attention during maneuvers near Zagreb after we took Yugoslavia. He thought I was an excellent officer. I am."

"Perhaps we are fortunate you are defecting," the President said with a gentle humor his visitor was too self-absorbed and too serious to notice. "I could use some excellent young officers, myself."

"I am ready to serve in any capacity you wish me," Ivan said solemnly. The President nodded and Ivan resumed.

"So. Yuri Pavlovich began to favor me. Perhaps he saw in me a vision of himself when younger; he has almost told me as much on several occasions. In any event, I was soon promoted to the secretariat of what you would call our Joint Chiefs of Staff—to the Strategic Rocket Forces, in fact, which is the most important segment of our armed forces. And he began with increasing frequency to include me in confidential meetings. I think I am"—he corrected himself, eyes looking bleak again for a second —"was, rather, almost in the classification of one of Yuri Pavlovich's private secretaries. I have learned much from this."

"Which is why you are here tonight," Mark said encouragingly.

"Which is why I am here tonight," Ivan agreed. "To tell you what I know, and to help prevent a great catastrophe for the world if I can."

"I understand that your desire to help prevent this catastrophe is your final motivation for being here tonight," the President said, "but what about all the other motivations? You appear to have acquired some regard for America, which is unusual in your country you will admit, and in the process to have rejected very substantially the training and teaching of your own country. I'd like you to tell me how this came about."

"There are some of us—" Ivan said, "more than you in the West will believe, I think—who have these same feelings. I do not know exactly where it begins—a moment, perhaps, when one's mind suddenly rebels and one thinks, America cannot possibly be as evil as they tell us."

"But he overcame it," the President suggested dryly.

"He did."

"But you did not."

"I thought I had," Major Valerian said earnestly, "but I found it had left its mark on me. It had weakened my faith in our system, particularly since I was now inside and could see and understand what was going on."

"Do you now think your system is as evil as you once thought ours was?" the President pursued.

"It is worse," Ivan said somberly. "It is much, much worse. And always we—those of us who no longer believe—have wondered why so many in America have been unable to see this, and have continued to pretend, after so many betrayals and examples, that our system has the same goals and the same desire for peace. It does not, Mr. President, believe me."

"I believe you," the President said, "but I am still puzzled how one who is raised from birth in your system can gain enough perspective to defect from it. It seems almost impossible."

"Yet it happens," Ivan said simply. "Other defectors have come to you, have they not? Even now, despite the persecutions of all these years, there are still within our borders many who protest. They are punished, but they persevere. It is one of the reasons that you must persevere."

"We will," the President told him. "Tell me—do you think all of the defectors who have come to us are sincere? Do you think there are none who have been allowed to escape—like yourself, for instance—simply so they can be in place when your country launches its final attack upon us?"

Ivan Valerian studied him very seriously before he answered.

"I think," he said slowly, "I *know,* that there are some who are false, who remain agents of my country. One of the things I have for you, in fact, is a list of those I know who are in this position. It would be useful for you to have this information, I think."

"Very useful," the President agreed.

"How will we know the list is truthful?" Mark inquired. "If you are a double agent you could simply be using us to eliminate sincere defectors who wish to help us. How do we know you are really genuine, yourself?"

It was his turn to come under Ivan's slow and careful scrutiny, and it was several long moments before he replied.

"You do not know," he said simply. "You have only my word, and your personal impressions of me."

"Which are good so far," the President remarked. "We have to take it step by step, I think."

"Exactly," Major Valerian said. "When I do not seem true to you, then you can stop believing me."

"We will keep that in mind," the President said.

"Please," Major Valerian said; and looked at Mark with a smile so full of genuine warmth that Mark could not refrain from smiling back.

"Very well," he said, "but you realize why we must be very, very careful."

Ivan shrugged.

"I do not blame you. It is only common sense."

"So you have become a defector," the President said, "and you have a list of those who, you say, have not really defected but are only here as agents in place, ready to support the Soviet Union when the time comes. Do you have anything else for us?"

Major Valerian took a deep breath and reached into his right coat pocket.

"Yes," he said slowly. "I have here the list of names"—he handed it to the President—"of those I know to be false defectors. And I have here"—he displayed a large manila envelope but did not yet yield it—"the secret general staff plan for the maneuvers ordered by Yuri Pavlovich which will begin two days from today, regardless of what you say or do."

"As long as they occur in lands occupied by, or friendly to, the U.S.S.R., or on the high seas," the President said, "then there is little we can do about them."

"It is what will come *after* that is important," Ivan Valerian said. "That is what I will explain you now. May I?" And getting to his feet, he drew a card-table from the corner of the room to its center and beckoned them forward.

"Now," he said, unfolding a map which he took from the envelope and opened upon the table, "you will be kind and listen to me, Mr. President and Mark? Come closer and I will show you what I bring you."

And for the next half-hour he did so, going over it all twice, slowly and in great detail, so that there could be no doubt. When he had finished the President straightened up, said, "Ouch, my aching back!" and shook his head thoughtfully.

"It is hard to believe," he commented, "but not unexpected, at least by me. How about you, Mark?"

"I find it *awfully* hard to believe," Mark said slowly. "It was not expected by me, and I am not at all sure how much credence you should give it, Mr. President. You might simply invite a reaction that—"

"I don't believe, with the Soviets," the President interrupted with a rare show of real impatience, "that there is such a thing as reaction. I think they move by an imperialist, expansionist plan which, as in the Cuban missile crisis, may take a slight detour but basically goes right on regardless of what we say or do. We may react to them: they do not react to us. They just do what they intend to do, and to hell with us and everybody else."

"You are correct, Mr. President," Ivan said somberly. "You are completely correct."

"I should still, however," Mark replied with some coolness, "move very slowly to react to something as unsupported as this."

"It will be checked out thoroughly by the most competent authorities we have," Hamilton Delbacher said, "and then we will decide where to go from there. Meanwhile, Major Valerian"—and he held out his hand to terminate the interview—"thank you very much for giving us this information." He walked over to his chair, pressed a button in the wall beside it. "Directly down the hall you will see two men seated on a sofa. They are from the CIA. They will conduct you to CIA headquarters across the river in Virginia, where you will be kept for a couple of days while they ask you questions about this plan and also, I am sure, about many other things concerning Yuri Pavlovich and your experiences in your homeland. You then will be taken to a safe place somewhere nearby where, with a little luck, you will find your wife and children waiting. After that, if all

goes well, I am sure the CIA will wish to make further use of your particular skills and knowledge. I may see you again myself. Good luck, and
many thanks."

"Thank you," Ivan said, obviously moved. "I cannot begin to tell
you—"

"Don't try," the President suggested with a smile. "Mark, I'd like to
talk to you a little further, if I may."

"Surely," Mark said. He found himself enfolded once more in the
bear hug and, this time, kisses on both cheeks.

"My friend," Ivan said fervently. "My friend! I hope we may meet soon
again."

"We will," Mark promised. "Best of luck."

"With two such good friends," Ivan exclaimed with a happy laugh, "I
will *be* lucky!"

After Mark had called to tell Linda, whom he could sense was nervous
and uneasy, that he would be home before long, he put down the phone
and turned to the President. Ham gave him an appraising look for a moment and asked him if he wanted a drink. He said he did. A couple of
minutes later, Mark with scotch on the rocks and the President nursing a
vodka martini, Mark asked, "Well?"

"What do you make of him now?" the President replied. "Do you think
he's for real?"

"I . . . *think* . . . so," Mark replied carefully. "He *seems* to be. I assume the CIA will have a pretty good idea after they've checked him
out."

"Yes. At your suggestion they've got a tape of the entire interview, and
there are experts over there who are able to analyze the sincerity or insincerity in a voice with quite amazing accuracy. So we'll see. Meantime he'll
be under wraps and soon reunited with his family, who, I happen to know
already, did get away safely. So the chances are better than even, I'd say,
that we have a new and valuable ally. What did you think of his information?"

"As I made clear, I'm very dubious and cautious about it."

"I'm a little less so. I've been studying their literature a lot the past two
days and it fits the pattern they've been projecting for themselves for at
least the past two decades. It ties in with *surprise,* which they stress in all
their military writings. Of course they present it as a fear that *we* will
surprise *them.* This is almost invariably followed by a discussion of the
desirability of surprise and a description of the great good it can achieve
for the one who uses it first—obviously designed to be instruction for
their own forces. Consistent as this is with that concept, I'm inclined to
believe it. Anyway: would you do me a favor?"

"If I can," Mark said cautiously. Ham Delbacher laughed.

"A sensible answer. I want you to call your pal Chuck Dangerfield of the AP right away and leak the story to him. 'A Soviet defector told highest American authorities today that the Soviets intend to—a source who did not wish to be named, present at the meeting, said the Soviet plan consists of—' et cetera. You both know the drill. Everybody nameless, but the plan spelled out—up to its final stages."

"Oh?"

"Yes, I think I'll save those for a while. And finish by saying that 'the highest American authorities' are taking the plan 'very seriously.' "

"What about my own doubts?"

"Express them freely. Tell him I suggested you call him and that *I* do take it seriously. Tell him I said if he really disbelieves it *absolutely*—and stress I used the word—then of course don't print it, and no hard feelings. Or balance it with some skeptical quotes from you and others on the Hill, if he likes. But try to get it into print. Will you do that for me? Present it just the way I said. Keep your own options open, but tell Chuck. I'd do it myself but I'd rather keep a little distance. O.K.?"

"Well—"

"You'll have a chance to raise all the hell you like. In the meantime, help your President, all right?"

"That's an old pitch," Mark observed with a smile.

"I'm making it," the President said cheerfully. "How about it?"

"Well . . ."

"Great," Ham Delbacher said, picked up the phone, consulted a large address book filled with many names, found Chuck's unlisted number, dialed it, and held out the phone. Mark smiled again, took it, and said, "Hi, pal," when Chuck answered with a sleepy, "Who the hell is this? I'm in bed."

"Enjoying yourself, I hope," Mark said. "Sorry to interrupt, but—"

And while the President listened with a benign smile, he proceeded to tell Chuck and the AP all about it.

"Do you believe it?" Chuck asked, long since wide awake and getting it on his tape recorder.

"A little—maybe. I'm really not sure."

"I'm inclined to," Chuck replied, to Mark's surprise. "It fits the pattern. Mr. Big wants it, right?"

"I'm calling from the Lincoln Study," Mark said. "Mr. Big is sitting here with his tongue hanging out."

"Put him on."

"O.K.," Mark said and held out the phone.

"Tape recorder off first," the President said firmly.

"Tape off," Mark relayed as the President took the phone.

"Done, Mr. President," Chuck said.

"Good. Sorry to yank you out of domestic bliss, but—"

"Why does everybody always assume that all I do is—" Chuck asked with mild indignation. The President laughed.

"If I were your age and had a wife as nice as yours is—and mine is—that's all I'd do too. Now the way to get into this, I think, is just the way Mark outlined it. 'A Soviet defector told highest American officials tonight that the Russians intend to,' et cetera. O.K., Chuck?"

"You think it's true," Chuck said thoughtfully.

"I honestly don't know. It's very possible. We've got to get it out in the open and raise as much hell as we can, in any event."

"All right. It's done."

And so it was, and this time it was not just Yuri Pavlovich who grabbed the world's attention.

DEFECTOR REPORTS SOVIETS PLAN SNEAK ATTACK ON U.S., EUROPE DURING MANEUVERS. AIDE TO SERAPIN SAYS RUSS WILL STRIKE NORTHEAST U.S., HIT EUROPE FROM EAST GERMANY AND BALKANS. WHITE HOUSE REPORTED CONVINCED TALE MAY BE TRUE.

The reaction, particularly in the United States, was about what the President expected. The pejorative word "tale" in the headlines was the tip-off to the attitude of the nation's most powerful publications. Fear was the prod but that of course could not be admitted. Disbelief, derision, skepticism, scorn, were the weapons. Scathing words poured upon the head of Hamilton Delbacher.

"There is something extremely fishy," the Washington *Post* observed acidly, "about this cock-and-bull tale concerning an alleged Soviet defector who has reportedly informed the White House that the Soviet Union will launch a massive first strike against us under the guise of upcoming worldwide maneuvers. Not since Lewis Carroll wrote *Alice in Wonderland,* one suspects, has there been a fairy-tale of quite this magnitude. And at least Mr. Carroll was delightful and amusing. This is pure horror stuff, straight from the worst grade D movie anyone ever imagined.

"First of all, there is the nature of the informant. He seems to be a Major Ivan Valerian, allegedly a 'close aide' of the new Soviet President, Yuri Serapin. We have this on the sole word of a story from the Associated Press purporting to quote 'the highest American authorities,' which presumably might mean President Delbacher himself. If so, we suggest it is quite possible he has been taken in, through inexperience and a certain urge to see his worst fears come true, by an agent, or double agent, of the Soviet Union. Until the country knows more about mysterious Major Valerian, it would be well advised, we think, to show a skepticism toward him which apparently does not exist at 1600 Pennsylvania Avenue.

"Secondly, and this is by far the most important consideration, there is no assurance whatsoever that the Soviet maneuvers will even be held. President Serapin was very careful not to set a specific time in his statement from Moscow yesterday. He deliberately left room for this country and our allies to make 'proper response.' The clear indication was that if we do so, the maneuvers will not take place . . ."

"Hamilton Delbacher," Walter Dobius wrote sternly, "is not content with shoving the country willy-nilly into a new arms race with the Soviet Union; he now must scare us to death as well, with a fanciful story attributed to a mysterious 'Soviet defector' who is supposed to be a former aide to President Yuri Serapin. According to this hazy and unsubstantiated source, the Soviet Union, under the guise of maneuvers, is going to launch an attack upon the northeastern seaboard of this country and upon Europe—simultaneously. Even given the present state of the Russian armed forces and missile capability, this would be an enormous, indeed impossible, mouthful for any power to chew. It also attributes to the Soviets a desire and capability for the most devious and deceitful actions —for sheer lies, in short. Such have occurred, perhaps, but only on isolated occasions and only in the pursuit of what the Soviets regard as their legitimate interests, close to home. Any such surprise move would hardly be consistent with the Soviets' constantly expressed desire for peace and harmony with us and our allies. It is simply impossible to accept that they would sacrifice all that in return for an enormous gamble that could only bring instant and overwhelming retaliation.

"The key to the latest horror story out of the White House," the New York *Times* said "—the so-called 'Soviet defector,' the alleged pre-emptive Soviet attack upon us under the guise of maneuvers—lies not in Moscow but in Washington itself.

"In his statement yesterday President Yuri Serapin gave a clear signal to President Delbacher and America's allies: if they make a 'proper response' to the announcement of Soviet maneuvers, then there will, in all probability, be no need for the maneuvers at all. There will instead be a new attempt to work out mutual problems by peaceful and constructive negotiation, rather than by the tired old dance of action and reaction which was touched off, initially, by Mr. Delbacher with his violently militaristic overreaction to the collapse of the disappointingly brief 'summit' between himself and Mr. Serapin at the UN.

"From that flowed, inevitably, Mr. Serapin's threat of maneuvers. We must all hope that Mr. Delbacher will not react as wildly to the tall tale he has been brought by a mysterious 'defector' but instead will take the opening offered by Mr. Serapin and return to the conference table, no matter how long or frustrating that process may be. To go in the other direction is to go straight toward world destruction . . ."

"Hamilton Delbacher," CBS's editorial commentator summed up the network attitudes, "has set the world upon a strange and fearfully hazardous course with his $10 billion emergency defense budget and his sleight-of-hand disclosure of a mysterious 'defector' who warns of surprise attacks and invasions by the Soviet Union. There is no verification of these from any other source, nor is there any reason to believe, simply on the common sense of it, that the Soviets would take so awesome and potentially fatal a step. They could not escape a dreadful mauling if they did; nor could America and indeed most of the Western world, escape similar devastation.

"President Serapin left the way open in his announcement of the maneuvers for a return to the negotiations President Delbacher broke off so impatiently last week. Mr. Delbacher should take him up on it. Elsewhere lies horror beyond belief . . ."

And so it went, in general, in newspapers all across the country and in most television programs monitored by the White House press office. As always, sight was being lost, either deliberately or through the habit of casual dismissal of unpleasant facts, of the Soviets' primary responsibility for creating the current situation. As usual, the United States, and particularly its President, were being blamed. The afternoon's debate in both Senate and House reflected the same attitudes, although there were an increasing number, it seemed to Ham Delbacher, who were beginning to come to his side.

"This is no time," the Speaker told a tense and troubled House, "to abandon the President to his critics. He is acting on what he believes to be the facts, and he is the only one who has *all* the facts. He needs our help, not our nagging." And although there were quite a few who sharply criticized what one of them called, "this tired old rally-round-the-flag defense of the President," a majority of both houses seemed to be lining up behind him.

Elsewhere in the world, particularly among America's allies, the reaction was not so favorable. Most of them were greatly alarmed: his phone was busy most of the day with presidents and prime ministers. And over at State, Chauncey Baron called to say that a steady stream of ambassadors was passing through his office to give their superiors' apprehensions added emphasis.

The coolest person he spoke to, as he had expected, was the Prime Minister of Great Britain, whose words were crisp and to the point.

"Mr. President," she said, "I just wanted you to know that we here are supporting you 100 per cent. This does not mean that if there were a chance for reasonable negotiations to resume, we would oppose such a move. On the contrary, we would urge it; changing the venue possibly to Geneva and broadening the panel to include myself and the NATO allies.

"Meanwhile, how serious is this defector of yours?"

"Not mine, Prime Minister," he said with a slight annoyance in his voice. "Yuri Serapin's. He was here last night for some time and I am reasonably well satisfied that his story is genuine."

"Or at least he believes it to be genuine."

"Yes," he conceded, "there is that possibility. He could be just a plant, carefully fed false information—'disinformation,' as they so delightfully call it—so that he might be sincere and convincing in what he told us."

"In that case, he might have been encouraged to play the role of defector, don't you think?"

"It could be, but I doubt it. I had a shrewd young Senator with me, and we both studied him very carefully. And both the CIA and FBI have checked him out very, very thoroughly during the night. He rings true to us over here."

"They wouldn't dare!" she exclaimed. "They would be utterly insane to launch any such attack!"

"Insanity creeps up on one when power comes," he observed. "Particularly in that society."

"Yes, surely not in yours or mine," she said with a chuckle. "What did you hope to accomplish by releasing the news? You have scared us all thoroughly, if that was the intention. Now we want to know what you plan to do about it."

"The motivation was to publicize it and scare *them* off their plan, if it exists. I thought there might be a world outcry against them. How naïve of me. Over here I'm getting the usual flack—the substance of the plan is being given the once-over-lightly: the fault is mine for daring to release it. I gather that's the general feeling abroad, too—or at least the vocal part of it. However, I can stand all that. Basically I wanted to have it on the record so that whatever I decide to do about it will be seen to have justification."

"And that is?"

"In due course," he said calmly. "There are several options . . . what do you suggest?"

"I think there may be considerable merit in the suggestion which seems to be the universal demand, to which I have already alluded—the option of a return to the conference table."

"Do you want to be mediator and try to set it up?"

"Very good. How about Geneva in five days?"

"Fine. Call me back. I'll be interested—to put it mildly—to know what progress you make."

"Right-ho," she said briskly. "I'll be back to you shortly."

He almost said, "Good show, old girl!" but confined his pleasantries to a cordial, "Thanks so much, Prime Minister. I'll be waiting." He gave her chances about 1 in 100, but she was a forceful and impressive lady and anything might help.

He was pleased a few minutes later when both the Chancellor of West Germany and the President of France called with the same idea. He referred them and subsequent high-level callers to the Prime Minister and turned to the problem he had been wrestling with ever since his interview with Ivan—what he actually *could* do, if it came right down to it.

The bleak answer was: not much.

If Serapin and his colleagues really were so insane as to push things finally over the brink, then the world would be at war by the end of the week, in all probability; and given the Soviet military emphasis on surprise (which they had lost), the advantages of first strike, their primacy in missiles, and atomic, chemical and space weaponry, the war would almost certainly be enormously devastating from the first. In the nuclear area the American arsenal was entirely adequate, but if he let himself be stampeded into using it—which the Joint Chiefs had already virtually advised this morning—then that would be the end of everything. He knew Serapin relied, as the Soviets had relied for three decades and more, on the reluctance of American Presidents to respond with this final, dreadful act. Therefore, although the Soviets could be said to have lost the element of surprise, the reluctance of America to actually commit atomic weapons had, in essence, restored it. They were left with the option of moving first because the only infallible method of victory was the method the Americans would not use.

He could call the Joint Chiefs right now, announce a speech to the nation for a couple of hours from now, and under cover of that the Soviets could be taken by surprise and blasted to perdition from Minsk to Vladivostok. But unfortunately, enough of them would have warning so that the Americans and most of the rest of the world would suffer the same fate. He was sure—or thought he was sure—that he would never resort to that. Yet if he did not, they, having no such compunctions discoverable anywhere in their official writings, statements or training manuals—on the contrary—very likely would.

It was a dilemma almost insoluble and so he returned, as he had all his life, to his practice when confronted by seemingly insoluble problems. He would take it day by day—in this case, hour by hour or even minute by minute—get everything in readiness, as the Joint Chiefs were doing for him at this moment, and then let his course be dictated by events as they developed.

He got up from his desk, went into his bathroom off the Oval Office and looked at himself thoughtfully in the mirror. He ought to be ashen-faced and trembling at this juncture, he supposed, but luckily for his country he was not the ashen-faced, trembling type. He could be as stolid as he looked, and thank God he was right now. "Hang in there, baby," he told himself wryly. "Only six more miles to eternity." Fortunately he had another strong lady on his side, and with the infallible instinct she had acquired during their shared years of political life, the phone rang and there she was, just when he needed her.

"Hi," she said from the TV room on the second floor. "How are things down there?"

"Probably a bit of livelier than up there," he said. "How are you?"

"All right. I have all three networks on. Bad as Lyndon Johnson used to be."

"Are they still after me?"

"They've calmed down a bit on that. Now they're mostly trying to stick to schedule, which I suppose is wise for the public nerves, with only an occasional special break to report anti-Soviet protests in London, or anti-American riots in New Delhi or something philosophical but fortunately pro-American from the Chinese. But I'm sure you get all these digests. The radio stations are much the same. There's no doubt there's a feeling of profound crisis, but everybody is trying, very nervously, to proceed as normally as possible. Which is good. And how about you, Mr. President?"

"I, too, am proceeding very nervously but trying to be as normal as possible."

"What are you going to do?"

"The Prime Minister called me from London a little while ago, and was just as direct as you are. She suggested a try to resume negotiations, I told her go ahead if she could do it. She's now in the process and will call me back soon."

"Oh," Elinor said hastily. "Then I'd better get off the line—"

"Oh no, they'll break in. Actually, what have you been doing?"

"Calling the kids."

He chuckled ruefully.

"That's suitably maternal at a time like this. How are they?"

"Ham and Cathy are laying in food supplies. Melinda and John and Debby and Robert are doing likewise. So are Beth and Jim. They all say there are hundreds and hundreds of people at the supermarkets and the gas stations. They all wanted to know if you would like them to come down here and join us. I said I didn't think so, that would look too much like panic in the Presidential family and make a lot of people even more terrified than they are already. They all agreed."

"Spartan mother of a Spartan brood!" he said with a chuckle. But the emotion he felt went far deeper and his eyes suddenly filled with tears. How many, many millions, all over America, frightened and inept, trying to do what little they could to protect their families! And why hadn't they, and preceding Presidents and Congresses, paid a little more attention to civil defense while they still had the time?

Improvident America! It never changed.

"Are you coming up for dinner?" she asked, breaking the silence that had fallen on them both.

"I think I'd better stay right here," he said. "Why don't you come down about eight? Order us something good but not too heavy from the kitchen and have them set it up outside here on the lawn. It's cooled down a little, hasn't it?"

"I doubt it very much, but it would be nice to be out."

"Yes, I've been chained here all day and probably will be all night, so—"

"Very good idea. I'll—"

"Sorry, Mrs. Delbacher," the chief White House operator broke in, "but I'm afraid I have the Prime Minister—"

"Oops, I'm off!" Elinor exclaimed and left the line. The Prime Minister, self-possessed and efficient as always, came on.

"Mr. President."

"Yes, Prime Minister. What's happened?"

"We have a consensus, I think. I've got West Germany, France, Spain, Portugal, Greece, the Scandinavians and even Ireland, which shows you the extent of concern. A very simple, short—not more than five sentences —appeal to you both to meet in Geneva 'at the earliest possible moment' to resume negotiations. And an added sentence directly to him to abandon the maneuvers 'which are giving such great concern to all peoples.' We'll have it released in two hours."

"Wonderful! You're a miracle worker."

"Just an underpaid but extremely competent secretary," she said cheerfully. "Ta!"

"Ta to you, too," he said with a laugh more relieved than he really cared to show.

But from there the day was all downhill.

In two hours, just as she had promised:

TEN CHIEFS OF STATE APPEAL TO U.S., SOVIETS TO MEET FOR GENEVA PEACE TALKS. URGE RUSS TO ABANDON MANEUVER PLAN. WORLD HOPES RISE.

Two hours after that:

SOVIETS REJECT PEACE APPEAL, BLAME U.S. FOR "DELIBERATELY INFLAMING CRISIS." SERAPIN SAYS PLANS "WILL PROCEED INEVITABLY AS SCHEDULED." WAR FEARS GROW.

And at seven-thirty, as he was preparing to clear his desk for a little while and join Elinor for dinner on the lawn:

MASSIVE SOVIET TROOP AND NAVAL MOVEMENTS BEGIN IN EUROPE, ASIA, SOUTH AMERICA, ARCTIC, ANTARCTIC, PERSIAN GULF, INDIAN OCEAN. MOSCOW SAYS "HISTORY'S MOST MASSIVE AND INVINCIBLE MILITARY FORCES ARE READY TO DO THEIR DUTY." WORLD AWAITS U.S. RESPONSE.

It was still very hot, very humid, but a little breeze was beginning to stir as they sat at a table under one of the giant old elms on the South Lawn. The hum of the city, always close to the edge of consciousness in the White House hemmed by busy Pennsylvania Avenue and E Street, was muted now in the long summer twilight. Traffic had diminished substantially, only a few taxis passed at the moment along E Street to the south; on the north Pennsylvania Avenue traffic was somewhat heavier as a few sight-seers drove slowly past, annoying the last of the homegoing traffic as their occupants craned to get a look at the great white mansion where their fate and that of their country was presumably being decided. On the east, where East Executive Avenue curved up to meet Pennsylvania, dividing White House from Treasury, the little mounds and rolling contours of the lawn were such that no one passing could see over them to the big gray-haired man and trim gray-haired woman who sat at the little table under the trees.

From their vantage point they could see south over the Ellipse to the Washington Monument, lighted now as the twilight deepened; beyond it, over Virginia, the last soft pinks and purples of sunset, fading fast. The first few stars were out.

The breeze was soft and gentle, nostalgically so. He smiled at Elinor, breaking the somber mood that had fallen upon them when they finished the light meal and sat back to sip the last of the wine.

"I think I'll get a few dairy cows and let them graze on the South Lawn," he said humorously. "Then it will really remind me of the farm."

"I wonder what they're doing on the farm tonight?" she mused. "Probably what we are—feeling the summer evening all around and refusing to believe that anything or anyone can possibly destroy such peace and harmony, or ever take it away from us . . . refusing to believe there could be such evil, in such a lovely world."

"Probably," he said. "That's probably just what they're doing. And then sighing and recognizing, as we all must, that yes, there is such evil and that, yes, it is intent upon destroying us and everything we cherish in this crazy, bumbling, idealistic country. How little they know us, these two-bit savages in the Kremlin who are so dedicated to our death! And how little they know us in these insane mobs who scream for our heads in the Middle East, Asia, Africa! America is so far removed from their ignorant stereotype that there's not even a remote resemblance. But they're all determined to bring down the stereotype, aren't they?" He sighed. "And thereby hangs my problem . . ."

"How are you going to solve it, do you think?" she asked quietly as the fireflies began to dance over the lawn and in one of the elms an owl complained softly, a small, sleepy, testy sound. "Do you know?"

"Not really," he said moodily. "Not at this moment. But it will come to me. It's got to . . ."

"Do you think they will actually attack us? Or is it all just a big bluff to knock us off balance psychologically and frighten the world to death?"

"Probably that."

"But if it isn't—"

"Then we go," he said simply. "Taking them with us, of course. That's why at heart I don't really believe what Ivan Valerian said. I think he believes it, and I'm sure all the Soviet contingency plans center around that or something quite similar at some time, but I don't really think it's going to happen at this time."

"You certainly got the world aroused, if you don't," she said with a rueful little laugh. "Maybe it would have been better to keep it quiet."

"No. No, I wanted the world to know the scope of the evil, if the plan does exist, and to enlist world attention and possibly support—sympathy is too much to ask—in making enough fuss about the possibility so that they will be persuaded to abandon any such madness, if they entertain it. Oh no, it's necessary to have the whole world in on this. Serapin made it very clear to me in New York that his mind is absolutely closed. Private appeals to him would do no good . . . world pressure may do no good . . . but it was the best weapon I had at hand."

"You must have some ideas what to do now, though. The maneuvers are beginning. You've got to do *something.*"

"Have I?" he asked with a wry smile. "How about masterful inaction? Go on about our business, ignore the maneuvers—"

"Nobody will let you do that, Soviets, the world, the media—it's going to be the main topic in the world during the next few days. You can't ignore it."

"Well," he said, folding his napkin neatly and placing it on the table beside his plate, as he had been taught to do on the farm long ago, "I won't. I do have some options and by morning I think I'll have decided which one to take. They wouldn't be starting with all this fanfare, after all the news about their purported attack on us, if they were really going to do it right away. So there's time."

"Don't miscalculate."

"I hope not."

They stood up as two servants started across the lawn toward them to clear away. He put his arm around her and they stood for a moment looking silently at the Washington Monument, rising white and strong into the deepening sky. Then they turned back to the White House and started walking slowly toward it, thanking the servants as they passed.

Again they paused and were silent, looking at the gleaming white building, repository of so many hopes, scene of so much travail, over so many years.

"America, America!" he exclaimed softly. "Why do you, who want to do so much for your people and the world, have such a hard time doing it?"

"Others in history have had a hard time," she said, squeezing his arm, "and they're still here."

"Yes," he said firmly, "and so will we be."

But exactly how, or with what remaining of the dream after it was all over, he could not be certain in that grim hour.

Yuri Serapin sat alone in his office studying the enormous map of the world on the wall facing his desk. His men were about to prove in the next few days that they did in fact have full control of all the approaches to all the continents and in many places were in effective control, direct or indirect, of the lands themselves. They now were indeed "history's most massive and invincible forces . . . ready to do their duty," and they were about to offer such a show of power everywhere across the globe that if weakling America entertained any idea of stopping them, weakling America would back away and give it up.

Across the lighted map long red lines were already leaping the seas and the continents: the Air Force. Out across the plains of eastern Europe, into the conquered satellites of southeast and southwest Asia, other red lines were pushing, more slowly, but at a rate, he knew, of at least one hundred, sometimes two hundred miles a day: the tank and artillery forces. Little lighted red dots clustered off Washington, New York, London, the west coast of Europe, the Panama Canal, Hawaii, San Francisco, Los Angeles, Seattle, the Bering Strait, the Mediterranean, the Strait of Hormuz, both ends of Suez: the atomic submarines. Blue dots moved toward strategic locations in the Atlantic, Pacific, Indian and Mediterranean Oceans and the Persian Gulf: the Navy. Looking like clusters of small diamond needles, the missiles pointed toward the United States and South America from Cuba and Siberia, commanded Asia and Africa from the Kurile Islands north of Japan and the bases in satellite Afghanistan and Iran.

The Soviet Union was everywhere, he told himself with an excited satisfaction, *everywhere*. And when everything was in place and the maneuvers under way, the world would fall in a week's time if he gave the word. And what could become of the dying capitalist state then?

If he gave the word . . . that was the question, of course, and that was for H. Delbacher and his advisers and the American Congress and American people to worry about. They knew one of the contingency plans now, but there were others. He had a dozen options already and when all of his forces were in place on maneuvers he would have a dozen more. Then the Motherland could literally strike in any direction at any moment—or in several directions at the same moment—or even in all directions at the same moment. It was that strong, and its enemies that weak.

Only one element marred this otherwise encouraging and delightful picture. He was forced to admit (only to himself, of course) that he had been somewhat startled, even somewhat dismayed, by the reactions so far of H. Delbacher. Yuri and his colleagues had become so used, in the last few years, to dealing with hesitant, uncertain, stop-and-go, threaten-and-back-off American Presidents that to find one reacting swiftly and strongly—and meaning it—was an unsettling novelty.

The typically strong statement from an American Chief Executive had been that of J. Carter in 1980, relative to the Persian Gulf:

"An attempt by any outside force to control the Persian Gulf region will be regarded as an assault on the vital interests of the United States of America. And such an assault will be repelled by any means necessary, including military force."

This drew great praise from his countrymen for his "dramatic change to a new and more forceful stand." TAKING CHARGE, *Time* magazine hailed him ecstatically on its cover. But within nine days he was saying to a group of editors and broadcasters in Washington (drawing the headline, typical of many, in the San Francisco *Chronicle:* CARTER WANTS HELP IN PROTECTING GULF):

"We can protect our interests there. Obviously we don't intend and never have claimed to have the ability unilaterally to defeat any threat to that region with ease . . .

"What is called for was analysis by all those nations who are there who might be threatened. We'll cooperate with them as they request to strengthen their own defense capability as they desire. We'll coordinate our efforts with nations not located in, but heavily dependent, even more than we, on an uninterrupted supply of oil from that region . . . We'll be arousing the consciousness of other nations in the world to condemn any threat to the peace of that region . . . I don't think it's accurate for me to claim at this time or in the future that we expect to have enough military presence there to defend the region unilaterally."

Astounded and delighted by this abrupt backing-away from his applauded "tough stand," Yuri and his colleagues in the Kremlin sighed a

sigh of relief and mentally sent J. Carter permanently back to the Futile
File where they had long since consigned him.

"What is called for was an analysis by all those nations who are there
. . . We'll be arousing the consciousness of other nations . . . We'll coordinate our efforts . . . I don't think it's accurate for me to claim *at this
time or in the future* [Yuri's emphasis] that we expect to have enough
military presence there to defend the region unilaterally . . ."

And the very next day his Secretary of Defense and the Chief of the
Joint Chiefs of Staff testified to the Senate Armed Services Committee
that there was no certainty the United States could win any battle with
Russia in the Persian Gulf area because it just didn't have the strength.
But, warned the Defense Secretary, one should not talk about U.S. weakness because that might reveal something to the Soviets—who by then,
of course, thanks to their spy network and the sophisticated computer
technology given them earlier, had exact U.S. military strength catalogued
and computed right down almost to the last bullet in the last gun.

And a day after that, unbelievably, came release of a Defense Department study showing conclusively that the U.S. was far weaker than the
Soviet Union in the entire Persian Gulf area.

The reaction in the Kremlin was delighted, contemptuous and completely scornful.

This kind of about-face and public confession of weakness was the way
to face down the Soviets?

"Not while you and I and K. Marx and V. I. Lenin govern Mother
Russia," Yuri had remarked jovially to a scornfully laughing, heartily
applauding Politburo.

But now here was H. Delbacher, and suddenly they were having to
revise their assumptions and analyses. They had always known that he
was no friend to the socialist revolution or to the Soviet Union, but they
had all expected that when he actually took office and was confronted
with the full burden of facts concerning Soviet superiority, he would drastically modify his views and become as hesitant, wavering and timorous
as others before him.

Not so, H. Delbacher. Yuri had really believed, at their aborted "summit," that the facts and his own stern and implacable approach would
give the new President pause and drastically change his stubborn refusal
to co-operate with what Yuri honestly regarded as history's inevitability.
He had been far more astounded than he allowed his colleagues to know
when he learned that H. Delbacher's response had been to rush back to
Washington, make a speech designed to arouse and rally his countrymen
against inevitable history's chosen instrument, and promptly commit the
U.S. to a $10 billion spurt in armaments. But after the shaken Politburo
had discussed the matter for almost two hours they were able to perceive,
as Yuri kept telling them, that this was all part of his own plan and that

from it would come the perfect opportunity to take a quantum leap toward the final battle that would decide the fate of all mankind.

In fact, Yuri persuaded them, the battle itself might not be necessary at all if they played carefully the hand that H. Delbacher had given them with his impulsive and precipitate action. They all had the feeling that they were taking perhaps the next-to-last step in achieving the final victory when they issued their joint statement characterizing H. Delbacher's move as "an action almost of war" and countered with the announcement of the maneuvers. At Yuri's suggestion they deliberately offered the bait of further negotiations.

Disclosure of a possible Soviet attack on the northeastern United States and Europe, both very high on the list of options, served to confuse and intimidate the dying capitalist world, but much to their annoyance and concern there came no direct response from H. Delbacher. Instead he used that bothersome British busybody, as Yuri considered her, to set up a group of minor heads of state to do it for him.

Again there had been an emergency meeting of the Politburo. Some tensions were developing there despite the power of Yuri's personality and position. Some dared express fear that he might be going too far in his gamble, that he might provoke the now suddenly unknown quantity of H. Delbacher into some rash and fearsome reaction much more violent than his initial one.

"Comrades," Yuri had retorted with a somber and menacing contempt, "the battle to decide the fate of all mankind is not for cowards. If anyone wishes to withdraw and abandon the socialist Motherland now, he is free to do so. But he need not return to this room . . . ever."

Nonetheless there had actually been four abstentions when the vote came; and since they were the four remaining members of the old guard, last advocates of caution, holding relatively minor ministerial posts and not carrying any great weight any more, he decided to ignore their opposition and let them live and continue in their posts. But he felt suddenly as he had one time on one of his KGB-accompanied vacations, mountain-climbing in Switzerland: very high and very far and relying entirely upon himself, which was thrilling and the way he secretly liked it to be.

So, without comment except for the single sentence, "The Council of Ministers of the U.S.S.R. rejects the impertinent suggestion of the British Prime Minister and others. Y. P. Serapin," he had given the final order for maneuvers and the die was cast.

He did not know, as he watched the red lines, red dots, blue dots and tiny glistening slivers moving on the seas and continents, whether the final outcome would occur at exactly the time he estimated or take exactly the form he presently planned: but he had no doubt that in due course it *would* occur—just as K. Marx and V. I. Lenin said.

There might be some slip-ups here and there, some waste motions and unnecessarily lost men and equipment, because even the forces of the socialist Motherland were human . . . but insofar as it was possible to train them, they were not human any longer. They were part of a machine.

Terribly excited inside in some deeply visceral way, but ice cold, calculating and calm in heart and mind, he sent them plunging forward across the helpless reaches of the earth.

BOOK TWO

BOOK FIVE

1

"Our ground forces have been transformed beyond recognition. Equipped with nuclear missiles, they can deliver powerful strikes at a great depth, destroy major enemy groupings of troops, seize important regions and quickly advance following nuclear strikes. The National Air Defense Forces have developed rapidly. Armed with various powerful surface-to-air missiles, all-weather supersonic fighter-interceptors, modern radar sets, high-speed computers and other equipment, they are able to successfully accomplish their missions. The capabilities of the Air Forces have risen immeasurably. They are equipped with long-range supersonic aircraft armed with missiles and able to launch strikes from great distances. Our Navy, the foundation of whose combat might is atomic submarines armed with underwater-launched long-range missiles and homing torpedoes, has grown into a truly formidable ocean-going force."

—*The Superiority of Soviet Military Organization,*
General Major M. M. Kir-yan

All of this the President of the United States was prepared to concede. But as he plodded doggedly on through one of his major tasks in these tense opening hours of the Soviet maneuvers—the reading of intelligence reports on the relative strengths of both sides—he found himself becoming bogged down in claim and counter-claim to the point where he felt the truth was becoming increasingly confused by argument. He had not been at his desk more than an hour on this first day of the new situation before he put in a call to his military aide, a bright young Navy captain named Bosserman, and directed him to prepare the Situation Room in the basement for a conference. Then he asked his secretary to get him the Secretary of Defense, Roger Hackett.

"Rog," he said, "what are the Joint Chiefs doing this morning?"

"I think going to the Hill to testify before the Senate Armed Services Committee," the Secretary said. "Why, do you want 'em?"

"I think it might be fitting, don't you?" Ham Delbacher asked, a trifle dryly. "Say forty-five minutes, in the Situation Room. I'll call Jim Elrod and explain it to him. He's one committee chairman who won't take umbrage at being pre-empted, I think."

Nor did he.

"Why sure, Ham—Mr. President," he said. "We can question 'em later in the week sometime if they're free. Just scoot us out of the way. Cancellin' the committee meetin' in favor of an emergency White House session will step up the sense of urgency on the Hill a bit, anyway, and maybe we need that."

"Reaction's pretty divided, isn't it?" the President inquired thoughtfully.

"It is up here," Senator Elrod said. "Startin' with my own household."

"You mean Mark isn't convinced yet?" the President said sharply. "What's the matter with that boy?"

"Oh, he's comin' round," Jim Elrod said, "but there's a certain amount of face-savin' goin' on. And not only Mark. A lot on the Hill and lots of 'em in the media are havin' to swallow a lifetime's rigid beliefs in a few hours' time. It doesn't come easy."

"I'm aware of that," the President said, again dryly. "The tone toward me is very mixed but I think concern for their own necks is beginning to predominate. Good old-fashioned fear can have a mighty accelerating effect on a man's making up his mind. And that's beginning to occur, I think. Meantime, the same old eternal rationalizing is still going on in some quarters."

"Oh yes, I saw 'em," Jim said with a snort. "Nothin' to be worried about in 'a few routine maneuvers,' so they tell us. A few routine maneuvers from Europe to the Bering Strait and from the Arctic to the Antarctic. Paradin' their whole might everywhere across the globe. Some maneuvers! Some routine!"

"Well, our friends in the media *are* scared," Hamilton Delbacher remarked with more tolerance than some of his countrymen deserved. "So they cling to their usual routine, like a cat does when it's disturbed. Ever notice that, Jim? Something out of the ordinary, and your average cat immediately starts cleaning itself, because that's familiar, *that's* routine, that means the world isn't suddenly disturbed but is still in its normal place. But maybe you didn't grow up on a farm like I did."

"I surely did," Jim Elrod said stoutly. "I most certainly did. We always had cats. But, here, now! Suppose I told people the President of the United States and I, facin' the greatest crisis this country literally has ever known, are sittin' here talkin' about cats while the Soviets move to their battle stations all over the world. *Then* you'd catch it!"

The President chuckled. Then his voice grew somber.

"It helps me," he said. "It preserves in my mind the illusion that your grandchildren and mine are going to be able to enjoy something of the same peaceful world we did in our early days. And in my heart, Jim, I don't think so."

"Nor I," Senator Elrod said, equally somber. "It's goin' to be mighty tight, Ham. Mi——ghty tight."

"Help keep the fires damped down as much as possible up there, O.K.?"

"We'll do our best for you. No particular legislation you need at this point, is there?"

"I think I have everything, thanks, but if not I'll let you know. Basically it's just a matter of deciding what I should do with it—and then getting the country to go along. I'll be calling you fellows down probably this afternoon, incidentally. A conference of all the leaders and major committee chairmen."

"You don't really expect a sneak attack, do you?"

"No. But I don't expect any categoric denial from them, either. It suits their purpose to have us worried about it. But I think publicizing the threat was necessary—it was sufficient to stop any possibility, however remote, of its occurring. And it contributes to that sense of urgency you were talking about, both here and abroad."

"Speakin' of which," Jim Elrod said, "I'd better get off the phone now and let you go back to work. Don't let the JCS fill you too full of tobacco juice about the ready state of our forces. We've received some reports lately that would curl your hair."

"I have them in front of me," the President said. "We're going to discuss them at some length."

And so they did, when the Secretary of Defense and the Joint Chiefs drove up two by two in their chauffeured limousines a few minutes later and he went down to the Situation Room to meet with them. Out of it emerged very little he did not already know. What he heard did not frighten him, because he literally had no time to feel frightened. But in him, too, it produced an urgency that even he had not felt up to now.

"Gentlemen," he said, when they were all seated across from him like schoolboys flanking teacher: Roger Hackett in the center; the chairman of the Joint Chiefs, General Rutherford "Smidge" Hallowell, U. S. Army, on his left; to the left of them General Martin "Bump" Smith, Chief of Staff, U. S. Army and Admiral Harman "Snooze" Rydecker, Chief of Naval Operations. On Roger Hackett's right were General Bartram C. "Bart" Jamison, Chief of Staff of the U. S. Air Force and General Robert "Gutsy" Twitchell, Commandant of the U. S. Marine Corps.

Despite their somewhat juvenile nicknames, mostly dating back to youthful days at the service academies, they were all highly intelligent and competent men. They were also, the President could see, as close to full panic as they had probably ever been. Because now the weaknesses, stupidities, misjudgments and miscalculations of other men—particularly

some recent Presidents of the United States—were suddenly falling on
their shoulders.

They were responsible for the bail-out and those gentlemen had left
them almost nothing to bail with.

For several moments Hamilton Delbacher studied their worried faces
and then decided to hit a note which, he told himself, he must strike in
his next address to the nation. He had an idea this would come very
soon: possibly even tonight.

"Gentlemen," he said quietly, "it appears we are all in this together.
For reasons with which we are all familiar, going back to decisions which
many of us opposed, we have very little at hand to meet the exact combination of ominous bluff and direct threat with which we are being faced.
The first thing I want to say to you is that you are not to blame for the
situation we are in. You don't deserve recriminations for it and you aren't
going to get them. Neither will it do any good to stop now to engage in
recriminations against those who are to blame. We have but one direction
in which to go, and that's forward; and one way in which to do it, and
that's together. All else sinks into unimportance now."

He paused and there were almost audible sighs of relief across the
table; so much so that he could not resist a slight smile, which was picked
up and expanded into a hearty laugh by Bump Smith of the Army.

"Wow!" he said, mopping his brow in mock relief. "That's good to
hear!"

After which they all relaxed and laughed; and suddenly it was as
though a great weight were lifted. The meeting assumed at once a businesslike and forward momentum which it retained to their departure an
hour later.

"O.K., Bump," the President said. "Suppose you start by giving us an
overview of the condition of the Army."

"Lousy," Bump Smith said promptly. "In one word. But by no means
irreversible."

"In twenty-four hours?" Admiral "Snooze" Rydecker of the Navy inquired. His colleague bristled slightly.

"We have more time than that!" he snapped. "By the time your tubs
get into battle formation—"

"Quiet!" Roger Hackett ordered, half-humorously but meaning it.
"You heard the President. Another thing we haven't got time for is inter-
service rivalries. Right?"

"Just wait until we march through Red Square," General Smith said,
also half—but only half—humorously. "Then we'll tend to you Navy
guys."

"You will never march through Red Square," the President said in a
tone suddenly cold and not at all amused, "unless this country is lucky
beyond belief. About all we can hope for is a negotiated peace, it seems

to me; and that is extremely problematical, since the Soviets are dedicated to a war to the death. *Our death.* In their minds it is literally *them
or us.* So let's stop the fun and games and get serious. Bump, I asked you
for a run-down on the Army. Now let's have it and no nonsense. All
right?"

"Yes, Mr. President," General Smith said meekly, and proceeded for
five minutes to discourse on fire power, throw-weight, storage facilities,
weaponry, expected body counts and the like, all of which were germane,
perhaps, on a certain slide-and-blackboard level but were, the President
knew, immaterial to what he was after now.

Finally he interrupted.

"Thank you, Bump, but I suppose essentially what I want is the answer
to this question: will your troops fight, and fight to win? That's all I want
to know about."

"Eliminate the drug problem, poor discipline, generally poor morale—
which accounts for maybe 25 per cent real bedrock," General Smith said
soberly, "and I think the rest will give a good account of themselves. Of
those about half will go because they're told. The rest will have to be
convinced, if they're to really put up the kind of fight that may be necessary."

"Do the same percentages hold for you, Snooze? And the Air Force?
And the Marines?"

"We're in a little better shape, maybe," Admiral Rydecker said, "but not
a great deal. Pride of ship helps, and since a few new ones are finally beginning to come on line from the '80–'81 budget, we have an increasing
amount of that. But, as Bump says, for the majority it's a matter of being
convinced. Our friends in Moscow are helping there. Navy recruiting stations are being besieged all over the country this morning."

"We, too," agreed Bart Jamison of the Air Force.

"And we," echoed Bump Smith, and Bob Twitchell of the Marines.

"Yes, at least that's one specific thing they've done for us," the President agreed. "They've proved to the country that the threat is real and a
lot of kids, bless their hearts, are turning out to answer. But this time it's
going to take more than that, I'm afraid."

"What do you mean, Mr. President?" Smidge Hallowell, the chairman
of the chiefs, inquired in his somewhat ponderous but thoughtful way. "A
civilian draft?"

"Something like that," the President said. "I haven't thought it through
entirely yet, but I'll have it by tonight, when I go on the air again."

"You're going on again?" Roger Hackett murmured politely. The President smiled.

"Friend," he said crisply, "I'm going to be on so often from now on
that you'll think my name is Bob Hope."

"Wish you had his money," the Defense Secretary said.

"It won't matter," the President said shortly. "If the Soviets succeed in what they want to do, it won't matter one little damned bit. Now: I want you gentlemen to go back to your offices and prepare for my immediate approval—let's say by 4 P.M. this afternoon—a plan for the political education of the forces. I want a political program worked out for every unit right down to virtually the smallest you've got. I want Soviet plans and ambitions explained to them, in detail and with documentation, and I want them to understand why we are probably going to have to fight to stop them."

"You can't politicize the armed forces!" General Hallowell said, looking genuinely shocked.

"They do," the President said grimly, "and we're going to also, at least to the extent of having the men understand *why*. The major task of education of course rests on me, and I'm going to do it in my speeches to the country. But I want an informed military and I intend to have one. Fast. That, too, should have begun decades ago, as it did with them, but at least it isn't too late to get a rudimentary but clear understanding established."

"But—" Snooze Rydecker began and trailed away as the President stared at him questioningly.

"On my desk by 4 P.M.," he said flatly. "Back to you by 5, in operation starting 0800 tomorrow wherever Americans are stationed throughout the world. Got it?"

"Got it," they agreed, looking at him as though he was something entirely new in Presidents; and as most Presidents had been in recent years, he was.

"I am also going to put you all on limited alert when I speak tonight," he added, almost as an afterthought. "And Bart and Snooze—I want that Air Force and Navy to dog those bastards' heels so closely all over the world that they'll feel they don't have a moment's privacy. All the satellites will be busy, too, of course, but I want them to see you guys. Be visible."

"They may shoot," General Jamison said.

"Shoot back," the President said bluntly.

"We haven't got the power to retaliate successfully if something goes wrong, I'm afraid," Admiral Rydecker said slowly. "Are you sure you want us to—"

"From this moment forward," Ham Delbacher said, "I want the armed forces of the United States to act as though they don't have a doubt in the world that they are superior and in full command of the situation."

A silence fell. Finally Roger Hackett ventured softly:

"That's an awful gamble to take, Mr. President."

"Yes," he agreed, deliberately turning to each in turn and looking him squarely in the eyes.

"Do you know of any better?"

And, of course, as they all acknowledged while the limousines whisked them back across the Potomac and deposited them once more at the River Entrance to the Pentagon, he was entirely right. It was a great gamble—but there was nothing better. And yet, as the group of reporters waiting at the great bronze doors surged forward to bombard them with questions, there came to each the same nagging worry: We may literally have a week or less. How do you restore morale and build up forces in that time? *How do you do it?*

"Mr. Secretary!" the reporters cried. "General! Admiral! General! General! Mr. Secretary!"

Roger Hackett raised a hand above his head, the clamor subsided for a moment.

"Ladies and gentlemen," he said calmly, "this is all quite pointless. We have, as you know, been to the White House. We have discussed the current situation at some length with the President. We have given him our views, he has given us his orders as Commander-in-Chief. We have come back here to put those orders into effect."

"What are they?" the AP demanded with some belligerence. Roger waved him away with a smile.

"Now, Bob," he said, "that's a great try, but you really don't expect to get anywhere with it, do you? His orders are his orders and you know perfectly well we aren't going to tell you. Everything will become clear as we go along."

"Are there any plans for counteracting the sneak attack, Mr. Secretary?" UPI joined in. Roger Hackett hesitated, then decided to answer.

"We do not anticipate such an attack. The cover's been blown on it, after all; we're alerted. There can't be any 'sneak attack,' now. We're ready for it."

"Entirely ready, Mr. Secretary?" the *Christian Science Monitor* inquired with some dryness. Roger Hackett smiled cheerfully.

"Quite sufficient to make any such venture completely unproductive from the Soviet point of view."

"Diplomats go abroad to lie for their country," the Washington *Post* remarked, *sotto voce*. "Others stay home."

"Now, see here!" the Secretary said, permitting a real anger to enter his voice, while behind him the members of the Joint Chiefs formed a solid line supporting him, an equal disapproval showing in all faces. "That remark is smart-ass and uncalled for. If you and your precious—if you and your newspaper come through this episode alive, you can thank the people who defend this country. It won't be any thanks to the likes of you. Gentlemen, let's head on in. We've got a lot of work to do."

And he stepped up to join his phalanx. They all turned on their heels and pushed on inside.

"That didn't help much," the New York *Times* remarked to the *Post*.

"Who cares?" the *Post* said indifferently. "They're all scared shitless anyway. They haven't got a plan and they know it."

"Then we haven't got a prayer and *we* know it," UPI tossed over her shoulder as she too went on inside. "So what do you make of that, genius?"

But his rejoinder, if any, was lost as they dispersed, some to go back to the press room and speculate, some to start checking their junior sources in the JCS staff, some to make camp in the Secretary's reception room. He was inside, his secretary informed them—alone. The members of the JCS had returned to their offices. There would be no top Pentagon meeting at the moment—though of course she couldn't guarantee that one wouldn't be called at any time. So, better stay in touch.

In the office of the chairman of the Joint Chiefs, to whom they had consigned by tacit agreement the task of drawing up what they were already referring to as "the political plan," General Rutherford "Smidge" Hallowell was facing a blank piece of paper with a big felt pen. The task was not monumental—he had drawn up dozens of troop training directives in the long years since West Point—and he expected to have it accomplished in less than an hour once he put his mind to it. Meanwhile that mind, one of the very best in the country, was wandering back over the White House meeting. For the first time he thought he saw a very faint glimmer of hope named Hamilton Delbacher; but whether it would be sufficient to bridge the frightening gap between American illusions and Soviet reality he could not at the moment say.

Smidge Hallowell—the nickname had started when the football coach at the Point had yelled, "Where's that little smidge of a fellow who wants to play forward?"—felt that the President might just do it—just—if he had a sufficiently strong team backing him up in all the areas where he would have to act. Going down the line of the team here in the Pentagon, he thought the JCS, on the whole, were about as competent a bunch of men as had ever held their respective offices: and thank God for that.

Starting with his own branch of service, the U. S. Army, he knew that both he and Bump Smith ("That guy sure bumps noses with a lot of people, but he gets where he wants to go.") were from exactly the same mold, with almost exactly the same record. The small-town backgrounds, Minot, North Dakota, in his case, Visalia, California, in Bump's—the outstanding high school records as students and athletes; the Point;

Korea, Nam, military attaché in half a dozen embassies in the more troubled areas of the world; the recurring bouts of desk time here in the Pentagon; the long, steady push upward, slightly more diplomatic in his case
than in Bump's rather abrasive approach to life, but equally effective; the
last few years of assignment as liaison to the Senate and House Military
Affairs Committees; assignment to the JCS staff, a last couple of years of
duty abroad, this time in Moscow; the command posts in quick succes-
sion, the last two promotions virtually tumbling on top of each other; the
JCS as Army chief of staff, and then finally, in his case, the appointment
as chairman. Bump was four years younger but he would get it too, in
due course. It was the Navy's turn next, then the Air Force, then the Marines. In the normal course of things, Bump might have to wait at least
another six—

He stopped himself abruptly. In the normal course of things! What
"normal course"? They'd all be lucky to be sitting at their desks a month
from now, probably; might even be lucky if there was any Pentagon or
any Washington to sit in. He shivered suddenly in the office's brisk air-
conditioning, and pulled himself back hastily from *that* particular preci-
pice.

He forced his mind to trace its way along the huge building's busy corridors, always a-move with the endless flow of military and civilian traffic
carrying the endless orders, directives, messages and memos that tied together the plans, hopes, dreams, ambitions of the military machine in all
its human and material aspects. The Pentagon always hummed with activity; important-looking people went hurrying by on what often appeared to
be, and often were, vitally important matters. He loved the feeling of
being at the vortex of it all, which he now was, just below the Secretary;
and with a civilian Secretary as pleasant, easygoing and willing to be
educated as Roger Hackett, he found the duty extremely congenial. Except, of course, for the situation with the Soviets, which now was passing
almost beyond the realm of control by either side into that dangerous
area of which he had received intimations in Korea and Viet Nam. There
war had taken on its own nature and sometimes overruled even the most
carefully drawn and carefully implemented plans of men.

The Soviets made a great deal of this in their literature, he had noted—
"the nature of war," particularly atomic war, dictating its own rules. It
was a concept they had embraced from the beginning with a great enthusiasm entirely different from the guilty, conscience-ridden hesitations of
the West. There was no guilt about it in the Soviet military mind as
represented in their official military papers: they *loved* the idea of atomic
war, and they were convinced that they could win it, too. For two decades and more they had been deliberately preparing for it; and not all the
"tactical atomic weapons" which the U.S. and NATO might have in place
in Western Europe could, he suspected, offer an adequate match for the

Soviets' arsenal *and the unhesitating enthusiasm with which they would use it if they saw the chance.*

This was the difference, he sometimes told himself. It came down to something as simple as: *the Soviets are killers and the Americans are not.* To this day there was an occasional lingering conscience-stricken reference to "the My Lai massacre" in which a tiny Vietnamese village was wasted. He doubted if anyone in the Soviet Union, aside from a few top military, ever heard of the slaughters in Afghanistan in which a thousand men and boys at a time were machine-gunned down, their bodies ground into the soil by bulldozers—in order, the Soviet officers in charge remarked sarcastically, "to give you a good potato crop next year." Who cared about such things in the Soviet Union? They would be done to Europeans, if it came to that; they would be done to Americans, if it came to that. *And nobody would ever know*—firstly because the Soviets didn't give a damn, and secondly because if such things ever occurred, the Soviets would then be writing the history and the record would simply be left blank.

But again he was face to face with horrors from which he tried to keep himself at a necessary distance if he was to function properly. He had been mentally on his way, he reminded himself, to the office of Admiral "Snooze" Rydecker ("I think I'll just take a little snooze between classes," he often used to tell his classmates at Annapolis; but he didn't snooze much these days, that's for sure.) Snooze and Bartram Jamison (who mercifully didn't need a nickname aside from "Bart") of the Air Force were right out there on the front line in this modern battle-age. In a way, though the over-all responsibility was Smidge's and the Secretary's, Smidge was glad he wasn't in his two colleagues' shoes. They were directly responsible, and that was considerably different.

But, as the President had said—the President was quite a guy, General Hallowell was beginning to believe, very kind and decent and also tough, thank God—neither commander could be blamed for the condition of his forces. The previous Administration had pursued such an erratic course toward the Soviets, zigzagging between spasmodic halfway (half-assed, Smidge thought to himself) military build-ups and wafted kisses of Christian love, that the sum total had been near chaos in the armed services and particularly in the Navy and Air Force.

"Hell!" Snooze had said bitterly in the Secretary's office a few years ago when he was Navy liaison to the Senate Armed Services Committee, "I can't tell what the fuck they're up to over there in the White House. One minute he's waving a big stick and the next he's offering Brezhnev an hors d'oeuvre on a toothpick. And we're the hors d'oeuvre."

"Must be confusing for them too," the then Chief of Naval Operations had offered philosophically. Snooze snorted.

"Those bastards made up their minds twenty years ago—hell, forty years ago—what they planned to do," he said, "and they're just going right ahead doing it. We're immaterial, except as an obstacle to be eliminated. *The* obstacle to be eliminated."

And now they apparently thought they stood within sight of their goal.

If they didn't make it, Snooze and Bart—and after that, Bump and his boys—would be the ones to bear the brunt.

This was as long as the war was confined to a recognizable battle front. If the Soviets adhered to all their official teachings since World War II, which there was no reason to suppose they wouldn't, they would overleap, or overrocket, the standard battle lines and go direct for the civilian jugular. At that point, God help the country.

But there he went again, he told himself angrily, getting gloomy; and there wasn't time or energy to waste on being gloomy. He had too much to do.

Before he got back to it, though—the blank piece of paper, the felt pen and the President's desire for an immediate political education program— he decided to do what he called "making the rounds." He picked up the tie-phone and dialed four digits.

"Hi, Gutsy," he said to General Bob Twitchell at the Marine Corps. "Just making the rounds. How you feeling?"

Gutsy thought for a moment and Smidge could envisage him rubbing his chin in his steady, thoughtful way.

"Not doing too badly for an old man," he said finally. "We're in pretty good shape. We could be better, and we damned well soon will be or I'll chew ass a bit around here. But on the whole, count us in. And you?"

"Making it," Smidge said. "Thanks and keep in touch."

"Any time."

"Bump," he said to his Army colleague, "just thought I'd make the rounds. The Old Man gave us a lot to think about, didn't he?"

"Who needs it?" General Smith inquired tartly. "I've got so much to think about, Janice and I have started sleeping in separate beds because I'm up ten times a night pacing the floor. I don't *want* any more to think about."

"Kind of an impressive guy, I thought."

"Oh, I've always thought so, clear back to Senate days. Got his hands full, though. So've we all."

"Going to be able to help him?"

"Are you kidding? Who has a choice? As I said this morning, the Army is ragged but right. We need a little time—"

"And we may not have it."

"We may not have it. Somehow I think we will, though. We've got to proceed on that basis. Meanwhile we're moving double-quick over here. It's going to be a long, hot summer. And it's half over already."

"O.K., Bump. Just making the rounds. Keep the faith."

"Hang in there, baby," Bump said crisply. "Give me another million men by tomorrow morning and I'll kiss your little twinky-toes."

But the ones Smidge really wanted to give them to were Bart and Snooze, along with about five hundred more ships of all types for Snooze, and about ten thousand more planes for Bart. He caught the admiral in mid-mouthful.

"Snooze," he said. "Just making the rounds. Eating at your desk?"

"Eating here now, eating here this evening, sleeping here tonight," Snooze said after an audible swallow. "Don't you think you'd better set up active command quarters here for us? We may be doing a lot of live-in commanding in the next couple of months."

"I'll tell them to activate the basement this afternoon. How's it going?"

"All right. He wants us visible, we're going to be visible. I've already sent out orders to get tracking missions going off Europe, the Atlantic seaboard, the Indian Ocean and the Bering Strait. My God, do you realize how much that still leaves uncovered?"

"I realize. Don't let it get you down. The Secretary's going to reactivate some of the moth-ballers this afternoon."

"Moth-ballers! Good Christ, that'll knock the Soviets right into the water. They'll be laughing so hard they'll all fall overboard. What a clever way to win a war!"

"We'll make it, now," General Hallowell said with a certainty he didn't feel, so thoroughly did he agree with the Chief of Naval Operations. "Just keep plugging, Snooze, you know that."

"Of course I know that," Snooze said, more calmly. "I'm not faulting anybody. We'll do what we have to, *you* know that."

"O.K. Just making the rounds. Let me hear any ideas immediately."

"Put the *Post* on observer station in a rowboat off Murmansk," Snooze suggested. General Hallowell laughed.

"Naughty," he said.

"But nice," Admiral Rydecker remarked. "See you around the plantation."

Bart Jamison, as General Hallowell expected, was in conference with his top aides, but came to the phone in a moment.

"Hi, Smidge," he said. "What can we do for you over here?"

"Just making the rounds, Bart," Smidge said. "Any special problems that need attention or help?"

"No," Bart said thoughtfully. "Nothing ten thousand additional planes wouldn't cure."

"That was my figure exactly," General Hallowell said, "but unfortunately I left mine all home in the play-pen this morning."

"Yeah," Bart agreed. "Me too. I'll give you the slogan for this war—if it's going to be one. *Buy time.* Not bonds, not USO's, not planes, even. *Buy time.* Because, brother, that's what we don't have."

"Maybe we can wangle a little," Smidge Hallowell said, "if *he* is very, very clever."

"And very, very lucky. We'll all have to pray for that. . . . Well, excuse me, Smidge, don't mean to be abrupt, but I've got to get back. We're working out a few ideas I'll buck along to you tomorrow. If tomorrow comes."

"It'll come," General Hallowell said with perhaps more confidence than he felt. "And with it, the time you need."

"You're a good chairman, Smidge," General Jamison said. "You know when to apply the optimism and the soothing sauce. I can use all I can get, right now."

"I'll keep it coming," Smidge Hallowell said. Although from what secret source or what undiscovered strength, he couldn't have said, right then. He didn't think he had much left, to tell the truth.

He turned from the phone. Facing him across the room, as it faced the President, the Secretary of Defense and State, the members of the Joint Chiefs—and Yuri Serapin—the animated map of the world continued to crawl with little lighted lines and dots. They were quite far out, now, he noticed with a strange sort of shuddering sigh; quite far out, and moving fast.

Ten gray, grim faces stared at him from around the long oaken table. Why would they not laugh, now that all their plans were under way at last, success guaranteed by history and the disarray of their mortal enemy? Why always so solemn and so somber? Now, in the supreme moment of all their lives?

"Comrades!" he cried, and he hit the table so hard with the flat of his hand that the older members of the Politburo jumped and the younger snapped warily to attention. "You are so *solemn!* You are so *somber!* You are so *grim!* Do you not see this is a time for laughing and celebration? We are moving forward everywhere while our enemies run about like frightened mice! Why will no one celebrate with me our inevitable victory? Come, come!"

A titter of nervous agreement ran along the table, but no one really laughed with him, so that his triumphant bark of amusement rang out overloudly in the dark, enormous room and almost seemed to hang in the air, suspended and visibly shredding before their eyes. Yet he knew they were with him completely. He could not be more certain of their loyalty.

"Comrades, comrades!" he chided again. "Do not tell me there are doubters among you? Do not let me suspect weaklings! It is going so well, comrades! *So well.* Watch the map, watch the map! We are on the move everywhere—*everywhere.* Surely," he cried with the charming smile he could assume when necessary, *"surely,* there is at least one pleased laugh in that!"

Then they did laugh, at first self-consciously, but then, as it went around the table, with increasing gusto until presently they were roaring, pounding one another on the back, gasping for breath, gray faces turning purple with the mass hysteria of it. The Minister of Defense at last managed to gurgle out a sentiment for them all.

"Yuri Pavlovich!" he cried. "Comrade President! You are correct, we should be laughing. Here we sit like so many dummies, when we should be laughing! Why is this? You have called us to this meeting to witness the marvelous progress of your ideas, which we have all approved, and we act like scarecrows and dummies! It is inexcusable, Comrade President. You, Yuri Pavlovich, are proving your magnificent leadership with every hour—no, every minute, *every second*—that passes. Every second carries the brave sons of the socialist Motherland closer to their battle stations, closer to victory over the pathetic Americans! We are with you, Yuri Pavlovich, Comrade President! We are with you!"

And inspired by his words they all burst out applauding and laughing hysterically once more. It was only when the uproar began to subside that Yuri spoke again with a softness that was suddenly extremely menacing.

"Yes," he said. "Why, then, must I *demand* that you join me in celebration?"

There was a sudden dismayed silence, during which they cast alarmed glances at one another and finally turned once more to the Minister of Defense, who looked desperately anywhere but at Yuri; but finally spoke, in a voice that noticeably trembled.

"Comrade President," he said carefully, "it is not that we do not approve and applaud your course. How could we do otherwise, having already voted you our support of it? It is just that—well, now that it is here at last it does not seem quite—quite—real to us yet. It is such an enormous event you have set in motion. It is taking us a little time to adjust to it. If you will forgive us, Comrade President."

"There is no time for adjustment," Yuri snapped. "There is time only for the sternest dedication to the Motherland and to the victorious outcome of the decisive battle to determine the fate of all mankind. We are only in the opening stages, that battle is not yet even joined, and some of you seem doubtful already. What will it be like when I give the decisive word to strike? Will there be cowards then? If so"—and his voice acquired again its menacing softness—"I warn you, they will not last long around me. . . . There is but one way for our victorious communist banners to go, now—forward. There is but one way for us to achieve the victory—together. Anyone who does not care to be present at the supreme moment of all history may leave now." And suddenly his voice rose to a shout that made several of them, he noted with satisfaction, literally turn pale. "NOW!"

Then there were indeed great protestations of loyalty, exclamations of faith, grovelings of appreciation and praise. How frightened of me they are, he thought with a sudden terrible, deep gratification. He might not have Stalin's name but he had his power and infinitely more; and now he was indeed supreme among them all. For the ordinary purposes of government the communist fiction could be preserved that he and his colleagues ran things together, that he was only the first among equals. In practical effect he was Czar of All the Russias, and they were terrified of him.

And so it should be, he told himself with great satisfaction. He was the most intelligent, the most decisive, the most powerful, the most worthy, the best. He would let them go through the motions of votes, resolutions, approvals for now; but when the final battle actually began, he would have them vote him Supreme Commander of the Armed Forces and Peoples, Leader of the Socialist Coalition, and from then on he would see the battle through until he was finally in place above the entire world, Supreme Ruler and Arbiter of All Mankind. (This was the title he had secretly chosen for himself.)

"Comrades," he said, abruptly terminating their nervous paeans of praise and encouragement, "I have called you to this meeting because I think it is time for a progress report on the maneuvers. I am pleased to see that you have followed my suggestion and have dressed in your uniforms as generals of the various branches of the armed services. We will wear these uniforms daily hereafter until the maneuvers are either over or, if necessary, have moved on into their decisive, pre-ordained further stages. I am especially anxious that we be seen in them everywhere in public, particularly by the foreign press. That is one reason I have asked you to accompany me in a few minutes to the press conference I have scheduled. I assume you will all be able to do this?"

"Oh yes, Comrade President!" they cried. "Oh, but certainly, Yuri Pavlovich!"

"Good," he said. "That is good. Comrade Minister of Defense, report."

"Yes, Yuri Pavlovich," the Minister, a flabby-faced toady of seventy who knew very well who the real Minister of Defense was, replied with an obsequious little bow. "As of ten minutes ago when I left my office to come to you, everything—and I mean everything, Comrade President— was on schedule throughout the world. Our satellites, as you know, are monitoring all the movements of all our forces, and I am proud to say that every single one is exactly where it is supposed to be with no more than a mile's expected deviation on land or an allowable five miles at sea, in the air and in space. Thanks to the computer technology we were so kindly allowed to purchase by the American J. Carter"—and he laughed with a complacent amusement in which they all joined—"we are exactly where we have planned to be. It is a great tribute to the training of our brave forces of the socialist Motherland."

"And, of course, to J. Carter," Yuri observed; and their laughter rose delightedly—and contemptuously—once more.

"What would we have done without him, Comrade President?" the Minister of Labor shot out. And again they were convulsed with laughter.

"Comrade Minister of Foreign Affairs, report," Yuri said; and the minister, a year younger than himself, whom he had nominated to his new office just three days ago, cleared his throat and bowed.

"As we all know, Comrade President," he said, "the reaction among our enemies, particularly in the United States, has been one of great confusion, disarray and, in some influential cases, despair. The only organized response has come, at the instigation of H. Delbacher, from our eternally busy lady in Britain, the Prime Minister. You know she gathered together a handful of leaders of minor states, France, West Germany, the like, to issue a joint appeal to you and H. Delbacher, requesting a return to the negotiating table. We all know your terse, magnificient response, which we endorsed. It was a trap and you were infinitely wise to stay out of it, Comrade President. We applaud you."

And he led the way as they did, with many murmurs of approval and assent.

"Therefore, diplomatically, there is little to report at the moment. No doubt there will be other similar attempts in the next few hours and days, as the U.S., the criminal conspiracy of NATO and the rest scurry about frantically attempting to halt our maneuvers. Yet what can they do? It is all perfectly legitimate. We are not attacking them."

"Not even a surprise attack through eastern Germany and along the United States northeastern seaboard?" Yuri asked dryly, and again they all laughed.

"There is nothing, I repeat, that they can do," the Foreign Minister said. "We are not infringing on their territory. We are not overflying their air space. We are not threatening them. It is a supremely clever move, Yuri Pavlovich, and it is all your doing! It was your idea! It was your genius!"

"And," Yuri Serapin said with great satisfaction as their eager applause once more anointed him, "*it puts us in place.* That is its supreme importance. If there should be the slightest provocation—or if it seems right that we should decide to create one—then we have them surrounded everywhere. Never have such armies marched, never has such an armada sailed, never have such airborne armies taken to the skies in all of human history. What can they do? They are helpless. Our busy British lady could not get us to negotiate now, but there will come a time, comrades. Oh yes! There will come a time. *We* will tell *them* when that time has come!"

He could not restrain himself from his characteristic short, sharp bark of laughter. They too crowed triumphantly at the thought of that happy day, and for several seconds the room rang with delighted reverberations.

"I am glad," Yuri remarked, rising from his chair, "that your mood is now more suitable to the present and future successes of our armed forces. There is nothing to worry about. You have but to watch the map. . . . And now, comrades, let us go to meet the representatives of the corrupt capitalist press. They no doubt will have many worried questions. We must see to it that their worries increase."

And amid more laughter and the exchange of many self-congratulatory remarks, they followed him down the long corridors to the great hall where the world's press had deliberately been kept waiting for over an hour for their appearance.

When they entered, Yuri in the lead, all wearing uniforms and full decorations, there was a gasp and then a great silence from the squabbling, impatient reporters, broadcasters, television cameramen, who filled every one of the five hundred seats and spilled over in more hundreds along the walls, along the back, even sitting up front on the floor below the rostrum which the Soviet President and his Politburo ascended.

Obeying his command as they had marched two by two down the hall, their faces were as grim, gray and implacable as they had been when he chided them earlier. There were to be no official smiles at this press conference. This was to be a Scare-the-World day.

On the wall behind them hung, yet again, the crawling map. For a full minute, while the hall rustled in uneasy silence, Yuri stood arms akimbo, back to them, studying it closely. Finally he exclaimed, *"Da!"* with great satisfaction, dropped his arms, turned back to the lectern and looked out upon their intent and apprehensive faces.

"Socialist comrades," he said in English, "and you who represent the imperialist press of the West and Asia: you have asked to speak with us. We are here. First I should like to make a brief statement on behalf of myself and my colleagues of the Politburo. It is this:

"The mightiest armies, the greatest armadas, the best-equipped and most deadly airborne forces in the history of mankind, together with history's greatest missile forces stationed in the most strategic places around the world, are now beginning the greatest maneuvers ever held. You can observe from the map that they are moving rapidly ahead with complete success and without meeting any opposition. This is only correct, because they are not engaged in war, even though some of our timorous capitalist friends would seem to want the world to think so.

"These are maneuvers designed to keep and to strengthen peace. They are maneuvers to make sure that no one ever again will dare to launch an unjust imperialist capitalist war. They are a guarantee to the whole world that the great peaceful coalition led by the Soviet Union, in co-operation with the Warsaw Pact and other friendly allies around the globe, *will keep the peace.* We will keep it *permanently,* because we are strong enough now so that it is impossible for anyone else to even dream of war. War would be suicide. We guarantee it."

There was a loud burst of applause, begun by the Politburo, taken up with great vigor by *Pravda, Tass, Izvestia* and the media representatives from the Warsaw Pact and allied countries. His expression did not change, but it pleased him greatly to note that several of the major correspondents from the West, such as the representatives of *Time* and *Newsweek* magazines, the New York and Washington newspapers, were sitting silent, glum and unhappy. It was not very grateful of him to feel this way toward them, since so many of them had been of so much assistance over the years, dutifully explaining and airily rationalizing away for their readers the ominous, ongoing Soviet build-up; but it was, of course, typical of Yuri and the philosophy he espoused.

The Western media's purpose had been served, now. They were no longer needed to help win acceptance for communist conquest. They had reverted to being just the hated enemy. Their only function now was to be frightened so that they might transmit their fear back to their corrupt imperialist country.

This was his purpose here this morning.

He dipped his head brusquely to indicate that questions were in order. The representative of the Associated Press raised his hand and stood up. He and Yuri had met years ago in Washington, there had been the usual intimate, flattering lunches at the Metropolitan Club, he had basked in Yuri's "friendship" like so many. All that was gone now.

"Yes?" Yuri demanded sharply, face expressionless. "What is it?"

"Mr. President," the AP said, attempting a small smile but obviously shaken by this hostile reception, "if the purpose of the maneuvers is strictly peaceful, why are they being conducted on a worldwide scale?"

"Because we wish to prove to the entire world that they are peaceful," he answered as though answering a child. There was a burst of raucous laughter from the communist press.

"But Mr. President," the AP persisted doggedly, "aren't the maneuvers being conducted on an unnecessarily vast and menacing scale—a scale that leads many people to conclude that their basic purpose is to be hostile and outright intimidating?"

"The West, and your country in particular," he said in the same contemptuous tone, "may assess them as they please. I am telling you what they are. If you wish to call me a liar, do so. It will not change the peace-loving nature of the Soviet Union or the peace-enforcing purpose of the maneuvers—which incidentally are coalition maneuvers of all the socialist camp, not just the Soviet Union."

"That, too, Mr. President," the New York *Times* said, on the defensive but not letting himself be intimidated, "arouses concern. Why must the entire coalition be involved? What are you planning, once you have ascertained from the maneuvers that everything is, from your point of view, ready for action?"

"Everything *is* ready for action!" Yuri snapped. "It is not just our 'point of view.' We could go to war in an hour, if we had to. The imperialist states should not forget this."

"*Do* you intend to go to war, Mr. President?" the Washington *Post,* a doughtier soul than his colleague in the Pentagon, demanded in a tone as sharp as Yuri's.

The Soviet leader snorted.

"Why should we do that? We would be fools."

"You would indeed," the Washington *Post* agreed in a totally unimpressed voice. "Then what is the purpose of this nonsense?"

At this there was a gasp of alarm from the Politburo and the communist press, an at first tentative but then wholehearted applause from the West. For a moment Yuri looked genuinely angry before he forced his expression into impassivity again.

"I would suggest to smart-minded and smart-talking reporters from corrupt capitalist nations," he said with the slow menace he found so effective with his colleagues, "that they not overreach themselves. They can be sent packing by nightfall. They can also help to aggravate an atmosphere in which they and their corrupt countries can be swiftly and decisively destroyed."

"Then you do contemplate the destruction of the United States and the West, Mr. President," *Time* magazine said. "It is part of your plans."

"We offer peace to the world," Yuri said calmly. "Those who interpret it as preparation for war are idiots."

"I am an idiot," *Time* magazine responded with equal calmness, "but I still would like to know why your maneuvers are, as you boast, 'the greatest in history.' What is the point? What is the purpose? Who are you trying to frighten?"

"Your President, H. Delbacher," Yuri said with an exaggerated patience as though he were indeed explaining to an idiot, "began by seeking to frighten us. It is not the Soviet Union who tries to frighten anyone, it is H. Delbacher who thinks he can frighten the Soviet Union. We met in New York, we talked: many of you same people were there. H. Delbacher professed not to be frightened himself, nor should he have been, for there, too, my talk, the talk of the Soviet Union and the socialist coalition, was only of peace. Nonetheless, H. Delbacher chose to be afraid, apparently, for he hurried hime to Washington and promptly announced to the Congress that he would spend $10 billion. And what would he spend them for? Why, he would spend them for a crash program of building weapons against the Soviet Union. We are to make no response to this? We are to applaud H. Delbacher when he launches an offensive against us? Ask H. Delbacher why we have gone on maneuvers. We have been forced by his insane adventurism to show him that we cannot be bluffed or intimidated."

There was another great burst of applause from Politburo and communist press.

"He said in his address to Congress, Mr. President," the Washington *Inquirer* said when it subsided, "that your words and attitude in your talk at the UN were so menacing to the United States and the free world that he felt he had no choice but to order an immediate build-up."

"That is a lie," Yuri said calmly. "My words were of peace, only of peace. How many lies must H. Delbacher and other leaders of the West try to tell before they accept the simple fact that the Soviet Union and the coalition it heads want only peace for all mankind?"

"Whose peace, Mr. President?" UPI shouted as the communist applause rose again. "On whose terms?"

The applause subsided swiftly to catch his answer.

"Peace for all mankind," he repeated. "Peace need not be defined—we all know what peace is. On humanity's terms! On what is best for mankind! Those are the only terms known to the Soviet Union! Those are the only terms the world can accept! What other terms are there?"

Again the applause of his colleagues and the communist press burst out with a wild and overwhelming enthusiasm. When it subsided he raised a hand and spoke in a contemptuous tone.

"Now, comrades! Has the corrupt capitalist imperialist press had a fair chance to ask me all the questions it wants?"

A great shout of *"DA!"* went up.

"Very well. Now, comrades, you may question me and perhaps we may talk, now, if our corrupt capitalist friends will permit us, along the lines of truth."

Again there was applause. And laughter—contemptuous, scornful, self-righteous, smug.

"Comrade President," an East German correspondent said, "is it not true that the war-monger H. Delbacher gave you no choice but to order maneuvers when he threatened the Soviet Union with his $10 billion 'build-up'?"

"He threatened us," Yuri said simply. "Only in reaction to his threats did we order the maneuvers."

"And is it not true, Comrade President," a Czech inquired, "that it is the purpose of the glorious Soviet Union and the glorious socialist coalition to bring only peace and harmony to the world?"

"That is our sole and only purpose," Yuri said solemnly. Some sort of muffled sound, not very clear, came from the area of the Western correspondents. A hissing began from the communists until he raised his hand again and silenced it.

"Comrade President," a Cuban correspondent asked, "what do you consider the single most menacing threat to peace in the entire world?"

"I do not like to say it," he replied. "It gives me regret to have to say it, but I believe the most serious threat to peace in all the world is the United States of America."

This time it was the communists who applauded furiously, the Westerners who booed and hissed. He let it run on until the applause grew so loud and vigorous, along with shouts of approval, that the annoyance of the West could no longer be heard.

"Comrade President," an Iranian correspondent asked when it had all died down, "is it not true that United States imperialist-militarist circles are planning a Third World War and that therefore your maneuvers are necessary and completely justified?"

"Such is my belief," Yuri said solemnly.

"Mr. *President!*" the New York *Times* cried with an indignation that struck his communist colleagues as very funny. Hoots and howls of laughter drowned him out and Yuri next recognized a correspondent from Afghanistan.

"Comrade President, is it not imperative for the peace and safety of all mankind that the imperialist-militarist circles of the United States be driven forever from the face of the earth so that all men may know peace and freedom and no more wars?"

"There can be no lasting peace as long as they remain in power," he said solemnly. Again there was a stirring from the Western group, but before anyone could respond a correspondent from the Philippines was on his feet.

"Comrade President, is such a thing as détente or 'co-existence' possible with the imperialist-militarist circles of the United States?"

He paused for a long moment during which the tension noticeably increased.

"So-called détente and peaceful co-existence," he said carefully, "may be possible with the oppressed peace-loving masses of the United States, but as long as they permit themselves to be controlled by the imperialist-militarist clique in power in Washington, New York and other centers of capitalist corruption there can be no such détente or peaceful co-existence. Only after they have rid themselves of imperialist-militarist control can détente or peaceful co-existence with the socialist coalition have any real meaning."

"Then, Comrade President," the *Tass* correspondent inquired, "must it not be a major aim of the Soviet Union and the peace-loving socialist coalition to bring the power of the imperialist-militarist circles of the United States to an end as soon as possible?"

Again he paused, deliberately, and the tension rose still further.

"We need not concern ourselves too much with that at this moment," he said finally, "because history teaches us that their collapse is inevitable through one means or another. . . . Now, comrades, that is sufficient for one morning. With your assistance I think we have given our friends of the corrupt capitalist press some idea of the truth as it exists in the world today. Let us hope they will report it truthfully to the oppressed peace-loving masses of the United States and to the imperialist-militarist circles in Washington, NATO and Asia.

"Meanwhile"—and he turned, hands once more on hips, to survey the restless map before turning back with a triumphant smile—"are not our great maneuvers proceeding splendidly?"

And so ended, to the biggest burst of applause yet from the communist group, his first and perhaps last press conference as President of the Soviet Union. An hour later the censors brought him copies of the first dispatches filed by the Westerners. He saw with grim satisfaction that their tone was exactly what he wanted it to be:

"MOSCOW—A sternly defiant President Yuri Serapin said today that worldwide Soviet maneuvers will continue on schedule and agreed with a Communist-bloc questioner that 'imperialist-militarist circles' in the United States 'are planning a Third World War.'

"Serapin told an hour-long Kremlin press conference that 'imperialist-militarist circles' in the U.S., NATO and unspecified Asian nations (clearly indicating the People's Republic of China) will inevitably have to bow to Soviet wishes if further détente and peaceful co-existence are to have any meaning. He described the United States as 'the most serious threat to peace in all the world.'

"Nowhere in the new Soviet leader's unprecedented press conference was there the slightest hint of conciliation or friendliness toward the United States and other nations that have expressed strong alarm concerning the nature and worldwide extent of Soviet maneuvers.

"Many Western observers at the conference believed it was President Serapin's deliberate intent to further increase world tensions and widen the gap between his country and members of the Western coalition led by the United States . . ."

And so it was, he thought grimly: and thank you for making it so clear to your stupid readers. It is good for them to begin to understand that they will soon face defeat in the final battle to decide the fate of all mankind.

Now, he thought contemptuously, we must see what the great leader H. Delbacher can say about it. Aware of the unimpeded progress of the little lines and dots further and further out across the globe, he predicted tartly to himself: not much.

But H. Delbacher, who had watched the televised press conference along with unnumbered millions across that same troubled globe, was not without words on the subject; and after meeting with Congressional leaders, again with the Joint Chiefs, and finally with his wife, he went on television himself at 9 P.M. Washington time for a brief message to his countrymen.

"My fellow Americans," he said in a quiet, conversational tone, deliberately low-key, deliberately pleasant-faced and confident, "I imagine that many of you earlier today, like myself, were privileged to hear direct from Moscow the words of the new President of the Soviet Union concerning the worldwide military maneuvers that are giving us all so much concern.

"I say 'privileged,' though I do not know how much of a privilege it is to be told that the United States is the single most menacing threat to peace in the whole world, that we are planning World War III and that history makes our imminent collapse inevitable.

"You know now what I faced in my private talk with Mr. Serapin—complete hostility, complete intransigence, complete lack of co-operation and complete threat. It is no wonder, then, that I decided to use at once the $10 billion defense emergency bill voted by the Congress. And it is, perhaps, no wonder that Mr. Serapin, apparently congratulating himself on having prepared a trap for me, decided to spring it in the form of maneuvers which obviously have been under planning in Moscow for many months.

"Such a true menace to world peace does not simply happen overnight. It happens"—and now for the first time his tone became personal, a genuine dislike and contempt for his adversary began to show through—"because a Serapin, and colleagues of his who feed his ego by telling him he is frightfully clever, find themselves so carried away by their own self-congratulations and self-hypnosis that they think they can play fast and loose with the peace of the world, and get away with it.

"This could prove to be a very costly mistake.

"The press conference many of us saw out of Moscow this morning was an exercise in imperial ego—an attempt, by lying, to blackguard the United States in the eyes of the world. In some ignorant places, this will probably succeed as it always has. In more sophisticated and intelligent parts of the world, it cannot succeed because it is not the truth.

"The truth is that the Soviet Union and the Soviet Union alone, seeking to frighten and intimidate the world into abject compliance if not outright surrender, has embarked upon a most dangerous course in these worldwide maneuvers. Apparently nothing is going to stop them.

"Neither, I hope, is anyone anywhere going to be unduly frightened by them.

"There will be no surprise attack on the United States in connection with them. There will be no attack upon Europe in connection with them. Timely exposure and publicity have removed these possibilities if they ever existed. What we are left with is a gigantic worldwide bluff; impressive in numbers, yes, but not impressive in any way that can possibly contribute to true world peace.

"However"—he paused, and in the Kremlin, in spite of their overweening confidence, and despite their growing personal annoyance with this stupid man who evidently did not know his country could be squashed like a bug, Yuri and the Politburo felt a sudden visceral tightening—"however. Lest there be any thought that the United States is asleep or unconcerned by this blatant threat to the stability of the world, I have ordered, as of half an hour ago, a limited alert of all our armed forces wherever they may be stationed throughout the world. This will, if necessary, be followed by a full alert.

"I am also sending to Congress tomorrow an urgent recommendation for a standby civilian service bill which will require every American over selective service age to give at least six months' duty to the country in whatever capacity he or she may be needed, should a real emergency arise.

"I have today reviewed with the Joint Chiefs of Staff the progress to date in putting into effect the new arms procurement program under the emergency defense bill. I can assure you it is progressing very well indeed.

"And finally, I have directed Chauncey Baron, the Secretary of State, to fly to Brussels tonight to request an urgent, immediate meeting of the NATO Council so that our efforts and those of our allies may be coordinated effectively in the face of the Soviet action.

"Therefore, my friends, be of good cheer. It is obviously the Soviets' intention to test our nerves, those of our allies, and those of the entire world. Some may be intimidated. The United States will not.

"Good night and God bless you."

WORLD TENSIONS ESCALATE AS U.S. GOES ON ALERT IN FACE OF SOVIET MANEUVERS. SERAPIN CALLS AMERICA MAIN THREAT TO PEACE, THREATENS DRIVE AGAINST U.S. "RULING CIRCLES." PRESIDENT REQUESTS URGENT NATO MEETING TO CONSIDER CRISIS. ALLIES DISAGREE ON BEST APPROACH TO SOVIET MOVES.

2

"Soviet military doctrine is the doctrine of a peace-loving socialist state and is diametrically opposed to the modern aggressive, reactionary military doctrine of the imperialist states, particularly the 'bloc' military doctrine of NATO."

—Marshal A. A. Grechko

Not only, Chauncey Baron thought as Air Force Two slanted down through a light summer overcast to land at Brussels International Airport, was this one more magnificent bare-faced lie by the creators of the military bloc known as the Warsaw Pact, but it was also a very strange picture of the condition of NATO. Where was this ominous, tightly unified NATO "bloc" the Soviets were always talking about? He had been associated with it, now, for the four years of his previous term as Secretary of State under an earlier President and the three years of his present one; and rarely had he known such a squabbling, disorganized, self-interested body of men and nations as called themselves the North Atlantic Treaty Organization.

Their disagreements were continual, their agreements few and far between; their desire to help the United States uncertain at best, their desire to have the United States help them voracious and unending. "Talk, talk, talk, take, take, take," one of the permanent U.S. ambassadors to NATO had remarked a few years ago when the United States was trying, without success, to organize a united front on the then latest Soviet aggression. Aside from the fact that they were all scared to death by the Soviet maneuvers, which might induce a brief and unusual state of co-operation, Chauncey Baron thought this would probably be a fully adequate description on this occasion also.

Nonetheless, he was here to go through the motions, and the first one was the arrival at the airport and the effusive greeting from the secretary-general of NATO. He cut his own remarks to the bone and within ten minutes was being driven off to American delegation headquarters. The formal meeting would be held tomorrow—the President had deliberately created his own urgency by letting it be known that Chauncey would fly home tomorrow night irrespective of whether the meeting achieved any formal result—and the minute he arrived at headquarters the phone began to ring. To each of his anxious callers he made essentially the same reply: the United States was here expecting to find a firm, unified, emphatic response to the Soviet maneuvers; he hoped such a response would be developed at the meeting; the United States was prepared to assist those who assisted it, and he hoped all NATO members would keep that in mind; he did not mean to be rude, but there were things he must discuss with his own delegation. And he would see them all tomorrow.

He then had a good meal with the current U. S. Ambassador and his staff, studied the latest dispatches on the Soviet moves and retired with a sleeping pill and a good mystery novel. There were international conferences at which behind-the-scenes negotiating sometimes accomplished a lot but he was under strict instructions from the President that this one was to be entirely on the record.

"I want the world to see the strengths, weaknesses, integrities, hypocrisies," he said when Chauncey came by to take the helicopter from the White House lawn to waiting Air Force Two at Andrews Air Force Base. "The KGB boys in the NATO secretariat would tell them all about it if it were closed, anyway, so there's nothing to lose. Plus the fact that I suppose the new government of Italy will be there. Let's let the world see for itself how they all perform when there's a call for united action against a real threat. It will be an instructive spectacle."

"First I have to get them to agree to an open meeting," Chauncey said.

"Demand it or leave," Ham Delbacher said calmly.

"Yes, sir!" Chauncey replied with a smile and left for Brussels reflecting that this kind of decisiveness had been absent from the White House for so many recent years that he had almost forgotten it was possible for a President to be so direct, decisive—and, well, Presidential.

Accordingly, when they were all in their seats (save for France, ostentatiously absent, as always, from NATO military discussions) precisely at ten the next morning, he raised his hand and was recognized by Norway, in the chair.

"Mr. President," he said, "the United States moves that this meeting be opened to the world media."

"Mr. President!" West Germany cried in startled dismay. "Mr. President, that is most irregular. We are about to embark upon a discussion of the highest and most secret nature and surely we cannot admit every curious person who may wish to eavesdrop upon our deliberations—it would defeat the whole purpose, Mr. President."

"There is nothing whatsoever secret about our meeting," the Secretary of State replied, face impassive but relishing every word, "nor is there any question about our purpose. The Soviet Union is suddenly embarked upon massive maneuvers throughout the world and we are here to decide what, if anything, NATO intends to do about it. Who is all this supposed to be secret *from?* The Soviets? It seems to me they know very well what they are about and what we are about. Who are we trying to hide from, the peoples of Earth who will have to suffer beyond imagination if war eventuates from Soviet miscalculation in this matter? Or who may well be saved if we take firm, united action right now before things proceed any further?"

"Mr. President," the United Kingdom said in his precise and quiet voice, "Her Majesty's Government are disposed to agree with the United States, providing only that we do not discuss in open session specific figures on comparative military strengths—even though"—he raised a cautionary hand as Chauncey Baron started to lean forward to his microphone—"even though I am quite aware, as is my good friend from the United States, that these figures are as well known to the Soviets as theirs are known to us. Spies and spy satellites are not idle on either side, and comparative strengths are known in very substantial detail. Nonetheless we think they should not be emphasized in public at this time. Will my distinguished friend from the United States accept that small caveat? If so, we are quite prepared to support his motion."

"My friend makes my essential point," Chauncey said with a smile, "which is that nothing much is secret anyway. But I am happy to accept his amendment."

"Mr. President," West Germany said, "we still do not like it. This is a matter of the utmost gravity and we should not rush headlong, it seems to us, into a public confessional of what our plans are."

"It is more a matter of how we arrive at them, I think," the Netherlands remarked. "It is more the processes of discussion and debate which should be secret, in our judgment. Therefore we would, I am afraid, find it impossible to support the United States motion."

"Mr. President," Denmark said, "that is exactly the point on which we agree with our American friends. We face, collectively and individually, perhaps the greatest threat we have ever faced from the Soviet Union. It is a time, as the Americans say, to stand up and be counted. Before the day is out there will be some official expression of the majority NATO view. How we vote will be clear enough; but we think the crisis is of such severe nature that we owe it to mankind to let them know *why* we vote as we do. Denmark is prepared to support the United States resolution, and is prepared to vote now."

"West Germany," its delegate replied doggedly, "is not convinced. The reasons that prompt certain governmental actions, as we all know, are sometimes best held secret from the general public, otherwise misunderstandings, arguments, conflicts, even protests, riots, even physical violence, can ensue. We do not mind a discussion as frank and comprehensive as anyone wishes, but we are very dubious about the wisdom of conducting it in public. My government believes we should at least have a hour or two recess so that we may consult privately together, and with our governments, before we take a vote on the American motion."

"We are back where we started," Chauncey Baron said, "and the United States regrets very much having to make its position so emphatic. But I must tell you that I am under instructions from the President of the United States to leave the meeting and return home at once if secrecy is not lifted and the proceedings are not held in open session."

There was a gasp of surprise, murmurings of annoyance from several members; but he proceeded somberly.

"Whatever others think, *we* think this is a situation of the utmost gravity. We think we owe it to the peoples of the world to inform them of everything we in NATO do to meet it. Mr. President, I move a vote on my resolution as amended by the United Kingdom, to wit, that our discussion be public and that we be debarred from discussing in public only the actual figures on the military strengths of the Soviet Union, which are known to us, and the military strengths of NATO, which are known to them. I so move, and request a vote."

"Second," said Luxembourg, quite unexpectedly.

"Moved and seconded," Norway said. "The secretary-general will call the roll."

"Belgium," said the secretary-general.

"No," said Belgium.

"Canada."

"Yes."

"Denmark."

"Yes."

"Greece."

"No."

"Iceland."

"Yes."

"Italy," said the secretary-general, and added, "The newly elected People's Republic of Italy has sent a representative to the meeting. He has informed me that he does not wish to vote in our deliberations but is here for the time being only as an observer."

"Another good reason for going public," Canada murmured, and was seconded by several wry laughs around the table, including one from Italy's new representative, small, shrewd-eyed, sharp-faced.

"Luxembourg."

"Yes."

"The Netherlands."

"No."

"Norway."

"No."

"Portugal."

"Yes."

"Turkey."

"No."

"The United Kingdom."

"Yes."

"The United States."

"Yes."

"West Germany."

"No."

"The affirmatives," Norway said gravely, while the tension slowly subsided, "are seven, the negatives six, and the motion is agreed to. I would suggest we take a half-hour recess while the doors are opened and the members of the media are allowed to take their seats and set up their photographic and television equipment. . . . Without objection, it is so ordered."

"Rather close," the Ambassador of the United Kingdom murmured in Chauncey Baron's ear. "Ra——ther close."

"Too damned close," Chauncey said. "If Italy had been smart enough to vote, it would have died on a tie. I suppose the closeness of the vote indicates we will now have a long wrangle, getting nowhere."

"Perhaps," the U.K. said. "Perhaps some of the reasons for these negative votes will come out. I doubt if any were prompted by support for the Soviets."

"Oh, of course not," Chauncey said. "But now of all times I wish we could be unanimous on something."

"We will be at the end," the U.K. said dryly, "after we've got it watered-down to the point where it's meaningless."

In precisely half an hour, when the last reporters and TV crews had squabbled their way into position in the press section and the television booths, Norway rapped his gavel and said:

"This emergency meeting of the NATO Council requested by the United States of America is now resumed. Would the Secretary of State wish to offer some preliminary remarks?"

"Remarks and a resolution, Mr. President," Chauncey Baron said. He paused for a moment, looked slowly around the table. Each flanked by his little flag on a wooden block, the delegates of NATO stared back at him with varying mixtures of impassivity, concern, sympathy or opposition. As Britain said, the end result would probably be meaningless. But it was important that the debate be known.

"Mr. President," Chauncey said in a thoughtful voice, "we are all aware that the Soviet Union yesterday launched massive worldwide maneuvers involving all branches of its armed services. We are all aware that prior to the start of those maneuvers, ten nations, including some members of NATO, addressed an appeal to the President of the U.S.S.R. to cancel the maneuvers and instead, with the President of the United States, go to Geneva and resume negotiations on the differences between our two countries. We all know that this appeal was accepted by the United States. We all know it was rejected by the Soviet Union.

"And the maneuvers began.

"As a result of that, the President of the United States has ordered various actions to place the armed forces of the United States in a condition of greater readiness. These actions are being taken under a limited alert and state of national emergency which the President proclaimed in a television speech to the nation. In that speech he also announced the request of the United States for this present meeting of NATO. His thought, and the hope of the United States, is that from this meeting there may emerge a strong consensus and condemnation of the Soviet maneuvers and a renewed request for their cancellation which will be firm enough to bring some reasonable compliance from those who control the Soviet Union.

"The United States believes, with one of the greatest of its founders, Benjamin Franklin, that, 'We must all hang together, or assuredly we shall all hang separately.' This was true of the original American states when they broke with Great Britain, it is true of every aggregation of states or nations that wishes to survive in the face of a common enemy, it has never been truer than it is today with regard to the remaining independent nations of the world vis-à-vis the Soviet Union.

"NATO was created to preserve the independence of all of us, and to serve as a shield for the free nations against the slavery, tyranny and ravenous imperialism of the Soviet Union. That imperialism has grown increasingly bold and open in the past few years as the United States and NATO have, admittedly, allowed their own strengths to decline. We do not like to face this fact in the United States, and it is quite obvious from past discussions and decisions here that we do not wish to face it in NATO. Nonetheless we all know it is true.

"Therefore the United States proposes the following resolution and asks for its immediate consideration:

"Whereas, the Union of Soviet Socialist Republics has launched worldwide maneuvers of a nature implicitly hostile to the well-being and survival of free nations everywhere; and

"Whereas, it is clear that these maneuvers are creating worldwide tensions that pose an immediate, direct and inexcusable threat to world peace; and

"Whereas, it is imperative that these maneuvers be terminated forthwith and immediately if world tensions are to be eased and the threat to world peace is to be ended; now, therefore,

"Be it resolved, that the member powers of the North Atlantic Treaty Organization do hereby deplore, condemn and oppose the continuation of the Soviet maneuvers and demand their immediate termination and the immediate withdrawal of all Soviet forces throughout the world to their regular home bases and areas; and further,

"Be it resolved, that the military high command of NATO be directed, and it hereby is directed, to prepare immediately all necessary plans to repel a Soviet attack launched under the pretext of these maneuvers; and further,

"Be it resolved that the forces of all member nations be put under immediate alert to take whatever action may be requested and deemed necessary by the NATO military command pursuant to this resolution."

He stopped, arranged his notes neatly before him on the table, folded his hands comfortably upon them and stared slowly around the table with a bland and immovable air.

"Mr. President," he concluded quietly, "I ask for an immediate vote on this resolution."

There was a silence followed first by a long, low whistle from the press section and then a torrent of babbling, excited voices throughout the room as his fellow delegates and their aides turned excitedly to one another, reporters dashed from the room to file their bulletins, TV cameras swung back and forth along the tense and agitated faces of the nations, coming to rest at last upon Chauncey's, impassive and imperturbable.

For several moments Norway made no attempt to restore order. Then he rapped sharply twice with his gavel and inquired in a carefully impersonal voice:

"You have heard the resolution offered by the delegate of the United States. Does anyone desire to discuss it before we have a vote?"

Thirteen hands, including Norway's own—and Italy's, which produced some laughter and some needed decrease of tension—shot up.

"Very well," Norway said with a slight smile. "I assume we should proceed in regular alphabetical order. Does the distinguished delegate from Belgium wish to—"

"Mr. President!" Italy interrupted. "Mr. President, before we enter into debate upon the corrupt and contemptible resolution of the imperialist United States—"

"Mr. President!" the United Kingdom cried angrily, "there is such a thing as decorum here and Her Majesty's delegation is going to insist upon it. The delegate of Italy is entirely out of order to use such language concerning a fellow member of NATO. Furthermore, the delegate of Italy is entirely out of order, period. He cannot have it two ways. Either he votes and participates or he does not vote and does not participate. He has already made his choice. I insist upon the regular order, Mr. President."

"Regular order!" cried several voices, all of them, Chauncey Baron

noted, from the group that had voted for his earlier resolution. Norway
hesitated for a second and Belgium, who had voted No, filled the breach.

"I have the regular order, Mr. President," he said calmly, "and I will
yield to the distinguished delegate from Italy providing there is some
valid purpose behind his request to speak. What is it, Ambassador?"

"State it without adjectives, please," Norway interjected with some
asperity. Italy's little fox—he was actually called this in the Italian press
—smiled cheerfully and waved to Belgium.

"I thank the distinguished Ambassador of Belgium," he said. "Bearing
in mind what I said earlier about the source of the resolution now before
us"—there was an admiring chuckle from somewhere in the press seats,
an answering hiss or two—"I wish to offer an amendment to that resolution, as follows:

"Strike all after the first word of the first paragraph, the word *Whereas,*
and substitute the following language:

"Whereas, the militant and aggressive action of the President of the
United States of America in ordering a $10 billion speed-up of American
defense spending, his placing of the armed forces of the United States on
a limited alert war footing and his other warlike measures and statements
to the American people have created a grave threat to world peace and,

"Whereas, the gallant, peace-loving leaders and peoples of the Soviet
Union and the socialist coalition are motivated solely by the desire to restore and maintain the peace so ruthlessly disrupted by the warlike actions and statements of the President of the United States; now, therefore,

"Be it resolved, that the member states of NATO deplore, abhor and
condemn the warlike actions and statements of the President of the
United States and applaud, endorse and support the brave and gallant actions of the peace-loving leaders of the Soviet Union and the socialist coalition in their desire to protect and strengthen world peace by opposing
this wanton attack upon it; and, further,

"Be it resolved, that the military high command of NATO be directed,
and it is hereby directed, to render immediately all possible assistance to
the armed forces of the Soviet Union and the peace-loving coalition of
socialist states; and that all member states of NATO place their armed
forces on alert to render such assistance to the peace-loving forces of the
Soviet Union and the socialist coalition in their attempt to halt the aggressive imperialism of the United States of America and repel the U.S.
threat to world peace . . .

"*That,* Mr. President," he concluded with a happily mischievous smile
he could not resist beaming down the table to Chauncey Baron, who
could not resist a wry little bow and answering smile in return, "is *my*
offering to the debate. I, too, like my friend from the United States,
would welcome an immediate vote."

There was general laughter and more scurryings from the press and TV sections. Norway said dryly:

"That, I do not think either of you is going to get, Mr. Ambassador. *Now* may we proceed in order? The distinguished Ambassador of Belgium, if you please."

"Mr. President," said the Belgium Ambassador, a tall and stately white-haired political veteran, retired to this honorary post by his party after thirty years' service in the parliament, "caught as I am between two stools, I think I shall sit upon neither. I do not like the American resolution as it stands, and while I think the Italian Ambassador, in his first participation in NATO since his party won control of his country in the recent elections, has contributed much-needed hilarity and amusement to our usually somber proceedings, I do not like his resolution either. Our task here today is obviously to modify and moderate the United States resolution. I consider it as unlikely that we need concern ourselves with the Italian resolution as that we should all burst out together in a chorus from *Aida*. It would be sensational, but it would not be a great contribution to world peace.

"In fact, I think, Mr. President, that it might expedite matters substantially if we do give the Ambassador of Italy his wish and vote at once upon the matter now before us, namely the substitute resolution he has offered. I so move, Mr. President."

"Second," said Portugal.

"Moved and seconded," Norway said. "The secretary-general will call the roll." And five minutes later, after Italy had cheerfully insisted upon voting despite his earlier abstention, and had been amicably allowed to do so without objection from anyone, Norway announced:

"The affirmatives are one, the negatives thirteen, and the substitute language of the delegate of Italy is rejected."

There was an ironic burst of laughter and applause, the Italian Ambassador raised his clenched fist in a communist salute accompanied by a big grin, and Norway said to Belgium, quite gravely:

"Now, Mr. Ambassador, let us return to the very serious matter before this council."

And suddenly, in an abruptly sobering change of mood they were brought up once more against the fact that it was indeed a very serious matter; and that behind the jolly antics of the Italian Ambassador there was a very grim, very unfunny, purpose: and behind the falsely amiable communist grin, quite possibly the death-mask of the world.

"Mr. President," Belgium said, "the resolution of the United States, with all due respect to the distinguished Secretary of State, does really tend, as our friend from Italy notes, to put the cart before the horse. It was, after all, the President's action in activating the $10 billion emergency defense bill which prompted the Soviet maneuvers, was it not?"

"No," Chauncey Baron said crisply, "it was not. It was the completely intransigent and threatening attitude of President Serapin at the summit meeting at the United Nations which prompted President Delbacher's decision. That was the horse, and it came before the cart."

"What proof do we have of that?" Greece inquired, and for a second Chauncey looked at him quite blankly.

"You have the word of the President of the United States," he said coldly; and when there was a snicker from the press section and a few other skeptical looks around the table, he added sharply, "And that is exactly why the President of the United States wished to have this meeting open to the media. There will be no lies coming out of this one; it is all here."

"Mr. President," Belgium said with equal sharpness, "*I* would not lie about what happens here."

"Some would," the Secretary of State said in the same cold tone, "and you know it. What else does the Ambassador wish to say about the U.S. resolution?"

"Only that much of the language is deliberately hostile in tone toward the Soviet Union and can only unnecessarily aggravate the attitude of that government and gravely affect its willingness to yield to our request and terminate, or drastically moderate, the maneuvers."

"Is the Ambassador proposing that we settle for a 'modification' of the maneuvers and not their termination?" Luxembourg inquired. "That would not accomplish so very much, would it?"

"It may be all we can get," Belgium said.

"It may be we cannot even get that," Denmark said bleakly.

"Well, Mr. President," Canada said, "if we are to start from that defeatist premise, then what purpose—"

"None," Italy interjected cheerily. "Really none."

"Her Majesty's Government," Britain said, ignoring him, "cannot accept that defeatist stance. We must at least try, I suggest to my friend from Canada."

"All right, then, let's try," Canada said. "Let's don't pussyfoot. The original language of the U.S. resolution suits us."

"It would never pass," Iceland observed, "and we all know that, too."

"Why not?" Canada demanded. "Because we are all cowards? Are we that afraid of the Soviets?"

"It is well to have the advice," the Netherlands said tartly, "of those who live three thousand miles further away than we do from the Soviet Union."

"I beg your pardon," Canada said, as tart as he. "If the distinguished Ambassador of the Netherlands will remember that the world is round and will consult his map thereof, he will observe that, as the missile flies, from Siberia across Alaska to the capital of Canada is about four thousand miles, or shall we say roughly three and one half minutes. Who is closest and who is farthest, these days? We are all close."

"And they are close to us," the Netherlands replied, "and while our NATO forces may have some problems, we too are capable of going great distances at great speed. So we have some leverage which my friend from Canada has forgotten, I think."

"Well taken," Canada agreed, more graciously. "I think you will concede my basic point, however."

"I do," the Netherlands said. "Essentially we have no argument, except —" He paused and looked around the table. "It becomes a matter of method. Whether we gain more by demanding or by conciliating. Is that not right?"

"It goes deeper than that," the United Kingdom said quietly. "It goes to a matter of will—and determination. Whether we have the will to enforce demands, if enforce them we must. Whether we have the determination to stand firm, if stand firm we must. It is there that the nations come to judgment, vis-à-vis the Soviet Union, and it is there that we must each of us search our consciences and our hearts and determine what approach we wish—or dare—to take. . . . Is not that," he concluded gravely, "the truth of it?"

There was a silence, an uneasy shifting, a studying of papers, a turning of heads in thought and consultation. Here and there an aide conferred with an ambassador, an ambassador murmured to his neighbor. The press section was very still, and in the television booths the cameras swung relentlessly from face to troubled face. Finally Denmark conceded with equal quietness:

"That is the truth of it. . . ." He leaned forward earnestly to his microphone and looked around the table. "Were Denmark," he said, "were Greece, were Norway, were Belgium, were any of us, possessed of strength as great as the Soviet Union's, then there would be no hesitations and no doubt of it. We would pass the United States resolution as quickly as we defeated the Italian joke. But none of us, no, not even collectively through NATO, is that strong. Or"—he turned politely, but with a quiet insistence not to be denied, to the Secretary of State—"am I mistaken? Is there one of us who possesses that sufficient strength?"

Again there was silence and now the entire room and all the cameras were concentrated on just one face. For a moment Chauncey Baron stared down at the papers in front of him. Then he raised his head, looked the Ambassador of Denmark in the eye and responded in a tone as grave as his.

"My answer to the distinguished delegate of Denmark is this: yes, the United States has sufficient strength to obliterate this world in five minutes—if we ever wished to do so *or if we ever found ourselves backed against the wall with no other choice*. It is precisely because we do not want to be backed against a wall, precisely because we do not want ever to be forced into making that frightful decision, that we are appealing to NATO and to all other independent nations of the world to join us in a sufficiently strong condemnation and warning to the Soviet Union so that it will never push us that far.

"It is our estimation of the facts that in these worldwide maneuvers and their potential sequel, the Soviet Union is coming within a hair's breadth of forcing us to that decision. It is for that reason that we have requested this urgent meeting of NATO and that is the reason I have submitted on behalf of my government the strongly worded resolution that I have. By each word that you diminish its force and its impact, by so much do you bring closer the ultimate action we all abhor. That is why we cannot willingly accept any modification of the resolution and why, if a majority here forces us to do so, you will be playing directly into the hands of the Soviet Union and bringing us a great step further toward the ultimate horror we all wish so desperately to avoid."

He paused and searched for a moment through his papers, extracted one.

"But perhaps," he said softly, "I should not say 'the ultimate horror we *all* wish so desperately to avoid.' Perhaps the Soviet Union is not so averse to it as we are. I quote from the official Soviet publication, *Soviet Military Strategy,* the words of Marshal V. D. Sokolovskiy. He says: 'The armed forces of the Soviet Union and the other socialist countries must be prepared above all to wage war under the conditions of the mass use of nuclear weapons by both belligerent parties . . . The preparation and waging of just such a war must be regarded as the main task'—*the main task,* I ask you to note, gentlemen—'of the theory of military strategy and strategic leadership.' And in *Problems of Contemporary War,* General Major A. D. Milovidov asserts: 'There is profound error and harm in the disorienting claims of bourgeois idealogues that there will be no victor in thermonuclear war . . .'

"That is what we face, gentlemen, a Soviet Union which has prepared for, expects to win and indeed would seem to be almost eager for, a thermonuclear war . . .

"The only way for humankind to win it is to stop it before it begins. The only way to stop it before it begins is to stop the power that welcomes it and believes it can use that horrible technique to conquer us all. The only way to do that is for the independent nations of the world to band together in such a strong expression of opposition, and such a readiness to respond, that the Soviet Union will not dare take that final, irrevocable step.

"The United States, I admit to you, has made extremely grave mistakes in recent years in permitting its so-called conventional forces to decline to the point where it must rely in a final conflict upon its nuclear strength.

But we have done so, and it will be several years before we can restore the conventional balance. Therefore"—and for once the world saw the bland mask of Chauncey Baron almost crack with emotion—"it is imperative that you support us wholeheartedly and completely in opposing the present war-preparing moves and associated diplomatic threats of the Soviet Union."

And again he placed his papers neatly together and visibly struggled to regain his patient, impassive air, while around him the room was hushed and still. He recognized the excited voice that was raised in reply before he even glanced down the table.

"Mr. President!" the Ambassador of Turkey cried in great agitation. "Mr. President, it is all very well for the Secretary of State to warn us of horrible things and demand our support for his inflammatory resolution which can only aggravate and annoy the Soviet Union. The Soviet Union sits on Turkey's border, Mr. President! It need not even use the threat of missiles upon us, Mr. President! A day's march only, which we would oppose desperately but could not under any conditions stop, separates ourselves and our liberty from being conquered by the Soviet Union.

"Turkey is willing to maintain its obligations to NATO by joining in a warning to the Soviet Union, Mr. President, but it must be a reasonable warning, a sensible warning, a warning which is not an ultimatum or which closes all doors. We cannot support the American resolution as now worded, Mr. President, we simply cannot. We are really too close. Really too close . . ."

His face was pale, his hands shaking. His voice trailed away into what appeared to be almost sobs and gaspings for breath, so great was his agitation. And again the room was still save for the whirring of the television cameras as they moved again from face to troubled face.

"May I say to my colleague from Turkey," Norway said at last, "that this, essentially, is Norway's position too. That accounts for the 'No' votes of our countries, and I suspect others, on the American motion to make these discussions public. We are entering here, as the Ambassador of Great Britain stated a few moments ago, the area of will and determination—and the reasons why some of us do not have it in such abundant measure as the United States appears to do. We did not think such a candid public discussion of weakness would do any good at all. We did not see how it could help.

"Nor do we see how the American resolution, so strongly worded, can possibly help. It seems to us that the American point is essentially well taken: the Soviet maneuvers are certainly not conducive to a peaceful and untroubled state of mind in the world, and certainly they could carry the potential of a Soviet surprise attack or, at the least, a major diplomatic offensive to bring pressure upon many of us who are comparatively small and weak or for some other reason such as geography are more easily subject to Soviet threats. So we are certainly in accord with the American purpose—and hopeful that it will have the desired effect upon the Soviet Union. But we, and I sense many others here today, do not believe it can be achieved"—and suddenly he looked quite sad as he emphasized —"*if* it can be achieved—by the harsh language of the American resolution."

"Mr. President," Chauncey Baron said, and he too looked sad for a second, though it was succeeded quickly by an expression stronger and more determined, "I thank the Ambassador from Norway and the Ambassador from Turkey—and the Ambassador from the Netherlands, earlier—for their informative attempts to clarify their position. I can see it, I can understand it, I can sympathize with it; nobody will feel any kind of displeasure or reaction from the United States, however this turns out. But before we fall like a lynching party upon the United States resolution, permit me to say a few more things which we believe are pertinent and extremely important to the discussion here.

"I would remind you, to begin with, of a man named Hitler and an event to which history has given the generic term 'Munich.' Some of us—though increasingly few, which accounts for many of the weaknesses in present attitudes towards the Soviet Union—lived through those times. Many of your nations were close to Hitler's Germany. Many of your nations opposed a strong, united stand against him. Many of your nations, frightened and uneasy, rationalized his actions, excused his ambitions, explained away his obvious drive towards world domination. Some of your nations, including the Soviet Union, which now preaches so piously of its peace-loving purposes but then saw a chance to fish with complete cynicism in troubled waters, were actually allied with him. Others were overrun and occupied either by Hitler or by the Soviet Union as a result of that completely cynical collaboration.

"And at any given point along the way, up to perhaps the last two or three months prior to the outbreak of World War II, it could all have been prevented by unshaken courage, determination and *unity*. It could all have been stopped by *the absence of fear*. And 30 million would have lived. Nations now slave under Soviet domination would be free. And the world would not again be facing a megalomaniac drive for universal conquest, this time on the part of the Soviet Union.

"Today four billion are at stake. And the freedom of all remaining independent nations is at stake. Earth itself is at stake. And again we quibble and squabble and rationalize and explain away the perfectly obvious drive for world domination which the Soviet Union, like Hitler, has always frankly announced and which, like Hitler's, has always been scoffed away by certain media, intellectuals and leaders of the West. It is all there, spelled out, just as it was by Hitler, just as it is in the official papers from which I read a few minutes ago. It is clear, simple, direct, uncomplicated, unabashed, on the record, completely in the open. The Soviet *Mein Kampf* was written by Marx and Lenin; they make no bones about it whatsoever. They have adhered to it without a single deviation for almost seventy years. It is only the Great Gullibles of the West who deny it, and that is basically, I believe, *because they are afraid of having to do something about it if they once admit candidly to themselves and the world that it exists.* They are cowards, intellectually and physically; and this is an era that is literally fatal to cowards.

"So, then, as I said before with old Ben Franklin: we hang together or we hang separately. Some of you say the United States resolution is too strong; I only wish it could be ten times stronger. We are now faced at last with what may well be the initial steps of the final implementation of the permanent and unchanging Soviet plan. We must condemn it in the strongest possible language, we must bring the military arm of NATO, and all our individual forces, to their highest state of readiness. We must act strong, think strong, *be* strong. It is the only way. Mr. President, again I request a vote on the resolution proposed by the United States of America."

"Mr. President," West Germany said, "it is now past noon. I wonder if our friend from the United States would not be willing that we have a luncheon recess of several hours which would give us time to eat and also to confer, perhaps, with our respective governments and with each other, before we have a vote?"

"Mr. President," Chauncey said, aware even as he spoke that he was beaten, compromise and weakening were too much in the air—but he must make the try—"my government would much prefer that we vote the American resolution up or down at once. There is no need to prolong this."

"Mr. President," West Germany said, "to some of us it does not seem an up-or-down situation. Will the distinguished Secretary of State really not consider—?"

"Yes," Norway agreed. "Would it not be best to—?"

He paused and they all looked at the Secretary of State. He returned the look slowly and for a moment did not speak. Which was his mistake.

"Mr. President," Italy said calmly into the silence. "I move that the meeting stand in recess until 4 P.M."

"Second," said West Germany promptly.

"All those in favor—" Norway said. Eleven hands went up.

"All those opposed—" The United States, the United Kingdom, Canada raised their hands.

"The affirmatives are eleven, the negatives three and this emergency session of the NATO Council stands in recess until 4 P.M.," Norway said promptly. The room exploded into sound as everyone stood, stretched,

talked. In the press section and the TV booths reporters and commentators began to send their reports around the globe.

U.S. BALKED IN KEY NATO VOTES ON STRONG ANTI-SOVIET STAND. MAJORITY FAVORS SOFTER APPROACH TO MANEU-VERS. AMERICAN CALL FOR ULTIMATUM, WAR FOOTING FOR ALL NATO FORCES, FACES DEFEAT.

And when the meeting resumed at four it was not too long coming:
and from the source which had accurately predicted the outcome when
the meeting opened at ten.

"I'm sorry," the British Ambassador murmured in Chauncey's ear, "but
an exhaustive check indicates the sentiment is exactly as I suspected."

"I know," Chauncey said glumly. "I didn't even have to check."

"You don't mind if I try to salvage what I can?" Britain asked. Chauncey shrugged.

"I suppose something is better than nothing, even if the something *is*
nothing. Go ahead. And thanks." The British Ambassador nodded and
raised his hand.

"Mr. President, before we vote on the American resolution, I would
like to propose substitute language, if I may."

"The Ambassador will proceed," Norway said, looking relieved.

"The first three paragraphs of the original resolution, if honorable
members will remember," Britain said, "read as follows:

" 'Whereas, the Union of Soviet Socialist Republics has launched
worldwide maneuvers of a nature implicitly hostile to the well-being and
survival of free nations everywhere; and

" 'Whereas, it is clear that these maneuvers are creating worldwide tensions that pose an immediate, direct and inexcusable threat to world
peace; and

" 'Whereas, it is imperative that these maneuvers be terminated forthwith and immediately if world tensions are to be eased and the threat to
world peace is to be ended . . .'

"I propose to substitute for these three paragraphs the following language, Mr. President—I shall read slowly, so that ambassadors may write
in the changes, if they like—to wit:

"Whereas, the Union of Soviet Socialist Republics has launched large-
scale maneuvers of a nature that could be construed as hostile to the
well-being of some other nations; and

"Whereas, some governments apparently believe that these maneuvers are creating an uneasiness which could, if continued, pose a possible threat to world peace; and,

"Whereas, it seems advisable that these maneuvers be curtailed or restricted as soon as possible if such uneasiness is to be removed; now, therefore—

"Do my colleagues find the language agreeable so far?"

"Much better," Turkey said with great relief. *"Much* better."

There was a general murmur of assent, equally relieved, around the table. The British Ambassador proceeded smoothly on.

"Now, therefore, be it resolved that the member powers of the North Atlantic Treaty Organization deplore the Soviet Government's desire to hold maneuvers on what might be construed to be an unnecessarily stringent basis at this particular time, and join in appealing to the Soviet Government to curtail or restrict these maneuvers at the earliest convenient date; and furthermore,

"Be it resolved, that the member nations of the North Atlantic Treaty Organization will observe with concern and await with interest, the response of the Soviet Government to this suggestion . . .

"That concludes my amendment of the American resolution, Mr. President."

With great difficulty Chauncey Baron managed to preserve the impassive expression with which he had listened throughout; but behind his hand as the British Ambassador settled back into his chair he murmured savagely, "My God! Why not scrap the whole thing? Or take Italy's?"

"The art of the possible," Britain whispered, unperturbed, "was never more difficult than right now. I ate no lunch, conferred steadily for three hours—I assure you this is even stronger than many of our colleagues wanted. But they will go along if no attempt is made to reinstitute your original language. I most earnestly advise you to go along too."

"I don't know," Chauncey said. "I just don't know."

"Gentlemen," Norway said, having watched with much interest, as did they all, this inaudible but obviously lively exchange, "does the delegate of the United States wish to comment on the amendment to his resolution before we vote?"

"I pass for the moment, Mr. President," Chauncey said, "and ask to be excused for ten minutes while I consult with my government."

And he stood up, bowed and left them expressing their apparently unanimous approval of the British compromise while he went out to a private office offered by the secretary-general and put through an emergency call to the White House. In a moment Hamilton Delbacher's calm voice bridged three thousand miles.

"Yes, I've been watching. Who hasn't?"

"And?"

"I'm disappointed, but I gather that if the U.K. did it, it must represent the consensus."

"So I'm told by the U.K.," Chauncey said.

"And have no reason to believe otherwise?"

"No reason to believe otherwise. He assures me it's even stronger than many of them want to go, but that they'll stand hitched if we don't try to reimpose stronger language."

"Then I guess we don't have much choice, do we?"

"It makes this meeting and NATO itself pointless," the Secretary of State said bitterly. "Pointless."

"We pretty well expected it, didn't we?"

"They'll come running soon enough, if anything happens."

"Of course," the President said, "but that isn't much consolation now. The only thing we can do is put the best face on it, I think, and accept it. But I think maybe a few more home truths wouldn't hurt."

"Gladly," Chauncey said grimly. "Gladly."

When he returned to the chamber he found Italy, tongue-in-cheek, expressing his great admiration for the modified language and for the United Kingdom's great diplomatic skill in devising it, and in securing such unanimous support for it.

"At least," he said archly as the Secretary of State resumed his seat, "I take it it *is* unanimous? Certainly our distinguished friend from America cannot help but be impressed by the sound reasoning and sensible approach of Her Majesty's Government in thus solving the dilemma he had created for us?"

And he paused and looked with a brightly challenging air at Chauncey Baron.

"When the new delegate of Italy has finished having his fun," Chauncey snapped, "I will make my comments on my own time. The fact that the new delegate of Italy is having his fun, I might point out, should give many members pause. If the Soviet Union's representative on the NATO Council is so pleased with what you are about to do, then—"

"Mr. President!" Italy cried indignantly. "Mr. President, I and my government resent that! I represent the free and independent government of the People's Republic of Italy! It is slander for the American representative to speak of me in that fashion! Slander!"

"I serve notice now, Mr. President," Chauncey said coldly, while the room buzzed with excitement, and the TV cameras swung wildly between their two angry faces, "that as soon as this present crisis is over, the United States will move formally for the expulsion of Italy from NATO. It is ridiculous to have it sitting here when it is nothing now but a Soviet stooge."

"Mr. President!" Italy yelled, his voice rising almost to a scream. *"Mr. President!"*

"At least I have taken the silly smirk off his face," the Secretary of State observed with a deliberately infuriating contempt. "And presently he and his communist-stooge country will be gone from here entirely."

"Mr. Secretary——" Norway began.

"Presently your insufferable imperialist country will be gone from us entirely!" Italy cried. "You will be gone from the entire earth entirely, I say to you, arrogant America! You will be gone from the entire earth!"

"That is exactly my point, Mr. President," Chauncey Baron said, lowering his voice to a calm but still contemptuous level. "There speaks the voice of communism, which would destroy every nation and every individual who dares defend the freedom of peoples and the independence of nations. And now, since I have the floor"—which he did not, but he simply ignored objecting murmurs, Italy's near apoplexy and Norway's nervous indecision about what he obviously regarded as a most unseemly and painful clash—"since I have the floor, I will make my position clear.

"Mr. President, it is obviously the consensus of this meeting that the language offered by the United Kingdom is preferable to that proposed by the United States. I am under instructions from the President of the United States to accept it without further argument. I will do so when we vote. Meantime, he has also instructed me to leave you with what we call 'home truths.' 'A few more of them,' he said. I am glad to oblige.

"The principle of unity and strength upon which NATO was founded is today being hopelessly, probably permanently, shattered. Put to direct test by the challenge of the Soviet maneuvers, we have failed to be either unified or strong. Member nations have given in to their fears. They have abandoned will, determination, courage.

"Yet if it be true that many no longer have sufficient armed strength to permit them, in their own estimation, to be brave, then what is left to them, Mr. President? What is left to NATO as an organization, and to individual members as states and peoples who wish to remain free and independent from communist domination? If we cannot stand together—*if we cannot abide by what is right, but instead knuckle under to the threats of history's greatest bully without even an attempt to stand firm*—then what is the future of ourselves and the world? Hopeless, Mr. President—hopeless. And in our heart of hearts, we all know it.

"The United States, with or without NATO, will continue to oppose the greatest threat ever made to individual liberty and national independence. When you all decide that you are frightened enough, let us know and we will of course do what we can to help you. We pray to God that you do not come to the realization too late for us to do you any good; because once we go, I say to you frankly, there will be no one—*no one anywhere in this world*—left who can save the principle of freedom. It will be all over. And our friends in Moscow, using all the means of modern technology and modern slavery which they now possess will see to it that freedom never—*never* is allowed to live again.

"Mr. President, the United States is prepared to vote on its resolution as amended by the United Kingdom. I would suggest we proceed forthwith."

And now even Italy was silent, and no one apparently wished to challenge his somber warning and so Norway once again instructed the secretary-general to call the roll. And presently announced:

"On the resolution of the United States of America, as amended by the United Kingdom, the affirmatives are fourteen, the negatives none, and the resolution of the United States as amended by the United Kingdom is unanimously adopted."

"Mr. President," the Secretary of State said before anyone else could speak, "I move that this emergency meeting of the NATO Council be adjourned sine die."

"Second," said the United Kingdom.

"All in favor—" Norway said, and fourteen hands went up. "It is so ordered."

And Chauncey Baron was up and away, pushing through the clamoring media, not pausing to speak to anyone, even though many tried to stop him to express some sort of jumble of regret, support and plea for understanding. In less than an hour he was airborne on the way home; and in Moscow Yuri Serapin turned to his colleagues and they gloated once again over the humiliation of the corrupt imperialist enemy that appeared to be already well on its way to defeat in the final battle that would decide the fate of all mankind.

3

"The 'maneuver' method of utilizing submarines—Under present-day conditions, the most active and expedient method of utilizing submarines consists in an organized move, at sea, of a grouping (or group) of submarines and single submarines, for the purpose of searching out the enemy and bringing their armament to bear upon him; or, alternatively, for the purpose of massing submarines in a chosen sector (or region) to deliver a strike against a given enemy objective . . ."

—*Soviet Dictionary of Basic Military Terms*

Next morning in the American media, and to some extent in Congress, as the President remarked to Chauncey when he came in for lunch, "we're catching hell." He managed to sound quite cheerful about it, but it was obvious that both he and his Secretary of State were more than a little disturbed by the general failure to appreciate—or even give a fair hearing to—the position they had taken in Brussels. The principal KGB agent in the Soviet Embassy was able to report with great glee to Moscow that many of the most vocal leaders of American opinion were lined up against their own country.

"It is unbelievable," he concluded his coded message, "but once again, it is true."

"We fail to see," the New York *Times* remarked in its lead editorial, "what has been gained by the exercise in failed ultimata that President Delbacher and Secretary of State Chauncey Baron put this country through at the NATO meeting in Brussels yesterday. It certainly did not frighten the Soviet Union, but it must have scared millions of Americans, including us. We cannot believe it was in the slightest degree necessary.

"From its opening moments, when the United States insisted upon having the meeting thrown open to the world press, to its final ones when the belligerently anti-Soviet resolution introduced by Secretary Baron was whittled down to an appropriately moderate form by the sensible intervention of the United Kingdom, the NATO meeting was a glaring lesson in how not to handle the present crisis.

"The United States professed fears of the Soviet maneuvers—maneuvers which are entirely legitimate and entirely beyond the right of this country to challenge as long as they remain either in Soviet-dominated areas or international waters—and proceeded to try to browbeat our fellow NATO members into going along with a hostile and inflammatory resolution against the Soviet Union. Wisely, NATO refused to follow the American lead. To do otherwise would have given unjustified and indeed unwarranted provocation to the Soviets. Do we wish to keep the peace with them or go to war with them? If the former, then we think the President should rethink his present course of action very, very carefully . . ."

"Rarely, it seems to us," said the most influential television commentator, whose avuncular reading of wire-service copy on the evening news for many years had made him the nation's "most trusted man," "has there been a clearer instance of how not to deal with the Soviet Union. Faced by worldwide Soviet maneuvers which he chooses to regard as being somehow a major threat to the United States and the free world, President Delbacher has reacted with near hysteria. He insisted on calling an emergency meeting of NATO; then he insisted that it be thrown open to the public; then he tried through Secretary of State Chauncey Baron to force through an extremely hostile and provocative anti-Soviet resolution. Naturally enough, since he had demanded an open meeting, the debate on the resolution—and its thoroughly justified defeat—were made known instantly to the entire world. Out of it all has come a new and sorry picture of the present condition of NATO; an entirely unnecessary, defeated but openly hostile, challenge to the Soviets which the Soviets cannot possibly forget; and a revelation of how weak the United States has become in dealing with its allies. And all of this is an answer to a real threat from the Soviet Union? We cannot believe it . . ."

"We cannot believe," the Washington *Post* said, "that the intentions of the Soviet Union, whatever they may be, can possibly be as dangerous to the world and to the United States as President Delbacher seems to think. The President's reaction from the first, in fact, has seemed very odd to us: the sudden implementing of $10 billion in new armaments; the 'sneak attack' scare, which has proved to be nothing but a figment of a defector's wild imagination; the call for an urgent NATO meeting, which went public at U.S. demand; an overly harsh U.S. resolution, which was rightly knocked down by our allies; the revelation of U.S. diplomatic weakness . . . why has all this been necessary? We cannot believe the Soviet threat has suddenly become sufficiently great to warrant such reckless and self-defeating moves . . ."

"We cannot believe—" said the Boston *Globe*.

"We may be naïve," said the Los Angeles *Times,* "but we cannot believe—"

"There are times," Anna Hastings wrote in the Washington *Inquirer,* "when the President seems to deserve the label placed upon him by some of his critics—'Ham-handed Ham.' We cannot believe—"

"We cannot believe—" said the New York *Post.*

"We cannot believe—" said the San Francisco *Chronicle.*

"We cannot believe—" said the Minneapolis *Tribune,* the Chicago *Tribune,* the New Orleans *Item,* the Dallas *News* and many and many another.

"The story of what has weakened United States policy for the past thirty years," the President observed with a sigh. "It ought to be on the currency: *'We cannot believe.'*"

"Because, as I told them in Brussels," Chauncey said, *"we do not want* to believe. Belief would be too terrifying. Leave us alone in our cocoon of self-delusion and deliberate denial of the facts, and we'll die happy."

"I can't believe," Hamilton Delbacher said, "that a majority of the American people agree with them. At least the mail that is coming in here is running about two to one in my favor. Those who disagree are very vehement, but those who agree are very positive. There's a gut instinct in the country that's suspicious as hell of the Soviets and scared as hell of their intentions. And that's in our corner. But," he said, "listen to this." And he pressed one of the two buttons, one red, labeled "S," one blue, labeled "H," on a little box that stood at the left-hand corner of his desk. The one he pressed happened to be labeled "S" and into the room flowed the mellifluous tones of James Monroe Madison, senior Senator from California, direct from the Senate floor.

"—close to absurdity," Jim Madison was saying sternly to his colleagues. "With all respects to our great President"—Ham Delbacher winked at Chauncey Baron—"I for one do not believe that this so-called 'crisis' warrants all the fuss that is being made of it. To my mind, Brussels was a fiasco and one that did us very little good. I ask you, Senators, what purpose was served by exposing all these divisions in NATO? What purpose was served by exposing our own weaknesses and everybody else's? If we are really supposed to be so terribly threatened by the Soviets, this spectacle must have given them great heart and hope. Great heart and hope! Yes, I will yield to my distinguished young colleague."

"Mr. President," Mark's youthfully determined voice came over, "does my distinguished colleague agree that there is any threat *at all* posed to the United States and our allies by this strategic deployment of Soviet forces literally around the globe? Does this deployment, taken in conjunction with the very belligerent and threatening statements made by President Serapin, mean nothing at all to him?"

"My colleague sounds a lot more alarmed now than he used to about the Soviets," Senator Madison observed in his customary arch tones. "Can it be he is taking counsel of his fears, now, after all those valiant speeches he made opposing the emergency armaments bill when he first came into this Senate? Is he now supporting what seems to be a rather warlike policy on the part of our great new President?"

"I'm sure the President appreciates your constant compliments," Mark said. "However, he knows what you think of him, I imagine, and I believe he is genuinely convinced that the Soviet maneuvers indeed represent a major threat to the security of this country and to the peace of the world. As for me, yes, I will say to my colleague, I am much more deeply concerned than I was three years ago about the vast increase in Soviet strength and belligerence since that time. I am not prepared to go quite as far as the President, yet, but in general I do approve of the moves he has made since the summit meeting in New York. I was there, you will remember, Senator, and it was my impression also that the intent behind these maneuvers is anything but friendly to us and the still independent nations of the world. And I admire the President's guts, I will say to the Senate, in bringing everything into the open. Why not? NATO's divisions and weaknesses are no secret. Maybe publicity will encourage a little closing of ranks."

"But the resolution finally adopted will not do anything to encourage the Soviets to back off, will it?" Jim Madison asked softly.

"We will have to see," Mark said, to some tittering from the galleries which came clearly over the Oval Office speaker.

"No signs of it yet, anyway," Senator Madison remarked.

"No signs of it yet," Mark conceded crisply.

"What would the Senator say to a sense-of-the-Senate resolution that we deplore the actions of the President in adopting a course of belligerence and threats toward the Soviet Union, and hope most earnestly that he will adopt a more moderate policy leading to resumption of peaceful negotiations and an end to the tensions between our two countries?"

"I would consider it the height of unfairness and naïveté," Mark said with the same sharp emphasis. "Why don't you deplore the Soviets for a change, Senator? Why are you always deploring America? And how do you get things so topsy-turvy that you say the *President* is being belligerent and threatening in this situation? And what makes you think, in view of Soviet responses so far, that there is any slightest chance of negotiations? People like you are remarkable to me. Your minds seem to function backward whenever the Soviet Union is concerned."

"Now, Mr. President," Jim Madison said angrily, "the Senator is coming very close to personal insult. And I don't like it, sir! No, sir, I do not like it! Mr. President, I send forward the language of the resolution I have just mentioned."

"God damn it!" the President exploded. "Now, who turned that damned mischief maker loose? As if I didn't have enough to worry about, without that kind of a fight on the Hill. God damn him anyway. Sheer mischief!" He picked up the phone and jammed a buzzer. "Get me Senator Hampton," he ordered, "as soon as he can leave the floor. I'll be in the family dining room with Secretary Baron. We're leaving right now. Thank you."

"Come on, Chauncey," he said, rising from his desk, a tall, heavy, slightly ponderous man, usually amicable, now annoyed, not without resources or options but beginning to find them being narrowed down rapidly by his countrymen. He turned at the door and went back to his desk: he had forgotten to turn off the Senate debate. Rick Duclos of Vermont and Bob Templeton of Colorado were coming to Jim Madison's assistance. He cut off their earnest young voices with a ruthlessly impatient finger before turning back to take Chauncey upstairs to join Elinor for lunch.

Unaware of their dismissal in the Oval Office, Rick and Bob went on for the better part of an hour, concentrating their arguments principally on Mark, whom they obviously regarded as having abandoned the "Young Turk" solidarity that had linked the three of them since they entered the Senate together three years before. He felt himself increasingly isolated by those who had been his allies since those early days; but with the stubborn integrity that had always characterized him he did not abandon his position nor did he abandon his increasingly strong defense of the President. By the end of the debate he realized he had come a long way from the opponent of bigger defense spending and general apologist for the Soviets that he had been. He realized that his beliefs had been profoundly shaken by his visit to New York and his chance to study Yuri Serapin and his colleagues close up. He had never thought them particularly nice people: now he felt them to be possessed by an unmitigated evil. And he too, like the President, was now convinced that there was no possibility whatsoever of any genuine negotiations for peace. He realized that the only negotiations, if any, would be on their terms, for the establishment of their kind of peace; and this, he knew with a sudden shiver as though a wind had passed across the grave of the world's hopes, was the peace of death for everything free men and independent nations held dear.

He had just resumed his seat after a final riposte to Rick Duclos, who had accused him of "betraying everything we believed in when we first came here," when Rick's son Pat, still a page boy and now in his senior year at Georgetown, came over and told him he had a telephone call in the Majority Cloakroom. He had a sense of instant replay when he picked up the phone and heard a familiar voice:

"Mark! I must see you!"

"Where are you?" he asked, guarded. "I thought you were a long way from here."

"Far enough. But I can be there tonight."

"At the house again?"

"The bigger house."

"Does the—does he know about this?"

"Surely. He has arranged it. He will tell you the time."

"I'll be there."

"Good. It will be good to see you again."

"You too."

"That makes me happy."

"Me too," he said; but he was not entirely sure of this when he hung up the phone and sat for a moment staring moodily at the scribbled-over wall of the booth. Who was "Margot"? What did "Chk. cte." refer to? What would Freud have made of that Senatorial doodle, small and neat, half-finished; or this other generous figure, vaguely pornographic? What had been running through statesmanly minds when they had transferred onto scratch pad and panel their casual telephonic artwork?

And what was on Ivan's mind now, that he should take the risk of leaving sanctuary and coming again to the White House? And, being in sanctuary, how was it that he had found out whatever it was he thought he had found out?

Mark and Linda had discussed their ebullient visitor several times since the night that had culminated in what the media now referred to scathingly as "the sneak attack scare." He was inclined to believe, she to be skeptical.

"It's possible," she had said just last night, "that *he* thinks he had valid information that the attack was planned. But he could so easily have been used—knowingly or unknowingly—as a plant."

"For what purpose?"

"To make us do what we did. Get everybody scared—and then make everybody turn skeptical when it didn't occur. And consequently lower our guard until some later date when it might suit them to really hit us."

"Yes," he agreed. "That idea has occurred to me. But it seems to me he was too genuinely concerned that night to be a plant—at least knowingly."

"A trained KGB agent, which he certainly is?" she demanded. "You're being pretty naïve, it seems to me."

"In any event, though," he pointed out, "if there was any thought of an attack, he did effectively stop it; or the President did, rather, by making an international issue of it and putting us on alert. So whatever he or his superiors intended, the end result was a help to us."

"Except," she reminded, "that the real end result was to increase the skepticism that is one of the main things they count on. Big deal, sneak

attack, everybody rushes around and gets very dramatic, and then—*nada*
—false alarm—the blahs—and the merry ha-ha from the media. That
may have been exactly what they intended, all along."

"Do they know us that well?" he asked, and then answered his own
question. "Yes, I expect they do. I expect they have people who spend
their entire lives psychoanalyzing the Americans."

"They've been planning on this for a long, long time," she said, eyes
suddenly bleak. "Markie, what's going to happen to the kids?"

"What's going to happen to all of us?" he responded. "If it ever happens, it'll all be academic anyway."

"We've become so used to horror in these recent years," she said, "that
I don't think we ever stop to realize what it could be like."

"Oh yes," he said, suddenly grim. "Oh yes. Every once in a while, not
very often, but underneath there in almost everybody's subconscious, it
lurks—the beast. Every once in a while there's a sudden flash of light
from Yucca Flat or Hiroshima or Nagasaki, and the human animal
freezes. Even they, though they train their military for, fully expect and
fully intend to win, an atomic war, must sometimes look into hell and
wonder."

"They're insane," she said in a near whisper. "Totally insane."

"Yes. And yet it's in all their official literature without any qualifica-
tion whatsoever: they do intend to wage atomic war and they do intend
to win it."

"Monsters," she said in an even lower whisper. *"Monsters."*

"Yes . . . and is Ivan one of them, even though he has professed to defect?"

"He has to have been for a good part of his life, hasn't he, otherwise he
never would have risen to the inner circle."

"I still think genuine defection is possible," Mark said. "The more
some of them find out about the outside world, the more doubts must
creep in. I think it could happen."

"Yes, but you like him. You find him attractive and charming and lika-
ble, which he is. Men are not very good judges of other men, when they
come on strong and are good Joes and macho and fit the masculine self-
image. It's the good-guy syndrome. We women are a little more objective
unless we're in love. And I'm not in love with your Ivan."

He laughed.

"Neither am I and he isn't my Ivan. But I'll admit I'm taking him
pretty much at face value, so far. I think it may still turn out that the information he gave us was correct at the time."

"And may be yet," she said unhappily. "Don't forget that."

"And may be yet," he agreed, suddenly somber, "and I'm not forgetting
it."

And now here was Ivan again, presumably coming out of several days of isolated debriefing at the CIA, a defector, completely out of touch with his own people but professing to know something else that had apparently persuaded the President to bring him back to the White House. Mark determined to be extra watchful and suspicious this time. When the White House called and said he was expected at nine he said, "Tell the President I accept with pleasure, have already talked to the guest of honor on the telephone and am quite skeptical this time." The President's secretary read it back to him, to be sure she had it correct. "That's right," he confirmed. "Tell him I said to underline 'quite skeptical.'" "All right, Senator," she said. "I suppose he'll understand what it's all about." "I think he will," he said.

And so he seemed to, as he rose from his desk to extend a hand of greeting when Mark was ushered into the Oval Office promptly at nine.

"Thanks for coming, Mark," he said. "I thought you really deserved to be in on this second go-round. Incidentally I switched on part of the debate this afternoon. Thank you for your stout defense of this old gray head. A lot of people would like to chop it off, I gather."

"That's one great advantage the Soviet leadership has, isn't it?" he said, shaking hands. "They don't have to worry about the opposition, because there isn't any; they don't have to worry about a free press, because there isn't any; they don't have to worry about an independent, democratic legislature, because there isn't any; they don't have to worry about any opinion other than their own, because there isn't any. They call this 'people's democracy'? They've got it made."

"It does give them a certain ease of movement," the President agreed wryly. "However, I'm used to our sloppy and inefficient free way of doing things, so I guess I'll just have to struggle along with it. Anyway, I do appreciate your support. It helps."

"Not on everything," Mark warned. The President smiled and gestured him to a chair near his desk.

"I know, 'not on everything.' I'm just being thankful for unexpected favors and playing it day by day. What do you make of this latest word from our friend?"

"He called me in the Senate this afternoon to tell me he was seeing us again. Calling from the CIA, I gather."

"He's been over there a lot in the last few days," the President admitted. "They thought he'd told them almost everything he knows, but this is apparently something new. You're right to suggest skepticism. How did he sound to you?"

"Chipper as ever. Not as though he had a great many cares in the world."

"We got his family out all right. They're in a safe house close by in Virginia, where he's been seeing them, so that probably accounts for it. But what can he have for us now? I can't imagine what's left."

"Nor I. How's everything going otherwise?"

The President frowned.

"They're continuing to move on out, of course. I give them about two more days to have everything in position all around the world. Then I suppose there'll be some well-publicized mock exercises—at least they'd better be mock—and after a couple of weeks, when they feel they've impressed the world enough, I suppose they'll withdraw and go on back home. After which we'll all be so impressed that we will presumably lie down and roll over like dutiful little puppy dogs, whenever they command. Except of course we won't. *I* won't, anyway. I don't know about some of the others, after the NATO show."

"Not so good, was it?"

"Maybe I shouldn't have forced the issue. On the other hand, why not? If it had all been glossed over with the usual hypocrisy, nobody would have been fooled anyway. From now on, I'm going to be strictly out in the open with allies and everybody. If they don't like it they can lump it. We have absolutely nothing to lose; and maybe, if we shock them enough, quite a lot to gain. This is just the beginning, I feel. This thing is going to spread far, far beyond just the Soviet maneuvers before we're through. There's a long way to go, yet."

"I just hope we can contain it," Mark said gloomily.

"We've got to," Ham Delbacher said grimly. "And one thing I do know: the old mincing, timorous, namby-pamby, humble-pie, walk-all-over-us methods of some of my recent predecessors are not going to work with the Soviets any more. What we can't do from strength we've got to do by bluff; and it's got to be a tough bluff, not a halfhearted, half-assed, oh-dear, I-didn't-really-mean-it kind of bluff . . ." He smiled without much humor. "I'm in process of establishing a hard-nosed international reputation for myself. It may be the sole defense of the United States of America, when you come right down to it."

Mark sighed.

"I hope it works."

The President snorted.

"Baby, it *better*." There was a rap on the door. He stood up, Mark following his lead, and called out, "Yes!"

"Major Ivan Valerian, Mr. President," one of the guards said, opened the door and stood aside. Ivan, in full uniform, looking as though he had stepped out of a band box after twelve hours' sleep, almost literally bounded into the room, exuberant and smiling. The door closed silently behind him as he paused dramatically, arms flung wide to embrace the world.

"Mr. President!" he cried. "My dear Mark! We meet again!"

"So we do," Ham Delbacher said, smiling in spite of a resolve not to respond too much. "Once again, you surprise us. Come in, Ivan, and sit down." And he held out his hand, which Ivan leaped forward to seize and pump with great enthusiasm before turning to Mark. Him he clasped in a great hug and kissed on both cheeks, so much like a big puppy—or a big bear cub, Mark thought dryly—that Mark could not refrain from a wink and a grin at the President over Ivan's shoulder.

"Now let me go," he said after a moment, disentangling himself with difficulty from Ivan's enthusiastic embrace. "You've made your point."

"I am not making a point," Ivan said cheerfully. "I am expressing my affection for my great friend in America, Mark Coffin, that great United States Senator who understands me so well!"

"I hope so," Mark said with a quizzical look at the President. "I certainly hope so."

"It is true," Ivan said complacently, not missing the look—he did not really miss very much, Mark remembered—and wagging his finger at Mark as at an erring schoolboy. "You need never doubt it! You understand me completely, my suspicious Mark! Except you do not understand yet, I think, that I am truly on your side. That is the problem, *nyet?*"

"That is the problem, *da,*" Mark agreed, again with a glance at the President.

"And your problem too, Mr. President!" Ivan cried. "I am surrounded by suspicious people, and all I wish to do is help the United States! Have I not already helped the United States? Is it not proven?"

"It is proven there has not yet been any sneak attack on the northeastern seaboard," the President agreed. "And I don't expect that there will be."

"Well!" Ivan said triumphantly. "There you are!"

"Where are we?" Mark inquired. "Why did you ask to see us again?"

"In good time," Ivan said, again wagging a monitory finger. "Good time. First I must tell you how well I have been treated by your famed American hospitality—never greater," he said with a sudden wryness of his own, "than when it is given to a defector from my country. But, be that as it may! Your men at the CIA, Mr. President, have been most sympathetic and most understanding—and, I must say, most thorough. I do not believe there is *anything* they do not now know about Ivan Ivanovich Valerian. I thought the KGB was thorough, but your CIA, Mr. President, knows when I go to the bathroom, I might put it. That is how thorough *they* are. But I do not mind it," he assured them lightly. "It is only to be expected. I should, in fact, have been suspicious had they not been so thorough, because this way I know you really want to find out everything about me so that I may be worthy of your trust and may become one of you. With my family"—he bowed with sudden gravity—"who are safely here, as you promised, and for that I thank you with all my heart." And he placed his hand over it dramatically for a second.

"How do they like it here?" the President asked, and their visitor's gravity dissolved in a sparkling smile.

"They are *happy*. *Happy*. The two little girls run about the countryside as though they were in our dacha in the country at home, and the little boy, who is also Ivan, has already tried to ride a pony. Not too well, I might say, but at least he has tried. They feel at home. And my wife— one of your CIA ladies took her shopping yesterday and she could hardly talk from excitement when she got home. She is quite a simple girl, you understand, but already I think she loves America. She cries some for her parents, but"—he dismissed it with a shrug—"that will pass. And perhaps"—he brightened—"perhaps someday it will be possible to see them again. Who knows what time will bring?"

"It may not be for a while," the President remarked, "as things stand now. But, as you say, who knows? Meanwhile, you asked to see us—?"

"Yes, yes! How stupidly I have run on, telling you of simple things when there are much more serious matters involved. I wish you"—and he abruptly looked very solemn and portentous—"I wish you to think of Cuba."

The President smiled.

"I do. Quite often, in fact."

"You will want to think," Ivan told him very seriously, "of how best to neutralize it *at once,* if need arises."

"We have thought of that for years," the President said. "Plans exist."

"Review them, strengthen them, be prepared to obliterate Cuba *at once,*" Ivan said, his tone in effect giving orders. "Look, let me explain you." And he stood up, took from his pocket, once again, a folded piece of paper, came around and spread it on the desk. Mark too got up, and once again the three of them stood side by side studying a piece of paper from Ivan Ivanovich Valerian. This time it was a hand-sketched but recognizable map of the Caribbean.

"Now," Ivan said, indicating the seas off Cienfuegos on the Cuban underbelly, "what have your spy satellites and underwater sonar sweeps discovered in this area so far?"

"Six subs," the President said. "All in place before on a number of occasions—what we have come to think of as the normal complement in that area. They come and go, never less than two, rarely more than six. Six it is now."

"As of when?" Ivan demanded.

"I don't know, exactly. I get these reports constantly, now that the maneuvers have begun. Last night, I believe."

"Tell them to look again," Ivan suggested. "There will be twelve by tomorrow morning, eighteen by tomorrow night, and by thirty-six hours from now, there will be twenty-four. All are missile carriers and all are fully armed. Thirty-six hours from now, when all Soviet forces are at their stations, you will find no other concentration of subs of this size anywhere in the world. I would expose them, Mr. President, and I would challenge them."

"Oh, I will if what you say is true," Hamilton Delbacher assured him. "You can rely on it. But what is this supposed to indicate, another sneak attack?" And despite himself he could not prevent a slight trace of sarcasm in his voice.

"Mr. President," Ivan said solemnly, "do not be fooled by what has happened—or has not happened, rather. If I had not come to Mark, and so to you, the first time—if you had not promptly made your public challenge before the whole world—who can say what would have been the case now? I think you would be missing many millions and I think America would at this moment be surrendering, Mr. President. Such was the full intention when I left Moscow. It is easy to mock what does not happen, as your press persists in doing; it would not be around to mock *anything* had we three not done what we did. I believe this."

And looking very solemn again and quite offended, he left the desk and moved back to his chair, where he sat down stiffly and stared at them with an uncompromising earnestness.

"I want you to understand me, Ivan," the President said, sitting down also as Mark returned to his chair. "There is no intention in this room to mock you or to discount what you have to say. There has been the thought in my mind, and possibly in Mark's, that you might have been sent to us originally to mislead us. Not"—he raised a hand as Ivan started angrily in his chair—"not deliberately on your part, I'm not saying that—you could have been misled yourself, so that you could have been sincerely and entirely convinced of what you were telling us."

"But to what purpose?" Ivan demanded, almost spluttering in his indignation. "To what purpose, Mr. President and Mark? What purpose?"

"To exactly the purpose that occurred when I made it public and nothing happened—a great rise in public skepticism, a great strengthening of all those within America who always discount any warning of any Soviet hostility of any kind, anywhere, any time. These people do not help the President of the United States, you know; they are great hindrances and serious obstacles to him in forming the foreign policy of the United States, particularly as it involves the possibility of doing anything strong and decisive to curb the Soviet advance. That could have been the purpose of your mission, whether you knew it or not. My conviction is growing that you did not."

"Thank you," Ivan said with a sudden sarcastic bitterness. "I have defected from my country, dragged off my family from their home, torn my wife from her parents—I thank you."

"I know," the President said calmly, "but you admit deceptions have been used by the Soviet Union, do you not? You yourself have participated in the preparation and carrying forward of some of them, have you not? You admit the United States has good reason to be suspicious of almost anything coming out of Moscow, do you not?"

There was silence while they stared at one another, neither the stocky young Soviet officer nor the older, pleasant-faced American President yielding an inch for several moments. Finally Ivan's eyes shifted to Mark's.

"Yes," he said at last in a low voice, "I admit those things. They are true. I can understand why you would not believe me. But, Mr. President!" And he swung back with great earnestness to Hamilton Delbacher. "This time I beg of you, do believe me again! It is true, Mr. President! It is a great peril to the United States! They never stop pressing, my people, you know that—never! Alert your Navy, keep the surveillance on twenty-four-hour duty, do not relax for one second! I beg of you, I beg of you!"

"We will do our best," the President said, standing up and once again holding out his hand, this time in firm but pleasant dismissal. "I wish to thank you, Ivan, for coming to us again." He hesitated for a second, then smiled. "Now, is there anything else? Will there be something later on, or is that all?"

"You mock me again," Ivan said, but smiling a little, and speaking more lightly now. "Twice I have given you warning of infinite danger to the United States. Is that not enough?"

"It is enough," the President said, shaking his hand with an extra, paternal warmth. "My best to you and your family, and I hope the CIA will not bother you too much more. I may send for you on my own, from time to time. I would like your thoughts on things as they progress."

"Thank you, Mr. President," Ivan said, beginning to sound fully mollified. He turned to Mark, who braced himself for the bear hug and the kisses. They came as expected, and after he pulled away Ivan laughed and clapped him on the shoulder.

"Someday when this is all over, Mark, you must teach me golf and we will play together."

"I'm better at tennis."

"I am *very good* at tennis," Ivan said with his charming smile. "Watch out! My love to your beautiful Linda."

"I'll tell her," Mark said. "She'll be pleased. Good night."

"Good night," Ivan said, drew himself up, saluted the President and then Mark with smart precision, turned on his heel and walked to the door. It opened smoothly before him and he returned to the protective arms of the waiting CIA without a backward look.

"Of great charm," the President said, "and great intelligence. A remarkable young man in many ways. I wonder if being a double agent is one of them."

"I wonder if we will ever know," Mark mused.

But three hours later, after he had gone home to Linda and they had hashed and rehashed the conversation until they were exhausted trying to analyze it, there came a very late phone call from the White House.

"I just wanted you to know," Hamilton Delbacher said, "that two fish just entered the pond. There are two more about an hour out, and we've picked up two more beyond that. Everything on schedule so far."

"I think he deserves to be told," Mark said.

"I've just talked to him," the President said with a rueful little chuckle, "I pay my debts. He was gratified for himself but afraid for us."

"So am I," Mark said.

"Well: try to sleep."

"You, too," Mark said fervently. "You, too."

In the Kremlin they were not sleeping. It had now been almost thirty hours since Yuri Serapin had found the chance to do so. He was beginning to feel quite groggy: he realized suddenly that although young in terms of Soviet leadership, he was no longer quite so young in terms of the calendar. It was the first time he had ever been required to confront this fact, and for a moment or two it struck him with a sharp dismay. But this did not last long. It vanished as quickly as it had come, wiped out by the excitement and euphoria of the great Soviet triumph so far.

It had been necessary to revise some plans, shift some others; but overall the maneuvers were proceeding exactly on time and producing exactly the effects throughout the world that he had foreseen in all the careful hours of study, planning and contemplation of alternatives that had preceded his order to put them in motion.

In the area most crucial to any final confrontation with the United States—Cuba—he had just been informed that American surveillance had been sharply increased in the past two hours. But what of it? The special submarine force whose composition and timetable he had personally worked out with the Navy was moving into place without a hitch and there was nothing the Americans could do about it—or, he told himself with satisfaction, dared do about it. His opposite number in the White House might make some public squawk, as he had about what the American media now chose to call scornfully "the sneak attack scare," but Yuri was confident he would receive the same treatment. And if protest came, he himself was prepared to meet it as vigorously and harshly as he had the earlier complaint.

What could Hamilton Delbacher do about it? The answer, Yuri was sure, was nothing.

He stared up at the huge lighted map and for a moment it blurred before his eyes. He really must get some sleep, and quite soon. He could allow himself, he thought, perhaps eight hours; by that time the desired correlation of forces would be pretty much complete everywhere around the globe, and it was quite obvious by now that no nation anywhere, singly or in combination, was going to be able to interfere. In fact, the NATO meeting had shown that none of them, except possibly the United States—and certainly it could not be said to be a nation united in this goal—had any desire to interfere.

"Our friends of the West!" he had remarked with jovial scorn to the Foreign Minister as they watched the tortuous NATO debate. "When in doubt, rationalize, when in fear, retreat. Pah! How can they possibly believe we still have respect for them? They are chickens scurrying about while the fox runs forward. Sooner or later none will escape, and they know it. Let them pass whatever resolution they please."

"We would prefer, however, a weak one, would we not, Comrade President?" the Foreign Minister had suggested in his timorously ubiquitous way.

"It will be weak," Yuri said flatly. "Trust them for that."

And so it was, and as he watched its wording fall into place under the skilled compromising hand of Britain, he could not resist a series of excited gratified chuckles that rose finally into a bark of delighted laughter while he pounded with clenched fists on his desk and shouted words of encouragement for the final vote as though he were urging on the Moscow soccer team in some politically motivated contest with some naïvely non-political team from the West.

"That is it, my little children!" he called out to them in a savagely crooning voice. "That is it, my sweet innocent little ones! Be gentle with Mother Russia and she will be gentle with you while she swallows you up! You will hardly feel it at all! You make it so easy for all of us!"

And not for the first time in all these recent hours, he had tossed back another quick shot of vodka, smeared caviar on a chunk of black bread and gobbled it down. One could not, however, live on vodka and caviar forever, even though these days of unimpeded progress were certainly vodka and caviar days, and he did not expect—until the final victory, now at last within sight—to enjoy such exhilaration and excitement again. He must very shortly leave his desk, eat a decent meal and go to bed. America and the West might think the maneuvers were the sum total of it. He and his colleagues knew that placing their forces in positions from which they could literally command the land masses and sea lanes of the world was only the start. Much more remained to be done and he must be fresh for it.

He had met scarcely half an hour ago with the commanding officers of Army, Navy, Air Force and Strategic Rocket Forces. He had played them and that huge lighted map like a conductor leading the sections of his orchestra through a gigantic pavan.

"I think we need more submarines here," he had suggested, indicating the seas off Norway, the Bering Strait and particularly Cuba. The Navy had jumped to obey.

"More planes to Yemen," he had said. "Two more squadrons to Nicaragua, more to the port on the Persian Gulf. We must be able to close the Strait of Hormuz in ten minutes' time." The Air Force had fallen all over itself to comply.

"A thousand more tanks to Poland," he had ordered, "the same to southwestern East Germany. If we decide on a pincers through Europe, it must be instantaneous and fully adequate." The Army had exclaimed at his great wisdom and the orders had instantly gone forward.

"All missiles must be flight-ready," he had told the Strategic Rocket Forces, "especially those in Cuba and Siberia. No exceptions." His orders were carried out at once.

There were moments when he felt like a god, so supreme and all-powerful was he becoming. For all practical purposes he was getting ready to go to war at once, though he knew the plan was far different; but let them think so, in Asia and the West. *Schrecklichkeit,* Hitler had called his policy: *frightfulness.* The beginning and end of frightfulness was fright. Let them eat it, breathe it, swallow it, be paralyzed by it. It would make all the rest so much simpler.

And although the forces of the communist Motherland and her Warsaw Pact and other allies scattered across the globe were now deployed on such a vast scale that only the extremely sophisticated computers that the U. S. President J. Carter had kindly permitted the Soviet Union to buy prior to Afghanistan could possibly keep track of them all, he still felt that simplicity was the key. They all had their orders; they were being monitored literally every second from Moscow; the orchestration could continue without danger of mistakes. The basic plan was classic in its simplicity. There was no slightest reason to doubt that it would be decisive.

He yawned, so deeply that it seemed he would never stop; squeezed a hand across his tired eyes, pushed back his chair from the desk, stood up.

"Yes, Comrade President?" his secretary said, rushing forward.

"Yes, Comrade President?" queried the Foreign Minister, the Defense Minister, the administrator of Civil Defense who had come in a while ago to discuss the evacuation of the Kremlin and the quiet unobtrusive movement underground of key defense factories that, begun long ago, was due to be finally completed in another month's time.

"Nothing, comrades," he said, gesturing them away with a smile. "I am just tired. It has been almost thirty hours since I have slept and I think I must do so or collapse."

"Yes, Comrade President," the Foreign Minister said with the rather coy archness which Yuri found basically irritating—but flattering, too. "After all, all depends, one might almost say, upon him who might in another era have been called, 'The Father of All the Russias.'" And to remove the stigma of this Czarist phrase, he immediately gushed, "You *are* our father, Yuri Pavlovich!"

"That is nonsense," he said gruffly, but they could see he was pleased. "I simply hope I am discharging my duty to the Motherland as you all would wish me to do. That is my sole desire."

"Oh *yes,* Yuri Pavlovich!" they cried in unison. *"Oh yes!"*

"Good," he said, starting to walk slowly toward the door. Before he could reach it, a young fellow whom he recognized as one of the Foreign Minister's junior aides hurried through and thrust a paper toward him.

"Comrade President," he said hurriedly. "Forgive me, but this letter has just come in from Washington. The American President H. Delbacher is—is being difficult again."

Which was why, Yuri thought with a sudden blind, exhausted anger, things might not go so smoothly after all. The fool might yet upset everything by being difficult and so bring the world crashing down upon them both.

He sat slowly down in the center of the room in a chair the young man had hurriedly pushed forward and began to read the message with a terrible scowl.

There was the usual stirring at the door. The East Room, more crowded with newspeople than it had ever been, hushed abruptly. Everyone rose.

"Ladies and gentlemen," the press secretary said, "the President of the United States."

He walked in with his slow but purposeful stride, placed a leather folder on the podium, looked up with a tired face but a pleasant smile, said the usual, "Please be seated."

He opened the folder, looked directly into the cameras and began to speak.

"I have this morning sent the following letter to the President of the Soviet Union, Y. P. Serapin. Copies will be available when you go out, but I shall read it slowly so that you may take notes now if you wish.

"'Dear Mr. President: Since I know that it is your foremost desire, as it is my own, to preserve and strengthen world peace, I must call your attention to a feature of the present Soviet maneuvers which in my judgment poses a most severe threat not only to that peace but also presents a direct challenge to the national interests and security of the United States.

" 'I refer to the unprecedented and extreme build-up of Soviet missile-launching submarines which is now under way in the waters immediately south of the island of Cuba.

" 'As you know, Mr. President, the normal complement of your submarines in that area has been between two and six for several years. That has apparently been, by tacit agreement, the number past American Administrations have considered acceptable in terms of what could be successfully neutralized in case some unfortunate misstep on our part or yours produced unexpected tensions in that area.

" 'I am now informed, however, of what you yourself already know: that the normal six has already been increased by six more as of this morning; that another six are on their way, roughly five hundred miles out, due to be in place by sometime early tonight; and that another six, bringing the total to twenty-four, will be on station by tomorrow morning.' "

There was a tense expulsion of breath among his hurriedly scribbling listeners.

" 'All of these are under our surveillance so there need be no dispute between us as to the total figure. It is known to us both, as I am now making it known to all through the public release of this letter. The number is twenty-four. Two dozen. Eighteen more than are normally hiding in our offshore waters near Cuba.

" 'I must ask you, Mr. President: why? And I must demand an explanation at your earliest convenience. I would, in fact, appreciate an answer not later than six hours from this moment at which you are reading my letter in the Kremlin. Otherwise immediate, widespread and unfortunate consequences could ensue.' "

There was a sudden commotion as the wire service reporters and a dozen others jumped up and raced out to the telephones to send in their bulletins. Every television camera in the room was trained upon the President's face, which looked unperturbed, calm and completely determined.

" 'Mr. President,' " he went on, " 'this new escalation of tension in connection with your maneuvers is solely and entirely your doing. These are not *our* submarines which are clustering suddenly just off *your* shores. This is a deliberate, calculated, bare-faced attempt to threaten and intimidate the United States. It is unacceptable; and I would remind you, Mr. President, that you now have a President in the White House who, when he says something is unacceptable, means it is unacceptable. There will be no equivocating, backing down, crawling or giving in by me. Those days, I hope, are gone from this White House permanently.

" 'Therefore, Mr. President, I suggest it would behoove you to give some attention to this communication and to give some serious thought to the immediate withdrawal of this excessive missile-carrying submarine force from our nearby waters.

" 'This would be truly in the interests of world peace, for which you profess some concern. Please give this matter your immediate attention. Very truly yours, Hamilton Delbacher.' "

There was silence for a moment while he folded the copy of the letter and placed it neatly in the folder. Then the room exploded. Thirty reporters were on their feet frantically shouting, "Mr. President!" He smiled and gestured to the Boston *Globe*.

"Mr. President," the *Globe* said, "is there some independent verification of the approach of these submarines and if not, do you feel justified in sending such a letter to President Serapin?"

"In other words," the President said, "am I a liar, and if I can't prove I'm not, should I dare address so august a personage with so awful a charge? Well, I think I know what I'm talking about and I think you had better accept it because I've given you all the verification you're going to get for the time being.

"The Pentagon will be releasing some sonar charts and some surface pictures before the day is out, I expect. But don't forget to tell your readers they may be fakes. . . . Yes?" He turned to the St. Louis *Post-Dispatch*.

"Mr. President," the *P.-D.* said, "assuming the submarines are coming to Cuba, as you say—"

"I do say," he snapped, suddenly openly angry, "so what do *you* have to say to that?"

"Very well," the *Post-Dispatch* said hastily, surprised and taken aback by his tone; though why he should have been, the President couldn't see. "What I mean is, what do you intend to do if President Serapin doesn't respond as you request?"

"There are several options," he said more calmly, "none of which I am going to disclose at this time. Let's see what he does, first."

"What alerted you to the presence of this Soviet task force—or war force?" Chuck Dangerfield asked, and the President thought he must have been talking to Mark and Mark had suggested Chuck provide an opening to mention Ivan if he wanted to. But Ivan in the media's eyes was the source of the "sneak attack scare." He decided not.

"War force, I think, is a good designation. We received indications something unusual was afoot, afloat, rather. It checked out. They're definitely there and more are coming."

"Would it be the same source who prompted the sneak attack scare?" the New York *Times* inquired. The President smiled.

"It could be any number of sources. Our surveillance hasn't been exactly idle since the maneuvers began. The ships are there."

"Mr. President," the Washington *Inquirer* said, "what do you consider to be their purpose in Cuban waters? Do you think *they* are planning a sneak attack?"

"I don't know whether it's attack or threat, but in either event it is not acceptable to me or to the security interests of the United States."

"Isn't it a little late, Mr. President," AP asked, "to be concerned about subs in Cuban waters? Haven't the last couple of Administrations virtually given them carte blanche by not protesting much earlier than this?"

"I agree with you," he said. "I would have done it differently, and I often argued in the Senate and as Vice President, as you know, that we react much more strongly than we have over the years. But we didn't, for reasons the history books will have to go into. The fact is, we didn't. But the circumstances were not quite the same either, of course. There never have been circumstances like these created by the Soviet maneuvers. We hope there never will be again, but meanwhile, we have to face them as they come. And this sudden boost in sub strength in Cuba—which quite literally is enough to blast the whole United States off the map if they all let go at once—is something that has to be faced. I can't sit by and let it go on without the strongest kind of reaction against it. That would be stupid, and it could also be suicide."

"Do you really think, Mr. President," the Los Angeles *Times* said, "that they would dare launch an all-out attack of that kind upon us? Aren't you possibly overreacting—again—to what may be just a routine Soviet exercise?"

"What you don't seem to realize," he said patiently, "is that nothing in this present situation is routine. We have passed beyond the routine with them, in these present maneuvers. This literally *is* the greatest mass military exercise in the history of the world, and its potentials for trouble are literally worldwide. Something could happen anywhere at any moment with this much hardware flying around—floating around—moving around. I'm sure Serapin thinks he has it under control, but there's always the human factor that even they haven't succeeded in controlling entirely. Somebody can still make a mistake. Particularly in something like this sub concentration, which is no mistake. You don't rendezvous twenty-four of them without having something in mind. And whatever it is, it bodes no good for us."

"How do you know that, Mr. President?" CBS inquired in his usual manner, which just skated the edge of insolence with a well-calculated nicety. "Aren't you, as my colleague from the Los Angeles *Times* puts it, possibly overreacting again? Why should we get so excited about it? They haven't offered any threats to us, have they?"

"The accumulation of everything Serapin has said to me, everything he has done in these maneuvers, the whole attitude, the whole idea, the whole exercise, is a threat," he said, still patiently, though he wondered how long he could keep it up. "If you were walking down the street near the Press Club and suddenly some individual came up to you, billy clubs hanging out of both pockets, guns in both hands and a knife in his teeth, you'd have a pretty good idea that he wasn't exactly friendly, wouldn't you? You'd have a gut feeling about it. If you were smart you'd begin to take steps to defend yourself."

"I think I'd run like hell," CBS said with a grin, and the room exploded into laughter in which the President joined.

"Good thinking," he said after it subsided, "but where are we to run to? We have to take a stand, otherwise we're going under, in my judgment. And unhappy though it makes some of you, it is my judgment which has to prevail in this matter as long as I'm in this office. Right?"

"Are you convinced, Mr. President," the Washington *Post* asked, "that American public opinion is unanimously behind you in your attitude?"

"Are you convinced it's unanimously behind you?" he shot back. "It's not unanimously behind anybody," he added with a smile that removed some if not all the sting from it, "and certainly you and your employers are doing your best to see that it's not unanimously behind me. But I think the majority is behind me, because I think the majority has that gut feeling I mentioned a minute ago. Americans know when they're threatened, whether their media do or not. They're threatened now."

"Will you release President Serapin's reply as soon as it comes to you?" UPI inquired.

"If it comes you'll get it."

"You have doubts that he'll reply, Mr. President?"

"It's a possibility."

"What would you do, in that case?"

"Read my letter. Consequences are mentioned."

" 'Immediate, widespread and unfortunate' " she quoted thoughtfully. "For whom, Mr. President?"

"Stick around," he advised dryly. "You'll be among the first to know."

"Thank you, Mr. President!" she said, and the conference was over. They streamed out in a babble of voices, a few last questions, which he ignored, tossed at him as he left. Chauncey was waiting just outside the door, where he had stood listening.

"The skepticism," he murmured in a dismayed tone. "The skepticism!"

"I hope they never have to find out how empty a thing it is," the President said grimly. "They enjoy it so. . . . Come on back to the office. Roger and the Joint Chiefs are coming over in about ten minutes. We can do some planning while we wait."

But after they had done their planning, and long after Chauncey, Roger and the chiefs had all gone back to their respective offices, he continued to wait for an answer to his letter to Yuri Serapin. It was not until the next afternoon, after the media had enjoyed another chance to denounce him as an hysterical war-monger, that a reply was forthcoming. It came from Yuri, but he had company. And it did not come from Moscow.

4

"The Soviet-Cuban cooperation of many years, dictated by the aims of Cuba's defense, comprises an inalienable right of two sovereign states. Any attempts to restrict this right are in crying contradiction with accepted norms of international intercourse and are absolutely unfounded."

—Pravda

The announcement of the press conference was made at 6 A.M. Washington time. It would be held promptly at 6 P.M. at the Presidential palace in Havana. All journalists, and particularly all American journalists, were cordially invited to attend. All visa requirements and all restrictions on the entry of American journalists were suspended for twenty-four hours. The Cuban Government would, if permitted by the Government of the United States, begin a regular half-hourly shuttle service, starting at noon, between Havana and Miami to transport any and all American journalists and any and all foreign journalists stationed in the United States. If the round-trip shuttle was not permitted by U.S. authorities between Havana and Miami, then arrangements had been made with the government of Haiti to permit the shuttle to operate between Havana and Port-au-Prince. Any American journalists or others who found themselves restricted by the American Government could, upon arrival in Port-au-Prince, be assured of immediate transportation to Cuba. The conference would be "of major importance."

Practically no one had a hunch how important it would turn out to be. But adding everything up, the Soviet submarines, the President's virtual ultimatum, the continued silence out of Moscow, everybody knew it had to be covered. Phones at the White House and State Department began to ring at 6:05 A.M. and when both opened for business at 9 A.M. they found themselves besieged by literally hundreds of clamoring press and TV reporters. The press secretary and the "State Department spokesman" hurried into the Oval Office, greatly agitated, as soon as the buzzer sounded through the White House to indicate that the President was at his desk.

"What should we do?" they demanded breathlessly, not even stopping to respond to Hamilton Delbacher's calmly cordial, "Good morning."

"Take a statement for immediate release," the President said, and dictated it to his press secretary off the cuff:

"In view of the situation now existing in the Caribbean, the President by executive order has directed that all visa requirements and travel restrictions to Cuba imposed upon American journalists and others stationed in the United States for the purpose of news-gathering be, and they hereby are, temporarily suspended until 0600 tomorrow morning. The President, like all Americans, is interested in the press conference announced in Havana and agrees with the Cuban Government that it should be fully and completely covered by the American media and all others who so desire.

"The President has directed the Air Force to make available immediately a sufficient number of unarmed troop transports to accommodate all holders of bona fide White House press passes, Congressional press cards or bona fide temporary special credentials issued by either agency. He assumes the Cuban Government will guarantee the safe transit of these planes while in Cuban air space and will make suitable provisions for safeguarding them on the ground in Havana.

"All wishing to take advantage of this transportation should be at Andrews Air Force Base not later than twelve noon. The planes will return from Cuba three hours after the conclusion of the press conference . . .

"Now take that back to State and have them draw up the necessary executive order lifting restrictions and get it back to me for signature within the hour," he told the department spokesman. "And," he added to his press secretary, "you get hold of Bart Jamison at the Air Force and tell him to have at least a dozen of his biggest troop transports on the line for take-off promptly at noon. I imagine it won't be just the peons who get to go on this one—every bureau-chief, publisher and editorial writer who can get to Andrews in time will want to go along. Issue credentials to everybody who has a valid claim." He chuckled. "I'd rather like to go myself. Wouldn't that be a sensation!"

As he said it a sudden little hunch flashed into his mind and was as instantly dismissed: surely Yuri wouldn't think of that. Then the hunch returned and nagged at him: on the other hand, maybe he would.

If so, the world's headlines belonged to Yuri this day.

But if Ham Delbacher was prepared for Havana's biggest sensation, not many others were; and when the U.S. transports—fourteen of them were needed, as it turned out—lumbered out of the sky to descend upon the airport in Havana, (their pilots nervously hoping that the President's confidence in a peaceable Cuban welcome was well grounded) exclamations of excitement and disbelief swept each craft as it came in sight of the tarmac below. Off to one side the huge Ilyushin jet rested, red hammer-and-sickle flag hanging limply from its nose in the suffocating heat and humidity. Around it a double cordon of armed Soviet troops from the local barracks stood guard. Both plane and men had an air of being in possession; which, of course, they were.

The next hour passed in a blur of reporters, typewriters, cameras somehow getting jammed into the dilapidated buses provided by the Cuban Government and being driven erratically off to the vast temporary press area set up under tents in the sports stadium. In the sweltering atmosphere tempers were short, territorial imperatives pressing; the sound of constant arguments in a dozen tongues enlivened the chaotic scene. Nearby a couple of run-down hotels had been set aside for natural needs, refreshments and the germination of gossip; and there the world's press hung around uneasily until 5 P.M., when the tired jitneys reappeared and began to shuttle them off to the Presidential palace on whose lawn some one thousand folding chairs had been set up. When the contingent from America arrived they found the first five rows solidly occupied by communist "press," whose superior air did not increase the love of nations; and it was a restless and combative group of reporters who were called to attention by a blast of trumpets precisely at 6 P.M. A sudden hush fell as the President of Cuba and the President of the Soviet Union suddenly materialized upon the wooden platform that had been set up in front of the palace. Immediately there was a great roar from the communist reporters, who rose to their feet, applauded and screamed, while in back of them the decadent democratic reporters yelled, "God damn it, down in front, you God damned motherfuckers!" and other pleasantries characteristic of the corrupt capitalist press.

Upon this scene Yuri Serapin and his smug, beady-eyed companion gazed with a happy satisfaction. It had not taken much preparation—one quick phone call between Moscow and Havana—and now the eyes of the world were literally focused upon them. How do you like this, my friend? Yuri asked savagely in the privacy of his mind.

He noted, somewhat to his own dismay, that in spite of his faith in history's inevitability, he was beginning to feel a more and more personal dislike for the President of the United States. This was not good for objective judgment and he shook his head as if to clear it. His eight hours of sleep had been achieved—just barely—before he was required to board his plane and leave Moscow. But it had not been a restful trip, undoing most of the good achieved, and he felt decidedly snappish. Which was not good preparation for the serene and all-commanding impression he wished to make. He spent the fifteen minutes of the Cuban President's seemingly endless and endlessly fulsome introduction telling himself sternly to relax; and by the time the last standing ovation had been elicited from the communist sector below, he was ready for them.

"And so," his colleague said in English with a final great flourish of his arms, "I present to you, and through you to the world, the most able and distinguished leader of mankind's eternal struggle for freedom, right and justice ever to appear on earth—His Excellency Yuri Pavlovich Serapin, President of the Union of Soviet Socialist Republics!" With great solemnity he gave him an *embrazo* on both cheeks.

"Did he walk over on the Atlantic?" a voice yelled from somewhere among the American press into the reverent silence that greeted this tender exchange between two great leaders. Smart dog, Yuri thought viciously: you will yelp another song before long.

Once again there were wild shouts and screams from the communists, polite but generally cordial applause from the West. He stepped forward to the podium, adjusted the microphone, shed his coat, rolled up his sleeves, mopped his forehead—evoking, as he had in New York, a little friendly chuckle at his simple humanity—and spoke in a firm and unhurried voice.

"Comrade President"—he said in English—"comrades of the great people's struggle for justice and freedom"—he said in Russian, arousing another wild cheer from the communist contingent—"my friends of the American and international press," he said, returning to English—"welcome to Havana. I had not thought to see you here."

"Nor we you," someone shouted, more friendly, from among the Americans; and there was a warm and encouraging wave of laughter, which he acknowledged with a broad smile and a quick little bow.

"We live in strange times," he replied, "and strange things happen. I would like to be greeting you in Washington on a friendly visit, in company with my good friend, your President. But alas"—his expression hardened—"your President is not my good friend. He does not feel for me those amicable feelings I hold for him."

"What kind of crap *is* this?" some irreverent reactionary American asked his immediate vicinity in a loud disgusted voice. He was promptly shushed, with many angry looks of admonition and disapproval.

"No, he does not," Yuri repeated. "In fact, as you know, he sent me yesterday a most harsh and unfriendly letter concerning the legitimate right of the Soviet armed forces to hold maneuvers *as* they please *where* they please. And he did not even do me the courtesy of sending it to me first. He released it in a press conference before I even knew what was troubling him. I had no choice but to reply to him in a similar forum."

Applause and cheers rose dutifully from his communist supporters in the first five rows.

"The forum best suited for that, it seemed to me, was this forum right here, in the very nation—the independent, free, sovereign nation—which is the scene of the event that seems to have agitated him so greatly. The great people's democracy of Cuba, of which we in the Soviet Union think so highly and with which we have such warm, close and intimate ties." He pounded suddenly on the podium. "Nothing and no one in this world dare disrupt those friendly ties! No one dares try to tell us what we may or may not do within our friendly alliance! That is"—and his voice assumed a mocking, sarcastic note—"completely and entirely 'unacceptable' to me and to the great Cuban nation, and if anyone ignores this there will be 'immediate, widespread and unfortunate consequences' for whoever tries it!"

At this his communist rooting section rocked with delight and at his side his Cuban vassal slapped his thigh, put back his head and roared with enormous, if somewhat calculated, laughter.

"No, my friends," Yuri said somberly when all the hilarity died down, "*no one* can disrupt the friendly ties between us and Cuba, and *no one* can thwart or interfere with the river of history as it flows on uniting and making strong our two peoples together. What is it the President objects to? I see from the newspapers—I simply had to have some sleep yesterday, so I was in bed, and they did not wake me, when his letter arrived— nor have I bothered to read it since—but I see from the newspapers and of course from one or two of my nervous advisers who persist in saying, 'Oh, dear, here is *another* letter from that American President' "—there was another delighted burst of laughter and cheering—"that Mr. Delbacher is concerned because we have sent a few submarines into Cuban waters. We have had a base here at Cienfuegos for many years. Right after the episode when President J. Carter made such a fuss about a 'Soviet brigade' here—but then thought better of it and swallowed his words when we told him they were nonsense"—again laughter, mocking and derisive from his rooting section—"we built a second pier for the handling of submarines at Cienfuegos. Neither J. Carter nor H. Delbacher nor anyone in between has objected to that expansion or to our continuous use of this base.

"Now we wish to station a few extra submarines here temporarily in connection with our maneuvers, and what happens? H. Delbacher acts as though he owns Cuba. He acts as though he can tell Cuba and the Soviet Union what to do. He acts as though, perhaps, he owns the entire Caribbean. He says our submarines are a threat to the United States. Have we uttered any threats with them? Have we used them in any way to bother the United States? *Have we?*"

He paused and stood, arms akimbo, staring at the press. A dutiful cry of "NO!" went up from the first five rows, echoed, to his obvious satisfaction, by a good many others scattered through the crowd.

"No, we have not! Nor will we! These famous submarines, my friends, are down there"—and he gestured southeast—"maybe 100 or 150 miles, but who knows what they are there for? *I* know!" And he struck his chest a thump. "And my admirals know! But H. Delbacher does not know! They may be just passing through, ladies and gentlemen! They may be just stopping for a little rest before proceeding on their way to the maneuvers. What right has H. Delbacher to challenge them? None at all! None at all!

"However," he said, and his voice abruptly became calm and reasonable—"Sweet as the suckling dove," Chauncey Baron remarked dryly to the President as they watched in the Oval Office—"However. If these submarines are such a worry to the President, then perhaps we should do something about them. Perhaps we should find out really why they are here and whether it is all right for them to stay."

He turned to his Cuban lackey and with an exaggerated politeness gestured him to the microphone.

"Perhaps, Mr. President, you will tell us how it comes about that our submarines are here, and how you and the great Cuban people feel about them. You, after all, are much closer to the matter than some other Presidents!"

And again to the accompaniment of laughter and applause he bowed low to the President of Cuba, turned to a chair on the platform beside him and sat down with an attentive and expectant air.

"Mr. President," the Cuban President said, "you know and I know—even if some other Presidents do not know—why your submarines are here. They are here because a week ago I sent you a letter requesting that they be sent here to defend Cuba from a surprise attack—a sneak attack, if you will—by the United States of America. You know, Mr. President, that the United States is always plotting such an attack. Now that this new President is in the White House, this new, belligerent, sword-rattling man, that danger has never been so great.

"Cuba is threatened, Mr. President! Cuba fears attack at any moment! Cuba has proof that such an attack is planned and ready! Cuba is afraid and Cuba asks your help! That is why your submarines are here, because we asked you to help us and defend us and you replied with all the brave strength of the great Soviet people and the socialist coalition. You sent your submarines to save Cuba from a sneak attack by the United States, as we had asked them to come, in a free exercise of sovereignty! We invited you as we have every sovereign right to do, and you have not failed us, Mr. President! Thanks to your submarines we are now safe from the dastardly planned attack, the dastardly planned crime of the United States of America!"

"God damned liar," Hamilton Delbacher said quietly.

"So are they both," the Secretary of State agreed. "But who gives a damn?"

Not their audience, obviously, for now all the communists and a good

many of the others, even including some few scattered Americans, were on
their feet cheering, applauding, shouting their approval.

"And, Mr. President!" Yuri's Cuban errand boy shouted as they
quieted abruptly to hear him conclude. "We want them to remain just as
long as you deem it wise for us to have them in our waters! Our waters
are yours, Mr. President! Our ports are yours! Our fuel, our supplies, our
people even, if you need them, are yours! We ask your submarines to
remain with us, Mr. President! You are our guests, Mr. President, your
submarines, your airplanes, your troops, whatever! They are all our
guests and we are proud to have them. *Nuestro casa es su casa!* Cuba and
the great Soviet people, forever! Communist solidarity forever! *Viva!
Viva!*"

And now not only many of the press but the enormous crowd that had
steadily grown beyond the police barricades that held them back a safe
quarter of a mile away were screaming with excitement and the world was
splitting with sound to the glory of Yuri Pavlovich and his servant in the
final decisive battle.

It went on for quite some time—almost ten minutes, the more objective
American reporters clocked it—before the Soviet President returned to
the podium. Once again he and his Cuban vassal solemnly embraced.
Then he held up his hand and a universal silence fell.

"Mr. President," he said solemnly, "as I wrote you in reply to your letter a week ago, the Soviet Union accepts with a feeling of great pride and
honor your invitation to assist Cuba in defending itself against the vicious
imperialist, anti-democratic designs of the new President of the United
States. We accept your invitation, issued freely as a sovereign act of a
sovereign state, that we station in your waters as many submarines as you
and we may deem sufficient to meet the vicious American threat. We will
always defend Cuba, Mr. President! We will always accept your freely uttered sovereign appeal for help! We will never abandon you! We will never
permit the dastardly schemes of the United States against Cuba to be put
into effect! Our submarines are here at your sovereign invitation for the
protection of Cuba *and—here—they—will—remain!*"

Again a great shout greeted his words. He let it run on with obvious
satisfaction, nodding and smiling. Then he raised a solemn hand and silence abruptly fell.

"However," he said, his tone now bland and reasonable, "we would not
want our good friend, the new President of the United States, to think
that this is done in any spirit of hostility toward him and his country. We
intend to continue our maneuvers just as we have planned them, and to
incorporate in them whatever movements of our submarines we may
deem advisable under all the circumstances. These decisions are irrevocable and no threats from outsiders can stop them. But we do not do so
in any spirit of hostility toward the United States. On the contrary, we

want to issue a formal invitation ourselves, and I now do it in the presence of all these witnesses:

"If there really are serious differences at the moment between the Soviet Government and the Cuban Government on the one hand, and the Government of the United States of America on the other, then His Excellency and I would be very happy to meet here in Havana with the President of the United States to discuss such differences and attempt to settle them.

"The President of the United States several days ago persuaded some other heads of state to request himself and myself to hold such a meeting in Geneva. For various appropriate reasons I rejected a meeting in that time and place. But now that I am here in Havana I am quite prepared to remain for as long as necessary if the President wishes to fly down for a meeting. It is only three hours or so, as you all experienced this morning. It can easily be done.

"The Soviet Government and the Government of Cuba would be more than happy to welcome the President immediately to Havana for this purpose. We join in issuing him this invitation here and now, and we await with hope and eagerness what we are sure will be his favorable and immediate reply."

Again a great surge of applause, laughter, shouts, approval.

"Ladies and gentlemen," he suggested, "why don't you join us in waiting for the President's reply? If the answer is yes, then the Cuban Government will of course immediately provide sufficient housing so that you may remain overnight and for as long as the Havana Conference continues. If the answer is no, then you will be taken back to your aircraft and may depart as scheduled for Washington."

There was general applause and as it died down some voice from the American sector shouted, "Where's the press conference? How about some questions?"

"The press conference is finished, ladies and gentlemen," Yuri Serapin said blandly. "Now we move on to the Havana Conference. Let us await the reply of the President of the United States."

There were sudden groans, catcalls, hostile yells from the area behind the communist bloc; but before they had time to coalesce into a really impressive roar of disapproval, the Cuban President leaped to his feet and began applauding. Obediently it was taken up by the communists in front, with countering shouts of approval and endorsement that effectively drowned out, at least for television purposes, the sharp disagreement in back. Eventually both sides abandoned the contest and settled down into a restless beehive of reporters getting up, stretching, using the temporary sanitary facilities on each side of the lawn, wandering around to talk to friends, gossiping and joking to pass the time.

And the time did pass. An hour of it, then another, then the start of another, while Yuri and his Cuban satellite sat on the platform and appeared to be exchanging amusing pleasantries without a care in the world. Two and half hours after Yuri's challenge a uniformed Cuban military aide dashed out of the mansion, raced up onto the platform, leaned down and blurted a breathless message.

For a moment the two leaders looked angry and upset, then there was a quick exchange; Yuri shrugged, got up and went to the microphone. Everyone froze. Absolute silence settled instantly over all.

"Ladies and gentlemen," he said, "the President of the United States is ready to reply, but he has requested that his answer be broadcast over these same microphones. It will take the technicians perhaps fifteen minutes to set this up. Please give us your kind patience for that time."

And he and his Cuban puppet left the platform at last to return to the palace and take care of their own needs, which for the past two hours, at least, had been a matter of much speculation in a bored press group without much else to talk about. They were back in ten minutes. A tense silence settled gradually again over the group as tropical twilight plunged abruptly into night and lights went on all around the area.

There were sudden squeakings, cracklings, other familiar sounds of technical equipment warming up. Someone said (it took them a startled moment to realize that it was the President himself), "Testing, one, two, three. Testing, one, two, three. Can you hear me, Havana?"

Again Yuri stepped to the microphones and replied politely, "You are coming through clearly, Mr. President."

"Thank you, Mr. President," Ham Delbacher said with equal politeness, his voice booming out across the silent crowd. "Your embassy here has finally delivered the formal version of your invitation, which has delayed me somewhat in replying. Also, I have been meeting for most of the afternoon with the Secretary of Defense and the Joint Chiefs of Staff and have not been free to give full attention to your proposal . . .

"Let me put my answer very simply, gentlemen: I can see no purpose to be served by such a conference. Accordingly I shall not come to Havana."

A great wave of boos and hisses arose, unanimously from the communist group, with less unanimity but considerable vehemence from some of his countrymen and many of their European and Asian colleagues. He continued unperturbed.

"If this were anything but an enormous propaganda extravaganza—and I do congratulate you upon its cleverness, gentlemen—then there might be some remotest chance that I would consider dignifying it as a serious proceeding by coming down. But obviously it is not such a serious proceeding. And obviously my presence would only be used to twist further and further obscure the legitimate purposes of the United States in objecting to the very clear and present danger to its interests and physical safety posed by your concentration of missile-carrying submarines in Cuban waters. No amount of pseudo-legitimacy gained by an ex post facto charade of invitation and acceptance can obscure that plain and simple fact.

"Incidentally, I might add that the emplacements of all your missiles on the territory of your Cuban satellite are known to us and as of this afternoon are now targeted and in our computers."

There was a gasp from the media, a sudden angry hardening of expression on the part of the Soviet President.

"I repeat what I said in my letter to you yesterday. Your concentration of submarines in Cuban waters is unacceptable to the United States. Immediate, widespread and unfortunate consequences will ensue very shortly unless they are removed."

["From 'could' to 'will,'" the New York *Times* noted. "He's getting tougher."]

"In the meantime, I have just issued an executive order declaring the United States in a state of national emergency and putting its armed forces on immediate full war alert."

Again the gasp, this time genuinely alarmed: they were finally beginning to take him seriously. Yuri and his Cuban errand boy exchanged furious looks and through many an American mind in the press corps shot the sudden worried thought: *Am I going to get home safely?* Followed by: *Hadn't we better get the hell out of here?*

"I appreciate your invitation, for it has given me the opportunity to again make the position of the United States clear before the same worldwide audience you have been entertaining this evening. But it has in no way altered my determination that this open threat to the United States and to world peace must be removed.

"Good night."

There was a decisive click! and he was gone. Immediately the press from Washington began to move hastily toward the staging area where the ancient Cuban buses were parked. As they did so, Yuri's Cuban lackey jumped up and literally leaped to the microphones. The last thing they heard as they crowded into the buses and urged the drivers to "Go like hell!" back to the airport was an almost incoherent string of obscenities and raving invective, punctuated at frequent intervals by the screaming promise, "You will pay for this, arrogant America! You will pay for this!"

Within forty-five minutes they were safely airborne and swinging north out of Cuban air space. The moment the last of their convoy lifted off the Ilyushin followed. Everybody was going home after the great extravaganza. Yuri Serapin said nothing to anyone but his expression was such as to make everyone in his party speak in whispers and tiptoe fearfully about the plane.

5

"*Détente creates a much more favorable international setting for each of the three revolutionary streams of our day—world socialism, the international working-class movement and the national liberation revolution—to achieve their goals . . . Détente is not only a* political *but also a* social *factor characterizing a new and important stage in the anti-imperialist struggle the world over.*"

—*International Affairs,* Vadim Kortunov,
May 1979

For the first hour of the flight to Moscow, he simply sat at his desk in the lavishly furnished executive cabin and stared out into the darkness over the Atlantic without any particular cohesion of thought or emotion. He had expected H. Delbacher to reject the invitation to Havana—in fact he had produced the idea of the invitation, completely on the spur of the moment, precisely so that H. Delbacher *would* reject it —but once again he had been unprepared for the defiant vigor of H. Delbacher's response. The man spoke as though he still commanded forces equal to, if not greater than, Yuri's own: and they both knew this was nonsense. He gave no indication of being a hesitant man or a frightened man or a man who had any intention whatsoever of yielding to obvious Soviet superiority. He acted, in fact, like a man who was both defiant and contemptuous of that superiority. It was the latter that particularly annoyed the Soviet President. Yet he knew that he must under no circumstances give way to his annoyance, or the great over-all master plan whose success was so crucial could easily be thrown off schedule. The consequences could be very serious for the planned conclusion of the final battle.

After an hour they brought him an excellent meal, which he found himself consuming with relish and a swiftly returning certainty. As soon as it had been cleared away he opened a briefcase, took out paper and pen and began to write. Half an hour later he punched the buzzer, a secretary hurried in and said, "Yes, Comrade President?" in a deeply respectful voice.

"Transcribe this immediately and bring it back."

"Yes, Comrade President! At once!"

Twenty minutes later she was back with it, neatly typed. He went over it slowly, making a handful of minor corrections while she stood at attention by the door. Then he looked up, smiled and nodded.

"Excellent, comrade. I want this radioed at once to *Tass* for immediate release to all information organs of the Motherland and to all foreign correspondents. Tell the radio officer to make it clear transmission in English, no code. And repeat twice."

"At once, Comrade President!" she said, saluted smartly and stepped out, closing the door carefully. Yuri touched another button to connect the plane's powerful transmission system to the cabin and sat back to stare out again at the darkness. In a moment the radio officer's slow, careful voice came over the intercom.

"'The President of the Soviet Union, acting with the complete agreement of the Politburo, deplores and deeply regrets the action of the President of the United States in summarily rejecting the proposal for a Havana Conference on the problems troubling relations between our two countries.

"'This invitation was issued in good faith by the President of the Soviet Union and the President of Cuba because the President of the United States had appeared to be unduly agitated by the presence of Soviet submarines in Cuban waters in connection with current Soviet maneuvers. Both the Soviet and Cuban Presidents made it quite clear at their joint press conference that these submarines are in Cuban waters solely and simply because Cuba requested Soviet protection against plans of the United States to launch a sneak attack upon Cuba. In the full spirit of socialist solidarity, the Soviet Union has responded with adequate forces to guarantee Cuba's safety from this planned imperialist blow to world peace.

"'Nonetheless, though he is the guilty party in this matter, the President of the United States saw fit to pretend in his statement of two days ago that the Soviet Union in the dispatch of these forces was somehow threatening or planning to threaten something of danger to the safety of the United States. How could this be, when it was the United States itself that was planning a sneak attack upon Cuba? The Soviet Union and Cuba wisely and correctly ignored the false protest of the President of the United States.

"'However, since the world desperately desires peace and since the President of the United States persists in misrepresenting Soviet intentions during current maneuvers, such agitation being itself a threat to world peace on his part, it seemed prudent and sensible for the President of the Soviet Union and the President of Cuba to seek a face-to-face meeting to try to set his foolish fears at rest. We also wished to settle any

other outstanding grievances, including his ridiculous fear of Soviet submarines in Cuban waters, even though they are there at the invitation of
the Cuban Government to protect it from the unwarranted designs of the
United States. Cuba is a sovereign power which has every right to issue
such an invitation to its long-time close ally and friend, the Soviet Union.
The Soviet Union is a sovereign power which has every right to accept
such an invitation. False, war-mongering, imperialist statements by the
President of the United States cannot change these facts known to all the
world.

" 'The President of the Soviet Union and the President of Cuba regret
with all our hearts the obstinate, irrational, peace-defying stand of the
President of the United States. Again he threatened "immediate, widespread and unfortunate consequences" if the submarines are not removed
from Cuban waters. They are there strictly for the protection of Cuba
against American adventurism. No threat is posed or has been uttered
against the United States by their presence, nor will it be. When the
threat to Cuba from the United States has subsided, they will be withdrawn.

" 'Until then, they will remain.

" 'In the meantime, the invitation to the President of the United States
to meet with the President of the Soviet Union and the President of Cuba
remains open. The President of the Soviet Union is prepared to return to
Havana at any time the President of the United States wishes to abandon
his false, war-mongering statements and decides to work for peace, as his
own people and the whole world desperately wish him to do.' "

The radio officer's level voice paused for exactly two minutes and then
began the first repeat.

And that, my friend, Yuri thought savagely, ought to give you a few
things to think about and a few more little problems to contend with.
You are of course entirely right as we both know, but I think this will assist your people in deciding that you are not.

And that, to considerable degree, was exactly what happened; though
on Capitol Hill the President seemed to be gaining some ground in his
own educational efforts.

The first headlines belonged to the President:
**PRESIDENT PUTS U.S. ON FULL EMERGENCY WAR ALERT,
INSISTS SOVIET SUBS LEAVE CUBA. REJECTS HAVANA SUM-
MIT, SAYS U.S. HAS RED MISSILES ON ISLAND "TARGETED."**
Within two hours he was relegated, if not to second place at least to
equal billing with Yuri's dramatic message from the skies:
U.S. ON FULL WAR ALERT AS SERAPIN DENOUNCES DEL-

BACHER REFUSAL TO MEET IN HAVANA. RED LEADER SAYS
SUBS WILL REMAIN IN CUBA. LEAVES SUMMIT DOOR OPEN,
URGES PRESIDENT STOP "WAR-MONGERING," WORK FOR
PEACE. DELBACHER HINTS SOVIET MISSILES MIGHT BE HIT.

Predictably, as Yuri had planned and intended, H. Delbacher's countrymen were heard from, in full voice.

Editorials in the major morning newspapers throughout the country
were almost unanimous in giving strong if occasionally rather indirect
support to Yuri's "war-mongering" denunciation.

"We cannot entirely endorse," said the Washington *Post,* symbolizing
the lot, "Soviet President Serapin's charge that President Delbacher is
'war-mongering' when he complains of the presence of an unusual number of Soviet missile-carrying submarines in Cuban waters. Nor, equally,
can we agree with President Delbacher when he issues a virtual ultimatum that the subs must go and simultaneously puts this nation and its
armed forces on a national emergency war footing.

"Both Presidents appear to us to be overreacting to the general sense of
crisis that seems to have swirled up around the worldwide Soviet maneuvers. Explanations of the crisis depend on which President one listens to.
Each is understandably intent upon blaming the other. Without taking
sides or presuming to judge one way or the other, we cannot help but
conclude that American hysteria may just possibly have done a little
more than Soviet heavy-handedness to inflame the situation. In that light,
President Delbacher's latest actions would seem to be a quite legitimate
excuse for the harsh language President Serapin has used to characterize
them.

"Whether Mr. Delbacher can be justly accused of actual 'war-mongering' is a matter, it seems to us, for the historians to decide. Yet it must in
all fairness be said that he has summarily dismissed the fact that the
Cuban Government did, indeed, invite the Soviet submarines to rendezvous off the island. Cuba's fears of a 'planned American attack' may be
exaggerated—although it is certainly no secret that the Pentagon has had
such plans, on the customary contingency basis, ever since the current
Cuban regime came to power—but nonetheless they seem to be real
enough to the Cubans. It should therefore come as no surprise to Washington if Cuba calls upon its huge patron for help. It is a perfectly natural
response to what is seen as permanent American hostility. Certainly the
President's statements in recent days have done nothing to lessen this
Cuban impression.

"As for Mr. Delbacher's ultimatum—he seems to be employing a lot of
them, these days—to the Soviets to withdraw their subs or suffer 'immedi-

ate, widespread and unfortunate consequences,' we might venture to suggest that ultimata very soon lose their effect if no one follows through on them—and if, in reality, there is very little with which to follow through on them. Both as Senator and as Vice President, Mr. Delbacher was very critical of taking strong stands without the wherewithal to back them up. To be fair to his consistency, he also constantly advocated building up the wherewithal at the earliest possible moment. But since this was not done to any great degree by his recent predecessors and their Congresses, then we would suggest the better part of valor at the moment would be a return to traditional diplomacy—a return, if you please, even to Havana, abhorrent as that seems to be to Mr. Delbacher.

"Little is to be gained by ranting and railing at the Soviet Union from a position of comparative weakness. We learned under Mr. Carter that such schoolmarmish tactics did not work in Ethiopia, Angola, South Yemen, Afghanistan, and Cuba itself during the so-called 'Soviet brigade crisis.' A lot of preaching was done but, lacking the sticks and stones to back them up, the pious words that came out of the White House never hurt the Soviet Union's bones. It went right ahead doing exactly what it had planned to do.

"We do agree with Mr. Delbacher that the subs in Cuban waters are part of a plan—the Soviets do nothing without one. But lacking sure proof that the plan is to use them against the United States, and apparently lacking the means to force their withdrawal without plunging the world immediately into war, we are afraid we must join President Serapin in suggesting that Mr. Delbacher tone down the threats and give serious thought to reappraising his curt and, we think, counter-productive dismissal of the Havana summit."

With very few exceptions, this was the general tenor of news stories and editorials, TV and radio commentaries, across the nation. They were supported by mass demonstrations, some few spontaneous, the rest inspired and arranged by various Soviet apologists and active Soviet friends, on a dozen major campuses. A full-page ad blossomed overnight in the New York *Times,* the Washington *Post,* the Washington *Inquirer,* the Chicago *Tribune,* the L. A. *Times.* Organized by Hollywood's most talented and most scatter-brained activist, it carefully ignored all other aspects of the crisis and devoted itself to admonishing HANDS OFF CUBA, MR. PRESIDENT! One hundred of Hollywood's most self-righteous and self-conscious added their well-informed, intelligent endorsements. And from certain unctuous academicians, famously smug and enlightened theologians, and the customary excruciatingly "liberal" fringe whose members will go to the Gulag still protesting the Soviet Union's gentle decency and tender love for humankind, there came the usual frantic interviews and condemnatory statements.

From overseas also, particularly from the NATO allies and from

France, hitherto aloof but finally deciding to play her usual wrecker's role, came statements of concern, alarm and criticism of the President's course. Several Asian allies also expressed cautious but profound misgivings. Only the People's Republic of China, cheerfully watching, issued a wholly benign statement praising "the courage and foresight of the American President as he struggles valiantly to defeat the imperialist hegemonists of the Soviet Union."

By twelve noon when the Senate convened, everybody was well primed for a knock-down, drag-out on the crisis that seemed to have increased dramatically in the past two days.

"Senators," James Monroe Madison said earnestly to his hushed and attentive colleagues, "it is with great regret that I call up the sense-of-the-Senate resolution I introduced two days ago and ask for its immediate consideration. But events of the past forty-eight hours have moved so swiftly, and the threat to world peace has escalated so fast, that I think for the sake of the country and the world we must make some attempt here in the Congress to urge the President to follow a more peaceable and constructive course."

"If the Senator will yield," Art Hampton, the Majority Leader, interrupted, "could he tell the Senate why he is not addressing his appeal at least equally to the President of the Soviet Union?"

"Well," Jim Madison said, sounding somewhat flustered. "Well. The Senator knows that our responsibility rests with the United States, does he not?"

"And the Senator knows very well that other appeals have been addressed to the Soviet Union, does he not?" Art inquired.

"Yes, I know that, Senator."

"And he knows they have always been completely ignored, does he not?"

"Yes!" Senator Madison admitted grumpily.

"So really he isn't addressing the Soviet Union because he knows it's useless, whereas addressing the President of the United States will at least embarrass the President, right?"

"Now, Mr. President," Jim Madison said indignantly, addressing Kal Tokumatsu of Hawaii, who happened to be occupying the chair, "I don't like that implication on the part of the distinguished Majority Leader. It is not my purpose to embarrass our great President. It is my purpose to help him restrain what seem to be his impulses to take a perhaps unnecessarily harsh tone toward the Soviet Union."

"Mr. President," Mark Coffin said, "if my able senior colleague from California will yield, has it occurred to him that the President may have information unknown to us which prompts him to feel that a stern and unyielding tone is not only necessary but absolutely vital if the Soviet Union is to be deflected from a course that poses great dangers to world peace?"

"It seems to me," Jim Madison said, "that the President has been very open about his reasons for acting as he has every step of the way."

"Then how can you condemn him for the way he has handled it, Senator?" Mark asked with some asperity. "If he has been that frank with the country, then certainly we probably know just about as much as he does. And doesn't it inspire you with small misgivings?"

"Now, Mr. President," Senator Madison said, "I also resent the remarks of my young colleague. Like everybody in America and everybody in this world—or the part we are associated with, anyway—I have plenty of misgivings. Plenty of misgivings! I only question the very frank and forthright, yes I might even say threatening, manner in which the President has seen fit to address the Soviet Union. It does not make for healing wounds or settling problems. I think you will concede that much, Senator."

"I concede that," Mark said, "but who said the Soviet Union has the slightest interest in healing wounds or settling problems? They profess to have, but they use language differently than we do—I've heard it called 'semantic infiltration' by some Sovietologists. 'People's republics' of course aren't people's republics, 'people's democracy' means the dictatorship of the Politburo and its leader, 'peace' means war, 'war'—if they win it—means peace to them, and so on. Sure, they'll heal wounds—their way—and they'll settle problems—their way. They'll spout 'co-existence' and 'détente' but to them the words mean 'doing it our way, deciding things on our terms.' 'Détente' is simply another means of winning, to them, and they say so with complete candor. We in the West persist in using words in the peace-hoping sense that we've been brought up to use them. We *must* understand that to the Soviets' they usually mean exactly the opposite. And they *always* mean: *to the Soviets' benefit and contributing to the Soviets' eventual triumph.* That basic meaning never changes. So I ask the Senator, why not be tough? They never yet have been deflected one iota in almost seventy years by any soft diplomatic words from us."

"If you are right, Senator," Jim Madison said soberly, "you open up a ghastly prospect for the United States and the world."

"*I* open it up!" Mark exclaimed. "*They* opened it up almost seventy years ago and absolutely nothing has changed their approach in all that time. Anybody who doesn't see that in the record is either unbelievably naïve or deliberately denying the facts."

"Mr. President," Clem Chisholm of Illinois said, "will the Senator yield?"

"My senior colleague has the floor," Mark said, "but if he doesn't mind—?"

"I yield sufficient time for the Senator from Illinois to conclude his interrogatory of the Senator from California," Jim Madison said and left his desk for a hurried and obvious trip to the men's room that produced a small titter from the crowded galleries.

"Mr. President," Clem said, handsome black face earnest and intent. "I find all this, coming from the junior Senator from California, very puzzling. I remember when he first came into this Senate three years ago, there wasn't a more determined opponent of excessive war spending and big-stick carrying than he was. Now he seems to be switching over pretty fast to the other side. I wonder if the Senator has any explanation he might enlighten us with?"

"I thought a Senator always had the privilege of changing his mind and his vote," Mark said with a smile at this old friend. "Sometimes one, sometimes the other and sometimes both together at one and the same moment . . . Seriously, I'll say to the Senator that I have simply become convinced, the longer I stay here and the more information I get about the Soviets, that they are up to no good and never have been. I've had time to study the record pretty closely and that's what it says. So I've changed. I don't apologize for what I believed then when I was relatively uninformed, or for what I believe now when I know considerably more. I'm sorry to part company with my old friend, but I don't honestly feel I have any other choice. Particularly in the last week or so, when the situation precipitated by the Soviet maneuvers has brought a lot of things to a head."

"Mr. President," Clem said, "I am not an apologist for the Soviet Union, but I do recall that the President came roaring home from his meeting with President Serapin in New York to put into effect immediately the emergency $10 billion fund, the so-called Elrod bill, which was passed here three years ago. This was followed by the activating of Soviet plans for worldwide military maneuvers, which now agitate everyone so. The American egg, you might say, hatched out the Soviet chicken. I cannot entirely blame Mr. Serapin for reacting as he did under the circumstances, just as I find it a little hard to view the Soviet maneuvers with quite the same alarm as seems to agitate Mr. Delbacher. We have had a 'sneak attack' scare, now we are having a 'Soviet subs in Cuba' scare. The first didn't come to much and I don't think the other will either. Therefore I'm inclined to vote for the resolution of our good friend the senior Senator from California."

"If the Senator will yield," Mark said patiently, "has it occurred to him that just possibly the sneak attack did not occur for the very reason that the President did make such a public issue of it? And that if the Soviet Union has had plans to use the unusual concentration of missile-carrying subs in Cuban waters—and these aren't toys, as the Senator knows, they are monstrously lethal weapons, far more than enough to vaporize instantaneously all the main population centers of the United States in a single co-ordinated attack that would be over in ten minutes—it may perhaps have had to change or at least delay those plans because the President is making such a public issue of them? I grant you they may still try to use them, either in open attack or as a blackmail weapon to force us to surrender, but at least the President has bought precious time, it seems to me."

"You don't have to grant me that they may use them that way, Senator," Clem said with a smile, "because I don't think they will. Have you had reason to think that this is their intention? Perhaps you know things we don't know."

"Not really," Mark said. "The President has pretty well laid it all out, it seems to me. Even Senator Madison concedes that. It comes down to interpretation of motives, and in interpreting motives one has to look at stated intentions and past record. When the record and the statements coincide exactly, as they have for almost seventy years, then it seems reasonable that one can proceed on the assumption that they will continue to do so."

"Not necessarily," Clem objected. "People change."

"Not those people," Mark retorted. "They never have and they never intend to. And this they tell us every day of their lives, and it must be as baffling to them as it is to some of us, why so many Americans refuse to admit it to themselves. It's all right there on the record for the world to see."

"In any event, if the Senator will yield," Art Hampton said, "there is no doubt whatsoever that the President will be seriously handicapped and hindered in dealing with them if the Senate is so foolish as to pass any kind of resolution criticizing or opposing him. Isn't that true?"

"In my estimation," Mark said, "it will most severely handicap him. The Soviet leadership presents a monolithic front to the world because it *is* monolithic—there is no democracy, no public opinion, no voice other than the Kremlin's. It is hard enough for an American President to deal with this without being hamstrung by opposition on the Hill. At this very tense moment he really does need our help. I would suggest to my distinguished colleague from California—whom I see just returning from his telephone call"—there was another wave of laughter and Jim Madison, re-entering the chamber, stopped dead and blushed to the crown of his bald head—"that he has plenty of channels, just as all members of Congress do, through which to make his views known to the President. He does not need to make a public issue of it through a resolution of the Senate. Even if defeated, as I think it would be—it would bring great cries from our own media and the world at large about how divided we are."

"Mr. President," Senator Madison said, "if I may reclaim the floor, which I think still belongs to me, let me ask my colleague, doesn't he think we *are* divided?"

"Certainly," Mark agreed, "but not as much by any means as a resolution passed here would tend to indicate to the world. I really do appeal to my colleague to withdraw it. It would just make mischief."

"It is not my intention to 'just make mischief,'" James Monroe Madison said stiffly. "It is my intention to restrain what seems to be the President's tendency to use big-stick diplomacy when really the stick we have isn't all that big. I think it's big enough, you understand," he added hastily, "to withstand anything the Soviets can bring to bear against us, but I don't think it's big enough to warrant this kind of—of—well, war-mongering."

"Score another for Yuri Serapin," Mark said dryly. "He's added something to the current vocabulary, I can see that. You have known Ham Delbacher for thirty years, Senator, and you know he's no war-monger. Firm in his approach to them, yes, but no war-monger. But you *have* to be firm with these people. It's the only thing they'll listen to."

"Nonetheless—" Jim Madison began stubbornly, but Jim Elrod interrupted before he could get into full oratorical flight.

"Let me ask the Senator, does he or does he not think we are in a very serious, very tense situation at this moment?"

"Why, yes, obviously I do," Senator Madison said.

"Then why," Senator Elrod demanded, "does the Senator wish to make it infinitely worse for all of us by tryin' to stab the President in the back?"

"Mr. *President!*" Jim Madison cried in startled indignation. "How *dare* my old friend from North Carolina use such a term to me? *I* don't wish to stab the President in the back—"

"Just tie him up, put a gag in his mouth and toss him in the Potomac," Jim Elrod said. "That's all the senior Senator from California wants to do. I agree with the Senator's colleague that it would be mighty helpful to the President and the general welfare of the United States if he would withdraw his pernicious resolution. It would really be a great help, Senator."

"It isn't pernicious," Jim Madison insisted. "It just makes sense that we urge him not to make a bad situation worse by issuing inflammatory denunciations and threats he probably doesn't intend to, or isn't able to, carry out."

"I think if he's able to, he will," Senator Elrod said. "You know him, Senator."

"Yes," Jim Madison said spitefully, "and that's what scares me."

"It does me too," Clem Chisholm agreed. "And I think a good many on this floor."

But when the vote came finally, shortly after 8 P.M., Jim Madison's resolution was defeated 62–37. It was obvious from the heated debate that continued all afternoon, however, that many of the favoring votes were responses to the traditional appeal to "stand by the President." Many who voted for the resolution expressed their misgivings about the President's course quite freely even though in the end they voted for him. It was a halfhearted endorsement at best, and although the White House issued no statement one way or the other, Art Hampton, Minority Leader Herb Esplin of Ohio, Jim Elrod, Jim Madison, Mark and Clem found a White House limousine waiting for them when the session ended. Twenty minutes later they were in the Oval Office facing a puzzled, annoyed but still determined President.

"Thanks for coming down," he said when they were all comfortably seated, drinks in hand, in the overstuffed chairs that formed a casual circle in one corner of the room. "Apparently I need enlightenment. I didn't listen to all the debate, but from what I heard there's some attempt to portray me as out of step with the Hill and the country. Am I really? Would you all rather I stopped sounding firm and started sounding meek and humble instead? Am I all wrong? Jim Madison? Clem?"

"Well," Jim Madison said uncomfortably, "I wouldn't go so far as to say you're all *wrong,* Mr. President, but—"

Ham Delbacher snorted.

"You couldn't have been much more specific. Was the resolution just your idea or are you getting any real backlash from the country? Clem?"

"I'm getting quite a bit," Clem said thoughtfully. "I wouldn't say it's exactly opposed to you, but people have great misgivings—not so much about standing up to the Soviets as about the methods you're using. There's a small but powerful minority left, of course, that can always excuse anything the Soviets do, but I'm speaking of the great majority who don't like them, who are afraid of them, but who seem to be fearful—as, frankly, I am—that by taking such an extremely strong stand, you may be risking an increase in pressure from them or even an outright confrontation. Nobody wants that."

"That's right," Jim Madison agreed.

"That's right," the President agreed. "But do you really think the strength of tone or the degree of opposition is going to make that much change in their plans? These people, as I told the Congress when I came back from New York, are literally bent upon the conquest of the world. They say so and they act so, and they have with increasing vigor ever since World War II without the slightest change in plan, purpose or performance. The alternative to standing up to them is to knuckle under to them. And that literally means the end of the United States and with it all that remains of human freedom in the world. The slaughterers of Afghanistan, Hungary, Czechoslovakia—and their own people—are not going to stop at any halfway measures. Yuri Serapin boasted to me that no country captured by communism has ever successfully broken free—there are just too many modern means of keeping them subjugated, starting with the murder of all their leaders, all their intellectuals, their press, all elements of any kind who might conceivably mount resistance or a successful insurrection. He boasted about their use of poison gas in Cambodia and Afghanistan and indicated it would be used upon us and anybody else who gets in the way, if necessary. *These are really not nice people,* gentlemen. They're as monstrous as Hitler and they're out to win. And you want me to act as though I were afraid of them! Get yourselves another President, someone who can surrender America gracefully. I can't."

"Nobody wants to surrender America, Mr. President," Clem Chisholm said mildly. "But is it that much of an either/or proposition?"

"Yes!" Ham Delbacher exclaimed. "For God's sake, *yes!"*

"In your opinion," Jim Madison said smugly. The President threw up his hands and shook his head in angry disbelief.

"In the opinion of everyone who isn't afraid to look at the record and the written philosophy of government, foreign policy and human oppression that backs it up," he said. "That's all."

There was a silence, broken finally by Herb Esplin.

"I think maybe the problem is, Ham—Mr. President," he said, "that while a lot of people agree with you, basically, they believe it can be solved without having to come to a direct confrontation that could mean world war and with it the destruction of everything."

"Includin', of course, the Soviets," Jim Elrod said, "though they're such monumental egomaniacs that they manage to convince themselves they'd survive. But I still think it's true what somebody said about 'em, that they want all the spoils of war without havin' to fight a war to get 'em."

"As many of us," Art Hampton said quietly, "want all the blessings of peace without having to make the sacrifices necessary to preserve peace. . . . I think you're in good shape, Mr. President, both in the country and on the Hill, despite the debate today. The end result is what counts and you won overwhelmingly. I'd ignore the debate and proceed as you're doing, if I were you."

"It's foolhardy," Senator Madison said stoutly. "I agree with you we shouldn't 'knuckle under' to them or 'surrender' to them, or any other of those pejorative terms you use in defense of your own position. Of course not! But I still think you can be less blunt, less hostile, less provocative, less—inviting of reprisals."

"You can be firm without issuing ultimatums," Clem Chisholm said.

"How?" Mark demanded. "How can he do that? If he wants to tell them he'll knock their blocks off if they don't behave, what can he say except that he'll knock their blocks off if they don't behave? 'Tut, tut!' and hit them with a wet noodle? I mean, after all, Clem, these are not history's most subtle people and the challenge they're presenting to us— openly, at last—is not a very subtle challenge. All they understand is strength."

"And we don't have much," Herb Esplin said softly.

"No," the President said, "that's right. But I sure as hell had rather sound as though I had strength than sound like some little two-bit weakling country with nothing to back me up. We may be behind at the moment in some things but we have considerable punch even so and I'm not going to sound or act as though we don't have any. You remember how it was back in the Fifties when the situation was reversed and they were behind. They boasted and threatened and shouted and bellowed every hour on the hour about how tough they were and what they were going to do to us if we overstepped the bounds. We're a lot stronger now than they were then, and in another two or three years"—he shook his head— "God! Two or three years!—we'll be back on a fairly equal footing with them. In the meantime, while I believe in being candid about it in sufficient degree to give the country the sense that it's really threatened— which it has to feel in order to get really cranked up again—I don't think it does any good to be too humble either. That's the last way to be successful in handling them, it seems to me."

"So you really called us down here," Clem suggested with a smile, "to convince yourself that what you're doing is quite O.K. Isn't that right?"

"Maybe," the President admitted cheerfully, "but then again, maybe not. I really would like your alternatives, if you have any. Tell me what I should do differently. I'm open to suggestions, Clem. And Jim Madison? What would you have me do?"

"Cool it a little," Clem said. "Instead of saying something is 'unacceptable,' say it 'causes serious concern' or 'great concern' or something like that. Instead of demanding withdrawal of the subs and threatening 'immediate, widespread and extensive consequences' if they aren't withdrawn, maybe something like 'consequences that could be disastrous for everyone' or words to that effect."

"In other words," the President said, "—words."

"Right," Clem agreed. "Words."

Again there was a silence while they all thought about this; but the President's basic expression remained stubborn and unconvinced.

"I don't believe they understand those kinds of words," he said finally, "I really don't. I think they've reached a point in their continuing build-up at which they aren't even listening to words unless they're shouted at them. And they have to be tough words, not gentle ones."

"I didn't say gentle," Clem objected mildly. "Just firm. Otherwise you give Serapin all the propaganda advantage. People want gentle words, you see. They may want to know something tough is underneath but they're scared to death of having to face right up to it."

"Facing right up to it," Ham Delbacher said grimly, "is what they have to do, nonetheless. I could talk softly, all right; I haven't been in public life for as long as I have without learning how. But I'm convinced that not only would that not impress the Soviets, it would also further encourage the American people to kid themselves a while longer; and the time for kidding ourselves is all gone, now. There just isn't any more of it left."

"So what will you do about the Soviet subs in Cuba?" Herb Esplin asked quietly, "which is still the question of the moment, after all?"

"What can he do?" Senator Madison demanded.

"More than you think, Jim," the President said. "Something that will absolutely horrify you, no doubt. Don't you think you'd better hustle up another resolution?"

"If necessary," Jim Madison said with dignity. "If necessary."

"Mmhmm. Well: one thing you can be sure of: there will be a response from me to his response. We've simply got to get those things out of there. They and the missiles that have been on the island all these years are directed straight at our jugular. The two together are 'decisive'—as they love to say—ten times over, as far as we're concerned. We can't fool around with them any longer."

"And how will you get them out?" Senator Madison inquired with a heavy skepticism.

"Not by saying 'pretty please,'" the President shot back. "Not by saying 'pretty please.'"

But what he would say or do he did not enlighten them further, although they pressed him on it vigorously a while longer. All he would say was that he intended to see Secretary of Defense Hackett and the Joint Chiefs first thing tomorrow morning to "go over things" and then would have a statement.

"I'm having luncheon guests tomorrow, too, you know," he said. "Five hundred of the nation's top editors, publishers, news commentators— daily press, periodicals, networks—across the board. I thought it would be good p.r. to get them in here and explain my position to them on a more intimate basis. They love to be told how important they are, you know. We're setting up in the East Room. I think that would be the ideal audience for announcement of what I'm going to do about Cuba."

"Don't we get even a preview?" Art Hampton inquired.

"Not a word," the President responded.

"Maybe he doesn't know yet, do you suppose?" Herb Esplin asked with his customary puckish air.

"Maybe not entirely," the President said. "But it's shaping up."

Around eleven that night, going over the day's events with Elinor as had been their custom every night of their married life, he told her what he had in mind. She put down her book and looked at him with a genuine concern.

"You're taking a fearful chance, Ham. Are you sure—"

"Not sure of anything," he replied promptly. "Except that I have to keep going forward. There's no chance to stop, hesitate, look around or look back. However, El—you don't really think I'd do this if I believed there was the slightest chance it would really mean a war, do you?"

"What else can it mean?" she asked tartly, "I think you're stretching the word 'slightest,' as in 'slightest chance' just about as far as it can go, don't you? I think there's a terrifically good chance."

"No," he said soberly, "I don't think so. I just have a hunch that this isn't the time. For all his bluff and bluster, I don't think Yuri Serapin is quite ready yet. Maybe if I can keep him sufficiently off balance for a while, the time will come and go and he won't be able to seize it. That's my hope anyway."

"You're taking a fearful chance," she repeated soberly. "A fearful chance."

"What is this whole situation we're in but a series of fearful chances? You wouldn't want me to give in, would you?"

"You can't afford to give in."

"So—"

But next morning, of course, he found Roger Hackett and the JCS as doubtful and apprehensive as she: and their opposing arguments much more vigorous and specific, since, as Snooze Rydecker remarked, "Our necks will be right out there on the line, Mr. President—ours in the Navy most of all."

"You're still thinking in terms of World War II, fixed fronts, 'behind the lines' and all that crap," Bart Jamison of the Air Force told him bluntly. "That kind of war is gone forever between the superpowers."

"Exactly," the President agreed.

But it was at times a heavy argument before they got to that point.

It began over breakfast upstairs in the family dining room. They arrived exactly on the dot at eight-thirty, as requested, and were ushered up immediately. Elinor stayed long enough to have the first cup of coffee with them, then excused herself gracefully and departed.

"Keep this war-monger under control," she advised them lightly, and there was a moment's nervous laughter before they realized she was parodying Yuri Serapin, and let their laughter relax. She paused at the door to give them a cheerful smile and departing wave.

"He really is, you know," she said. "You'll find out."

And so they did, as he described for them what he wished to do and saw from their increasingly long faces that they had anticipated nothing like this. There was a long, thoughtful pause before anyone responded. It was Roger Hackett who spoke first.

"Mr. President," he said cautiously, "that is a rather strong reaction, is it not?"

"Strong as could be," he agreed cheerfully.

"And not one that leaves much room for maneuver," Bump Smith of the Army remarked.

"Or much chance to back out gracefully if they call our bluff," Gutsy Twitchell of the Marines agreed.

"And a very poor position to be in if your calculations suddenly fall apart and we have to put up or shut up," Smidge Hallowell, chairman of the JCS, added. "You're practically inviting war to begin, Mr. President. I'm not sure I could conscientiously support that."

"Nor I," said Admiral Rydecker for the Navy.

"Nor I," said General Jamison for the Air Force.

"Nor I," said the others in almost a single voice.

He looked thoughtfully from face to face.

"So we come down once again to how serious we think they are, and how much we believe what they say."

"Serious enough to put twenty-four subs into Cienfuegos," Snooze Rydecker said glumly. "That seems serious enough to me."

"Plus all the missiles, atomic warheads, neutron bombs, canisters of nerve gas, bacteriological toxins and other more conventional weapons they have there," General Smith said. "That island's so crammed with stuff it's a wonder it doesn't sink. That seems serious enough to me."

"To say nothing of the money it all cost," General Hallowell said. "A mighty big investment, for a bluff."

"Is it?" the President asked sharply. "Compared to the investment of actually fighting? Having it there for blackmail purposes is nothing compared to the cost of actually fighting a war. They'd be getting off cheap."

"Who's to fight?" General Twitchell inquired. "Who'd be left here after the first ten minutes? Cockroaches and horned toads, I'd say."

"That's assuming everything they sent got through," the President said, "and nothing we sent did the same. I'm not presupposing we'd do nothing, you know."

"We'd do what we could," General Jamison said, "and that would be plenty, at least as far as the Air Force is concerned."

"Well, the Navy, too, of course," Snooze Rydecker said somewhat stiffly, responding at once to this challenge from the Navy's eternal rival, more aggravating than any foreign antagonist.

"The Army wouldn't be exactly idle," Bump Smith said emphatically.

"The Marines would do superbly whatever is asked of them," Gutsy Twitchell pointed out matter-of-factly.

"Very commendable of you all," the President said with a smile, "and just what I'd expect. However, you still all have great misgivings as to whether we have the strength to do it, right?"

"Yes, Mr. President," Roger Hackett said firmly, "we do. And we thought you did, from previous conversations on the subject."

"Oh, I do," he admitted. "I haven't changed. Nothing yet would justify that."

"Then if you'll permit me, Mr. President," the Secretary of Defense said, "what has changed? Certainly not their strength, which is now upped to twenty-four subs. Certainly not ours, which isn't really upped by much of anything, as yet. I don't mean to be argumentative, but what exactly do you have in mind when you propose something as rough as this?"

"I have in mind the mind of a communist in Moscow. He has shown himself to be a very tough animal and a very great gambler . . . but not, I think, one quite yet bereft of all his senses. I believe that he's on the way; I think he's well along to becoming a megalomaniac as complete as Hitler or Attila the Hun. I think what we've all feared for years would happen in Moscow is happening: something's breaking inside the guy with his finger on the button. But I don't think he's there yet. I don't think he's quite sure yet that he's *really* got us where he wants us. He thinks he's almost there—but not quite, as I interpret him. Therefore it's bluff for bluff, will against will; and I don't doubt my own. We have nowhere else to go, gentlemen. Where's our alternative? If I don't stop this latest gamble then we *are* lost—you know that. You don't want me to back down. I *can't* back down. If I did we'd be beaten anyway; so what can I do but take a stand?"

"Moscow doesn't have the only great gambler," Smidge Hallowell murmured, but with a smile that saved him from insolence.

"And thank God for that," Bart Jamison said with sudden conviction. "Damned if we do, damned if we don't, so damn it, let's do *something*. I'm with you, Mr. President. The Air Force will do whatever we have to do. But maybe we won't have to do anything."

"Our necks will be right out there on the line if we do, Mr. President," Snooze Rydecker said. "Ours in the Navy most of all."

"You're still thinking in terms of World War II, fixed fronts, 'behind the lines' and all that crap," General Jamison said. "That kind of war is gone forever between the superpowers. The guy in Pocatello, Idaho, is as much on the front line as one of your wagons, Snooze, or one of my B-52s, or Bump's squadrons or Gutsy's platoons. Ain't no hidin' place down here, boy. We's all *it,* if it comes to that."

"Exactly," the President said. "Exactly. So—you're on full war alert. Theoretically, you're ready to meet whatever's coming—and I hope to God you are. Because I'm going to handle this as I've told you. Have I picked up any support but Bart?"

Again there was silence; again they looked to Roger Hackett to answer for them all.

"Theoretically, Mr. President, we're for your plan 100 per cent. Actually and in fact"—he smiled—"we're for *you* 100 per cent. If you do what you say you're going to do—and we believe you—most of us think the risks are enormous. On the other hand, as Bart says, and as you say, the risks of doing nothing are probably equally enormous. And as you and Bart believe, maybe the risks don't exist at all. Maybe it will work. Maybe your friend Yuri will back down." His face became more serious. "We can't stop you from trying it and it's our duty to back you with everything we've got. After all, you are the Commander-in-Chief."

"I'd rather not put it on that basis," Hamilton Delbacher said, "but, of course . . . that is the fact. As long as I can count on you, that's the important thing." He stood up. "Thanks for coming by. Have a good lunch, wish me luck with mine. I'm going to give my editors a lot to think about, too."

"I'm not going to eat lunch," Admiral Rydecker said with a rueful humor.

"What are you going to do, Snooze?" General Jamison asked as they shook hands with the President and started out.

"Ha," Snooze said. "I'm going back to the Pentagon and pray like hell."

And this, although he did not admit it to anyone but Elinor, was what Hamilton Delbacher did too for a few minutes after they left. There was a sudden rather strange pause in his day: everything became hushed. The phone did not ring, his secretary did not enter, nothing broke the silence of the big white room. He returned to his desk, sat down, dropped his head on his hands, realized suddenly how tired he really was from the combined physical and mental strain of recent days. At first he had to fight to clear his mind deliberately of all the frightening, nagging possibilities that kept pounding at it; then suddenly it was an utter blank; a great calm flooded in. As he had been taught to do on the farm so many years ago, he began to pray silently to a God who had never really failed him in times of crisis; for several minutes peace descended. . . . Then abruptly, the phone rang, the buzzers sounded, the world started up again and rushed forward; but inside, the peace remained. He was doing his best for a good people in a good cause; he was literally trying to save the world from the endless night of a universal communism hostile to every instinct of freedom and decency that lifted humanity above a mindless animalism. He could not be mistaken in this, or it was indeed the end of all.

He gathered his notes together, put them in his coat pocket, called his secretary to say he would be back at his desk by 2 P.M. and started walking slowly along toward the East Room. Two guards fell into step unobtrusively behind him. Thus escorted he went forth once more to contest with Yuri Pavlovich for control of the battle, and of the minds of men.

The East Room buzzed with earnest talk, subdued laughter, the clink of silverware and glass. Many faces he knew looked up at him where he sat in the center of the long table on the dais, flanked by suitable dignitaries. Five hundred of the media's finest, he thought wryly, most of them out to do him in politically and psychologically if they could. Here among them were the great rationalizers and excusers who had done so much to aid, with their unfailing skepticism, the rise of Soviet imperialism. Here were the powerful, the pompous and the portentous who, because they could not face the implications of what they had helped to create, turned with savage fury upon all who dared to point it out. Here were the genuine fools who did not see the facts, and the frightened clever who saw but deliberately denied them. Here were the creators of the slogan, "We cannot believe," which the President said should be on the coinage.

They believed now, most of them, but even in the midst of their fright and their terror, false and arrogant pride was still prompting many of them to deny it still. They will really believe it in a few more minutes, he told himself grimly; although, as usual, they will save face by turning their fury not upon the Soviets, who have caused it, but upon me, who am responding.

Because he knew so well, from so many lesser crises in the past, exactly what their reaction would be, he was less amicable and more terse than usual in his brief social exchanges with the publisher of the New York Times, on his right, and the president of NBC, on his left. They did not appear surprised by this, conceding that he did, indeed, have much on his mind these days. In any case, there was really only one vital topic to talk about, and since he could not be expected to discuss that until he addressed them all, there wasn't much to discuss anyway. The publisher of the New York *Times* ran through in five minutes his plans to make a "survey trip" of Western Europe next week—"Good luck," said Hamilton Delbacher— and the president of NBC outlined in five minutes his plans to fill his fall schedule with "more comedy and laughter—people want *fun,* nowadays" —"Yes," agreed Hamilton Delbacher, "it's a fun time, sure enough"— and after that, both fell silent. The President seemed not only preoccupied but almost hostile. They would show him when the time came, but for now they decided to hold their fire for the question-and-answer period they hoped would follow whatever he had to say. It couldn't be much— probably just another illogical defense of his own dangerously warlike policies. They ate heartily and prepared themselves, along with many of their colleagues in the room, to let him have it.

Forty-five minutes after they began eating the President turned to the publisher of the New York *Times* and asked, "Do you think we can begin now? I have a few things to say and then I expect you'll all want to cut me up into little pieces."

"Oh no, Mr. President," the New York *Times* responded, blushing a little in the face of this direct challenge. "I'm sure it won't go like that."

"Why don't you introduce me now?" the President said with a wry smile, "and we'll find out."

"Will you take questions after?"

"Oh yes. Until two o'clock, when I have to get back."

The New York *Times* got to his feet, rapped on his glass with a spoon. The East Room quieted abruptly.

"Ladies and gentlemen," he said, "colleagues: We meet in one of the gravest moments that has ever faced our country and thanks to the very generous invitation of the man on whose shoulders the burden mainly falls, we are privileged to be here to get his views firsthand. The President tells me that he will be happy to accept questions after he has made an opening statement, so you can be preparing some good ones for him. We all know from long experience that Hamilton Delbacher can handle them. Ladies and gentlemen, the President of the United States."

Then they were on their feet and for a few moments a real, emotional warmth and sympathy for him and his enormous burdens filled the room. The applause was genuine, the cries of encouragement were genuine. While it lasted, he and they were united against the common danger. Then the applause died down, they took their seats, the room became silent again. Bright, inquisitive, challenging, the media's finest remembered that they were supposed to maintain their self-created "adversary position" towards their President, and dared him to say a good word for himself.

"Ladies and gentlemen," he began slowly, adjusting his notes on the lectern that had been placed before him, "thank you for coming. I thought it might be of mutual value, in what our friend from the New York *Times* has correctly described as 'one of the gravest moments that has ever faced our country,' for us to meet and discuss our responsibilities. We both have them: I to handle the crisis as your President as competently as I can—*you*"—and his head came up in a look as challenging as theirs—"to support your government loyally and faithfully against the enemy, bearing in mind that you have a perfect right to criticize *providing it is constructive criticism and providing you have viable alternatives to offer instead of just negative obstructive ranting.* I know some of you do not feel that this is your responsibility, but I believe it is and I believe the majority of our countrymen agree with me."

There was murmuring across the room, some of it approving, some hostile and angry. He smiled without much humor.

"I did not expect unanimity on that, and you have not failed me. Nonetheless, it is something for you to think about. Particularly since the crisis, already extremely grave, is about to become more so."

There was an abrupt end to the murmuring, a sharp increase in the attentiveness; above all they were newspeople and from his tone and somber expression it was obvious that something big was about to happen. He let this sink in for a moment or two, then went on.

"Within the hour, I shall send the following message to the President of the Soviet Union. There are as yet no copies released. I am giving you the chance to be reporters again. I hope you won't mind too much. The message reads:

" 'Dear Mr. President:

" 'I am in receipt of your message of yesterday, sent from your official plane, concerning your response to my suggestion that the unusual aggregation of twenty-four Soviet missile submarines now in Cuban waters be withdrawn and dispersed to other areas of your well-publicized maneuvers.

" 'You have made very clear your intention that these submarines "will remain" at or near your naval base of Cienfuegos in Cuba.

" 'You will remember that in my first communication on this matter, repeated to you in my direct broadcast to you during your visit to Havana, I stated that "immediate, widespread and unfortunate consequences" would occur if the submarines were not removed. More recently I changed this to *"will occur."*

" 'You apparently are adamant in your position that they "will remain" despite my very clear and unequivocal statement.

" 'Therefore, Mr. President, you leave me no choice.' "

"Slower, *please!*" somebody yelled and he noticed with a grim satisfaction that no one was trying to stare him down now. They were all too busy scribbling.

"Right," he agreed pleasantly: and waited.

"O.K.!" somebody else shouted after a couple of minutes. He proceeded more slowly:

"'I must again demand that your unusual and threatening group of twenty-four missile-carrying submarines be removed from Cuban waters and dispersed to other areas of the world.'" There was a gasp, which he ignored. "'If this process is not begun within twenty-four hours from 1400 Washington time today, then I will regretfully but without hesitation bring to bear upon this situation the full might of United States arms, including—'"

"Slower!"

"All right . . . 'including a sea and air blockade of the island of Cuba.'"

There was a great gasp—exclamations—expletives—groans—some small stubborn scattering of applause. He ignored it all and went on.

"'I suggest you consider with great care what your response will be. The fate of the world may very well hang upon what you do. It is now your responsibility, Mr. President. I am discharging mine consistent with the safety, security and vital national interests of the United States of America, which is only ninety miles from Cuba and is most directly and direly threatened by your inexcusable aggressive act.

"'Signed, Hamilton Delbacher.' That concludes my—"

But he was unable to finish, nor did he have to accept any questions. There was a sudden unanimous rush to the doorway, a dash down the Great Hall of the White House, frantic cries of "Telephones! Telephones! God damn it, where are the telephones?"—and a hasty scurrying of guards to assist in the search.

He stood for a moment surveying the empty room, the overturned chairs and tables, the chaos left behind. Only one member of his audience remained, seated to his right at the end of the head table.

"Well," he said to Chauncey Baron, "the die is cast."

"God help us all," Chauncey said quietly. "But," he added with a small but unperturbed smile, "I am convinced He will."

PRESIDENT PLEDGES "FULL MIGHT OF U.S. ARMS" TO BLOCKADE CUBA IF SOVIET SUBS NOT GONE BY TOMORROW. WORLD WAR III FEARS SOAR THROUGHOUT WORLD AS DELBACHER ISSUES FINAL DEMAND. ANTI-AMERICAN RIOTS FLARE IN MANY CAPITALS. STUDENTS MARCH ON MAJOR CAMPUSES. "PEACE VIGILS" DRAW PROTESTING THRONGS TO TIMES SQUARE, LAFAYETTE PARK. PANIC BUYING HITS FOOD STORES AS THOUSANDS CLOG ROADS OUT OF D.C., NEW YORK. SHOCKED WORLD AWAITS SOVIET RESPONSE.

And waits . . . he thought grimly . . . and waits . . . and waits . . .

He held an emergency Cabinet meeting in the afternoon and had Roger Hackett explain in more detail to his colleagues exactly how things would develop in the event the Soviets did not respond. No word came . . .

At 6 P.M. the directors of the CIA, the FBI, the National Security Agency and the chiefs of intelligence of the military services gave him the latest information received on what was happening in Moscow. There were many comings and goings in the Kremlin, apparently much confer- ring in the office of Yuri Serapin, but no unusual activity in the field. Most of the maneuver forces were apparently on-station now. None seemed unduly active at the moment. And no word came . . .

There was a state dinner for the visiting President of Zimbabwe at 8 P.M. Two hundred guests came, chatted nervously, danced uneasily after- ward in the East Room—long since cleared of its overturned chairs and tables but still, for many, holding a palpable atmosphere of menace and doom that made them very uncomfortable. And no word came . . .

He checked again at 11:30 P.M. with the JCS: everything was on full war alert, as he had ordered. Roger Hackett recommended that he leave Washington secretly and go to the tunnel-honeycombed mountain that was to be Presidential headquarters in case of atomic war. He refused and he and Elinor, after their usual review of the day during which she agreed completely with his decision, went to bed. And still there was no word.

"I hope we get some sleep," she remarked as he turned out the light.

"Now I lay me down to sleep," he responded, beginning it almost as a joke but suddenly finding it wasn't so funny, "I pray the Lord my soul to keep. If I should die before I wake, I pray the Lord my soul to take."

"Amen," she said, and it was no joke for her either. "Do you expect him to reply?"

"Not if he withdraws them. If he doesn't then I expect a reply at the very last moment. What it will be, I don't know. It may be an attack or it may be an offer to negotiate. In either event he'll keep the world scared to death and guessing up to the very last minute. He's that kind of man."

"Nice."

"A peach," he agreed. "A very decent, compassionate, worthwhile sort of fellow who I hope will rot in hell forever when he gets there. Mean- while I intend to get a good night's sleep, having left word I do not want to be disturbed unless Doomsday actually arrives. And if I die before I wake—well, I won't go where Yuri's going. I'm sure of that."

"So am I," she said firmly, "and I refuse to worry about it any more."

"That's my girl," he said as he kissed her good night. "Sleep well. Whatever it brings, tomorrow will be a busy day."

Yet neither of them drifted off for quite a while. Like almost everyone everywhere they were profoundly worried by Moscow's silence. He could only hope, grimly, that his antagonist was feeling some worry also. He could not imagine even that ruthless ideologue not being shaken by the ultimatum, and by the certain knowledge, now, that the President of the United States was an opponent just as tough as Yuri knew himself to be.

6

"Therefore, in time of war, politics must often conform its actions with this fact: to what degree do these actions favor the achievement of strategic results, which in the final analysis lead to the accomplishment of political aims in war."

—*Soviet Military Strategy,* Marshal V. D. Sokolovskiy

At that very moment, in fact, the President of the Soviet Union was sitting in his office remembering this quote from Marshal Sokolovskiy and attempting to fit it into his mental picture of the man who was indeed proving himself to be a very tough opponent. Even though he knew that H. Delbacher was operating largely on bluff—even though he *knew* American arms were incapable of supporting an ultimatum of any kind, let alone the ridiculous threat of a blockade of Cuba which H. Delbacher must understand would mean instant Soviet retaliation in full force—still H. Delbacher's defiance gave him pause. It made him hesitate. It created worry. It upset his plans. It made him ask himself: does H. Delbacher know something we don't know?

This uncomfortable thought was indeed bothersome, and though he fought against its implications and refused to let them really upset him, still—

Once more, as he had done a dozen times in the past three days, he went over the latest comparative figures. As had been the case for several years now, the balance was heavily in favor of the Soviet Union. As of this day, the situation was heavily in favor of the Soviet Union. His forces were now fully distributed around the globe, not only in Cuba but in many other strategic places for which Cuba played, as planned, the role of decoy and smoke-screen. No doubt nearly all of these emplacements were well known to American intelligence, but the fuss centered on Cuba, as he had intended it should. But did that mean that H. Delbacher was playing a similar game? Did he, too, have secret sources of strength, secret dispositions of forces, that Yuri and his comrades had yet to discern or understand? It would be so typical of what they had to contend with from America as they strove unceasingly to make the world safe for all peace-loving, anti-imperialist, anti-capitalistic peoples. It made it so hard sometimes to carry out the Soviet Union's non-aggressive, anti-war, peace-loving policies.

Hated, despised, treacherous America! How much easier life would be if those blindly avaricious people could only understand how vital peace, détente, co-existence and the triumph of the Soviet Union actually were to the future of mankind! If only, just once, they could co-operate and not stubbornly stand in the way of history's inevitable tide!

But that, he knew, would never happen. They were too ignorant, too grasping, too conditioned by their greedy past and even greedier imperialist present. Everywhere they tried to thwart the will of the Soviet Union, which was history's will; everywhere they attempted to destroy peace, détente, co-existence; everywhere they defied *him,* to whom history had given the great task and glory of presiding over the final liquidation of all that combination of avarice and deceit which, calling itself "democracy," was only imperialist capitalism's last and most sinister disguise before it came finally to an end, to be absorbed for all time by the Soviet Peace.

He sighed. A great burden and a great responsibility were his. He knew he would discharge them successfully. Meanwhile, what to do about H. Delbacher and his insane, misguided defiances that might blow the world up before Yuri had a chance to save it?

His eyes wandered where they always did in these hectic days, to the lighted map of the world crawling now from pole to pole and sea to sea with the little twinkling symbols of Soviet power. He felt an excited visceral thrill. How powerful his country was! How powerful was the socialist coalition it led! How powerful *he* was!

But he had better review everything once more with the heads of the armed forces, just to make sure: and also to tell them what he had in mind as answer to H. Delbacher's latest ridiculous gesture. Half of H. Delbacher's twenty-four-hour ultimatum had run out. He was in no hurry to answer it yet—he knew to the minute when he would—but meantime it would not hurt to check everything one more time.

He buzzed his secretary and gave him instructions to order the chiefs of the armed forces to be here in fifteen minutes. Then he sat back and again watched the map while he thought contemptuously of the men H. Delbacher had to advise him, contrasted with the men who carried out his own orders.

During his time in Washington he had met three of the future Joint Chiefs of Staff, all then serving in relatively minor posts in the Pentagon, and he was not very impressed.

General Jamison of the Air Force, Admiral Rydecker of the Navy, General Smith of the Army: known then, as now, in the disrespectful, absurd American fashion, as "Bart, Snooze and Bump." Imagine the top military commanders of a great power—or now not so great, he reminded himself quickly—being called Bart, Snooze and Bump! Now joined, in their very responsible positions, by "Smidge" and "Gutsy." It was like something from a Walt Disney cartoon, such as he had seen when he and his lump of a wife had visited Disney World in Florida on one of their educational trips around the country. Uncle Sam and his Five Dwarfs, he thought contemptuously: Bart, Snooze, Bump, Smidge and Gutsy. The nicknames alone were enough to indicate that fatal informality of the Americans that made it so impossible for them to organize themselves seriously to meet any real threat. Imagine—he really could not—the chief of the Soviet Air Force, the Army, the Navy and the Strategic Rocket Forces—being named Bart, Bump, Snooze and Gutsy. And their staff secretary, or possibly the Minister of Defense, being known as Smidge. Gutsy Krelenko! Snooze Andreyev! Bump Valenko! He suddenly burst out laughing, something he had not done in—how long? Days, weeks, months, years? How like the Americans! How *like* them! And how much more serious—indeed, one might truthfully say, grim—were the stolid quartet that now entered his office and came forward to take seats at the big conference table beneath the map, giving him quick, formal nods and quick, formal handshakes.

Here were his right-hand men in the conduct of battle, all in their sixties, each a veteran of at least forty years in the armed forces and the Communist Party, each a comrade absolutely serious, absolutely dedicated, absolutely unsmiling and relentless in pursuit of the common goal of destroying forever the flippant, arrogant, irreverent, disrespectful United States. Marshal Andrei Andreivich Krelenko of the Air Force. Marshal Vladimir Alexeivich Andreyev of the Army. Admiral Anastas Nikolaivich Valenko of the Navy. Marshal Gavril Petrovich Shelikov of the Strategic Rocket Forces. Not all the Barts, Bumps, Snoozes, Gutsies and Smidges in the world, let alone in America, could match such a lineup for the Motherland!

He was proud of them and it showed. Seeing this, they relaxed somewhat and even allowed small, tentative smiles to cross their phalanx of solemn faces.

"Comrades!" he said. "We meet much, these days. I thank you for coming to see me once again."

"It is our pleasure, Comrade President," Admiral Valenko replied, "as well as our duty."

"We also expected," Marshal Shelikov said, "that you might wish to consult with us in view of this latest stupidity from the American President."

"It does not worry me in the slightest," Yuri said.

"No," Marshal Andreyev agreed. "It does not worry us, either."

"It is foolish," said Marshal Krelenko.

"Child's play," agreed Admiral Valenko. "What could he possibly be thinking of?"

"He could be thinking of the great, overwhelming power of the United States," Marshal Andreyev said with a heavy mockery.

"Its endless submarine fleets, its many thousands of surface ships," said Admiral Valenko.

"Its missiles and satellites, so much more numerous and more powerful than ours," suggested Marshal Shelikov.

"Its many fleets of airplanes, filling the skies with such darkness that one cannot see from the Kremlin to Red Square," Marshal Krelenko offered; whereupon they all laughed, harsh, contemptuous, smug, overwhelmingly self-satisfied.

Abruptly, however, they cut it short, because it was obvious from Yuri Pavlovich's expression that he did not find this heavy-handed humor agreeable. He looked, instead, severely disapproving. Their response was instant silence. It was as though he had turned a faucet and dried them up completely. For a moment it seemed they hardly breathed. What was wrong with Yuri Pavlovich?

"Comrades!" he said sharply. "H. Delbacher does not worry us. I did not say we must regard him and his country as jokes. The United States, while we know it to be inferior in every category of conventional arms and trailing some distance behind in numbers of missiles, still possesses quite enough nuclear power to destroy the Soviet Union completely. In fact it can destroy the world completely. That is why it is so dangerous that such a madman as H. Delbacher has been elevated to the Presidency. His actions, while they do not impress us, nonetheless should be accorded a healthy respect. He will fall, and in due course his nation will fall, victims of history's inevitable decisions. But he does not yet know this. He thinks history's inevitable judgment can be reversed. This prompts him to issue warnings and threats and promises of stupid yet wildly dangerous actions such as a blockade of Cuba. Who knows what he might do, if we push him too hard, too fast? There is a timetable for the United States: we must not open to H. Delbacher the possibility of upsetting it by some foolish action that would destroy us all."

"Comrade President," Admiral Valenko said cautiously, "if you will recall our discussions of a month or so ago, I believe we expressed certain —reservations, one might say—concerning the wisdom of such a large and openly displayed gathering of submarines at Cienfuegos."

"We wondered if it was entirely wise, Comrade President," Marshal Andreyev agreed, more strongly.

"I believe we raised the question: will it achieve the objective of restraining the Americans?" Marshal Krelenko concurred, yet more confidently.

"Agreeing entirely with your purpose, Comrade President," Marshal

Shelikov confirmed with a smooth self-assurance, "we yet wondered: is this the proper time?"

For a moment, confronted by their united attempt to shift responsibility and always aware that in the Soviet hierarchy one must protect oneself on all sides on all occasions, Yuri simply stared at them without expression. Then a fearful scowl shot across his face, he stood up abruptly and glared down upon them. Instinctively they shrank back: they were suddenly not so smart-aleck, so confident, so dangerously disrespectful.

"Are you trying to tell me, comrades," he asked, and his voice in contrast to his face was deliberately soft and gentle, "that you actually *opposed* my decision to send the submarines to Cuba?"

"Oh no, Comrade President!" Marshal Shelikov replied, his voice sounding shocked but, Yuri thought, with the faintest undercurrent of mockery still detectable in it. "We simply expressed our opinions. Naturally we would not *oppose* your order, even though—" His voice trailed away and Yuri snapped:

" 'Even though,' what?"

"Even though we did, as we have said," Admiral Valenko responded stoutly, "have some doubts."

"Why did you not express them much more vigorously, comrades?" Yuri asked, and now his own tone was openly sarcastic. "Your second thoughts seem stronger than your first thoughts. It would have been such a help to me. All along I have thought you were giving me your full support in the Motherland's great battle to decide for all time the fate of mankind. Instead I find you tiptoeing about filled with doubts and tremblings. All the courage seems to be in H. Delbacher. I had not thought I was depending upon cowards! Disloyal cowards!"

"Comrade President!" Marshal Andreyev cried indignantly. "We are not cowards, nor are we disloyal! We serve the Motherland in every way, and we have served her, all of us, for four decades and more! It does not become you, Comrade President, who are younger than any of us, to doubt our loyalty to you and the Motherland and to accuse us of cowardice when we simply state, as we should, the situation as we see it from our respective responsibilities."

"True," Yuri said, suddenly calm, resuming his seat and speaking in a matter-of-fact voice. "I should not criticize you for expressing your opinions, and I apologize if I spoke too strongly. Nonetheless, it is necessary for me to know at all times that I have the full support of the armed forces, since we are in a period of great tension and delicacy where one false step could jeopardize everything the Soviet Union has accomplished over almost seventy years. Do I have that support?"

He gave them a sternly challenging look, and as he had suspected, they virtually fell over each other expressing assent. He felt a sudden deep contempt for them all; his attitude toward them was permanently changed. He knew now that he must watch them all the time and, when the opportunity came, remove them as quickly as possible and replace them with younger officers unquestionably loyal to him and him alone. But this he of course dissembled entirely.

"Let us leave it, then," he said, "that you did have certain questions about the dispatch of the submarines but that I resolved them for you, and that when I asked for a formal endorsement of my proposed plans, you did indeed express your full and final approval. Is that not correct?"

"Perfectly correct, Comrade President," Marshal Krelenko said in a relieved tone of voice.

"Completely correct," Marshal Andreyev said.

"We did so agree," said Admiral Valenko.

"With our full and unyielding support," said Marshal Shelikov.

"In the highest spirit of the Motherland," added Marshal Krelenko.

"Very good," Yuri said, still somewhat severely, but seeming to relax. "Then I think we may proceed with our discussion of the situation as it now exists without further distractions brought on by anti-socialist expressions of wavering and doubt. Our great cause has no room for them, comrades. We must act and think positively in the true spirit of the Motherland. And so we return to H. Delbacher . . ."

"Yes," Marshal Shelikov said. "How seriously must we take his ultimatum, Comrade President?"

"Any ultimatum is worth taking seriously," Yuri said, "if the individual issuing it is under sufficient pressure. He may be in a state of mind that makes it impossible for him to be impressed by reality: therefore he may suddenly exceed the bounds of sanity and react in some wholly irrational way. Such a one is H. Delbacher. I do not think we can minimize his threat, though I do not believe under normal conditions he would follow through with it. These are not normal conditions for him—or for us either, for that matter—and so I do not believe we can minimize the possibility that he may suddenly do something completely irrational."

"Then we must be completely prepared to retaliate," Admiral Valenko said.

"If the situation remains as it is," Yuri Serapin said, "that is so. Let us proceed on the assumption that this is the case. I should like each of you to give me his estimate of the likelihood that H. Delbacher will proceed with his ultimatum, and if so, what each of your commands can do. If he does so, the climactic battle will immediately begin and must be pursued with the greatest vigor to its inevitable conclusion. There will be no turning back at that point. Comrade Marshal Shelikov, perhaps it is you as commander of the Strategic Rocket Forces who should speak first."

"I am inclined to think," Marshal Shelikov said slowly, "that H. Delbacher will proceed to do what he has threatened. He has shown many signs of unbalance in these recent days. There is every evidence of a tension approaching, as you say, insanity. Certainly anyone who has so little comparative strength of arms and yet issues such an ultimatum cannot be considered sane. Objectively he must be declared insane and totally irrational. Therefore we must expect him to do as he threatens unless some factor now unforeseen prompts him to withdraw or modify his statement.

"I should think that at a given time, say one hour before the expiration of his ultimatum, we should without further comment or warning launch an immediate nuclear missile attack upon the major cities of the United States from Cuba and from other suitable locations, some in the air and on the sea, still others undersea, also those in space, that we now have ringing the North American continent."

Yuri nodded.

"Comrade Marshal Krelenko? What will the Air Force do?"

"Firstly," Marshal Krelenko said, "I agree with Comrade Marshal Shelikov's appraisal of the state of mind of H. Delbacher. There is every evidence, to my mind, of genuine paranoia. How can he possibly feel that our submarines are threatening the United States? It strikes me as quite absurd. Someday they may, of course, but at present, as I understand the plan, there is no such intention—particularly now that he and the Pentagon have been fully alerted to their presence. To do anything with them now, in the absence of his ultimatum, would be entirely opposite to plan. Now that he has issued the ultimatum, however, it must be taken into account.

"I also agree with Marshal Shelikov's proposal of an attack, and I can only say that the Soviet Air Force stands ready to do whatever is asked of it in such an eventuality. Like you, Comrade President, we realize that this battle, if it is begun, will be the decisive one. It is what we have trained and planned for, for many years, as you know; and while this may be a little previous to what we had expected for the start of hostilities, we are prepared to fight it, win it and survive it."

Again Yuri nodded.

"Comrade Admiral?"

"I too," Admiral Valenko said, "concur in the estimate of H. Delbacher. He is obviously unbalanced, under great tensions, perfectly capable of doing such an irrational thing as to try to make his ultimatum valid. We have no doubt that is what will occur unless he withdraws, for some reason, his threat.

"Like the Air Force, we too are thoroughly trained and prepared for nuclear war, and we also fully intend to co-operate with all forces of the Motherland to win it and survive it and make permanent the triumph of Soviet arms and the socialist coalition."

"And Comrade Marshal Andreyev?"

"On behalf of the Army," Marshal Andreyev said, "I, too, must agree

with the judgment on H. Delbacher. He is obviously suffering great paranoia, is unbalanced probably because he has come so suddenly and
recently to the White House, and shows all the signs of an immature, inexperienced, virtually insane individual. Therefore we cannot rely on his
common sense and good judgment, which if they ever did exist obviously
do not exist now. We must be prepared accordingly.

"I too favor an attack at least one hour prior to the expiration of his
ultimatum. The Army's entire training since the ending of the Great Patriotic War has concentrated, as you know, on the nuclear aspects. The
principal emphasis of the Army has always been upon successfully conducting, winning and surviving an atomic war. The principal purpose of
the Army has been all the time to fight such a war successfully and
emerge from it with enough of the Motherland still intact so we can
rebuild our society and establish our permanent rule of the earth. We do
believe that this can be done and we are ready for it.

"We are also prepared, with the aid of our friends in the Air Force and
certain sections of the Navy, to carry such a war immediately to the
heartland of America, to strike aggressively into the depths of the continent by parachuting in tanks, troops, ammunition and supplies to begin
the immediate occupation of the key areas that will already have been
devastated by our atomic and particularly by our neutron bombs, and by
biological warfare ruthlessly and totally applied. These areas will be incapable of resistance or recovery, and we shall take them at once.

"Yes, I would say in every way the Army is ready for any task that is
asked of it in the event that H. Delbacher goes through with his insane
and hopelessly doomed threat."

"Thank you all, comrades," Yuri Serapin said. "You have fully
justified the faith the Motherland has, and I have, in your great abilities
and your readiness to defend our country and the socialist coalition
against the unwarranted, imperialist-aggressive policies of the United
States and of H. Delbacher in particular. Your loyal support is a great inspiration to me, as I know it will be to all our loyal troops . . .

"Like you, I had thought that the climactic battle to decide the fate of
all mankind would come at a somewhat different stage of our present situation. But if it becomes necessary that it begin within the next twelve
hours, then it is heartening beyond description, comrades, to know that
you and the gallant men of our armed forces are fully prepared and
ready. It strengthens me as President and Commander-in-Chief more than
I can describe to you . . ." He paused and a musing faraway look came
into his eyes.

"Everything you have said about preparations to fight and win nuclear
war," he said, "has truly been the basic plan of the Soviet Union ever
since the development of the nuclear weapon and the missiles and other
systems with which to deliver it. All of our official military literature, as

you know, since the conclusion of the Great Patriotic War has been devoted to that end and that end alone. We have not been like the bourgeois ideologues of the West who have always been afraid of nuclear war and have also insisted that 'no one could win.' This is nonsense, comrades. We will win it, as we have long planned and intended. It is history's command and we will fulfill it.

"Not, of course, mind you," he said, almost as if talking to himself, reviewing his own ideas, strengthening his own determination, while they watched him like four impressed and somewhat overawed schoolboys, "that we would prefer it that way. If one can win the rewards of war without having to fight, that is so much the better. We have been proceeding actively along that path, steadily driving back the United States, steadily weakening it, ever since the ending of the Great Patriotic War, with great overall success. Aided by the cowards, the fools, the wishful-thinking skeptics who have always aided us in America, we have brought their country to a position of near paralysis. Now comes the last thing we had expected from their recent history, a strong and defiant President.

"We have been spoiled, perhaps, by too many weaklings, so afraid to challenge us, so willing to go on shouting about the United States being 'the strongest power on earth,' while all the time they have known as we have known that its strength was steadily declining. It is only the American people who have been fooled by this; and they have been fooled because they wanted to be—*because they have lost the imagination to grasp what we have done, and the will to fight to stop it.*

"Against this over-all triumph, our own few failures here and there, such as being ousted from Egypt and North Yemen, miscalculating how much it would take to win our eventual and inevitable victory in Afghanistan, fade to nothing in history's balance. Our chief and never-changing objective—to destroy the United States permanently because it is the last and *only* real obstacle to the final conquest of the world—has come ever closer, day by day, month by month, year by year. Adding it all up, comrades, we have been successful beyond our wildest hopes.

"Only"—and he smiled wryly—"to find in our way as we near the final mile of our long road the figure of one stubborn and obviously insane man who happens to be the present President of the United States. How ironic if he forces our hand at this late date! The result will be the same, it is entirely inevitable, but it will not be so easy as we planned.

"However, there are several ways to trap a wolf and perhaps I shall think of one—or perhaps"—he smiled upon them with graceful flattery— "one of you may think of one, yourselves, before our friend's foolish 'ultimatum' has expired today. If you do, advise me at once and it will be fully considered . . .

"I appreciate your suggestions that we use surprise to launch a first strike before his deadline arrives. Surprise and the first strike, as you also know, have been implicit in all our preparations from the beginning. But that may not be necessary. The time for it may arrive, but perhaps it is not yet. Please hold yourselves ready to consult with me again ten hours from now. By that time I shall have met with the Politburo and a final course of action will have been decided. Unless I hear from you further with other ideas, you will of course be fully informed at that time.

"So, comrades!" He stood up, held out his hand, which they obediently shook. "Thank you for your support, your advice, your readiness at any moment for the final battle. We are prepared, I believe, for H. Delbacher." He gave his short, sharp bark of laughter. "More than he for us, I think. My grateful thanks, and the thanks of the Motherland, to you all."

And having thus calmly and cold-bloodedly made things ready, if need be, for the probable deaths before sundown of half or more of the earth's population—for that, he told himself, is how suddenly and how completely it will come, if it comes—he saw them to the door and returned to his desk; his mind also made up to get rid of them all immediately after the battle, if it occurred; certainly within the next few weeks, if it did not.

Seated again at his desk, eyes fixed once more upon the map of a world alight with the signs of Soviet power, he made himself dwell for a time on the only weaknesses he could see in his own country and the socialist coalition he commanded. There were not, he told himself smugly, very many.

There was basically, of course, the fact that the Soviet Union which seemed so monolithic to the outside observer—and was monolithic, insofar as its political governance and the dictatorship of the Communist Party and himself as its head were concerned—was in actual fact a leftover czarist conglomeration of fifty-three distinct peoples and nationalities dominated and controlled by the Great Russians of the Russian "republic" whose capital was Moscow. These Russians were threatened by the birthrate: the next largest group, the Islamic peoples of the southern and southeastern Soviet "republics" seemed likely to overtake and surpass them within the next few years. Other subject states and peoples within the Soviet borders, while smaller, were also increasing steadily. The dominance of the Russians was more and more dependent upon the control of the party, the KGB and the armed forces. Yet this was not a truly major worry: that control was absolute, and as long as the party, the KGB and the armed forces remained the ruthless instruments of suppression that they were—and neither he nor any other Soviet leader had the slightest intention of ever permitting otherwise—then the unity of the U.S.S.R., though uneasy, would remain. Certainly it would remain for all practical purposes of warring upon others. There was in this diversity no more real hope of a break-up for outside enemies than there was for the Union's own subject peoples. If anything the diversity made war against the outside world more likely; for, even if there were no overriding ideological drive to conquer the world, war itself was the opium of the peoples that would still their rebelliousness and hold them all together.

Agriculture—agriculture was a problem, admittedly; it seemed to be perpetual problem, he thought with a sigh. But as long as the Americans were willing to sell grain and other foodstuffs to the power that wished to destroy them, that power would manage to feed itself and keep going. Meanwhile it constantly attempted to improve its agriculture. But it would certainly not falter simply because of a nagging but relatively soluble problem in that area.

Industry—consumer goods lagged; shortages there seemed to be perpetual. But war industry—that was another matter. Everything else had been deliberately sacrificed to that, and its production records justified it. Tanks, planes, subs, missiles, satellites, ships, biological and chemical warfare—they came off the assembly lines as they had for years, each year's record growing over the last. Not for us, he thought with satisfaction, the American concentration on achieving the absolutely perfect this, the uttermost sophisticated that, the most completely intricate something else, each one costing more and more, the defense budget unable to keep up with the pace of Soviet spending because of the American passion for the biggest, the most overdeveloped, the best. Soviet war industry began with a much bigger proportionate share of the national budget than the American, and its emphasis was on producing workhorses, not fancier and fancier gadgets. That was perhaps the basic reason why the United States had sunk to second place some time ago: too many gadgets. Cheap, simple, utilitarian and deadly, Soviet armament flowed off the production lines in a flood the gadget-hypnotized Americans could not overtake. (This also included space, where Soviet experimentation had continued at a frantic and highly sophisticated pace while the U.S. space program suffered from steadily declining interest and steadily decreasing funds.)

Furthermore, he thought with equal satisfaction, the very nature of the Soviet approach to treaties and international agreements gave them an advantage virtually impossible to overtake. Partly it was the difference in basic vocabularies, in which "peace" meant "a gathering of one's forces," "détente" and "co-existence" meant "factors for speeding up social and political change in the anti-imperialist cause." No word was ever fully kept, no promise was ever fully maintained, no treaty "agreement" or "understanding" was ever entirely unviolated. Deceit, betrayal, lying and double-dealing were standard practice. The final objective, world conquest, was everything. Achieving the worldwide death of democracy and freedom justified all.

And to guarantee and meld it all together there was the final ingredient: American willingness to believe in the good faith of the Soviet Union, American unwillingness to face up, until too late, to the reality of

Soviet ambition and completely conscienceless deceit, American desire to deliberately deny the only too obvious facts of Soviet imperialism, Soviet ambition, Soviet greed. American decency, if you like—a blind, stubborn, deliberately unseeing determination to cling to a vision of a decent world in the face of eternal Soviet indecency and betrayal. Yuri did feel some slight glimmer of respect for this, but he daily thanked whatever fates there be, because it made his task and his country's so very much easier.

He concluded, as he sat there contemplating the lighted worms and twinkling dots and shining slivers, that things were really in very good shape, all around. He did not for a moment believe that much of mankind would be annihilated this day, because he had a plan that he would presently set in motion, just before it was too late, just before H. Delbacher "pushed the button," as his countrymen liked to say, just before the world finally went into convulsions because of the sheer tensions it was living under. He had his plan, and in due course it would be implemented.

Nine hours later, exactly one hour before H. Delbacher's deadline, having met with the Politburo and received its ecstatically relieved approbation, consulted once again with the service chiefs and received their humble admiration, he buzzed his secretary and instructed him to get a certain number overseas.

Far away in a city he considered the modern Sodom and Gomorrha— but enjoyable, he had to admit, enjoyable and exciting, too—a shaky old hand picked up the receiver and a shaky old voice responded with a babble of gratitude and tearful relief to the calming words of Yuri Serapin. There was, after all, A Way Out.

Thus did the world, forgetting as usual the never-ending record of Soviet betrayals, regard it; and thus did it embrace it, with wild rejoicings from pole to pole and sea to shining sea.

So, too, did H. Delbacher, not so uproariously and not before he had come as close as he would ever wish to the actual start of hostilities in the Caribbean. And not with any great rejoicings, though he could almost physically feel his own continent convulsed with relief, and from lands beyond the seas seem almost to hear the distant roar of humanity letting go its fearful tensions.

He had not realized, quite, how great those tensions had become until the clock crept on to the last few hours before his deadline was to expire. As he had expected, and predicted to Elinor, there was no response whatsoever from Moscow and no movement whatsoever of the submarines at Cienfuegos. Everything seemed frozen exactly as it was. Intelligence continued to report the steady scurryings to and from the office of the Soviet President, but nothing more.

He waited: his country waited: the world waited. But it was not, on any side, an idle waiting. Insofar as they were able, the nations went on alert, began to sandbag their public buildings, began to send their troops to battle stations, began the ancient—and in this age of instant annihilation, futile though still automatic—rituals of preparation. In the United States, demonstrators rioted from Lafayette Square opposite the White House to Union Square in San Francisco; students spilled out onto campuses in frightened anger and despair; newspapers, TV and radio frantically issued their appeals for moderation and denounced him, sounding very much like the marshals in the Kremlin, for his "hasty, ill-advised, close to paranoid impulsiveness—almost, one might say, actually unbalanced, if not on the verge of real insanity." And from overseas a steady stream of telephone calls from his counterparts in other lands, suggesting —urging—pleading—begging—demanding—that he stop now, withdraw his ultimatum, save them all before it became too late.

Of the range of these, two were typical: the lady of Westminster and the President and Benevolent Protector for Life of the central African despotism of Gorotoland.

The British Prime Minister's call came in three hours before the ultimatum was due to expire. She sounded self-possessed but an undercurrent of genuine tension rippled through her words despite her obvious attempts to restrain it.

"Mr. President!" she said, "I must say you have us in a state, over here."

"Prime Minister," he said, "believe me it is as nothing compared to the one I'm in."

"Nonsense," she said, trying to sound lightly chiding but not quite achieving the lightness she desired. "I'll wager you're as cool as an iceberg in the midst of all this turmoil you've created."

"*I've* created?" he responded sharply.

"Sorry," she said quickly. "Sorry, sorry! My error. You will not challenge 'helped to create,' however, will you?"

"No, I won't challenge that. Providing it is kept in mind that this is as though you suddenly discovered twenty-four Soviet subs just off the Isle of Man, all of them with missiles pointed directly at Number 10. If your natural and inescapable response to that was similar to mine, then you could be said to have 'helped to create' a situation. Right?"

"They may be there this moment, for all I know," she said, still striving for a lighter tone. "If we discover such, I may very likely do the same. That, however, does not solve our dilemma at the moment, does it. The question is, where do we go from here? Straight to perdition in another three hours? Or to the negotiating table?"

"That," he said calmly, "is up to our friend in Moscow. Personally I
see nothing to negotiate until the submarines are removed; and if they
are, then the reason for negotiating is removed also. Have you heard from
him? Are you calling to convey some message?"

"None whatsoever," she said crisply. "I am calling to speak to the only
man who has the sense, and the power, to do something to alleviate the
present situation. I am calling you to urge that you either extend your ultimatum or withdraw it entirely, in order to allow time for mediation of
the dispute."

"Again," he said patiently, "I can see nothing to mediate while the
subs remain in place. There must be some concession to the safety of the
United States, after all. I take an oath to that effect, you know; it is part
of my personal responsibility, as the safety of Britain is yours. I would
not ask you to abdicate that responsibility."

"I am not asking you to abdicate it," she said with a sudden sternness
of her own. "I am simply asking you to be reasonable."

"I am trying to be," he said, "but I am not getting much co-operation
from Moscow."

"You may not. It is quite possible. But that does not mean that both of
you must go insane. You still have a duty to be reasonable, whatever he
does. Mr. President, I beg of you: do not do what you contemplate. It
would be too horrible—beyond words. It could literally mean the end of
the world. Surely sane men can find a way out of this."

"In spite of my domestic critics," he said with a wry return of his customary good humor, "who consider me completely and entirely insane by
now, I believe there *is* one sane man involved in this crisis. But whether
my opposite number can also qualify for that designation in terms of any
test you can name, I am not so sure."

"This is perhaps the greatest test there is, right now," she said. "Match
yourselves against it and determine which of you is sanest. But in any
event, I beg of you again—and I may tell you that I received a call from
Her Majesty a few moments ago, and she authorized me to tell you she
adds her plea to mine—*please,* Mr. President, draw back. Your responsibility is too great, the potential too awful. We beg of you: think it
through once again. If you do, we are convinced you will agree."

"Tell Her Majesty I appreciate her thoughts, as I appreciate yours. I
promise you both I will think again. I would also like you to do something for me."

"Anything. I cannot of course commit her, but for myself: anything."

"Pray for the United States," he said. "And, if you will, use your great
persuasive powers immediately to bring the same message to the other
party. That's only fair, is it not?"

"I shall call him immediately, although I must tell you frankly, Mr.

President: I do so with very little hope that he will listen. I think it still comes back to you. But I will try."

"Thank you, Prime Minister," he said gravely. "You can do no more . . ." thinking, as they said good-by, *I wonder if she got my message and if she will transmit it as sent* . . . but still determined, though increasingly tense, to go ahead if she did not, or if his message was ignored.

That was typical of the tone of the more reasonable calls he received from more than one hundred heads of state in these last, increasingly tense hours. Then there was the other type.

"Mon!" screamed the wizened little killer who had finally, with Soviet and Cuban help, ousted the hereditary ruler of Gorotoland, "Terrible Terry" the M'Bulu of Mbuele, and established central Africa's most virulent and ruthless communist dictatorship. "Mr. President, mon! What you mean, tryin' to destroy the whole wide world, mon! We don't like that down here! We goin' to catch it like everybody else, mon, Mr. President, sir! What you mean? What you mean, mean, *mean?*"

"Mon," Hamilton Delbacher replied, keeping his voice calm in the hopes this would induce a similar abatement of the torrent from Africa's heartland, "Mr. President, mon, why don't you address your appeal to President Serapin? You know him, he's the man who put you there. It would be a great help to the world if you would say these same words to him."

"I can't reach him, mon!" the People's Hero and Eternal Guiding Light replied in the same hysterical voice. "I've tried but I can't reach him! He had me as his guest in Moscow not six months ago, too!" he added in an aggrieved tone. "He told me I was a friend of his. Now I can't talk to him. So I'm talking to the only one I can, Mr. President, sir! I'm talking to you, mon! My people down here, they're going crazy, Mr. President! They're making magic and stopping everything dead in its tracks. Nobody's farming or tending cattle or keeping up the people's revolution. It's a crime, Mr. President, mon! A bloody crime!"

"I agree with you," he said, "but I still think you must talk to President Serapin. All he has to do is withdraw his submarines from Cuba. It is very simple. You, as his friend, must tell him that he is stopping the people's revolution in Gorotoland. That will make him think and change his ways, I'll wager."

"Mr. President!" cried the Glorious Defender and Father of Everything, slipping, the President noticed, into rote-English of perfect clarity, "now you make a joke with me! You, the imperialist racist capitalist warmonger who have created this crisis to pursue the sinister colonialist aims of the United States! You, the murderous leader of capitalism's imperialist racist designs upon the socialist coalition everywhere! You, the deceitful and unprincipled manipulator of the bourgeois imperialist racist campaign to recapture control of the oppressed millions of Africa! How dare you, sir! How dare you!"

"Oh, come now," the President said. "Who taught you how to say all those good things about my poor self and my poor country? They are not true, Mr. President; not true. I invite you once again to try to reach Comrade Yuri. He placed you where you are. Without him you would be nothing. Remind him of that, Mr. President. Remind him! He will tell you what to do."

"I will tell *you* what to do, mon!" the Golden Planet and Gleaming Star of the People's Revolutionary Heaven cried, his voice sailing up into hysteria again. "I will tell you, murderous American! Go to hell, mon, Mr. President, sir, that is what I say to you! Go to hell forever, hateful American! You will be utterly destroyed, utterly! You and your arrogant country will be wiped from the face of this earth, imperialist capitalist war-monger, mon! Fuck you, mon, horrible colonialist aggressor! Fuck you!"

"Thanks for your call, Mr. President," he said cheerfully. "Always good to hear from such a fine intelligent representative of the people's revolution. Don't forget what I said: call Comrade Yuri. He will listen to you, I'm sure of it."

He hung up with the outraged cries and wild obscenities of the Sacred Elephant and Unmitigated Universal Mind Who KNOWS ALL While Showering It on the People still erupting from the telephone.

Half an hour after her first call, the Prime Minister called back.

"I got through," she said dryly, but with a certain note of triumph too. "I was Received. And I conveyed your message. I pleaded with him exactly as I did with you. I quoted Her Majesty also, I repeated your words exactly as you said them. I assume that was what you desired."

"What was his response?" he asked, conceding her shrewdness by ignoring it.

"None, and I expected none. But he listened very closely and with much more respect than I anticipated. I would say he was thinking. I would also guess he is going to announce some dramatic way out, though I would also guess it is exactly what he has planned all along. I don't know why I suddenly feel less apprehensive, but I do. I think this has been an exercise and it is now nearly over. I doubt that I contributed much to it, but I'm glad I've been involved."

"So am I," he said sincerely, "and I thank you very much. Now let's hope you're right."

And in due course they found out she was; though as it turned out she had somewhat minimized her own part in it.

FLASH SERAPIN ASKS SECURITY COUNCIL MEETING.

BULLETIN—MOSCOW (UPI)—President Yuri Serapin of the Soviet Union today urgently requested an emergency UN Security Council meeting to discuss President Delbacher's ultimatum on Soviet submarines in Cuba.

He issued a public appeal to the President to "cancel or at least suspend" the ultimatum in return for the immediate withdrawal of six of the twenty-four submarines alleged by the President to be present at the Cuban port of Cienfuegos, reportedly a long-time base for Soviet subs . . .

" 'Alleged' by me to be present!" the President snapped, angrier than any of his Cabinet had ever seen him, when he called them together twenty minutes later. "Cienfuegos 'reportedly a long-time base for Soviet subs.' 'Alleged!' 'Reportedly!' Jesus Christ, these piranhas of the press! And six subs out of twenty-four! Eighteen left, when five or six with the missiles they have aboard are quite enough to devastate the country from end to end. God *damn!*"

"And yet, you know," Elinor spoke up quietly, because she knew no one in the Cabinet might dare to, "you really don't have any choice, do you?"

He looked at her, still furious, for a long moment. Then his face gradually relaxed, as did they all, until finally it had regained a semblance of its normal easygoing amicability.

"No," he agreed with a rueful smile. "I guess I don't. I asked the Prime Minister to transmit my message—'There must be some concession'—she was smart enough to realize what I meant and *he*"—the ruefulness deepened—"*he* was smart enough to seize upon it and give me just enough of a one so that I can't logically refuse it . . . I guess," eyes becoming somber, "that I've lost every round so far, haven't I?"

"I think the world, which often misses such subtleties, isn't going to see it that way," Chauncey Baron objected, though his heart was hardly in it. "He challenged you—you issued an ultimatum—he ran to the UN, withdrew some subs, appealed to you to suspend the ultimatum. He blinked first. In a propaganda sense, I think you've won this round. Now if we can just keep the momentum rolling in the UN—"

The President snorted.

"That snake pit for biting the United States? Good luck, Chaunce. You'll be carrying the ball."

"*You* should," Elinor said quietly, and they all silently considered that for a while.

"Yes," he finally agreed. "I think I should."

PRESIDENT ACCEPTS SERAPIN PROPOSAL, "SUSPENDS" ULTIMATUM "PENDING UN DECISION." WILL HEAD U.S. DELEGATION. SPY PLANES CONFIRM SUBS LEAVING CUBA. WAR TENSIONS EASE.

And so, now, the wild hosannahs, and the dancing in the streets.

And in the Kremlin, the vodka-toasting, the jubilation and the effusive congratulations to Yuri Pavlovich for having played his game exactly right. The Politburo and the general staff stood in line like dutiful schoolboys to shake his hand, swear yet greater allegiance, express an admiration and fervent respect beyond any he had so far received. The Minister of Foreign Affairs, in a moment of impulse prompted by a secret hint from Yuri himself, even went so far in the midst of the hilarity to propose a toast to, "Yuri Pavlovich, President for Life!" A great roar of agreement went up but was jovially dismissed by the object of all the attention.

"No, no, *no,* comrades!" he modestly protested. "Your approval is enough! Let us not go overboard! One step at a time, and we still have far to go. I may fail you dismally in the next few weeks."

To which there were cries of, "No, no! Never! Yuri Pavlovich our great socialist leader! Yuri Pavlovich, genius, great commander of the coalition!"

Shooing them finally out the door, drunk, happy, awed and impressed by his overwhelmingly clever move toward final checkmate of the hated enemy, Yuri Serapin returned to his desk and resumed his favorite position, seated, chin resting on folded hands, eyes glued to the glowing map of the world. How now did he bestride it like a colossus! How supreme, how powerful, how shrewd, *how clever!* What a giant of the socialist revolution! Not even V. I. Lenin in all his mummified glory, not even K. Marx with all his ideas that had germinated such monstrous fruit, could ever loom larger in the pantheon! He, Yuri Pavlovich Serapin, had claimed his place, supreme, inviolate, first among equals, greatest of them all.

For this, he admitted to himself with an ironic amusement that he would make clear to him at some appropriate point in the coming days, he must partially thank that egregious fool, H. Delbacher. Yuri had planned no "concession" save his exactly timed and superbly diversionary appeal to the UN. But H. Delbacher really must have been more afraid than Yuri thought; he had really had Yuri fooled. When *he* mentioned "concession," Yuri, who had been mentally preparing himself for the world's—and his colleagues'—instant interpretation that he was somehow afraid of the ridiculous figure in the White House, knew that he still had the whip hand after all. He still did not quite dare play the bluff to the end without compromise, because H. Delbacher might be just insane enough to do exactly as he had promised, which was the last thing Yuri wanted even though he knew the socialist coalition was far and away the stronger, and could handle it if it came. Still it was with great relief that he had heard the word "concession" from Britain's bustling Boadicea; he must thank her, too, sometime.

The rest of the inspiration, however, was his: if he offered H. Delbacher *anything* it would place the President in such an awkward position with the world that he would have to accept it and pretend himself satisfied. He could not in all conscience (*he* could have, Yuri thought scornfully) refuse what outwardly appeared to be a major concession indeed, the removal of a powerful Soviet striking force, under challenge from the United States. He wanted a concession, Yuri gave him a concession: a paltry one, as H. Delbacher well knew, but one which he could not refuse when under such pressure from the world to find a way out of the confrontation that seemed to loom so horribly ahead.

So Yuri had made his concession, 6 out of twenty-four, and still, as H. Delbacher knew, enough was left behind to destroy the United States in ten minutes' time. The world knew this too, of course, when it stopped to think; but it had been so terrified, and suddenly was so relieved, that nobody wanted to think. And Yuri, instead of appearing to be the one on the run, was now riding the crest of the wave as the man who had made the brave concession, sought the statesmanly way out, and saved the earth.

When they met in New York—for he, too, had decided to head his delegation; and so had Britain's lady, and so had many another throughout the world—it would be Yuri who overshadowed all. His genius—he was willing to accept the word—had permitted him to seize the tide of fortune at its flood. There was no doubt who would dominate the "gathering of giants," as the ever-busy American media had already dubbed it in headline, news story, editorial and commentary. "Giants!" One giant from Moscow, one pathetic would-be giant from Washington, and the rest a gathering of pygmies, he thought sarcastically; but the media *would* create their fantasies. He intended to give them much opportunity in the days ahead.

In the meantime, the world rejoiced; and he too rejoiced, though only in the privacy of his office and in the few hours he was able to find to see Ekaterina, who like all women—all paradoxical, he had long since decided—appeared to find him more and more boring in this, his greatest hour of triumph so far. They were getting to be like old married people, he told himself; they were much too used to one another after seven years. By mutual agreement the UN meeting had been set for two weeks from now—both new Presidents needed a rest, it was explained, so hectic had been their brief tenures in office. Perhaps the ten days he and Ekaterina were planning at the recently finished Presidential villa near Sochi —"the Czar's latest palace," the modern-day serfs murmured as his gleaming convoy of armored limousines screamed by—would bring regeneration. At least it would bring sheer physical collapse, which was what he very badly needed at this moment. And it would give the world time to turn and re-turn, polish, buff and burnish, the image of Yuri the Peacemaker that he would take with him to New York.

He lifted the special phone, heard its subdued ring at the beautiful antique-filled apartment just beyond Red Square.

"Are you alone?" he asked. A scornful laugh responded.

"Am I ever anything else?"

"I can join you now."

"Please do. Possibly I shall be entertained."

"Possibly," he said, his voice instantly sharpening to meet hers.

"You can try," she suggested, and laughed again, deliberately trying to unman him.

"I shall," he promised grimly, breaking the connection without farewell; and for a moment felt a familiar stirring. But it was prompted by anger and little else, and was gone as abruptly as it came.

He wondered, as he left his office with all the pomp and bustle that usually attended his comings and goings—guards snapping to attention, rifles clicking, the great barbaric torches he had ordered because they pleased him with their reminders of the past, flaring down the ancient, dark and bloody corridors of the Czars—whether it was worth it. Or whether anything was worth it, even the earth-shaking triumphs of that great genius and leader of the Revolution, Yuri Pavlovich Serapin.

Something of the same mood, had he but known it, had descended upon his antagonist as he too prepared for what the White House press office always liked to refer to as "a working vacation" at Camp David. In his case the mood was not induced by anything as clichéd as a mistress— and certainly not by a wife, for Elinor was as loving, shrewd and supportive as ever, as she strode beside him toward the just-landed helicopter that would whirr them away to the Presidential retreat in Maryland's Catoctin Mountains.

There was only a vague malaise, an underlying uneasiness and dissatisfaction; brought on, he supposed, by the knowledge that he had indeed been bested by his opponent this time around, and would need to keep all his wits about him if he and his country were not to be bested again in what he had called "that snake pit for biting the United States." He realized that Yuri had met him shrewdly, both in his appeal to the UN and, more damaging still, in his clever and meaningless withdrawal of the six subs from Cuba. Yuri was coming to New York as the great hero, he as the war-monger who had only at the last moment accepted the urgent appeal of the great peacemaker to avert the world's catastrophe. Once again Yuri, who had created the crisis, had emerged as Yuri who had, at least for now, assuaged it; and so overwhelming was the world's relief that it was only the heroic Yuri who was left in the collective minds of humanity to reap all the psychological gains and propaganda benefits. And eighteen subs still remained at Cienfuegos.

He had wondered, ever since Serapin had issued his appeal to the UN and announced his withdrawal of the six, whether he himself could have handled it differently. Regardless of an outcome less than satisfactory, he did not see how. The subs were a brazen, direct and taunting threat to the safety of America, and as such they had to be acknowledged and acted upon by the President. If he had not demanded their removal, all would still be there; and there would hang about them a damaging miasma of contempt and anger for a President who could not protect and defend his own country—even from those who were always most vociferously critical of any President who seemed to be even remotely contemplating that post-Viet Nam shibboleth of the late Seventies and Eighties, "military force."

They wanted him to defend the country, all right—there wasn't much argument there. Except they didn't want him to defend it by any means that involved pressure or force or action—the only means, in the final analysis, that counted with the nation that posed the greatest and most relentless threat to the United States.

This was a paradox that had to be solved—or ignored—by any President worth his office; and while there had been some in recent years who had thought they could do the job by a series of empty pious platitudes and constantly shifting evasions of responsibility, he was not one of them. Things had to be met, he met them; and in this particular situation there probably could have been no other outcome given the shrewdness and the grim unyielding hatred of the Soviets.

Now the UN lay ahead: and there, he knew, America faced the usual uphill battle to wangle even a decently favorable compromise out of that ragtag and bobtail aggregation of larger powers and minipowers. He was glad he had decided—or Elinor had decided for him, rather—that he himself should lead the delegation; he was glad that Yuri and the rest had followed his lead. To some degree he felt the same contempt Yuri did for the tiny, powerless, often troublemaking specks that appeared side by side with the superpowers and the greater powers in the glass palace on the East River; but among them there were some reasonable men and some who really could contribute something intelligent and constructive to the world's problems. Not those such as the Golden Planet and Gleaming Star of the People's Revolutionary Heaven of Gorotoland; on that dark continent, not only dark in native color but sometimes apt to be dark in intelligence, apparently utterly without illuminating sense, there were quite a few like him. But there were others who compensated, and he was glad they would be there. He also felt that face to face in the focus of the world, he would make a better showing and be better able to handle his opponent.

He welcomed this interval at Camp David with a heartfelt relief and anticipation such as he had rarely known in all his long public life. He had, as he expressed it to Elinor, "hit the Oval Office runnin'" and he had never had time to stop running since. Very few if any of his predecessors had ever had such an initiation; the pressures had begun immediately and ever since they had been unrelenting. An uneasy world had abruptly escalated into one that appeared to be on the brink of final disaster; one thing had tumbled upon another until he had finally remarked wryly one morning, "If it's Tuesday, it must be chaos."

Through it all, he felt, he had managed to stay astride a constantly shying horse, though very often it had not been easy. Everything had been subordinated to foreign policy; domestic matters had been allowed to go by the board. Congress had dawdled along without any prodding from him, waiting to find out what he wanted in domestic legislation: he had not had time to formulate a program and tell them. "Keep the machinery going and pass any minor bills that seem to need attention," he had told Art Hampton and the Speaker. "We'll stick to the budget and the appropriations bills as they stand, for the time being." They had nodded and done their jobs like the veteran troupers they were. He would have most of them up for consultations in the next few days.

He had not even had time to give more than passing thought to perhaps his major domestic task at the moment: the nomination of a Vice President to fill his own now-vacant place. This worried him, potential target for any crank with gun, bomb, stick or stone who might not approve of his conduct of foreign affairs. Fortunately, perhaps, he had also had very little time to move among the public, which simplified the problem. This trip to Camp David would be his first real venture out of the White House since taking the oath, except for the "summit" and his talk to Congress. He realized with a reflex of pleasure that he really was a kid out of school this morning. For the first time, almost, he was not "the prisoner of the Oval Office." A sudden sharp olfactory memory of pines heightened his anticipation. How glad he was, he thought as the helicopter gained altitude and below them the beautiful Mansion and its neatly manicured grounds dropped away, to be leaving it behind for a while.

"What do you plan to do while we're there?" Elinor asked.

"Work. Work, work, work—and work."

"No play?" she chided.

He smiled.

"A little," he said. Then his expression sobered. "Not much."

"I think you'd better manage as much R. and R. as you can, my boy," she advised, "because you surely aren't going to get much for the rest of the summer."

He smiled again.

"Oh, UN sessions don't last long. A day or two, a speech or two, and we'll be out of there."

"Ho, ho," she said. He grinned.

"Ho, ho and double-ho. A guy can dream, can't he?"

BOOK THREE

"As long as capitalism and socialism exist, we cannot live in peace. In the end one or the other will triumph. A funeral dirge will be sung either over the Soviet Republic or over world capitalism."

—Joseph Stalin

For ten days the world's top news stories bore the datelines "Sochi" and "Camp David," and from them both came a series of headlines that traced the opening skirmishes of the diplomatic battle ahead:

SIXTEEN AFRICAN LEADERS GIVE SERAPIN UN BACKING . . . NATO DELEGATION VISITS PRESIDENT, EXPRESSES "UNDERSTANDING" . . . WARSAW PACT GIVES SERAPIN "COMPLETE ENDORSEMENT" IN UN FIGHT . . . FRENCH SEEN LEANING TO SOVIETS . . . BRITISH PLEDGE SEARCH FOR "REASONABLE COMPROMISE" . . . INDIA SEEN LEANING TO SOVIETS . . . CENTRAL AMERICAN RED STATES PLEDGE VOTES TO SERAPIN . . . BRAZIL, ARGENTINA, CHILE BACK U.S. . . . AUSTRALIA, NEW ZEALAND SUPPORT DELBACHER . . . MEXICO SAYS "UNDECIDED" ON UN CLASH . . . JAPAN BACKS U.S. . . . RADICAL ARAB STATES MAY SUPPORT SERAPIN . . . NEUTRAL BLOC COULD DECIDE VOTES IN U.S.-SOVIET BATTLE . . . THIRD WORLD GROUP IN SECRET CAUCUS ON UN CRISIS . . . PRESIDENT CONFERS WITH CONGRESSIONAL ADVISERS ON PROPOSED UN RESOLUTION . . . SOVIETS PLEDGE ATTEMPT TO SECURE FULL CONDEMNATION OF U.S. . . . CHINA OFFERS "SYMPATHETIC AND BENIGN OBSERVATION" OF CRISIS.

("Whatever the hell that means," they remarked in both Sochi and Camp David.)

And of equal importance in shaping the future, although by now a little further down the front pages and a little less prominent in the news broadcasts, just as Yuri had hoped they would be:

SOVIET WORLDWIDE MANEUVERS SPREAD. OTHERS' LAND AND NAVAL FORCES WARNED OFF PRACTICE AREAS. NO TIME LIMIT SET BY MOSCOW.

For both Presidents these were busy days, though perhaps the busier for the President of the United States. His prediction to Elinor of "work, work, work—and work" was not borne out quite so stringently as he had assumed, but there was enough to occupy most of the hours of the day. He managed to set aside an hour and a half before dinner during which he and his wife took a brisk walk around the compound, concluded it with the one martini they allowed themselves, and then either had dinner served in the Presidential lodge without company or appeared in the dining room to eat with whatever guests might have been asked to remain overnight. The helicopter shuttled back and forth between Washington and Camp David on a regular schedule twice a day, and it was only four days out of the ten that they were completely by themselves except for staff. He had arranged that these would come at the end of the visit and so they had a little time to themselves in which to do literally nothing. He found that he could use it.

When their stay was over, he had put together his delegation for the UN, which in addition to himself and Ambrose Johnson of Alabama, continuing the tradition of a black as permanent American Ambassador to the UN, included the Secretary of State, the Secretary of Defense, Senate Majority Leader Art Hampton, Senate Minority Leader Herb Esplin, Mark and Representative Bill Lapham of Virginia, a quiet-spoken, highly intelligent young minority member who had entered the House the same day Mark entered the Senate. The President told his press secretary to tell the media, whose members appeared faithfully twice a day for briefings, that Mark and Bill were added "because the President felt it would be well to have two younger viewpoints on the delegation. Also, he likes them and regards them as being fully worthy of such an important assignment." The media, after analyzing everybody closely, concluded that it was "a basically conservative delegation" that could be "counted upon to back the President wholeheartedly in whatever he proposes."

Ham snorted.

"Of course they will," he remarked to his wife. "I wouldn't appoint them otherwise, would I?"

He realized with amused surprise that this was the first time since he took office that the pejorative word "conservative" had been used to characterize him. It was such a media pet that he supposed they must all have been too disturbed by events to have had time to think of attacking him with it. From now on, no doubt, the whole crisis would, if at all possible, be pictured as a battle between "conservative" Delbacher and "liberal" Serapin, in an attempt to move the conflict—for the comfort of the public —smoothly out of the area of "the life-and-death struggle between the two opposing systems," which the Soviets bluntly and accurately and always called it.

But he would remember that fact at all times because he knew Yuri would. The American President could not slip in this matter: his opponent was not only waiting to take advantage of slips, he was ruthlessly set upon creating as many opportunities for them as he possibly could. Nothing had been changed in the slightest by their little moratorium, which the naïve world chose to regard as a reprieve. It wasn't a reprieve for anything: it was "peace, a time for gathering one's forces."

On other matters he moved closer to a decision on a Vice President, telling Art and Herb he would nominate one very shortly. He worked out with them necessary budget cuts in more than two dozen programs, wasteful but popular, that had been dear to the heart of his predecessor. He called in the Joint Chiefs again to urge them to speed up the emergency procurement plans under the Elrod Act, and to remind them sternly that despite the outward easing of the crisis they must not allow their forces to relax vigilance for even a moment; and, not entirely to his surprise, received a secret communication from the villa near Sochi.

This was transmitted to him by a special messenger, disguised as a butcher's helper, who came in with a truckload of meat one morning. His arrival had been prearranged in a secret telephone call from the Soviet Ambassador in Washington and he passed through the unsuspecting reporters hanging around the gate as smoothly as his master could have wished. It was apparent that no visit from the Ambassador himself was possible at this moment; the endless speculations and the worldwide repercussions would have been enormous and completely confusing to the issue. The message could very easily have been transmitted by radio, but the President was sure that in the devious and conspiratorial Soviet mind this would only have opened up possibilities of interception, publication, and so on. This way was primitive and simple, and for that reason, possibly, worked like a charm.

"Dear Mr. President," Yuri wrote. "Once again we are going to meet at the United Nations in New York. I am glad that you have accepted my proposal. The event should be a great contribution to peace.

"I wish to point out that I have taken the initiative to break the deadlock between us by requesting this meeting and by withdrawing six of the submarines previously stationed in the port of Cienfuegos in the sovereign nation of Cuba. I have thus eased worldwide tension and satisfied your fears of some fictitious and mythical 'sneak attack' upon your territory.

"Therefore it seems only right that you should make some gesture of similar nature in return.

"Your country is presently still in a state of national emergency and your forces are still on full war alert.

"Would it not be a suitable gesture, I ask you, Mr. President, if you would contribute to the easing of tensions prior to the meeting of the Security Council by cancelling the state of national emergency and returning your forces to a normal, non-warlike condition of readiness?

"The Soviet Union is not in a state of national emergency, Mr. President. Our armed forces are not on full war alert. Indeed, most of them are far from home conducting peaceful maneuvers.

"Therefore, can you not take these two actions I suggest, as your matching contribution to making the atmosphere in which we are to meet a more peaceable and productive one?

"I am sure the world would welcome and applaud this.

"Yours sincerely,

"Y. P. Serapin
"President and Chairman of
the Council of Ministers,
U.S.S.R."

His first impulse was to pick up the phone, get through to Sochi, chuckle heartily and say something like, "Yuri, old buddy, who the hell do you think you're kidding with this hypocritical crap?" But that, of course, was not how it was done. Yuri was making one more shrewd propaganda ploy, and probably was already releasing it to the press over there, after all his two-bit spy-melodrama theatrics with the butcher man over here. He had best be nimble, best be quick, Ham Delbacher thought, and ten minutes later stood before the panting group of reporters who had come scampering from all directions to the Presidential cabin.

"I have here," he said, holding it up, "another of those propaganda transmissions from Mr. Serapin which he loves to send me in his unceasing attempts to embarrass the United States of America. In fact, looking at the record, that seems to have been his sole unchanging purpose throughout this entire episode.

"We'll get some copies made for you in the next half-hour, but briefly, he suggests that since he has appealed to the UN and withdrawn six out of twenty-four submarines from Cuba, leaving eighteen highly dangerous death-machines there, I should reciprocate, as my contribution to peace, by putting an end to the state of national emergency and cancelling the war alert I ordered for the armed forces.

"I come from the farm, you know, and this strikes me as the usual Soviet tactic of offering an outhouse for a cow barn. Neither is very appealing, but one is certainly very much larger than the other.

"He points out that the Soviet Union is not in a state of national emergency, nor are its forces on war alert. They are simply strewn all over the face of the globe, in excellent position to strike anywhere and at anytime they please, and now actively practicing those 'maneuvers,' if such they be, which began this entire crisis.

"As long as those forces are on the prowl, and more specifically as long as eighteen missile-carrying submarines, fully loaded and ready to strike instantaneously against the United States, remain in Cuba, I will under no circumstance return the United States or its armed forces to a normal peacetime condition. Let him call his forces home and I will cancel my orders. As long as they stay where they are, my orders stand. And no amount of propaganda gimmicks out of the Soviet Union," he added with a visible annoyance and contempt, "are going to change that quid pro quo." He started to turn away, then turned back. "I do wish to thank him, however, for enabling us to return this controversy to what it is really all about, namely the worldwide maneuvers which he has tried to obscure and make the world forget about, and the direct threat to America posed by the very large concentration of subs in Cuba. Those things are the issue, and I thank him for returning the world's attention to them, as it should be. They are what the UN must stop."

"Mr. President!" thirty frantic voices cried, but he turned away again and walked out the door, closing it firmly behind him; pausing only to murmur to his press secretary as he passed:

"Has he released anything yet?"

"Nothing yet, Mr. President," the press secretary replied with satisfaction.

"Thank God for once he wasn't so smart," the President said. "This time he gave me the jump and I took it."

And so, for some reason he never did learn, he seemed to have done; because it was not until almost an hour later, long after the bulletins had gone out and the headlines had been written, that Yuri's letter was released from Moscow. Inevitably it took second place, and inevitably the President had achieved what he had felt it imperative to do: return the maneuvers and the remaining subs to center stage.

PRESIDENT REJECTS SECRET SERAPIN PLEA FOR END TO EMERGENCY, WAR ALERT. DENOUNCES CONTINUING WORLD-WIDE SOVIET MANEUVERS, REMAINING SUBS IN CUBA. PLEDGES TOUGH UN FIGHT TO STOP BOTH.

That was what happened, the Soviet President thought with a frustrated anger, when you trusted dunderheaded, unimaginative, stupid civil servants to do your bidding as fast as you wanted them to in this racing world. He had been lying in the sun alongside the villa's enormous swimming pool, eyes closed, mind drifting, when suddenly the idea of yet another message to the hapless H. Delbacher had flashed into his head. This was one of his better ones, he congratulated himself, putting the President once more in an awkward and embarrassing position, making him seem once again to be the belligerent one, the chief obstruction to the world's desperate desire for "peace."

Yuri had picked up the pen and pad that were always at his elbow and begun furiously scribbling. Ekaterina, sunning on an air cushion, had rolled over and yawned lazily in his face.

"What is it, Comrade?" she asked with deliberate mockery. "Another Communist Manifesto?"

"A letter to Delbacher," he said tersely, not bothering to look up, pen hurrying across the page.

"Oh, that poor man!" she exclaimed in the same mocking way. "Every day another letter, another message, another embarrassment from clever Yuri Pavlovich! How does he stand it, I wonder? It must be terribly frustrating for him."

"I hope so," Yuri said crisply. "Do you mind not talking until I finish?"

"I do," she said, stifling another yawn. "It is the most animation I have seen you show since we arrived at this boring place. I wish to enjoy it to the full. Why are you writing poor Delbacher this time?"

"*Please,*" he said angrily. "I am trying to organize my thoughts."

"It is a deliberate process?" she inquired innocently, opening a bottle and spreading suntan lotion luxuriously across her already deeply tanned breasts. "I thought these things came full-formed to you without further thought, inspired by your great genius which guides us all daily to new triumphs of the Revolution. I did not realize the Little Father of All the Russias had to stop and *think*. It is a revelation, actually."

"Ekaterina Vasarionova," he said sharply, "I do not like to be called that, even in jest. It is an insult to the collective leadership and I will not have it."

"The collective leadership does not presently consist of very clever men," she observed in an offhand tone. "Yuri Pavlovich is far more intelligent than they are. He is beginning to be far more powerful than they are. They are beginning to be far more afraid of him than he is of them. Does not their humble respect warrant some such august title?"

"You know very well why that title can never be used again in Soviet Russia!"

"Even if it is true?" she asked, giving him a long slanting look from the gray-green eyes that had once seemed to him to contain the sun, stars and moon combined. *That* nonsense had stopped at least four years ago, but by then custom, habit, inertia, not wanting to have trouble or conflict while he successfully negotiated his final moves to the top, had let the arrangement continue.

"It is *not* true!" he hissed, keeping his voice low lest some of the servants—spies, all spies, he was sure, KGB internal agents reporting back everything they could to the Politburo, whose members, even though afraid of him, made sure they knew all they possibly could about him, all the time. "I forbid you ever to say that again! It simply is not safe and *I will not have it.*"

"Oh, ho!" she said with a triumphant little laugh. "Even the Little Fa—even the distinguished President, Chairman and Hero of the Revolution does have his limits, then! I had not been aware it was possible. Except," she added dryly, "in certain—areas—shall we say."

He gave her a sudden glare.

"Again, I warn you," he said, and turned back deliberately to his note pad, scratched out a word, revised a phrase, made busy work for himself as though he were dismissing her completely from his mind. She laughed and rolled over.

"Will you put some oil on my back, please?"

"I am writing a letter to H. Delbacher!" he exclaimed. "Must I tell you ten thousand times!"

"Only once. But will you put some on my back, please."

"Ekaterina Vasarionova," he said very softly as he flung down his pen and pad, came over, sat down beside her on the concrete lip of the pool and began very slowly and insistently to comply with her request, "what were you, when I found you?"

"And abandoned that cow of a wife?"

"Stop that!" he ordered so sharply that she jumped; and accompanied it with a sudden hard slap across the buttocks that made her jump again and even cry out a little, more from surprise than anything else. They exchanged many savage blows verbally nowadays, but very, very rarely did she succeed in provoking him into physical retribution. He always felt himself diminished when she did. "My wife is not your concern," he added roughly. "Keep your dirty tongue off her."

"It is not dirty," she said with dignity. "It *does* tell the truth, and I suppose that is hard to take when one is surrounded by sycophants as you are."

"You will tell me the truth, then," he said, continuing to apply the lotion with a hard but even hand to her back, buttocks and legs, "when I repeat: What were you when I found you?"

"I was a clerk in the decoding section of the Ministry of Foreign Affairs," she said calmly, "making a few paltry kopeks a week."

"And what are you now?" he continued in the same even tone.

She uttered a scornful little laugh.

"I am the private property of the leader of the collective leadership, which does not believe in private property but whose members nonetheless do pretty well for themselves, I must say."

"Peasant!"

"Not really," she answered calmly. "My father still has a very nice little farm near Gorky. He is not permitted to keep much of what he grows, nor does he receive very much money for it, nor is he permitted to leave it even to come to Moscow to see his daughter, who in turn is not permitted to leave her beautiful prison-apartment in Moscow to go and see him. But still he is not a peasant nor am I a peasant."

"How would you like to go back to the farm and try being one, however?"

She rolled over and sat up, tossed back her long blond hair, gave him a steady look and laughed.

"I should be perfectly happy," she said calmly. "When are you going to let me go?"

"Ekaterina Vasarionova," he said again, becoming aware with a genuine annoyance that the sun, the heat, the nearness of his naked body to hers, and quite possibly the argument itself, were beginning to give him an erection, "you know that I could order you killed and in a moment's time—no, perhaps not a moment, that would be less than you deserve— you would be killed."

"I know that you could have me turned into a vegetable or tortured until I became a mindless blob of nothing," she said coolly, reaching out with a gesture of quite ineffable irony to begin playing with his distended flesh. "But *you* know that as long as I had breath left in me and mind left to think I should despise you for doing it and be superior to you with my despising. Do you not, Yuri Pavlovich? And are there not pleasanter things you might do to me?"

"Get away!" he exclaimed harshly, knocking her hand aside, retrieving himself, his pen and his note pad and returning to his chair in one quick panther-like movement of disliking and distaste. "Now, be silent! I must complete my letter to H. Delbacher."

"Don't let yourself become too small," she advised, rolling back on her stomach and stretching luxuriously in the sun. "You will not be writing the letter forever."

"Long enough," he said still harshly, "unless you will be silent and let me concentrate."

"Read it to me when you've finished," she suggested, sounding suddenly sleepy. "Perhaps I can improve upon it."

Which she did not do. But nonetheless he read it to her, as he did many of his speeches and proclamations: because her mind was very intelligent and very shrewd and sometimes she did have excellent suggestions. And she was perhaps the only person he knew, now, who was absolutely unafraid of him. That was why, he thought as he finally joined her on the air cushion, the habit of seven years would probably not ever be broken.

An hour later the letter was typed and ready for release. He gave it to his secretary to transmit to the Foreign Ministry in Moscow, along with exact instructions on how it was to be presented to H. Delbacher. Simultaneously it was to be released to the foreign press. But when the foreign correspondents' stories got to the censor, something went wrong with his careful plan.

Some new man apparently was on the job, some overly cautious fool who was too frightened of his own shadow—or of Yuri's—to take upon himself the responsibility for giving the automatic approval all of Yuri's statements were understood to receive. Instead this individual went to his superiors, precious time was lost, the co-ordination collapsed, the President received it before the press and now his tart and clever response was filling the ears of the world while Yuri's shrewdly designed gambit was being relegated to secondary place. He determined that the fool responsible would be found and by tomorrow would be on his way to a collective in Sibera, there to think back for the rest of his days upon the comfortable life he might have led in Moscow had discretion not overcome him at the wrong moment.

These things happened, Yuri reflected with an annoyance that lasted really for quite a long time, so involved did the situation somehow seem to be with his mixed-up relationship with Ekaterina. Even in the efficient Soviet state, these things did happen. Human error could still creep in. Perfect plans could still go astray. Even the Little Father, he told himself wryly, could be thwarted by human nature and its unplanned errors. It had happened before during his long party career, and no doubt would happen again; except that now, with the outlines of the final battle beginning to take shape under the guise of maneuvers, it was imperative that everything proceed with the exact efficiency demanded by the state.

Perhaps internal exile would not be sufficient punishment; perhaps the culprit should be shot.

In any event, he and his opponent were going to arrive in New York on a relatively equal basis, for the moment—were going to enter the arena, he actually thought of it, with some half-amused yet romantic echo of history while gladiators, lions, Christians, *imperialist capitalist racists* became all tangled up in his mind for a second. He would not have quite the propaganda edge he had planned upon, but he was not overly concerned: it would return. If one added the members of the United Nations who were genuinely frightened of the Soviet Union to those who were actual satellites and sympathizers, plus those who had received enough financial and military aid to consider themselves under real obligation, then you began with a very sizable number of votes.

The pledges of support he had received this past week far outnumbered those that had come to Washington. He had his own resolution ready for introduction and he was sure H. Delbacher had his. As far as either of them had indicated, this was to be simply a major debate and review of the situation; but he knew they both were determined, as he suspected were most members of the UN, to have a definitive decision of some kind put on the record at its conclusion. The vote, like most UN votes, would have no binding effect, but psychologically and in a propaganda sense it might well be the most important the UN had ever cast. Even if it were simply an exchange of vetoes, debate would indicate what might happen when the issue was referred to the General Assembly, as it certainly would be. Of the final outcome there, Yuri had no doubt.

Meanwhile the maneuvers would go on, the eighteen subs would remain at Cienfuegos, and in the United States the national emergency and war alert would continue. In the house of democracy the termites would gnaw on, aided by the inevitable tides of history as they swept the two powers toward the confrontation which one of them regarded as perhaps the last chance for peace and the other regarded as the final decisive battle for the control of all mankind.

"The Soviet Union considers it one of the great tasks in the world to work toward the total dismantling of all remaining institutions of imperialists and racists."

—*Radio Moscow, March 6, 1980*

It was estimated by the New York City police that a crowd of at least 200,000 filled UN Plaza and spilled over into adjacent streets to watch the leaders of the earth arrive at 3 P.M. for the Security Council's fateful meeting. Forty-seven presidents and prime ministers, many of them from Africa and Asia, had decided to come to New York; for many from lesser states it had become a matter of prestige and national bombast to participate in the Western media's quickly labeled "gathering of the greats." Many of them, such as Gorotoland's Sacred Elephant and Unmitigated Universal Mind Who KNOWS ALL While Showering It Upon the People, had impoverished their treasuries, probably for years, to bring with them parties of as many as one hundred, take dozens of suites at the Waldorf-Astoria, hire fleets of limousines and even, in the case of another tiny African speck, a twenty-five-piece band to accompany the appearances of its National Redeemer and Lifetime Emperor. It was true that the opening stages of the contest would take place in the Security Council, but no one expected this to last more than a week. It would then go to the General Assembly where the veto powers of the five original Council members, China, France, the U.S., the U.K. and the U.S.S.R., did not apply. That was where the majority of smaller powers would have their chance. They intended to be well prepared for it, enjoying meanwhile all the attendant delights of New York and the privileges conferred upon them by their almost universally poverty-stricken, oppressed and helpless peoples.

The real movers and shakers, in customary contrast, had arrived two days before with somewhat less fanfare and plunged immediately into the incessant lobbying that forms nine tenths of the UN's business. The Prime Minister of Great Britain was the first of the major power leaders to arrive. British delegation headquarters immediately became a crossroads for constantly arriving and departing spokesmen for most of the governments of the Commonwealth and former Empire. They knew Britain's case and which side her leader would be on, but the Prime Minister put it to each of them in her usual blunt and emphatic manner. She was not sure she won over any votes, but at least, as she told Hamilton Delbacher when he arrived and paid a courtesy call a day later, "They know where we stand —they know the *right* thing to do. Whether or not they will do it"—her voice took on a faintest hint of regret for the days when Whitehall could guarantee that they would—"at least *they know*."

In similar fashion the President was aware that the former French colonies were meeting with the French President: Ham had observed that the offspring of both empires often came home for consultation and advice in times of trouble. He did not know what the French President was telling them, but he supposed he was counseling the same sort of neutral-against-the-United-States attitude that usually characterized the French. He had never heard from the French leader in these recent days; an occasional spiteful remark surfaced in the press, tossed off at some political gathering or impromptu interview in Paris. The general idea seemed to be that Hamilton Delbacher was overreacting ridiculously to the Soviet challenge and should be as calm and self-possessed as the French, say, always were about everything. "Maturity" was the word that seemed to recur. These pin-pricks were standard to French-American relations in this era; born of jealousy, filled with an insistent spite, harking back, no doubt, to the World War II record of their own sad failure and then their rescue by the Americans, which could simply not be forgotten or forgiven by the French. How sharper than a serpent's tooth, he thought wryly, is the ingratitude of nations that have been helped. This did not dismay or discourage him; but he did feel some annoyance now and then.

He also was the recipient of a number of visits and calls during his first twenty-fours in New York. Some were nations such as Japan, normally a good American ally, now wavering uncertainly, some were frankly avowed enemies such as Angola. Some called to comment, some to commit, some to curse. He did not seem to be picking up many votes. Demonstrators gathered virtually around the clock at American headquarters, some with placards saying GO HOME, WAR-MONGER or DOWN WITH CAPITALIST IMPERIALISTS, others urging GIVE 'EM HELL, HAM or STOP THE RED MURDERERS.

Twelve hours after his arrival, the familiar Ilyushin landed at JFK and Yuri and his delegation—the Foreign Minister, the Defense Minister, the military commanders—joined "the gathering of the greats." Tension rose steadily—it was rather like an American political convention, the President thought, the arrival of each new candidate increasing the level of excitement—as tomorrow's opening session approached. Yuri too was greeted at Soviet headquarters with enormous crowds and placards.

Bearers of critical placards had been efficiently roughed up and shoved back by plainclothes KGB agents before he got there, so that he was greeted with STOP THE CAPITALIST IMPERIALISTS . . . HAIL THE DEFENDER OF WORLD PEACE . . . CRUSH U.S. RACIST WAR MACHINE and the like, all encouraging, all friendly, all convincing him that America was far more divided than it perhaps actually was.

There was no doubt, however, that it was sufficiently divided in his favor so that his task at the UN was greatly simplified. The usual chorus of critics was slamming away at Hamilton Delbacher, from the National Council of Churches to the Council of California Kooks (honorary chairman, Sacramento). He was too impulsive, too belligerent—too concerned about maneuvers which were after all Soviet business, and submarines in Cuba which after all were the prerogative of the two countries involved and no real threat to the United States. Uneasy feelings may have been troubling them on this last point, but the way to overcome those was simply to drive them away by blustering ever more loudly against the President. If there *was* any menace—and you could get ten to one at the National Press Club bar in Washington that it was all a figment of Ham Delbacher's conservative, reactionary, ignorant mind and imagination—then it was best not to think about it and to go right on pretending that it did not exist. It was much more comfortable that way. The deadly level on which the two Presidents were contending was unknown and almost inconceivable to these wishful-thinking people. Off to their readers, viewers and listeners went a steady flood of soothing treacle, interrupted only by frequent spurts of acid splattered on the occupant of the White House.

Yet he was heartened by the fact that here and there among the lot there were a fair number who saw the situation as he did; who did not draw scathing editorial cartoons or write hysterically funny columns depicting him as the world's greatest dunce running scared by the shadow of a minuscule, laughable and virtually non-existent Soviet threat. There were some, particularly in the smaller newspapers and media outlets, who supported him despite the raucous put-downs of their peers; and there were far, far more among the citizenry who, by letter, wire and telephone call to the White House let it be known that they, too, saw the Soviet advance as he did and applauded him for standing firm despite great risks.

And yet, of course, he had not stood as firmly as he wished. He had, in a sense of which he knew his antagonist would take every advantage, given way. He had accepted not even half a loaf when he accepted the withdrawal of only six submarines. He regretted now that under the pressures of the moment and the world's desperate fear of war he had not at least demanded removal of twelve more and reduced the force to the original six. Not that this would have helped much either, basically, but it would have given him the psychological advantage. But Yuri had been too clever for him on that point, of course. By waiting to the last moment to reply he had made further ripostes impossible: the President had no option but to agree at once or be faced with having to follow through on his ultimatum. As Yuri accurately surmised, he had no desire to do this.

So much for playing cat-and-mouse at the highest level. The task here in the UN would be much simpler, an out-and-out, head-on battle for votes, an open debate which might possibly slow down, perhaps reverse, the Soviet drive to world domination.

So mused Hamilton Delbacher, knowing perfectly well that nothing at all except sheer brute superior force would stop the Soviet drive to world domination or the grimly dedicated campaign of Yuri Pavlovich Serapin to bring it to victorious fruition. And his White House predecessors and their encouraging supporters in the media, academe, the arts and a hodge-podge of sundry assorted naïve opinion-makers had left him precious little of that.

So the 200,000 gawkers gathered on the fateful day, and into the UN complex by ones and twos and sometimes—in the case of the National Redeemer and Lifetime Emperor and his twenty-five-piece band, a good many more—the leaders and other official spokesmen of the nations made their way to the chamber of the Security Council; and there, around the green baize table, the permanent members took their seats—

The People's Republic of China
France
The United Kingdom
The United States of America
The Union of Soviet Socialist Republics
—along with the ten members who were chosen on a geographic basis to serve two-year terms. At this time they were:
Cameroon
Eire
Egypt
Greece
India
Iraq
Nicaragua
Seychelles
Tanzania
Tonga
The presidency of the Council rotated month by month, and by the luck of the draw this month's President was Prince Koahumahili of Tonga, an amiable brown giant who stood six feet eight inches tall, had weighed 305 pounds stark naked this very morning before breakfast on his special set of scales, and was known as "Koa" to everyone around the UN where he had served as his tiny nation's ambassador for the past

three years. He was easygoing, amiable, fair-minded and firm, and was, as Chauncey Baron murmured to the President when they took their places, a good break for the United States. India, Nicaragua, Iraq or even France might not have been so evenhanded in presiding over what was almost always a sharply disputative group. It certainly would be this time.

Before it could degenerate into this, however, much was made of the formal entry. Because of the high-ranking nature of several heads of delegations—India, too, had sent her lady, and Egypt her statesman-idealist—it had been arranged by the protocol officer that each delegation should enter separately from the area to the left of the circular table where Prince Koa already sat, accompanied on his left by the Secretary-General.

The permanent members were introduced first.

"The People's Republic of China!" the protocol officer announced loudly, and there was a burst of applause from the more than two hundred media representatives who sat in the press section, and the other heads and representatives of states not on the Council, who with wives, staffs and other encumbrances, filled what would normally be the public gallery. Down from their glassed-in booths along both walls above, the translators gossiped, the radio broadcasters chattered and the television cameras panned back and forth across the solemn, attentive faces, making much of the formal entries.

The P.R.C.'s Vice Premier, Ju Xing-dao, entered with five subordinates and took his seat, small, wizened, bright-eyed, seventy-eight years old and as lively as a cricket—a very wise and very sly cricket, as Chauncey remarked, continuing his thumbnail sketches for the President's benefit.

"The Republic of France!" the protocol officer informed the world. The President of the Republic entered, also with five aides, and took his place, peering about through old-fashioned pince-nez with his usual lean and prepared-to-be-disapproving air.

"The United Kingdom!"—and the Prime Minister, in a feminine but businesslike blue dress with a single red rose for adornment, entered with four aides and took her seat. Again applause, this time a little more polite, but generous nonetheless.

"The United States of America!"—and the President, looking like the portly, amiable, no-nonsense grandfather he was, entered with his delegation of seven. Much applause, some hearty, some polite; and this time, also, a commingling of boos and hisses that brought a sharp glance from the Secretary-General and a sharp rap of the gavel from Prince Koa.

"The Union of Soviet Socialist Republics!"

And in came Yuri, grinning like an expectant prize-fighter with his six-man delegation marching quick-step behind him, he and the Ministers of Foreign Affairs and Defense in dark gray business suits, the marshals and admiral (on his orders) sans uniforms, deliberately and equally drab. As they took their seats alongside the U.S. delegation—being careful to leave a suitable space between—there was a sudden surge of excitement, shouts of greeting from satellites and friendly countries, the biggest applause of all; and again a stern look from the S.-G. and the emphatic "thunk!" of Koa's gavel.

One by one the rest came in, all greeted with about the same level of polite applause except for Egypt's President, wearing a flowing, blue gelabayah beautifully embroidered with gold, as if to emphasize his Arabness; and India's Prime Minister, who seemed to float in a mist of silken sari, green and red and gold and sparkling with a thousand tiny spangles as though she herself were a jewel, except for her dark, hook-nosed face and dour look. For both of them there was a loud com-mingling of applause and boos, and again the gavel from Prince Koahu-mahili . . . and so, finally, the Council settled down to work.

"This emergency meetin' of the Security Council will be in order!" Prince Koa said, banging the gavel in an extra-portentous way; and si-lence settled abruptly on the room.

"We convene today," he went on in a businesslike tone, "to consider the urgent appeal of the President of the Soviet Union that we do so." He glanced down at a paper the Secretary-General passed over to him. "Every member of the Council with the single exception of the People's Republic of China"—there were sharp looks at Ju Xing-dao, who twin-kled blandly and stared down at his freckled old hands, clasped before him on the table, as though they held the secrets of the universe—"has reserved time to speak. Normally we would, as the Council knows, pro-ceed in alphabetical order, but since the President of the Soviet Union did not make his request for a meetin' specific, only that we have a meetin', I think it might be bes' and mos' efficient if we hear from him first, to ex-plain. If there is no objection—? Very well, Mr. President"—he leaned forward informally, hand on chin, which even in the midst of the growing tension in the room, brought a chuckle—"explain."

But he had been too optimistic and spoken too soon. There had been a hurried whispered consultation between the President and Secretary of State. Now Chauncey Baron leaned forward quickly and raised his hand.

"Mr. Chairman," he said. "I don't mean to shatter your hopes for a quick conclusion of today's business, but I think that's impossible any-way. Therefore I think it would be best if we adhere to the alphabetical order in which we usually speak. The subject is obviously the present cri-sis brought about by the scope of the Soviet maneuvers and by the threat of Soviet submarines to the United States. If members have already re-served time to speak, they obviously have the subject well in mind. I sug-gest we proceed in the customary way."

Half a dozen hands promptly went up, half a dozen voices clamored, "Mr. President!"

Prince Koa looked slowly around the table and shook his head with a rueful little smile.

"On this one," he said, "I think maybe I'd better seek the wisdom of the Council."

In the booths above, the radio and television commentators explained to their worldwide audience in the six languages of UN translation—Arabic, Chinese, English, French, Spanish, Russian—the significance of this initial controversy. Whoever spoke now, they said, would obviously have the propaganda advantage of the first news stories—conferred by their own reporting, though they did not put it quite that candidly.

"The distinguished delegate of Eire," Koa said, selecting the one he thought would be the least self-interested among those who sought recognition.

Ireland's white-haired, kewpie-faced delegate, whose advanced years, a pipe and a carefully cultivated air of slow-puffing wisdom had won him great status in the press as "the UN's philosopher-statesman," cleared his throat carefully, tapped out his pipe, looked solemnly and with great deliberation around the table ["For God's sake, you old phony, come *on!*" the AP hissed to his seat-mate, *Le Monde,* in the press section] and finally condescended to speak.

"It seems to me, Mr. President," he said in his lovely brogue, "that we are already confronted here with a rather serious question, don't you know? A rather serious question. If the distinguished delegate of the Soviet Union speaks first, as some would prefer, including"—he chuckled comfortably and went, "Tap! Tap! Tap!" with his pipe—"the distinguished delegate of the Soviet Union, then obviously he will clarify the situation for us, just as the President suggested. If, however, the first alphabetically designated delegate, who I believe"—he peered with great care at the duplicate of the speakers' list, which had now been distributed by the clerks to all delegates—"is our good friend from the Dark Continent"—everyone visibly winced—"Cameroon, then that will delay coming to grips with the main burden of our problem here, which may be, as the distinguished Secretary of State of the United States puts it, the responsibility of the Soviet Union"—there was an ominous stirring from the Soviet delegation. He shot them a sudden expansively twinkling smile—"or it may lie elsewhere. That, we will have to discover for ourselves." He seemed for a moment to lose his train of thought; tapped his pipe again slowly three times; murmured, "Ah, yes!" to himself, and concluded brightly, "Therefore, Mr. President, I am of the opinion that it is a very difficult decision for the President and one on which he should perhaps seek the wisdom of the Council."

There was a moment's silence, into which Cameroon suddenly contributed a half-suppressed giggle; whereupon the whole room exploded into relaxing laughter for a moment. Eire beamed around the table, looking very philosopher-statesman and pleased with himself.

"Yes," Koa said. "Well. That surely puts the whole business in perspective, all right. I thank the delegate. Does anyone else—"

"Mr. President," Yuri said in English with no attempt to conceal his impatience, "why are we wasting time like this? The President's first instinct was entirely right. I asked for the meeting, I obviously know why I asked for it, I obviously am the one to open the debate with an explanation of my position. It is as simple as that. I suggest I proceed as directed by the President. Now, Mr. President—"

"Mr. President!" Chauncey Baron said sharply. "The United States does not intend to have the Soviet Union bulldoze this meeting. If President Serapin does not wish to abide by our regular procedures then it may be necessary to seek 'the wisdom of the Council,' as my friend from Eire puts it."

Eire, who had just started to drift off into a pleasant doze, woke with a start, grabbed his microphone and said in a loud voice: "Mr. President, I request a vote of the Council!"

["Oh, oh!" the St. Louis *Post-Dispatch* murmured in the press section. "You should have gone slower, Chauncey."]

"Not yet, Mr. President—" the President of Egypt protested, but Koa, seeming suddenly impatient himself, banged the gavel and said in a firm voice, "What is the pleasure of the Council on the request of the Ambassador of Eire?"

Several hands shot up, clamor again besieged him. This time he chose Greece.

"Mr. President," Greece pointed out, "there is nothing before the Council to vote upon. Therefore if the distinguished delegate of the United States wishes to propose his point of view in the form of a motion—? Or the distinguished delegate of the Soviet Union similarly—? Or perhaps, in the interest of saving time, we should simply let the President decide? But something must be before us if we are to vote, is that not right?"

"Quite right," the President of France agreed in a how-stupid-can-you-be? tone of voice.

"The President will tell you frankly," Prince Koa said, with a chuckle that evoked amused sympathy from many, "that the President intends to stay out of the crossfire as much as possible durin' this debate. If you want a vote, members of the Council, then you've got to move somethin'. That's obvious, as the distinguished delegate of Greece says. Who wants to do the movin'?"

"I move—" Chauncey Baron and Yuri Serapin began together; stopped abruptly and looked at Koa, who shrugged; everybody laughed, though tensions were now rising and the laughter was no longer so amused.

"Mr. President," the Seychelles said in a clear, level voice, "I move that the delegate of the Soviet Union be allowed to proceed."

"Second," said the Prime Minister of India.

"Moved and seconded," Koa responded promptly. "Any further debate?"

For a moment there was a tense silence. Koa banged the gavel.

"Good! Mr. Secretary-General, if you please?"

"Cameroon!" the S.-G. said in his grave, old man's voice.

"*Oui,*" Cameroon said promptly.

"China!"

"Abstention," Ju Xing-dao chirped in his light little voice. There was an immediate buzz of talk and speculation.

"Eire!"

"Ummmm," Eire said slowly, tapping his pipe. "Y—es."

"Egypt!"

"No!" Egypt said promptly.

"France!"

"Abstention," the President of the Republic said as though it were a bore to articulate even that. The buzz of talk increased.

"Greece."

"Yes."

"India!"

"Yes, certainly," she said with a deliberate offhand indifference.

"Iraq!"

"No!" Iraq said spitefully, an echo of all the recent Soviet advances in the Arab world, which had cooled this once-snug friendship. He and Yuri exchanged cold glances.

"Nicaragua!"

"*Sí.*"

"The Seychelles!"

"Yes, of course."

"Tanzania!"

"In the interest of expediting only—yes."

"Tonga!"

"Same reason," Koa said. "Yes."

"United Kingdom!"

"No!"

"United States!"

"No," Chauncey said quietly.

"U.S.S.R.!"

"Yes!" Yuri said triumphantly.

"On this procedural matter, to which the veto of the permanent members does not apply," Koa announced after a moment's study of the Secretary-General's tally, "the noes are four, affirmatives nine, two abstentions. A majority of nine is required by the rules on procedural matters, and the motion of the delegate of the Seychelles is passed. The President of the Soviet Union will continue."

There was a loud burst of applause and pleased outcries from his supporters in audience and press.

[SECURITY COUNCIL UPHOLDS SOVIETS IN FIRST VOTE, the headlines said. HEAVY MAJORITY DEFEATS U.S.]

"Now, Mr. President," Yuri said, leaning forward to his microphone, "if we may proceed without further delays and obstructions by the United States, I for one should like to get on with this important matter. Because of its urgency, and in order to expedite our consideration of it, I shall speak in English so that there will be no delay for translation.

"Mr. President"—and abruptly his tone became stern and emphatic—"does the world really need explanation of what needs no explanation? Is there any doubt why we are here? Is anyone anywhere on this earth unaware of the crisis that brings us here—a crisis created by the imperialist—capitalist—[each word a bullet]—racist circles of the United States of America? Is anyone anywhere ignorant of the crimes of the United States in these recent days? Is anyone—"

"Mr. President," Hamilton Delbacher said quietly, and his audience, many just settling back to hear with relish another stinging attack upon the United States, tensed again—"if the President of the Soviet Union will yield to me—I really must object to his language concerning my country. We know what the world thinks of my country. Or at least we know that the world knows what he thinks of my country. Is anyone —anywhere," he asked, deliberately mimicking, "in doubt? Surely we can maintain civility for a little while longer. I know it is fragile, but we might at least give it a chance."

"Yes," Prince Koa said, "I am inclined to agree."

"Mr. President!" Yuri interrupted, voice rising sharply. "The Soviet Union will not stand for the mockery of this—this—"

"The title is 'President of the United States,'" Ham Delbacher said crisply, not looking at Yuri, seated a scant five feet away, "and I would appreciate it if that is how I am addressed. And referred to. Either that or 'the delegate of the United States.' Or 'the distinguished delegate.' After all, I might say 'this murderer from Moscow,' and you would not like that."

["Wow!" the New York Times exclaimed softly to the Daily Telegraph in the press section. "Wow-ee."

["It's going to be a rough night at Mach II," the Telegraph murmured back. "Fasten your seat belts and have the stewardesses bring us all another drink."]

"Mr. President!" Yuri spluttered, but Prince Koa beamed down comfortably upon him and interrupted.

"Don't know as I'd appreciate that much myself," he agreed. "Maybe the President of the Soviet Union should be a l'il mo' careful. I have a feelin' he's goin' to get responses from the President of the United States."

"Responses!" Yuri snapped scornfully. "How can he respond to the truth about the imperialist capitalist conspiracy led by the United States if he does not engage in infantile insolence? He has nothing else to argue with. The facts will not support him. History does not support him. Two thirds of the nations on the face of this earth do not support him. How can he—"

"Mr. President," Hamilton Delbacher said, "I am not aware of your rules here, but in the Congress of the United States we can demand a 'return to the regular order,' which means that all extraneous nonsense and pointless name-calling stops and the debate returns to the point at issue. It might be well if we did that here."

"I'm afraid," Prince Koa said with a chuckle, "that in the United Nations our rules are subject to change without notice—and nobody *does* notice, very much. I can urge the delegate of the Soviet Union to watch his language, but I can't order him to do it. Perhaps it is better anyway if we let him express himself as he pleases and we will then know better what he's like. You're both new here. We have a lot to learn about you both."

Ham Delbacher smiled.

"You are right, Mr. President. Let him proceed as he pleases. It *is* very enlightening. I reserve the right to interrupt and correct the record at any point, however."

"Mr. President," the Prime Minister of India said sharply to Koa, "there must be some order here. Delegates cannot interrupt one another all the time. That would be sheer chaos."

"Mr. President—" the President of Egypt began; but Koa banged down the gavel and looked suddenly stern.

"One thing I *can* do," he said, "is keep everybody from talkin' at once. The distinguished Prime Minister of India has a very good point and I thank her for it. Mr. President of the United States, sir, you will kindly refrain from interruptin' the delegate of the Soviet Union. On the other hand, Mr. President of the Soviet Union, you will kindly refrain from givin' Mr. Delbacher *cause* to interrupt. This is goin' to be a long evenin', probably a long week, maybe who knows a long month, so let's at least start with some kind of order. Agreed? Agreed. Mr. Serapin, go on."

"Thank you," Yuri said, giving Ham Delbacher an angry glance. "If I *am* interrupted further I shall speak in Russian and the President may then argue with the translator if he likes . . . Now, Mr. President, let me review the circumstances which bring us here.

"Both the President of the United States and myself have come to the top executive positions in our two countries very recently—within days of one another. This being so, I moved at once to try to resolve the outstanding differences between us, which have caused concern to many peoples of the earth and particularly to our own peoples. I invited him to meet me here at the UN so that we could get to know one another a little and begin informal preliminary discussion of some of these issues.

"I hoped that our talks would lead on to a constructive approach by the United States to the solution of these problems. Instead, what happened?

"We only had one brief private talk together. Before I could even begin to explore with President Delbacher the areas of disagreement between us, he had returned to Washington and immediately ordered a $10 billion increase in defense spending. Does anyone doubt that it was directed solely and entirely against the Soviet Union?

"He made no bones of it. He went before Congress and told them that my country and I were threatening the United States and the world with conquest and domination. How dramatic, Mr. President! How exciting for Mr. Delbacher! . . . How frightening for the world.

"Confronted by this abrupt warlike action, dictated no doubt by the capitalist imperialist circles which control the United States and seek to police and conquer the whole world—"

There was a stirring from Ham Delbacher, a lifting of the gavel by Prince Koa.

"—at least," Yuri said smoothly, "that is how we see it, and I am sure how many others at this table and in the United Nations also see it."

There was a burst of applause and Koa brought the gavel down hard; but it took a moment for the approving sounds to die down. Yuri and his delegation, and many others, looked pleased.

"Confronted by this warlike action, we in the Soviet Union felt we had no choice but to put in motion plans for maneuvers which we had been contemplating for some time, but which now seemed absolutely imperative for the safety and security of our country. Surely no one of you, faced with my responsibilities and the sudden threat offered by the United States, would have done otherwise."

He looked sternly around the table. Again there was a scattering of applause from the audience. Several of his colleagues, notably India, Nicaragua and France, nodded firm agreement.

"These maneuvers, however, seemed to upset the ruling circles of the United States, and so Mr. Delbacher, as their agent, began a campaign of threat and bluster against us which really has no place in the reasonable discourse which should occur between civilized states. We had always been led to believe, by its own claims, that the United States was one of these, Mr. President. Indeed," he interjected dryly, *"the* most. We are finding this belief increasingly difficult to maintain."

There was laughter from many in his audience and in the media, particularly those from satellite and supporting countries. He seemed pleased with this, but when Ham Delbacher smiled amicably too, it seemed to excite him.

"Yes, Mr. President!" he said sharply. "I see the President of the United States smile, but I do not think his smile makes much sense in view of the danger he has brought upon the world. Look at the inevitable consequences of his actions! We are here today because of him. The world stands at the very brink of war because of him. He and the imperialist circles of the United States would like to have war, Mr. President, but we will defeat them. The UN will stand together and defeat them! Our votes here will show him that the imperialist racist war-mongering capitalist circles of the United States do not dominate this world of ours, no matter how much they wish to!"

"Mr. President!" the Prime Minister of Great Britain said sharply, "I must protest this kind of language, I really must. The distinguished delegate of the Soviet Union surely can make his points without resort to this kind of propagandizing. All it does is inflame an already intensely aggravated situation. It is no help to our discussion here. It is no help to his own cause. It simply confuses the issue. Can he not desist?"

Prince Koa looked across the table at Yuri.

"You have heard the lady."

"I heard that I have been asked to refrain from telling the truth," Yuri said coldly. "I am afraid that I cannot oblige."

And again his supporters in the audience and among the communist media applauded vigorously. The Prime Minister shrugged with an air of disgust, pursed her lips contemptuously and looked away.

"Yes!" Yuri cried, his voice rising suddenly. "I see the Prime Minister smirking and mocking! I see her making fun of me and my country, Mr. President! I warn her not to smirk and mock too much! We can crush Great Britain and all her outdated pretensions like *that!"*—snapping his fingers—"we can crush anyone like *that!* And that includes—" Admiral Valenko leaned forward hastily and put a hand on his arm. He shook it off angrily, but subsided as Hamilton Delbacher leaned forward to his microphone.

"Does it?" he asked softly, giving the Soviet leader a stony stare. "I would urge the distinguished delegate of the Soviet Union not to be too quick to put it to the test, Mr. President. Not too quick."

"Now, Mr. President," the President of Tanzania said to Koa in an annoyed tone, "it is time that this Council resume its deliberations on an adult basis, instead of listening to delegates bickering like two schoolboys daring one another to cross a line. I *must* request we get on with it, Mr. President. *Please!*"

"I would suggest to the delegate," Ham Delbacher said, "that he address himself to the speaker who has the floor."

"I am addressing you both," Tanzania said.

"I know you are," Ham Delbacher said tartly, "and I resent it. I refuse to accept equal blame for something I am not a party to and I serve notice on you all that from now on I shall challenge every slur upon my country or myself that comes from anyone at this table. I have had enough of this damnable nonsense, and it is going to stop."

There was a gasp from the audience. Tanzania blinked, flushed, looked angry, started to speak, thought better of it, subsided. Prince Koa uttered a heavy sigh that was almost a groan, so openly and naïvely heartfelt that it broke the tension. Everyone laughed, quite genuinely for a moment.

"Well," Koa said as the laughter subsided, "you mus' admit this is a heavy load to carry, distinguished delegates, a heavy load. I'd rather be lyin' under a coconut tree or out catchin' fish, any day. Now, wouldn't you?"

Again there was laughter, this time accompanied by applause, even Yuri and the President relaxing enough to join in. Koa shifted his enormous bulk and approached the microphone again with a determined air.

"Now if we can get on with it, and if the Soviet delegate can restrain himself a little bit, it *would* be helpful. Mr. Serapin?"

"Delegates will remember," Yuri resumed as though nothing had interrupted his narrative, "that there then occurred the famous 'sneak attack scare' promulgated by the ruling circles of the United States, in which the President found himself suddenly alarmed by a traitor from my country who informed him that we were about to attack Western Europe and the northeastern seaboard of the United States. This was to be the greatest wave of horror since the Golden Horde swept across the steppes, I gather. The West was to go down before us like a bowl of jelly, all in one day's time, I gather. It was to be a marvelous spectacle. I only wish," he said dryly to the amused titters of his supporters, "I could live to see it. It was nonsense, utter nonsense!

"But the ruling circles of the U.S., and Mr. Delbacher as their agent, were apparently terrified. Great hullabaloos were raised in the world press. Taking the word of a worthless defector, who is no longer recognized as ever having been a citizen of the Soviet state—and incidentally kidnapping his wife and three children, to use them as weapons to force him to sing the tune of the capitalists—"

"That is not true," the President interrupted. "The defector asked us to give them asylum and we did. Otherwise they would no doubt have been thrown into real captivity, or perhaps even killed, by the kind government of my kind friend."

"The facts are there," Yuri said indifferently. "The world will interpret them. In any event, there was no attack on Western Europe or the northeastern seaboard of the United States, was there? Nothing happened, is that not right? *Nothing at all occurred.* So much for the scare stories put out by the ruling circles of the United States and their agent. Lies, all lies!

"So, then." He paused and took a drink of water. "What happened then? Apparently the 'sneak attack scare' was only sufficient to scare the President of the United States and his imperialist backers and allies. It did not really scare the world, or anyone else with any sense even though Mr. Delbacher put his country and armed forces on partial alert. It did not even scare the American people sufficiently. Many of them could not believe it at all nor do they to this day. They were not willing to accept the war-mongering schemes of the President. Some other means must be found to keep the world properly worried and the American people—or some of them—in the proper warlike mood. So next came the 'submarines in Cuba scare.' That one was a masterpiece, Mr. President! *That* one really shook the world! That one gave everyone a case of nerves and brought us all, in due time, to this table. But that, too, was nonsense. All nonsense!"

"Not quite," the President remarked crisply, and this time Yuri leaned forward, turned to Koa and snapped:

"Mr. President! Am I to be allowed to speak here or not? I demand the end of these interruptions!"

"Seems to me," Koa said, a trace of impatience in his voice, "the distinguished delegate of the United States has been keepin' pretty calm under some pretty strong provocations. Maybe the delegate of the Soviet Union would just proceed?"

For a moment Yuri obviously contemplated making a major fuss of it; then as obviously he thought better and continued.

"Very well. When the imperialist ruling circles of the United States and their agent, Mr. Delbacher, found they were unable to terrify the world and their own people sufficiently with the 'sneak attack scare' they turned to the 'subs in Cuba scare.' And what did that consist of, Mr. President?"

"Subs in Cuba?" Koa inquired innocently and added, when Yuri gave him a sudden sharp look, "Well, you asked me, Mr. President."

"Yes, subs in Cuba!" Yuri snapped. "But subs have always been in Cuba! They have been in Cuba ever since agreements were signed with the late President J. Kennedy in 1963. It has always been known we have subs in Cuba. See, we have subs in Cuba." He smacked the table suddenly with the flat of his hand. "Subs in Cuba! And from *that* comes all this fuss!"

And he made a wide expansive gesture with both arms that took in the solemn-faced delegates watching him intently around the table, the press and diplomats watching in the ranks of seats above, the television cameras and the whole wide world watching, from Barrow to Buenos Aires, from Hong Kong to Lusaka.

"Our subs are in Cuba because we have a treaty with the sovereign Cuban nation giving us those rights! We are both sovereign peoples! We have our sovereign rights! I do not think even Mr. Delbacher, who has issued so many ultimatums since taking office that he has become the President of Ultimatums, would deny that we have the legal right to have our submarines in Cuba. It is absolute and irrevocable. I deny absolutely the power of any capitalist imperialist circles to change that legal situation. It is there. It cannot be changed. It will never be changed! Never, never, never!" And again he slapped his hand on the table, so abruptly and so hard it made several of his fellow delegates jump.

["The shoe will be next," the Washington *Post* murmured to UPI. "No," UPI predicted, "he's not Khrushchev, he's too smooth for that. But I'll admit he's getting close."]

And so he seemed to be as he paused for a moment, took another sip of water and appeared to be gathering himself together for a new burst of indignation. Instead his tone changed abruptly: completely reasonable, completely thoughtful, completely calm.

"Now, Mr. President," he said quietly, "we come to the antics of the new President of the United States—the President of Ultimatums, as I have called him. Why, does one suppose, is he so excessive and so violent in his approach to world affairs? Why is he so hostile to the Soviet Union? Why is he so determined to create a world war between us—a war which he and his country could not possibly win, which none of you could possibly win, against the might of the Soviet Union? We are not seeking such a war, Mr. President and my fellow members of the United Nations. We wish to live in peace with everyone. It is not our purpose to interfere in the internal affairs of anyone. We have never done so, except when peoples struggling to be free of imperialist aggression and domination have invited us to come to their side and aid them. Why should we change now into such horrible warlike monsters as Mr. Delbacher tries to describe us? It is absurd. It is hysterical. And because Mr. Delbacher possesses nuclear weapons and apparently intends to use them if he can find an excuse, it is all terribly dangerous to world peace and to the welfare of all peoples . . .

"Submarines in Cuba, which we have every sovereign right to send and Cuba to receive . . . and what happens in Washington? We invite him to Cuba but he will not come. Instead he issues another ultimatum. He says we must take them out, these subs which have been using Cuban ports by clear legal right, and clearly understood acceptance of the United States,

since 1963! Only once, by President R. Nixon, was there protest. All subsequent Presidents have accepted their presence. But Mr. Delbacher says
we must change the pattern of our maneuvers—*our* maneuvers, Mr. President: I emphasize that because it apparently cannot be emphasized too
much to imperialist circles who seem to think they have some strange
right to interfere in *our* maneuvers. He says that if we do not remove the
subs and thereby change the pattern of *our* maneuvers, there will be
dreadful consequences of some nature he does not specify. At that point,
as you know, he also placed the United States in a condition of national
emergency and its armed forces on worldwide war alert. Then he issues
an ultimatum that we must remove our subs and change our plans in
twenty-four hours' time or there will be these awful consequences.

"Well, Mr. President and fellow members"—and he too sighed heavily
—"confronted by this—not having the slightest idea of what the true nature of this man may be, or how far he might actually go in his threatening
madness—and bearing in mind always the Soviet Union's responsibilities
toward world peace and the well-being of all peoples—I decided to take
the action which has brought us here today.

"I could not risk that this man might actually do what he said he would
do—I could not risk that he might actually plunge the world insanely
into nuclear war—I could not have such a horrible thing as nuclear war
on my conscience! So, as you know, I gave orders that six of our submarines should be withdrawn from Cuba, even though we have a perfect
right to station them there; and I appealed for an emergency meeting of
this Council to see if there might not be some way in which the United
Nations could restrain this individual who threatens to plunge us all into
total destruction on the basis of his fantastic fears and charges about
what Soviet intentions are supposed to be.

"In due course, after all who wish have had a chance to speak, the Soviet Union intends to introduce a formal resolution to pave the way for
this.

"Statesmanship and a decent regard for the world—for *saving* the
world, Mr. President," he said solemnly, his voice dropping to a lower,
somber level to which some listened as if hypnotized, while others, including the American and British delegations, paid tribute with quizzical
smiles to a master performer. "Statesmanship and saving the world! These
are what prompted me to bring us together here today to restrain this
mad war-monger of the United States and the capitalist imperialist racist
circles which he heads. He wishes to destroy the world, my fellow
members! *Do not let him do it.*" His voice sank even lower, a near whisper now. "I beg of you, *do——not——let——him——do it!*"

And he sat slowly back, an exalted expression on his face, while suddenly the room burst into an excited roar of applause and approving
shouts in which not all joined, but quite enough to give the watching

world the impression that a new savior had indeed been conferred upon a grateful universe.

"Mr. President," said Nicaragua with smooth reasonableness, "we have had a long session and I imagine many delegations are weary. I move that the Council stand in recess for dinner until 9 P.M. tonight."

"Don't let him—" the British Prime Minister leaned over and whispered urgently to Hamilton Delbacher, on her right. The warning was unnecessary.

"Mr. President!" he said loudly into the roiling room, which instantly quieted for his words. *"MR. PRESIDENT!* The American delegation demands the right of immediate reply to these scurrilous lies and slanders, this deliberate hiding of the truth! We DEMAND it, Mr. President!"

And he glanced angrily around the table, daring anyone to deny him. Yuri shifted in his chair, but the President cast him such a furious look that not even he quite had the nerve, though he could not resist a deliberately smug little smile as he sat back.

Prince Koa took his time, in the absolute silence that then ensued, to hoist himself closer to his microphone. Grasping it firmly in a huge, pudgy hand, he said with a deliberate softness:

"Why, that seems perfectly reasonable to me . . . Mr. President, if— you—please!" And banged down the gavel in his other hand so hard that it expressed very well an accumulation of contempt and dislike for Yuri Serapin that no words probably could have.

For several moments Ham Delbacher did not speak, carefully arranging the notes he had taken during Yuri's talk, and his own prepared remarks, side by side on the green cloth before him. Then he came to a decision, passed the prepared text to Chauncey Baron, glanced slowly through his notes again, then leaned forward comfortably to his microphone and began to speak in a quiet, level voice:

"Mr. President, I thank you for the chance to reply immediately to these lies and slanders while they are still fresh and before they can appear unchallenged in the press. I appreciate the courtesy, which would have been denied me by the errand boys of the Soviet Union had they had their way."

Nicaragua gave him a nasty look and there was a hiss from somewhere in the gallery. He did not glance up as he responded.

"There speaks the voice of the mindless. It is what the decent must contend with, in this age."

The hissing grew for a moment and he turned to Koa with a thoughtful look.

"It is like a ghastly schoolroom, is it not, Mr. President? We hiss, or we applaud, or we boo, or we exchange verbal brickbats with one another, but Death's-head stands behind every chair. The lives of almost five billions of people are in this room; they are truly what is at issue here. Yet it is like some gruesome gigantic children's game; and like a children's game, what we destroy here can probably not be put back together, ever again . . . *if* we destroy it . . . But, perhaps," he said—and the room was once again absolutely still—"we will not destroy it—if we are brave—and if we find the truth and face the truth—and do what must be done.

"Mr. President, we have been privileged to listen today—and I hope the whole world has paid close attention, for it has been very instructive —to a supreme example of Soviet lying. It has been presented to us by a master—a man so adept at this and all other aspects of Soviet deceit that he has risen, at an unusually early age, by a bloody path to a bloody eminence. There he sits," he said, inclining his head slightly to the right but not looking at him, "and there is what not only the United States, but the freedom-loving peoples of the world as well, must contend with. Let us strip him down as though he were a piece of machinery—which, essentially, he is—and see, as we say in America, what makes him tick."

"Mr. President!" Yuri cried angrily. "What is this? I demand to know what kind of rules these are and what kind of body this is, which permits such—such—"

"Mr. President," Koa said sharply, "you are out of order! You spoke here as you pleased and called the delegate of the United States whatever you wanted to call him, and got away with it. Now it's his turn. You be silent, Mr. President, sir! You let him talk now!"

And he banged the gavel again, and this time there was quite a heartening burst of applause across the room for the cause of Hamilton Delbacher.

"But—" Yuri began again, and again Koa banged his gavel.

"Silence!" he thundered—and being a big man, he had a big voice when he wanted to to use it. "Silence, now, and let the distinguished President of the United States speak on!"

["Ooops!" the L. A. *Times* murmured to the Boston *Globe*. "There goes Tonga." "It'll never be missed," the *Globe* assured him. "Never be missed. Imagine having a clown like that chairing the Council at a time like this!"]

"Thank you, Mr. President," Hamilton Delbacher said, consulting his notes and speaking in a matter-of-fact tone. "Let me take the lies of the Soviet President section by section. His initial comment was to the effect that 'the crisis that brings us here' was a crisis created by 'the imperialist —capitalist—racist circles of the United States of America.' There was a reference to 'crimes of the United States in these recent days,' followed by a reference to 'the imperialist capitalist conspiracy led by the United States.' There then followed a rather lengthy discussion of how Mr. Serapin, being always interested in easing world tensions in his great devotion to world peace, invited me to a meeting here at the UN immediately after we both took office. At that meeting, I failed him badly and

everything has gone wrong since. I think I had best pause here and answer these lies first.

"I am not afraid to say, Mr. President, that I bear some joint responsibility for the crisis that brings us here, in that I did, of course, react to
the threats to world peace and specifically to the United States posed by
the worldwide maneuvers of the Soviet Union and particularly by the
great increase in Soviet submarine strength in Cuba. Pursuant to my oath
of office to preserve, protect and defend the Constitution of the United
States, I did not see that I could do otherwise. It was obvious—it still is
obvious—that the worldwide disposition of Soviet arms which has now
occurred as a result of the maneuvers—the fact that they are there *right
now,* in position to strike swift surprise blows not only at us but at all of
you without exception—posed and poses a very serious threat to this
country, as it does to everyone. It does not take much intelligence to see
this, nor does it take a great deal of foresight to see that the time to oppose these warlike maneuvers of the Soviet Union is before they decide to
strike somewhere, not after.

"My concern about the maneuvers came against a background of our
aborted summit talk here at the UN. I found Mr. Serapin absolutely intransigent, absolutely unyielding in his view that the Soviet Union has an
historic mission to conquer and to rule the world. He made absolutely
clear that this has always been the aim of the Soviet Union, that it has
never deviated from that aim for a moment, and that it fully intends to
accomplish that aim at the earliest possible moment. He made it very
clear that he thinks that moment is approaching with great rapidity and
will be accomplished, if his country can possibly do it, very soon. He
made it very clear that he does not have the slightest doubt that his country can do it. It was against that background that I was forced to assess
the scope and purpose of the Soviet maneuvers and the open and deliberate threat to this country posed by the sudden concentration of submarines at Cienfuegos.

"I did, as Mr. Serapin has said, order an immediate $10 billion emer-
gency expansion of American military capabilities, and I did place the nation on limited national emergency and our armed forces on limited war
alert. I would have failed my responsibility to my people had I not done
so, and so would any of you who failed to take similar action in a similar
situation."

He paused and took a drink of water. His audience was quiet, following
with close attention.

"There was no 'imperialist capitalist conspiracy' led by the United
States in all this. There are no 'imperialist capitalist racist circles' in the
United States responsible for my actions." Suddenly he slapped the table
as hard as Yuri had. He was rewarded with twice the reaction, since no
one expected him to be physically emphatic.

"I am responsible for my actions! *I* am the President of the United States! And it is my judgment that these lying charges, coupled with world-threatening Soviet maneuvers and the open challenge of Soviet subs in Cuba, must be defeated and turned back, for the sake of the safety of the entire world—particularly those parts of it which are still free from Soviet domination and which, like ourselves, intend to remain so . . .

"I believe, however," he said, "that there is, in these charges of the Soviet Union, something fundamental to the character and the actions of its President and those others, several with him today, who help guide its destinies. I do believe that Mr. Serapin, although he spent sufficient time in America in his younger years to know better, really does believe to some degree in 'imperialist capitalist racist circles' in the United States. I think he really does to some extent believe in an 'imperialist capitalist conspiracy led by the United States.' How scathing and how clever some of our domestic critics become when some Americans talk of 'communist conspiracy'! Yet in Moscow, I think, the 'imperialist capitalist conspiracy' is just as much a bugaboo to some minds, and by some just as sincerely believed . . .

" 'Communist conspiracy' is not what worries me, so much as it is the terrifying communist conviction that history has given them an inevitable mandate to assume dominion over the entire earth and force everyone on it to enter their cheerless, hopeless, inhumane, mind-crushing, life-crushing slave state. Combine that with the enormous military machine the Soviet Union has built up over the past couple of decades—far exceeding, as we all know, any possible necessities of self-defense—and one really has something to be concerned about. And the United States and its present President *are* concerned about it; and that, too, is why we are here at this table today . . .

"Mr. Serapin concluded by saying that I am 'determined to create a world war between us,' which he says the United States could not possibly win—adding as a gratuitous and deliberate threat, 'which none of you could possibly win.' He says flatly that it is not the purpose of the Soviet Union 'to interfere in the internal affairs of anyone,' and he claims it has never done so 'except when peoples struggling to be free of imperialist aggression and domination have invited us to come to their side and aid them,' thereby neatly obliterating the history of Afghanistan, Hungary, Czechoslovakia, Cuba and other states where puppet pro-Soviet regimes have been established for the sole purpose of inviting the Soviets to come in . . .

"He says the Soviet Union has a sovereign right to send subs to Cuba, and Cuba a sovereign right to invite them, arguing that it has been understood ever since President Kennedy and the Cuban missile crisis that Soviet subs in Cuba were acceptable to American Presidents—even though now he has tried to send twenty-four in there instead of the usual six or so that come in and out. He appears to be saying that the withdrawal of a paltry six of these is enough to make the remaining eighteen innocuous, and he expects you—and me—to believe it. You may be that gullible," he said with a sudden tartness, "but having in mind the safety of the United States, which I know concerns some of you not at all, I am not.

"And finally Mr. Serapin says that, confronted by my warning to remove the submarines at a time certain, he became suddenly a noble, peace-loving soul, made the great sacrifice of withdrawing six submarines, and besought this Security Council to meet and try to find some way 'to restrain this individual who threatens to plunge us all into total destruction.'

"Such is my own desire, Mr. President. But he and I happen to have a different individual in mind . . .

"And he concludes, O pious thought, with the slogan, 'Statesmanship and saving the world!' which he says must guide the Council to 'restrain this mad war-monger of the United States and the capitalist imperialist racist circles which he heads.' He tells you that I wish to destroy the world, and he beseeches you with thrilling passion, 'Do——not——let——him——do it!'

"Well, Mr. President, I do not say that he is mad, nor do I say that he wishes to destroy the world. But I do say that he has been conditioned from childhood by the Soviet state to believe that Soviet conquest of the world is inevitable and is to be accomplished in his lifetime by whatever ruthless and deceitful means are necessary; and I do say that if this happens it will destroy the world as the human spirit has known it and that this, in terms of the free mind, free spirit, free inquiry, free lives, free destinies, the freedom to be happy—just the plain, simple ordinary, humanly enjoyable aspects of human living—would be a tragedy as great, if not greater, than its physical dissolution.

"Therefore the United States will also present a resolution to this body and if need be to the General Assembly later on; and we invite the adherence of all who understand the implications of this fateful confrontation and the infinite values of human living that hang upon its outcome . . .

"And now, Mr. President," he concluded quietly into the hush that for him, too, whether they agreed with him or not, was as attentive as that given Yuri, "it *has* been a long session and delegates I am sure wish a substantial break before proceeding further. I now move adjournment until 10 A.M. tomorrow."

"Mr. President," the Prime Minister of India protested, "why must we have this delay? This is an urgent matter. I myself wish to speak—"

"Yes," Prince Koa agreed. "You and the Prime Minister of Britain both wish to speak this evening."

"Then why," she said, adjusting her sari so that it floated like a golden cloud and shaking the many bracelets on her arms so that they rang and tinkled in the silent room, "can we not adjourn for dinner until 9 P.M. and then resume? My colleague from Britain and I can at least dispose of our comments for the record at that time. After all, we were given to understand there is some urgency here."

"I bow to the perspicacious and entrancing Prime Minister of India," Ham Delbacher said with a pleasant smile, and did so, a gesture she returned with a somewhat grudging but nonetheless pleased smile of her own. "As always, she makes sense—"

["Oh, boy," the London *Times* murmured to the *Daily Express*. "Is old Ham learning fast!"]

"—and I think her suggestion is an excellent one, providing it has the agreement of our equally delightful lady from Britain?"

["Oh, come now!" the *Daily Express* agreed.]

"Entirely," the British Prime Minister replied with a quick smile. "An excellent idea!"

"Good," he said. "Mr. President, I amend my motion to an adjournment to 9 P.M. this evening."

"Without objection," Koa said swiftly, using the gavel again, "it is so ordered!"

And the room exploded into a hubbub of talk, gossip, laughter, relaxation, as the delegates moved slowly out (Yuri carefully, the President casually, managing to ignore one another) and the media rushed off to file their stories, jabber into their microphones, face their cameras with informed and gravely portentous commentary.

SOVIET, U.S. HURL ANGRY CHARGES IN FIRST COUNCIL MEETING. BOTH PROMISE RESOLUTIONS TO SETTLE CRISIS. SESSION TO CONTINUE INTO NIGHT. BRITAIN, INDIA, CHINA REPORTED WORKING ON COMPROMISE.

There was not, however, any sign of this at 9 P.M. when the Council reconvened and the two ladies took their turns at the microphones. If compromise there was, it was still being born somewhere in the depths of the UN—the initial resolutions, after all, had not yet been introduced and probably would not be for another two or three days—and in the meantime, both were maintaining their positions without sign of acknowledging alternatives, let alone secret compromise. Ju Xing-dao remained, as before, silent, smiling, gently interested and obscure.

"Possibly," Prince Koa suggested as the delegates once more settled into their seats around the table, a few showing signs of having dined not wisely but too well, but most as serious and alert as they had been at the morning session, "we might now revert to the alphabetical order, if that would be agreeable to the Council? . . . Very well. The Chair would like to say that it is his intention, if this meets with Council approval, to hold consecutive sessions this week until this matter is disposed of. We are now approaching August, and August in New York is not a month of charm, as we all know. We shall be here, of course, because this will undoubtedly go to the General Assembly, but at least we can get our work in this body completed as expeditiously as possible."

"Hear, hear!" said Eire heartily, twinkling around his pipe. His sentiments were echoed generally from floor and galleries.

"Therefore, it is contemplated by the chair that we will have morning sessions at 10 A.M., afternoon sessions at 3 P.M., and if members so desire, night sessions beginning at 9 and lasting at your pleasure, every day except the weekends. It is foolish to punish ourselves too much, yet the seriousness of the situation demands of us, it seems to me, that we stick pretty close to our hoein' and get it over with. Agreed? Agreed. Now. On the list of speakers, I think we can accommodate comfortably maybe two in an evenin' and you know we have our two for tonight. In fact, Mr. Secretary-General, I believe you tol' me it was not more than two hours after Mr. Serapin's request for a meetin' that you received a cable from our charmin' lady from India askin' to be placed on the speakers' list for openin' day, and perhaps not more than half an hour after that when you got one from our charmin' lady from the United Kingdom. So order of request is same as alphabetical in this case, so that's how we'll do it tonight . . . I would like to present to the Council, and to our watchin' and listenin' audience aroun' the world, the beautiful and distinguished Prime Minister of India!"

"Thank you, Mr. President," she said in her strongly accented, cultured English, disposing her sari—a misty purple one now, set off by golden bracelets and enormous ear bangles of the same metal—carefully about her chair and settling herself comfortably at the microphone. "You are too kind with your generous words about 'beautiful and distinguished,' but I accept them even so." And she gave him a pleasant smile before she turned back to the microphone and her face turned stern to suit her words.

"Mr. President, Mr. President of the United States, Mr. President of the Soviet Union, my sister Prime Minister, distinguished delegates: It is with a humble spirit that I speak to you tonight. Although I represent, as you know, the second largest aggregation of human beings on the face of this earth, we do not possess the military power that might be expected to go with such size. Therefore India made the decision some years ago— some decades ago—that our influence in the world, if there was to be any, must be directed more along spiritual and persuasive lines than along the military lines of the crisis which bring us together now. We do not believe in threats and ultimata. We do not believe in belligerent gestures and warlike acts. India believes in peace and will always be found working for peace."

[In the diplomatic gallery the Ambassador of Pakistan murmured something behind his hand to his aide, but it was too quiet to be heard by their neighbors. His aide smiled and nodded with a wry expression.]

"Therefore, Mr. President, there can essentially be no doubt where India stands in this present controversy [pronouncing it as the British, con-*trah*-ver-sy]. It is not on the side of those who would make war. It is on the side of those who would make peace."

She paused, shifted her sari; gold bracelets and earrings clinked and tinkled.

"It is, therefore, on the side of the Union of Soviet Socialist Republics."

[There was a rustling and stirring in the press section as several wire service reporters swung out of their seats and hurried up the aisles to go to the press room and file their bulletins.]

"I must apologize to my good friend—whom I wish to be my good friend, though I have not yet had the pleasure of a talk with him—the President of the United States, if this seems somewhat harsh and inimical to his point of view. I am afraid he has given me little choice."

And she looked solemnly at Hamilton Delbacher, who looked solemnly back. He did not look at Yuri, but was told by Chauncey later that his face was completely expressionless.

"Mr. President, in a situation of such gravity—the gravest, perhaps, that the world has ever faced—certainly that this body has ever faced—I think it is incumbent upon each of us to state the reasons that have prompted the position taken by her—or his—country. I have no hesitation in stating India's.

"Leaving aside the sequence of events which the President of the United States has used to justify his position, what is the essential reality that faces us? It is that the Soviet Union, in perfect accord with its sovereign rights, is conducting maneuvers of its forces; and that in conjunction with those, it has, at the invitation of its ally Cuba, stationed certain submarines at a Cuban base. All of this is perfectly correct according to international law, the practice of nations and the treaty between these two sovereign states. Therefore because the President of the United States believes he saw something in the eyes of the President of the Soviet Union, or psychoanalyzes his youth and training, or considers his attitude to be something or other, does not change the situation."

There was a spatter of applause and amusement. For the first time her stern expression relaxed, she permitted herself a small smile. Then she became stern again.

"The Soviet Union is not making war on anyone. It is not issuing ultimata to anyone. It is not telling the United States where to move its
forces or saying that it cannot go here or go there. It is doing none of
these things. It is simply acting as a sovereign power, threatening no one.
All perception of threats, and all violent acts in response to supposed
threats, come from the President of the United States. Why is he doing
this, Mr. President? We have heard his explanation, but to me it does not
seem to make much sense."

Again there was applause, stronger now. Hamilton Delbacher, who had
decided already that there was no point in interrupting this determinedly
one-sided presentation, kept his face carefully impassive, staring thoughtfully down at the table top, chin on folded hands, a slight pursing of the
lips his only reaction.

"Mr. President," the Prime Minister said, her tone changing now to one
almost of pleading, "can we not persuade the President of the United
States to abandon these policies which, in the estimation of India and I
think many others here, can lead only to world disaster and destruction?
Is there nothing we can do to convince him that his fears are groundless,
that he is only seeking trouble where none exists? Surely there must be a
way out of this impasse without saber-rattling, gun-shaking, war-mongering, threats, ultimata, all the paraphernalia of war that could instantly destroy the earth if we were such fools as to permit it to break out."

Again applause, much stronger and more fervent now. She looked
straight at the President of the United States, turning upon him the full
and very considerable strength of her somber and determined personality,
addressing him directly as though they were alone at some personal summit in Washington or Delhi.

"Mr. President," she said earnestly, "I do beseech you—think better of
this! You and your country are not threatened. World peace is not threatened—except by your own hasty and ill-advised actions. There is no necessity for saber-rattling and war-mongering, no necessity for threats and
ultimata! The Soviet Union is not threatening you or anyone! Can you
not see this?

"Mr. President, you have a great chance to be the world's savior in this
situation if you will only exercise it. It is you who began this, it is you
who can finish. The conscience of the world demands it of you, if you
have conscience yourself, and I think you do. Abandon your inflammatory armaments build-up. Abandon your national emergencies, your war
alerts and your threats and ultimata. Accept the facts of the world as they
are, that is all we ask of you. The Soviets are maneuvering: they have a
right to do so. They are positioning submarines, perhaps: they have a
right to do so. In due course the maneuvers will end. In due course the
submarines will go. In due course, all will be as it was again. Why then

must you, in a moment of fear and impatience, perhaps precipitate the very thing you wish to avoid?

"Certainly we of the world wish you to avoid it, Mr. President! *We* do not wish to be caught in the middle should your unfounded fears of the Soviet Union lead you to precipitate war. We do not wish this. And we do not wish war upon you. It could only destroy your country—it could only destroy the Soviet Union—it could only destroy us all.

"We beg of you—reconsider! Withdraw your violent actions! Withdraw your threats to peace! Let us live, Mr. President! Let us live!"

And to a final burst of applause, now almost a roar, she drew her lovely sari about her, adjusted her bracelets and earrings once again with a cling! and a ping! and settled back in her chair, darkly severe face aglow with what appeared to be genuine earnestness and exhortation.

From the President there came no response save a long, slow, impassive look which conceded nothing, promised nothing, said nothing. The cameras picked it up and sent it flashing across the world. No one who saw it knew what, if any, impact her words had made upon him.

Yuri Serapin got up from his seat, came swiftly over and clasped both her hands in his with a grateful bow.

"Thank you," he said, voice clear and carrying in the sudden abrupt hush. "The world owes you more than we can ever express."

"Thank you, Mr. President," she said with a graceful little bow in return. "I gladly do what I can to help."

And again the applause welled up and rolled over them both while the cameras turned and the reporters reported and the cause of Hamilton Delbacher went down while the cause of Yuri Serapin rose high.

Against this background the Prime Minister of Great Britain had her work cut out for her, and she obviously knew it as she cleared her throat, tucked in a stray hair, looked about her with a pleasant smile while the hubbub gradually diminished. Hr female colleague looked at her with an expression which, among many old, remembered, bitter things from history's cupboard, carried also one clear message for the present, as blunt, concise and triumphant as though she had said it aloud: *Top that, if you can!* A mind equally as intelligent and determined as hers knew it could not; the British Prime Minister began along a different tack. The Council and its audience settled down again into a fascinated silence as two strong ladies met in battle.

"Mr. President," the British Prime Minister said in a calmly reasonable voice. "Prime Minister, Mr. Presidents, distinguished delegates: my personal congratulations to you, Prime Minister, for a brilliant and effective rhetorical presentation of things as you see them. It will come as no surprise to you or anyone that I do not agree with much that you say, but I cannot fault your effectiveness. I only wish I were equally unhampered."

"By what, Prime Minister?" the Indian Prime Minister inquired softly. "The same forum is now yours."

"But I, you see," her colleague explained pleasantly, "am constrained by the facts. It is difficult."

"I am sure you will overcome them," the Prime Minister of India remarked with equal pleasantry. "Please proceed."

["Meow, meow!" the *Daily Mail* whispered to the *Christian Science Monitor* as the audience erupted in discreet but delighted laughter. "Prime Ministers Have Hair-pull at UN," the *Monitor* whispered back. "Mercy, what a story!"]

"Mr. President," the Prime Minister of Great Britain said with a jolly laugh that cost her considerably more than she showed, "I will acknowledge a hard hit—a hard hit! I only hope my poor stodgy logic will suffice to at least hold my colleague at bay until I can state my case. She is formidable, Mr. President; but so, I think"—and her tone became abruptly serious and unamused—"are the facts which she has neglected to mention in her most effective comments . . .

"Mr. President, it may be because of India's geographical location—the fact that she is separated from the Soviet Union by other states—but somehow there seems to be a psychological separation too. The Soviet Union manages to have this psychological advantage with many of her sympathizers in this world. She seems a lot farther away than she actually is, in this day of missiles, jets and instant annihilation.

"To us, psychologically, and to Europe in general, I think, she seems much closer. And to the United States, of course, the Soviet Union, possessing as she does the client state of Cuba ninety miles off the tip of Florida, and Siberia being only fifty-five miles across the Bering Strait, she seems close indeed. Actually, there are no distances these days. Everyone is neighbor to everyone and only in the farthest reaches of Africa, South America and the Antipodes, perhaps, is there really geographic space to separate weaker nations from the seat of the world's troubles.

"That seat, I might say to my colleague from India, is not in the United States of America, easy target though America is. It resides squarely and implacably in the Kremlin in Moscow and other states are right to look to it as the fount and focus of the great majority of the world's problems. This is how the United Kingdom regards it, and I make no apologies for that because I think it conforms quite closely to the facts—those facts which I do not intend to 'overcome,' but to use as they deserve to be used in my comments here tonight.

"Light though my colleague makes of it, there is much to be said about the importance of the training received by Soviet leaders as it bears upon the destiny of the world. That destiny, they are taught, is to be conquered by and permanently subjected to the rigid and unbreakable control of the Soviet system. It is not a destiny that I think my friend would like to contemplate for India, any more than I would for Britain. Yet the attempt to impose it is what ultimately confronts us all unless we can somehow persuade the Soviet Union to halt its drive in this direction.

"There is much more at stake here, as I suspect the previous speaker knows, than the legalistic application of surface facts. It is true that the facts, stripped down to the bare bones she offers, would appear to favor the Soviet Union. It does have a right to hold maneuvers, of course, as do we all. It does have the right under its treaties and understandings with Cuba to station submarines at the Cuban base. The President of the United States has acted on what he perceives to be potential and implicit threats to his country rather than on actual statements out of Moscow— other than those statements, of course, which have incessantly and un- swervingly proclaimed for seventy years that communism intends with ab- solutely determination to destroy all capitalist states and bring us all under the absolute domination of the Soviet system.

"This is not something that I for one contemplate with equanimity and pleasure I might say to my colleague from India, even though it seems to concern her not at all."

"It is not the issue here!" the Prime Minister of India snapped, and there was some agreeing applause.

"I beg to differ," the Prime Minister of Great Britain said calmly. "It is, quite essentially, the only issue."

There were boos, and a sharply disagreeing glance from her Indian col- league, but she ignored both.

"In the judgment of Her Majesty's Government, there is a deep and most disturbing threat not only to the United States but to all of us in these worldwide Soviet maneuvers. Why worldwide, in the first place? Why is it necessary to distribute Soviet arms across the face of the globe so that the entire map seems to be bristling with them at this very mo- ment? Is it not deliberately to cow, to frighten, to intimidate and terrorize the rest of us? What else is their purpose, Mr. President? Let me halt here and ask the Soviet President direct: what actually is he contemplating with these maneuvers, if it is not to frighten and intimidate us all?"

And she paused to turn to Yuri and await his reply. For several mo- ments it seemed he would give none, staring straight ahead and ignoring her question; then he thought better of it and spoke, though grudgingly.

"The lady is giving us a very dramatic picture of her version of the world, Mr. President," he said, "done in very harsh and dramatic colors. I have no comment to make upon it. She has the floor."

"You beg the question, Mr. President," she told him tartly.

"You exaggerate it, madam," he said. Prompt laughter and applause re- warded him. She flushed but stood her ground.

"I do not exaggerate the fear you have aroused in many well-informed and aware people throughout the world. I ask you again, why are you deliberately trying to intimidate us?"

"I am not trying to do that," he said, tone almost sullen now. "If you see it that way, that is your problem. I pity you and the President for being so timid, Prime Minister. Fortunately others have much stronger nerves than you."

"My nerves are strong enough," she snapped, "but I am not a fool, Mr. President. Nor are you. You know perfectly well what you are doing and your refusal to tell us why only serves your purpose by making perceptive people more uneasy. Why will you not tell us?"

"Mr. President," the Prime Minister of India said, jingling her adornments and frowning severely as she placed a hand on her microphone, "must the British Prime Minister bully the President of the Soviet Union? He has answered her sufficiently. Can she not carry on?"

"Very well," her colleague said, "then he will not answer. That is what stands on the record, if that is the way you both want it. He refuses to tell us why he is deliberately threatening and intimidating the world with these maneuvers. Thus does he lend complete credence to the actions of the President of the United States, who like any intelligent human being must act on what experience tells him of others and their intentions, no matter what innocence they may pretend.

"The President was obviously not mistaken in his judgment of Mr. Serapin. Mr. Serapin obviously has other plans for his egregious maneuvers which are cluttering up the skies and the seas and as many lands as he can reach around the globe. They are not necessary for the defense of the Soviet Union, they are not made imperative by any threatening act by anybody. They are the evil brain-child of Mr. Serapin and his colleagues in the Kremlin, for some purpose that deserves the world's condemnation and the world's united opposition, if the world knows what is good for it. I am not so sure it does, but—"

"I am not so sure that it needs to be lectured on that by Britain," the Prime Minister of India interjected swiftly. There was laughter and applause.

"Possibly not," her colleague agreed, flushing, "but neither should it be bemused by the half-facts and carefully obfuscated presentation of the delegate of India. Foreign ships have but to appear at the island of Diego Garcia, thousands of miles away, and India squeals like a stuck pig. Yet twenty-four Soviet submarines, any handful of which, bristling as they are with missiles, could hit America, appear on the underside of Cuba perhaps two hundred miles all told from continental United States, and you scoff and are horrified because the President becomes concerned and takes drastic action to get them out. I say thank God the United States has a leader again who is capable of taking strong action."

"As long as we are able here to stop it from becoming *too* strong," the Indian Prime Minister again interjected dryly.

"My colleague persists," the British Prime Minister said coldly, "in being frivolous with a matter of the utmost gravity. There *is* no peaceable excuse for the concentrating of Soviet submarines in Cuba. There *is* every reason for the President of the United States to react as swiftly and strongly as he has. It is the hope of Her Majesty's Government that a majority of the United Nations, perceiving that peace is indivisible in this day and age, and that when one of us is threatened all of us are threatened, will stand together to oppose the imperialistic actions and ambitions of the Soviet Union. Certainly we are ready to do all we can to bring about such unity.

"Mr. President, Her Majesty's Government cannot protest and condemn too strongly the Soviet maneuvers which have cast fear into the entire world. We cannot protest and condemn too strongly the deliberate flirting with world disaster which has prompted the sending of excessive numbers of submarines to Cuba. Both must be opposed as vigorously and strongly as can possibly be by peace-loving nations of the world.

"Let us endorse and give full support to the actions of the President of the United States, who has taken the lead in trying to halt both these terrible threats to peace. Let us transfer this burden where it properly belongs, to the United Nations, and by doing so, remove both Soviet intimidation and the possibility that United States may be forced into a reaction so extreme that it can only end in the calamity none of us wants.

"There must be a middle ground. It is up to us to find it. Honorable delegates should remember that the Soviet maneuvers continue and that the President of the United States has only 'suspended,' not cancelled, his ultimatum. We do not have much time to indulge ourselves in rhetorical games. Let us work together to find a solution both sides can adhere to: otherwise, we are all lost."

And she pushed her microphone aside and sat back, grim-faced. A fair amount of applause responded, but it was obvious once again that it was not friends of the United States who dominated the audience.

Prince Koa leaned forward and started to lift his gavel; the earnest voice and clipped British-African accent of the President of Tanzania stopped him.

"Mr. President," he said, large earnest eyes even larger and more earnest behind their heavy glasses, "I know it may possibly upset the schedule you outlined earlier, but I think, as a relatively neutral party to this dispute who represents perhaps many other neutrals, that I should like to speak at this point. With all respect to the two Presidents and the two charming Prime Ministers, possibly I can end our discussion this evening on a more positive and impartial note than has so far been achieved. I should like the opportunity to try. It is, after all, not yet 11 P.M."

"Is there objection?" Koa asked, looking around the table. No one objected, most nodded. "Mr. President, you have the floor."

"Thank you," the President of Tanzania said. His face became solemn, his tone grave. He was obviously aware that history's eyes were upon him, and he was obviously determined to conduct himself in a manner worthy of its regard.

"Mr. President, what do we start with here? Let us admit it: we start with two, equal wrongs.

"Yes!" he said emphatically as both Yuri Serapin and Hamilton Delbacher stirred uneasily. "Two, equal wrongs. We have heard the two principal partisans, the Presidents, state their positions; we have heard two strong advocates, the Prime Ministers, each defending the position she favors; but we have heard nobody say: both sides are wrong.

"If it is wrong for the Soviet Union to hold worldwide maneuvers and take actions with submarines which the President of the United States chooses to regard as hostile, then it is also wrong for the President of the United States to react so violently, to seek enormous arms build-ups, to order national emergencies and war alerts, to issue an ultimatum which, had it not been met with such statesmanlike forebearance by the President of the Soviet Union, might already have caused, at this very moment, a universal incineration. If there are condemnations and united oppositions here, then it seems to Tanzania, and I think possibly to other neutrals, that they must be applied across the board to both sides. Only out of such an evenhanded approach can there come a sensible compromise.

"And it does seem to us, Mr. President, that sensible compromise is the only solution. Peace cannot be preserved by the superpowers growling at one another like hyenas over a fallen zebra. It must come down to what each regards as vital to its own safety. And both must be prepared to yield on that point to the common good of all mankind. It is only thus that peace can be secured. And that is our task here in the United Nations and most particularly in this Security Council.

"It may be true, Mr. President, as President Serapin would have us believe, that maneuvers of such a vast worldwide scale are necessary to the safety and security of the Soviet Union. It may be true that treaties and understandings permit the stationing of submarines in Cuban waters within very easy striking distance of continental United States. But neither of these two things is exactly conducive to world peace, as witness our being here tonight. Nor, on the other hand, does the United States response to them appear to be the ideal way of handling the situation, either.

"It may be true, as President Delbacher tells us, that he felt that he detected in President Serapin a harsh and implacable attitude which, taken together with military actions of the Soviet Union, gave President Del-

bacher cause for alarm. Yet that can hardly be said to justify such extreme reactions on President Delbacher's part, actions which really almost would have come, in earlier times, as the result of an actual state of
war. Yet we do not have a state of war today, Mr. President. Nobody has
taken that step. Presumably nobody wants to. Certainly the great majority of the United Nations does not want anybody to. It is up to us to prevent it, then, by the most effective means we can.

"Under some circumstances, this might be by a simple appeal to both
parties to exercise restraint and self-control; but we have often had occasion in this Council to observe how far that gets us. It will have to be
something stronger than that, and there is already, one sees by the evening papers, the possibility of a compromise being talked about by some
delegations. Tanzania welcomes such efforts and will do everything it can
to assist in bringing them to fruition. But more than that, it seems to us,
is needed a change in attitude on the part of both the superpowers if the
world is to emerge from the shadow of their constant bickering and constant jockeying for power. That is the only way to really lift the burden
from the backs of mankind. There has to be a change of heart.

"President Delbacher and his partisan, the distinguished Prime Minister
of Great Britain, say that this change of heart must occur most extensively and noticeably in the Sovet Union; they say the attitude of the Soviet leadership and the training of the Communist Party create an
unyielding and implacable desire for world conquest. Yet there are other
ways of looking at it, and of looking at them.

"There are many of us, Mr. President, who believe that there is an
equally distasteful attitude in the ruling circles of the United States. I will
not use derogatory adjectives in the manner of President Serapin, because
I am not an ideologue and I am not speaking in an ideological sense—but
there *are* ruling circles in the United States, and many of us believe that
they, too, have long been engaged on a form of conquest. Not colonial
conquest in the old sense, or even in the sense the Soviet Union would
imply—or even in the sense"—he paused and looked thoughtfully at Yuri
Serapin, who was following his words with close attention—"that the Soviet Union sometimes practices." Yuri frowned and there were a few obedient hisses from the audience. "Rather, I mean principally in an economic sense, in the taking of commercial advantage, in the spread of
American ways and attitudes, inescapable perhaps with the spread of
commercial conquest, yet no more palatable to many of us than any other
kind of colonialism . . . We think, as I say, that there are two sides to it,
and that two wrongs do not make a right."

Here he received his first round of applause; looked very pleased for a
second; then resumed his dignified air and continued.

"Attitudes on both sides must change, Mr. President, but I recognize
this is a long-term proposition and perhaps beyond our scope or authority

here, except to urge. I think both sides understand that we do." He looked from President to President, but both remained impassive. He sighed audibly and went on to his conclusion.

"Mr. President, obviously both the United States and the Soviet Union must be encouraged to compromise their terribly dangerous differencs in the matter now before us. Each must abandon rigidity—arrogance—arbitrariness—hostility. Each must regain a sense of responsibility to the world community. Each must exercise restraint. Each must yield position to some degree in order to further the common good.

"The world expects this from them, Mr. President. The world has a right to demand it. As our deliberations proceed this week, let us be always alert to note signs of this, and to use them in the furtherance of our common desire for peace, in which I know both contending powers join and for which each must be prepared to sacrifice some degree of advantage."

And looking pleased with himself, and with the renewed applause that greeted his hopeful and well-meaning conclusion, he sat back and smiled earnestly around the table.

From neither President, even then, did his views receive recognition, aside from a slight bow and smile, somewhat ironic, from the President of the United States; and a polite but still impassive tap-tap of hands, supposedly applause, from the President of the Soviet Union. For a second the President of Tanzania looked obviously disappointed; then his expression, too, became impassive as if to say: Well, I tried. It is not my fault if they will not listen. His brief moment of conciliation passed, worth no more in the media than a casual line—"The President of Tanzania urged moderation in a brief address to the Council as the evening session ended."

For end it did, on a motion from a rather surprising quarter, even though there was some disposition to continue on for another hour or two.

"Members of the Council," Prince Koa said, "I think we can congratulate ourselves that we have accomplished a good deal today—five speakers so far, ten to go. Perhaps tomorrow we can all finish up and then we can get down to the resolutions. I'm assumin'," he added with a smile, "that it'll be 'resolutions,' plural, so we'd best get at 'em as fast as possible, because we'll be a while gettin' rid of 'em, I have a feelin'."

"Mr. President," the Greek Ambassador said, "it is still not 11 P.M. Perhaps in the interests of progress, one or two more might like to speak this evening—?"

"Mr. President," the Seychelles said, "I should like to avail myself of the privilege if it is agreeable to the Coun—"

"Mr. President," Ju Xing-dao said in his gentle little voice with its undercurrent of what appeared to be chuckling good humor. Instantly the room froze into silence.

"Does the distinguished delegate of China wish to speak tonight?" Koa inquired. "If so, alphabetically he has precedence over our friend from the Seychelles."

"No, Mr. President," Ju replied, "not at all. We are all exhausted now, I believe. We have accomplished much, true, but the ears are somewhat weary from it, do you not think?"

And he beamed around the table to the accompaniment of quick, sycophantic laughter that welled up obediently from the audience, hanging on his every word.

"Whatever the members desire," Koa said.

"I for one," Ju said in the same jolly-chipmunk way, "desire my rest. Mr. President, I move we stand adjourned to 10 A.M. tomorrow, as you suggested. I will say now, incidentally, that the People's Republic of China *will* speak very briefly tomorrow. Very briefly. It is our earnest hope that others will do the same so that we may proceed forthwith to the substantive business of this emergency meeting."

"I second that," Koa said amicably. "Does anyone second the motion to adjourn?"

"Second," said the Seychelles and several others.

"Without objection, so ordered," he said, and gave the gavel a final bang as they all rose, stretched, started their babel of tongues and on the wave of it washed themselves out the door.

Twenty minutes later, relaxing in the Presidential suite of the Waldorf-Astoria, the American delegation agreed that no discernible trend had yet developed—"except the usual one of criticism of the United States," Chauncey Baron amended with a wry smile.

"Of which," Hamilton Delbacher agreed, "there will be considerably more tomorrow. But on the whole I didn't feel that we did so badly. I would assume the balance lies somewhere along the lines Tanzania was putting forward. The usual plague on both your houses."

"That isn't enough," Mark said. "There's got to be an outright condemnation of the Soviet Union, sufficiently strong to make them think twice."

"Well," Chauncey replied, "there isn't going to be. The last time anything close to that happened was Afghanistan, and you saw how scrupulously they obeyed that: sloughed it off as though it had never happened and went right on slaughtering Afghanis. There's nothing to indicate they'll be any more co-operative this time."

"Except," Art Hampton pointed out, "that the ultimatum then goes back into effect."

"Does it, Mr. President?" Roger Hackett inquired.

There was silence while he swiveled his rocking chair and stared thoughtfully out over the lighted chasms of Manhattan. How many there had followed the session today? A great many, he imagined, though many others had probably already ceased to worry, turned their backs on it, assumed with a sigh of relief that since the UN was debating it, the pressure was off, the crisis eased, war no longer an imminent threat. For himself, he felt no lessening of tension whatsoever and this was obvious when he finally swiveled back and turned a candid and troubled gaze upon him.

"I think it must, don't you? How else are we to retain credibility?"

"Even credibility at the cost of world war?" Herb Esplin asked quietly, his irreverent humor for once put aside.

"Even that," the President said. "I'm sure you understand that all of this has been, essentially, an exercise in building up my credibility. I have *acted as though* I had sufficient force to back up everything I have said. I have *acted as though* we were indeed, as my predecessor and his predecessors were so fond of saying, 'still the strongest power in the world,' even though it is no secret to anybody that those words are now some way from actual fact. I have *acted as though* I could issue an ultimatum and make it stick. It has all been quite deliberate. The risks have been extreme, but the risks of doing nothing and *acting as though* we were weak, ill-prepared, incapable of strong action and unable to make good our commitments would have been even greater—in my judgment, which has had to be controlling."

"And do you think, Mr. President," Representative Bill Lapham asked, "that this has been sufficient to bluff them?"

"It brought Serapin here," the President pointed out.

"And left eighteen of his subs still in Cuba," Congressman Lapham said.

"I have hopes we can get the rest of them out, now that we've got the process started."

"Not on the basis of today's debate," Ambrose Johnson remarked gloomily.

"No," the President agreed, "but I just have an idea, once all the fine statements are made for the record and we get down to the horse-trading, that there will be very strong pressure by such as our lady from India, for instance, to get further concessions from him."

"And from us, what?" Herb Esplin inquired.

"Full cancellation of the ultimatum," Ham Delbacher said. "Ending the state of national emergency. Dropping the war alert. Possibly even cancelling the orders for new military equipment under the Elrod bill."

"Are you prepared to yield all that?" Mark asked sharply. The President smiled.

"Inch by inch," he said, "if at all. . . . No, I'm not prepared to yield on everything. One or two of them, I might, to some extent. It's soon going to be a contest between friend Yuri and me as to how cosmetic we can each afford to be. But I'm determined to get those subs out of there."

"Essentially," Art Hampton said, "isn't their presence there cosmetic in itself? If they aren't in Cuba they'll be somewhere else in striking distance. And if not, then there's plenty of other things to take their place."

"Yes, but they're the symbol. And so are the maneuvers themselves, of course. As a matter of fact—" He paused.

"He won't abandon those," Chauncey Baron predicted. "If that's what you're thinking."

"He might," the President said, "if he thought there was sufficient quid pro quo."

"Then you *are* prepared—" Mark began, but Hamilton Delbacher smiled and lifted a cautionary hand.

"I'm just thinking out loud, now. Lots of things could happen before this is over. Meanwhile, Chauncey, how are you coming on the language of our resolution?"

"I've got the bones," Chauncey said and, referring to a sheaf of handwritten notes, read them the rough draft.

"If anybody has any ideas, give them to me," he suggested at the end, "and we'll kick it around and try to work them in. I don't suppose we'll be offering resolutions until day after tomorrow."

"Better be prepared for tomorrow," the President said, "knowing our friend's propensity for grabbing the headlines. In fact, I think you'd better table it tomorrow morning when we convene."

"O.K.," the Secretary of State agreed with a smile. "There goes a good night's sleep. Roger, want to help me?"

"Sure," the Secretary of Defense agreed. "Want to go back to delegation headquarters?"

"O.K.," Chauncey said. "We'll have to round up a secretary at this late hour, but I suppose that can be done."

"I used to be a court reporter in my misspent youth," Congressman Lapham said with a smile. "That's how I worked my way through University of Virginia Law School. I'll volunteer."

"Good man," the President said. "Get it back to me at 9 A.M. I'll see the rest of you at 10."

"We must turn in too," Art Hampton said as they all rose. "Ten more speeches to get through tomorrow."

"I may skip it after I hear China," the President said. "A lot of things from Washington are piling up already."

But when he learned, in a telephone call that came shortly after they left, what China was going to say, he decided possibly he had better plan on attending the full session. The gentle little voice, full of some secret amusement, did not have anything particularly amusing to convey.

Nor did it encourage the President of the Soviet Union, either, as he prepared methodically for bed at Soviet headquarters. He had read over the latest dispatches from Moscow, received from his military associates their reports on the excellent progress of the maneuvers, now fully activated around the globe, and had been pleased to hear that the six subs withdrawn from Cuba had successfully made their landfall at the secret Soviet base on the Caribbean coast of Soviet-controlled Nicaragua. There they were resting, all missiles targeted on the United States, until the next move might develop in the global game he was playing with Hamilton Delbacher; an effective little covey, to be called upon if needed.

Appraising the day just concluded, Yuri Serapin could see little cause for worry and much for satisfaction. He had always considered the Indian Prime Minister a ruthless and generally unpredictable woman, but fortunately her hatred of the West was such that Moscow had never had to do very much to secure her support for most Soviet ventures. She had been uneasy about Afghanistan and, much as she despised Pakistan, unnerved by constant Soviet pressure there and on her own Rajasthan; but as long as communist activities were not too openly obvious outside her borders or too subversive within, she appeared to be convinced that India could remain untouched and immune. Meanwhile she looked with the blandest sympathy upon all Soviet adventures elsewhere, provided only that they sufficiently hurt the West. He was quite confident, perhaps a little too much so, that on this occasion as on many others, she would be found willingly and forcefully supporting the communist point of view. Certainly her remarks in the Security Council had indicated as much.

He did not, therefore, put too much stock in the gossip of the Delegates' Lounge, already leaking into the press, that India, Britain and possibly China were working together on some sort of compromise resolution. He did not honestly see what such a resolution could be, or how it was possible to reconcile such differing positions as those of himself and his antagonist in the White House. He would admit it to no one, but he had secretly been much more impressed with the President today than he had on their first meeting a month ago. There was a new assurance and confidence. A certainty of power as firmly seated as his own; yet what did it matter, when all was said and done? He still did not command the power that Yuri did; and since Yuri had no intention whatsoever of being bound by what the UN decided if it in any way hindered or embarrassed him, there was nothing to worry about.

The problem really was how to make what the UN did conform to

long-range Soviet intentions; and this he did not deem such a major problem, either. He had his plan as carefully mapped out as though he were in
a chess game, and little the UN, or the United States for that matter,
might do could effectively change a move of it.

It would not, however, look well in the eyes of the world if the resolution adopted here to "solve" the present crisis were to emerge too obviously critical of Soviet actions or in too obvious conflict with ultimate Soviet purposes. He assumed the United States would introduce a resolution
harshly critical of himself and his country; similar in essence and tone, no
doubt, if not in exact wordage, to the one he had prepared, before leaving
the villa at Sochi, for introduction against the United States. There would
ensue another debate, and there would be votes that would reveal the essential majority sentiment. Whatever the words might say, he was sure
the votes would reveal that the sentiment was still what it had long been
despite occasional waverings such as had occurred with Afghanistan: an
uneasy mixture of respect, admiration and fear that added up to sometimes tacit, more often outright, compliance with Soviet aims.

His colleagues had given him the enthusiastic approval he was beginning to accept as his due, when they had returned to delegation headquarters after tonight's session. He had been praised for his effectiveness,
his powerful logic, the inescapable truth of the things he had said concerning the erratic course of the American President; and he had been
heartily and effusively congratulated for the clever way in which he had
appropriated for the Soviet Union the leadership of the world's desperate
desire for peace and stability.

"You will receive the Nobel Peace Prize, Yuri Pavlovich!" the Defense Minister had assured him jovially.

"When we take Sweden," he had responded with a confident laugh, "we
shall see that it is *always* conferred on a Soviet citizen."

There was no slightest doubt in his mind or theirs but that he meant
exactly what he said.

Well: Peace Prize or no, he thought he had very effectively obliterated
the arguments of H. Delbacher, answering every one in detail before
H. Delbacher even had a chance to present them to the Council. Thus the
American President's presentation had been in some sense anti-climax,
made further so by the shrewdly objective and enlightened remarks of the
Indian Prime Minister. The British Prime Minister had tried to refute the
logic of the Soviet position, as endorsed by India, but her arguments, he
could see and she could see, had influenced no votes and served only to
show up the weakness of Britain's position and America's. It was what
Britain deserved for being America's—what had H. Delbacher had the
nerve to call Nicaragua?—America's "errand boy." When the Soviets
took Britain, he also reflected, things would be different there, too.

He felt suddenly very tired. He should write Ekaterina a note, probably, but she would be following it all on television anyway. Her admiration for his cleverness, which she occasionally admitted, would only be surpassed by her feeling that she could have been even more clever, had she had the chance. She never would, but he did not minimize her contributions. They were a good team. There was nothing now to keep him from divorcing the cow he had married and putting Ekaterina beside him on—yes, he would say it in the secrecy of his own mind, where not even the KGB could hear him, or even imagine he would have such frighteningly subversive thoughts—the Throne of All the Russias.

That was virtually what he occupied now, and his hold upon it was becoming tighter every day. Once he had brought off the brilliant scheme he was planning here at the UN and followed it with the even more brilliant one he had devised for the world, well—perhaps: perhaps. Certainly there would be nothing to stop him then.

Into this pleasant bedtime reverie the tiny voice of Ju Xing-dao broke with shattering unpleasantness. It was all very soft and gentle, filled with its customary secret amusement, but like H. Delbacher, Yuri found in it nothing amusing. The conversation was most wary, circumspect and polite, but the import was unmistakable.

When we take China, he promised himself savagely when the chuckling little voice had whispered away to nothing in his ear, things really *will* be different.

3

"There is no doubt that American strategists intend to make even more active use of Peking in the struggle against world socialism and to create with its aid a kind of second front against the socialist community."

—*Radio Moscow, 1980*

"Recently [1980] Washington has been yielding increasingly to the temptation to play the China card. This is a risky game for those who start it, but it is also dangerous for the cause of peace. Peaceloving states must draw the appropriate conclusions from this for their policy and their security, and they will do so."

—Andrei Gromyko, Foreign Minister

This morning an extra tension gripped the room when the Security Council reconvened. It had been a busy night and an early morning for many members of the UN. There had been much telephoning, conferring, meeting for late drinks or early breakfast. A great air of self-importance surrounded some of the more colorful delegates; one could almost literally feel the world slipping about as it balanced precariously on their self-appointed shoulders.

"So I told the Prime Minister— . . . I said to President Delbacher— . . . President Serapin told me confidentially— . . . The Secretary of State indicated clearly to me— . . . I understand from the Chinese delegation that— . . ."

Nine tenths, or probably all, of these significant conversations had never taken place, of course; but it was all part of being a member of the UN: you made yourself sound just as important as you could, and everyone you spoke to received your remarks with as much skepticism as you received his. It made for excitement and a feeling of being at the center of things; and since the great powers generally kept their own counsel and ignored the nervously earnest self-importance of their smaller friends, it didn't really matter much anyway. It made for delicious gossip and it made every one feel very important. And that was vitally necessary. At the UN it was very important to *feel* important, whether one was or not; and usually most weren't.

On this occasion, however, when the issue was of such literally earth-shaking proportions, and when it was almost certain to go to the General Assembly before it was finally decided, many would probably be as important as they thought they were before it was over. There would be a lot of lobbying for votes, much courting of the undecided. It was quite conceivable that sooner or later President Delbacher *would* make promises or utter threats, Ju Xing-dao himself might even condescend to whisper a few fluting obscurities in one's eager ear. Although the end result might be meaningless except in terms of headlines and propaganda, this was one occasion when everyone might be, momentarily at least, as important as he or she liked to think.

And more specifically today, the world would hear its first words from the new delegate of the People's Republic of China. By one of those strange coincidences history sometimes provides, the fiercely silent, fearfully intense, years'-long struggle within the Central Committee in Beijing had come to a head just days before the changes of leadership in Moscow and Washington. It had spilled briefly into print and then subsided without the world really knowing what had happened; except that a few of the old faces were gone, some new ones were suddenly introduced to China and the world, and speculation was given intriguing fuel. But nobody really knew what it portended, just as nobody really knew much about Ju Xing-dao.

Nor, of course, was he or anyone else in his intensely secretive land about to enlighten them. He remembered very vividly his humble beginnings in the tiny village in Shansi Province, the near starvation of his family, his own meager education, his decision to join the cause of Mao Zedong, the Long March, the days of glory, the sweet rewards of power; but those things were his business, he felt, not the business of foreign devils. Up and down like so many he had floated on the tides of party politics, narrowly escaping death on numerous occasions, first from the forces of Chiang Kai-shek and then from his own colleagues in the Politburo. He had been banished twice to internal exile far out in the Gobi; twice had been recalled to power, this time, he hoped, permanently. He was getting too old, at seventy-eight, for the turmoil in which he had lived since adolescence. Now he hoped to remain where he was until such time as his ancestors called him home.

His colleagues in Beijing had given him his instructions, though by now they all understood one another so well that there was little need for formal words; and he had departed for New York determined to conduct himself with all the circumspect shrewdness learned in a hard school where self-preservation often depended upon the proper attitude stated at precisely the proper time. He had learned long ago that timing was everything, and now China was confronted with the ideal situation its leaders had hoped for and sought to encourage for many, many years. The hated Soviet Union and the easily fooled United States had finally met head-on; and in their confrontation, as his long-time friend/enemy the present Premier had remarked just before Ju left for New York, "Opportunity flowers like the daffodil in spring." This was not one of the Premier's more original thoughts, though the Premier thought highly enough of it to have it plastered on posters throughout the city—just the aphorism, of course, no reference to the two powers that prompted it. It did sum up the world's crisis. Ju had been sent to New York to make the most of it.

He felt a secret, old man's amusement, not harsh or vindictive, just amused, when he thought of how naïvely and earnestly the Americans had embraced their "China connection," how savagely and bitterly the Soviets had denounced Chinese "hegemony" and armed their 4,500-mile, largely indefensible border against it.

Who knew where China stood? Only those who analyzed with neither naïve optimism nor jealous fear understood what China wanted. Very few seemed able to discern it, or to accept it if they did. Underneath the bland smiles to Washington, the harsh snarls at Moscow, China wanted chaos. It was the only climate for a power very far from being industrialized, far from capable yet of meeting the military challenge of a Soviet Union top-heavy with armaments.

Ju was not in New York to conciliate: he was there to wreck. Nothing else made sense for China now, and nothing else had made sense at any time since the first naïve American President, R. Nixon, had convinced himself that a few nice words and a few military baubles really could wipe out millennia of contempt and superiority toward all things foreign. Words, words, smiles, smiles: China had spewed them forth with the best of them, but at heart not a single Chinese attitude, prejudice or policy had changed. Let the foreign devils destroy one another. China would do what she could to set them on each other.

For the time being, however, dreams must be encouraged, self-delusions played upon, pretenses maintained. Not now, perhaps never, would the basic aim of Chinese policy be stated with such blunt candor. Why should it be? Now, it would ruin ultimate plans; later, it would be unnecessary. The daffodil in spring was not a shy or unobtrusive flower; it would be noticed soon enough—when, the Middle Kingdom hoped, it was far too late for both eternally despised enemies to save themselves.

Meanwhile American tour groups descended upon China and burbled their way through its schools, factories, monuments and swarming, curious people—"Always smiling, so happy, so welcoming, everybody *so* nice"—and in Beijing the planning went on, and in New York Ju Xingdao prepared to speak. His country, like Yuri's, was not afraid of atomic war; his country, like Yuri's, had every intention of winning it. The only difference was that his country, unlike Yuri's, had absolutely no intention whatsoever of fighting it. Others would do that. They were ready, and he was prepared to encourage them. The first step was to establish a high moral position.

Prince Koa rapped his gavel, uttered Ju's name: the charade was about to begin. His wispy little voice, amplified so that it spread sibilantly through the room, began the brief but devastating statement with which China intended to lift itself above the battle. The rest, he thought to himself with a happy inward smile, would follow in due course.

"Mr. President," he said, "the People's Republic of China has sought permission to speak at this early hour today so that we may make clear at once our position regarding the unfortunate crisis which has brought us here.

"We condemn without reservation the warlike actions of both parties to this dispute. We demand without hesitation the immediate end of Soviet maneuvers, the immediate withdrawal of Soviet submarines not only from Cuba but from all other areas of the world, we deplore and denounce the warlike actions of the United States, we demand the withdrawal of the American ultimatum, we abhor the warlike declarations of various emergencies by the American President, we regard the proposed emergency build-up of American forces as a direct threat to world peace, and we demand that both powers cease instantly and utterly all actions which could lead to war."

He paused and there was a startled murmur from his audience, followed by the stir of reporters hurrying out to file bulletins. China had been expected to condemn the Soviet Union and perhaps slap the wrist of the United States, but no pundit or pontificator had foreseen this wholesale condemnation of both. This was plague on both your houses with a vengeance. Already the "Third World" could be sensed gleefully preparing to rally around a new champion.

"Mr. President," Ju whispered on, his normally smiling little face a mask of stern disapproval, "imperialists and hegemonists have much in common. They are, in fact, the same, whether they be in Moscow or Washington. Humanity universally abhors, condemns and despises them. The People's Republic of China says to all peace-loving nations: do not be fooled by the claims of either. Both wish to pull the wool over your eyes. Both wish to use the present crisis for their own despicable ends. Both wish to use this United Nations meeting to hide their true purposes. Both hope to obscure their warlike ambitions and advance their antihumanistic goals. The world must not allow this.

"The United Nations and all humanity must condemn both parties. We must give no quarter to universal crimes against mankind committed by both parties. We must condemn both parties for the world criminals they are.

"The People's Republic of China invites all peace-loving humanitarian states to join us in this wholly worthwhile and justified endeavor."

And he sat back, folded his hands before him upon the table and stared down at them with a resumption of his usual bland and uncommunicative little smile. The room exploded in a rush of excited sound and argument which went on until Koa finally rapped sharply with his gavel.

"Well," he remarked with a wry smile. "Well, *well*. There is no doubt where the delegate and his government stand, anyway. Do either of the governments attacked wish to exercise the right of reply at this time? President Delbacher?"

Hamilton Delbacher shook his head.

"No, thank you, Mr. President. I think the extreme exaggeration of the delegate's attack is its own answer. The United States has no desire to dignify it with any comment now. We only hope the People's Republic of China may find itself in a more positive and constructive role before our meeting finally concludes. We would welcome it."

"President Serapin?" Koa said. Yuri leaned forward, tossed a terse, "We would also welcome it," into his microphone and sat back.

["There's the signal for compromise," UPI murmured to the AP. "Oh, sure," the AP said. "We'll get to it, but not before everybody has had his hour in the limelight. Do you think we can get through nine more speeches today?" "Late," the UPI predicted, "but we'll do it."]

And so they did, in a long, turgid discussion that seemed to drag interminably through the morning session, the afternoon session and an evening session that ran past eleven, when Koa finally concluded its formal portion with a brief pro-American statement from Tonga. The "debate," which in customary UN fashion consisted mostly of set speeches, revealed an almost even division of opinion.

France, as was expected, offered much the same type of condemnatory speech as China and Tanzania, though her President managed to find France's own special middle ground between Tanzania's rather mild denunciation and Ju's brief and all-encompassing blast. French jealousy and dislike of America competed as usual with French wariness and mistrust of the Soviet Union; a rather garbled attitude emerged, but the best guess after the President's acrid presentation seemed to be that France would probably abstain in the final voting. One could never, however, be sure of the French, and a large question mark through the word "France"—both crossed out heavily and then as heavily repeated—filled the doodles of Hamilton Delbacher as he sat patiently through the day. After China's severe tongue-lashing, made even more impressive because it had been delivered in Ju's fading little voice, he had decided he had best remain in case of further surprises. There were none, but the tension in the room mounted sharply nonetheless as Koa prepared to make the concluding address of the evening. The resolutions had not yet been introduced and there was much speculation in audience and media as to when and how they would be. No word had leaked from either the Soviet or American delegation. Who wanted to risk the first vote? Who would be maneuvered into it? Win or lose, the result would have a major effect on world opinion and a probably decisive impact on the General Assembly later on.

The stage was thus set with unusual drama for the Tonganese presentation, and Koa made the most of it as he hunched his enormous bulk forward and seemed almost to cradle his microphone in his arms as he talked.

"Ladies and gentlemen," he said shortly after 11 P.M., "I suppose after all these dramatic and excitin' speeches we've heard here today, and also considerin' the late hour, that you don' want to hear what little Tonga has to say. But little Tonga sees things in its own way, and maybe it's just as valid a way as somebody else's. So I'll proceed . . .

"What Tonga sees, from 'way down there in the South Pacific ocean, is that just yesterday there appeared off our shores two Soviet battleships and three Soviet submarines. They're there today and I might pause here to ask the distinguished and noble President of the Soviet Union how long they plan to stay? It makes us a little nervous, havin' them off there. We never thought Tonga was of value to anybody but us, bein' so small and so far away down there, but nonetheless, there those Soviet ships are. How long, Mr. President? And to what purpose?"

He paused and turned to look with a politely attentive air at Yuri Serapin, who stared impassively back.

"Well?" Koa repeated, his tone noticeably sharper. "I asked a valid question, Mr. President, and I want an answer. As truthful as possible, please."

"What right has the delegate to demand an answer," Yuri snapped, face flushing, "and in that tone? Soviet ships are there because Soviet ships are there. They are part of our maneuvers. I am not responsible for every ship, every plane, every tank, every missile, every division. I do not know specifically about the ships the delegate complains of. I cannot know everything."

"That's a surprise," Prince Koa said softly, "I could have sworn you did. Well, I'll tell you this: we'd appreciate it if those ships would move on, Mr. President. You can move them away from Tonga, if you will. We don't like 'em. Can we have your co-operation on that?"

["I say!" the *Daily Mail* exclaimed. "Good for him, the nervy bastard." "He's posed a nice problem for Serapin," the Miami *Herald* agreed. "Will Big Brother be tough or give in?"]

For several moments it appeared that Yuri was not sure himself. He leaned back, whispering behind his hand to Admiral Valenko, who leaned forward to converse with him earnestly. Then Yuri turned to his microphone again.

"Orders will be sent tonight," he said in a voice without emotion. "The ships will leave Tonganese waters immediately. The Soviet Union does not wish to be in the position of threatening or seeming to threaten anyone. The Soviet Union works always for peace."

There was an immediate outburst of excitement and talk, some scornful laughter, some defensive applause, some boos.

["Talk about nervy bastards!" the Miami *Herald* exclaimed.]

"Good," Koa said. "Are we to assume, then, that the same will apply to the submarines in Cuba and to the flotilla off Bombay?"

"What flotilla off Bombay?" the Indian Prime Minister demanded harshly, surging forward to her microphone with a tumultuous jangle of rings, bracelets, loops of gold. *"What flotilla off Bombay?"*

["The Americans must be feeding Koa their intelligence reports," *Tass* exclaimed in an aggrieved tone. "How awful," murmured the Washington *Star.*]

"The twenty submarines offshore there," Prince Koa said with a bland innocence as Yuri gave him an angry, quickly masked glare. "Surely the Prime Minister knows?"

"I do not know!" she snapped. "Mr. President, I want those vessels removed at once! At once, do you hear me?"

"Madam—" Yuri began, but she interrupted, voice shrill with indignation.

"At once! Give me your word right now and get them out of there at once! At once, I say! At once!"

For a somber moment Yuri stared straight at her. Then he spoke in a cold, dead-level voice.

"Madam, you need not screech. The submarines will be removed."

"Where?" she demanded. He replied in the same tone.

"Elsewhere in the Indian Ocean," he said; and when she opened her mouth to protest again, he snapped with a sudden anger, "Madam, just because India's name was given the ocean by the British as a matter of geographic convenience does not mean that it belongs to you! The Soviet Union will move its submarines out of your offshore waters but after that it will move them where it pleases, as a sovereign independent power. It may be in the Indian Ocean or it may not, *but it will be where we say it will be.* Is that clear, Madam?"

"Well—" she began, still sputtering, "I—I—"

"You were discussing Tonga's views, Your Highness," Yuri said, ignoring her and turned deliberately to Koa. "Have you further surprises for us?"

[REVEAL RED SUBS OFF INDIA, the headlines said. "They're so

arrogant now that they don't give a damn if they offend their own friends, do they?" the British *Guardian* muttered in an alarmed tone.]

"No, I don't expect I have further surprises," Koa said, amicably. "Two's enough for now . . . So, ladies and gentlemen, I was saying that Tonga does not like to be involved in these maneuvers any more than India does or the United States does, or anybody. We don't like Soviet ships skulkin' about, Mr. President of the Soviet Union. We don't like the potential you have developed this very moment for takin' action against anyone it suits you. That's not peace-keepin' and that's not peace-makin'. That's war-makin', sure as we sit here. That's what the maneuvers are and that's what the subs are. And Tonga sides wholly and entirely with the President of the United States in his condemnation of this and his wish that these maneuvers be terminated and the subs removed, not only from Cuba, but from India and everywhere . . .

"Tonga does not agree with Tanzania and those others on the Council who feel that blame can be equally applied in this matter. Most certainly Tonga does not agree with the distinguished delegate of the People's Republic of China, who seems to feel the United States is every bit as bad as the Soviet Union and every bit as responsible for creatin' this crisis. We do not believe this, Mr. President. We believe it is a crisis 70, maybe 80, maybe even 90 per cent created by the Soviet Union for its own purposes. We do not know what those purposes are, but we suspect they may not be as easy to figure out as they would seem on the surface. We don't expect any immediate attack on anybody by the Soviet Union as a result of this. But the question is, when will attack come? Tonga doesn't doubt that it will, and we're thankful we're down there where we are, although if people start throwin' atomic bombs at each other no doubt some radioactivity will come driftin' down someday, and there goes Tonga just like everybody else. Includin', I might add, the Soviet Union.

"Yes!" he said firmly as Yuri started to protest. "Includin' the Soviet Union. I know you have a theory in Moscow, Mr. President, that somehow the Soviet Union can survive an atomic war. I know that's your comfortin' theory—comfortin' to you. But you're fools, Mr. President. You're goin' just like Tonga and everybody else if you start this damnable craziness, this insanity. Wait and see.

"And now," he said, ignoring Yuri, who had one hand up for recognition and was slapping the table rhythmically with the other. "I'm about to conclude and then I'm goin' to recognize somebody for the purpose of introducin' a resolution. Everybody's had a chance to talk, we need somethin' substantive in front of us now, otherwise we'll be here all summer and we haven't got the time for it. At least I haven't: I want to go home and swim and fish a little before it all comes crashin' down.

"Tonga supports the American position entirely. We want the maneuvers ended and the subs home—period. There can be no certainty of

world peace until the Soviet Union gives up its crazy ideas of world conquest and goes home. Anythin' we in the United Nations can do to encourage that we must do, in the estimation of Tonga.

"And now the Chair sees the distinguished President and delegate of
the Soviet Union askin' recognition for the purpose of introducin' a resolution and the Chair recognizes him for that purpose."

"That is not my purpose, Mr. President!" Yuri said angrily. "My purpose is to protest the lies of the delegate of Tonga. The Soviet Union
does not wish to introduce a resolution at this time—"

"You're recognized for that purpose," Koa said bluntly. "Want it or
not?"

"We do not wish to introduce a resolution at this time," Yuri repeated
in a furious voice.

"Mr. President?" Koa asked, turning to Hamilton Delbacher. But he
shook his head.

"I repeat, then, President Serapin—"

"Mr. President," Yuri said, grating out the words, "I do not know how
often the Soviet Union must make its position known to fools and dunces,
but I have told you—"

"Mr. President!" the Indian Prime Minister interrupted in a voice as
harsh as though she were back home scalding the opposition in the Lok
Saba, "How much longer must we waste time on this childish tarradiddle?
Somebody is going to introduce a resolution. No doubt two somebodies
are going to introduce two resolutions. Why must we play these infantile
games about it? The Soviet President is a grown man. Let him act like
one! He has the floor, let him introduce his resolution and stop acting like
a spoiled brat, Mr. President! Who cares who has a temporary parliamentary advantage, the votes will be all the same! Get on with it!"

And she turned and glared at Yuri Serapin with an expression of contempt that gave Hamilton Delbacher a momentary flicker of hope that
she might bring India over to his side, though he knew this was nonsense:
she would run true to form when the votes were cast. Her blind passion
against America would guarantee that.

For several moments there was an almost frightened silence in the
room as she and Yuri tried to stare one another down. Neither succeeded.
Their eyes were still locked in furious encounter when Yuri finally said in
a voice choked with anger:

"Very well, Mr. President, the Soviet Union introduces the following
resolution and asks for its immediate consideration."

And taking the paper which his Foreign Minister leaned forward and
thrust into his hand, he exchanged a last angry glare with the Prime
Minister and began reading in a voice that became progressively quieter
and calmer as he proceeded:

"Whereas, the United States of America has sought to intervene directly and inexcusably in the relations between the sovereign states of the U.S.S.R. and the Cuban People's Republic; and in this instance and on many other occasions running back for at least three decades has shown itself to be a constant and continuing threat to world peace and to the stability and well-being of peace-loving nations everywhere; and,

"Whereas, no other nation on earth has committed so many vile and inexcusable imperialistic crimes against the freedom, liberty, independence and self-determination of free peoples everywhere;

"Now, therefore, be it resolved by the Security Council of the United Nations that the United States is, has been, and is hereby declared to be, the major enemy of freedom and world peace now existing on the earth; and,

"Be it further resolved, that the Security Council calls upon all the peace-loving, freedom-loving peoples of the earth to unite against the earth's worst criminal state, the United States of America, and to unanimously condemn, defeat and overthrow the ruling circles of the United States of America for their innumerable imperialistic crimes against humanity and the cause of world peace."

There was a stunned silence when he finished. He might have expressed the sentiments of many, but no one before had ever gone this far in the United Nations in condemnation of another power, particularly the power that had saved so many of them in far-off, long-gone World War II and had done so much since to try to restore them to national health and well-being. In some way no one could quite define, it was as though some fundamental rupture had been made in the very fabric of the UN itself. No one thought for a moment that the Soviet Union's extraordinarily harsh language would be approved as presented; it was recognized instantly that something much different would have to be found; but the mere fact of its enunciation gave it a weight and ominous power that disturbed and frightened even the Soviet Union's most determined apologists.

"This could well mean the end of the United Nations itself," the Ambassador of Norway whispered excitedly to the Ambassador of the Netherlands; and his was not the only mind into which this shattering thought leaped. If the United States left at this moment, not only would the United Nations lose its major financial supporter, but it would also lose all reason and pretense for continued existence. The fragile gloss of a so-called common purpose, the cause of world peace—so fervently proclaimed, so rarely honored—could no longer exist if any of the major powers withdrew. And this was aside from the even more catastrophic consequences that could ensue if the United States left without some resolution of the fearsome crisis that had brought about their emergency meeting in the first place.

But, as usual, the United States did not fail them. Like most whose reputation is invested in a failed dream, the United States even under Hamilton Delbacher was not about to abandon it unless absolutely forced to: it was as committed to maintaining the pretense of a "United" Nations as anyone else. But there was one thing the President found encouraging about the harshness of the Soviet language, at any rate: it justified his own. He raised his hand when Yuri finished, was recognized and proceeded to deliver his own thoughts in a calm and level voice.

"Mr. President," he said, while the room remained tense and hushed to hear him, "the United States wishes to offer the following resolution in the form of an amendment to the Soviet resolution just offered, and requests its immediate consideration:

"Strike all in the Soviet resolution after the word 'Whereas' in the first paragraph and substitute the following:

"Whereas, the Union of Soviet Socialist Republics has embarked upon worldwide maneuvers which are unwarranted by any reason of its own security and which directly and openly threaten the security, peace and well-being of nations throughout the entire world; and,

"Whereas, the Soviet Union has specifically directed a major threat to the United States of America by concentrating a wholly unnecessary and overtly hostile force of missile-carrying submarines in Cuba; and,

"Whereas, the Soviet Union has steadily expanded the size, scope and striking abilities of its armed forces in recent decades for no purpose reasonably associated with the needs of self-defense; and,

"Whereas, this build-up has created an overwhelming aggressive threat to world peace and to the security and well-being of all freedom-loving peoples everywhere; and,

"Whereas, the Soviet Union in recent decades has become the major aggressive force threatening peace in virtually all areas of the world, through indirect subversion, direct invasion and the constant threat of armed blackmail and open war; now, therefore,

"Be it resolved, that the Security Council of the United Nations demands the immediate termination of Soviet world maneuvers; the withdrawal of all Soviet submarines from the waters of Cuba, India and wherever else they may be concentrated around the globe, and the immediate abandonment of all Soviet aggressive, subversive or warlike ambitions against any nation whatsoever; and, further,

"Be it resolved, that the Security Council herewith condemns the Soviet Union as the major existing threat to world peace and calls upon all members to unite in opposing Soviet imperial designs and ambitions, wherever and whenever they may be found, anywhere on earth."

This brought an even deeper silence, although, aided by the impact of Yuri's words, the impact of these was a little easier to take. Next time, he thought wryly, they could probably toss a declaration of war at each other and it would be regarded as routine business, so quickly did the human mind become accustomed to the horrors of the abyss in this atomic-ridden world. Nonetheless, they now had something to think about; and it did not come as a surprise when the Prime Minister of Great Britain raised her hand for recognition and said quietly:

"Mr. President, I believe it is time for the Council to take a needed recess of substantial length during which we may rest, consider and hold those private consultations within and among governments which do so much to advance the work of the United Nations. We have all expressed ourselves, we are all on record, and now we have the two contending resolutions before us. We need time to consider their diametrically opposed objectives. Obviously both could use substantial amendment. This must be found in private discussions, not in the public forum. Therefore I move that the Council stand in recess for the balance of the week, reconvening next Monday at 10 A.M."

"Mr. President," Yuri began angrily, "this world is in a terrible crisis because of the United States! Mr. President, the Government of the Soviet Union objects to any such attempt by the lackeys of the United States to close off debate just as we reach this crucial moment! Mr. President, the Soviet Union proposes—"

"Oh, for heaven's sake!" the Prime Minister of India interrupted with a loud and emphatic irritation. "*Stop this nonsense!* Mr. President, India seconds the motion of my distinguished colleague!"

"Question!" Eire cried, pipe waving, blue eyes popping, white hair standing up about his head in a halo of agitation. "Question, question! Vote, vote!"

"All those in favor," Koa said rapidly, "all those opposed, the ayes have it, the Council stands adjourned until Monday at 10 A.M."

And down came his gavel, leaving Yuri still openmouthed and shouting for recognition. Instantly he stopped shouting, his face smoothed into its customary stolid half-Asian mask, he turned and began an intent discussion with his Defense Minister as they stood up and began to move slowly out. This scene was over and his ever-restless, ever-clever mind was already preparing for the next.

So, too, was that of the President of the United States, who inevitably found his preparations conditioned to some degree by the reactions of his countrymen and the media. He had flown back to Washington Wednesday morning and now, twelve hours and a lot of routine business later, was sitting in the Lincoln Study with a dozen newspapers spread before him and a television set on. He had not gone so far as Lyndon Johnson, to the point where he had three sets in place so that he could watch three news broadcasts at once, but he was switching channels rather briskly. Elinor, having addressed the party's National Women's Club at noon with a firm and emphatic defense of her husband's policies, was seated in the tiny room's other reclining rocker. They had eaten there and now the TV trays had been cleared away by the staff and they were alone. From every corner of the land came word that they were not alone emotionally, psychologically or politically. The advice he was receiving was, in fact, a tidal wave, and it had begun with the networks first thing in the morning. By now they had their comments well organized, well practiced and well frozen. They were giving him some charity, but not much. Inevitably, as American Presidents usually seemed to do in the American media when they clashed with the Soviets, he was emerging as a bit more of a villain than his opponent.

"Thus the two resolutions," said CBS's commentator, "equally extreme, equally harsh, equally violent. Both appeal to the UN to do something it is organizationally, legally and psychologically incapable of doing, which is to call to book one of the superpowers which could extinguish it in a moment by the simple act of withdrawing, were the members to be so foolish as to indulge in the kind of condemnation both Presidents seem to desire.

"It is hard to believe they actually do desire this; rather, this appears to be part of the propaganda game both are playing at this fateful Security Council meeting. Such an approach is perhaps to be expected from the Soviet Union, which never misses an opportunity to try to place this country in a bad light. It does not so easily become President Delbacher, who might have been expected to proceed with more decorum and restraint. Much as he disapproves of the Soviet Union, its maneuvers and its dispatch of submarines to Cuban waters, one wonders whether this head-on assault is the best way to bring about the objectives of ending the maneuvers and getting rid of the submarines. Since President Serapin has already, in fact, removed some of the submarines and has resorted to peaceful methods of settling the dispute by turning to the United Nations, one wonders why the President of the United States has deemed it necessary to be still so harsh and warlike in his approach.

"Obviously neither resolution could be adopted as it stands; much modification and amending will have to be done. The President, one suspects, has made this task far more difficult by his harsh and completely condemnatory attitude."

"It's you again," Elinor said. "You're at fault, you naughty boy."

"Certainly," he replied with a smile, though he could not escape feeling some annoyance. "Who else?"

"It seems to us," said NBC's earnest soul, "that the position of President Delbacher, while admittedly taken under great provocation from the Soviet Union, has probably made it more difficult to find an equable solution for the present crisis. As the President of Tanzania pointed out, two

wrongs do not make a right, and it seems to us that this applies quite obviously and forcefully to the situation in the United Nations. That sometimes difficult body has not been aided by the competition in epithets between the Soviet President and our own. It instead finds its task much
more difficult. Since no one expected President Serapin to make it easier,
it should have been incumbent upon President Delbacher, in our estimation, to lean over backward in his attempts to be conciliatory. Instead, he
has come out swinging in a situation that unfortunately demands the
greatest of diplomatic skill and tact. It will not be surprising if this sets
back very substantially the UN's efforts to find a solution.

"One expects exaggerated and inflammatory statements from the Soviet
Union: such harsh tactics are an integral part of the communist arsenal.
One does not expect them from the United States. It is a pity the Presi-
dent saw fit to use them, for they aggravate much and settle little."

"Even if true," he said; and Elinor responded dryly, "Oh, what has that
got to do with it, anyway?"

"Now the UN," ABC's pedantic philosopher remarked, "finds itself jug-
gling two hot potatoes instead of one, and for this President Delbacher
would seem, unhappily, to carry the principal blame. He had two options
in presenting his resolution to the Security Council: he could either attempt to match the harsh and inflammatory language of President
Serapin, always a difficult task when dealing with a professional communist, or he could opt for the language of diplomacy and come up with
softer words that might have made the same point but with less provocative emphasis. A softer position might have opened the way for compromise. As it is, there will be compromise—the UN has no choice—but it
may be less favorable to the United States than it would have been if Mr.
Delbacher had been more restrained in his language.

"President Serapin's attempt to pin all the responsibility for the world's
tensions upon the United States would surely have backfired with all but
the most ill-informed and incorrigibly anti-U.S. members of the UN—"

"Of whom," the President remarked, "there were at last count one
thousand three hundred and seventy-eight out of a membership of a little
more than one hundred and fifty—"

"—but now he will gain at least some sympathy and support, if only in
reaction to President Delbacher's harsh words. It is unfortunate that the
American President saw fit to meet charge with charge and epithet with
epithet. The Soviets are more skilled at this, and they start from a
broader base of support, including deep-seated skepticism about American motives. It is not statesmanship but futile time-wasting to seek to
beat them at their own game. President Delbacher would seem, unhappily, to have made matters worse instead of better."

And not surprisingly, that was the conclusion of the newspapers as
well, from the New York *Times'* and Washington *Post's* clucking wonder-

ment about the wisdom of his course to the San Francisco *Examiner*'s more free-swinging, editorial columnizing about his "having shown a diplomatic ineptitude reminiscent of Jimmy Carter."

All in all, he remarked to Elinor as he switched off the TV and tossed the papers in the wastebasket, he appeared to be the Peck's Bad Boy of the media—again.

"Perhaps they rationalize it that they *expect* the Soviets to do these things and they don't *expect* us to," Elinor said. "Within the permissible bounds of expectation, any Soviet effrontery or outrage is therefore perfectly recognizable, acceptable and assimilable; they can shrug and say, 'Oh yes,' and hurry on to something else. But when we do it—when *you* do it—it is considered out of character, out of phase, surprising, startling, affronting and worthy of condemnation. Do you suppose that's it?"

"I'd like to think so," he said, "and about most of them, I do. But there are some I really wonder about . . . In fact, I really wonder about them all at a time like this, when the Soviets are so blatantly and ruthlessly doing something that really does jeopardize the safety of this country, and indeed of the whole world. How can they switch so fast? They were beginning to sound really scared last week—still critical of me, of course, but really concerned about Serapin's plans. Now suddenly they're back on target—namely me—and his responsibility seems to be pretty much forgotten."

"I think they feel they can *do* something about you," she said. "They know they can't do anything about him."

"But doesn't that tell them something about him?" he inquired. "Don't they see the implications of it, for this crisis and for the future?"

"We come back to the same old thing—they don't want to see it, because the implication is that if they see it they would have to do something about it. And they don't want that. So consciously or subconsciously, depending on the individual, they deny it."

"I don't want it either," he said grimly, "but they can thank their lucky stars I have the responsibility to face up to it."

"And the guts," she said. "Don't forget those, old dear. What do you think is going to happen on the resolutions?"

"Much watered-down language offered by Britain and India, I suspect, with possibly an assist from China, for all its apparent harshness toward us both. I think I'm going back up tomorrow morning, incidentally. Want to come?"

"Sure. Why are you returning so soon, isn't Chauncey minding the store sufficiently?"

"Oh yes, he's fine. He and Mark and the rest of them are seeing a lot of UN members right now. But just as we were breaking up last night, Ju looked over at me and came as close to a wink as I imagine Chinese diplomacy allows. I rather expect to be approached, quite soon now, for private discussions. The People's Republic of China and I have a little getting acquainted to do, too, you know. So I think I'll be there."

"It wouldn't be simpler to have him fly down here—?"

"I'm sure he wouldn't. Dignity and protocol, you know. Also, he *is* seventy-eight and an old man, though still a very bright one, I think. I don't mind. I just wonder how we're going to arrange it so the whole world doesn't know, though."

"Maybe he'll want it to know."

"Maybe," he agreed. "China moves in mysterious ways her wonders to perform."

"Watch out for him," she cautioned. "I don't feel they're really all that friendly, even now."

"He certainly didn't sound it yesterday," he agreed with a smile.

"That was window dressing, of course. But fundamentally, I don't think they're on our side. They're up to something."

And possibly she was right, though Chinese-U.S. friendship was now a great article of faith in all the best circles.

When they went along to bed they found two copies of the early edition of next day's Washington *Inquirer* neatly laid out for them on the counterpane.

CHINESE MEET WITH SERAPIN, the headline said. JU HINTS POSSIBLE COMPROMISE TO BREAK U.S.-SOVIET CLASH. SAYS HE WILL ALSO SEE DELBACHER.

"Yes, sir!" the President said, coming to attention with a mock salute, "I shall be there, sir!"

When Chauncey Baron called two minutes later, he was ready for him.

"Yes, Chaunce," he said, before the Secretary of State could say more than hello. "Tell the old man I'll come to his headquarters or he can come to my suite at the Waldorf, whichever suits him."

"He says he'll come to see you," the Secretary said.

"No! Really? That's a concession."

"An evenhanded one. He went to see Serapin too."

"Well," Ham Delbacher said, "I don't wish Yuri any bad luck, of course, but I hope he was as thoroughly baffled as I expect to be."

This, indeed, he was, had the President but known it; and as Yuri also prepared for bed and mulled over a very full day capped by a very peculiar performance by the delegate of the People's Republic of China, he did not know exactly what to make of it.

It had begun Wednesday as he was finishing lunch, which he had consumed in the company of his four military advisers. It had been a pleasant meal during which they had discussed the progress of the maneuvers, now moving smoothly all across the world, and had congratulated themselves on how successfully the submarines had been transferred to the secret base in Nicaragua. So far there had been only two minor mishaps in all the vast deployments of men and weaponry; a sailor in Task Force Australia had fallen off a destroyer and been almost instantly consumed by sharks; and two helicopters taking off from one of the five aircraft carriers assigned to Task Force East Africa had collided, causing the total destruction of one craft and the loss of three airmen. Otherwise, not another one of the many millions of men and women involved and not another piece of equipment of any kind had been lost anywhere in the world.

"Comrades," he said and meant each heartfelt word, "you have created a magnificent exercise worthy of the Motherland and true to the spirit of K. Marx and V. I. Lenin. All socialist states and peoples will be forever grateful to you. You have proven beyond the slightest doubt that the armed forces of the Soviet Union, the Warsaw Pact and all associated states of the socialist bloc are at their absolute peak and are now supreme on all the seas and continents without the slightest possibility of challenge. We are truly invincible. The bourgeois capitalist imperialist warmongers of the West and their hegemonist encouragers in Asia are absolutely beyond salvation now. It remains only for us to decide the day and hour."

"Will it be soon?" Admiral Valenko asked and they all looked at Yuri with a genuine eagerness whose true socialist spirit he treasured almost beyond words, even though he no longer really trusted them personally.

"My dear comrades," he said, "if I could only tell you how deeply thrilled and moved I am by your obvious desire to move forward speedily to the completion of our sacred task. Never have I been so pleased and so happy, never have I been prouder of our millions of gallant servicemen and women and particularly of those fine men—you, comrades, *you*—who lead them in this glorious hour. How I would like to say to you, 'Yes! Yes, comrades! Let us strike at once at corrupt, dying America, let us obliterate from the face of the earth this very day the cruel and crafty hegemonists of Beijing! Let us rid humankind forever of their imperialism, their corruption, their insane crimes against the well-being and future of all peace-loving, freedom-loving peoples everywhere! Let us strike! Let us strike now!' *But*"—and he held up a sudden cautionary hand, for his four listeners were starting from their chairs, uttering incoherent sounds of excitement and eagerness under the hypnotic whiplash of his words—"*but*, I cannot say it yet. No, comrades"—as they sank back down again, faces disappointed and uncertain but still alight with inspiration and anticipation—"not yet. We must proceed very carefully and cautiously, now. We must get through this charade at the United Nations first, for it too is all part of the plan. Gently we will lead them on, slowly but surely we will guide their steps, with shrewdness and with skill we will draw over their eyes the veil of wishful thinking and of hope, bit by bit we will confuse, mislead and baffle them, until finally they have been persuaded that there is no more danger and all is peaceful and settled again in the world. *Then*, comrades," he said, and his voice dropped to a low and thrilling note. "you may come to me and ask, 'Will it be soon.' For *then* I will have the answer for you that history has made inevitable. *Then* there will be nothing ahead for us but complete and total victory in the final battle that will decide the fate of all mankind."

He concluded so quietly, in such a soft yet penetrating half-whisper, that the hairs literally rose on the backs of their necks, and into the eyes of marshals and admiral there sprang tears of true socialist fervor and devotion to their glorious cause. A world without America! A world without China! A world with nothing in it but peace-loving, freedom-loving, mindless, thoughtless, dutiful, *obedient* people! How marvelous it would be! How magnificent a tribute to K. Marx, V. I. Lenin, F. Engels and all the leaders since whose demonic, ruthless destruction of the human mind and human liberty had brought them finally to this glorious day, this pinnacle of invincible, unchallengeable power! How great were they! How great, how supreme, how magnificent above all was their new leader, who had been selected by history to guide their final triumph! How glorious was Yuri Pavlovich Serapin!

It was just at that moment, injecting a note of the humdrum everyday, that the special phone had rung at Yuri's elbow.

"*Da?*" he said sharply, for he could see how swept away they were and he resented any slightest thing that could break their adoring mood at such a moment.

"I am sorry, Comrade President," his secretary said in an apologetic yet excited voice, "but the delegate of the People's Republic of China is here in the office and wishes to see you."

"Ju Xing-dao?" he demanded in a voice of such startled disbelief that the idolatrous murmurings all around him sank suddenly to breath-held silence.

"Yes, Comrade President," his secretary said. "He says it is imperative to see you—if, he says, that would not be too much of an imposition and not too inconvenient for you."

"No, no," he said hastily. "Not at all, certainly not! Tell him I will be there at once. Offer him tea—vodka—whatever he wants. I shall be there immediately."

"I have offered him things already," his secretary said. "He will partake of nothing but tea. Which he brought himself, in a small silver pot."

"What is he afraid of?" Yuri asked sharply. "That we will poison him?" His tone became wry. "Yes, probably he is. Very well, tell him I will be there in ten minutes . . . Comrades, you gather what has happened. The representative of the Asian hegemonists has come to see me. I have not asked to see him. *He has come to see me.* You will excuse me, but I must dignify this visit, I must honor this old man, I must see what treachery he is plotting against the Motherland and the peace-loving peoples of the world. Wish me luck!"

"We do, Yuri Pavlovich!" they chorused fervently. "Be careful, Yuri Pavlovich! He is a devil! Have him searched. He may wish to do you bodily harm!"

"Comrades, comrades!" Yuri chided. "You know perfectly well every visitor is thoroughly screened. He is carrying no concealed weapons, believe me."

"But in his teapot—?" Marshal Krelenko suggested.

"Only tea, I am sure," Yuri said with a smile. "Anyway, I shall not drink it if he offers. I shall offer him vodka instead." His smile broadened. "Without poison. I am much too interested in what he has to say." He pushed back from the table, stood up; they followed his lead. Solemnly he shook hands.

"Thank you all for your magnificent reports of progress in the field," he said gravely. "Thank you for your loyal and heartening support. All moves well for the Motherland and the socialist cause—thanks to you."

"Thanks to *you,* Yuri Pavlovich!" they assured him, handclasps hard and lingering, eyes again misting with emotion.

It was all very satisfying for him, and after they had gone he stood alone for several moments before he went down to the floor below to greet his visitor—head up, back straight, eyes glowing, pride, arrogance and power in every line. Let the old yellow man threaten, bluster, praise or damn, Yuri Pavlovich did not care. He was ready, and more than ready, for anything the hegemonists of East or West might try to do.

Consciousness of power was still in his eyes when he opened the door and entered his office, and he was glad that the old man should see him so, still relatively youthful, at the peak of his physical powers and political authority, challenging, dominant, unmoved and unyielding. Their two nations had been, and were, as close to war as—well, as the Soviet Union and America—although not on quite such a dramatic level; and he was fully prepared to be as harsh and hostile as his visitor wished to be. True to form, however, Ju Xing-dao looked at him with a smile of quite extraordinary—and quite meaningless, Yuri knew—gentleness. He made no offer to shake hands nor did Yuri; only bowed very low. This was to be a Chinese visit, Yuri saw with a secret inward amusement: even to the extent that the old man, abandoning the drab uniform of his bastard-communist state (that betrayal of Moscow and everything that true communists stood for!), was dressed in a flowing yellow robe that made him, too, look very mandarin and imperial. Except for the sweet smile, of course, and the humble scraping that meant not a thing.

"Mr. President," he said in his wispy, half-whispering old voice. "You do me great honor to see me at such short notice and in so unexpected a fashion. I must extend my deepest apologies for my rather abrupt informality. I had intended to give you much more formal notice, but I have been engaged all morning with other delegations, and . . ." His voice trailed away, he bowed humbly again.

"And you were not sure I should receive you if you sent advance word," Yuri finished for him. "Please be seated, Vice Premier."

"Thank you," Ju said gently, easing himself carefully onto one end of the enormous sofa that stood against the window. Yuri seated himself with equal ostentation at the other. The famous teapot appeared from somewhere up Ju's sleeve and took its place on the coffee table in front of them.

"You have come prepared, I see," Yuri said with a wry humor. "Our Russian tea is not good enough for you."

"Oh, perfectly good," Ju said with his roseate little smile. "Perfectly good. I simply happen to prefer my own."

"Understandable," Yuri said. "My luncheon companions, who are our top military men, thought perhaps you might be afraid that we would poison your cup if we served it to you. Conversely, they thought you might poison my cup if you should offer it to me. That is military men for you."

"Very suspicious people," Ju agreed. "Very suspicious. The thought would not occur to either of us."

"Never," Yuri said cheerfully. "So, you shall drink your own and I, if I wish any, will drink my own. And thus will the relations between our two nations be preserved on an even and harmonious level."

"Ah!" Ju said with a sigh. "Would that they could!"

"It is not our doing, Vice Premier," Yuri said with a sudden harshness. "It is not we who threaten constant war and seek always to cause trouble along the border."

"No?" Ju murmured softly, an expression of surprise coming into his eyes. "We could have sworn it was."

"Well," Yuri said, harshness deepening, "you are mistaken. As you very well know."

"We cannot keep track of everything," Ju pointed out gently. "Ours is a very big country."

"Ours is bigger," Yuri retorted.

"But not in people," Ju replied, still gently. "We have many, *many* millions more than you do."

"And we have many, *many* more sophisticated weapons and a much, *much* more developed industrial capacity," Yuri mimicked. "But," he added impatiently, "this schoolboy bickering gets us nowhere. Why did you come to see me, Vice Premier?"

"Because it seems to us, Mr. President, that there must be a way out of this impasse between you and the United States which threatens to explode the whole world."

"That is bluff on their part," Yuri said flatly.

"And it is not bluff on yours?" Ju inquired. Yuri shook his head, expression severe.

"Even with your relatively unsophisticated intelligence devices, you know the status and capabilities of our armed forces."

"Not so unsophisticated as you think," Ju replied with a sudden trace of amusement. "Not quite."

"Then you know even more about us," Yuri said, undisturbed.

"We must try to be impressed," Ju agreed like some wry little chipmunk. Yuri's instant anger turned to astonishment at his next question. "How do you propose to handle the hegemonists in Washington?"

For several moments Yuri looked at his visitor with a deliberate lack of expression. The word "hegemonists" was the last he had expected to hear the presumed enemy of the Soviet Union use concerning the presumed friend of China. "Hegemonist" was a very bad word in both their lexicons. He was literally astounded to hear it in this context. A great discretion descended upon him. Just what *was* the Chinese game, anyway?

"If they are, as you say," he began cautiously, "hegemonists—"

"Indubitably," Ju said firmly. "Have you any doubt?"

"None. But we have assumed for some years now that you did."

"We have not been prepared to condemn as violently as some others," Ju said delicately. "Nonetheless, there have been moments . . ." And again his whispery little voice trailed away.

"You have not indicated them to us," Yuri said bluntly. "Official visits, trade missions, diplomatic and cultural exchanges, coupled with continuing and usually extreme denunciations of the Soviet Union—what were we to think? What, in fact, am I to think right now, Vice Premier? That China has suddenly changed her spots completely? Even a Chinese tiger cannot change that rapidly, can it?"

"You are skeptical, Mr. President," Ju sighed gently, spreading his spidery old hands in a gesture indicating frustration, hopelessness, the difficulties of making Yuri understand—or possibly, Yuri thought dryly, just indicating that he felt like spreading his spidery old hands. He was not convinced for one second but had no intention whatsoever of showing it.

"Then," he said with a deliberate boyish eagerness, "dare we hope that China at last—Vice Premier, *dare we hope?*"

"On a long journey," Ju said, suddenly going into what Yuri categorized contemptuously to himself as his Ancient Sage Performance, "there must always be a first step."

"How true," Yuri said gravely. "How true. And the first step, I take it, is that we may dare to hope that China—?"

"Even hope should not be entered upon without caution," Ju murmured.

"Hope, most of all, should be entered upon with caution," Yuri said, his tone suddenly matter-of-fact. "Then I take it we must not hope. China is still hegemonist. China still covets the East. China still sides with the capitalist imperialist war-mongers of Washington. China still hopes to goad us into destroying one another so that China may ultimately inherit the world. China is still our enemy."

"Mr. President!" Ju exclaimed, crumpled old face suddenly showing genuine anger, whispery old voice suddenly raised to normal level. "Now who is it who is goading! You play games with me! I shall leave!" And he made as if to rise; except, Yuri noticed, he made no gesture toward reabsorbing his silver teapot, which remained small, exquisite and untouched, upon the coffee table.

"Now, Vice Premier," he said soothingly. "Long journeys are begun with one step but not, I would hope, ended with one stumble. I apologize if I have sounded suddenly too harsh. But you must admit your words have taken me completely by surprise. It is perhaps no wonder if I express my feelings with more of our famous Soviet bluntness than your equally famous Chinese courtesy. Please sit down again. You interest me very much."

"Well," Ju said, still sounding huffy but face returning to its normal cheerfully meaningless smile, voice sinking again to its wispy, confidential note as he slowly resumed his seat. "Well. Very well. But you must not startle me so again."

"Never," Yuri promised solemnly. "It is a serious matter. The most serious we could possibly discuss. What is China proposing?"

"China is proposing that when the hurricane blows, prudent men aid one another to build a shelter."

"I gather Britain and India wish to build a shelter," Yuri said in an indifferent tone. "Does China wish to help them? Surely that needs no approval from me?"

"Ah," Ju said, "but of course it does, if the shelter is to be successful. And if it is successful, then what happens when the storm is over?"

Yuri gave him a thoughtful look and decided to fall back upon what he had always considered one of the most useful obfuscating phrases in the English language.

"That depends."

"The world will not be the same after this particular episode," Ju observed with sudden directness. "One of you or the other will be substantially diminished in the eyes of the world."

Yuri snorted.

"The eyes of the world do not matter. Power is what matters. The eyes of the world can see who has it. Is there any doubt in your mind, Vice Premier?"

"The journey runs through mountains as well as desert," Ju replied softly. Yuri almost laughed in his face, but managed with some effort not to.

"Let us hope there are springs along the way so that all who wish may refresh themselves," he said, and this time it was he who started to rise. "Thank you for coming to see me, Vice Premier. It is always interesting to learn the views of China—"

"Oh, but," Ju protested quickly, "you have not heard them yet, Mr. President! No, not yet. Please be seated once more. China wishes most earnestly that you will truly understand."

"*So*," Yuri said, sitting down again with a no-nonsense firmness. "What is it, then, Vice Premier? I am a busy man and there is much to do. I have many appointments, others wish to speak with me. China desires— what?"

"Sometimes," Ju said with a sudden intimate little smile, "one finds that the journey—"

"Vice Premier," Yuri interrupted with a deliberate harshness, "no more journey and no more aphorisms, if you please. What does China want and what does China intend to do? Straightforwardly, and with no thoughts of Confucius, Ju Xing-dao or even Mao Zedong to confuse the issue, if you please. Otherwise, good day."

And he stared at his wizened little visitor with an expression impassive, unimpressed and determined.

"Mr. President," Ju said finally, "China thinks that possibly it is time to consider a strengthening of relations and a renewal of friendship between our two nations."

"Very well," Yuri said, outwardly calm but inwardly so torn between excitement and absolute disbelief in the old scoundrel that he could not have exactly defined his feelings if his life depended upon it. "Let us discuss this honestly and straightforwardly as two comrades of the socialist camp should do in the face of threatened attack by the capitalist imperialist hegemonists of Washington."

"Good," Ju said in a normal tone of voice, and from his other sleeve two tiny silver cups and saucers miraculously appeared. "May I serve you tea?"

But what their subsequent discussion really meant or what it really all added up to, Yuri thought as he clambered finally into bed and found himself with Ju in some strange dream of walking through a hurricane over endlessly expanding deserts toward endlessly retreating mountains, he could not really say.

Nor could Hamilton Delbacher, reviewing his own talk with the old man next day in his suite a few blocks away in the Waldorf-Astoria. No more than Yuri did he believe for a second in the sincerity or truthfulness of his visitor; yet the words were persuasive enough and the friendliness apparently sincere. If Ju could be believed, the United States could now expect far more than the "interested and benign observation" of the crisis that Beijing had promised, to everyone's confusion, some days ago. But that was if Ju could be believed. Who, but Ju, knew?

Who but Ju knew? the President thought wryly: I'm a poet and don't know it. But Ju knew who? But who knew Ju? Who but Ju knew who Ju knew?

And what the hell could anybody rely upon, with China?

He uttered an impatient sound, then began to smile to himself. He, too, had been given his share of aphorisms and had concluded his interview in much the same mood and spirit as Yuri. Which of course, though they never compared notes and were unaware of one another's bafflement, was undoubtedly what Ju intended all along. But who but Ju knew?

In any event, the old man appeared in his yellow robes and produced his teapot promptly at 11 A.M., after a spokesman for the Chinese delegation had telephoned and requested that no one else be present at the interview. This gave a certain initial air of secretiveness to something that was almost a media circus when one of the longest and sleekest black limousines in all of New York City's rental services drew up with a flourish at the hotel door and some two hundred shouting reporters and cameramen sought to provoke the slight little figure who got out into some kind of statement. There was none: only a flutter of hands, a cherubic smile, a shrug and a slow, shuffling progress, shielded by police and Secret Service, to the guarded elevator leading up to the Presidential suite. Safely ensconced therein, Ju turned and waved at his clamoring pursuers being held back by a uniformed cordon. For a moment there was a genuinely amused smile on the ancient crafty face; then the doors closed and he ascended. When the door opened on the equally guarded floor above he commented appropriately on this.

"Whenever one meets with the President of the United States," he said with the most discreet of chortles while Ham Delbacher carefully shook his bony little hand, "one feels one is that much closer to heaven."

For a moment the President tried desperately to think of some appropriate celestial rejoinder to this; found none; and burst into a laugh.

"Mr. Vice Premier," he said, "you have the definitive word. I'm at a complete loss; I can't possibly answer that. Thank you for coming to see me."

"It is my pleasure," Ju said softly as the President led him into his private rooms and closed the door behind them, "And, of course, it is my duty. I do not say it is an easy one, but every journey must begin with the first step."

"Let us hope two friends arrive at the end of the journey still walking together," Ham Delbacher said, congratulating himself with an amusement he carefully concealed that this was not such a bad rejoinder, given the context. Ju seemed to think so too.

"You know, then, some of our ancient sayings," he observed with a satisfied air. "They contain much wisdom."

"China itself contains much wisdom," the President said with hearty approval. "We can all learn from China. What, may I ask, did China learn from the Soviet Union yesterday?"

"You Americans!" Ju said with an amusement of his own, quite genuine for a moment. "You are always so hasty. Would you like some tea?"

And from their wicker cradle in the voluminous folds of his sleeve he produced his magic pot and brazier and placed them on the coffee table, producing from somewhere else a match to start the fire, and from the other sleeve the two tiny silver cups and saucers.

"Did Yuri Pavlovich drink from this very cup?" the President asked, picking one up in his big hand and turning it admiringly in the light from the window.

"I do not know which one," Ju said, "but, yes, he did condescend to have tea with me."

"Then I must do likewise," the President said, making a mental note of the word "condescend" and the rather testy tone in which it was uttered. "I am sure it will greatly improve my understanding of what you have to say."

"Excellent," Ju said. "First, we must let it heat up."

And folding his hands, much as he was used to doing in the Security Council, he concentrated gravely on the teapot until suddenly it gave a tiny, unexpected little fluting and he said, *"Ah!"* with great satisfaction and poured the tea.

"Now," he said, after they had consumed the first cupful and were started on the second, "let us consider the journey we have to make together."

"By all means," the President said. "It is over rather rough terrain, I'm afraid."

"Mountains," Ju said airily. "Deserts. But there are springs along the way to refresh the traveler, and at the end two friends *may* still find themselves walking side by side."

"I hope so," Hamilton Delbacher said. "That *may* make things easier, all around."

"You have doubts?" Ju asked quickly, giving him a sudden shrewd glance.

"Until I know where China stands I shall certainly have doubts," Ham Delbacher said. "Where does China stand?"

"China," Ju said in a reproving tone, "stands where China has always stood—for peace."

"Who doesn't?" the President inquired dryly. "How does China propose to go about achieving it?"

"That is not now a question for China," Ju observed. "It is now a question for America and the Soviet Union."

"But we need help," the President pointed out. "Perhaps China can give us that help."

"The feeble trumpet blast does not inspire the winning charge," Ju murmured, his half-whisper so pronounced the President almost had to cup his ear to hear it.

"Who's feeble?" the President inquired, perfectly aware of what his difficult little visitor meant but determined to make him state it.

"You say *'perhaps'* China can help," Ju said, pouting slightly. "Why *'perhaps'*?"

"I have no assurance at this moment that China will help at all," the President said tartly. "The last I heard from China was a broad-ax attack in the Security Council upon me, my decisions and my country. Why should I have any expectation that China will help?"

"Somtimes cold winds are necessary to produce a beautiful spring," Ju remarked.

"Yes," the President said dryly, "and sometimes they wither everything and nothing comes up in the spring. What do your ancient sayings indicate about whether China is with us or against us?"

"Petals unfold one by one," Ju observed in a remote little voice.

"Yes," Ham Delbacher said, "but I haven't got all summer to sit around and wait for them. This crisis needs solution now. Is China satisfied with the knowledge that twenty Soviet submarines are off Shanghai and another twenty scattered in the waters from Canton on north?"

For just a second Ju looked truly startled, dismayed and alarmed; then the mask came down again. But he spoke now, the President noted, with an extra caution.

"This is interesting news to us," he admitted. "We assume it is true."

"You may assume so."

"Can you protect us from them?" Ju asked, and now the shrewd old eyes were very sharp, very bright and very intent. It was the President's turn to be cautious. He decided instead to be honest—a mistake, he realized much later, but appearing to be a good idea at the time.

"Only in the context of a general war that might draw them away from you to concentrate on us," he said. "If war does not break out, then I assume them to be no real threat to China at this time, and perhaps never. But if China is contemplating amendments to the resolutions now before the Council, I think it might be well for China to consider the American position that all Soviet maneuvers should be terminated and all Soviet submarines should be withdrawn, wherever they may be. We have already spelled it out. Now we need your support with many nations that listen to you and tend to follow your example. After well over a decade of friendship with China—if that is what it is—we might perhaps have a right to expect that; particularly if you yourselves are under threat also."

"He did not tell me that," Ju whispered, almost as though talking to himself.

"He did not tell you much, I suspect," the President said crisply. "China should restudy the question of exactly who is her friend in this situation and be guided accordingly."

"China has many friends," Ju said with a sudden severity. "It is by not taking sides that China has what influence she has. We can be no help to you if we antagonize them all."

"Play the middle ground, then," the President said bluntly. "Just don't forget that it is where your strength is."

"China does not forget," Ju said. "China remembers everything."

"It is convenient to have such a memory," the President replied. "Mercifully, we are not quite so bound to the past."

"Yes," Ju remarked, "America forgets too much. And too easily."

The President sighed, suddenly grave.

"You are entirely right. But what, then, can we expect from China?"

"China has, in general, enjoyed our closer association," his visitor observed.

"So have we," the President said, "though I am a little disturbed that you choose to put it in the past tense. Are we not still enjoying it?"

"An old man's slip of the tongue," Ju said with a sudden cheery smile. "China *has* enjoyed, China *does* enjoy, China"—he paused and then gave his host a teasing, twinkly glance—"*will* enjoy, our association."

"That's better," Ham Delbacher said, laughing in spite of himself at this playful—or was it?—play-acting. "But," he added, swiftly and deliberately changing mood again, "you still have not told me, Vice Premier, where China stands now, at this moment, on this issue; and that of course is what concerns me most. Is it true you are joining Britain and India in trying to work out a compromise?"

"Ah!" Ju said, his smile becoming man-to-man. "Those *two—determined*—ladies! They are, as you Americans say, 'something else.' Dare I venture into such a den of lionesses? I am not so sure."

"Haven't they already come to you?" Ham Delbacher inquired.

Ju lifted his hands and shook his head in amazement.

"Mr. President!" he exclaimed. "You know *everything!*"

"Well, I know they saw you last night. Everyone knows that."

"Not the press," Ju said with a satisfaction that most leaders of government on his level seemed to share. "But obviously American intelligence."

"We keep ourselves informed," Hamilton Delbacher said, "though under some handicaps. In any event, did you decide anything?"

"As the petals unfold," Ju said, reverting to what the President thought of as his Ancient Wisdom Bit, "the nature of the flower is revealed."

"Yes," the President agreed. "Well: what is it going to be, rose or stinkweed?"

"I am not sure we have anything called 'stinkweed,'" Ju said with his cherubic smile, "but I perceive the meaning, I believe. All will become clear on Monday when the Council meets again."

"And what can we expect for the long haul, Vice Premier?" the President asked in a bluntly pragmatic tone. "We have had an intriguing conversation but I am faced with practical matters. Once again let me try: is China for us or against us?"

There was a pause during which his astute little visitor stared into his teacup as though he were finding the future, as perhaps he was. Then he glanced up, a sidelong, oblique glance. His voice was still almost whisper-soft.

"Our two countries have a very strong enemy. . . . We have perhaps not done enough . . . together . . . to prepare for him . . ."

"How should we prepare for him together, Vice Premier?" the President inquired, much intrigued but not really expecting much save more aphorisms.

"We should prepare for him," Ju said in a suddenly normal tone that surprised Hamilton Delbacher with its vigor and practicality "thus—"

And he proceeded to talk without a break for the better part of fifteen minutes; at the end of which Ham Delbacher found himself, as anticipated, as uninformed and uncertain as before.

"So you see," Ju said with an air of satisfaction as he concluded, swooped up his teapot and accouterments and rose to his full five feet in preparation for departure, "that is what we suggest and that is what we propose. For the danger is mortal."

"Yes," the President agreed, accompanying him to the door. "And when the wind ripples the pool one can hardly discern the outline of the trees."

"But when the wind settles," his visitor replied promptly with a bland little smile, "it is as though a perfect mirror reflected the start of the pathway through the woods."

"Yes, Vice Premier," Hamilton Delbacher said dryly as he shook his hand and ushered him into the elevator which was waiting, door open. "I shall certainly remember that."

"Good!" Ju replied with a sudden flashing smile. "Then we shall progress!"

The doors began to close, he waved and bowed. The doors closed and he disappeared below.

"God knows," the President of the United States said aloud to the empty room. "God only knows!"

Well over a decade since the Nixon visit.

And still only God knew.

The remainder of the week hurried by in a blur of meetings, conferences, discussions and constant rumors that spread out from the Delegates' Lounge across the globe via news reports and television programs that served to keep the world thoroughly confused yet at the same time oddly reassured. The crushing sense of immediate doom that had surrounded the opening session and second day of the Security Council meeting had been alleviated substantially by the general business-as-usual aspect of national leaders squabbling over the circular table. "At least they're talking, not shooting," millions told one another in the comfortable cliché of half a hundred succeeding steps on the downward slope of Western power. The subsequent days of familiar consulting, conferring and general scurrying-about, so characteristic of the UN in times of crisis, had brought the matter down still further toward the commonplace. Newspapers and television were doing their best to keep the public informed, constantly running pictures of the Soviet maneuvers, courtesy of the U.S. and British Governments, which released as many of their satellite photos as were deemed consistent with national security secrets—and also courtesy of the Soviet Government, which, significantly changing past patterns, released a great many pictures of its own to give deliberately an impression of overwhelming strength operating everywhere.

Yet somehow, as always, repetition of such scenes began within hours to produce the boredom of the accustomed; and so world tension—and attention—slumped further. The problems of inflation, crime, domestic concerns, national politics, began to dominate the headlines once more; the crisis, while still featured everywhere and continuing to hang in the background, ominous and potentially explosive still, nonetheless began to take on the aspects of an accustomed everyday, almost friendly thing.

Soviet warships touched at Caribbean islands, and in addition to such places as Granada and Jamaica, where communist-controlled governments turned out their citizens by the thousands to wave greetings and throw flowers at the sailors, such nominally neutral or pro-American mini-states as Haiti, Curaçao and the Bahamas proved equally cordial. The troops and tanks rolled back and forth across the communist-held terrain of Eastern Europe, and across neighboring western borders the thump of enormous guns could sometimes be heard; the inhabitants soon settled down and began to take it all in stride. Now and again a Soviet plane or medium-range missile would streak across some neutral air space, always promptly apologized for and explained by Moscow as "a standard tactical error which will not occur again"; when it did, nobody paid any particular attention. Soviet subs were sighted, described, commented upon, forgotten in a day, off all the major seaports of the globe; within a day or two their distant ominous stumpy black cones had become familiar sights to swimmers and sun-bathers in Miami, Cannes, Ostia, Blackpool, Vogliamini, Durban, Sydney, Manila, Vancouver, Papeete and many another seaside resort. Only vague, quick-dying attention was paid. Within seventy-two hours the maneuvers were a habit, a feature of life, a part of the way things were. Since the United States and its new President seemed to be calming down about it too, along with everybody else—or at least, since the President's ultimatum was "suspended" and neither side was making any new warlike sounds—the crisis also was rapidly becoming a habit, a feature of life, a part of the way things were.

Aside from their consistent use of pictures, and the fact that nobody quite dared take it off the front pages or out of the evening news because it was editorially recognized that the potential was still there, the media too contributed heavily to the general slacking-off of interest. In the age of instant and exhaustive information about virtually everything, the ever-adaptable human mind performed another of its miracles of accepting the initially unacceptable—this time the last, final and most unacceptable of all. An almost soothing note began to enter the headlines, editorials, columns and commentaries—a sort of "hush, hush, children, go to sleep and don't worry about the boogeyman" theme began to creep, at first tentatively and then with growing confidence, into the pontifications of even those, not too many, who had at first agreed with Hamilton Delbacher that the greatest threat to peace the world had ever known was indeed upon them.

Now there was an almost universal application of rationalization, a relaxation, a near-unanimous attitude that hysteria had now given way once more, thank God, to commonsense. The world, after all, would be here tomorrow. The Soviets, after all, were not ten feet tall—even though it did have to be admitted that in many areas of military preparedness they might be about nine and a half. The United States, after all, was still "the greatest power on the face of the earth"—even though it was increasingly hard for those who claimed this to cite specifics in support of their confident contention.

It was as though a growing sigh of relief could be heard around the globe: everybody was still here, and life could settle down again to its placid, unthinking, normal rounds.

All of this took place between a Wednesday and the following Monday, so amazing is the willful blindness of humankind when it wishes to deny the obvious and inescapable evidence of its own peril; and nobody on earth could have been happier about it than Yuri Pavlovich Serapin and his colleagues of the Politburo, for this was exactly what they desired and exactly what their shrewdest psychologists had told them they could anticipate and rely upon.

Particularly had this been the conclusion of the shrewdest and most experienced staff members of the American Institute in Moscow. Its director, who was not a betting man but who had literally spent an adult lifetime of more than forty years intensively studying the Americans, had actually put down a sizable sum of money with his colleagues to support his contention that the Americans, or at least a majority of them, would be the very first to revert to business as usual. A careful perusing of the American media and a thorough study of reports from KGB sources all over the United States confirmed him handsomely in this. He pocketed his rubles with a grim satisfaction that was reflected throughout the party hierarchy.

Reports coming in from all over the world were exactly the same: the Soviet presence was becoming more "natural" and more accepted every day. The world didn't really want to argue about it. And thus becoming easier every day—and thus much less likely to necessitate actual war to achieve the ultimate goal—was the final battle.

Which might not need to be a battle at all, if things continued as they were going.

Unhappily for Hamilton Delbacher and his colleagues of Cabinet and Congress, this fact was apparent to them as well; and underlying what seemed to be the endless round of conferences and meetings that he, Chauncey Baron, Roger Hackett, Art Hampton, Mark Coffin and the rest were having with other members of the United Nations, there lay the gnawing realization that popular support was slipping away—that each day the uses of habit, the refuge of denial and the refusal to admit perilous facts were sapping their position and making their enemy ever stronger. Infuriating to them all, and particularly to the President, was the knowledge that they were locked into the time-frame that was doing so much to assist their opponents. There was no reason for him to ask for an earlier convening of the Council, no excuse to go before the cameras and rally renewed backing for what appeared to be a universally sagging cause. The recess until Monday proposed by the British Prime Minister with his full approval had seemed a good idea at the time—so many things, in the story of recent American decades, had seemed to be good ideas at the time. A fiercely determined, grimly united and unflaggingly aggressive purpose in Moscow had one by one destroyed them all.

The President was reminded sometimes of an old Hereford bull they had on the farm when he was a child. In his last year of life the old bull for some reason had developed a fierce antagonism for a huge maple tree near the barn. Day after day he would charge that maple tree: day after day, exhausted at last, he would snort, paw the ground one last time and turn away. Would he himself, the President wondered grimly, be like that old bull? Would he, too, keep charging until he, too, eventually had to paw the ground and snort and turn away, taking with him the hopes and dreams and precious, still-to-be-realized things that were America?

It could not be.

It could not be.

Yet it was with an increasingly heavy heart and worried mind that he found himself on Monday taking his seat once more at the Council table while the audience and media chattered and gossiped . . . and the television cameras swung in upon his carefully expressionless face . . . and the babble of a hundred tongues presaged the joining of the battle, once again.

4

"Peace and détente can be reliably insured only in a persistent struggle which rebuffs imperialism's aggressive forces."

—*Pravda, March 9, 1980*

"Détente does not at all abolish, nor can it abolish or alter, the laws of the class struggle."

—Leonid Brezhnev, 25th Party Congress

Once again they were all in place, once again they faced one another around the fateful circle. Once again tension rose in the room like a palpable thing. Here, at least, no one had relaxed, nor had the issue dwindled or diminished. Death's-head still, as Hamilton Delbacher had said, stood behind every chair. The outcome of their deliberations might be no more substantial than words and phrases, but on the preponderance of sentiment expressed in those words and phrases much of the future would depend. Here, at least, the fate of the increasingly relaxed world was taken seriously still.

During the days since their last meeting, most of the heads of state had remained in New York. The President of the United States had made his one quick trip to Washington. The British Prime Minister, the Canadian Prime Minister and the President of France had all flown home briefly to attend important parliamentary votes, but all had quickly returned. Yuri Serapin, the Prime Minister of India, Ju Xing-dao and the rest had remained in New York. Many private meetings, many lengthy discussions, had occurred each day. The offices, conference rooms, corridors, Delegates' Lounge and Delegates' Dining Room of the United Nations had provided the venue for innumerable private meetings, voluble discussions, deals and counter-deals. The media had kept the tally as best its members could: the "Third World" had met on such and such a day, the Arab states on another. Western democracies had conferred and issued calls from an uncertain trumpet. Communist colonies, satellites and client states had conferred and issued rigid declarations of solidarity. Every public coming and going of a head of state had been faithfully chronicled;

some of their more secret conferrings had also been reported. Millions of words of analysis, conjecture, speculation, had poured forth from printed page and television tube. Behind it all, in secret meetings successfully concealed from the media, in private telephone calls and handwritten notes which even the busy intelligence services of the major powers sometimes failed to intercept, the business of consultation went on.

The British Prime Minister, exhausted from her parliamentary battle and one-day turn-around in London but still wearing her bright smile and cheerfully determined air, had managed to meet on the night of her return with her sister Prime Minister from India. Public disagreement was abandoned temporarily for a most candid discussion: it did not appear that the one lady was quite as rigid, or the other quite as naïve, about the Soviet Union as their formal declarations had indicated. The beginnings of understanding, the formulation of strategy, began. Ju Xing-dao, retreating into his tightly guarded headquarters and publicly venturing forth no more after his visits to the two contending Presidents, nonetheless let it be known discreetly that he would gladly talk to any delegates who cared to come to him. More than a hundred did, and while none found himself or herself any more enlightened than Yuri Serapin and Hamilton Delbacher, still the old man managed to gather about himself an aura of leadership, a consensus of attention, which guaranteed him considerable strength in the negotiating ahead.

The President of Tanzania, seeking to rally his fellow Africans in similar fashion, found himself thwarted and annoyed by this, as did those heads of Arab states, most notably Libya and Saudi Arabia, who sought to establish competing positions of leadership. In most cases they found that China's delegate had been there ahead of them. Many nations they had expected to defer to their points of view responded with a frustrating, "We intend to wait and see what China does." Late on Sunday afternoon, after their staffs had conferred for three straight days to work out an absolutely secret time and place, the Prime Ministers of Britain and India actually managed to meet in complete secrecy with Ju themselves—the one other time, and this completely unknown to the media, when he had left his well-publicized retreat. (Nor had it been known to their fellow delegates: Ham Delbacher's shrewd guess had been strictly a lucky shot.) Again there was practical talk of compromise and strategy; and a decision, in one of the moments when Ju deemed it advantageous to speak plain English, as to the timing and procedure to be jointly followed. Both Prime Ministers took this to be in good faith, though both remained basically as skeptical of China's intentions as the two Presidents were.

Later the gist of their discussion was transmitted with the greatest discretion, again unbeknownst to the media, to the Presidents. Both expressed gratitude for the hard work expended on behalf of a solution to the crisis; neither gave any indication how he would treat the proposal in open meeting. The two ladies, and presumably Ju, were not surprised by this. They remained hopeful that they had found a way out, though both were aware that no one would know for sure until the Council actually met.

And now it was meeting and once again Prince Koahumahili, vast bulk draped this time in native skirt, plus a Western-style coat and open-necked shirt, which made him a somewhat incongruous but obviously comfortable figure, called them to order.

"Ladies and gentlemen of the Council," he said, looking with an amiable smile around their circle of solemn faces, "I hope you all have had a pleasant recess in this emergency session of the Security Council, which is now hereby again in session. I know it's been busy for everyone and perhaps profitable for some. Even Tonga has been busy, which has kep' me from bein' bored. I think I realized this week for the first time how really serious this issue is, when many of you have been in touch with *me*. When Tonga gets a call"—his smile broadened, the solemn faces relaxed as he wanted them to, a ripple of laughter swept the room—"you *know* it's serious. . . . Now, then, Mr. Secretary-General, perhaps the best way to begin would be for you to read us the language of the Soviet resolution and then the language of the United States amendment. We've got 'em printed right here before us, but perhaps you could start it off in that official way for the record? If nobody objects? . . . Nobody does, I see, so please proceed."

"Yes, Mr. President," the Secretary-General said gravely, looking distinguished and statesmanly as always with his black, fine-featured face and silver hair. "As the Council directs. First, the Soviet Union." And he proceeded to repeat the bitter words, which somehow now, in his solemn tones, seemed even more shocking than they had the first time:

" 'Whereas' "—the faces of Yuri and his delegation were absolutely expressionless, as were those of the Americans. ["Instant Stonehenge," the London *Times* murmured to the St. Louis *Post-Dispatch*]—" 'the United States of America has sought to intervene directly and inexcusably in the relations between the sovereign states of the U.S.S.R. and the Cuban People's Republic; and in this instance and on many other occasions running back for at least three decades has shown itself to be a constant and continuing threat to world peace and to the stability and well-being of peace-loving nations everywhere; and,

" 'Whereas, no other nation on earth has committed so many vile and inexcusable imperialistic crimes against the freedom, liberty, independence and self-determination of free peoples everywhere;

" 'Now, therefore, be it resolved by the Security Council of the United Nations that the United States is, has been, and is hereby declared to be, the major enemy of freedom and world peace now existing on the earth; and,

" 'Be it further resolved, that the Security Council calls upon all the peace-loving, freedom-loving peoples of the earth to unite against the earth's worst criminal state, the United States of America, and to unanimously condemn, defeat and overthrow the ruling circles of the United States of America for their innumerable imperialistic crimes against humanity and the cause of world peace.' "

The Secretary-General paused, took a sip of water, gravely placed one paper on the table in front of him, gravely picked up the other. Absolute silence held the room save for the ghostly just-audible murmur of the six simultaneous translations coming through the earphones attached to every chair.

"And the United States:

" 'Strike all in the Soviet resolution after the word "Whereas," in the first paragraph and substitute the following:

" 'Whereas, the Union of Soviet Socialist Republics has embarked upon worldwide maneuvers which are unwarranted by any reason of its own security and which directly and openly threaten the security, peace and well-being of nations throughout the world; and,

" 'Whereas, the Soviet Union has specifically directed a major threat to the United States of America by concentrating a wholly unnecessary and overtly hostile force of missile-carrying submarines in Cuba; and,

" 'Whereas, the Soviet Union has steadily expanded the size, scope and striking abilities of its armed forces in recent decades for no purpose reasonably associated with the needs of self-defense; and,

" 'Whereas, this build-up has created an overwhelming aggressive threat to world peace and to the security and well-being of all freedom-loving peoples everywhere; and,

" 'Whereas, the Soviet Union in recent decades has become the major aggressive force threatening peace in virtually all areas of the world, through indirect subversion, direct invasion and the constant threat of armed blackmail and open war; now, therefore,

" 'Be it resolved that the Security Council of the United Nations demands the immediate termination of Soviet world maneuvers; the withdrawal of all Soviet submarines from the waters of Cuba, India and wherever else they may be concentrated around the globe, and the immediate abandonment of all Soviet aggressive, subversive or warlike ambitions against any nation whatsoever; and, further,

" 'Be it resolved, that the Security Council herewith condemns the Soviet Union as the major existing threat to world peace and calls upon all members to unite in opposing Soviet imperial designs and ambitions, wherever and whenever they may be found, anywhere on earth.' "

"That, Mr. President," the Secretary-General concluded quietly, "completes my reading of the two resolutions now before the Council."

"Thank you, Mr. Secretary-General," Koa said with equal decorum. "Are there requests for special order in the speakers' list today?"

"The delegate of the People's Republic of China has requested that he be allowed to speak first, Mr. President, followed by the Prime Minister of Great Britain and then by the Prime Minister of India."

"Is there objection?" Koa inquired as the room suddenly buzzed with anticipatory sound. "The United States and the Soviet Union do not—?"

"Not at this moment, Mr. President," Hamilton Delbacher said crisply.

"The Soviet Union passes for the moment," Yuri Serapin said in almost the same breath.

"Very well," Prince Koa said. "The distinguished delegate of the People's Republic of China has the floor."

It took him, characteristically, several seconds to claim it, during which he shifted in his chair, positioned his microphone in front of him first in one place, then in another, adjusted his yellow robe around him with all the delicacy and precision of the Indian Prime Minister with her sari, cleared his throat softly, folded his hands, finally looked from face to face with a sweetly benign and gentle smile.

"Mr. President," he said in his whispery old voice, so frail-seeming this morning that they all leaned forward instinctively and strained to hear, "it is a great honor for China to be allowed to open this concluding stage of the debate in the Security Council on this most grave and serious matter. I wish to thank my distinguished colleagues the Prime Minister of Great Britain and the Prime Minister of India for permitting my country this honor. In our recent private discussion"—he could not resist a mischievous glance toward the press section, many of whose members obliged him by looking at one another with startled, upset, why-didn't-we-know-about-this glances—"it was agreed among us that I should present our conclusions. Insofar as it falls within my poor powers as a user of the English language, I shall be happy to do so.

"Mr. President, there is a saying in my country"—this time it was Hamilton Delbacher who could not resist glancing at Yuri Serapin, and for a tenuous moment there was a brief gleam of shared amusement— "that he who would calm the sea must first pacify the storm. Such is the hope of the two charming Prime Ministers and of my old, unworthy self. But first we must determine the nature of the storm."

He paused and again looked about the circle of attentive faces. Eire waved him on encouragingly with his pipe.

"We are now agreed, I think," Ju said, "at least the two Prime Ministers and I are agreed, that there is indeed a mutually shared responsibility for the storm. Yet we consider that it is not, perhaps, equally shared—that it is, perhaps, a little more tempestuous on the one side than on the other."

["Here we go again," the Chicago *Sun-Times* said with some disgust. "America the Scapegoat, once again." But Ju surprised him.]

"Despite the initial reactions of the Prime Minister of India and myself, our severity perhaps prompted by our great alarm over the possible consequences of the current situation, it is perhaps, as our colleague from Britain says, somewhat more the responsibility of the Soviet Union than it is of the United States."

There was an intake of breath in press and audience, a surprised look from Yuri, an even greater attentiveness given Ju as he went half-whispering on.

"We do not wish to be understood, however," he added with some renewal of severity, "as saying that it is exclusively, or by any means entirely, or by any means excessively, or by any means extremely, or overwhelmingly, the responsibility of the Soviet Union."

["Clear?" inquired the *Daily Telegraph*. "Crystalline," replied the Washington *Star*.]

"On the other hand," Ju said, and even his colleagues from Britain and India began to look a little restive, "it cannot be said to be exclusively, or by any means excessively or overwhelmingly, or indeed extremely, the responsibility of the United States, either. It is just that in our estimation, it is more obvious that it is, indeed, somewhat more the responsibility of the Soviet Union . . . perhaps."

"Mr. President," the Prime Minister of India said with a frown, "I do not wish to interrupt the distinguished—"

"Therefore, Mr. President," Ju continued blandly, "it has seemed to us that the way out of this is to offer still a third alternative to the, shall we say, somewhat extreme language offered by both the President of the Soviet Union and the President of the United States. We realize that under orderly parliamentary procedures this would normally have to come after votes have been taken on the two contending resolutions, and would have to be then introduced as an amendment to whichever proved to be the winning one.

"But, Mr. President, in practical fact we all know that neither resolution will be adopted because in each instance the veto will be exercised by the opposing power. Therefore essentially we face an exercise in futility which I believe a majority of the Council would rather not endure. I do not speak for the Soviet Union or the United States, but I am quite sure, from many discussions I have had this week, that most of us would prefer to expedite this as much as possible. Or," he added dryly, "do the honorable delegates of the U.S. and the U.S.S.R. wish to delay in order that they may exchange further comments upon one another's shortcomings?"

And he peered like a solemn little owl at the two Presidents.

"Mr. Delbacher?" Koa inquired.

"The United States has no wish to delay this matter," Hamilton Delbacher said. "Soviet worldwide maneuvers and the disposition of Soviet submarines in waters adjacent to many of us indicate the extreme urgency of the matter. If the three powers think they have devised a method of expediting it, by all means let us consider it at once."

"Mr. Serapin?"

"The imperialist racist adventures of the United States, which have brought the entire globe to the very edge of war at this very moment," Yuri remarked in a spiteful tone, "are certainly not decreasing or diminishing. Yes, I say, let China, let Britain, let India, let anyone, come forward with a means of instantly stopping American aggression. We welcome it, Mr. President."

"It might necessitate," Ju said softly, "the abandonment of both the Soviet and American resolutions. We wish to make this very clear at the outset."

"Of course we can make no promises on that," Ham Delbacher said crisply, "until we hear the wording of your resolution."

"Nor we," Yuri said.

"You shall hear it," Ju said with equal tartness. "It is quite simple and direct."

["That's a change," the *Christian Science Monitor* murmured to *U. S. News and World Report*. The two Presidents, both smiling slightly, obviously thought so too.]

"It reads," Ju said, ignoring them, "as follows:

" 'Whereas, the world now faces a situation of the utmost gravity involving a most serious threat to peace created jointly by the military actions of the Soviet Union and the response thereto of the United States; and,

" 'Whereas, resolutions now before the Security Council do not seek a compromise or peaceful solution but seek rather to enlist the Security Council and the United Nations openly on one side or the other, to the detriment of the cause of world peace, and in a way that could very likely inflame rather than diminish the threat to peace; and,

" 'Whereas, it is obvious that because of the veto, no solution of the crisis can be reached on the basis of the two opposing resolutions now before the Council; now, therefore,

" 'Be it resolved, that the Security Council desires to be, and hereby is, discharged of its responsibility in this matter' "—there was a stir of excitement—" 'and calls upon the General Assembly to begin immediate consideration of it, looking toward a solution that will:

" 'First, define with equal justice the joint responsibility of the United States and the Soviet Union for the creation of the crisis and the attendant threat to world peace;

" 'Second, call upon the Soviet Union to curtail immediately its present peace-threatening worldwide military maneuvers, including widespread deployment of submarines, and restrict them to those lands and waters adjacent to its own territory which are legitimate subjects of concern for Soviet security;

" 'Third, call upon the United States to abandon all those actions which have contributed to world tension, specifically the projected increase in United States military spending; the national emergency and war alert declared by the President; and the ultimatum of the President regarding the presence of Soviet submarines in the territorial waters of the sovereign state of Cuba; and further,

" 'Be it resolved, that the Security Council, having discharged itself of its responsibilities and having called the matter to the attention of the General Assembly, with recommendations, does hereby declare this emergency session to be adjourned, and it is so adjourned, sine die.'

"That is all, Mr. President," Ju concluded gently and sat back, folding his hands once again on the table as many reporters rushed out to file bulletins and from audience and Council members alike there came an explosion of excited chatter.

Across it rang a repeated shout of "Mr. President! Mr. President!" from the President of the Soviet Union: and presently, aided by Koa's vigorous use of the gavel, reasonable silence was restored. Yuri's words tumbled forth in angry spate.

"Mr. President," he cried indignantly, "what kind of parliamentary trickery is this! What plot is being cooked up here by China, Britain and India! It is typical racist imperialist plotting, Mr. President! The capitalists and the hegemonists have formed an unholy alliance to thwart the desires of the world's peace-loving peoples! They have conspired with the United States behind the Security Council's back to attempt to restrict the Soviet Union in the free exercise of its sovereign powers in defense of the peace and security of all mankind! What a sinister thing is this, Mr. Chairman! What a trick! We will have none of it! *None of it!*"

And he slapped his hand hard on the table and glared around, red-faced and apparently furious.

"Mr. President," Hamilton Delbacher said quietly, raising his hand for recognition. "If I might—?"

"By all means, Mr. President," Koa said, and the last vestige of sound abruptly trailed away.

"Mr. President," Ham Delbacher said, "first of all, I wish to thank the Vice Premier and the two Prime Ministers for their sincere and responsible attempt to find a solution for the very desperate crisis that confronts us. It is with the greatest reluctance that I also must demur. Their attempt to sidestep the issue and send it immediately to the General Assembly is very clever, but it does several things, in my opinion, that tend to violate the mandate and the purpose of the Security Council.

"First, it deprives us of our right to vote on this desperately important issue. Secondly, although it purports to 'call upon' the General Assembly to take up the issue, it in fact directs the General Assembly to do so. Not only that, but it specifically directs the General Assembly to do certain things and arrive at certain conclusions. And it then attempts to foreclose the Security Council entirely by coupling these recommendations with a motion to adjourn, which theoretically makes this a procedural matter not subject to veto, and theoretically not subject to debate—although I think that there is going to be substantial debate on it, nonetheless . . . Thus the three-power or C.I.B. resolution, as I might call it for easy reference, verges on illegality—if there is such a thing, in UN procedure. At least it verges on violating the rules, such as they are, and it also is an attempt to assume a dominance and a direction over the General Assembly which the Security Council does not have and which the General Assembly should rightly resent.

"There are in addition a number of substantive points and conclusions in the resolution with which the United States does not agree. I get the impression"—he smiled amicably at Yuri, who scowled back—"that the delegate of the Soviet Union also finds himself in some disagreement. Since the co-authors of the resolution have deliberately placed it, with their motion to adjourn, in a sort of no-man's land between procedural matter and substantive resolution, I don't know at the moment whether the United States will veto it or simply join what I hope will be the majority in voting it down. In any event we are opposed."

"Mr. President," the Prime Minister of Great Britain inquired politely, "perhaps the Chair could give us a ruling as to which category he believes our resolution falls into?"

"I was wishin'," Prince Koa said with a rueful grin that brought a fleeting answering amusement from around the table, "that nobody would ask me that. But since the lady has—and since I *am* presidin'—and since this is obviously an important turnin' point in this matter—and since it's now almost noon—I'm goin' to take it on myself to adjourn this particular session to 8 P.M. this evenin' so that there will be ample time for me to ascertain the general mood of the Council before I make my rulin'. Does anybody want to disagree with that? If so, the floor's open."

He paused and looked slowly around the table while the tension mounted dramatically. The Americans and Soviets conferred among themselves, the British and Indian Prime Ministers sat in determined immobility, Ju contemplated his hands and perhaps considered ancient wisdoms, other delegates shifted in their chairs and whispered earnestly to one another. But no one spoke. Finally Koa glanced at his watch.

"Very well," he said comfortably, "one full minute has now gone by, and nobody's said boo. Without objection this emergency meetin' of the Security Council stands adjourned until eight o'clock tonight."

He was immediately besieged by the media as Council and audience moved slowly to the doors. But with an amicable laugh and a mock-astounded, "Imagine little ol' Tonga bein' so important as all this!" he elicited their laughter, and on the surge of it, got himself safely away without letting anyone know what he intended to do.

There ensued a busy few hours for all the delegations, particularly those of the five powers directly involved. Each was in contact with Koa at some point during the afternoon, but he remained as pleasantly non-committal with them as he had been with the press. They all knew he had spent a couple of hours with the Secretary-General in the S.-G.'s office on the thirty-eighth floor of the Secretariat Building—"studyin' precedents," he told the AP—but that was all anybody knew. Later he appeared in the Delegates' Lounge at 6 P.M. and had a drink with Tanzania and Egypt, after which they all went up to the Delegates' Dining Room where they were joined for dinner by Cameroon and Eire. But despite frequent approaches by the writing press, requests to appear on the evening televi-sion news programs, and many urgent appeals for information from members of the General Assembly, he turned them all off with jokes and humorous evasions, and kept his own counsel. Not even his dinner com-panions were able to penetrate his amiable demeanor, as the President of Egypt confided to the President of France. Everybody agreed that Koa was certainly being mysterious, even as each of them scrupulously kept his own secrets and told no one of his own plans.

Despite the general closemouthed atmosphere, it was apparent to the two Presidents as they lobbied busily during the interval that there was substantial sentiment for the ruling Koa was probably going to give. Both Ham Delbacher and Yuri Serapin deployed their delegations through the UN like troops in the field; both looked ahead to the General Assembly debate even as they themselves argued earnestly with fellow delegates on the Security Council. The President of the United States assigned Mark and Congressman Lapham to the South American delegations; permanent U. S. Ambassador Ambrose Johnson was assigned to Africa, Chauncey Baron took the Asian nations, Roger Hackett the Europeans, Art Hamp-ton and Herb Esplin the Middle East. Their paths frequently crossed those of the Soviet Foreign Minister, Defense Minister, the three marshals and Admiral Valenko. No words were exchanged as they met one another in corridors, committee rooms, offices, Delegates' Lounge and dining room. The Soviets were grim and intent and the Americans, after a few attempts at scrupulously polite nods, gave up and ignored them as they themselves were ignored. In his hotel suite the President either tele-phoned or received in person all the members of the Security Council. In his office at Soviet headquarters, Yuri did the same. Each perceived what he thought was a glimpse of the prevailing mood, though none of their callers or visitors was other than completely discreet. At that point in the day, no one was committing him or herself one way or the other.

Meanwhile, both Presidents were receiving reports on the progress of the Soviet maneuvers, which were going steadily ahead throughout the world as though the UN did not exist—a fact that did not surprise Hamilton Delbacher, and to Yuri Serapin seemed the most natural thing in the world. After all, the UN had objected to Soviet actions before, most notably in Afghanistan, and the Soviets had learned from that and many other episodes that all they need do was keep calm, ignore the UN and proceed exactly as they planned to proceed: presently the UN would subside. The Soviets could then consolidate their conquest, plan their next, or make whatever other undermining move seemed called for in their unrelenting war upon the world. Anything to weaken the capitalist imperialist enemy, Yuri thought with satisfaction. Everything was going exactly according to plan.

In the Arctic the combined submarine and ski-troop exercises were entering their second stages. In Eastern Europe the trucks and tanks (built with the kind assistance of those sophisticated computers whose purchase had been so generously permitted by J. Carter) were roaring over the landscape with terrifying efficiency. In the skies over Asia and South America armadas of bombers and fighter planes, ignoring the feeble protests of the helpless nations below, were occupying others' air space with split-second precision. Missiles in European Russia, Siberia, Cuba, Nicaragua, Grenada and half a dozen other launching sites were being raised, lowered, moved, shifted about with clockwork regularity. Off the shores of many unsuspecting lands in the Caribbean, Indian Ocean, Mediterranean, North Sea, Sea of Japan, Atlantic, Pacific, the submarines were methodically plodding their way through maneuvers beneath the seas. Day by day, hour by hour, Soviet forces were becoming more skilled in the use of their vast and arrogant armament; and Yuri's long-range gamble was coming closer and closer to success.

Meanwhile within continental United States and Alaska, in Hawaii and Puerto Rico, in NATO-land in Western Europe, in the South Pacific and in one or two remaining dots in what used to be the "American lake" of the Caribbean before it became the "Soviet lake" of the Caribbean, a Navy inferior in numbers and an Army inexperienced and in many specifics underequipped were conducting modest and restricted maneuvers under the umbrella of a diminished Air Force. Out on the plains of the upper Midwest MX missiles were being moved about from hole to hole with great diligence, bringing smiles to the faces of men in Moscow who hardly gave a damn for what they called "the children's game," because their own missiles were so far ahead in numbers, warheads and precision targeting. In the Pentagon the Joint Chiefs were being told every day by eager juniors how marvelously sophisticated their future weapons were going to be; but, being experienced old-timers, the sheer cold logic of numbers oppressed them all. "Look!" Bart Jamison finally snapped when two of his brightest aides were burbling on about the ultra-ultra-ultra sophistication of the latest projected U.S. fighter plane. "I can count! You have two of the God damned things in mock-up and the rest won't be ready until 1991, for Christ's sake! Do you really think anybody in Moscow gives a fuck right now?"

There were great and wondrous plans going forward in many clever minds in the Pentagon for the building of bricks without straw; but the Joint Chiefs of Staff, being knowledgeable and weary at the game, and bearing upon their shoulders the terrifying responsibility, grew daily more concerned and more depressed.

Nonetheless, a stand had been taken by their Commander-in-Chief and a front had to be maintained. Also, amid all the tangle of outdated equipment, slipping numbers and plans for yesterday's war, there were still the elements of a strong and viable fighting force. It was their job to drive it into shape, and slowly but surely they were doing so. The crisis had given them new power, new authority, new urgency; they were putting in twelve-, fourteen-, sixteen-, sometimes twenty-hour days, and all down the chains of command their dedication and determination were being felt. If the confrontation could just be avoided awhile longer—if plans on the drawing-board (always "on the drawing-board") could be brought to fruition—if the good Lord in His wisdom would just grant them *time*— then a respectable showing, perhaps even a winning one, could still be achieved. Thus they alternated between gnawing despair and bred-in-the-bone confidence that "good old American know-how" would yet achieve one more miracle. The road ahead was very hard and very long. And they did not know, in this hectic hour of crisis, just how much time they still had in which to travel it.

In his Waldorf suite, the President had his moments of suddenly feeling the same way; and one of these afflicted him just as he was preparing to go down to meet his limousine and be transported, with due panoply of state, back to the Security Council at 8 P.M.

He had taken his stand, he was fighting his battle; he, too, was in his way attempting to make bricks without straw. Here in this house of the nations, launched with such idealism (combined with such low, crafty, self-interested cynicism on the part of all the great powers as they suavely jettisoned Hope and blandly crowned King Veto in its place), he was prepared to use whatever weapons he had, including King Veto, to protect and preserve the United States of America and the safety of the world.

Perhaps that order was the wrong one, he thought as he squared his shoulders, adjusted his jacket, straightened his tie; perhaps it summed up what was wrong with the United Nations and indeed with all the endeavors of nation-oriented man. Everybody came first: nobody was subordinate to the overriding need of humanity for justice, and for peace. His opponent thought that justice and peace could be achieved by destroying the United States; everything in Hamilton Delbacher cried out that preservation of the United States was necessary to justice and to peace. He had no desire to destroy the Soviet Union, only to live with it in non-competitive, non-aggressive, non-infringing ways; and such, he knew, was the desire of the overwhelming majority of his countrymen. But it could not be done as long as the Soviet Union was constantly plotting, pushing, conniving, subverting, expanding, conquering, empire-building, dedicating itself with cold-blooded determination to the conquest and enslavement of the world.

Its leaders made no bones of this intention. They proclaimed it, with what amounted to a monstrous glee, on every possible occasion. Why should anyone else, virtually guaranteeing self-destruction, pretend that it was not so? It was so. The entire ideology, the entire training, the entire leadership of the Soviet Union announced it openly. They were history's greatest killers of the dream—the dream of human decency, freedom, the simple right of life-to-be-lived, by everybody everywhere.

None of this was for Yuri and his friends. They had much starker purposes than that. And so they had to be stopped, not because any sinister "capitalist imperialist racist" conspiracy wanted to stop them, but just because they *would not leave other people alone*. It wasn't enough for them to enslave their own vast country, which was a crime monstrous enough: they had to go after everybody else. *They just would not keep hands off.* They could not be happy until they had finally forced the world to showdown. And now, almost, they had.

He sighed, because in these closing years of the twentieth century it was not an easy thing to be President of the United States, the land Abraham Lincoln, with his remarkable prescience about so many things, had called "the last, best hope of earth." Now it truly was, in a way old Abe could never have foreseen. Nobody else had the strength, worn and tattered though it was; nobody else, really, had the will.

And did the United States and its confused, uncertain, well-meaning people? Yuri and his friends didn't think so, which was why they were pushing so hard and so fast now. He himself was not so sure, but one thing he did know—*he* did. And as long as he, who sat in the White House, did, then there was hope. If he, or any future President, ever lost that will, then there would be no more hope for the free mind, the free heart, the free spirit, anywhere—*anywhere*—to the utmost reaches of the earth. The final death of the mind would occur and endless night would descend and reign forevermore.

Well: he told himself. It was not here yet, by God, and he was determined it never would be. Yuri and his fellow slave-masters were determined it would, he and his easygoing, basically goodhearted countrymen were determined it would not . . . It will, it won't, it will, it won't . . . It was not an immediate clear-cut decision, though the time was coming very close when it might be just that simple. Up to now it had been a slow, gradual process compounded about equally of growing Soviet strength and shrewdly calculated planning on the one hand, and on the other declining American strength and more or less willful blindness on the part of those who governed America and controlled its public opinion. He was in a position to arrest the decline and attempt to overcome the blindness; but his opponent was in a position to increase the strength and speed up the shrewdly calculated planning. Behind this propaganda roundelay at the UN lay the grim bare bones of their struggle. The vote or votes tonight were one more part of the conclusion that was beginning to fall into place. He was not entirely sure how the debate would go when it resumed, but he told himself grimly that the United States under his leadership would not give up, no matter what.

Equally determined, and much more confident of the outcome, the President of the Soviet Union also entered his limousine at about the same moment to travel the short distance to the United Nations, its curved row of flags drooping listlessly in the sweltering summer twilight.

"The Council will be in order," Koa said inside the brightly lit, air-conditioned chamber, and upon crowded table and overflowing gallery a restless, uneasy silence finally settled. The clock stood at twenty-two minutes past the hour of eight, and everyone was aware it would record a very much later hour before the evening's work was done. The wire services and television networks had alerted extra crews in anticipation of a session running well past midnight; reporters without such backups were prepared for a long and weary vigil. Most of the delegates had a patient, dogged air; they expected to be exhausted and they looked resigned to it. Koa took note of this: trying, as he always did, to introduce at least a little relieving humor into the proceedings. The odds against it were usually heavy and seemed even more so tonight. But he tried.

"Distinguished delegates," he said, "at least we can be thankful for one thing: we're not out there in that oven New York turns into in the summer. We're nice and cool and the only heat that's goin' to be generated here is goin' to come from ourselves. I expect that's plenty, but maybe we can hold it down a little. Let's try!"

And he beamed around the circle of solemn faces, but found therein a wan support, at best.

"Anyway," he said, *"I'll* try, though I expect I'm goin' to make some of you mad at me right off the bat. Not that I want to, but just because that's how it's goin' to be."

["For God's sake, you old coconut-milker," the New York *Daily News* muttered to his neighbor, the Minneapolis *Star,* "get *on* with it!"]

"As you all know," Koa went on comfortably chatting, "I have spent the past few hours conferrin' with most of you, and many others besides, about the decision I'm about to announce here tonight. I believe most of you have been conferrin' too. I think, but of course I don't know, that many of you may support me. I know some won't . . .

"After talkin' at length to our distinguished Secretary-General, here, and after studyin' all the precedents"—he paused, suddenly serious and deliberate—"I have come to the conclusion"—he paused again—"that in response to the question raised in our last session by our distinguished lady from Britain, I should rule as follows"—and again he paused, milking the moment, as the Minneapolis *Star* muttered to the New York *Daily News,* as though it were the biggest coconut that ever came off the tree—

"Inasmuch as the so-called three-power resolution offered by the People's Republic of China, India and the United Kingdom does contain specific substantive conclusions, directions and admonitions, it might well be considered a substantive matter. But in view of the fact"—the first reporters began to start from their chairs, and above in their booths the television cameras whirred in upon fifteen keenly intent faces—"that its authors have chosen to conclude it with a motion to adjourn—and in view of the fact that certain practical considerations involvin' the veto do indeed enter in here—" ["*Christ,*" the *Daily News* exploded in a savage whisper, "hurry up!"]—"it is the rulin' of the Chair that it is indeed a procedural matter, that the veto does not apply, and that accordingly the Chair now declares this emergency session of the Security Council to be adj—"

But he was not, of course, to get away with it so easily; nor did he, of course, expect to. He had dragged out his final words very slowly in anticipation of exactly what would occur; and when it did, he sat smiling patiently until some order had been restored and they were back on track again.

The first interruption came, almost simultaneously, from the two Presidents, followed rapidly by the two Prime Ministers.

"Mr. President!" Yuri Serapin cried indignantly, "the Soviet Union wishes to protest the ruling of the Chair!"

"Mr. President," Hamilton Delbacher exclaimed with equal vigor, "the United States must protest the ruling of the Chair!"

"Mr. President!" cried the Prime Ministers of Britain and India together, "Vote! Vote!"

Ju Xing-dao smiled gently, eyes fixed vaguely on some distant ink-brushed landscape only he could see.

"Mr. President," the President of France remarked with rather spiteful reasonableness above the hubbub that filled the room, "if there is disagreement with the ruling of the Chair, should it not be expressed in an orderly fashion? There are means of doing so, after all."

"I move," the British Prime Minister said quickly, "that the ruling of the Chair be approved."

"And we ask for an immediate vote," the Indian Prime Minister supported her with equal speed.

Ju Xing-dao came back from wherever he was to nod solemn agreement.

"You have heard the motion of the delegate of Great Britain as perfected by the delegate of India," Koa said with surprising rapidity. "All those in favor—"

"NOW JUST A MINUTE MR. PRESIDENT," Ham Delbacher said in a voice that produced the result he wanted. Koa stopped, blinked, then suddenly grinned.

"Just tryin' to save a little time," he said cheerfully. "But," he added, unable to resist a little sarcasm, "we've got lots of it, I guess, even if the Soviet Union is movin' all over the world and even if its submarines are threatenin' the United States and even poor little Tonga 'way down there. So I guess the President of the United States can take all the time he wants. The Chair recognizes him for as much as he wants of it."

"Thank you, Mr. President," Ham said dryly. "I'm overwhelmed by your generosity, as I am by your desire to expedite matters. But that still does not remove from this resolution the features which are repugnant and unacceptable to the United States. Nor presumably, those which are repugnant and unacceptable to the Soviet Union."

"We will discuss those on our own time," Yuri said coldly, without looking at him.

"I'm sure you will," he replied calmly. "Mr. President, the United States cannot accept the thesis that this crisis has been 'created jointly' by the Soviet Union and the United States. The escalating of this situation to a state of worldwide crisis is directly attributable to the maneuvers of the Soviet Union and their implicit threat of aggression to many lands, particularly the United States. This has not been a joint creation. It has been the sole responsibility of the Soviet Union. That is our first and most basic quarrel with the so-called 'compromise' devised by China, India and Britain.

"Secondly, we cannot under any circumstances accept the subparagraph designated 'third,' which urges the General Assembly, I quote, to 'call upon the United States to abandon all those actions which have contributed to world tension, specifically the projected increase in United

States military spending; the national emergency and war alert declared by the President; and the ultimatum of the President regarding the presence of Soviet submarines in the territorial waters of the sovereign state of Cuba.'

"I cannot believe that the Prime Minister of Great Britain, in particular, really means it when she lends her endorsement to such language, aware as she is of the dangers to all peace-loving peoples implicit in the Soviet maneuvers, and knowing as she does that the strength of the United States is a vital element in the defense of all independent nations. I admire the urge for compromise which has always distinguished the United Kingdom, but in this instance I think the urge has overleapt the facts."

"Mr. President," the British Prime Minister responded with some asperity, "heartily as we support the United States in its basic position, there is such a thing as practical reality. It is in an attempt to allow for it that I have joined in this endeavor with my colleagues from India and China. They have conceded substantially as regards the responsibility of the Soviet Union and the call upon it to curtail immediately its worldwide maneuvers. I have made equal concessions as regards the United States. I would remind the distinguished delegate of the United States that there are worse bargains possible, given the present climate in the United Nations toward his country. I urge him to support this resolution."

There was a burst of applause from the audience, composed today, as previously, of a preponderance of Soviet satellites and sympathizers. She ignored it and so did he.

"Mr. President," he said calmly, "I am not going to be deflected into a debate on this matter with my good friend from Britain. I understand and appreciate her motives in what she has done, but the fact remains that the three-power resolution, compromise or no, still contains major items unacceptable to the United States. History shows that there is no point in agreeing to the slightest concessions to the Soviet Union because its leaders will simply regard this as a sign of weakness and will ride over you wherever they can. This is historic fact.

"As for my part in this, Mr. Serapin's own attitude accounted for my orders to increase military spending in this country; his maneuvers prompted my declaration of national emergency and military alert; his deliberate deployment of submarines as a threat and a testing of the United States prompted my ultimatum for their removal. And his token gesture of removing a measly six," he snapped with a sudden surge of anger that abruptly tightened the tension in the room, "does not remove the necessity for my ultimatum, nor does it decrease by one iota my continuing intention that they will *all* be removed before we are through with this. . . .

"No, Mr. President," he concluded more calmly, while Yuri permitted himself to look openly furious and a sibilant wave of hisses swept the audience, "the United States will not vote for this resolution. Perhaps if it could have been presented as a simple transfer to the General Assembly without attempting to insert condemnations and prejudgments, we might have. But we cannot in its present form, and I detect no indication that its authors wish to amend it. Therefore our negative vote on the motion to uphold the ruling of the Chair is inevitable."

He pushed aside his microphone and sat back while members of the press again bestirred themselves to hurry out and file additions to their running stories on the debate. Yuri raised his hand and an attentive silence immediately fell.

"Mr. Serapin," Koa said with a patient sigh that provoked some amusement and a sharp sidelong glance from Yuri.

"The Soviet Union," Yuri said, "cannot vote for this so-called 'compromise resolution' which in reality is no compromise but condemns the just position of the Soviet Union and is an insult to peace-loving peoples everywhere."

There was a murmur of approval, a scattering of applause. He made his favorite table-slapping gesture.

"Yes! An insult to the peace-loving peoples of the world! A blow to world peace! An insult to us! An attempt to place us on the same footing with the rascist imperialist war-mongers which we *cannot and will not* accept! *'Joint responsibility,'* when it is the capitalist imperialist circles of the United States that have chosen to seize upon our perfectly legitimate maneuvers as an excuse to embark upon a new arms race, a new attempt to inflame and upset the world!

"Our maneuvers hurt no one, Mr. President. They harm no one. They are a threat to no one. They are our sovereign right. Our ships and troops are greeted with friendliness everywhere. No one is afraid of them except the United States. No one makes a fuss about them except the delegate of the United States. No one attempts to use them as an excuse for warlike gestures except the delegate of the United States. He is too timid, Mr. President. He is too frightened for the serious and responsible office he holds. He is afraid of our shadow. He thinks it will eat him up. He will scare himself into blowing up the world if we permit him to!"

There was a wave of laughter, a new round of applause. At some cost, Ham Delbacher managed to remain impassive.

"Mr. President," Yuri went on with heavy sarcasm, "he must calm himself. He must give up his foolish fears. He must not see bugaboos and hobgoblins under the bed. He must be brave. We will not hurt him . . .

"But, Mr. President"—and his expression turned abruptly severe, "neither will we vote for this abominable 'compromise,' so-called, which has been brought here by China, India and the U.K. There *is* no 'joint responsiblity.' There *is* no reason for anyone to 'call upon' the Soviet Union

to stop its maneuvers. We will not stop our maneuvers, Mr. President. Why should we? Neither will I go further"—he paused and repeated his words—"neither will I go further than I have in withdrawing submarines sent at their request to protect the Soviet Union's brave ally, the sovereign state of Cuba." He slapped the table again, a crack that made them jump. "Six is enough, Mr. President! Six is enough! If the President of the United States does not like that, let him plunge the world into war, Mr. President! Let him! We are ready for him!"

And he leaned forward, turned to Hamilton Delbacher and gave him a savage look as the audience gasped. Obviously holding himself under tight rein but still impassive, the President ignored him, looking straight ahead.

"No, Mr. President," Yuri said flatly, turning back to a somber Koa. "We will never vote for this resolution. Or for the motion to uphold the ruling. Never, never! We call upon all peace-loving peoples to join us in repulsing this dirty imperialist racist trick!"

"Mr. President!" the Prime Minister of India cried angrily. "Am I dirty? Am I imperialist? Am I racist? Do I indulge in 'tricks'? For shame on the delegate, Mr. President! For shame! For shame!"

"Oh, Mr. President!" Yuri cried, turning to her, arms outstretched. "I beseech my dear friend from India, do not let the capitalist war-mongers come between us! Do not fall for their games! No, the Prime Minister is not imperialist, she is not dirty, she is not imperialist, she is not racist! But she has been duped, Mr. President! She has been fooled by the hegemonists and the lackeys of the racist imperialists. Her intentions are of the best, but she has permitted her good heart and her genuine desire for peace to blind her to the game that is being played here! I beg of her, join me in voting down this resolution. It is not your handiwork, Prime Minister! It is the handiwork of those who are enemies of India and the enemies of peace! Join us and all of India's true friends. Vote no! Vote no!"

"Mr. President," the Indian Prime Minister said icily, "I suggest we now terminate this drivel on all sides and permit the Security Council to work its will. I move we vote, Mr. President. Now!"

"I second that, Mr. President," the British Prime Minister said with a matching coldness. "We have had quite enough, I think."

"Well, you know," Koa said, hunching himself forward to his microphone, "I think you ladies are quite right. If there is no further debate—"

"Vote!" many Council members began shouting, and "Vote! Vote!" the audience took it up.

"The Secretary-General will call the roll!" Koa bellowed, banging his gavel furiously until a modest semblance of order was restored. Solemnly, as always, the S.-G. complied.

"People's Republic of China!"

"Yes," Ju murmured, so low that many demanded nervously of each other, "What? What?"

"Yes!" he repeated, somewhat louder, and the Secretary-General nodded.

"France!"

"Oui," the President of France said in a tone that added, *You idiots.*

"The United Kingdom!"

"Yes!"

"The United States!"

"No," the President said calmly. Many in the audience cried: *"Booo!"*

"The Union of Soviet Socialist Republics!"

"No," Yuri said sharply. Applause rose dutifully from satellites and sympathizers.

"Cameroon!"

"Oui," said Cameroon, looking important.

"Eire!"

"Yes," Eire said solemnly, shifting his pipe. "I should say so! Yes!"

"Egypt!"

"Yes," the President of Egypt said quietly.

"Greece!"

"Yes."

"India!"

"Yes!" she said, sounding impatient.

"Iraq!"

"Yes!" giving Yuri a spiteful look.

"Nicaragua!"

"Sí!"

"The Seychelles!"

"Certainly."

"Tanzania!"

"Yes."

"Tonga!"

"You bet!" Koa said with relief, and though the mood was anything but light, he managed to lift it a little.

The Secretary-General handed him the tally and he made the formal announcement:

"All members of the Security Council having voted, and the veto not applying on this issue, there are two votes No, thirteen Yes and the resolution offered by the People's Republic of China, India and the United Kingdom is approved."

"Mr. President," the President of Tanzania said quietly, "I move this emergency session of the Security Council stand adjourned sine die."

"It's already in the resolution," Koa pointed out with a smile, "but I'm thinkin' like you, Mr. President: we'd better nail it down. It is so ordered, and this session is now *absolutely finished!*"

And for the last time he brought down his gavel and the room erupted into controversial, combative, cantankerous sound, members, press and audience still arguing heatedly as many reporters dashed out to send their final bulletins—SECURITY COUNCIL DUCKS WAR ISSUE, SENDS CRISIS TO ASSEMBLY WITH INSTRUCTIONS TO CONDEMN BOTH SOVIETS AND U.S.—and the chamber of so many sharp contentions fell gradually quiet, leaving only clerks to gather up papers and janitors to vacuum carpets, straighten chairs and leave the empty table in order until the next time—if there was to be one—when its occupants would meet again to debate the troubles of the world.

The political columnist of the Washington *Post,* who for many years had been the best in the country, analyzed it for his extensive readership in a special article that was syndicated the following Sunday in the United States, thirty-seven major foreign countries and the Kremlin, where perhaps fifty citizens of the Soviet Union were permitted to read it. They were, however, the fifty who mattered, and thus it reached nearly all the important personages in the world. Few who had been directly involved in the Security Council debate found cause to disagree with his conclusions. He was a thorough reporter, an extremely well-informed man and a sound and responsible analyst; and he had been able to talk to all of the principals before they returned temporarily to their capitals to await the session of the General Assembly, now expected to begin within two weeks, on or about August 15.

Only the Vice Premier of China and the President of the Soviet Union at first remained elusive; and since the columnist assessed Yuri's motivations with the political instinct acquired in many years of experience, and since the President of the United States and the Prime Ministers of Britain and India all agreed in what they told him of their general impressions of Ju Xing-dao, he did not think his article would suffer from the absence of the two difficult gentlemen. It was part of their act, as he told his editors, to *be* difficult: he could go ahead without them. But at the very last moment, on Tuesday afternoon after the vote, both surprised him by sending word that they would see him. Concealing his surprise and instinctive skepticism, he hurried off first to the headquarters of the People's Republic of China and there secured the first and, as it turned out, the last, exclusive interview ever granted a Western newsman by the tiny little figure who represented so many millions of the earth's inhabitants.

The first thing the columnist noticed as he was ushered into Ju's presence by an obsequiously hushed assistant was his dress: the mandarin robe was gone, the drab blue-gray uniform of the P.R.C. now enclosed the frail form of the Vice Premier. Gone also was the whispery, almost inaudible voice: Ju seemed to be speaking in quite a normal tone, perfectly clear and perfectly distinct. Gone also was the air of deliberate remoteness, the allusions to ancient wisdom and other obfuscating mannerisms.

"You will have tea," he said immediately upon shaking hands, gesturing toward the handsome porcelain set already in place on the cocktail table in front of a huge sofa, to which he also gestured.

"Yes, thank you," the columnist said, seating himself carefully toward one end of it while his host poured him a cup, inquired politely, "Milk? Lemon? Sugar?" obliged his request for lemon and sugar and then seated himself with equal care at the other end.

"I would have had them serve us," he explained, "but it just means another person in the room to upset the mood. Mood," he added with a sudden charming little smile, "is so important, do you not think?"

"Indeed I do," the columnist agreed; and ventured to remark, "Yours seems to have changed somewhat since last night, Vice Premier. I take it you are happy with the results of the vote."

"Frightful people!" Ju exclaimed with a sudden show of annoyance. "Frightful people, both! Between them they have practically set the world at war. At least we were able to stop that."

"Stop it or just delay it, Vice Premier?" the columnist inquired. "It seems to me you have only achieved a breathing space."

"Ah," Ju agreed, "but within the breathing space there can be a chance for cooling. They will not fight now."

"Are you sure?" the columnist asked. "The world certainly hopes so."

"I am sure," Ju said in a tone of such positive certainty that his guest could not refrain from asking one of those questions that made him such a good reporter.

"Why?"

It was then that the first little insistent nagging of doubt began to come into the columnist's mind, and, through his mind and the article it produced a few hours later, into the minds of many influential people around the world; for Ju did not answer at once, and when he did it was with another smile and a little shrug.

"They will not be able to."

"But why not?" the columnist persisted. "What is to stop them, really? Surely not the UN, Vice Premier. We all know how effective that is."

"Perhaps not the UN," Ju conceded, "though I think the UN has helped—will help, even more in the General Assembly, perhaps, than in the Security Council. No, perhaps not the UN . . . but you will see. It will be impossible."

"But I still don't understand—" the columnist began. Ju cut him off, politely but firmly.

"All things are understood in time," he remarked. "It is your business to watch, learn and analyze. You must do so."

"I'm trying," the columnist said. "I had hoped to find enlightenment from you."

"Alas," Ju said, spreading his hands wide in his characteristic gesture, "I am sorry you feel I have disappointed you. Perhaps in time . . ."

"Yes," the columnist said, deciding to drop it. "What do you see happening in the immediate future—in the General Assembly?"

"I would hope an overwhelming vote for the position of my country, India and the U.K."

"To be followed by—?"

"On the part of the U.S. and the U.S.S.R.?" Ju smiled. "Rather more compliance by the U.S., as always, than by the U.S.S.R. Your country always tries so hard to be nice and always feels so guilty about being not nice."

"But not so the U.S.S.R."

Ju shook his head.

"Not so the U.S.S.R. Yet I think there will be some withdrawing if only to make the world feel easier."

"But there will be no real cause to feel easier," the columnist suggested. His host shrugged and frowned.

"Perhaps. Perhaps not. It is hard to fathom what goes on in the minds of the foreign devils in Moscow."

"The foreign devils in Moscow," the columnist echoed thoughtfully. He smiled. "Suddenly the conversation turns Chinese."

"An old habit," Ju said, also smiling, as suddenly as he had frowned. "An old phraseology. Do not let it concern you. It is an outdated state of mind which no longer dominates our thoughts."

"Oh, I know," the columnist agreed quickly, while again a tiny warning flag went up in his mind. "I understand perfectly. After all, I have been to China. I know what it is today."

Ju beamed.

"Then we understand one another."

"Indeed we do," the columnist said heartily, thinking, *Yes, possibly we do. I wonder—*

"Good," Ju said comfortably. He stood up and extended his hand, tiny figure as straight as though he were twenty-eight instead of seventy-eight. "I thank you for coming to see me. It has been most courteous."

"My duty and my pleasure," the columnist said, rising also. "It has been very helpful for my article."

"Do not be too positive in your writings," Ju advised with a sudden twinkle. "Trust time. It tells."

"What will it tell, Vice Premier?" the columnist asked with a blunt directness. "What will it tell about China?"

"It will tell that China is there," Ju said, taking his arm with surprising strength and leading him toward the door. "That is one thing that never changes."

"But where?" the columnist persisted as the door opened and the ubiquitous humble one appeared to lead him downstairs.

"Ah, where?" Ju echoed, and suddenly he was his public self again. "Ah, yes, where? It is a question."

"It may be *the* question," the columnist said; but with a wave, a last gentle smile and a low, amused bow, Ju stepped back and closed the door.

O Cheshire Cat, the columnist thought, come back, come back! But he found that the interview, for all its brevity, had given him a great deal to think about. He spent a lot of time doing it before he sat down to write his article.

In the meantime there was his appointment with the President of the Soviet Union. He expected no subtleties here, and got none; though he had to trust his instinct to give him certainties. The ones it came up with were not exactly reassuring.

But to begin with, all was smiles and pleasantries.

"Come in, my friend!" Yuri exclaimed expansively when the columnist had penetrated some four layers of security and arrived in Yuri's office in the company of the stolid and forbidding woman who had accompanied him from the heavily guarded entryway on the street below. "It has been a long time since our last luncheon at the Metropolitan Club in Washington!"

"Too long," the columnist agreed. "Those were interesting days."

"Not half so interesting as these, however," Yuri observed with a hearty laugh.

"Not half," the columnist agreed. "Thanks, in large part, to you."

"With assistance," Yuri said, still chortling. "With assistance from your H. Delbacher, this big new President who orders me about so fiercely."

"He is not a very fierce man, really," the columnist observed. "May I sit down, Yuri—Mr. President?"

"Yes," Yuri said with an elaborate sigh, "thank you for the title. I suppose we must have these little honors when circumstances change. Yes, do sit down. But you have not changed, my friend! You have only grown younger."

"Life seems to be agreeing with you, too, Mr. President," the columnist remarked as they took armchairs by the window facing one another. "You seem to be thriving on crisis. And, of course, on power."

"Power! I wish I did not have it! I wish I could lay it down! But my duty to my country and to the glorious socialist cause—"

"Yes," the columnist said dryly. "I can imagine how difficult it must be for you."

"Not at all," Yuri cried with a sudden bark of laughter. "I love it, old friend! *I love it!* As you know perfectly well, so you need not tease me."

"Back there when we had those lunches," the columnist said, "when you were telling me all those plausible, false, misleading things about the Soviet Union's peaceful intentions—"

"You saw through me even then!"—with another bark of laughter.

"—were you planning, even then, to become President one day?"

"Anyone who becomes leader of my country—almost *any* country," Yuri said, suddenly serious, "usually has to think many, many years in advance. Sometimes not, in some countries, sometimes there are coups and surprises. But not in yours and mine, my friend. In them, one thinks —and thinks—and thinks. But tell me: did it never occur to you in those days that I might someday come to power? Did it not occur to you even once? Tell me so! It will flatter me!"

"I thought so," the columnist said truthfully, "from the first day I met you, Mr. President. You have not surprised me in the least. Nor, I may say, are you surprising me now."

"Again, you see through me! What is it you see?"

"I may be a bit cynical," the columnist said, "but I see a deliberate, determined attempt to frighten the rest of the world into acquiescence while you scientifically proceed to destroy the United States, if you can possibly do so."

"And?"

"And having destroyed the United States, to then take control of the entire world, just as communism has always intended to do."

"For shame!" Yuri cried. "I never thought you were one who believed in such hobgoblins! You did not formerly write in that vein."

"I did not believe it then," the columnist said. "Lately, I have become more convinced."

"But your paper does not support you in this," Yuri said shrewdly. "I still read the *Post,* you know."

"I did not say I was completely convinced," the columnist remarked mildly. "I just said I have become more convinced. And I think the paper as a whole is much more skeptical of Soviet intentions than it once was."

"But it desires peace so badly," Yuri said. "How can anyone who desires peace possibly be suspicious of our policy, which has always been to support and extend the peace of the world?"

"Yes," the columnist said without inflection. "One is aware."

"But surely, old friend, you cannot deny it! Particularly in the case of your belligerent new President. Already the *Post* has written things very critical of his actions toward us in these recent days. You yourself have been quite sharp in your columns. Why have you done so, if you do not believe in our peace-loving intentions?"

"It is one thing," the columnist said, a trifle stiffly, "to deplore actions by a President of the United States that seem ill-advised and apt to lead to exactly the clash that all Americans—including, as you call him, H. Delbacher—wish to avoid. It is another to wholeheartedly embrace Soviet actions and intentions as being universally kindly, sincere, peace-loving and good. You will note that very few in the American media have gone so far as to do that. In fact none, that I know of."

"Well, my friend," Yuri said cheerfully, "as long as your criticisms of the President remain as strong as they are, we are quite satisfied. You do not need to embrace us wholeheartedly as long as you condemn him so harshly. That is quite enough for us, thank you. Why did you wish to see me?"

"Not to revive memories of the Metropolitan Club, that's for sure," the columnist said. "How long are you going to maintain this threat against the world?"

"What, the maneuvers? As long as we wish. The world does not seem to be unduly agitated, in spite of all the talk here."

"How do you figure that? It seems to me there is a great concern."

"Really? The pace seems quite leisurely. Now that we have gone through our little charade in the Security Council—and, as always, my friend, you must not quote me too directly, you know, I must rely on your discretion as I used to do in the old days in Washington—but in any event, now that we have gone through the performance, everything seems to have slowed down abruptly. The General Assembly apparently does not intend to meet for another two weeks—"

"I understand that was at your direct request," the columnist interrupted.

"And the President's," Yuri said promptly. Then he laughed and covered his mouth in mock surprise and chagrin. "But now I have confirmed it for you! You heard just a rumor, you were 'fishing,' as you say, and now I have let the bear out of his cage."

"It was neither a rumor nor an error," the columnist said, smiling a little in spite of himself. "I have my sources and you have your plans, and I expect I am supposed to be part of them, as always. You're a great manipulator of the media, that hasn't changed. If anything, you're better than ever. Why do you want the delay?"

"There is a possibility of some personal contact with your belligerent Mr. Delbacher."

"And time to complete the maneuvers?"

Yuri shrugged.

"Perhaps, perhaps not. There is no need to hurry them. Their aim, after all, is to bring the armed forces of the socialist camp into the highest possible state of readiness in relation to the general correlation of forces in the world. I can tell you that in confidence."

"I doubt if it is exactly news," the columnist remarked. "Why else would you be holding them? It also gives you additional time to exercise pressure on all the doubtful nations. Of which there are a great many, I find, in spite of the vote in the Council and the probable vote in the Assembly."

"But the main thing of course is contact," Yuri said. "And possible compromise in the only possible context where it can matter—namely between us, outside the UN."

"Has he indicated that is why he also wants the delay?"

Yuri smiled.

"I would suggest you ask him. He has apparently told you about me, possibly he will tell you about himself."

"I want you to tell me," the columnist said, ignoring the gambit. "Then I will have it confirmed beyond all possible doubt."

"I should like a compromise," Yuri said slowly. "Tell him that. I am sure you will be in close contact."

"Possibly," the columnist said, "if I think there is any point in it. If I decide there is any truth in what you say."

For a moment he feared he had gone too far: the Soviet President's eyes snapped with a sudden anger. Then he thought better of it, and laughed.

"My old friend's tongue remains as sharp as his typewriter. Why would I lie to you?"

"That is something," the columnist replied, "that I haven't quite determined, yet, in this particular instance. Generally, I know why. To confuse the issue. To take the world's mind off what you're doing. To advance whatever your ultimate purposes are."

"To conquer the world?" Yuri cried with great sarcasm. "But of course! To conquer the world! What else does the big bad Soviet Union want to do, if not to conquer the world? Oh yes, my friend, we are fierce. We are terrible. We are under other beds besides H. Delbacher's, I see, even yours, my old, good, frightened friend! Watch out for the Soviet bear, my friend! Watch out, watch out!"

"Yes," the columnist said, unimpressed, "I intend to. I can safely say in my article, then, that you and the President have secretly requested a delay in the General Assembly meeting so that you may confer privately on a possible compromise, which in the opinion of the Soviet President must be along exactly the lines the Soviet Union dictates. Right?"

"What other lines are there?" Yuri inquired blandly. Then he leaned forward with another bark of laughter and slapped the columnist's knee.

"You are so gullible, my friend! You are so easy to fool, even after all these years of being Washington's best political columnist, even after all these years of knowing me! You really think I am a threat to your precious country! You really think I want to conquer the world!"

"Yes," the columnist said in the same unimpressed way. "I really think *you* think you can. I'm not saying that *I* really believe it, but I am certainly convinced that you do."

"Very well, then," Yuri said, and suddenly the laughter was all gone, the eyes no longer smiled, the columnist could see they were cold—cold —and he felt an increasing chill in his heart. "Very well, then, listen to me. Your pathetic country is nothing, now—nothing! You no longer have the military strength—you no longer have the will—you no longer have the *character*. Fifteen years ago when we were meeting for lunch at the Metropolitan Club, I had some respect for your country; I despised it and feared it but I still had some respect because it still had the only things that matter between nations, and those are strength—character—will. *Strength! Strength! Character! Will!* You do not have them now, my friend. Tell H. Delbacher that, if he wants to see me! Tell him that!"

There was a silence for a moment; but the columnist was brave as well as intelligent, and a loyal, determined man.

"I am sure you already have told him that," he said quietly, while Yuri studied him very carefully, "no doubt several times. And no doubt you will tell him again if you meet. But I don't think it will impress him much, any more than it impresses me. You are ahead of us in many areas, there is no doubt of that, and you have been for the past five or six years, in spite of the claims of previous Presidents. But that is one thing I will say for this one; he doesn't claim we are 'still the strongest power on earth.' But he thinks we can be again and he is determined that we will be. Meanwhile, I would suggest to you, Mr. President, that you never make the mistake of thinking he is afraid of you, because he is not. He is willing to make one more try to talk to you because he is a decent and hopeful—and, yes, peaceable and *peace-loving*—man. But don't try to bully him again, or it will be as pointless a meeting as I already think it's going to be."

"Write it, then!" Yuri said spitefully. "Write it that way, without hope, and see the effect it has on the world. You have a great audience. Frighten them to death! See what good it will do you. It will only make it easier for us—if, as you say," he added scornfully, "we are really the great menace to peace you say we are! Such awful, devious people!"

And abruptly he stood up, abruptly the mood changed. The columnist, unsmiling, stood up too.

"My friend," Yuri said expansively, offering his hand, which the columnist had no choice but to accept, "do not believe all your own bugaboo thoughts! Do not help create hobgoblins! We are strong and we are tough and we do not intend to take nonsense from the United States. But we have no designs upon the world. We do not wish to destroy the United States. We do not want to conquer mankind. It is nonsense! We want peace—peace—*peace!* It is all we have ever wanted, it is all we will ever want. Try to understand, and this all will seem much better."

"I think I do understand," the columnist said, extricating his hand. "I think I understand very well. Thank you for seeing me. It has been interesting to revive our old friendship."

"We must always be friends!" Yuri cried. "Our countries must always be friends! It is the only way there can be peace."

"On your terms," the columnist said.

Yuri laughed once more.

"Oh, of course," he said lightly. "Whoever wants anything else? But I think possibly H. Delbacher and I can reach a reasonable accommodation when we meet. Have faith! Wait and see!"

"I shall wait," the columnist said as his stolid guide reappeared to usher him out the door, "but as for the faith, I'm not so sure."

Yuri uttered a last burst of laughter, good humor apparently entirely restored, and waved him cordially on his way. Then he called in Marshal Krelenko, Marshal Andreyev, Marshal Shelikov and Admiral Valenko for a progress report. Everything around the world was continuing to go right on schedule, everything was moving perfectly according to plan.

The columnist went to the Waldorf-Astoria for his second visit in two days with Hamilton Delbacher; found the President preparing to return briefly to Washington, told him the gist of his talk with the Soviet President; was given Ham Delbacher's response; and went swiftly back to his hotel room to write his article, which was part news story, part analysis. His editor in Washington told him to let it run, instructed that it be made the lead story on page one, and alerted the syndicate to distribute it immediately.

It began with a couple of scoops, telling the world for the first time that the two Presidents would meet sometime in the next ten days or two weeks, prior to the convening of the General Assembly, and disclosing that they had requested the delay in the Assembly meeting for just this purpose. It then went on to analyze both nations' positions, which the columnist found had changed very little. Try though he did to sound optimistic, it obviously did not come easily. On the basis of some thirty-seven interviews bridging the whole spectrum of United Nations opinion, he predicted that the C.I.B. resolution would probably be the basis for the General Assembly's final decision on the matter; though he did raise a question that none of his fellow commentators was astute enough—or perhaps gloomy enough—to consider. He did it in such a guarded way that very, very few of his readers caught it. Most preferred not even to contemplate its possibility.

A frightening suspicion was beginning to grow in his mind but he did not dare express it in so many words at this time lest it help to precipitate the very thing he was worried about. The only two people he confided it to were his wife and the President. The latter admitted grimly that the thought had occurred to him, too, but that they must cling to the hope that it could not possibly be. The columnist concluded his article with these words:

"Several things remain unclear about the exact background of the events that have occurred so far at the UN, quite aside from the central U.S.-U.S.S.R. confrontation. The initial harsh condemnations by Britain of the Soviet Union and of America by India and China, for instance, only to be followed by the noticeable softening of their positions as indicated in the C.I.B. resolution. The almost carefree attitude with which the Soviet President is ordering continuation of the maneuvers even though they make the entire world uneasy. The apparent certainty on the part of President Delbacher that he can secure a removal of all, not just six, of the Soviet submarines in Cuba. The calm certainty of the Chinese delegation that war would be 'impossible' despite the head-to-head confrontation of the U.S. and U.S.S.R. The fact that many delegations (not those on the Security Council) are acting in a fashion that indicates that they do not really take the Soviet threat seriously.

"As far as this correspondent can ascertain, there is not much consistency in many UN quarters regarding what to do about the crisis.

"Fear of Soviet military blackmail is balanced by a sneaking admiration for the Soviets because they are embarrassing and trying to intimidate the United States, a power many lesser nations do not like—for emotional reasons, often irrational, which they cannot sensibly define. At the same time there is a genuine fear of potential Soviet world dominance, together with an uneasy feeling that the time may be slipping away in which to make some kind of accommodative acceptance of Soviet influence and that perhaps it may soon be too late to do so.

"Against these conflicting tides of world opinion the President of the United States must attempt to maintain his equilibrium, national safety, and the influence of the United States. The President of the Soviet Union is in an ideal position to keep on the pressure and scoop up the fruits of his alarmingly aggressive policies as they fall helplessly if not willingly from the tree.

"We are in that most dangerous of all times for the United States—that period of American weakness and Soviet strength which has been predicted for many years by serious American politicians, analysts, government figures and military men—the Soviets' 'opportunity gap.' President Delbacher is striving desperately to persuade his own country, the Soviets and the world that the opportunity does not really exist—that it is as dangerous now as it was a decade ago for the Soviets to unleash their world-dominating adventurism. He may be able to do it by sheer courage, strength of personality and a military machine which he has started to up-grade with desperate urgency. Or it may already be too little and too late. The cumulative errors of the years of sloth, inattention, disbelief in Soviet intentions and sometimes deliberate cutbacks by recent Presidents eager to pose as 'peacemakers' may prove too much to overcome.

"Much—very much—hangs upon the outcome of the President's meet-ing with Mr. Serapin, upon what happens in the United Nations, and upon what course the two superpowers follow thereafter. The mind can-not yet fully grasp the importance of the next few weeks and months.

"Perhaps it dare not."

Which was about as strong, priding himself on being a calm and objec-tive reporter, as he felt he could be. But to the President he had expressed it with considerably more candor:

"Personally, I'm scared as hell."

And in a blinding moment of honesty as bleak and devastating as his, the President had answered quietly:

"So am I. But the responsibility is mine, and I must go ahead."

This he prepared himself to do as he returned to Washington for the hurrying handful of days remaining before he must again face Yuri Serapin and all the spiteful and envious nations, usually "Third World" or Arab, whose ignorant, often illiterate leaders, disbelieving the menace that steadily advanced upon them, looked forward with varying degrees of pleasure and anticipation to what they too hoped would be the demise of the United States.

Whether they actually had any conception at all of what this would mean for the world, the cataclysmic social and political upheavals, the enormous readjustments, the inevitable end of their own independence, he had no idea. Certainly it was not apparent in their attitudes or their conversations as reported by Mark and the rest after their extensive canvassing of the General Assembly. A disturbing number of the reactions they found were strictly emotional. Responsible judgments were rare among them.

There were, of course, some generally reliable friends such as Britain, which could usually be relied upon; and there were others, such as India, which did not want America's destruction (too many dollars still flowed freely outward from that still-naïve and bountiful source) but simply its humbling, who could be counted upon to provide some moderation. The C.I.B. resolution, while he could not accept personally its thesis of equal

U.S.-Soviet guilt (but might have to, politically, when the final vote came), was proof enough that there were some forces of compromise at work. He would feel much easier if China were more understandable in intention, but the wisest thing seemed to be to accept its actions at face value and hope for the best. For the time being, at least, it appeared to be adhering to its general policy of favoring the United States over the Soviet Union, and for that—while it lasted—one could only be grateful.

Back in the White House, confronting a desk piled high with legislative and other matters, he reached a decision he had been considering for some days and put in a call to Art Hampton, who also was once more back in his Senate Majority Leader's office, getting caught up.

"Arthur, my boy," he said, "how's the legislative schedule been going up there in your absence?"

"Not too badly," Senator Hampton said. "The appropriations bills seem to be in good shape, and at the moment there seems to be general agreement that everybody must stand behind you and not rock the boat with any more critical resolutions such as Jim Madison tried to put over a couple of weeks ago. There seems to be a really serious appreciation of what's at stake—even though everybody tells me, and my own mail bears it out, that there's a certain amount of let-down noticeable in the constituency. That inevitable tendency to relax—that earnest desire to believe that everything's really all right—that don't-worry-it-can't-possibly-be-that-bad attitude that always dominates American thinking—and the thinking of most democratic nations, in fact. Here it is again. You saw the latest poll this morning. The percentage that believe that 'the present crisis with the Soviet Union is improving' is now 63 per cent against 37 per cent who feel 'the present crisis with the Soviet Union is getting worse.' It was just about reversed a week ago. People adapt so damned fast. It's amazing. And dismaying."

"It is that," the President said. "What I called you to suggest may turn it around again, though."

"Yes?"

"I think it would be helpful in many respects if we didn't have the distraction of Congress until the General Assembly debate is concluded. I think a recess, specifically linked to the crisis in so many words from you, would serve to re-establish a lot of the attention and seriousness that seem to be draining away. It would also free you fellows on the delegation to come back for the Assembly debate without having to worry about the Hill. I think it would be a good practical move."

"And a very good psychological one," Art Hampton said. "You're an astute operator—but, then, I always thought you were. What about the Vice Presidential nomination?"

"I'm still thinking."

"Better make a decision soon, if I may be so bold. Why don't we recess a week from today, and you send it up to us that same day? That will give everybody time to get used to it and think it over by the time we come back into session. It should move fast after that, providing you choose someone halfway decent."

"At least halfway," Ham Delbacher said with a chuckle. "Perhaps even two-thirds."

"I'm not worried," Art said. "One indication that the media at least are taking the crisis seriously—they've practically forgotten we don't have a Vice President at the moment. There's been hardly any speculation."

"The less the better," the President said. "You will put in the recess resolution this afternoon, then."

"It will be passed by nightfall."

"Good. I'll get on the horn to the Speaker right now and see if the House can't be as obliging."

"There'll be a little fuss on both sides of the Capitol," Art said comfortably, "but we'll work it out. Anything new from abroad today?"

"Nothing from Yuri, if that's what you mean. But I imagine he's planning, planning, planning. So am I."

"It will be needed."

"Want to accompany me when we meet?"

"Sure," Senator Hampton said, sounding surprised. "If you think it would be a help."

"I think it might."

"O.K. Let me know when."

"Will do," the President said. "Thanks for the recess."

"My pleasure," Senator Hampton said, "I find us very distracting at the moment, myself."

And amid mutual chuckles they hung up. His call to the Speaker proceeded with equal ease; and by nightfall, just as Art had predicted, both houses had voted to recess until the conclusion of the General Assembly debate, "having in mind the great gravity of the present crisis and wishing to leave the President completely free of legislative concerns so that he may concentrate without distraction upon its speedy and satisfactory solution." This was after a flurry of sharp debate in both houses and the firm commitment that they would be called back immediately if the crisis worsened. There still remained a small but vocal group who refused to believe even now that the situation was indeed as grave as the President said it was—or at least did not approve of some of his methods of handling it. In any event, they were overwhelmingly voted down. The impact on the country was as effective as the President had hoped. Two days later another poll showed that public concern had risen again sharply. So also, though he did not know it until they met, had the concern, and consequent belligerence, of the President of the Soviet Union.

That was still off in the future a week or so, however, and in the meantime he was able to sign whatever minor bills were on his desk; review the military situation extensively with Roger Hackett and the Joint Chiefs of Staff; entertain the President of Chile and the Prime Minister of Thailand on state visits arranged several months before by his predecessor; approve Chauncey Baron's plans to begin to lay the groundwork for his promised move to expel the "People's Republic" (the subversion-by-semantics of the English language and the democratic cause! It never stopped—and very effective it was, too, he had to admit) of Italy from NATO: and to return to the farm with Elinor for a brief three-day visit that also drew in their children and grandchildren and gave him some firsthand sense of how the more deeply concerned of his countrymen were holding up under the possible imminence of nuclear warfare.

If his children were any indication, and there was ample proof in the media that they were, a great many Americans, while frightened, were proceeding with admirable practicality and self-control to take whatever precautions they could without giving in to panic. The initial runs on foodstuffs, gasoline, tires, clothing, picks, shovels, axes, had died down, the frantic buying had virtually disappeared. People were still buying heavily in canned goods but in general their purchases were orderly and not excessive. Many of those who had the space were digging the shelters that might have been dug years ago, others were joining in the construction of community shelters: still others were skeptical of this altogether and chose fatalistically to take their chances. With few exceptions there were no unpleasant situations created by national tensions. Those who chose to take the crisis very seriously were doing whatever they could think of to protect themselves, those who chose either from fear or conviction to regard it as a temporary nightmare certain soon to pass seemed to have adopted a tolerant attitude. There was a conspicuous feeling of unity, fairness and mutual helpfulness in the air.

"After all, Daddy," as his daughter Beth remarked, "nobody's going anywhere. We're all right here, if it happens. We might as well keep calm and just do what each of us thinks best."

"I do think, though," he said, "that the shelter program should be made mandatory for everyone. I've asked Mark Coffin to put in a bill."

"To be ready for the next time," Beth said with a wry smile that changed to something more somber as she watched her children pushing one another in the swing that hung from the limb of the maple tree that the old bull used to challenge.

"I hope not," he said gravely, "but I wouldn't guarantee it."

"How much depends on you," Elinor observed and he shivered suddenly as though someone had walked over his grave—or the grave of the world, he did not at the moment know which.

"Too much," he said. "Too much."

"But you won't fail us," his son-in-law Robert said with a quiet certainty that touched him deeply.

"Not if I can help it," he said. "The good Lord willing."

But whether He was remained an open question in the President's mind as the days rushed by toward his return encounter with Yuri. From around the world press and media reaction reaching the White House in the next few days disclosed an uncertainty as deep as his own. Leaving aside the entirely predictable denunciations by the Soviet and satellite organs, the hysterical insane rantings of such as Iran and Libya, the cautious questionings of the British and West Germans, a note of growing pessimism concerning the chances of any kind of accommodation with his opponent was noticeable around the globe. These were tossed aside impatiently by vacationing millions but were evidence enough of the way informed opinion regarded the chances of achieving anything. This agreed with his own assessment.

It had not, in fact, been his idea that he and the Soviet President meet again. This, he supposed, was one of the reasons the Soviet and satellite press had been instructed to unleash their bitterest personal attacks upon him. Yuri did not want it to appear to his own people or to the world that another meeting had been his initiative, nor did he want any softening of feeling toward H. Delbacher. On the former point, indeed, both *Pravda* and *Izvestia* flatly declared it to be "the meeting sought by the imperialist leader, H. Delbacher . . . the meeting arranged at the supplication of the imperialist racist, H. Delbacher . . . the meeting being held at the placating request of the leader of the forces of capitalist aggression, the spokesman for the military-industrial complex, H. Delbacher."

At first H. Delbacher had thought idly of having Chauncey Baron convey a protest to the aging Soviet Ambassador in Washington, but then had thought better of it. The Ambassador himself, as had been proven on numerous occasions going back at least as far as the Cuban missile crisis, was one of the world's most consistent cold-blooded liars himself; and as for the communist press, it always lied. There was no truth in it, as history also proved—another reason, the President supposed with an ironic weariness, why the Soviets wanted to conquer the world: so that they might rewrite its history just as they had Russia's. Then everything would be just what they said it was and generations to come would absolutely never know that history had ever been any different. How neat—how clever—how terrifying, if you really stopped to think it through. How much more reason to confine Soviet communism to its own sad land if one possibly could.

What had actually happened was that in the evening of the day he had arrived back in Washington from the UN—the same day Yuri had arrived back in Moscow—a call had come most unexpectedly over the hot line. He could not escape a sudden tension, a sudden almost agonizing excitement. The thing, after all, was not used every day—it had been a long time. In context of what they were going through, it could mean something very ominous. Instead it was Yuri Pavlovich—not the joker, the jester, the sardonic sophisticate of many moods but Yuri Pavlovich the hostile statesman, very cool, very correct and for once very terse.

"Mr. President!" he said and Ham Delbacher could not resist a dry, "The same."

"Yes," Yuri said. "Very well. Since your desire to delay the General Assembly meeting has been granted—"

"Yours too," the President said with equal coldness. "I believe we both made our wishes known to the Secretary-General and the President of the Assembly." (Libya this month, which appalled him, but there was nothing he could do about it.)

"True," Yuri conceded. "We did. Delay has been granted. Therefore it seems an opportune time for us to meet again."

"The idea has occurred to me," the President said. "But it isn't necessary. Basically, I thought it might be a good idea to have a cooling-off period. What do you think another personal meeting could accomplish?"

"We would not know until we met."

"I don't think it would accomplish very much. I don't know whether it's worth getting the world's hopes up and then disappointing them again."

"They aren't very high," the Soviet President pointed out with some dryness. "And I doubt if they would be noticeably affected if we did not accomplish much. Nonetheless I think we should try."

"I suppose I would be charged with all sorts of heinous crimes against humanity if I refused," Ham Delbacher said with equal dryness.

"It would be easy to portray you as not co-operative," Yuri agreed.

"You must know I am completely skeptical of your good faith and completely mistrustful of your motives."

"We share a common complaint," Yuri noted with a trace of humor. "I think, however, that the world rather expects us to make this attempt and would be disappointed if we did not. In any event, I would like it to occur."

"Why?"

"There may yet be some compromise available."

"Nonsense," the President said, suddenly sick to death of deceit and hypocrisy.

"If you say so," the Soviet President said equably. "However—"

"Very well," Ham Delbacher said abruptly. "Where and when?"

"I shall be returning to New York three days before the Assembly is scheduled to convene on our dispute."

"So will I. How about the day following our arrival? Say 3 P.M.?"

"Very good," Yuri agreed. "Where?"

"I suppose the Secretary-General's office again."

"Too public. I find the media very tiresome, as I am sure you do. I was thinking of Fabrizio Gulack's penthouse in River House."

"Yes," the President said, a mental picture the Soviet-loving old humbug flashing into his mind, "you would."

"He told me he could guarantee complete privacy."

"I'm sure. What has the old fool ever seen in you people, anyway? Have you been blackmailing him all these years?"

"We do not do such things," Yuri said, and for a quick-dying moment they were amused together—except that the knowledge that the Soviets had indeed used blackmail on many, many people over the years really wasn't funny. So the President stopped laughing.

"He loves to rub elbows with history," Yuri said. "Particularly ours. He admires what we have accomplished."

"Some of it with his help," the President remarked.

"He does not hold the Order of Lenin for nothing," Yuri said with a smug chuckle. "It is agreeable to you, then—3 P.M. at F. Gulack's penthouse?"

"As good as any," the President agreed without enthusiasm.

"Good. Good-by."

"Good-by."

And that was how it came about. The columnist, being a very responsible reporter, called him Thursday before his article went to bed for Sunday's edition of the *Post*.

"I can say there will be a meeting?" he asked when he had finally convinced the chief operator he should speak directly to the President, and the President had agreed.

"You can."

"Can you tell me where and when?"

"No."

"Can you give me a fill-in later?"

"Possibly."

"O.K. What you've given me is good enough for now. Many thanks."

"My pleasure," the President said, and it was. He had never liked the *Post* much but he liked some of its people a lot, and most particularly this earnest, hard-working and absolutely fair-minded writer.

This was the brief exchange with Yuri which was now appearing in *Pravda* and *Izvestia* as his "supplicating" and "placating" request for a meeting. He could not imagine what new threats Yuri could produce that he had not produced already, or what further there was to talk about; but since the Soviet leader had opened the way, he determined he would present a few things himself.

First and foremost, because they were the immediate issue, were the submarines. It had taken American spy satellites and American double agents in Nicaragua about six hours to trace the six missing vessels to their new hideaway after leaving Cuba. This was no improvement at all, in the President's mind; and the eighteen remaining in Cuba, as he had publicly declared, were still as much of a menace as ever. He determined to raise this, and other things. He might as well, for he did not expect Yuri to be in any kindly or compromising mood when they met in Fabrizio Gulack's apartment. He was mentally preparing himself, in fact, for another round of bitter denunciation in which *Pravda*'s master would show him where its invective came from. If that was the way it went, he determined, he would simply walk out and leave his opponent sputtering.

He suspected that this might well be the outcome, particularly after he had gone through another equivocal episode with his and Mark's pet defector. He had received a CIA report on Ivan two days ago. He and his family, under assumed names, were living on a farm near McLean, Virginia. The owner was a retired agent who from time to time took on heavily accented foreign help that seemed to appear from nowhere, stay awhile and then disappear again, to be absorbed into the mainstream of American life somewhere across the country, usually far from Washington. In Ivan's case, he was still going regularly to CIA headquarters for debriefings and was apparently continuing to furnish what his interrogators considered worthwhile information. He had been subjected to numerous tests and cross-examinations designed to ascertain his own nature and the nature of his defection. It was the judgment of the chief agent in charge of these that both were probably genuine, though a decision was still being reserved. The KGB was very thorough in its training, particularly of double agents, and there was a code on his file which indicated that testing was to continue at moments when he was most relaxed and least expectant, for at least a year. Somewhere he might still slip up; a casual comment or indirect inquiry long after immediate pressures had eased sometimes tripped up the best of them. So far, however, he had passed with flying colors. He was the President's only immediate contact with Yuri and his inner circle, and it seemed a good idea to talk to him again. The President also decided to call in Mark, since Ivan seemed to have a genuine liking for him and had selected him as his initial American contact.

The idea came to him after dinner one night two days before he was scheduled to return to New York. Linda answered the phone.

"Hi," he said. "This is Ham. Is your distinguished and able husband around?"

"Hello, Mr. President," she said with a real cordiality, having known him as one of her father's closest Senatorial friends ever since she was in her early teens. "No, I'm afraid he's out doing his civic duty tonight. He's gone to a Boy Scout meeting with Markie—or Mark Two, I should say.

He's getting very dignified now that he's pushing ten, and that's the only way I can distinguish between him and his father when I yell for them."

"I never knew you yelled."

She chuckled.

"Frequently. Sometimes in rage, sometimes in love. I think they've learned to distinguish which it is and either hide or come running, as the case may be." Her tone changed to one of serious concern. "How are *you?* How are you bearing up under all these pressures?"

"Not badly," the President said. "Fortunately I've always been able to drop off at a moment's notice and sleep like a log regardless of my problems. This seems to have continued. So far."

"And during the day?"

"I haven't started biting my nails—yet—and I only twitch slightly on one side. The White House physician thinks he can probably take care of that if he amputates my right leg. Otherwise, I'm in good shape. I'm curious to know, though"—and he too became serious—"how you, as—well, not as an average housewife and mother, because Jim Elrod's daughter will never be average—but *as* a housewife and mother, are bearing up. Does the threat of atomic war keep *you* awake at night and give you the heebie-jeebies in the daytime? And how about your friends?"

"I think by now we're pretty philosophical," she said, sounding like his daughter Beth. "After all, here we are and nothing much can change that. We aren't going to run away, certainly. Most of my friends in the neighborhood are building shelters in the backyard, and so are we. Also we've all laid in a lot of extra canned goods, first-aid supplies and medicines. But aside from that, that there isn't much you can do. As for worrying, it comes and goes, depending on how seriously you take it all. I take it very seriously, being so close to it as wife and daughter; I think most people in political Washington do. I'm not so sure about others. My maid, who is a very bright woman, shrugs and says, 'I reckon Mr. President goin' take care of that, so I'm not worryin'.' I'm sure there are many, many millions who feel the same way. It puts a lot of responsibility on Mr. President."

"Who knows it," Ham Delbacher said, "and is doing his damndest."

"I know you are. I just wanted to be sure you're holding up all right."

"Pretty well so far, as I say. It may get worse."

"Yes," she agreed bleakly. "I for one fully expect it to . . . Is there a message for Mark?"

"Yes, there is. I suppose even my phone is tapped by somebody—particularly by the Soviets, after our then Administration obligingly gave them that hill in Northwest Washington on which to build their new embassy, whose elevation, as we were warned at the time, permits interception of virtually all phone calls in the District of Columbia."

"'As we were warned at the time,'" she said with considerable bitterness. "Why in the *hell,* if you'll forgive my unladylike language, have we never listened to all those warnings about all those things?"

"Willful deafness . . . deliberate blindness . . . 'Don't tell us, we don't want to know . . . Let us sleep, perchance to dream.' "

"Perchance to die, you mean," she said. "Well, forgive me. I didn't mean to interrupt. I get into this mood once in a while—like every hour on the hour. But it's bad to give in to it."

"Yes," he agreed gravely. "Mr. President tries not to . . . But back to Mark. Since I'm probably intercepted, tell him that his friend the chess player will be here tomorrow night at nine, and he's welcome to attend if he wants to. In fact, I'd like him to."

"How is his friend getting along?"

"Passing with high marks so far. You're a smart judge of character. What do you think of him?"

"I don't know," she said slowly. "There's been no contact here since that first night. My impression then was of a very shrewd, very clever, very alert, very confident mind. Whether he prefers the west wind or the east, however, I couldn't say for sure. Perhaps whichever blows his way?"

"I'm beginning to think it's more than that. And so are others. Some trust has been created."

"He's good at that."

"You're suspicious, lady."

"Women are," she said, not entirely humorously. "It's a matter of survival. I'd say, 'Be careful,' except that you've always been one of the most careful men I know."

"It's referred to in the local press as 'plodding' and 'humdrum,' " he said cheerfully, "but it's a worthwhile trait. Tell Mark I'll be expecting him."

"He'll be there," she promised.

"Good night, Linda dear," he said, feeling fatherly.

"Good night, Uncle Ham," she said with a little laugh, harking back to years long gone. "My love to Elinor. How is *she* taking it, by the way?"

"You know Elinor. Rockbound coast, granite hills, and all that. She's giving chins-up speeches and interviews practically every day, as you know. The old New England backbone is stiff as a ramrod and thank God for it. I don't know what I'd do without her. I really don't."

And he really didn't, as he went finally to bed shortly before twelve and found her sitting up, carefully perusing the early editions of the Washington *Post* and Anna Hastings' Washington *Inquirer.*

"Anything new?" he asked as he started to get ready for bed.

"Oh, nothing much," she said, peering ironically over her glasses as she liked to do. "The usual old boring stuff about imminent atomic war, the shortcomings of President Delbacher and even, now and then, some hint of the shortcomings of President Serapin. Apparently the French are

being very busy at the UN trying to line up votes for a substitute version
of the C.I.B. resolution."

"The French are always busy trying to line up something that they can
claim to be distinctively and exclusively French. We're aware of their
efforts. But I think the Chinese, British and Indians have it pretty well
sewed up. If there's to be any compromise resolution, that will probably
be it—or at least it will provide the basic framework."

"What do you know that the papers don't know that I should know?"
she inquired as he went into the bathroom. He laughed over his shoulder
as he closed the door.

"Give me five minutes and I'll tell you All."

"Five!" she called presently.

"I didn't mean for you to monitor me that closely," he said with a
chuckle as he emerged. "I don't really know very much. Things have been
pretty static for the moment. I have arranged another talk with young
Valerian. And Mark."

He related his conversation with Linda. Elinor nodded.

"I haven't met the man myself," she said as he clambered into bed,
"but just from what I sense, I have a feeling I'd agree with Linda."

"Well, it can't hurt, and he may come up with something else interesting. He has a lively mind, anyway, and it isn't going anywhere. There's no
way he can communicate with them now even if he is a double agent,
which I don't really think."

"Well. Watch him."

"Oh, sure. Are you through reading those predictable rags?"

She yawned, took off her glasses and snuggled down beside him.

"They're both rather kindly to you today. Make the most of it."

"Assist me," he said, turning off the light and turning to her.

"Mr. President," she said with a chuckle, "you've been so busy this
past week I thought you'd never ask."

"You can always volunteer," he murmured in her ear.

"I'd rather have you ask."

"O.K., so I'm asking, I'm asking."

"Oh, shush," she said with a last chuckle. "I'll never have a better
offer, and you know it."

"Yes," he with a comfortable little chuckle of his own, "and thank God
for that. I'd hate to have to start competing again, at my age."

Mark arrived next evening just before nine, having driven by circuitous
routes—because one never knew, in the suspicious world the Soviets had
created, who might be spying—to the East Gate and having been admitted to park inside. Again he found the President in his favorite Lincoln

Study, newspapers, news digests, Pentagon reports and CIA papers stacked beside him on the floor.

"Now, here's an interesting thing," he said, not bothering to shake hands but simply gesturing Mark to a chair with comfortable familiarity. "From the CIA."

"Oh?"

"Yes. Someone has arrived from Beijing to see Ju Xing-dao."

"And?"

"That's all so far. The only intriguing thing is that he arrived in New York three days ago, holed up in a small hotel down in the Thirties, ordered room service, didn't stir until this morning and then proceeded to delegation headquarters."

"So?"

"Well, nothing, except that he did not take a taxi, he walked—wearing a very nondescript outfit, just part of the crowd. First over to Fifth and up Fifth for a while, then back to First, then over to Park and a couple of blocks there, then back to Fifth and in and out of several stores, apparently just a casual shopper, then back over to the East Side and so finally to the delegation, where he slipped in with a group of secretaries whose passes were all carefully checked. His was not. He then went up to see Ju, and there the trail stops. But why all the camouflage and zigzagging? Why all the anonymity? It puzzles."

"And impresses. The CIA must really be on the job, to track him that closely. There must be some special message Beijing didn't want to entrust to code."

The President smiled.

"That was wise of them. Yes, I suspect that's it, myself. The question is, what?"

"Isn't there some way to find out?"

"Oh, he'll be apprehended on some excuse—shop-lifting, probably—if he attempts to get back to his hotel. His room has already been searched —nothing there. And he'll be interrogated—by the police, ostensibly— and there'll be nothing there, either. So we'll just have to await developments. But it's interesting."

"Very," Mark agreed.

"Keep thinking about it," the President suggested. "You may get a flash of something. Let me know if you do."

"Surely. You don't suppose our friend tonight would have any idea?"

"I doubt it. And I wouldn't tell him all those details anyway. But obliquely, maybe . . . we'll see. I think I hear him coming." He stood up as a sound of footsteps, almost in march-time, came down the polished hardwood floor and halted smartly outside the door. There was a soft, respectful knock.

"Come!" the President said.

"Major Ivan Valerian," a voice announced. The door swung open. Face beaming, arms outstretched, Ivan surged into the room.

"Mark!" he cried, complete once again with bear hug and kisses on both cheeks. "I have missed you, my friend! And Mr. President—!" a vigorous, pumping handshake and again the delighted beaming. "How well you look! How well, in spite of my difficult country!"

"Ivan," Mark said, returning the embrace with some adeptness, now, "it is good to see you."

"Major," the President said, returning the handshake, "you are looking very well too. Apparently they are treating you all right in Langley?"

"First rate!" Ivan said. "First rate! May I sit down?"

"Please do," the President said, giving Mark an amused glance. Ivan of course did not miss it.

"Please tell me," he said, suddenly serious, springing back from the chair he had started to take. "Am I too forward? Am I disrespectful? Perhaps I am being too familiar, perhaps you wish me to remain standing as befits your great office—?"

"Ivan," the President ordered amicably, "sit down. You will not be in any doubt when I am concerned about my great office. Right now I want you to make yourself at home. How's your family?"

"Thank you," Ivan said, easing himself into one of the leather armchairs with elaborate care. "I am glad I did not—my family is very well, thank you, *very* well!"

"They are liking it better here?"

"First rate!" Ivan said, which they took to be his latest colloquial acquisition. "Absolutely first rate! My wife, she still cries a good deal, you know, women are so sentimental. It is her own family she misses. My children are fast becoming little Americans. My boy is riding horses very well, now, the girls are watching television and beginning to ask for toys. Mr. President," he asked, quite seriously, "what is a Merry Mary and a Happy Herbie?"

"I'm not sure," the President said with a smile. "I don't really have the time to follow television much these days except the news. But I suspect they must be dolls, aren't they, Mark? Your kids ought to know."

"One of the banks is giving them for opening a savings account."

"How much?" Ivan inquired.

Mark smiled.

"Five hundred dollars, I believe."

"Ah!" Ivan sighed. "I cannot yet open a savings account, since you have not yet given me a new legal name. What shall I tell the children?"

"I think the bank will probably give me two sets for nothing if I ask them politely," the President said. "Let me see what I can do. It will be my personal contribution to Soviet-American friendship. Which, God knows, needs a few contributions right now."

"Yes," Ivan agreed, suddenly somber. "And if I may say so, Mr. President"—he paused delicately—"it is not entirely the fault of Yuri Pavlovich, if you will forgive me."

"Very true," the President agreed promptly. "It is not entirely the fault of Yuri Pavlovich. *Some* of it is the fault of Yuri Pavlovich, however. Is that not correct?"

"Oh yes," Ivan said. "Oh yes! Seventy-five per cent, I would say, is the fault of Yuri Pavlovich. I warned you before, Yuri Pavlovich is not a nice man, though he can smile and be clever, sometimes. He is a tough man, Yuri Pavlovich. A very tough man. But, then," he added with a sudden smile, "you, too, Mr. President, are a tough man."

"I can be," the President said, also smiling, "but I don't like to be. That may be a difference."

"It is a difference," Ivan agreed. "Yuri Pavlovich *likes* to be. He enjoys it. It is how he became President and Chairman of the Council of Ministers. Sometimes he smiles, sometimes he kills; always, he arrives where he wishes to go."

"Will he this time?" Mark inquired. Ivan gave him a long, thoughtful look.

"I do not know, yet. So far, he is not doing badly."

"He did not win approval of his resolution," Mark said.

"Nor did you, Mr. President," Ivan said, turning to him directly, "if you will forgive me. The C.I.B. compromise was better for Yuri Pavlovich than for you. It asks you to give up more things."

"That is true," the President said, "though Yuri Pavlovich seemed to be as opposed to it as I."

"A game," Ivan said scornfully. "He acts. Always, he acts. You must go through several layers of wool to find Yuri Pavlovich. He was not so displeased with it, though he made his big scene."

"Yes, I was aware he was doing that," the President said dryly, "as I suspect many others were too."

"Not all, though," Ivan said gloomily. "Many, many millions all over the world believe Yuri Pavlovich is sincere. They believe he speaks for my country. And that *it* is sincere. They do not know my country."

"I think I have a fair idea," the President said, "and I have tried to act accordingly." His tone sharpened suddenly. "Is that why you say I am responsible, along with Yuri Pavlovich, for the way things are? Because I have responded to his threats and bluster and blackmail?"

"No, Mr. President," Ivan said simply. "Because you have not used all the weapons I gave you."

There was silence for several moments while the President studied him closely and Mark studied them both. Finally Mark spoke.

"I have to confess, Mr. President," he said slowly, "that I, too, have been puzzled by that. Ivan gave us the entire strategic plan last time we talked; and you have only made public part of it, and that not in any great detail. I—don't understand."

There was silence again while Hamilton Delbacher, chin propped on finger tips, looked off into space a long, long way. At last he sighed heavily.

"Do you have any concept at all—but of course you do—of the enormous weight of world skepticism that America has to fight? Your people, Ivan, have been so persistent and so clever over so many years in creating a climate of suspicion and mistrust of the United States that it is a barrier almost impossible, now, to surmount. We in this nation have always had a general feeling of live and let live toward other nations, including yours; yours has been consciously and cold-bloodedly devoted for almost seventy years to our destruction. A never-ending flood of statements, speeches, items of 'information'—or 'disinformation' as your own people more accurately call it—has poured out of Moscow, each designed with the ultimate overriding aim and purpose of destroying the United States and thereby advancing the Soviet conquest of the world. The lies of Moscow are so innumerable, so literally endless, that they are like the sands of the sea; and they have been pouring out upon us for close to seven decades. To fight this is not completely impossible—quite yet. But it is very nearly so. The purpose has almost been accomplished. The world has been brainwashed to such a degree that it is only very rarely, now, that the truth can get through. We must first fight our way through many, many years of lies. It is not easy.

"Therefore I have not used all you gave us that night—the final plan, after this phase is over—because it has been all I could do to win even minimal acceptance of the idea that these maneuvers are designed to threaten us all. That they do have a sinister purpose. That there is an underlying terror. That they are not simply, as Serapin manages to convince too many, 'the sovereign right of a sovereign nation.' That there is a plan, and that he is in the process of working it out even as he uses the sounding-board of the UN to try to convince the world that it is not so. And he has almost succeeded, as witness the vote.

"It is only because I don't think even the most ignorant and most insanely jealous nations would quite dare to join in a demand that the world unite to 'overthrow' the United States that I think the Soviet resolution has been defeated so far. I don't quite think they will dare to pass it in that form in the General Assembly . . . but I am not entirely sure. Certainly it has only been by the most intensive work, aided by some few brave smaller friends in the world, that we have been able to hold the barrier against it. It is only because China, India and Britain have some sense of responsible diplomacy left that a compromise of any sort was offered, and passed.

"So I have not used all you gave us that night, Ivan. Nor have I used too many details of the maneuvers, except as it seemed effective to do so piecemeal during the Security Council debate—the subs near Bombay for instance. I will confess to you frankly that I was not entirely convinced of their truth, until our own intelligence confirmed them. You will understand that, and not be offended."

Ivan nodded, somber-faced.

"By the same token," the President continued, "what you told us about the ultimate plan, the over-all concept, I have not used *simply because no one would have believed it*. It has taken subs off Tonga, subs off India, Soviet planes violating the air space of a dozen helpless nations, dummy missiles 'accidentally' crossing borders and the rest, to even win acceptance for the limited things I have revealed about it . . .

"Mark and I have never discussed it. I know he has never mentioned it to anyone"—Mark shook his head—"but I know he has wondered about my strategy. But there has had to *be* a strategy, and we do not know yet that the concluding things you told us are true. If they are, then the time will come, probably toward the end of the Assembly debate, when I will use them. But I haven't been able to up to now: Soviet lies for so many years have been just too effective to overcome with my unsupported word. It has all had to develop step-by-step, just as Yuri planned, though he perhaps did not foresee that I could work in that framework too. Perhaps toward the end his plan and mine will coincide and I can make use of his intentions to save the situation. It is a slim hope, but it is perhaps the only one I have, insofar as the UN is concerned.

"You must be patient with me until then . . . All right?"

Again there was silence while he and Ivan looked at one another.

It was the younger man's eyes that finally dropped.

"*I* be patient with *you*," Ivan said at last, and for once sounded humble, and genuinely so. "Who am I to—? . . . But I do assure you, Mr. President—I do beg you—believe me. Believe me! What Yuri Pavlovich plans is what I told you. I did not lie to you, about that or anything. So far, all has been proven by events. So will that be. Use it when you can, and do not wait too long. Believe me!"

"When I can," the President said, rising to his feet. "When events support me. When I think there is belief. When it is possible . . ." He held out his hand. "Thank you for talking to us again. I hope all continues to go well with your adaptation to America. It is a difficult time to join us."

"I am glad with my choice," Ivan assured him, shaking his hand fervently. "I am glad I am here. It is to help the world!"

"Good," the President said. "We must hope so. Good luck."

"Thank you, Mr. President. And Mark! My friend Mark! We have not had a chance to talk, but I hope we will meet again before too long. Perhaps our families can meet too."

Mark smiled.

"Linda would like that."

"My wife too," Ivan said. "Good-by, Mark! I will see you soon!"

"I hope so," Mark said, submitting to the inevitable envelopment. "Take care."

"And you too, Mark! And you, Mr. President!"

And the door opened, his CIA escorts surrounded him and he was taken off, waving back at them as he went.

"Well, I don't know," the President said with a sigh, sitting back down again. "Close the door and stay for a minute. What do you think about the papers he gave us?"

Mark sighed too and resumed his chair.

"I think they're probably true. The rest has been. And it's in character for the Soviets."

"Yes," Ham Delbacher said somberly. "If I can just convince—enough."

"Events will have to help you. As you say, you can't do it alone."

"No, I cannot," the President said, "and that's for sure . . . Do you realize something? We never did ask him about China."

"I doubt if he knows," Mark said; and in this he was quite correct—the interesting thing being, though there was no way for him to be aware of it, that Yuri Serapin did not know, either.

So the day came for the President to return to his hotel in New York; and presently with great fanfare his shuttered limousine roared off behind a police escort to American delegation headquarters. Five minutes later he and Art Hampton, riding in an inconspicious but armored blue Buick sedan with no escort save four highly armed Secret Servicemen, set off for River House and the apartment of America's most equivocal millionaire, Fabrizio Gulack.

During their brief ride through New York's dead-summer doldrums, he and Art exchanged the usual baffled comments everyone always made about Fabbie Gulack, who despite his name was a third-generation American, offspring of the family's original Polish strain plus the Italian mother his father had met during a trip to Rome to expand the family business. This was heavy machinery, principally farm equipment, and with it the Gulacks had done very well by the time young Fabrizio reached an age to join the firm. This was at twenty-three and by the time he assumed full control at thirty-five when his father retired things were going even better. World War II, Korea and Viet Nam gave the company an enormous boost, for it went promptly into war production during World War II and Fabbie (a nickname he hated but whose recognition value he appreciated) went to Washington to join the Lend-Lease Administration furnishing equipment to America's allies. This made him a regular visitor to Washington (he maintained an apartment for many years just off Dupont Circle) and since he happened to be assigned by Franklin Roosevelt to the Lend-Lease division handling heavy equipment for Russia, it also made him a regular visitor to Moscow (where he maintained another apartment near the Kremlin).

His main base in recent years had been River House but he still traveled constantly to both capitals, particularly Moscow, which he referred to as "my second home." He was doted upon with great care by the Soviet Government, whose leaders regarded him as their pet American millionaire and heaped upon him many honors to insure that he would continue to act as a conduit between themselves and all the starry-eyed, flap-minded, flim-flammable dupes like himself who unknowingly did the Soviets' work in America.

If there was a rally for Soviet-American friendship anywhere in America, Fabbie usually picked up the major portion of the tab. If there was a full-page ad in the New York *Times* extolling the Soviet Government and denouncing the American, Fabbie was there with checkbook and generous heart wide open. If the Hollywood Fringe wanted to hail and grovel at the feet of the glorious Soviet, Fabbie was sure to support them with everything he had. If there were delegations to be sent to investigate "United States crimes against the people" of Iran, Timbuktu or Cloud-Cookoo Land, Fabbie was sure to be included, and no one was more bitter against his own country than he. If Soviet diplomats were expelled from the United States for plotting against the government, Fabbie was always in the picket line, banner held high, roseate, cherubic face sure to appear on front page and television screen across the nation.

Gulack Equipment Company was awarded many millions of dollars' worth of contracts by the Soviet Union, mostly for a type of truck body that could be easily converted into a tank—a line of production the company had stayed in after the end of World War II, it was such a salable item all over the world but particularly in the U.S.S.R. and the Warsaw Pact nations. He had been one of those instrumental in persuading J. Carter to permit the sale of sophisticated computers to the Soviets which had done so much both to speed up their tank production and to tighten their ruthless hold upon their own people. While those same people were hounded, enslaved, crushed, murdered, Fabbie loved Moscow and had a wonderful life there. It was so nice to be rich—and a buddy of the Kremlin. For all these activities he had been rewarded by the Soviets with many rich contracts for his company and many honors, culminating in the Order of Lenin, for himself. In interviews which he gave freely at the slightest stirring of a reportorial pencil or the slightest glimpse of a microphone he constantly extolled the virtues of the Soviet system and deplored the "crimes and excesses" of the United States.

At the same time, such was the curious tolerance of J. Carter and several of his predecessors, (and such was Fabbie's politically valuable standing with the likes of the New York *Times,* the Washington *Post,* etc.) that he continued to be invited to White House dinners, high-level conferences and intimate gatherings of Presidents and their friends. He enjoyed, as was often said of him, the best of both worlds. But, then, a millionaire always did—particularly one who so obviously had such a clear, objective and truly intelligent understanding of what the world of the later twentieth century was all about.

It might be a desperately dangerous world for millions—nay, billions—of its inhabitants, but for Fabbie Gulack, it was a ball. He was, as the proprietor of the Washington *Post* once cooed, "An old doll!"

To some of this—at least the White House part of it—Hamilton Delbacher intended to put a stop. He did not know what hold the Soviets had on Fabbie—blackmail of some sort, he suspected, recalling Yuri's grisly humor on the subject—but he did not want him around his White House and had so instructed the social office and his top political aides. He was sure Fabbie had already heard about this, and so was prepared for a cool reception. Instead the old fraud greeted them as effusively as though they were Marx and Lenin themselves.

"Mr. President!" he exclaimed when they had proceeded unnoticed through the servants' entrance to the service elevator and been whisked up to his beautifully furnished twelve-room hovel overlooking the East River. "And Art Hampton! What a pleasant surprise! And what a thrill to think you will be having such an historic meeting right here in my humble abode!" (Fabbie came of a generation that sometimes still talked like that.)

"It's humble, all right," the President agreed, surveying the original Picassos, Monets, Derains, oriental rugs and Aubussons, the underlying blue-on-white carpet from Red China, the items of antique French and stark modern Danish furniture that surprisingly set each other off very well, the étagères filled with original Fabergés. "It must be hell to live in a slum like this."

"Now you're making fun of me," Fabbie said, laughing along with him.

"It's so proletarian," Senator Hampton remarked. "Is it possible to sit down in one of your chairs?"

"Certainly," Fabbie said, taking one himself, "and you, too, Mr. President. Any one. You must admit, Art, it really isn't very grand compared to *some* people we know."

"Some people you know, maybe," Hamilton Delbacher said. "But we move in simpler circles, Fabbie."

"Even in the White House?" Fabbie inquired archly.

"Even in the White House. We have our antiques, but it's still relatively simple. The Czars would be quite at home here."

"They would never be permitted in!" Fabbie said with a sudden stern disapproval. "They were enemies of the people!"

"Yes, yes," the President agreed, also taking a chair. "You're not, that's for sure."

"I should hope not!" Fabbie exclaimed more cheerfully. "I love to move among them when I am in Moscow. I love to see their natural, simple life . . . which we in this country," he added with a certain wistful sorrow, "have grown so far away from with our harsh, selfish, materialistic ways. It's always money, money, money in America—always crass, material comforts. We have lost the old simplicity that made us strong. We can no longer relate to the workingman."

"Some of us can't," the President said, glancing around the ornate apartment, "but thank God *you* can, Fabbie. It's comforting to know someone understands."

"I do," Fabbie agreed with satisfaction. "And they understand me. That, I venture to think, is why His Excellency the President of the Soviet Union has requested the privilege of meeting you here—and why it has been my own very *great* privilege to agree."

"Where is His Excellency?" Ham Delbacher inquired. "Is something keeping him?"

"Nothing I have been informed of," Fabbie said, looking concerned. "I'm sure he would have called if—possibly just traffic, do you suppose?"

"Could be, if he's coming in an unmarked car like we did," Art Hampton said.

"I assume he is," Fabbie said. "This is supposed to be *extremely* hush-hush, I understand."

"It is," the President said. "Can we count on your discretion, Fabbie?"

"As deep as the sea, Mr. President! As silent as the grave!"

"Oh, I hope not," the President said. "But no tattling to the *Times,* O.K.? No secret little phone calls to Anna Hastings and Kay Graham. All right?"

"On my honor," Fabbie said, placing his hands, dramatically crossed, upon his breast. "On my respect for the Soviet Union. And the United States, of course."

"Of course," Hamilton Delbacher agreed. "How does this situation strike you, Fabbie?"

"Shall I be diplomatic or speak frankly?"

"Frankly, frankly. We understand each other, I think."

"I don't know whether you ever will really understand *me,* Mr. President."

"Nope," the President said crisply. "I'm afraid not, Fabbie."

"Well, it's too long to explain now," Fabbie said with a fatherly smile, "though someday perhaps I will. I believe in peace, you see. I really believe in the brotherhood of man. I really think nations can live together in loving harmony. I really think decency and tolerance toward one another will prevail."

"Is that why most of your profits come from tanks?" the President asked innocently. Fabbie gave him a sudden sharp glance.

"If the strength of the peace-loving Soviet Union is the only way to keep the peace of the world," he said severely, "and my tanks contribute to that, then I make no apologies. I consider it God's work."

"Well, good for you," the President said ironically, though looking slightly stunned. "Good for you, Fabbie."

"Thank you," Fabbie Gulack said serenely. "I know you don't really understand my feelings, but thank you."

"You really think the Soviet Union is peace-loving and we are not," Senator Hampton said in a bemused tone. Fabbie stood his ground.

"Well—yes. I'm afraid that is what I do believe."

"And, conversely, that Yuri Serapin is entirely in the right in this crisis and I am entirely in the wrong," Ham Delbacher said.

"Not entirely," Fabbie said calmly, "in either case. But certainly far, far more in his case than in yours."

"I see," the President said. "Well, I guess that tells me."

"You asked," Fabbie reminded him. "It is *so* tragic for the world that you cannot see his side of it. He wishes only to save the world from needless pain and bloodshed. Peace is his sole desire. Believe me."

"He has told you that."

"Oh yes. We are *good* friends."

"Apparently so. Well, it's nice you could furnish us a suitable place, anyway."

"I hope peace will grow here in my house," Fabbie said solemnly as they heard the first faint trembling of the service elevator coming up. "I hope my house, and both of you, may be so blessed. And you too, Art."

"Thank you, Fabbie," the President said as he and Senator Hampton stood up and turned toward the service entry. "It's good to know you're on our side."

"I did not say that!" Fabrizio Gulack said sharply. "I am on the side of peace!"

"So are we."

"And so is he," Fabbie said reverently as the elevator door opened and the President of the Soviet Union, accompanied by a single guard, stepped into the room. His eyes lighted up when he saw Fabrizio; he ignored the other two completely.

"Fabbie!" he cried delightedly and, stepping forward, swallowed the old man up in the usual bear hug and kisses on both cheeks, lifted him off his feet, spun him completely around and set him carefully back down. "My old friend and companion, my dear old colleague! How marvelous to see you again! It has been long, too long! And how marvelous of you to loan us your beautiful home for this meeting which we hope will do so much for world peace!"

"It is my prayer," Fabbie said, a bit breathlessly. "It is my only prayer."

"And mine," Yuri said. "Now," he said, abruptly businesslike. "Perhaps if you wish to accompany my guard, he will take you wherever you want to go while we talk."

"I am simply going downstairs to my bedroom and take a nap," Fabbie said. "I am an old man and I always nap in the afternoon. The guard may wait in the kitchen, if he likes. I told the servants to leave some sandwiches and cake. And vodka, if he wishes."

"Vodka!" Yuri cried, exploding into laughter. "You know us too well, Fabbie! But of course he will have vodka! Is there any for us?"

"The liquor cabinet," Fabbie said, showing them, "is here by the window. You are welcome to anything you like."

"Good!" Yuri said, turning to them for the first time. "That is all right with us, gentlemen, eh?"

"Fine," the President agreed, telling himself, *I'm damned if I'm going to be the first to offer to shake hands.*

"With me also," Art Hampton said, taking his cue from the President in all respects.

"Good, good," Yuri said with satisfaction.

"Well—good-by, then," Fabbie said rather uncertainly and Yuri suddenly looked and sounded quite impatient.

"Yes, yes," he said. "You may go, Fabbie. We will call you later."

"Yes," Fabrizio Gulack said hastily, stepping hurriedly into the elevator after the guard. "Yes, yes. Of course."

"Well!" Yuri said when the door had closed, surveying them coldly up and down. "We may sit down, I suppose."

"It would probably be more comfortable," Hamilton Delbacher said evenly: and so without further ceremony they did. And no one ever did shake hands.

For a long moment there was silence as they simply stared at one another. Yuri spoke first.

"You have me at a disadvantage," he remarked. "Why is Senator Hampton with you?"

"I invited Senator Hampton to accompany me," the President said, "for a reason even he does not know; because just before I left the White House I gave orders that there was to be delivered to the Secretary of the Senate"—he glanced at his watch while Art Hampton tensed in his chair—"just about now, my nomination of Senator Hampton to fill the now-vacant office of Vice President of the United States."

"Ham, you shouldn't have!" Art Hampton said, genuine surprise, genuine protest and a dawning pleasure commingling. "You really shouldn't have! I'm not worthy of—"

"You're worthy," the President said, "so let's don't argue about it. I want you—I need you—you're it. But don't thank me. It's a hell of a job and no pleasure if you have to move up, as I have. Particularly with—"

And he gestured, with only slight humor, toward Yuri, sitting across from them with a quizzical expression.

Yuri nodded.

"Yes," he said wryly. "I am, as usual, the villain. I will congratulate you, however, Senator. Perhaps if you *do* have to 'move up' someday, as the President puts it, you and I can get along more peaceably than he and I have done—so far."

"Perhaps," Art Hampton said, adjusted and non-committal already, possessed of the long-time politician's ability to accommodate to rapid change without missing a beat. "Perhaps so, Mr. President. But I do not think that will happen any time soon."

"I would not be so sure," Yuri said sarcastically. "There may be poison in the vodka. My guard may return and machine gun the President down. All sorts of horrid things may happen. It is all one can expect from those horrible Soviets . . . Well! Enough nonsense. I will accept your presence then, for I understand why the President brought you. May you contribute some sensible modifications to his determinedly war-threatening policies. Though I must confess I do not see much hope of it."

"Nor," said Art Hampton calmly, "do I. I think you may safely consider us as of a single mind in this matter."

"A good choice, Mr. President," Yuri said, still sarcastically. "You have provided yourself with a potential successor and an exact mirror. It must be a comfort to you—though I wonder if the duplication will be approved by your countrymen. Many of them seem to have been hoping for someone more—reasonable."

"There hasn't been too much comment, actually," the President remarked, "as you very well know. I think the majority will agree. Despite certain loud voices we're all familiar with, the polls seem to indicate general support for my policies."

"52 per cent to 48 per cent in Gallup this morning," Yuri said promptly. "Not a very wide margin."

"But sure to grow as the full implication of Soviet behavior sinks in," Ham Delbacher responded, more confidently than he felt. "Unless you change Soviet behavior. I assume you have requested this meeting to tell me that you will."

"I have requested this meeting," Yuri said sharply, "to find out if some sense has finally penetrated the top levels of the American Government during the past ten days. Already it appears that it has not."

The President shrugged.

"Why should it? Your policies are as vicious and threatening as before. Your maneuvers are still proceeding throughout the world. Your lies are still flooding the airwaves. Your subversion of peace is everywhere. You have done nothing to ease this crisis since the Security Council adjourned. You noticed Gallup had another question this morning: 'Is your faith in Soviet good will in the present crisis increasing or diminishing?' What was the percentage on that, Mr. President? You saw it."

"Due to the untrue anti-Soviet propaganda of yourself and your government," Yuri said coldly, "it was 82 per cent 'diminishing,' 12 per cent 'increasing' and 6 per cent 'undecided.' So much for the truthfulness of the great American Government!"

"So much for the commonsense of the American people," the President retorted.

"And thank God for that," Senator Hampton added.

"They are fools and idiots!" the Soviet President spat out. "They are the victims of the lying propaganda of a lying government! How can they think the truth when you will not let them have the truth! It is criminal, a crime against humanity, that you and your government lie so! *How can you do it?*"

And he glared at the two Americans with such apparent sincerity and such apparent righteous indignation that for a moment it took their breaths away. But not for long, because the last restraint finally snapped in Hamilton Delbacher. So much hypocrisy—so much lying—so much cheating—so much deceit. Suddenly and forever, it was beyond all bearing.

"You are obscene," he said quietly, though the quietness cost him a great deal to maintain. "You are, I think, the most vicious human being to walk this earth since Adolf Hitler."

"And Joseph Stalin," Art Hampton interjected.

"And Joseph Stalin," the President agreed. "Your statements are a lie. Your government is a lie. Your life is a lie. Your whole being is a lie. Nothing you say has the remotest resemblance to the truth as decent people know it, anywhere—anytime—any way. You wish to turn the world upside down and make black white, white black, yes no, no yes, the truth forever banished and the lie forever triumphant. You are Evil. Evil—Evil —*Evil*. I cannot begin to tell you the contempt I feel for you. It goes beyond capacity."

He stopped, breathing heavily now, Art Hampton white-faced at his side. Yuri too at first flushed, then paled, then flushed and paled again. At last he spoke, in a husky voice that was a shred of his normal vigorous tone.

"And I am winning, Mr. President," he ground out, barely audible. "That is what you cannot stand: I am winning—*we* are winning. And there is . . . nothing . . . you . . . can . . . do . . . to . . . stop us. So . . . rave on . . . Rave . . . on . . ."

He stood up, an obvious physical effort, his whole body shaking with a terrible rage.

"I should . . . not . . . have come. It is . . . pointless. You are determined to . . . destroy . . . yourselves. We shall be . . . delighted . . . to help. It . . . is . . . inevitable. History has . . . always . . . told us . . . so. Now—*now* we know . . . it is . . . going . . . to . . . happen . . ."

He turned and walked slowly, still in the grip of his terrible emotion, to the spiral staircase that descended to the floor below. With a great effort he straightened his shoulders, steadied his breathing, stood so for a long moment, then called sharply:

"Vaslav! Gulack!"

From below the guard responded instantly. A second later Fabrizio Gulack's alarmed old voice came up:

"Yes, Yuri Pavlovich? What is it? Is something wrong? Are you through already?"

"We are through," Yuri said with a sudden harsh, humorless laugh. "We are *through*."

"You have achieved peace?" Fabbie cried eagerly, puffing up the steps, the guard just behind.

"We have achieved *nothing*," Yuri replied. He spoke rapidly to the guard in Russian, the man stepped through the serviceway and touched the elevator button. The door opened.

"Well—" Fabbie began uncertainly. "I hope I may see you again—?"

"Yes," Yuri said, turning on his heel and starting out.

"I hope—I hope—" Fabbie began. Then his earnest old face crumpled toward the start of tears. "Oh, dear, I do *so* hope everything will be all right!"

"Ask them," Yuri spat out without turning his head as he stepped into the elevator. "They are so superior they know *everything*."

And the door closed and he and his guard were gone.

Again there was silence, while Fabbie stared at them, at first with bewilderment, then with comprehension, followed by an obvious and swiftly growing anger.

"You have offended him!" he cried. "You have refused to co-operate with him! You have destroyed the world's only hope for peace! *In my house! You have destroyed peace in my house!* How could you? Oh, how could you?"

"Fabrizio—" the President began, but Fabbie would have none of it. He drew himself up to his full, frail height and pointed to the elevator with a trembling finger.

"You have destroyed peace in my house," he repeated, near hysteria. "In my *house*. Now, you get out! You just get out! *Right now!*"

"Yes, sir, Fabbie," Hamilton Delbacher said quietly. "We most certainly will . . . And now," he asked wryly as the elevator began its slow descent to the armored car, the Secret Servicemen, the clamorous world, "do you still want to be Vice President with me?"

"Certainly," Art Hampton said. He sighed. "But we don't have an easy road ahead."

"Did I do the wrong thing?"

The Senator shook his head.

"It was inevitable, sooner or later . . . *Somewhere* there still has to be a place for the truth in this world."

The President looked grim.

"Let's hope we can bring a little of it into the General Assembly. There may never be another chance."

BOOK FOUR

"You will wheedle no favors out of aggressive circles through complicity with them. It whets their appetite."

—*Izvestia, May 1, 1980*

And so once again, after an interval that had not, insofar as the media could ascertain, changed many opinions, the diverse representatives of the world's conglomeration returned to their posts in Turtle Bay and the General Assembly of the United Nations was called to order at 3 P.M. by Libya, in the chair. Again it was the media's "gathering of the greats." They all were here: none wished to miss the climactic meeting. Outside it was muggy, overcast, oppressive. The thermometer was close to 100 degrees Fahrenheit with humidity to match. The weatherman was predicting thunderstorms but no cooling trend. The air-conditioning, as usual, was turned up too high, but even if it had been exactly right, the sense of depression conveyed by the weather would have crept through the walls anyway, an insidious and all-pervasive thing. Tempers were edgy, patience short. Moments after Libya, represented by a short, dark, wiry individual of high-bridged nose and high-handed demeanor, crashed down the gavel with great force and importance, the skies opened, the rain descended, lightning began and crack after crack of thunder rolled across the city.

It was all, as the President remarked to Ambrose Johnson, the permanent United States Ambassador, just too pat for anything.

"God wants somebody to be impressed, all right," Brose Johnson agreed with his engaging grin. "Let's hope it's the Soviets."

"I'm afraid the Soviets are impressed now only by Serapin's hatred of me," Ham Delbacher said, and told the Ambassador the gist of their conversation at Fabbie Gulack's: not a hint of which, by some miracle, had reached the media. He supposed Fabbie must be too crushed to talk.

Ambrose Johnson, who had been president of Howard University in Washington before the President's predecessor had persuaded him to take leave a year ago and become Ambassador to the UN, listened with frowning concentration. Occasionally he shook his head and a soft cluck of dismay escaped him. But when the President concluded he nodded firmly.

"I'm glad you did it. I'm glad you did. It's about time somebody called him on all those lies, and you're the only one who could do it. I couldn't."

"Why not?" the President inquired. "Not that I would want you to, but—"

"That's it," Brose said. "It isn't my place, for one thing; it's the sort of thing that could only occur on a mutual level. And also, it would sacrifice a lot of my constituency in Africa, and the 'Third World,' which I've been trying patiently to build up over the past year."

"They like you in Africa," the President commented, while Libya continued to rap sporadically for order, and slowly, in twos and threes and casually chatting groups the members of the General Assembly, many dressed colorfully in native costume, continued to drift in the doors to take their seats amid a hum of greetings, jocularity and argument.

Brose Johnson nodded.

"Yes, I think they do. There's always the assumption, particularly on the part of whites, that just because they're black and I'm black, Africans are automatically going to like me. But they don't—and frankly"—he grinned again—"there are plenty of them I don't like either. It takes more than skin color to make buddy-buddies in this world organization. And there's more to it than that. They're Africans and I'm an American and that means I'm two hundred years away from most of them—and ahead of them, too. In fact, sometimes I think it's two thousand. Quite a few of these fellows are right out of the bush. I can point out a hundred or so right here and now who go back home, take off their fancy New York duds and start sacrificing animals and drinking cow-blood an hour after they get off the plane. All I do is go home, take a shower, change into my sports-shirt and slacks and go play golf." And suddenly, a rich and infectious sound, his laughter boomed out, and many around them, turning to look, smiled and waved and gave him cordial greeting.

"But obviously you've managed to convince a lot of them that you're a friend," Ham Delbacher persisted, "and that's good for us."

"Oh yes," Brose said. "I've got a lot of pals . . ." His expression sobered. "But that doesn't necessarily mean it's good for *us*. They're very adept at separating me from the United States in their own minds, even though I never make any attempt to encourage them in it. In fact, if anything, I feel I've got to go further than most to convince them I *am* American and do support American policy in every way. Still, some of them don't believe it. It's a constant challenge."

"And now, I suspect, a constant burden," the President said. Brose paused to wave across the room to a couple of members of the Ethiopian delegation, then turned back with a smile.

"Not one I can't handle," he said cheerfully, "even though you are free to relieve me at any time, of course. You have my resignation on your desk."

"Yes," the President said somewhat ruefully, remembering the seemingly endless hours he had spent during his days in Washington sifting, resifting, accepting, rejecting. Hundreds of officials of the late President's administration had sent him similar missives. He had changed some two hundred so far, and his personal stamp was beginning to appear on the face of government. But there was a long way to go and no time, now, to complete the task. It would have to wait until the crisis eased. Meanwhile, he had no intention of relieving Brose Johnson and told him so.

"Well, I'm pleased," Brose said. "Frankly, I like it here, even when I am being given hell for what my President is doing." He sighed suddenly, as Libya in the chair cried out in exasperation, "Will the delegates *please* take their seats so this extremely important session can begin!"

"What's the basic problem?" Ham Delbacher asked, interested to see if the Ambassador's diagnosis agreed with his. It did.

"The basic problem," Brose said, "is that our friends in Moscow have succeeded in convincing a lot of people, particularly the semi-literate ones that I deal with a lot, that nothing the United States says is true. This is because for many decades, beginning with F.D.R. in World War II, there was a great attempt by Americans to convince Americans that the Soviet Union was nice and decent and pure and holy. It was felt necessary to do that in order to overcome the memory of previous decades filled with their deceit and our perfectly justified mistrust of them, and make ourselves believe that they were capable of being honest allies whom we could wholeheartedly help. When we had saved them with our Lend-Lease supplies, without which they could never have withstood Hitler and which they have never repaid, they simply took it from there, conning the gullible among us by continuing to pretend friendship with the one hand while tearing us down savagely with the other all over the world. Partly through naïveté and partly through a dislike for unpleasantness, we never really counter-punched. So there are millions and millions all over the globe who are convinced we're history's biggest villains, and they'll never think otherwise. Meanwhile, the Soviets really *are* history's biggest villains and you can't get even a lot of our own powerful people to gather up enough guts to admit it. So we stumble on. It makes for a tough time on the firing line . . . Anyway, I'm glad you told off Serapin. He's one mean, vicious, slimy, slippery, two-faced, evil son-of-a-bitch."

The President smiled.

"I take it your friends won't believe that."

"Oh no," Brose said with some frustration. "To a lot of these dopes here he's the great savior of the human race, the great peacemaker, the embodiment of mankind's hopes. Mr. Goody Two-Shoes. Oh, there've been little flurries now and then, Angola, Mozambique, South Yemen, Ethiopia, Afghanistan, Iran, Nicaragua, El Salvador, Grenada—quite enough evidence for any halfway intelligent man to see. But they don't see. Or if they do—and here's the further complication—we've let the Soviets get so strong that everybody's scared to do anything about what they do see. And since *we* haven't had the foresight or the guts to do it, why should any of *them* risk *their* necks attempting? They all think they're going to have to try to get along with the U.S.S.R. pretty soon, anyway, because a great many of them are convinced that it won't be long before we're out of the picture altogether. So why rock the boat? They think the Soviet Union is as inevitable as the Soviet Union thinks it is. And that's half—hell, more than half—the battle, right there."

"So you don't really see any hope of turning them back in this place, then."

"Assuming they'd listen," Brose said, "which they won't, there might be the slightest shred of it. But they won't. And I'm not so sure they'll be asked to. I'm beginning to think the vote against them on Afghanistan— and their response to it—was one of the major turning points of history. They were almost unanimously condemned—and they paid no attention whatsoever. Next time, the vote against them was less, the acceptance of their defiance easier. Next time, a little easier. Time after that, still easier. And so on. That was their test and the test of the world. We tried then, pretty damned late and pretty damned feebly. Some people didn't go to the Moscow Olympics, but a lot of people did. And basically, so what? The Soviet military machine went right on building, the Soviet Empire kept right on expanding. The things that really count didn't change at all. They kept going ahead, we kept falling behind. And here we are."

"And here we are," Ham Delbacher said, as Chauncey Baron, Roger Hackett, Mark, Bill Lapham and Herb Esplin came in together and immediately became the focus of many eyes as they walked up the aisle to join them. (He had asked Art Hampton, as Vice President-designate, to remain in Washington this time.) The next few moments passed in greetings as everybody shook hands, exchanged trivia, settled down. At the podium, Libya was still pounding away. It was now three-thirty and in typical UN fashion, approximately half the delegates were now in their seats.

"So," he said, sitting down and turning again to Brose, "your whole picture is pretty gloomy, I take it."

Brose gave him a sidelong glance.

"Isn't yours, Mr. President?"

Hamilton Delbacher nodded.

"Yes. But we've still got to fight like hell."

Brose snorted.

"If you think I don't—"

"Oh no," the President said quickly. "I know you do, and I'm grateful to you, and proud of you, for it. I think I'll let you carry the ball here for a while, as a matter of fact." He looked wry. "I'll save myself for Yuri."

"You'll need all your strength," Brose remarked with a grim half-smile. "Look at that! And listen to it!"

The President of the Soviet Union was coming up the aisle toward them, his delegation scowling obediently along behind him. His hands were raised above his head, he was applauding vigorously, in the Russian style. A great roar of welcome and answering applause rolled toward him from all over the chamber. He was carefully not looking toward the American delegation as he approached with his men to take their places alongside, separated by three empty seats, but to everyone else he was showing a smiling, almost exultant, face. And so he should be exultant, Ham Delbacher thought, recalling the small smattering of applause that had greeted his own entry a few minutes earlier. So he should. He was obviously among very many friends.

Presently he and his delegation were seated, the applause died down. But the tension in the big chamber, with its huge murals by Léger looking like scrambled eggs on the walls, its blond wooden paneling, blue carpets and upholstery and its garishly bright lighting, hard on the eyes and hard on thought, had suddenly risen to a level from which it did not recede.

The two antagonists were now in place. The drama was about to begin.

It was another ten minutes, however, before Libya was finally able to secure the decorum and order he had been so noisily seeking. Prince Koa came in, grinned and waved at the friendly applause that greeted his enormous, colorful bulk. The British Prime Minister entered with her Indian colleague, the former in her usual trim dress, her colleague as usual in floating sari, this one a startling deep blue set off by more gold jewelry. They were talking earnestly and paid no attention to the stir their joint arrival caused as they parted company before the podium and proceeded to their respective delegation areas. The press section was overflowing, many reporters standing along the sides and at the back. The public galleries were full once again with diplomats, wives, relatives, friends and those very few members of the general public who had been able somehow to wangle tickets. These included a frail, earnest and very determined-looking Fabrizio Gulack.

At the very last moment, causing his own special stir, Ju Xing-dao slipped quietly in with his delegation from the area behind and to the left of the podium, and took his seat to the accompaniment of a surge of excitement and a quick scattering of applause.

Gradually the delegations settled down, the room became reasonably quiet, a rustling, vibrant hush descended. Libya drew a deep breath, gave the gavel one more furious bang! and declared, too loudly and in a voice filled with tension:

"The delegates will be in order! This special emergency meeting of the General Assembly of the United Nations is now in session!"

As if on cue, the Lord delivered a sudden enormous thunderclap that literally shook the building. There was a spontaneous and hearty outburst of laughter from all over the floor. It was the last real merriment of a long, contentious afternoon and evening.

"We are seized here today," Libya said, using the legal language of one who had graduated from Columbia Law School on an American-sponsored scholarship before going home to devote his life to raising hell against America, "of the resolution sent up to us by the Security Council two weeks ago. To put the matter in perspective I think, if the Assembly agrees, that I should first like to ask the Secretary-General to read the resolution, in order to refresh our memories of it; and then to ask its three co-author states, the People's Republic of China, India and the United Kingdom to speak briefly in explanation before we begin full debate. If that is agreeable . . . very well, Mr. Secretary-General, if you will please read, sir."

"Yes, Mr. President," the Secretary-General said in his usual quietly dignified manner.

["That guy is worth his weight in image to this place," the Washington *Star* had once remarked to the Seattle *Times*. It summed up what they all thought of his unfailing air of grave, paternal statesmanship.] "The so-called C.I.B. resolution of the Security Council reads as follows:

" 'Whereas, the world now faces a situation of the utmost gravity involving a most serious threat to peace created jointly by the military actions of the Soviet Union and the response thereto by the United States; and,

" 'Whereas, resolutions now before the Security Council do not seek a compromise or peaceful solution but seek rather to enlist the Security Council and the United Nations openly on one side or the other, to the detriment of the cause of world peace, and in a way that could very likely inflame rather than diminish the threat to peace; and,

" 'Whereas, it is obvious that because of the veto, no solution of the crisis can be reached on the basis of the two opposing resolutions now before the Council; now, therefore,

" 'Be it resolved, that the Security Council desires to be, and hereby is, discharged of its responsibility in this matter and calls upon the General Assembly to begin immediate consideration of it, looking toward a solution that will:

" 'First, define with equal justice the joint responsibility of the United States and the Soviet Union for the creation of the crisis and the attendant threat to world peace;

" 'Second, call upon the Soviet Union to curtail immediately its present peace-threatening worldwide military maneuvers, including widespread deployment of submarines, and restrict them to those lands and waters adjacent to its own territory which are legitimate subjects of concern for Soviet security;

" 'Third, call upon the United States to abandon all those actions which have contributed to world tension, specifically the projected increase in United States military spending; the national emergency and war alert declared by the President; and the ultimatum of the President regarding the presence of Soviet submarines in the territorial waters of the sovereign state of Cuba; and, further,

" 'Be it resolved, that the Security Council, having discharged itself of its responsibilities and having called the matter to the attention of the General Assembly, with recommendations, does hereby declare this emergency session to be adjourned, and it is so adjourned, sine die.'

"On the strength of the final paragraph of this resolution," the Secretary-General said, "the resolution was ruled by the President of the Security Council, Prince Koahumahili of Tonga, to be a procedural matter and thus not subject to veto. His ruling was upheld by the Council on a vote of thirteen Yes, two No, and the Council accordingly adjourned, passing the matter, with instructions, to this Assembly."

From five different places across the floor there came instant cries of "Mr. President!" as Nicaragua, El Salvador, South Yemen, Ethiopia and Mozambique simultaneously ("And no doubt by prearrangement," the President murmured to Brose Johnson, who nodded) demanded recognition.

For a moment Libya hesitated and there were instant cries of "Regular order!" from Britain, India, China, Brazil and Canada. Still Libya hesitated, mightily tempted to let the debate begin with a mass denunciation of the United States; but somehow the emphatic tones of the British Prime Minister, given a penetrating clarity by years of talking down the opposition in Parliament, managed to pierce the clamor.

"Stick to your word, Mr. President!" she cried. "Come on, now, stick to your word!"

For a second Libya glared at her, openly annoyed by the reminder. Then with an obvious reluctance he decided that his image and some vestige of self-respect required him to comply. He brought down the gavel sharply and the clamor ceased.

"In line with my earlier statement," he said in his sibilantly accented English, "I shall call on the three so-called C.I.B. powers to explain their resolution. The Assembly will be in order!"

There was a moan of disapproval but, like Koa in the Security Council, he enjoyed his gavel and down it came again with an authoritative crack! that produced a return to reasonable silence.

"The People's Republic of China," he said, and with a slow dignity, amid renewed buzzing and excitement and the craning of many necks to observe his stately progress, the tiny figure of the Vice Premier seemed to float gently down the aisle with an almost excruciating slowness to the foot of the podium, where he bowed low to Libya and the S.-G., turned and bowed low to the Assembly, and then turned again to mount the steps to the lectern with the assistance of several guards.

After they had adjusted the microphone for him, and had swiftly pulled out from under the lectern a small footstool which was not visible from the floor but was always kept there in readiness for the Assembly's shorter members, he took his place—his head, still just barely visible, seeming to float almost disembodied behind the microphone. Upon it there appeared a gently benign but enigmatic smile; the political columnist of the Washington *Post* recalled his Cheshire Cat comparison and an involuntary smile touched his lips. Ju was certainly giving it all he'd got, this afternoon. Hamilton Delbacher braced himself for more Ancient Wisdom. He was pleasantly surprised when Ju appeared to be speaking in a clear and straightforward manner uncluttered by aphorisms.

"Mr. President," the Vice Premier said in Chinese, his voice reverting to its wispy half-whisper which even the UN's extensive electronics could not amplify much beyond minimal audibility, "let us think of what has happened in the past two weeks. Two weeks have passed, and still there is no war. Two weeks in which nothing has changed in the world as regards the U.S. and the U.S.S.R., and still there is no war! I think we of the United Nations can take much credit for that. There are those who scoff at us for our ineffectuality, but they will notice that still there is no war!"

There was a roar of applause, some scattered cheers. Yes, they told themselves with satisfaction. Yes, it is true, there is no war. Nothing has changed, of course, the threat of war is just the same, but there *is* no war. There were many mutual exchanges of congratulation before the delegates settled down again, many of them pausing only long enough to turn up the volume on their head-sets to bring in Ju's translated words more clearly.

"Mr. President," he said, turning slightly to Libya, "what may we conclude from this? I think we may conclude that actually the two powers most intimately concerned do not really want war. They are anxious to avoid it. They welcome the interposition of the United Nations between themselves and that last, most awful step. They wish to compromise their differences, and they wish our help in doing it. I venture to predict, Mr. President, that our efforts will be blessed with success."

Again he was rewarded with applause, warm, heartfelt, comforting.

"It was for this reason that my colleagues, the two most able and charming ladies of India and Britain, and I, devised the compromise resolution which concluded the Security Council meeting and brought this matter to your attention. As the Secretary-General has said, there was no hope, given the presence of the veto, for the passage of either resolution offered by the U.S. and the U.S.S.R." His face suddenly became stern, his tone likewise, "Nor should there have been! They both were much too harsh! They both were ridiculously harsh! Neither should ever have been offered! It was best they die!"

This time, too, there was applause, though much weaker than before. Obviously some members were not so sure about this; but whether they were hesitant about the American demand that the Soviets withdraw their maneuvers to their own security areas or whether they were hesitant about the Soviet demand that the world unite to "overthrow" the United States was not clear. No doubt there were plenty who favored one or the other, but how many for each there was no way, as yet, to tell. Hamilton Delbacher hoped there never would be.

Ju paused to take a drink of water, then continued.

"There is of course as we all know, no compulsion upon the General Assembly to accept the recommendations of the Security Council. The Assembly may start entirely *de novo,* if it pleases—from the beginning. But it did seem to us, in the Security Council, that true peace must require the objectives we listed: a fair judgment of joint responsibility of the two superpowers, a withdrawal of Soviet maneuvers to legitimate areas of their own security, and an end to the U.S. emergency military build-up, the U.S. state of national emergency and war alert, the President's ultimatum concerning Soviet submarines, which is only suspended and still hangs like the sword of Damocles over the peace-hoping world.

"There is a saying in my country—"

["Ah!" the *Daily Telegraph* murmured in the press section. "At last!"]

"—that each journey begins with a single step. But we have no time for single steps. We must take giant leaps"—he smiled and a faint little chuckle wafted from the loud-speakers across the room—"giant leaps *forward,* if you like—when the world is poised on the very edge of such disaster as war between the superpowers would bring upon us. Therefore it is the hope of the sponsors of the Security Council resolution that our deliberations here in the General Assembly will follow something of the course we have outlined. It is our earnest prayer."

And abruptly he turned and bowed to Libya and the Secretary-General, and started slowly down the steps of the dais, holding out his right arm for assistance which was speedily provided.

There was a surprised silence for a moment: he had ended so quickly and without much of an exhortation. Then a wave of polite applause swept across the chamber as he returned to his seat.

"Nothing new there," the President remarked in the American delegation.

"What did you expect?" Chauncey Baron inquired.

"Based upon our talk together a couple of weeks ago," the President said, "I expected something more actively friendly to the United States."

"Did he say so in so many words?" Ambrose Johnson asked.

"Well—no," the President admitted. "Not exactly."

"I've learned you have to watch the P.R.C.," Brose observed. "They're very tricky."

Glancing down the long curved table at the Soviet delegation, the President decided that its members were exchanging a similar opinion. Yuri looked puzzled and annoyed, the others stern-faced and upset. Obviously they had been expecting more. Perhaps both he and Yuri, the President decided, should be thankful the Vice Premier had chosen not to take sides today. Perhaps they both should hope most strongly that he and his country never would.

"India!" Libya announced with a sharp rap of his gavel, and like some glowing blue butterfly the Prime Minister arose from her seat, face preoccupied and unsmiling, and came gracefully down the aisle and up the dais to the lectern. In the flurry of Ju's departure someone had forgotten to put the footstool back under the lectern. There was a distinct clunk of wood on wood as the Prime Minister took her place at the microphone. On the floor this brought puzzled looks, but Libya and the Secretary-General could see that she had simply booted the footstool back where it belonged with one swift, well-placed kick. With equal matter-of-factness she adjusted the microphone for herself, brushing away the aides who sprang to help. With equal matter-of-factness she started to speak.

"Mr. President," she said, tossing the slightest of bows in his direction, "I shall attempt to be as brief as our colleague from China. The so-called C.I.B. resolution is self-explanatory. It may not please all, or even a majority. Nonetheless it seemed to us in the Security Council that it furnished the best basis for compromise, providing anybody will pay attention to it."

This bluntness brought some snickers, which she ignored.

"India, for one," she went on, "has had enough of this crisis. We want to get on with the work of the world and with our own work, which God knows is serious enough considering all our problems. We do not want to see the world tied up any longer while the two superpowers play games with the future of humanity. We want this crisis ended. We want to get on with life. We want to be left alone."

There was a wave of applause, perfectly genuine and for once completely united, across the chamber. Hamilton Delbacher and Yuri Serapin were seen to be applauding with equal sincerity and vigor. The nations were united in the simplest but most fundamental of human desires. Immediately thereafter the mood collapsed.

"Now, Mr. President," the Prime Minister went on in her rapid manner, "what is the quickest way to assure this? It is to place the blame

squarely where it belongs, namely on the United States in the first instance but on the Soviet Union in the second"—there was a beginning of
applause, which surprised and pleased the American delegation—"and
then an immediate curtailment of the Soviet maneuvers, which are unnecessary, and an immediate stop to all the warlike measures of the United
States, which are not only unnecessary but completely foolish."

Again applause, somewhat stronger. It was now the turn of the Soviet
delegation to look pleased.

"Yes!" she said sharply. "Applaud if you like! Boo if you like! The fact
remains that the Soviet Union is not threatened by anybody, so these maneuvers are nonsense. It is also a fact that the United States also is not
threatened by anybody, so its actions are also nonsense. It is we, the rest
of the world, who are threatened! We, all the big powers and the little
powers who are in the way of this collision course between Moscow and
Washington. That is who is threatened, Mr. President. And we want it to
stop!"

Again, applause. Her severe expression did not change, she gave her
bangles a shake and plunged on rapidly to her conclusion.

"India will consider with the utmost sympathy any resolution offered in
the General Assembly which sets forth these points. It was the opinion of
my delegation that in the Council we must join in some form of 'compromise,' but we did so only to speed the matter here so that definitive action
might be taken. Now it is time to really come to grips with it. This is the
place. India does not want to quibble here about compromises, India
wants action to stop this threat to the entire world which comes directly
from the United States and is only increased by the persistence of the Soviet Union in these ridiculous maneuvers. Stop them both, we say! It is
the duty we owe to humankind, of which I represent more than any of
you here with the exception of my colleague from China. Our millions
want peace, America! No more excuses, Russia! We want peace now!"

And with a toss of her head, a flip of her sari and another jingle-jangle
of her jewelry, she swept down the dais and back to her delegation like
what she was, a stern-faced Indian matriarch, while the chamber exploded into wild applause in which the few boos and hisses were
swallowed up completely. Only the television cameras in the booths
above, zeroing in on the equally stern-faced, unapplauding U.S. and British delegations and some few others across the floor, carried any indication that approval was not unanimous. And the disagreement did not appear very substantial.

"The United Kingdom!" Libya called when some semblance of order
had been restored, rather more in spite of than because of his own vigorous gavel-bangings for the past five minutes.

The British Prime Minister walked briskly down the aisle, up the steps
of the dais to the lectern, bowed briefly to Libya and the S.-G. and began

to speak without further preliminaries, her face almost as stern as that of her predecessor.

"Mr. President," she said, "members of the Assembly: I regret that my colleague from India has seen fit to disrupt the mood of compromise that our colleague from China and I had hoped to maintain here in opening this debate in the General Assembly. I cannot agree with all her harsh words and her attempt to place the heavier blame on the United States. However, perhaps it is as well to bring all differences of opinion into the open in the beginning. Perhaps real compromise can follow.

"I shall make no attempt to conceal from you the extreme gravity with which Her Majesty's Government continue to regard the present situation. Nothing, as the Vice Premier said, has changed since the Security Council ended its deliberations two weeks ago. Soviet military power is now emplaced over the entire globe, in the air above and on and under the seas below. The United States is pushing ahead with its emergency military build-up, the states of national emergency and war alert still exist, and the President's ultimatum on Soviet submarines in Cuba also still exists, though, as he chooses to put it, 'suspended.' The entire situation remains as explosive as before; the slightest spark could touch it off. One Soviet jet flying off course, one American officer or serviceman responding overhastily to an accidental blip on a radar screen, would hold the entire world in pawn. One slip and one only, for whatever reason, and we all are lost. It is time to return to that realization and proceed with the gravity it should induce in all of us.

"Against that background, harsh partisanship for one side or the other, some holiday feeling that this is the time and the occasion to have one's innings, real or imagined, with the United States, or the time to bait or harass the Soviet Union—all that is utterly out of place now. This is the gravest of matters, worthy of the most solemn and responsible consideration. It is no time for easy applause or easy booing. It is time for maturity, for statesmanship, for the most careful and cautious approach. We walk along the edge of the abyss of Armageddon. One tiniest slip and over we go with unimaginable consequences and absolutely irretrievable loss.

"Here, one word to our friends from the Soviet Union." She paused and looked straight down at Yuri Serapin, who stared impassively back. "A repetitive word, but necessary. There is a conviction, often expressed in official Soviet literature and the statements of many Soviet leaders, that atomic warfare is inevitable, that it is not something to fear and that it can and will be won, if it comes, by the Soviet Union. This," she said crisply, "is insane nonsense. It is nonsense that puts the entire world in jeopardy, because it removes the last restraint that intelligent men everywhere recognize as requiring them to keep the peace. If the Soviet Union does not feel this restraint, then God help us all. But just don't forget that the obliterating consequences include the Soviet Union as well.

"And to the United States I would say: you are not alone. There are many of us here—"

There were some derisive hoots, some scornful laughter. She looked annoyed and stood her ground.

"There are many of us here," she repeated with a slow and deliberate emphasis, "who are your friends. The lunatic fringe can take care of the lunatic fringe, but the responsible nations of this world know full well that in a world without the friendship and help of the United States they would be lost. Many of us have criticized you in the past, and sometimes quite harshly; yet basically, with many of us, this has been of a nature somewhat like that of some of your own domestic critics: it is because we have expected so much of you, and sometimes have been disappointed. With my country, and I think with a good many of the more responsible members of this body"—again there were boos and hisses but she dismissed them with a toss of the head and went on—"our basic appreciation for the ultimate good of your national purposes, and our thanks for your fantastically generous help on many occasions has remained undiminished. We have from time to time criticized; we have never been so foolish as to completely and mercilessly condemn. We, after all, are not perfect, either. Nor is anyone"—the boos began again, dutifully, from communist-bloc nations and their sympathizers. Yuri and his colleagues remained expressionless—"nor is anyone else on this floor who presumes to completely condemn the United States, or to engage in such ridiculous extremes as to demand that the United States be 'overthrown.' Statements like that are beyond the realm of reason. If sincerely stated and sincerely adhered to, they would make the achievement of a sensible compromise here beyond reach under all circumstances."

("Who said they want compromise?" Brose Johnson murmured; and the President nodded. "And who said they were not sincere?" he asked.)

"Members of the Assembly," she continued, "it is not by such extreme positions, on either side, that we will defuse this crisis and return the world to normalcy. [BRITISH ASK "RETURN TO NORMALCY," the next batch of headlines said; and the phrase instantly became the media shorthand to describe the position of the United States and its supporters.] It is only by seeking a sincere and genuine compromise. This will, at the minimum, require a drastic curtailment and drawing-in of Soviet forces from their present far-flung positions around the globe. It will also require a relaxation of tensions, an end to ultimatums, from the United States. It may also require some curtailment of the American emergency arms build-up.

"These will not be easy, for either power. But consider the alternative.

Consider the alternative! And then ask yourselves if there is any route other than genuine compromise that the world—and the two powers most directly involved—can safely pursue."

She turned briskly, bowed again to Libya and returned to her seat, head high and smile fixed, while a smattering of applause rippled across the room.

It was followed by a temporary release of tension, a rustle and chatter of subdued talk as the Assembly waited for Libya to speak. The Secretary-General handed him a sheet of paper, he put on his glasses and studied it carefully.

"Members of the Assembly," he said, "we have, to this moment, sixty-three nations that have placed themselves on the speakers' list." There was a deep and universal groan. "There are indications that even more may wish to speak before the debate is concluded." The groan was repeated. "Therefore the Chair must respectfully request that all members keep their remarks as brief and pertinent as possible.

"Although neither has requested precedence on the list, it seems only fitting to the Chair that the Assembly should hear first from the two contenders in this issue. In a sense, we are sitting as a court of appeal, and while legally, of course, we have no such jurisdiction, in a psychological sense it is not too extreme to describe us so. Therefore if there is no objection by a majority of the Assembly—which would of course," he reminded them with a severe expression, "necessitate a vote and delay proceedings even further—it is the desire of the Chair to hear first from the United States of America and the Soviet Union. Does either have a preference to be the first speaker?"

He paused and looked expectantly down at the two Presidents. Neither responded.

"Is it to be left to the arbitrary decision of the Chair?" Libya asked. There was a tense silence, broken finally by the British Prime Minister, speaking from her seat.

"Mr. President," she suggested, "obviously there are some advantages in being the first speaker, just as there are advantages in being able to offer detailed rebuttal. But since neither of the delegations wishes to express a desire in the matter, why don't you do something as simple as draw straws? Or flip a coin, perhaps?"

There was a scattering of laughter, surprised and approving—and relieved to have something to laugh about at such a moment. It was carefully noted that both Presidents joined in, and so after a moment Libya also smiled, rather thinly, and turned to the Secretary-General.

"Mr. Secretary-General," he said, "I think a coin is simpler. I must confess that at the moment I do not have—that is, would you happen to —could you loan me—"

There was another outburst of laughter, really amused this time, but in-

stead of accepting it gracefully he looked quite upset, promptly pulled out
his wallet and waved it angrily for them all to see.

"I *have* money!" he snapped. "I simply do not have a coin! It is nothing unusual! Mr. Secretary-General!"

["He *is* uptight," the London *Times* murmured to the Chicago *Tribune*.
"Absolutely no sense of humor whatsoever." "Which bodes no good for
us," the *Tribune* replied.]

"Yes, Mr. President," the S.-G. said, handing over a quarter. With
some difficulty, Libya tried to flip it, lost it; it rolled away toward the
edge of his desk. The S.-G. caught it skillfully and handed it back.

"If I might suggest, Mr. President," he said blandly, "it might be well
to ascertain which side of the coin each nation wishes."

"Heads!" Yuri cried, while the Assembly laughed again and Libya obviously grew more and more annoyed.

"Tails!" Ham Delbacher agreed amicably.

This time, with an obvious effort, Libya tossed the coin and managed
to have it fall directly in front of him.

"Heads!" he announced triumphantly. "The leader of the peace-loving
nations, His Excellency the President of the Soviet Union, will address
you!"

"Mr. President—" Japan started to protest his encomium, but was
drowned out by the roar of applause and whistles that greeted Yuri as he
came jauntily down the aisle, hands raised once more, clapping, above his
head.

"Are we going to get this act every time?" Ham Delbacher whispered
to Brose Johnson.

"I don't know," Brose whispered back, "but obviously I'm not going to
get my chance to speak today. You'll have to reply to him."

"We'll see."

Yuri surveyed them for a moment from the footstool, which made him
about five feet ten and permitted him to look satisfactorily down upon
them.

"Mr. President of the Assembly!" he said. Earphones everywhere
across the floor were switched hurriedly to the Russian channel, the big
room quieted rapidly as the television cameras in their booths above
zoomed in on his somber, now wholly stern and uncompromising face.
"Mr. President of the United States! All other Presidents, Prime Ministers, leaders of nations! I appeal to you in the name of truth! Not the
so-called truth of Western hegemonists, racists and imperialists, but the
truth of honest fact—the peoples' truth, which so many of you represent!"

Applause, warm, supportive, encouraging, welled up from the floor and
many places in the gallery. He gave a short, quick, satisfied nod and

surged ahead, emphasizing his remarks from time to time with his usual gesture of an openhanded slap on the surface of the lectern.

"Members of the Assembly, I have listened with great interest to the authors of the so-called C.I.B. compromise with which the Security Council chose to terminate its recent futile meeting, instead of denouncing and condemning the dangerous, war-mongering United States and its blood-thirsty President, as it should have done."

There was a murmur of hostility from the friends of the United States, a scattering of boos quickly drowned in applause from the friends of the Soviet Union.

"Oh, let them boo," Yuri said with what appeared to be a sudden offhand indifference. "Their lies do not concern us. It is the truth we are here to determine, and the truth which I am here to defend.

"There has been talk here by two of the co-authors of the C.I.B. compromise, the Peoples' Republic of China and the United Kingdom, about apportioning equal blame between the United States and the U.S.S.R. for the crisis situation which confronts the world. Only the Prime Minister of India, our good friend, has said honestly what the truth is—that there can be no equal apportionment of blame because the United States is chiefly and principally to blame, while the Soviet Union has consistently and determinedly sought to preserve and strengthen the cause of peace. How can there be 'equal' blame for that, members of the Assembly? It is like comparing the wolf and the chicken. One destroys peace, the other tries to build it up. How can anyone try to say they are equal?"

He paused and took a drink of water, while dutifully from the floor arose the applause of his supporters.

"The new President of the United States has told his Congress, and you, that I and my colleagues are determined to destroy the United States of America, which is"—his voice took on a heavy note of sarcasm—"so helpless—and conquer the world, as well. What a big task, my friends! Did you ever know a nation that could do it? No, not even the mighty United States, whose President has ordered various alarms and alerts of one kind and another, and has begun an emergency plan to increase the United States' already enormous military strength. For what purpose, my friends? Surely you must have wondered! Is it to protect the United States from this horrible Soviet Union which the new President fears so intensely, or is it to mask some sinister scheme to extend U.S. imperialist racist control to all the lands and seas until no one anywhere is safe? That is where you should look, I suggest, my friends—to the U.S.! Not to us! Not to the peace-loving Soviet Union, which is only conducting maneuvers as it has every sovereign right to do!

"The next thing I knew, he was seeing submarines—I almost said 'under the bed,' but they were not even under his bed, that big bed in the White House!" There was sudden delighted laughter and applause. "They were—where, my friends? In the sovereign nation of Cuba, which had requested their presence there for protection against the imperialist adventures the new President of the United States was already plotting and planning. They were sent there because Cuba was threatened—by the United States of America! By this foolish power that still thinks the Caribbean is an 'American lake,' when it has not been for at least the last five or six years!" [A great cheer went up from the Caribbean and South American nations, even those, like Brazil and Argentina, disposed to be friendly to the United States, for this was one infallible appeal to chauvinism they could not resist.] "This very power whose new President claims that *it* is threatened by us! How many threats within threats within threats can there be, my friends? Surely that is too big a story even for our American friends, who are noted for exaggerating somewhat!"

Again laughter—amused, scornful, sycophantic—welled up to reward him. Again he gave the short, sharp, self-satisfied nod.

"The Soviet Union"—and again he slapped the lectern, hard and sharp —"will never abandon its Cuban ally! It will never abandon any ally— unlike the treacherous United States! It will never deny the appeal of any freedom-loving people who wish protection against the racist imperialists of America! Never! Never, never, never will the Soviet Union refuse the call of freedom!"

And once again applause, excited, exuberant, encouraging. He paused with a grimly satisfied smile to allow it to run its course.

"Members of the Assembly!" Yuri said. "Do not listen to the lies and silly statements that come from hegemonist imperialist circles of the United States! They cry about Soviet military build-ups, yet it is only because their own military build-up threatens us—and threatens you—that we have undertaken the strengthening of our forces. That has been our only purpose.

"We have known from the beginning that we must always be vigilant against the sinister plots and schemes of the United States. Always, they have opposed us, except for the brief period of World War II and even then, behind a pretense of friendship, they were secretly placing themselves in a position to take over the world later on. But we fooled them, my friends! We were not so weak and helpless as they thought! We won the Great Patriotic War against Hitler and the fascists and then we began immediately to prepare ourselves for the inevitable conflict we could see ahead between the socialists camp led by the Soviet Motherland and the capitalist imperialist camp led by the United States! We had saved the world from Hitler but we knew the task was not finished. We knew we would eventually have to save it from the United States imperialists as well.

"And so we made ourselves strong.

"*And we are strong.*

"We can protect ourselves, and we will protect you as well, from the plots and designs of this new President, who still hopes, in the face of all the facts of history, that the United States can take over the world using the pretext of a so-called 'Soviet threat to mankind.'

"How absurd it all is, my friends! How ridiculous! Have we attacked any of you in these recent days? Have we seized anyone's territory or launched any missile strikes? Have we used the atomic bomb on any of you?"

There was a roar of, "NO!" He responded with a short, sharp nod of satisfaction.

"Such nonsense is farthest from our thoughts, members of the Assembly! Such thoughts are the imaginings of madmen! If our forces have done anything, aside from carry out perfectly legitimate maneuvers and practices, it has been to interpose themselves as a shield between you and the hegemonist imperialist circles of the United States and its war-seeking new President, who had rather issue ultimatums and threats than sit down for the peaceable solution of difficulties. We have not threatened you— we have protected you! It is clear to any but the greatest fools and madmen!

"We are proud of what we have done to save you from America! We are glad we are strong enough to do it! We are grateful for your friendly response to our efforts!

"The pledge of the Soviet Union is this: we will always be here, your shield and your protector!"

There was a great excited surge of shouts and applause, in which the vigorous boos and jeers and angry rejoinders of America's friends were lost in the uproar.

The President looked across at the British Prime Minister and both shook their heads in disbelief.

"This is absolute insanity," he said quietly to Brose Johnson, who nodded in agreement as he looked slowly around at the many wildly excited, applauding delegates.

"The world turned upside down," he said. "But," he noted grimly, "the inmates are eating it up. They are absolutely loving it."

"I think if you don't mind," the President said, "that I will handle the reply myself."

"I don't think you have any choice," Brose said.

"Members of the Assembly," Yuri said, and abruptly his voice dropped, his demeanor became solemn and earnest. ["He acts," Ivan had said scornfully, "always he acts. You must go through several layers of wool to find Yuri Pavlovich."] "Enough of such musings upon the sad and dangerously misguided nation whose imperial ambitions we must stop. The world *knows* we must stop them. The only question is, how?"

"Bomb them!" someone in the Ethiopian delegation shouted loudly, only to be instantly silenced by his startled fellows. But for all that, there was a low murmur of approval and a death's-ghost of applause that moved swift and grinning across the assemblage.

"No," Yuri said, "we do not desire to bomb them, though if it is their purpose to use such weapons against us and against the world, we would not hesitate."

This time the murmur grew and the applause became a little more solid, though no one quite dared go as far as Ethiopia in vocalizing it. Perhaps he would not have if he had not taken a couple of martinis too many in the Delegates' Dining Room for lunch. But many, too many, were secretly glad that he had, for he expressed a hatred many shared.

"No," Yuri said again, voice grave and contemplative now. "First we must exhaust all possible means of thwarting their imperialistic desires which are available to us here in the United Nations. And that bring us to the question: how we can best express and enforce that intention?"

He paused, and abruptly silence settled on the room as everyone adjusted dials, amplified translation channels, prepared to hear the Soviet proposal which now was about to be placed before them.

"My delegation and I," Yuri said, "are agreed that the basic framework of the so-called C.I.B. resolution is probably the most practical and possible for us to follow here in the General Assembly. However," he said, just as many press people half-rose from their seats, preparing to dash out and file their bulletins and just as the television cameras came in close upon his now calm and statesmanly face, "it is not acceptable to us unless amended. Our proposal is as follows:

"Firstly, since the final paragraph calling for this Assembly meeting is now moot in light of our presence here, we propose as a simple matter of parliamentary neatness to strike that paragraph from the resolution."

"Without objection, I believe we can consider that done," Libya said, bestirring himself, for the first time since Yuri began, from the half-smiling, half-dazed, obviously all-worshipful glow in which he had listened to his remarks. No one had applauded the Soviet Union and booed, hissed and jeered the United States any more vigorously than the occupant of the Chair. By any standards of civilized debate it had been a shameful performance; but the American delegation and its friends had decided unanimously and without any consultation that it was hopeless to protest.

"For the same reasons," Yuri said, "we suggest striking the first, second, and third paragraphs, all having to do with the deliberations of the Security Council and its reasons for shifting the responsibility to the Assembly."

There was a rustling of papers as everyone turned to his copy or her copy of the resolution, read it over, and agreed.

"Without objection," Libya said again, this time remembering to bang his gavel, "it is so ordered."

"Now," Yuri said, "we come to the heart of it."

There was an instant heightening of tension, an intent listening to his next words.

"The Soviet Union," he said slowly, "offers the following resolution based upon the resolution of the Council:

"Whereas, the world now faces a situation of the utmost gravity, brought about by the inexcusable overreaction of the United States of America to the entirely legitimate military maneuvers of the Soviet Union undertaken in pursuit of its entirely legitimate security interests; and

"Whereas, this overreaction of the United States has taken the form of peace-threatening, war-inviting military alerts, arms build-ups and an entirely unnecessary and unjustified ultimatum by the President of the United States to the Soviet Union; and

"Whereas, this course of conduct by the United States, if permitted to continue, poses the immediate and overriding possibility that it may plunge the world into a universal war of unknowable but undoubtedly cataclysmic scope; now, therefore,

"Be it resolved, that the United Nations hereby completely and totally and without exception condemns the warlike policies of the United States which pose the gravest possible threat to world peace; and,

"Be it resolved, that the United Nations welcomes and encourages the efforts of the Soviet Union, as represented in its present military maneuvers, to protect the peace-loving nations of the world from the threat of atomic war posed by the actions of the United States; and

"Be it further resolved, that the United Nations hereby calls upon the United States to abandon forthwith and immediately its war-threatening emergency military build-up, its declarations of national emergency and war alert, and the ultimatum of the President regarding the legitimate presence of Soviet submarines stationed in Cuban waters at the request of the sovereign government of Cuba; and,

"Be it finally resolved, that the United Nations recognizes, applauds and wholeheartedly approves the constant efforts of the Soviet Union to strengthen and defend world peace, and to encourage the unity and friendship of all peace-loving states against the aggressive threats of the United States."

There was a movement of surprise from the American delegation and quite a few others at the sheer audacity and effrontery of the final paragraph with its all-encompassing claim of Soviet purity and its blanket condemnation of the United States. At least this time, the President thought wryly, Yuri had not gone so far as to demand that the UN "overthrow" the United States, though probably that would come too in due course.

"Mr. President," Yuri said, looking about with satisfaction before he sat down, "I request an immediate vote on the Soviet resolution."

There were protests of "Mr. President!" from many places across the floor; the United States, its President was pleased to see, still had some friends. So, however, did the Soviet Union, and before Libya could recognize anyone, someone—it appeared to be Nicaragua—cried, "Second!" and an immediate chant of "Vote! Vote! Vote!" began. It was accompanied by banging on desk tops, yells, whistles and stamping of feet, and for a few moments it made quite an impressive spectacle for the television cameras, which was the intention. Partisan as he was, however, Libya was not quite that stupid; and after he had let it run for several moments and made sure the cameras had recorded everything they wished, he brought down his gavel several furious times and turned with a cold politeness to the tall figure of Ambrose Johnson, standing at his seat and saying patiently, "Mr. President . . . Mr. President . . . Mr. President," from time to time.

"Members of the Assembly!" Libya shouted, and after a few more scattered yells of "Vote!"—some boos, some jeers, some claps, some cheers —the Assembly finally quieted down. "Members of the Assembly," Libya repeated, "you have forgotten already that it was decided that the United States should speak following the Soviet Union. Obviously the United States has the right of reply and obviously we cannot vote until we hear its rebuttal and hear what, if anything, it offers as a counter-proposal. The Soviet resolution is duly moved and seconded, but it will not be voted upon until it arises in regular parliamentary order."

"It is suspended, like his ultimatum!" Ethiopia's martini-drinker cried, and again the room filled with raucous laughter.

"The Assembly will be in order!" Libya snapped, finally beginning to sound impatient. "The Ambassador of the United States."

"Mr. President," Brose said dryly, "I am simply holding the floor until this distinguished body is ready to get back to serious business. If it now is, I should like to present to you the President of the United States, who will state the American position."

Again there were jeers, cheers, boos, applause as Ham Delbacher's tall, portly figure came with an almost placid dignity down the aisle to the dais and up the stairs to the lectern. Yuri also had forgotten to replace the footstool, and in the excitement of the moment none of the guards had remembered to do it either. Without a word the President stooped down, grasped the stool and lifted it high for the room to see. Then he placed it carefully inside the lectern and resumed his full six feet three. Again there were some jeers but more laughter. For a second Yuri shot him a venomous look while he stared impassively back; then he arranged a sheaf of handwritten notes in front of him, placed a hand firmly on each side of the lectern, leaned forward slightly and began in a level, unhurried voice.

"I was talking recently," he said in an informal, almost conversational tone, "with one who knows the President of the Soviet Union very well. He said, and I quote: 'He acts. Always he acts. You must go through several layers of wool to find Yuri Pavlovich.' I think, members of the Assembly, that this afternoon we have been privileged to witness one of his more astounding theatrical performances. What he said may have had very little, or no, relation to the truth, and the layers of wool may still be undisturbed but I think we can all agree that it was, indeed, astounding."

More boos and jeers, drowned out this time by applause and laughter from those who either favored the United States, or, more likely, as the President suspected, welcomed any chance to join together in the safety of a group to mock a man of whom many of them were desperately afraid. And this, Ham Delbacher further suspected, even though they might very well turn right around and vote with Yuri when the time came.

"It was a rather disorganized speech," the President went on, "filled with bombast and fury and those official fictions which he has offered so many times to justify his desperately dangerous and completely inexcusable threat to the peace of the world. So my notes in response are a little disorganized too. But let me take up his points as he made them.

"Leaving aside the standard Soviet rhetoric about the 'dangerous, warmongering United States and its bloodthirsty President' "—he paused and chuckled, a comfortable, grandfatherly sound—"I *do* look very bloodthirsty, don't I?—and going to the heart of it, he began by complaining that the so-called C.I.B. resolution calls for apportioning equal blame for the present crisis between our two countries. He feels this is not right—it should blame the United States entirely. I agree with him that it is not right—it should blame the United States a little. It should blame the Soviet Union very, very much."

Again the boos and hisses, again scattered but vigorous applause for him.

"He then proceeded," the President continued, "to review what he referred to—no doubt in jest—as 'the facts' that led up to the crisis. And he told you that I am obsessed by the conviction that he and his colleagues are determined to destroy the United States and conquer the world. And with his by now well-known and famous sarcasm he added, 'What a big task, my friends! Did you ever know a nation that could do it? No, not even the mighty United States . . .'

"Well, you know, my friends, he was quite right—at least as far as the United States is concerned. It is a big task and I agree, I doubt if the United States could do it. But I know someone who thinks he can and that is Yuri Pavlovich Serapin with his sick giant of a country"—the boos began to rise—"whose leaders think they really do have some sort of phony mandate from history to destroy the United States and conquer the world. That is who he thinks can conquer the world, my friends, and that is what he has now set out to do."

The boos by now were so loud that they had drowned out his supporters' applause; but the amplification was sufficiently strong to carry his voice above the tumult as he repeated firmly: "That is what he has now set out to do.

"He accuses me of what seems to him undue concern," he went on calmly when the uproar began to die down a little (with no help from Libya, whose busy gavel was conspicuously at rest during the President's frequently interrupted speech), "because there were some eighteen additional missile-carrying Soviet submarines sent to Cuba a couple of weeks ago. I warned him they must be removed and ultimately some were—six, which were shuttled across a few miles of Caribbean to the secret Soviet base on the west coast of Nicaragua, which was no removal at all in any real military sense."

There was a moment's startled stir, immediately suppressed, in the Soviet delegation. They did not give American intelligence services much credit and were sometimes surprised at their discoveries.

"The removal of six submarines out of twenty-four," the President said somberly, "and those only to another nearby communist base which is just as much a threat to us as Cuba, is not satisfactory to the United States. Cuba is in no danger from us—"

There was a loud hoot from Cuba, jeers from many others, but he continued unperturbed.

"—no danger from us. But we are indeed under threat from the twenty-four Soviet missile submarines presently in the Caribbean." He paused and then went on with a slow and deliberate emphasis. "It is a threat I am determined to remove."

Again the jeers and boos, but this time a little more uncertainly. It was beginning to dawn on them that he meant it.

"The rest of the Soviet President's remarks," he went on, "were filled with the same kind of spurious charges, the same devious arguments, the same insincerity—the same lies—that he and his colleagues always present to the world. They are like a group of squid in the sea, always retreating behind a cloud of inky lies whenever the truth approaches them.

"Well," he said and his tone became hard and unyielding, "the truth is approaching them right now, and I want them—and I want those of you who are either their friends, their satellite slaves, or their terrified potential targets, to pay attention to what I have to say. We are not engaged in childish games of boo-and-applaud here. As I said in the Security Council, death's-head stands behind every chair—yours as well as mine. So pay attention, if you please. I want you to understand the American position."

There was an uneasy rumble, an outcry, literally choked in mid-word, from somewhere in the Ethiopian delegation, the quickly suppressed start of boos and hisses. All this ended very quickly this time, and even Libya sat up, suddenly alert, and prepared himself to gavel down anything the President might say that could be considered provocative or harsh to the Soviet Union. As if he sensed this movement behind his back, Hamilton Delbacher turned around suddenly and addressed him.

"I will advise the Chair," he said, a new and ominous coldness in his voice, "that I would appreciate it if he would lay aside his gavel while I speak. He gave every encouragement to the President of the Soviet Union to say as many vicious things as he could think of concerning me and my country; and I do not intend to have him try to gavel me down when I exercise the right of reply. Is——that——clear?"

And he stared at Libya, who looked surprised, then furious; but whose eyes presently were first to shift away.

"That is clear," he mumbled, in a voice so low and indistinct that the President said sharply:

"Speak up, man! *Is that clear?*"

"Yes," Libya almost shouted in the hate-filled voice of a would-be cheat caught out. "Yes, yes, yes, yes, *yes!*"

"Very well," the President said, with a deliberately menacing calm. "You remember that . . . Now," he said, resuming his conversational tone and turning back to the now hushed and thoroughly attentive Assembly, "let me proceed with my discussion of the lies of Yuri Pavlovich."

"Mr. President!" Yuri shouted furiously, rising at his seat.

"I have the floor," Hamilton Delbacher said with a sudden fury apparently as great and blinding as Yuri's own (he too was something of an actor, though bred in a more democratic school). "I have the floor! *I have the floor!* The Soviet delegate lied and lied and lied about me and my country. I have a right to answer those lies, *and I will.* I would suggest the Soviet delegate resume his seat. He is," he added on a sudden inspiration, "making himself a laughing-stock. We shall all begin to laugh at him shortly. I would suggest he sit down before he is laughed down."

The prospect of this, as he had shrewdly surmised, was too much for Yuri. With an angry scowl he resumed his seat. A collective sigh of released tension came from floor and galleries. It was followed by an attentive silence as the President paused to reshuffle his notes and give himself time to recover breath. Then he resumed in his former calm and steady tone.

"We had reached, I believe, the Soviet submarines in Cuba, and what a futile, empty gesture was made by the President of the Soviet Union when he graciously condescended to move six of them to Nicaragua. Members of the Assembly, surely the intelligent and realistic among you know that this had no real strategic significance. Absolutely none.

"Nor does all this talk of the Soviet President about how peace-loving and protective his country is, how eager it is to gather you all within its great big fuzzy, furry, lovable arms and just protect you to death from the big, bad United States, that ravening beast that presently, as of course you all know, is engaged in worldwide maneuvers that threaten everyone . . . Yes, to hear the Soviet President tell it, that is what is happening in the world. What childishness! What nonsense! What a ridiculous attempt to pull the wool—Yuri Pavlovich's wool—over your eyes.

"What a lie!"

"Mr. President!" Yuri shouted, rising again at his seat. Hamilton Delbacher ignored him. Instead he turned slowly around and stared at Libya in the Chair. Their eyes held for a long moment, the President's quite impassive, Libya's savage with anger and frustration.

The President kept staring, as the room gradually grew quieter—and quieter—and quieter.

"Mr. *President!*" Yuri shouted again.

"The delegate of the Soviet Union," Libya finally jerked out in a choked voice, "will—take—his—seat. The delegate of the United States —has—the floor."

"Thank you, Mr. President," Hamilton Delbacher said serenely, turning back to the lectern and ignoring Yuri, who remained standing for a few more seconds, then slowly took his seat.

["If looks could kill," the *Christian Science Monitor* murmured to *Newsweek*. "If looks could kill, man," *Newsweek* murmured back with a chuckle, "dat ole Pres'-dent of ours, he *daid*."]

"Following various phony gestures," Ham Delbacher resumed, "such as the shifting of six submarines and the grandstand stunt of the invitation to a so-called 'summit' in Havana, the President of the Soviet Union finally decided to buy time by bringing the matter here to the United Nations. He then proceeded to introduce an extremely harsh and implacable resolution—he actually let himself get carried away to the point where he called upon this body to 'overthrow' my country, an attempt to impose Soviet fantasies upon the rest of the world which I am confident this body would never approve at any time in any form, even if it did not face an automatic U.S. veto.

"We also introduced a resolution calling upon the United Nations to demand the termination of Soviet maneuvers, withdrawal of Soviet subs from Cuba, India 'and wherever else they may be concentrated around the globe'; the abandonment of Soviet designs upon all nations; and asked the UN to condemn the Soviet Union as the major existing threat to world peace and urged its members to unite in 'opposing' Soviet designs and ambitions throughout the world. We did not, at any time, call on anyone to 'overthrow' the Soviet Union.

"This U.S. resolution, too, of course, faced veto, by the Soviet Union.

So the Council moved on to the C.I.B. resolution which is now before you, and then adjourned. Actually, as you know, the Council never did vote directly on the substance of the C.I.B. resolution but only on up-holding a ruling of the Chair.

"During the past two weeks both the President of the Soviet Union and I have had, as you know, conferences with many world leaders. We have also had another private meeting"—there was a sudden stir of excitement —"which got nowhere and accomplished nothing because of the arrogant intransigence of Mr. Serapin"—the stir died as rapidly as it had arisen— "and so we start here today virtually afresh.

"I shall not, like the President of the Soviet Union, spend a lot of time denouncing his country and his personal character, as he did mine. Soviet purposes are all on the record, as candidly and completely as Adolf Hitler's were in *Mein Kampf*—for all who are brave enough and honest enough to accept them for what they are, a cold-blooded plan for the de-struction of the United States and the conquest of the world. It is only wide-eyed Soviet apologists who deny this. The Soviets themselves, I will say for them, have always been completely candid and completely honest in their intentions, if not in the methods they use to achieve them. Per-haps this is because they early decided, shrewdly enough, that if the truth is monstrous enough it may be freely stated because very few people have the imagination and the guts to bring themselves to believe it."

He paused, looked straight out at them. His tone turned somber.

"If the United States goes down, my friends, you go with it. Not a one of you will be left as an independent nation. You will join the ranks of Latvia, Lithuania, Estonia, Hungary, Czechoslovakia, Rumania, Bulgaria, Afghanistan, South Yemen, Ethiopia, Grenada, Nicaragua, Angola, Cuba —I shall not bore you with the rest of the list because you all know it. Some of you are on it. More of you will be. *All* of you will be before the century is out, unless the Soviet conquest is contained and turned back. There is no easy solution for it, no cowards' way out, no ducking, no dodging, no evasion, no easy, comfortable escape. If the Soviet Empire is permitted to continue to expand unchallenged, you will be gone, as inevi-tably as they say you will. Make no mistake about that. They tell us what they intend to do and they are going to do it as surely as you and I share this chamber today—unless the process can be stopped.

"And when all is said and done, fellow nations of the earth, there is no way to stop it—except stop it.

"Therefore, for what it may be worth in contributing to the process—it is not the solution, for it is only words, but even words may be of some help in the cumulative opposition that must be gathered together—the United States also wishes to introduce a resolution. It reads as follows:"

Again he paused and the tension sharply increased.

"In the resolution introduced today by the Soviet Union, strike all after the words 'Whereas, the world now faces a situation of the utmost gravity,' and substitute the following:

"brought about by the decision of the Soviet Union to engage in worldwide maneuvers in areas, and to an extent, far beyond any rational needs of Soviet security; and

"Whereas, these maneuvers have brought about the emplacement of Soviet air, sea, naval, missile and space forces in many areas throughout the globe that directly threaten the security of many other nations; and,

"Whereas, the emplacement of these forces, including submarine forces in Cuba, Nicaragua, near India, Europe, Hawaii and many other maritime areas not directly or remotely connected in any way with the needs of Soviet security, poses a direct threat to world peace; and

"Whereas, the disposition of all other types of Soviet weaponry is equally threatening to other nations and to world peace; now, therefore,

"Be it resolved that the United Nations condemns the Soviet maneuvers; declares the Soviet Union's present policies to be a direct and open threat to world peace and to the safety and security of all nations; and calls upon the Soviet Union to withdraw immediately to areas within its own borders, or to contiguous areas with which it has suitable treaty arrangements, all of the military forces and weaponry, of whatever nature, which presently threaten world peace and security."

["Why did he mention space weapons?" UPI asked Chuck Dangerfield. "Does he know something we don't know?" "Apparently," Chuck replied. "I noticed Yuri jumped when he said that. He didn't think anyone saw him, but he did."]

"Members of the Assembly," the President concluded, "that is the proposal we put before you. I ask for an immediate vote."

The response was exactly what he had anticipated, and of course exactly what he wanted.

The boos and hisses rose, the protest burst out. India was indignant, Iraq aghast, even Canada, New Zealand and Monaco were inclined to be upset. Fifteen minutes later, after all had expressed themselves with varying degrees of support from the floor, Hamilton Delbacher said, with a patient air of bowing to the inevitable, "Well, members of the Assembly, if it is your desire that a vote be postponed so that all may have a chance to consider, consult and confer on the two resolutions, I suppose the United States must reluctantly agree. I would hope the Soviet Union would see fit to do the same. Mr. President, I move that the Assembly stand adjourned until 3 P.M. on Thursday, which will allow us two and a half days to make whatever arrangements we desire."

Brazil started to say, "Second!" but before he could get it out, the President of the Soviet Union was once again on his feet demanding:

"Mr. President!"

"The distinguished President of the Soviet Union," Libya said promptly, ignoring Brazil, who had been on his feet first.

"Mr. President," Yuri said, "that is much too short a time for adequate consultations and decisions. The President of the United States is so fond of amendments, he should not object to mine. I amend his motion of adjournment to read that we adjourn to 3 P.M. one week from today. That is a much more comfortable time."

"Without object—" Libya began, but Ham Delbacher did appear to object, and vigorously.

"Mr. President," he said sharply, "in any responsible parliamentary body, a motion to adjourn is not subject to debate or amendment, but I suppose in this, as in many other things, this organization is unique. I want to point out, however, that even if the Chair arbitrarily rides roughshod over normal procedure, it does not change the fact that an adjournment of one week means that the Soviet Union has yet another seven days in which to conduct its maneuvers, practice its secret military exercises and continue its blatant threat to world peace. I thought we faced an emergency here, and that speed was of the essence. How can members in good conscience delay a swift solution? What is to prevent me, for instance, from reinstituting my demand, setting a date that I assure you will be much less than one week, for removing all Soviet submarines from Cuba and the Caribbean? What devious motivation does the Soviet President have for seeking this delay? Some new surprise for us? If so, I assure you I can probably offer you one or two myself."

"Mr. President," the Prime Minister of India said with a disapproving sniff, "it is repetitious, this. It reminds me of what we have been through a dozen times already, threat and counter-threat between the two superpowers. What is wrong with a one-week delay? The Soviet Union is not threatening anyone. Its maneuvers are being conducted peaceably, whatever President Delbacher says. There is no undue strain upon the world if we wait a few more days until we meet again. It might be good for us. A cooling-off period. Why is it such an issue? If President Delbacher wants to declare another ultimatum, then *he* will be the warlike one, not President Serapin. Does he really wish to do this?"

Ham Delbacher started to retort, "But President Serapin is the one conducting the maneuvers!" but the Prime Minister's bland ignoring of this fact was for the moment so breathtaking in its ability to deny reality that he gave up before he began. But he was confirmed in his decision that he would do several things before they met again; and after he had withdrawn his objection as he had planned to do, and after Yuri's motion had been passed unanimously, he called his press secretary and had him issue an announcement from the White House.

Before the members of the Assembly finished their gossiping and conferring over their good rich meals in New York's finest that night, the news was on TV, and in the headlines that greeted them on the streets:

PRESIDENT CALLS CONGRESS BACK FOR SPECIAL ADDRESS ON EMERGENCY. WHITE HOUSE HINTS POSSIBLE NEW SUB ULTIMATUM, PROMISES "NEW DISCLOSURES" OF SOVIET PLANS.

And sure enough, to the surprise of few, particularly not Hamilton Delbacher, (though he was a little surprised at his countrymen's co-operation) within another couple of hours more headlines:

SERAPIN ACCEPTS THREE-NETWORK TV BID TO ANSWER PRESIDENT AS "PUBLIC SERVICE." SAYS HE "MUST TELL WORLD, AND ESPECIALLY AMERICANS," THE TRUTH.

Worldwide tension, which had dropped substantially in the two weeks since adjournment of the Security Council, rose sharply once again.

2

"Surprise—One of the basic conditions for achieving success in battle . . . Surprise is achieved by the use of various ways . . . by leading the enemy into error concerning one's own intentions, by preserving in secret the plan of battle, by speedy action, by hidden artificial maneuvers, by the unexpected use of the nuclear weapon . . ."

—*Soviet Dictionary of Basic Military Terms*

Yet the tension in the President's mind, he was pleased to note, was not noticeably increased; or if it was, he did not realize it. He arrived back in Washington that same evening, having decided to return immediately after the Assembly adjourned at 7 P.M. He would be back in New York soon enough, he had no doubt (though it proved to be sooner than he anticipated) and meanwhile there was a lot to do in the capital.

First came a quick call to the Speaker and to Jim Elrod, who as Majority Whip had moved informally to take over Art Hampton's duties as Majority Leader while Art awaited the formality of brief hearings before his certain confirmation. The reaction to his appointment had been virtually unanimous from Hill and country; the only quibbles were the usual, from the usual high and mightily self-important sources—doubts as to whether it was entirely wise to have a Vice President "so closely tied to the strong, if not actually belligerent, policies of President Delbacher"—an occasional portentous questioning of whether the Soviet Union, "already dismayed and alienated by President Delbacher's aggressively stated antagonism, might not see in this choice of a Tweedledum, Tweedledee Vice President a signal that it must gird itself to face the continuing, unrelenting hostility of the American Government"—the wonderment as to whether "the world at large may not see in this nomination of a 'strong' Vice President the certitude that U.S. policy is going to continue along its present risky and intransigent road."

But in general there was a commonsense reaction from most of the influential smaller papers across the nation.

"In a way that is perhaps not realized in the Lower 48," the Anchorage

Times said, "we up here in Alaska are directly on the firing line between our country and the Soviet Union. In fact, only some fifty-five miles bridges the gap between continental U.S. and continental U.S.S.R., only a mile and a half the distance between our Little Diomede Island and their Big Diomede. Soviet planes violate our air space virtually at will, and always have; reports of Soviet subs lurking off our shores are nothing new to us. To us, it is an encouraging thing to have a strong Vice President, such as Senator Hampton will be, alongside the strong President that Hamilton Delbacher is proving himself to be.

"Our only regret is that while the President has devoted so much worry to Cuba, he hasn't devoted a little to us. As usual, we're Washington's forgotten orphans. Sometimes it is a temptation to shout, 'Hey! Look right over here, Mr. President! That's no whale, that's a submarine!' Maybe Senator Hampton can take it upon himself to keep Mr. Delbacher reminded. Somebody ought to . . ."

And the Omaha, Nebraska, *World-Herald,* understandably a little less anxious from the middle of the continent, but equally complimentary to the nominee:

"We have known Art Hampton here in his native Nebraska for a long, long time—for all of his fifty-nine years, in fact. In all that time, first as city councilman, then Mayor of Omaha; then as Congressman, next as Senator and finally in the highly responsible post of Majority Leader of the Senate, he has proved himself to be a man of calm courage, unfailing integrity and unshaken commonsense. These qualities, plus a steady nerve and an unflinching purpose under political fire, would seem to qualify him amply for the office of Vice President of the United States and co-partner with the President in a time of utmost gravity for this country, its freedom and all its institutions.

"There is no slightest indication that he will ever be called upon to fill the highest office, and since we approve wholeheartedly of President Delbacher's policies in meeting the Soviet challenge we see no reason, save the Lord's, why there should be any change in that office. But it is comforting to know that if such an unhappy eventuality should ever occur, Art Hampton of Nebraska would be waiting to step forward as steadily and courageously as Ham Delbacher of Pennsylvania has done in like circumstances."

There were no signs of any substantial number of adverse votes, the Speaker and Senator Elrod assured the President, though there "might be a few of 'em who like to get their names in the papers and make a little fuss on TV," as the Speaker put it—they might make a *pro forma* protest. Basically it looked like almost unanimous confirmation.

And as for calling Congress back to hear him speak on the crisis, well, if that was what he wanted, he of course had the constitutional right to require their co-operation and they would be very happy to give it. When did he want them? Day after tomorrow? "Say the word and we'll crack the whips," Jim Elrod said with a chuckle. Half an hour later the President issued the formal call and within two hours after that 535 men and women were beginning to drive or fly back to Washington. It was a psychological move the President now considered necessary. Two weeks ago it had seemed advisable for his own concentration to have them off his hands for a bit. Now it suddenly seemed preferable from the standpoint of shoring up public concern and public support to have them back and to address them directly again on the crisis. He hoped the significance was not lost upon the world nor upon the one mind in the world that he desired most to impress: that of Yuri Pavlovich Serapin.

And indeed it was having an effect—but certainly not the one stupid H. Delbacher had hoped for, Yuri thought contemptuously as he too waited out the week's hiatus (destined to be shortened drastically by himself, though he had not thought of it then).

When the invitation had come from the three networks as soon as the President's address was announced, Yuri had immediately cancelled plans to fly home and had informed them that he would be delighted to appear. Nothing in the world could have been more helpful to his cause than this unexpected and really quite astounding offer to go over the President's head and speak directly to the American people and to the world.

The networks had reached the decision to invite him, so they announced in a joint statement, because they felt that "in this time of extreme crisis, it would be a profound public service to bring his views directly to the American people.

"Those views have been presented indirectly since the start of the crisis, particularly in the extensive coverage of the United Nations debates. Yet there is no substitute for a face-to-face presentation which only television is equipped to provide. President Serapin is one of the two most important leaders in the world today. The President of the United States will be addressing the Congress, the American people and the world. It seems to us both an obligation and also the highest form of public service to bring you as soon as possible thereafter the contrasting views of President Serapin, so that all may judge for themselves.

"Public service is the overriding purpose and duty of American television. We believe that we have always consistently maintained a high level of responsibility in that regard. It is in furtherance of that continuing responsibility that we have invited President Serapin to appear."

If the last paragraph sounded a trifle defensive, it was; and for a day or two there was a fairly sizable amount of the kind of criticism the networks had known they would receive. The usual reactionary fuddy-duddies, the usual foolish hysterical souls who persisted in believing that the Soviets meant exactly what they said about destroying America, were upset and alarmed by this voluntary, gratuitous offer of a worldwide public platform from which Yuri could propagandize his views. There was even a one-day sensation of a news story, purporting to quote "reliable sources within the agency," which claimed that the Administration, working through the Federal Communications Commission, had tried to bring pressure on the networks to cancel the invitation.

This story had been floated through Washington in the usual casual fashion, starting in the National Press Club bar, by the disinformation officer of the KGB at the Soviet Embassy. It had immediately been seized upon by the media. No proof was offered, because there was none; but it had done its effective bit to arouse suspicion of H. Delbacher and create sympathy for Y. P. Serapin. Leading editorials immediately denounced the FCC, impugned the President, praised the networks and hailed "the opportunity for President Serapin to present his views fairly and squarely to the American people."

"Squarely, all right," Ham Delbacher remarked dryly to Elinor. " 'Fairly' is quite another matter."

"They are so—so—" Elinor sputtered in helpless disgust, but fortunately he was able to shrug it off with a smile.

"I won't be tongue-tied, myself," he promised. Nor was he, when the time came.

Meanwhile, having arranged his appearance before Congress, he called in Roger Hackett and the Joint Chiefs of Staff and reviewed the military situation thoroughly once more before he sat down to prepare his speech. There was nothing new in their detailed overview of the world except that Soviet forces were, if possible, even more deeply entrenched and strategically positioned now than they had been at the time of the JCS's last full-scale report a week ago. All twenty-four subs were still in the Caribbean, of course, those in Nicaragua as combat-ready as before despite their move. The forces off Bombay and Tonga had been "withdrawn," as Yuri had promised they would be when brought under direct public pressure in the Security Council, but only a modest hundred miles out. They were still hovering around Hawaii, in the North Sea, the Mediterranean, the southern Indian Ocean, north and south Atlantic and their many other duty posts. Contrary to the good-natured but nonetheless genuinely worried concerns of the Anchorage *Times,* the JCS were well aware that another ten were regularly patrolling beneath the surface of the Bering Strait and above the Arctic Circle in the Beaufort Sea, within seconds' striking distance of the oilfields at Prudhoe Bay and the Alaska oil and gas pipelines.

And all through the Pacific and Indian Oceans, wherever there was a landfall, they surfaced, to be joined by the many battleships and aircraft carriers of what was now far and away the world's largest Navy, to make well publicized visits to independent island mini-states and remaining colonial dependencies. There was no excuse to deny them permission to land and no force to prevent them even if anyone wanted to. (As many, helpless in the face of overwhelming power, did.) The sight of smiling Soviet sailors, necks circled with flower leis, being greeted by excited throngs of happy brown-skinned natives, was now an almost nightly sight on television. It was great propaganda and a great bonus. The world, while still uneasy in many places, was more and more accustomed to the Soviet presence as an almost normal part of life.

In New York, Yuri's colleagues continued their diligent lobbying— their paths frequently crossing that of the Americans, who were doing the same—while he too worked with his military and diplomatic advisers on his speech. He had a good idea of what his antagonist would say, of course: their knowledge of one another's positions was by now quite comprehensive. He was able to block out the basic points he wished to offer in rebuttal. He did not know the specifics, so knew he would have to rely at times on his considerable skill at impromptu debate; but having defended himself so often in the Politburo, sometimes against really mortal challenges, he had no doubt of his ability to handle anything H. Delbacher might say. He also intended to arrange the opening few moments of his presentation in such a way that they would make much of his statement for him.

For the rest, he would rely on what he knew was his considerable charm and persuasiveness when face to face with Americans, or indeed anyone, who wished desperately to believe in his good will and peaceable intentions. This desperate desire *to believe* was what he counted upon, above all. H. Delbacher, he told himself with grim satisfaction, would have a long way to go ever to overtake him there. After some indecision, he had told the networks he wished to go on the air half an hour after the President concluded. This was a gamble, but he was confident he could handle it.

The President was scheduled to speak before Congress at 9 P.M. of the third evening after the Assembly adjourned. At 3 P.M. that afternoon the phone rang in the Soviet President's office and his secretary announced a familiar name, one of the very few who had standing permission to get through.

"Fabbie!" he exclaimed, thinking *What does the old bore want now?* but never forgetting for a second how very much Soviet successes were due to the fervent support of the capitalist Fabrizio Gulacks of the world.

"Excellency," Fabbie said—he was always very formal, though they had known one another for the better part of thirty years—"I know you have a great deal on your mind at this moment—"

"No, no," he said soothingly. "Not at all. My speech is prepared. I am ready for him."

"Good!" Fabbie said, and his tone was startlingly venomous for a moment. "I hope you are! I simply called to wish you luck. You deserve it."

"Thank you, Fabbie," Yuri said gravely.

"And I am very glad I was able to arrange it for you with the networks," Fabbie added firmly. "It's only fair."

"*Did* you!" Yuri exclaimed, quite startled. "I should have known you were responsible. How were you able to do that?"

"I have some friends in important places," Fabbie said, sounding satisfied with himself. "They owe me a few favors. Also, it *is* fair, and the networks, you know, have an innate sense of fairness. They have always been very fair to me. I have been on their shows many times. And I have always taken occasion to put in a good word for the country, too."

"I know you have, Fabbie," Yuri said, assessing correctly which country he meant. "And we are very, very grateful to you. In fact, I am thinking about possibly recommending you for a second Order of Lenin—"

"Oh, Comrade President!" Fabrizio Gulack cried, quite swept away. "How marvelous! Oh, I cannot thank you enough!"

"Nonsense," Yuri said with a jocular sternness. "Certainly no one deserves it more."

"Oh, I know," Fabbie said, "but still I am overwhelmed, Comrade President! I am positively overwhelmed!"

"As I am overwhelmed by your great generosity and foresight in arranging my appearance tonight," Yuri said smoothly. "*I* cannot thank *you* enough. It will permit me to answer his capitalist imperialist lies almost the moment they have left his mouth. It is a priceless opportunity."

"Yes, it is," Fabbie agreed solemnly. "He is *so* vicious in his lies, and *so* hostile to you. It makes peace virtually impossible."

"It doesn't make it easy."

"He was positively gloating after you left my apartment," Fabbie said angrily.

"Oh?" Yuri said. "What did he say?"

"It wasn't so much what he said," Fabbie told him. "It was his *attitude*. He was *most* disparaging of you. *Most*."

"Yes?" Yuri said, voice becoming cold. "I do not think so much of him, either."

"It was inexcusable," Fabbie said indignantly. "Absolutely inexcusable. I ordered him to leave at once."

"And did he?"

"Certainly. It's my house. But I thought his attitude horrible."

"It was very unpleasant to me," Yuri observed, and suddenly, beyond his power to control, his mind flooded with a blinding anger as he recalled the humiliations heaped upon him by his opponent, his contemptuous denunciations in public, even worse his personal attack in their private talk—his referring to him as a "monstrous man," the unforgivable comparison with the fascist murderer and enemy (after being ally and friend) of the Motherland, A. Hitler. It had been a wonder that he, Yuri,

had been able to be so shrewd and restrained in the calculated use of his
anger subsequently in the Security Council. But there, of course, he had
to be, as he must be tonight on television also. But he realized suddenly
and finally that this report from Fabbie was the last straw. There was no
need for further tolerance of any kind toward H. Delbacher.

It was obviously utterly futile to hope that the stupid fool could be persuaded to yield peaceably to history's inevitable decisions. He could only
be beaten down by sheer force because he understood nothing else.

He had no respect for history's imperatives. Much more unforgivable,
he had no respect for Yuri Serapin.

He was impossible to deal with, impossible to forgive. He had no place
in the new world coming. From the moment he took the oath of office as
President it had been inevitable that he would be the first to be eliminated when the United States surrendered. Now Yuri knew he would take
great pleasure in personally supervising his death. And, he told himself
with a mixture of anticipation and excitement that almost became sexual
for a second, it would not be an easy one.

He realized that Fabbie was concluding some comment which, in his
sudden rage, he had been unable to hear.

"—millions of us agree," Fabbie was saying.

"What?" Yuri asked. "I'm sorry, Fabbie, your earlier words revived my
most unpleasant memories of my talk with H. Delbacher. For a moment I
could think of nothing else."

"I can understand," Fabbie said with great sympathy. "He is an impossible man. I was saying that it will be a great pleasure and relief tonight
to hear your comments on world peace with which so many millions of us
agree. Someone must stop our impossible President. I think he must be
insane. Absolutely insane!"

"I am trying," Yuri said grimly.

"We shall be praying for you," Fabbie assured him fervently. "Millions
of sensible peace-loving Americans will be praying for you!"

"I shall try not to fail you," Yuri said with a nicely calculated note of
simple dignity. "My eternal thanks to you again for arranging my appearance. It could be a turning point for all of us."

"I hope so," Fabrizio Gulack said. "Oh, I *hope* so!"

And he hoped so too, Yuri thought grimly as the gushy old voice faded
away in burbling farewell. Because if it were, then it would not be long
before he could put into operation the concluding stage of his plans for
the launching of the final battle that would decide the fate of all mankind.
He was becoming impatient for this, he realized, which might or might
not be a good thing. It was so tantalizingly close; yet it must be done with
great precision and care.

As for his opponent, the last hours before he entered the long black
limousine that would take him swiftly along the national mile of Pennsyl-

vania Avenue where so many had passed before him in portentous cavalcade to Capitol Hill were spent with his wife. They dined alone at seven
in the family dining room on the second floor, then retired to the glassed-
in Truman Balcony for a final review of his speech.

How many times, he thought as he glanced over at the neat, spare
figure, the shrewd intelligent eyes, the still-beautiful face under its cap of
tightly curled gray hair—the wryly humorous "New England look"—had
he relied on Elinor in crucial moments of his career. How many, many
times.

A proposed appearance, a scheduled speech, a contemplated political
stand, a legislative decision, a television talk show—even, sometimes,
what to wear, how to act with certain people—he had sought her advice
on them all. Invariably he had found it to be sound. He had been born
with a sure political instinct and so had she. Both had been much developed by their years in public office. "Their" years because in a very real
sense they had always operated as a team and the voters of Pennsylvania
had always accepted them as such; "theirs" because love and compan-
ionship had steadily deepened to the point where they agreed on nearly
all major matters of state and family, knew each other's thoughts most of
the time, often anticipated each other's remarks, generally gave each
other the soundest advice that each received. Now in this climactic moment of his personal contest with Yuri Serapin for the collective mind of
humanity, he knew he needed to test his reactions against hers as he had
perhaps never needed to before.

He did not expect at this stage that she would suggest any major
amendments or additions, because he had consulted her steadily over the
past three days, as he had six others: Art Hampton, Herb Esplin, Jim
Elrod, Mark Coffin (because he liked his mind and felt he needed a
youthful view of things), Chauncey Baron and Roger Hackett. In separate talks, and once yesterday afternoon when they had all come down at
five for a general discussion and Elinor had joined them, they had gone
over the major points he wished to make, analyzing, suggesting, phrasing
and rephrasing in the search for the most effective possible presentation.

He had very briefly considered a formal protest to the networks when
they announced their invitation to Yuri, then had abandoned the idea at
once with the feeling that it would only increase Yuri's already certain
audience of millions—no, billions, since Yuri's speech, like his own,
would be carried worldwide by satellite. Instead he had settled only for a
single sentence when the KGB disinformation officer's "pressure on the
networks" story had surfaced in the New York and Washington papers.
The White House press secretary had said: "If the American networks
wish so generously to give the President of the Soviet Union worldwide
exposure for his attacks upon their country and upon the freedom which
makes their broadcasts possible, that is their privilege." This had

prompted lengthy and defensive editorial commentaries, all ordered directly from the executive offices, on the evening news shows. But since each one repeated the White House statement several times in the course of denouncing it, the President felt he had arranged a fair exchange.

After the final discussion yesterday afternoon, he had eaten a quiet supper with Elinor and then retired to the Lincoln Study with his portable typewriter and the two-finger peck he had picked up long ago, and had rapidly typed out his first draft. He had then edited it line by line in his neat printed script and sent it to his secretary, standing by in the Oval Office, for immediate transcription. An hour later it had come back to him and he had gone over it once more before retiring, making further word and line changes, shifting a paragraph here and there, underlining phrases and checking points that he wished to emphasize. The same process had occurred twice more this morning, after which he had practiced the speech three times and then laid it aside to tend to other business. At widely spaced intervals this afternoon he had run through it aloud three more times, then had laid it aside until he faced the Congress.

Now he handed it to Elinor and sat back to study that familiar face as its owner read quickly through the final draft of the words with which he hoped to place Yuri Pavlovich and his cold-blooded plans in the merciless perspective they deserved.

When Elinor finished reading, she placed the text beside her on the sofa from which she faced the Ellipse and the Washington Monument, folded her hands quietly in her lap and said nothing for a few moments. It looked hot outside, and it was. It had been a very warm day even for mid-August in Washington, and now the beautiful old trees on the South Lawn looked drab and almost wilted as they stood listlessly in the heavy humidity of the lingering twilight. Giant thunderheads were gathering in the west over Virginia, aflame with the last dying of the sun; possibly his address would be underscored by nature as dramatically as the Security Council meeting had been. It would be interesting and fitting if it were.

"Well?" he asked finally.

"You've added some new material."

"Yes."

"From whom, Major Valerian?"

"Yes. These were things he told me in our first talk."

"And Mark heard them too. Does he believe them?"

"He does."

"Will the country and the world?"

He frowned.

"That, my dear, is something I could not tell you. Do they believe me about anything? I don't know. And I can't stop to ask."

She smiled ruefully.

"No, that's for sure. If they do, it's a very effective speech. If they don't—"

"Then they don't. In any event, it has to be done."

"What do you think his response will be?"

"Just what it's been right along, I suppose. Indignation. Denial. Counter-attack. More lies. If those people ever told the truth it would be a rare day in suburban Siberia. But I don't think it's in them."

"I think many of them," she said, "undoubtedly the great majority, believe implicitly what their leaders say. After all, the truth has simply never been allowed to penetrate. They are born in the dark, live in the dark, die in the dark, except for those few diplomatic, scientific, athletic or professional people who are allowed a little travel and some slight glimpse of the Western world; and the KGB guards them like hawks and it's a few and far between who get away. So I suppose one can't blame them too much."

"I don't blame the Russian people," he said. "They're helpless, as you say. But I do blame the leaders like Yuri, because he's been here, he knows what the truth is, he's deliberately manipulating the ignorant in his own country and everywhere else. There may be a root of sincerity in his personal beliefs somewhere, but not when it comes to the United States. He knows us. He's spent a lifetime studying us—they all have, preparing for the great day when they think they're going to bring us down."

She reached out a hand and took his.

"Are they?" she asked quietly.

He sighed and stared for what seemed a long time out across the Ellipse at the Washington Monument, now lighted, a pure, untroubled, pristine needle soaring serenely against the glowering sky.

"I can't tell you," he said finally. "I just can't tell you . . . Not if I have anything to say about it—and I do. But how effective I can be if this situation continues much longer without a break—I don't know. I can't do it alone, that's for sure. I need the country behind me and allies behind me, and a weight of international pressure that will really make him stop and reconsider . . . If it isn't too late for him to do that . . . and that's a question, too."

"Well," she said. "No one can say you're not doing your best."

"I'm trying," he said with an almost rueful smile. "I'm sure as hell trying."

From the other side of the Mansion they could hear the first sounds of exhausts and motors revving up: members of the police motorcycle escort that would soon accompany them to the Hill were getting into formation in the front drive. Distantly also there came a puzzling and unexplained murmuring, as of many people.

She stood too, turned to face him, placed the master copy of his speech in his hands and then drew his head down to hers and kissed him firmly.

"Now," she said, with the unexpected, characteristic switch to jauntiness that always endeared her to him, "get in there and give 'em hell!"

"Yes, ma'am!" he said with a chuckle, feeling suddenly much better about things for no good reason except the one her presence and support always gave him. "I shall do me best."

Ten minutes later they were in the limousine, the motorcycle sirens were screaming, they were on their way to the Hill. As they swung out the East Gate and turned south to go around the Treasury into Pennsylvania Avenue, a most unexpected and touching sight greeted them. On both sides of the Avenue, five, ten, twenty deep in some places, their fellow citizens flanked the entire route. A great many were carrying flags which they waved at the Presidential party when it passed; and from start to end of their quick ten-minute ride down the Avenue, which had been cleared of all traffic for their passage, a continuing roll of cheers, shouts, whistles, applause kept them company. Many, no doubt, disagreed with him, many were worried and afraid; but the national instinct to support the President in time of crisis had brought them out to speed him on his way. Elinor was quite frankly crying when they reached the House side of the Capitol, and it was all he could do to maintain his own composure. The reception inside did not do much to help: hardly an inch of space left in the House chamber, so tightly were members, galleries and spectators packed in—hardly a dry eye in the house, as he told himself in an attempt to hold onto steadying humor, as everyone rose with a great, prolonged roar of welcome and support.

When Elinor had been safely seated in the Family Gallery with Lyddie Bates, Linda Coffin and Art Hampton's daughter Jane, who would be his official hostess; and after he himself had been formally introduced by the Doorkeeper and the Speaker, and the great roar of greeting had been repeated in the set, traditional way, he stood for a moment looking thoughtfully up at the television cameras that peered down from the galleries; a tall, heavy, dignified, pleasant-faced man, obviously troubled, but also obviously undaunted. The moment was intensely dramatic, but he knew he was not. Just plain old homespun Ham Delbacher, he told himself with a recurrence of wry self-humor—but exactly what his country needed at this particular moment of this particular time.

When the cheering and applause had finally died down and the members of Senate and House, Supreme Court, Cabinet, JCS, diplomatic corps, relatives and spectators had resumed their seats and the chamber had settled into a tense and waiting silence, he turned and shook hands gravely with the Speaker of the House and the President Pro Tempore of the Senate. Then he turned back to the lectern and opened the black folder containing his speech.

"Members of the Congress," he said quietly, "my fellow countrymen and all those everywhere on earth who may be watching or listening at this moment.

"The American nation meets tonight to take counsel together on what is certainly the most serious challenge we have faced since the founding of the Republic, more than two hundred years ago. It is a challenge that goes directly to our life as a free people; to the beliefs and principles upon which our country was founded and by which we strive, however imperfectly, to live; and to the fundamental freedom without which all human life becomes barren and sterile, and Earth a mere dot of animation drifting without love or beauty through the universe.

"This challenge is posed by another power, the Soviet Union, whose beliefs and principles are the direct antithesis of ours; whose ultimate, unchanging, freely expressed goal is our own destruction as a free nation and its own final dominance over all the nations of the earth; and whose leaders desire and actively seek to obtain the complete and final exchange of the diversity and independence of the free mind and the free spirit for the rigidly controlled slave mentality and slave life that have for almost seventy years been the fate of the unhappy Soviet peoples and the peoples of their satellite and captive fellow communist states.

"One nation, and one only, stands in the way of this, and that is the American nation. Others may want to, others may wish to contribute strength and co-operation to the common cause of thwarting Soviet designs and preserving freedom in the world, and their assistance we welcome eagerly and always. But that alone is not decisive. In the final analysis there is just one nation the Soviets *must* destroy if they are to achieve their mad dream of universal and perpetual conquest. And that is our own.

"You are all familiar with events of recent weeks which have occurred since the death of the late President and my own accession to office. My term began with an invitation from the President of the Soviet Union, Yuri Serapin, who after many years of training as a rigid communist ideologue and a murderous contestant in the jungle world of the Kremlin hierarchy, finally achieved his personal goal of becoming President of the Soviet Union just days ahead of my own oath-taking.

"We met, as you know, at the United Nations in New York. We talked —or rather, he did, mostly—of how invincible and overwhelming the Soviet military machine is and how I should quickly and voluntarily surrender the independence of the United States and any hopes there might be of saving the independence of the free world. His threats did not impress me and I told him so.

"And so we parted, not amicably: and you are all familiar with the events since then which have culminated in the meeting of the United Nations General Assembly, now in temporary recess. Both nations have introduced resolutions condemning one another and asking United Nations support in opposing what each regards as the peace-threatening activities of the other.

"Around the world Soviet maneuvers go on, and here we continue our arms build-up, our national emergency and our hopes that sanity may yet prevail in the world so that the Soviet conquest may be first halted, then turned back, then sensibly abandoned.

"Otherwise," he said, and his face and voice were somber, "the prospects for both of us, and for humanity in general, are bleak."

He paused and took a sip of water. He had received no applause so far and had expected none. There had been almost no interruption, save an occasional murmur at the bluntness of his language, to break the intent silence of the chamber. He was not surprised that his bluntness startled them: he intended it to, and he hoped it was also startling and giving pause to the one individual among the world's billions to whom his words were most particularly addressed.

"They are bleak," he resumed, "because the Soviet plans for what they like to refer to as 'the final battle that will decide the fate of all mankind' between communism and the free nations do not stop with the maneuvers now in being. They extend beyond that."

He paused, flipped the pages in his folder, extricated a manila envelope, held it up. Now the chamber was swept by a surprised and buzzing excitement, the television cameras zoomed eagerly in.

"In this envelope," he said, "are the official Soviet plans for what they refer to herein as 'the maneuver beyond the maneuvers.'

"They envisage the deliberate creation of an incident which will give them the excuse to close immediately all the major waterways of the earth, thus stopping world commerce dead in its tracks and instantly halting the flow of necessary fuel and food to the United States and to all other still independent powers."

There was a gasp, commingled of shock and disbelief, and he knew it was echoed a billion-fold around the globe. So he went on as he had intended, in a firm and quiet voice.

"These papers will be released to the media immediately upon the conclusion of my address, so that all of you, believers and skeptics alike, may judge for yourselves. There is no purpose of invention here, and no intention on the part of *this* President to conceal. These papers come from a source the Government of the United States believes to be reliable, and we give them credence.

"If we are correct in this conclusion," he said slowly, "and if such an incident occurs—and if it is then followed by an attempt to thus strangle the United States and the remaining independent nations of the world— there can be only one result."

He paused again, face set, suddenly no longer the kindly grandfather but a stern, implacable man.

"We must—and we will—retaliate. The consequences, I leave you to imagine . . ."

And yet again he paused, while a shuddering murmur of talk and consternation passed through the chamber.

He replaced the envelope, closed the folder, put it aside, leaned forward earnestly to conclude.

"My friends of the Congress, my fellow countrymen, men of sanity and intelligence everywhere—I appeal to you.

"The United Nations General Assembly is to reconvene in four more days. It is in many ways a fragile and unsatisfactory instrument, yet it is the only one we have for mobilizing, in one place and with one voice, the collective conscience of humanity. We *must* pass a resolution condemning Soviet imperialism. We *must* pass a resolution calling for the end of the maneuvers and the restoration of a peace-saving balance in the world. We *must* pass a resolution demanding the withdrawal of Soviet forces to their own borders. We *must* pass a resolution demanding an end permanently to Soviet adventurism and the insatiable outward thrust of Soviet conquest.

"In return for these things I am prepared to pledge a drastic curtailment in the emergency arms build-up of the United States; an end to the state of national emergency; a termination of the war alert, a cancellation of the ultimatum concerning Soviet submarines, since under the conditions I propose the Soviet subs will no longer be there. I am prepared then to move on at once, within the framework of the United Nations, or in whatever general forum the nations may wish to set up, to a general disarmament program, mutual guarantees for maintaining all borders, the right of self-determination and independence for *all,* a universal permanent peace guaranteed by *all.*

"These are the things that sane men everywhere desire. The first and immediate place in which to establish them is the UN General Assembly already scheduled to reconvene. I return to New York to fight for these things. I appeal to men of good will everywhere to join me in this task."

He picked up the folder, turned and shook hands once again with the Speaker and the President Pro Tem; the chamber erupted in warm, generous, overwhelmingly approving applause. He smiled and waved to Elinor, Lyddie and Jane in the Family Gallery, started slowly down the steps. Outthrust hands grabbed for his as he went up the aisle, enthusiastic congratulatory thumps besieged his back. As he left the chamber members and guests were still standing, wildly applauding; on television screens across the globe the American flag rippled against a cloudless sky to the portentous strains of the national anthem. He remarked to Elinor when she and Lyddie—whom they had invited, along with Art and his daughter, to come back to the White House to listen to Yuri's speech with them —that he thought he had given him a few obstacles to overcome in capturing world support. His own exposure of Soviet aggressive plans plus his offer to curtail the American arms build-up and his call for a general disarmament conference would give Yuri a tough lead to overcome.

"Not that I doubt that he can do it, you understand," he said as they drove back down the Avenue past even greater crowds than before. (The thunderstorm had miraculously held off, to hit with a bang half an hour later, about midway in Yuri's talk, which was possibly more fitting.) A television set had been brought to the Truman Balcony, and to it they speedily repaired when they reached the Mansion. There was just time for one of the butlers and his wife to bring in sandwiches and for the President to mix drinks for himself and Art and pour wine for Elinor, Lyddie and Jane, when the last instant analyst of the networks concluded his interpretation of what the President had said. The screen went dark for a moment. The silence was followed by a hushed voice announcing, "Ladies and gentlemen, we bring you an address by the President of the Soviet Union." This was followed by Yuri's own choice for an opening.

In the Truman Balcony they concluded with sudden relief, and a delighted crow of laughter from Lyddie, that in contrast to the President's concluding remarks, Yuri had not made a very good choice. But this was only their opinion. It would not be known until the reconvening of the General Assembly, probably, whether Yuri's approach or the President's had been more effective with the country and the world.

First came a long shot of a Soviet aircraft carrier, escorted by a dozen battleships, plowing some distant sea. Next, a blur of Soviet jets flashing across the screen. Next, Soviet tanks rolling full-tilt across an open field somewhere in Eastern Europe. Next, a Soviet missile roaring off the pad (thoughtfully labeled "TEST LAUNCH ONLY" to reassure the nervous while intimidating the timid). Next, a shot of the newest Salyut space station. (There were now ten in orbit around the earth, carrying God—or the devil—knew what. Missiles armed with poison gas and bacterial agents, U.S. intelligence sources believed.) Two cosmonauts waved and grinned broadly. Next, a long shot of several troop divisions marching stern-faced through an ancient unidentified city square. ("Kabul?" Art Hampton asked dryly, "or Prague?" The President responded with equal dryness: "They believe in foreign travel. It could be anywhere.") Finally in the distance, a Soviet warship standing off a palm-fringed island; close up, the island's grinning inhabitants greeting with leis and kisses smiling Soviet sailors who jumped onto the sand from a gently rocking motor launch. And at last, fading slowly in as the joyous meeting of brave young heroes from the steppes and dusky willing maidens from some sunny clime faded slowly out, the earnest, thoughtful, open-faced and

guileless visage of the President of the Soviet Union, statesman, philosopher, friend to all mankind—except, as he speedily made clear, the President of the United States.

"Good evening, my friends of America," he said in his heavy accent,
with a pleasant smile. "Good evening, peace-loving peoples of the world.
I hope you all have just listened to the speech of the President of the
United States to Congress because"—and abruptly the smile was gone, a
somber earnestness took its place—"it is to his not very accurate remarks
that I wish to reply tonight.

"Yes, my friends, not very accurate. Not accurate at all. Coming very
close, in fact, to the deliberate lies of which he is always accusing me.
And certainly no contribution to world peace nor to a solution of the crisis which his own inexperienced fears and impulsive overreactions have
brought upon the world.

"There have been so many versions"—the smile returned, briefly—
"*so* many versions of our initial meeting in New York, that I must, as you
say in this beautiful country where I spent four most pleasant years in our
Embassy in Washington, set the record straight. I know Americans, as I
know the peoples of the world, and I know they are honest and they want
honest talk. You can tell them the truth but you cannot tell them lies. Yet
their own President seems unaware of this! He does not know this! It is
amazing. And it is frightening. He has so much power to destroy the world.

"We met and talked in New York, yes. I pointed out to him certain
facts concerning comparative military strengths of the United States and
the Soviet Union. I explained why the Soviet Union in recent years has
increased its strengths to a point where the correlation of forces weighs
heavily, now, in our favor. I placed the responsibility for this squarely
where it belongs, upon the imperialist adventurism of the United States
military-industrial complex. I said the truth: if we did not fear constant
U.S. expansionism and pressure, constant U.S. plots against world peace
and the well-being of freedom-loving peoples everywhere, we would not
have felt the necessity to increase our armed forces to their present
overwhelming strength. If we felt for one moment that we could trust the
word of the U. S. Government or the U. S. President—who do not, I am
afraid, truly represent the honest and truthful American people—then we
would have no such need. But, my friends, how can we, after the record
of recent decades? How is it possible?"

["Oh, dear, poor puzzled fellow!" Elinor exclaimed. "How difficult it all
is for him!"]

["He's a liar," Lyddie Bates said emphatically. "But a mighty shrewd
one."]

["Yes," Ham Delbacher agreed, "and there's our problem."]

"My friends of America," Yuri said earnestly, "and peace-loving peoples everywhere, it is only because of U.S. racist imperialist adventures

that we have built up our strength. It is to protect ourselves—*and to pro-tect you*—that we have far outstripped the declining military forces of the United States. The socialist bloc rejects entirely the concept of 'world po-liceman' which imperialist ruling circles of the United States are con-stantly trying to take for themselves. But we do feel that there is a need for a shield—a world shield of peace, you might call it—"

["You might," the President agreed.]

"—against the imperialist racist war-mongers of the United States.

"That shield of peace," Yuri said—and if it was possible for him to look any more earnest, he managed—"we gladly provide for all peace-loving, peoples. Even you, my friends of America."

["How's that?" Art Hampton asked. Ham Delbacher raised a caution-ing hand.

["Wait. It will all become clear."]

"I say that," Yuri said, "because I know from the many, many expres-sions of support I have received in these recent days that many Ameri-cans—a *great many* Americans—are very disturbed and upset by the strange course followed by President Delbacher. They do not understand him. They are terrified of his adventurism. To them he is a bringer of war, not the defender of peace he just tonight again proclaimed himself to be. They wish to oppose his course, but they are helpless.

"I say to them, and to you, peace-loving peoples of the world: Do not be afraid, because the Soviet shield of peace is so strong that not even Mr. Delbacher can push it aside. He can strike against it but he cannot move it. It is too strong for him. So he will presently have to recognize that he cannot start a war just because he does not like me. He will real-ize that he must make peace with us and co-operate with us, as all peace-loving peoples everywhere know they must do if war is to be banished forever from the earth. This is what all people want. We promise it to you, even to President Delbacher. But he must stop his reckless peace-threatening reactions against us if this is to be the case.

"He told you tonight that I threatened him with Soviet arms if he did not 'surrender' the United States to us. How absurd! How ridiculous! Who can believe it? Instead, he threatened *us,* my friends. And he went straight home and proved he meant it, by ordering the enormous emer-gency build-up of American arms which is only just beginning and which cannot, in fact, be ready in time to stop us—if," he added smoothly, "there were any slightest truth to his fears that we are somehow going to try to 'overthrow' the United States and 'conquer the world.'

"It is true, yes, that I did use the word 'overthrow' in the resolution I presented to the United Nations Security Council, but that was only a gesture on my part because I wanted to try to put some sense into the worried brain of this new President who seems so afraid of us. Is anyone else in the world so afraid of the Soviet Union as your new President? If so, let him step forward and say so. We are reasonable people! We will offer him some vodka and we will all laugh about it! I only wish," he said, and actually looked a little wistful, "that Mr. Delbacher could be so easily persuaded to calm his fears. A drink of our Russian vodka might be a great help to him!"

And he chuckled heartily for a moment before resuming in a comfortable, reassuring tone.

"No, I just used the word 'overthrow' to try to bring Mr. Delbacher to his senses. I knew, of course, that no such resolution could pass the Security Council. I knew the United States would veto it if it came to a vote, and anyway, I intended to withdraw it at that moment. I just hoped to show Mr. Delbacher how foolish it all was. 'Overthrow'! Who could possibly overthrow the United States? It is crazy, my friends. Absolutely crazy!

"But Mr. Delbacher has gone all the way with *his* craziness. Arms races, national emergencies, war alerts, ultimatums about Soviet submarines, which Cuba has an absolute sovereign right to request from us and which we have an absolute sovereign right to furnish to them. These are Mr. Delbacher's crazinesses. You do not hear him talk much about his responsibility for them. He just blames them all on us. How easy, how convenient! What would he and other war-loving American leaders do without us! They would have nothing to justify their own threats to peace.

"So Mr. Delbacher neatly turns the world upside down and the face of the villain changes. Suddenly it is the Soviet Union, and Mr. Delbacher is completely innocent. And then he tops it all by disclosing a big secret to the world: now we are plotting to create an incident and close the waterways of the world so that the helpless United States and its allies in the imperialist camp cannot even get a drop of oil or a crumb of bread. We are going to do all that! Does Mr. Delbacher realize how many planes, ships, troops it would take to do that? Does he realize what an effort it would be, even for the Soviet Union, which is now the world's greatest power—as well as its greatest shield of peace? And does he not realize how much fuel our present maneuvers, which are necessary to stop the spread of military-industrial adventurism in United States circles, are costing us? I will tell you frankly, my friends"—and he did look very frank—"it may be necessary to curtail these maneuvers very soon—"

["He's going to back down," Elinor said excitedly. "He's going to back down!"

["Maybe," her husband said skeptically. "May be."]

"—because of just exactly this cost in fuel and material. *Our* fuel supplies, too, are not so perfect as we would like them to be. We are in better position than the United States, yes, because we have loyal peace-loving allies in Iran, Saudi Arabia and other Persian Gulf states with whom we have established close friendly ties in recent years—but we still do not own the world's oil, though Mr. Delbacher seems to think so, with his scare stories about shutting world waterways. We would not expend our supplies on such nonsense even if we wanted to. I have learned from news reports just in the last few minutes that Mr. Delbacher has apparently given the press some so-called 'documents' very cleverly forged by the CIA about all this. That does not prove anything except that the CIA has some clever forgers on its staff. The documents are nonsense. They mean nothing. What is easier to forge than documents? What is easier to use for this purpose than the CIA?"

["And what is easier to smear than the CIA," Art Hampton inquired, "since our own people have done so much to create automatic suspicion of it everywhere?"]

"No, my friends," Yuri said, "do not believe these fantasies dreamed up by the CIA. Do not be taken in by forged documents or the worried dreams of President Delbacher. Water will still run through the Strait of Gibraltar, the Panama Canal, Suez. We will not drown ourselves trying to turn them off. Do not be afraid, President Delbacher! You will still get your feet wet if you step in them! Though if you did"—and for a moment he let his eyes and voice and face grow cold—"we might then find it necessary to use our shield of peace to pull you out and dry you off and send you back to North America, which is the only place where America belongs. It does not belong out in the rest of the world, trying to start imperialist adventures damaging the chances of world peace for which the Soviet Motherland has always fought and for which it will continue to fight until all threateners have been sent packing!

"May I conclude, however, by astounding President Delbacher? I am going to agree with him. If he will really stop the emergency arms build-up he has ordered—if he will really cancel emergencies and alerts and ultimatums where he has no business giving ultimatums—if he will really abandon adventurism and place America truly in the peace-loving camp —then I will be more than happy to join him in a world disarmament conference. We have always advocated this, for many, many years. His approval is a little late, but we applaud it. I will also be happy to join him in guaranteeing borders, protecting the independence of all freedom-loving peoples, establishing a guaranteed and lasting peace.

"What else has the Soviet Union ever advocated? What else have we ever done?"

["He is unbelievable," Jane Hampton said in a wondering voice. "But," her father said grimly, "many will believe."]

"Join me, President Delbacher!" Yuri exclaimed fervently, leaning forward into the cameras and releasing all the force of an extremely forceful personality. "Join me in the great struggle for world peace! You are the only obstacle! Stop your futile attempts to blame me, give up your dreams of conquest! Join me for peace, Mr. President! Join me and together let us free the world from fear—forever!"

And he sat slowly back, the "Internationale" thundered out as ponderously across the world as "The Star-Spangled Banner" had done and slowly, slowly, his earnest face—frank, open, honest—faded, still supplicating, from the screen.

For a long moment there was silence in the Truman Balcony.

Finally Hamilton Delbacher gave a prolonged and heavy sigh.

"That," he said softly, "is a hard act to follow . . . But, God *damn* it!" he added with a rising anger, "*somewhere* in this God damned topsy-turvy, messed-up world we live in there must be *some* place for the truth!"

But for the moment, feeling, like the world, the impact of his antagonist's virtuoso performance, he was not very sure exactly where it was.

Next morning reaction from America and the world showed him that it was not in many places. Both he and Yuri were given much credit from influential sources for their desire for peace, but from very, very few did there come the clear, unequivocal endorsement of his own position that he had hoped to secure a short few hours ago when he and Elinor had traveled through cheering throngs up the Hill he knew and loved so well to appear before the Congress of the United States. And from very few did there come much attempt to put the claims and assertions of the Soviet President into perspective with the facts.

"We cannot help but admire, even though we also deplore, the skillful manner in which President Serapin last night responded to the address of President Delbacher to the Congress," the New York *Times* said. "There may have been some spurious claims made by Mr. Serapin, some assertions of Soviet purity and disinterest that do not jibe exactly with what is going on in the world, but over-all, the force and effectiveness of his presentation are hard to discount.

"Unhappily, the assertions by President Delbacher of Soviet intentions and general duplicity seem equally hard to accept at full face value. We do not agree with President Serapin that the President of the United States is a 'war-monger' or a leader of the so-called 'military-industrial complex' in 'imperialist adventurism,' as President Serapin phrased it in typical Soviet fashion. But neither can we really accept President Delbacher's claims that the ultimate Soviet goals are the 'overthrow' of this country and the 'dominance' of the world. To some extent we agree with Mr. Serapin that this shows an exaggerated fear of Soviet aims on the part of Mr. Delbacher.

"The end result, in our opinion, is to give neither President the best of the argument, and to leave unanswered the question of which has the better right to claim the world's support in the confrontation which still, after more than a month, hangs unresolved over the world.

"As for President Delbacher's claim that the Soviets intended to create an incident that would give them excuse to close off the world's principal waterways, we find ourselves unable to avoid something of the skepticism with which President Serapin treated this. Not only would this be an impossible task for even the world's mightiest military machine—which we do not think the Soviet Union is, despite its President's boast—but when Mr. Delbacher offers so-called 'documents' to back up his statements, we, like Mr. Serapin, grow suspicious. The media has examined these documents very thoroughly since they were released following the President's speech. They appear authentic, but as Mr. Serapin says, the CIA is very good at forging documents. A serious doubt of their authenticity remains.

"To both Presidents, however, we must give congratulations for their apparent agreement that the crisis should be defused, that a general disarmament conference should be held, and that there should be universal guarantees of borders, self-determination and peace for all nations. It is true that President Delbacher went much further than President Serapin —there was no offer of Soviet withdrawal or 'curtailment' of arms such as the Chief Executive offered for American arms—but there seemed an equal sincerity in agreeing upon the peaceable course proposed by President Delbacher. For that, we think both leaders deserve the support and gratitude of the world . . ."

"If we were to judge the results of last night's long distance debate between Presidents Delbacher and Serapin," the Washington *Post* said, "we would have to give the edge to the Soviet leader, even though Mr. Delbacher spoke with a directness and sincerity that in some places did not seem to be present in the more pyrotechnic remarks of Mr. Serapin.

"Nonetheless, Mr. Serapin made points which to us seem valid. We agree with him that President Delbacher has overreacted to worldwide maneuvers which the Soviet Union has every right to conduct. We agree that he has been much too strong in his response to the perfectly legitimate stationing in Cuba of Soviet submarines whose presence is sanctioned by many years of tacit acceptance by this government and which are there at Cuba's sovereign request. We think his hasty and—given the length of time required—rather pointless 'emergency build-up' of American arms has only inflamed the situation. We think his claim that the Soviet Union wishes to 'overthrow' this country and exercise 'dominance' over the world has long since been discredited by every reasonable and non-hysteric American—as it has now again been discredited by Mr. Serapin himself. And we, like Mr. Serapin, remain highly skeptical of documents purporting to show Soviet plans for an adventure so enormous in size, and so impossible of achievement, as the closing of world waterways. Nor are we disposed to be any less suspicious than he of the possible influence of the CIA—which no one can prove, but which in many minds will take more than White House denials to disprove.

"At the same time, however, we cannot accept all of Mr. Serapin's assertions about American 'imperialist aggression,' Mr. Delbacher's alleged 'war-mongering' or the claim that the Soviet Union's own enormous military build-up in recent years has been solely for the purpose of providing a benevolent 'shield of peace' for the world. That may be the sincere and ultimate goal, but along the way the leaders of the Kremlin have occasionally given way to the temptation to use it for other, more sinister purposes. There seemed to us a certain disingenuousness about Mr. Serapin's remarks in this regard; although over-all his presentation clearly showed a sincere devotion to the ideal of world peace and stability that matched Mr. Delbacher's own.

"In any event, it was good to find both Presidents in agreement on the need for general world disarmament, the self-determination of nations, the guarantee of borders and the guarantee of peace. Perhaps starting from there it will be possible, first through the United Nations General Assembly when it reconvenes on the crisis, and through some more general forum later, to arrive at that goal of lasting accommodation and harmony that all nations desire . . ."

Only a few voices put matters in the perspective Hamilton Delbacher had hoped to see. One of these was the *Post*'s own political columnist:

"In judging the statements of the American and Soviet Presidents last night," he wrote, "certain significant items should not be forgotten:

"1. Mr. Serapin's generous explanation of the enormous Soviet military build-up of recent years—that it was designed partly to protect the homeland but even more to create a 'shield of peace' for the world—must be placed against such things as Afghanistan, Ethiopia, Angola, Nicaragua, El Salvador, South Yemen, Iran and a whole further cavalcade of formerly independent nations who today are the unhappy victims of Soviet outward expansion far beyond the homeland and far beyond the bounds of 'lasting peace.'

"2. Mr. Serapin's assertion that Mr. Delbacher '*must* make peace with us and co-operate with us, as all peace-loving peoples *know they must do* if war is to be banished forever from the earth [italics added].' It seems fair to point out that the Soviet definition of peace is *peace on Soviet terms,* and that in the minds of Mr. Serapin and his Kremlin colleagues, it is obviously all other nations who *must* 'make peace with and co-operate with' the Soviet Union, not vice versa.

"3. Those of us who covered the United Nations Security Council debate in which Mr. Serapin introduced his resolution to 'overthrow' the

United States were not aware of the jocular, cautionary purpose of it which he so cleverly described last night. It seemed dead serious at the time.

"4. Mr. Serapin described the difficulties his worldwide forces are having with fuel and said the Soviet maneuvers 'may' have to be curtailed because of this. He did not, however, say they would be.

"5. Mr. Serapin pulled out an old chestnut—the CIA—to discredit the documents President Delbacher released last night. The suspicion of forgery may or may not be legitimate. Nonetheless, the mention of the CIA automatically guaranteed disbelief on the part of many, and absolved the Soviet Union automatically in their minds of any charges that they would deliberately create an incident to permit certain lines of military action. History does not discredit this idea as cleverly and conclusively as Mr. Serapin was able to do with three magic initials.

"6. Mr. Serapin, though he purported to embrace President Delbacher's call for general disarmament and other steps to guarantee world peace, in no way matched the President's offer to dismantle military forces and cancel preparatory moves. There was no slightest pledge of Soviet withdrawal or reduction in Soviet forces.

"Mr. Serapin's performance was an extraordinarily skillful exercise in propagandizing American and world opinion. Mr. Delbacher's was an earnest attempt to place the truth before the country and the world. If this were an Academy Award contest, Mr. Serapin would take the Oscar. Unfortunately the prize is very much greater than that—and it appears Mr. Serapin may still take the Oscar if his statements are not matched against his policies, and his policies against the preservation and survival of individual freedom and world peace."

Which, the President thought, was a fair statement of it; but, then, it agreed with him, and that was probably why.

Comments from world leaders were more cautious than those of most of the world media, and split along predictable lines. The inevitable disagreement between the statements of the British and Indian Prime Ministers was indicative of how it went right down the line.

Of major leaders, only Ju Xing-dao refused all comment whatsoever, which left both Soviet and American Presidents in a state of considerable puzzlement. This, they knew, was the intention; and since there were indications that many of the "Third world" nations would follow Ju's lead in the Assembly, both felt they must approach him once again.

He remained elusive until the night before the Assembly reconvened, at which time he came with great secrecy to see them both. With both he proved equally obscure and tantalizing; until almost midnight, when he telephoned one of them back and in extremely guarded terms hinted to him of a future much different than he had seriously considered or planned for.

Three hours later this became a fundamental factor in all events and calculations when, in a thousand drowsing newsrooms, wire-service news tickers suddenly went wild with a

FLASH—RED SUB DOWNS U.S. PLANE.

followed in ten minutes by a more complete

BULLETIN—MOSCOW CLAIMS U.S. "SPY PLANE" DOWNED BY RED SUB IN INDIAN OCEAN.

and half an hour later by another

BULLETIN—SERAPIN CHARGES U.S. SPY PLANE "VIOLATES AIR SPACE OF SOVIET MANEUVERS" AS RED SUB DOWNS JET NEAR DIEGO GARCIA.

and half an hour after that by yet another

BULLETIN—WASHINGTON SAYS RED SUB USED TACTICAL NUCLEAR WEAPON TO DOWN U.S. JET. SEVEN CREWMEN LOST.

and finally, at 5 A.M., the night's last and perhaps most fateful

FLASH—PRESIDENT TELLS U.S. FORCES: "IF APPROACHED BY ANY SOVIET FORCE, SHOOT ON SIGHT."

3

"Disinformation: Propagation of false information about one's forces and plans of action for the purpose of misleading the enemy. Means of disinformation may be: radio, press, simulated troop relocations, etc."

—*Soviet Dictionary of Basic Military Terms*

And so, at 3 P.M. that afternoon, the General Assembly reconvened with considerably more on its mind than just what suddenly seemed to be a rather minor crisis—Soviet maneuvers and American reaction—when placed beside an extremely major crisis—an actual exchange of fire, with resultant American casualties, between the two superpowers.

And an ultimatum that *was* an ultimatum from the President of the United States.

For once in its rather casual career, nobody in the Assembly was late for the meeting. Not only was Libya able to crash down his gavel exactly at three, but every single delegation had been in its place for half an hour impatiently waiting for him to do so. The galleries and press section were filled and overfilled, the television cameras swooped and snooped incessantly from face to face, the translators cleared their throats nervously, an almost physically painful miasma of tension and excitement gripped everyone. A constant buzz of conversation, nervous, agonized, fearfully dismayed yet somehow deliciously apprehensive, filled the chamber. What *would* happen now? What *could* keep the world from blowing up?

In the time between 2:30 and 2:55 P.M., only two major figures were absent; and they, of course, were the two that everyone wanted to see. Not by agreement but simply on the basis of separate but equally shrewd judgments of effect, neither Hamilton Delbacher nor Yuri Serapin had entered with their grim-faced delegations. Their mutual absence gave rise to the wildest rumors, which swept the hall in a constant stream, crisscrossing the floor from delegation to delegation with a speed not quite that of light but seeming almost to approach it. They were having a secret meeting—they were refusing to have a secret meeting—Serapin had returned to Moscow—Delbacher had returned to Washington—Serapin had issued exactly the same order to his forces that Delbacher had given to his—Delbacher had reconsidered and withdrawn his order—Serapin had reconsidered and ordered cancellation of the maneuvers—Congress was in revolt against Delbacher—the Politburo was about to censure Serapin—and on and on. At least twenty-five rumors for twenty-five minutes, only one of which, as it turned out, was true; or "true."

Finally, just as the clock neared 2:58 and it seemed that no one could physically take any more rumors or any more tension, there was an excited stir in the area to the left behind the podium, and from it there emerged the short, stolid figure of the President of the Soviet Union, followed exactly one minute later by the tall, somber figure of the President of the United States. This time there was no applause, no cheering or booing, no greeting of any kind for either. Absolute silence held the chamber as first Yuri, then Ham Delbacher, both staring straight ahead without expression, came up the aisle to their respective delegations, turned and bowed to the Chair, and took their seats, a scant few feet apart.

A great cumulative sigh of held-in breath and pent-up emotion broke the stillness. Seconds later Libya brought down the gavel.

"Members of the Assembly," he said, voice trembling slightly, "this emergency session on the Soviet-U.S. crisis is now reconvened." He paused and cleared his throat nervously. "As you all know, it is now a somewhat different crisis—a *much* different crisis, and in some ways a much more serious one . . . In view of that," he paused again and again cleared his throat, unable to rid it of its burden of choked excitement, "the Secretary-General and I have decided—somewhat arbitrarily, but I hope the Assembly will agree—to put aside, at least temporarily, the list of speakers previously scheduled for this day. Instead, if agreeable, I should like to call first upon the President of the United States, as the aggrieved party—"

Yuri slapped his palm, suddenly and hard, on the table. Without exception, everyone jumped.

"Mr. President," he cried, "I object! The Soviet Union objects! *We* are the aggrieved party. *We—*"

But for once he had lost his friend in Libya, and Libya, unmoved, stood his ground.

"—upon the President of the United States as the aggrieved party," he repeated, voice growing stronger. *"Then* upon the President of the Soviet Union, to respond. And then upon the Prime Ministers of Britain and India, who have been so active in seeking a solution to the over-all crisis. And then upon the Vice Premier of China, who also has been very active. After that, we will resume the list of previous requests for time. Is that agreeable to the Assembly?"

He looked defiantly first at Yuri and then out upon his fellow delegates; and with a great and unanimous shout of *"Yes!"* the Assembly responded.

"Very well," he said with a new-found strength from such support,
while Yuri glowered, just on the thin edge of open theatricality, around
the room—"that is the Assembly's will, and that is how we will proceed.
Mr. President Delbacher, will you come forward, please."

Again the room stirred with excitement, then became tensely quiet as
the President stood up slowly, accepted a document from Roger Hackett,
another from Chauncey Baron, and walked slowly down the aisle. A
whisper or two, a nervous cough here and there—nothing else broke the
silence as he reached the podium, bowed to Libya and the Secretary-
General, climbed the steps to the lectern, placed the two documents
neatly before him, looked out impassively for a moment across the room
and then began to speak.

"Mr. President," he said, "Mr. Secretary-General, members of the Assembly:

"At 1400 yesterday afternoon, local time, 0200 our time, a routine observation flight consisting of one small unarmed jet plane was launched
from the deck of the United States aircraft carrier *Harry S. Truman* near
the island of Diego Garcia in the Indian Ocean. It carried a crew of
seven.

"The purpose of this mission was to maintain eye and radar contact
with a sizable force of Soviet battleships and submarines conducting maneuvers some one hundred and fifty miles south of the island and approximately one hundred miles east of the carrier.

"The mission was a continuation of routine contact flights which were
begun three weeks ago and have continued hourly around the clock ever
since. No Soviet objection has ever been raised to these flights.

"Personnel on this particular mission, as on all previous missions, were
instructed specifically that they were in no way to approach, overfly or
otherwise interfere with the Soviet force. Their purpose was to be strictly
and entirely one of observation.

"Pursuant to these orders, the American jet flew to within approximately ten miles of the Soviet force, having previously notified the Soviet
commander, Admiral Viktor C. Golovin, that it intended to do so, and
was on a routine, peaceful observation flight. Admiral Golovin did not at
first respond.

"Pursuant to orders, the jet circled the Soviet force, which was riding at
anchor with no planes in the air, at an approximate distance of ten miles.
The jet was moving at a slow rate of speed as indication of peaceful intent and it was reporting constantly to the *Truman.* No hostile reaction
was evidenced by the Soviet force. In fact, at the conclusion of the first

observation run, Admiral Golovin did break radio silence with these words:

" 'Good morning, Americans. You are welcome to observe our peaceful maneuvers conducted in the cause of peace-loving peoples everywhere. [There was a nervous snicker from somewhere in the press section.] We would appreciate your maintaining your present distance. Thank you.'

"The commander of the United States mission, Lieutenant Colonel Emory C. Standiford of Manchester, New Hampshire, immediately responded: 'Thank you, Admiral Golovin. We are on a routine observation flight. We appreciate your friendly gesture and will maintain our present distance for one more pass, which will conclude our mission.'

"Pursuant to this promise, the United States jet, still moving slowly, did make one more circle flight around the Soviet force at the same distance of approximately ten miles, after which it intended to return to the *Truman* and conclude its mission.

"However—" He paused to take a sip of water and looked out somberly once again across his audience. Tension suddenly rose to an almost unbearable level. "However, no sooner had the American plane turned and headed away, still slowly, from the Soviet force, than a lone Soviet submarine, the atomic missile-bearing craft *Alexandr P. Savkin,* stationed some forty miles from its closest sister-ship in the main Soviet force and lying directly between the U.S. jet and the *Truman,* surfaced and fired upon the jet with a single surface-to-air tactical atomic weapon.

"Despite immediate evasive action initiated by Lieutenant Colonel Standiford, the Soviet atomic missile scored a direct hit. Lieutenant Colonel Standiford, the six members of his crew, and his plane, were instantly lost.

"So concludes," he said quietly, "the report submitted to me by Secretary of Defense Roger Hackett, as submitted to him two hours ago by the Chief of Naval Operations, Admiral Harman Rydecker."

There was a sigh of released tension, quickly reinstated as he went gravely on.

"Word of this incident was released to the media by the White House press secretary immediately upon receipt, approximately 0300 our time this morning.

"It was followed, as you know, by various claims from the"—and suddenly his voice dripped contempt—"individual—who heads the Soviet Government and its delegation to this Assembly. The claim was made that the unarmed U.S. jet was a 'spy plane,' though it was unarmed and carried only routine radar equipment. The claim was made that it 'violated the air space of Soviet maneuvers,' though prior to and after the radio exchange between Admiral Golovin and Lieutenant Colonel Standiford, the U.S. jet maintained a distance of ten miles from the Soviet force at all times.

"The most startling and novel claim of all was that there even *is* such a thing as national 'air space' that can be violated over a military force on the high seas. If such a thing could be said to exist, the U.S. jet did not violate it. Since it does not exist, save in time of war when it can be enforced by counter military action, the U.S. jet did not by any stretch of imagination—or fabrication—violate it.

"But the Soviet force did respond with a military action. And it was done, I would point out, in exactly the false, duplicitous and sneaking way which Soviet military training and Soviet leaders consistently and constantly advocate. It was entirely consistent with Soviet training and Soviet practice as confirmed by the historical record over many decades.

"It was an act of war, and it was as an act of war that my advisers and I decided to treat it."

He paused again, lost in thought for a moment, remembering the hectic conference with Roger and the Joint Chiefs at the White House before he issued his order. Only Smidge Hallowell, the Chairman of the JCS, and Gutsy Twitchell of the Marines had held out at first, dubious, worried and uncertain. Bump Smith of the Army, Bart Jamison of the Air Force, and Snooze Rydecker of the Navy had been instant advocates of an even stronger response than he—or they—had been prepared to make. Snooze Rydecker in particular had been almost incoherent with fury and pain over the attack on his Navy and the loss of his men.

"Left to you, Snooze," Bump Smith had remarked, sympathetic but more objective, "we'd have the missiles on their way to Moscow right this minute."

"You're God damned right," Snooze had snapped before he finally calmed down. "I wouldn't leave a stick on a stick or a stone on a stone."

"It may be just as well, then," the President had remarked, sympathetically also but also with more caution, "that I'm the one with the so-called 'finger on the button.' Five buttons," he added with a smile, looking from face to troubled face. "But my response won't be equivocal, I can assure you."

He proceeded now to tell the Assembly how it came about.

"Confronted by this deceitful and despicable action by the Soviet military force off Diego Garcia," he said gravely, "which, given his statements to the world, it soon became apparent was done with the full knowledge and approval—and, we have sound reason to suspect, on the direct order —of the individual who heads the Soviet Government, I had several options.

"One was to ask Congress to declare war at once and simultaneously launch an all-out attack upon the Soviet Union.

"Another was to launch an immediate attack upon the Soviet force off Diego Garcia, using all the weapons available to the *Truman* and its sister vessels, without a declaration of war.

"And another was to do what I finally decided was most fitting and most responsible, and that was to issue the order I did at 5 A.M. this morning, and then to bring the matter immediately here.

"In my order, as you know, I directed all American forces everywhere to shoot on sight at the approach of any Soviet force, meaning by that aircraft, seacraft, undersea craft, land forces, missile forces and space forces, of any nature whatsoever.

"I did not, you will note, order American forces to go out in search of Soviet forces, nor did I order them to deliberately seek confrontation with Soviet forces. I am not yet quite prepared"—he paused and repeated the phrase so that even the most stupid delegate from the most backward country would catch the "quite"—"I am not yet quite prepared to take upon myself the onus of that kind of action, which would of course lead inevitably to war. *But I am determined that American forces of peaceable intent will not be wantonly attacked by the Soviet Union again.*

"*I am determined that we will not again be stabbed in the back with a deceitful, duplicitous, absolutely unprovoked sneak attack.*

"And I am determined," he added, "to persuade this Assembly that it must at once, clearly, firmly, unequivocally, *strongly,* without quibble or quaver, condemn the Soviet Union for this action and demand that it cease immediately all such actions and that it cease also that which makes them possible, namely the worldwide Soviet maneuvers which are now entering upon their fourth week of inexcusable threat to world peace . . .

"Accordingly"—he rearranged the papers on the lectern, placed Chauncey Baron's on top—"the United States has decided to withdraw its pending amendment to the Soviet resolution presented to this Assembly last week and present a substitute amendment, as follows:

"In the resolution introduced by the Soviet Union, strike all after the words, 'Whereas, the world now faces a situation of the utmost gravity,' and substitute the following:

"brought about by the decision of the Soviet Union to engage in worldwide maneuvers in areas, and to an extent, far beyond any rational needs of Soviet security; and

"Whereas, these maneuvers have brought about the emplacement of Soviet air, sea, naval, missile and space forces in many areas of the globe that directly threaten the security of many other nations; and,

"Whereas, the emplacement of these forces, including submarine forces, in Cuba, Nicaragua, the Indian Ocean, Alaska, Hawaii and many other maritime areas not directly or remotely connected in any way with the needs of Soviet security, poses a direct threat to world peace; and,

"Whereas the Soviet Union directly and deliberately attacked an unarmed aircraft of the United States flying in open air space in the Indian Ocean, with resultant loss of the aircraft and seven lives, thereby prompting the President of the United States to issue an order to all American forces to shoot on sight when approached by any Soviet force of whatever nature and,

"Whereas, this deliberate act of Soviet aggression against the United States and the United States response thereto, have brought the world to the very brink of war; now, therefore,

"Be it resolved, that the United Nations General Assembly totally and unreservedly condemns this act of Soviet aggression against the United States and demands the immediate withdrawal of all Soviet forces, of whatever nature, from all non-Soviet areas of the world; and furthermore,

"Be it resolved, that the General Assembly of the United Nations hereby establishes a United Nations Observer Force of six members, said members to be appointed by the Secretary-General equally from the armed forces of the United Kingdom and India; and further,

"Be it resolved, that the said United Nations Observer Force is hereby directed to report back to the Secretary-General within forty-eight hours whether or not the above-demanded withdrawal of all Soviet forces to Soviet areas has begun and is being carried out; and be it further

"Resolved, that all member nations of the United Nations hereby pledge themselves to give all assistance requested by the United Observer Force in ascertaining whether or not such Soviet withdrawal is actually taking place; and, finally,

"Be it resolved, that if the demand of the United Nations General Assembly is not honored by the Soviet Union, and if the United Nations Observer Force finds itself unable within forty-eight hours to report that the Soviet withdrawal is taking place, then this Assembly shall reconvene for the purpose of establishing a United Nations Command charged with bringing to an end the Soviet threat to world peace represented by continued Soviet maneuvers."

He put down his paper, looked for the last time at the members of his audience, faces solemn and intent, earphones tuned to the English channel held tightly to many ears.

"Such is the new and final United States resolution. If it passes, then, of course, my various orders to American forces prompted by the Soviet maneuvers and by today's unprovoked and unprincipled attack upon a defenseless American plane, with the resultant loss of seven American lives, will be withdrawn and the world, one hopes, will be able to settle down and return to peace and normalcy. If it is not passed . . . then," he said, and quite beyond his control a heavy sigh escaped him, "the United States will have to consider . . . other things."

And taking up his documents, he turned again, bowed to Libya and the S.-G. and went slowly back up the aisle to his seat, while all around the room remained hushed and deathly still.

And so it remained when, a moment later, Libya brought down his gavel, announced, "The President of the Soviet Union!" and Yuri, face equally somber and unsmiling, rose from his seat and walked, through equal silence and tension, to the podium: bowed low in his turn to the Chair and the Secretary-General; pulled out the footstool and put it carefully in place; stepped upon it and turned to address the Assembly.

"Mr. President," he said, "Mr. Secretary-General, members of the Assembly:

"You have just heard an account of the incident which occurred off the island of Diego Garcia at approximately 0200 this morning, our time, which is typical of the lies told by the capitalist militarist circles of the United States and their representative. It is filled with falsehoods. It is not the truth. It is not the way it happened. It is all lies.

"For the past three weeks, as the representative of the imperialists told you, United States planes have been making hourly reconnaissance flights, repeatedly violating the sovereign air space of the Soviet forces stationed southeast of Diego Garcia. These flights have been borne with great patience by the Soviet forces. Contrary to what the imperialist spokesman has told you, these planes have been equipped not only with radar but with the most sophisticated weapons capable of making an instantaneous surprise attack upon the Soviet forces."

There was a stir in the American delegation, but it could be seen that the President of the United States was sternly ordering silence upon his colleagues; and no interruption came.

"The Soviet forces," Yuri went on, "have suffered with great patience these provocative acts by armed planes of the United States imperialist forces. No protests have been made—for three weeks. No annoyance has been shown—for three weeks. No shots have been fired, no weapons employed—for three weeks. Is that not long enough for men to be patient, I ask the Assembly? Is that not long enough for us, or for any of you, to accept unchallenged these constant hostile penetrations of our sovereign air space?

"Is it not long enough to be spied upon and threatened by planes camouflaged as simple observers but in reality carrying devastating weapons of the imperialist forces?

"Mr. President," he cried, voice suddenly rising, "what does the spokesman of United States militarist circles think we are made of? What does he think he can get away with? *Who does he think he is?*

"At last, Mr. President, it was determined by the commander of the endangered Soviet forces, Admiral V. C. Golovin, and"—he paused and ground out the next words in a heavy and unyielding voice—*"and by myself*—that it had gone on long enough. Admiral V. C. Golovin *and myself* determined together that this deliberate provocation by capitalist militarist forces of the United States must stop. Accordingly, we so advised the American forces. We made clear to the commander of the U.S. task force, the commander of the aircraft carrier *Truman,* that we would no longer tolerate such spying. We warned him of severe consequences if such flights continued."

Again there was an angry stirring in the American delegation, but no voice was raised. This time, however, the President, grim-faced, slowly shook his head from side to side.

"Oh yes, Mr. President!" Yuri cried. "Oh yes! The representative of the imperialist forces of the United States may shake his head and pretend it is not so! He may make a big show of his head-shaking, Mr. President! But it does not change the truth! It does not make truth into lies, or lies into truth! It does not change the facts!"

Again Ham Delbacher slowly shook his head, this time with a profound wonderment that such things could be. Again Yuri responded.

"He shakes his head, Mr. President! A big show! But we notified the commander of the *Truman*. We warned him of the gravest consequences. We told him what would happen if U.S. spy planes armed with terrible weapons continued to spy upon us and violate our air space. We gave fair warning. And the imperialist forces of the United States, which think they can push around everybody on this earth and make them jump to America's tune, they ignored our warning and continued their provocative aggressive action against our peace-loving forces.

"But even then, Mr. President," he said more quietly, voice and manner now earnest and appealing for justice, "even then, we did not deliberately trap and shoot down an innocent American plane, as the imperialist representative would have you believe. I do not care what the *Truman* may have reported. It is easy to fabricate radio conversations, Mr. President! It is very easy to fake voices and conversations!"

["You ought to know," Chauncey Baron muttered bitterly; but only the President heard him.]

"Admiral Golovin did not welcome one more American spy plane—the *last,* Mr. President, that I think will dare to violate our sovereign air space and our maneuvers. No, he did not welcome it. He did say that we were conducting peaceable maneuvers on behalf of the peace-loving peoples of the earth. And he said, thinking it was language Americans would understand, '*Keep your distance.*'

"But, Mr. President"—and now he was all earnestness, all sincerity, while his audience listened with rapt attention, some convinced, some overwhelmed by what they believed to be the sheer lying audacity of it, but all completely silent—"what did the American imperialist spy plane do? It flew nearer. It kept on its course. It flew close to our forces, it encircled them twice. Naturally this alarmed Admiral Golovin. Naturally he took steps to see that his command would be protected. He is one of our best naval officers, members of the Assembly, he would not do a stupid thing. He notified the *Savkin* that the American plane might be about to attack and he ordered the *Savkin* to take appropriate action. Appropriate action, Mr. President. So the *Savkin* rose from its position five miles from the main body of our force—five miles, not forty, it was not hiding—and fired. It is too bad seven young men were lost, Mr. President, but we could take the provocation no longer. We are not at war, but what could we do against such frankly imperialist threatenings, really such warlike things? We had no choice but to protect ourselves. We had no choice but to stop the imperialist aggressors. And we did."

He paused and in his turn took a sip of water; then resumed in the same intent, earnest manner.

"So what did the spokesman of U.S. militarist circles do, Mr. President? He issued an order to the forces of imperialism telling them that from now on they must 'shoot on sight' at the approach of any Soviet force. Now he is threatening *all* Soviet forces, all over the world, whatever their nature, wherever they may be. And he cries peace, Mr. President, he cries peace. He shouts war and he cries peace. It does not make sense. It is insane. And then he comes here and lies to you to excuse himself and make it seem all right. What falsehoods, Mr. President, what lies!

"Nor is that enough for him. He must try to get this Assembly to endorse American imperialist spying and aggressive provocations. He must try to get you to condemn Soviet peace-keeping maneuvers and demand their withdrawal all over the world. He seeks to conceal the aggressiveness of war-loving imperialist forces while at the same time asking you to drive back Soviet forces which try to keep the peace for all peace-loving peoples. And he wants this Assembly to set up another spy committee to see if we have complied. And if we haven't, then he threatens 'other things.'

"What 'other things'?" the Soviet President cried. "What 'other things'?" And suddenly, unexpectedly, a savage sarcasm entered his voice. "What 'other things' is the United States capable of, Mr. President? Does anybody know? What 'other things' does this mighty imperialist force think it can do to us? We will tell him, Mr. President! Nothing! *Nothing!* It is so weak it can do *nothing!*

"Mr. President," he said dropping the sarcasm, instantly again the earnest, fervent, humble pleader, "we must ask the Assembly, do not believe these lies of the imperialist racist spokesman. Do not demand the end of our peace-loving, peace-keeping maneuvers designed to protect all peoples. Our maneuvers will end soon enough, do not worry about that. It is the aggressive imperialist circles of the United States you must worry about. They are the real threat to the peace of all peoples. Do not condemn us, fellow members, do not demand *we* withdraw! It is not *we* who threaten you. We seek only your interests, only the peace! Only the peace! Vote with us, not against us! That is where true peace lies!"

And he turned solemnly, bowed low to Libya and the Secretary-General and, still amid silence, his words not having aroused the wild approval he obviously expected—in fact, not having roused anything at all but more of the same tense silence that gripped the entire Assembly this day—he walked stolidly and without expression back to his seat.

"The Prime Minister of Great Britain," Libya said, and still the silence held as she came down the aisle in her turn, bowed, ascended the podium and turned to them with only a single sentence that astounded and excited them all.

"Mr. President," she said, "Mr. Secretary-General, members of the Assembly: after consultation with my Indian colleague I find that we are in entire agreement on recent events, and therefore the United Kingdom will pass at this time in deference to Her Excellency, the Prime Minister of India."

Now the silence did break and suddenly the chamber was filled with excited sound as many voices gabbled and speculated across the floor.

In the midst of the sudden uproar the British Prime Minister bowed briefly again to the Chair and started for her seat, while from hers the Indian Prime Minister arose and started to the podium. They met halfway, exchanged terse nods, went on to their respective destinations. The excitement, and the tension, rose still further. Libya brought down his gavel, the Prime Minister of India reached the podium, bowed and took her place at the lectern. Her acquiline face was somber and severe; today it was set off by brilliant greens and golds and shimmering things that suggested butterflies on a spring day. There was nothing springlike about her harsh and earnest tones.

"Mr. President, Mr. Secretary-General, members of the Assembly:

"I thank my colleague from Britain for her courtesy and confidence in thus yielding to me. We do, indeed, agree.

"It is impossible for us, and I think for many in this body, to accept the version of events just given us by the President of the Soviet Union."

There was a gasp of surprise and even greater excitement, an anticipatory stir throughout the chamber. Yuri looked stunned for a second, then made his face, with a skill born of long practice in the Kremlin, into a mask of instant impassivity. Hamilton Delbacher for the first time began to look a little more relaxed and like his normal self.

"We do not see much point," she went on, "in flinging about words such as 'lies' and 'falsehoods.' Neither are we much impressed by such slogans as 'capitalist imperialist,' 'racist imperialist,' 'imperialist racist' 'war-mongering,' 'peace-loving' and all the rest of them. We *are* interested in the truth of it, and we do believe that most of it in this instance lies with the President of the United States of America. And we think this does not bode well for the peace of the world or for those who are genuinely and without artifice seeking to preserve it."

There was a movement in the press section, many reporters hurried out

THE HILL OF SUMMER

to file bulletins. She paused for a moment to accommodate the flurry of their departure, then went on in the same severe, uncompromising tone.

"Obviously something happened near the island of Diego Garcia— whose use as a base and a potential item of conflict between the two superpowers, incidentally, we have always pointed out and protested vigorously. The account of the President of the United States has to it the ring of truth. It is typical of what we know of America. It is also typical of what we know of the darker side of the Soviet Union. It makes sense. It is not based on bluster. It rings true. The account of the President of the Soviet Union, I regret to say, does not. Incidentally," she added with an extra severity, "the concept of 'sovereign' air space over an intruding force on the high seas is so much poppycock.

"Mr. President, I think this incident illustrates very clearly the danger in the Soviet maneuvers which some have pointed out from the beginning. India, it is true, earlier on defended the right of the Soviet Union to hold these maneuvers and deplored what seemed to us the rather hysterical overreaction of the President of the United States. Yet even then we were aware that the maneuvers created a dangerous hazard to peace, simply because the emplacement of so many Soviet forces everywhere around the world creates many, many possibilities of either inadvertent or deliberate collision. Just by being there, they are a hazard to world peace. It is obvious."

["Then why in the *hell*," Chauncey demanded *sotto voce*, "didn't you say so in the first place?"

["Be thankful for favors," the President told him with a relieved lightness in his voice. "Just be thankful."]

"Now the collision has come," she continued, "and without judging entirely the basic question of who is right or who is wrong, we think the preponderance lies, as I have said, with the United States. But by the same token, no one can condone, either, or welcome, the response of the President, which certainly anticipates and makes probable still further clashes which can only escalate, and very quickly, into the kind of final clash we all dread.

"Therefore, there is only one thing to do with the Soviet forces whose presence is so provocative: get them out of there!"

For the first time in the session there was a burst of genuine, convinced, supportive applause. It was led by the U.S. delegation but many others picked it up and carried it across the floor. Yuri's mask did not change for reasons best known to himself; but the President was sure that he could not be very happy about it.

"Get them out of there!" the Prime Minister repeated, and her expression became even more severe. "And at once! It is the only way to prevent more of these cliff's-edge episodes. It is the only way to save the peace.

"India does not approve of every single word of the American amendment, but in view of today's events we now find ourselves in entire
agreement with its basic thrust. Mr. Delbacher has pledged himself before
all these witnesses and the world to withdraw his own ultimatums, declarations, orders, alerts, tensions, if the Soviet maneuvers are ended and Soviet forces withdrawn. There is no reason to doubt his word—it would be
foolish of him to do otherwise—and he appears to be an honest, if somewhat overreactive, man."

Hamilton Delbacher in his new-found euphoria, half-rose and bowed,
with a slightly ironic but appreciative smile. The Prime Minister actually
relaxed and smiled back, and from many places across the floor came
muted but complimentary amusement. Things, he told himself with a
great feeling of relief, were getting better by the moment.

"India will vote for the American amendment," she concluded firmly,
"and we urge you to do the same. If it passes, as we hope it will, we will
then expect"—and she looked straight down at Yuri, who returned her
look without acknowledgment of any kind—"that the Soviet Union will
honor it and begin the immediate return of its forces to their home stations. The Soviet Union has made a mistake, but we are providing the
way it can be rectified with honor. We are disposed to believe in the basic
peaceful purposes of the Soviet Union and we trust it will not disappoint
us."

And to a final wave of genuine, grateful, and apparently almost unanimous applause, she left the podium and strode swiftly back to her seat.

"We are making great progress," Libya remarked, his tone sounding so
surprised that there was a real burst of laughter and applause from everyone save Yuri, who still sat silent. He was now, however, projecting a
definite impression of thinking—or, perhaps, Thinking. It was obvious—
or at least he was making it appear obvious—that the proceedings were
giving him much to contemplate, and that he was, actively, contemplating. For the first time all those who favored him, all those who feared
him, began to feel that possibly, just possibly, a most significant event
might be in the making. No one, quite yet, dared put too much reliance
on this; but it was in the air, everywhere. The growing excitement in the
Assembly was transmitted via television, radio and printed word to the
watching world.

First, however, there were the Vice Premier of China and the many nations waiting on the speakers' list. Ju Xing-dao said what he had to say
with amazing brevity and no Ancient Wisdom, and stepped down.

"Mr. President," he said after he had come wraith-like down the aisle,
made his obeisance, and stepped carefully up on the footstool. "The People's Republic of China also agrees with our colleague from India. We
have come too close to disaster this day—too close. The President of the

United States, and his countrymen, in our estimation, are showing great restraint; but how much longer, Mr. President, can they do so?

"It is time now for the Soviet Union to abandon its maneuvers, which by now are certainly complete and serve no further purpose. It is time for it to take its forces home, where they belong. It is too dangerous to leave so much armament lying about the world." [A tiny but definite gleam of satisfaction flashed across the face of the President of the Soviet Union, and was as swiftly gone. Those few who saw it were baffled, and could not understand why.]

"The People's Republic of China also supports the American amendment and urges the same course upon all its friends of the 'Third World' and elsewhere. China, too," he said, and his voice lost its customary whisper and emerged with startling clarity and force, "expects the Soviet Union to obey."

And bowing low once again, he floated gently down the steps and up the aisle to his seat, while from all around the chamber there came further and even more openly approving applause.

For a few moments after that, Libya conferred with the Secretary-General. Loud conversation, relaxing laughter, speculation, gossip, excitement filled the enormous hall. Both the Soviet and American delegations talked among themselves with considerable animation, watched closely by all. Rumors raced again across the floor. Television cameras and radio were busy and in their seats members of the printed media exchanged shrewdly cynical jests that relieved the tension and got them ready for the unknowable, but by now increasingly possible, conclusion.

All this ended abruptly when Libya brought down the gavel. Instantly the room was still and tension ruled again.

"Members of the Assembly," Libya said, "it has occurred to the Chair that in the interests of expediting a decision on this most grave matter now before the Assembly, some members who have signified their intention of speaking might be willing to forego that right. The Chair," he added hastily as there was a murmur from the floor, "does not say this with any wish to foreclose anyone who feels he or she has something vital to contribute to a solution ["Doesn't everybody?" CBS murmured.] but it is just a suggestion. Are there members—?"

He paused and looked expectantly around the chamber. Mexico held up his hand, stood at his seat, reached for a table microphone.

"Mr. President," he said, "Mexico is of the opinion that the issue has been stated very clearly by the five previous speakers, particularly by the Prime Minister of India. Mexico is ready to vote and accordingly we withdraw our name from the speakers' list."

"Mr. President!" cried Thailand from across the room. "Mr. President!" cried Argentina, Canada, West Germany, Iceland, Spain, Portugal and several dozen more.

"I thank the Assembly very much," Libya said fifteen minutes later. "The speakers' list has now been reduced voluntarily to eight. I congratulate the Assembly—I think we can all congratulate one another"—and for the first time he smiled, a genuine and quite appealing smile—"upon our mutual restraint. Now if the remaining speakers will only be brief—"

There was laughter and applause; and surprisingly they were.

Of the remaining handful, only the President of Cuba, unable to restrain his famous penchant for endless speeches, went on at any length, shouting, declaiming, letting his voice sink into a confidential rumble, sending it shrilling into near hysteria, pounding the lectern, knocking over his water glass and generally, as Egypt remarked with distaste to his neighbor Eire, carrying on. His half-screaming, half-growling, all-pyrotechnical defense of "the great leader of the socialist camp, the great peace-loving leader of all mankind, His Excellency the President of the Soviet Union" did not greatly impress. But the last speaker, one of the great leader's uneasy own, did. He spoke from his seat, very briefly, in difficult but well-educated English, and it was generally considered later that he had probably convinced the last few undecided votes that still remained.

"Mr. President," Rumania said gravely, and once again the Assembly hushed abruptly to listen, "Mr. Secretary-General, fellow members of the Assembly:

"It is with regret, but with firm—determination—in the best interests of the—socialist coalition—and all truly—peace-loving peoples—everywhere—that Rumania joins—India, China, Great Britain, Mexico and—many—others—in support of the—American—amendment.

"We do not accept all the—statements—in that amendment concerning the—various—alleged crimes of the—Soviet Union; we have—reservations—about those, and it is with—reservations—that we will vote Yes. But we do accept the basic purpose of it, which—is—that the Soviet maneuvers have now gone on long—enough and that Soviet forces—must be —withdrawn—from around the globe—if we are—to avoid—other—confrontations—of the type that very closely—almost—plunged the Soviet Union and the—United States—into war—this morning.

"The world cannot risk—this, Mr. President. It is—terrifying—to contem-plate. Sanity must now—prevail.

"I speak, Mr. President, for—Rumania—only. But many have said—to me—today, since the—episode—was announced, that they agree even though some—of them—may find that of—necessity—they will have to vote—in the neg-a-tive. So Rumania, although subject—to—some—of the same—restraints—is happy—to speak—for them.

"Mr. President, Rumania urges all—our—friends—in the 'Third World' and—elsewhere—to join us—in support of this—amendment. We believe it—to be—absolutely—im-per-a-tive—for world—peace.

"Mr. President, I suggest we—now—vote."

"Is there objection?" Libya asked quickly.

"Second!" the Indian Prime Minister called, and a dozen more supported her.

"Very well," Libya said in a tone so openly relieved that a few actually laughed despite the by now fearfully heavy tension.

"The vote occurs on the substitute amendment of the United States to the resolution offered by the Soviet Union. Mr. Secretary-General, will you please call the roll."

And gravely, quietly, mustering every last ounce of his enormous dignity, the Secretary-General did, raising his classical ebony head from the roll to repeat after each nation the "Yes!" or "No!" with which each announced its vote on perhaps the most important matter ever to come before the United Nations.

In the television booths, in the press section and at literally every seat across the floor, the running tally was being kept. As it moved slowly toward the middle of the list, tension and excitement grew—and grew. It was obvious from the first few votes which way it was going to go, but by the time the S.-G. called out "Malawi!" and Malawi answered "Yes!" in a firmly defiant voice, it was apparent that it would be a landslide. And it was then, of course, that a voice from the floor cried loudly, "Mr. President!" and a stocky, familiar figure rose from its seat and started determinedly down the aisle.

Abruptly the S.-G. halted, Libya looked up startled from his tally.

"For what purpose," he asked, voice unsteady with the universal excitement that was suddenly almost unbearable, "does the delegate seek recognition?"

"To address the Assembly," Yuri replied with a light, jaunty, almost cheery air. "What else?"

"It is out of order for the delegate to interrupt the roll call—" Libya began, but with a great roar of "LET HIM SPEAK!" in which the President of the United States, the ladies of Great Britain and India, and even the Vice Premier of the People's Republic of China were seen to join, the Assembly shouted him down.

"All right, all right!" he cried finally as the uproar began to subside a little. "If that is your will! The roll call is suspended so that we may hear the President of the Soviet Union!"

And lightly, jauntily, almost cheerily, Yuri raised his hands and clapped them vigorously above his head as he hurried to the podium, up the stairs, onto the footstool, and, turning from a quick bow to Libya and the S.-G., delivered with an irony only they could see, turned to face the Assembly.

Instantly, as though he were the hero of the day, which he now set out to transform himself into, a wild tumult of applause, supine and sup-plicating, hurled itself at his feet.

Do not be harsh with us, O Master! it seemed to say. *We are your friends—your friends—your friends! Do not be angry, do not be harsh! Master, be kind to us! Be kind to us, O powerful one! You have fright-ened us so much, O infinitely wise one! Now be kind!*

And so he was, giving them first a calm and beneficent look and then proceeding to speak in an emphatic but quietly reasonable tone.

Yuri the Turbulent was gone.

Yuri the Statesman had returned.

Breathless they hung upon every word, which conveyed what so many of them wanted so desperately to hear.

"Members of the United Nations," he said solemnly, "I shall be very brief.

"It is obvious from the roll call so far that the American amendment has the overwhelming approval of this body. Therefore I pledge to you that the Soviet Union will immediately begin steps to implement it."

A great shout of relief, a rolling thunder of applause, came up from the floor. Again he raised his hands, this time without changing his solemn and respectful expression, and clapped them solemnly together in re-sponse.

"Orders will be issued immediately for the withdrawal of Soviet forces to their regular stations within our borders, or to those areas immediately contiguous where we have treaty rights to position them."

Again the great shout, again his solemn, clapping response.

"Although we cannot bring back to life men who have died in an un-fortunate accident, we hereby apologize to the Government of the United States for our part in the regrettable occurrence and we pledge that we will make every attempt to assist the bereaved families of the brave American airmen."

Again a great shout, filled with tender congratulations and warmest sympathy—for his wonderful gesture, the American delegation sensed, not for the bereaved families of the brave American airmen.

"We regret our part, also, in creating this whole unpleasant series of events that has so disturbed the world, and we shall seek hereafter to speed the process of achieving worldwide peace by every means at our command."

And once again, forgetting what his government always meant by peace —"A time for gathering one's forces," and forgetting the overwhelming means he *had* at his command, the chamber shook—the great shout rolled—and never was such a wonder seen.

Solemnly still, he turned and bowed again, expression nothing but com-pletely suitable and respectful now, to Libya and the Secretary-General, and started to turn away. Then, shaking his head with a little self-mocking smile at his own forgetfulness, he turned back quickly to the microphone.

"In view of the decision of the Soviet Union," he said swiftly, "we move that further roll call on the American amendment be dispensed with, that the vote so far be expunged from the record, and that the American amendment and the Soviet original both be immediately withdrawn and the debates thereon be also expunged from the record."

For just a second there was a hesitation. Then someone began to shout and clap and in an instant there came once more the great hysterical surge of all-conquering approval, endorsement and applause.

Into it the President of the United States found himself shouting futilely to the Chair. Only those nearest him could catch a few words—"totally irregular—don't you realize—cancels official UN Observers—UN Force—leaves no adequate check on Soviet promises—we cannot accept—"

Across the room here and there—the Prime Minister of Great Britain, the President of Egypt, Prince Koa, a few others—were also on their feet, shouting much the same things. But the Assembly had made up its mind, and the applause for Yuri turned with instantaneous speed to jeers, boos, shouts and angry denunciations for them. Their voices were drowned out, their protests lost. It remained only for the uproar to die down just a little, and Libya shouted as loudly as he could into his microphone:

"All those in favor of the motion of President Serapin—"

"YES!" roared the assembly of the nations, angry and hopeless "Noes!" from here and there drowned out.

"Mr. President," the Indian Prime Minister shouted into the tumult. "I move the Assembly stand adjourned sine die on this issue!"

And before Libya could even put the question, "YES!" roared the multitude again.

On the podium for the last time, Yuri raised his hands high and clapped them victoriously together as hundreds of delegates swarmed forward in a mass attempt to surround and embrace him—while on the floor, abandoned now, the President of the United States, his somber delegation, and those scattered few other delegations who supported them, looked at one another in grim-faced dismay as the media in all its forms told the watching world what it so desperately wanted to hear.

NO WAR! CRISIS OVER! SERAPIN SAVES PEACE! SOVIETS BOW TO UN PRESSURE, PROMISE WITHDRAWAL OF WORLD-WIDE MANEUVER FORCES!

And few heard, and few believed, the hollow laughter of history as the word "promise" was sent reeling still further toward nothingness in the lexicon of man.

4

"Americans, of course, cannot but think over how their stormy romance with China will end when the Chinese find themselves sufficiently strong in order to speak as equals."

—*Izvestia, June 1, 1980*

"Recently Washington has been yielding increasingly to the temptation to play the China card. This is a risky game for those who start it, but it is also dangerous for the cause of peace."

—*Pravda, February 6, 1980*

And so the world was jolly and happy, and from Bangkok to Birmingham and from Youngstown to Yalta everybody, figuratively and in many cases actually, danced in the streets. A carnival atmosphere swept the globe: the nightmares and bugaboos were gone, the frightful fears and terrors were banished, the dreadful demons of atomic war and Soviet conquest were exorcised. Pope Yuri ("That guy could be elected Pope!" the publisher of America's most influential newspaper had exclaimed admiringly, and, "Yuri Serapin could probably be elected Pope, so great is his worldwide acclaim today," the paper's top columnist had begun his post-crisis editorial musings) reigned supreme. Few voices anywhere were raised in skepticism and doubt, and those were swiftly hooted down. All over America, all over the world, private citizen, government leader and media pundit alike joined in the hallelujah chorus. **NOBEL PEACE PRIZE FOR SERAPIN?** the headlines queried; and resoundingly from around the globe came again the reverent, reverberant "YES!"

And in the White House, confronted by the shattering of a policy and the great leap forward of the enemy of all that America was supposed to believe in and hold dear, the President of the United States pondered late and long as how best to proceed from here.

For a few hours after he had left New York, seen off at JFK by hun-

dreds of clamoring reporters to whom he had given nothing but a quizzical smile and a brief, ironic wave, he had been overcome by a feeling of
profound depression. He had been greeted in Washington by the Cabinet,
several hundred more reporters, his wife, his children, Art Hampton
(about to be confirmed Vice President by the Senate) and the other
leaders of the Congress—and a noticeably small handful of his fellow
countrymen, whose numbers were contrasted everywhere with pictures of
the hundreds of thousands who completely filled Red Square to greet the
triumphal homecoming of the President of the Soviet Union.

Ham Delbacher's words of arrival had been businesslike and matter-of-
fact, unlike the self-preening oratory from Moscow ("It was like the Second Coming compared with a George Washington's Birthday Sale in
Woodward & Lothrop's bargain basement," one press writer put it) and
he hoped they did not convey too many of his inner feelings.

"My countrymen," he said gravely, "it appears that the world's crisis
has eased, and we must now turn ourselves to the task of working genuinely and unceasingly for peace. The proof of the pudding is in the eating,
and the world must now watch closely to see whether the Soviet Union
does indeed follow through on the promises of its President to the United
Nations."

"Will you, Mr. President?" someone shouted from among the reporters,
and he shook his head irritably as though he were the old bull by the
barn shaking off a fly.

"It takes some time to dismantle a crisis," he said with a certain
sharpness, "just as it takes time to create one. The present one, quite
likely the worst the world has seen, is not unusual in that respect. I did
pledge myself and the United States to a certain course of action and insofar as events make it possible—"

There was a sudden hoot of skeptical laughter but he brought his head
up sharply and it instantly ceased—"insofar as events make it possible,"
he repeated firmly, "I shall carry out that course."

"When can we expect that, Mr. President?" someone called in a carefully respectful voice, and he shook his head impatiently again.

"As soon as we begin to see evidence that the Soviet Union is indeed
withdrawing its worldwide forces. Even though the General Assembly saw
fit at the last moment to abandon the creation of an observer force to
supervise the withdrawal, there are other means available to monitor it.
We shall employ them, as we do, and as they do, constantly, to monitor
one another's actions. When they start going home, I shall start dismantling our crisis posture."

"South Africa reported this morning that a huge Soviet force passed
around the Cape of Good Hope this morning and is sailing north toward
Europe and, presumably, home to Murmansk," the AP said.

He nodded.

"Presumably. Yes, we have those reports. They are also moving in force in the Indian Ocean, toward Suez and presumably toward the Black Sea. In the North Sea there is also movement toward Murmansk. South Seas flotillas are on the move, overflights of many areas have ceased. Yes, they are moving."

"Well, then—" someone began impatiently. He interrupted with equal impatience.

"We shall see," he said sharply. "We shall see. I am not going to move hastily until I am really convinced. Seven young Americans are dead because they trusted a Soviet commander. Don't forget that, in all your hosannahas."

"But surely, Mr. President," CBS said, "one thing—American forces are not going to shoot Soviet forces on sight now, are they?"

"Not if they refrain from hostile action."

"Are *our* forces coming home, Mr. President?" ABC asked dryly, and with equal dryness he replied:

"They really haven't been much of anywhere, you know."

Which resulted in more condemnation from some editorialists, commentators and pundits, for his "negativism"—his "undue suspicion"—his "fanatic fear of the Soviet Union"—his "unwillingness to accept the Soviet retreat in the spirit in which it is offered."

In that last, he thought, the writer unknowingly, either with the arrogance of the truly uninformed or the deliberately denying, had put his finger on it.

He *was* accepting the Soviet withdrawal in the spirit in which Yuri offered it. He knew Yuri knew this. But the world did not. That was his problem.

So overwhelming was global approval, so desperate the worldwide need (including the apparent need of the great majority of his fellow Americans) to *believe,* that even the ordinary prudence he was trying to maintain in the face of almost universal acceptance was nearly impossible. Even his countrymen did not want him to be prudent, now. They wanted him to join them in forgetting. They just wanted to relax and have a good time and put it all behind them as soon as possible.

Which, he knew, was of course exactly what Yuri was counting on.

So he brooded, for a long time when he got home to the White House, sitting on the Truman Balcony staring out over the Ellipse to the Washington Monument and the gentle wooded hills of beautiful Virginia. He sat there for a couple of hours, in fact, so long and so uncharacteristically that Elinor, worried, appeared at last to urge him to come have a drink with the children in the Green Room and relax for a while before dinner.

"It will look better tomorrow," she said, rubbing the back of his neck gently in the old, familiar gesture. "You'll manage."

He looked up gratefully, took her hand and smiled for the first time since leaving New York.

"I know I will," he said. "The blues are just temporary. But it *is* discouraging. I feel as though I've been pushed 'way back down the hill and now I have to start all over again . . . And maybe they're all correct. Maybe I should give in and go for peace at any price. They seem to want it, no matter what the price really is."

"You'll have to concede something to that," she said, practically. "Better to do it gracefully than be dragged kicking and screaming. And perhaps he'll act in good faith."

"Perhaps," he said, gloomy again. "Perhaps. But I wouldn't bet on it."

So for the better part of a week he tried to put a good face on it. Step by step, to the happy plaudits of the press and most of the public worldwide, he began, as he put it, to dismantle the crisis. First he cancelled the shoot-on-sight order. Then he cancelled the national emergency and the armed forces alert. And finally, upon receiving assurances from American intelligence and reports from a dozen satellite scannings of the Caribbean, he cancelled his submarine ultimatum in the face of reasonably conclusive evidence that the subs were gone from Nicaragua and that only two of those that had been in Cuba still remained at Cienfuegos.

But despite much pressure inside Congress and out, he did not cancel or notably curtail the plans for the emergency arms build-up, the draft call-up or the civilian service bill. He took off the "emergency" label and began to refer to them casually to his questioners in Congress and the media, as "a planned and orderly modernization of the armed forces and our civil defense." Two, he thought grimly, could play the game of semantics; and the one thing he could not do, after such a rigorous challenge, was abandon what now seemed an absolutely imperative increase in over-all American strength.

Sometime toward the end of the week, he asked Mark if he could contact Ivan for him for a last check to ascertain whether the jovial major knew any slightest thing more about the plans of his former superior in Moscow. The CIA arranged a meeting at Langley. Mark stopped by the White House an hour later.

"He says he knows nothing more," he reported. "And I think"—his eyes grew faintly troubled, he was still obviously not entirely satisfied—"I *think*—he's telling me the truth. Insofar as he knows it."

"Yes," the President said. "Well . . . I guess we have to accept that."

"Yes," Mark agreed slowly. "I suppose."

But on Friday morning, just before the start of the long Labor Day weekend, everything changed again with an ominous, if not to him entirely surprising, abruptness.

From American intelligence, and coincidentally within the course of the next two hours from British and Japanese intelligence, and also—via muffled long distance telephone call from amiable Koa, far down in Tonga in the South Seas—he began to get disturbing reports.

Many, many Soviet ships, subs, planes, tanks, troops, mobile missile launchers and the like, had indeed gone home; but many more, including the ten Salyut space stations, apparently remained. Ten of the subs that had departed Cuba and Nicaragua, an entirely sufficient number, were now concentrated at the secret Soviet base in El Salvador. Others had just been discovered in the North Sea, Indian Ocean, Pacific, and Atlantic. The Soviet fishing fleets in many areas seemed suddenly to have expanded in numbers, and some of the small vessels appeared to be curiously top-heavy, carrying suspicious objects on their decks that could be cargo of some sort or could be camouflaged tactical nuclear weapons. On the border of Western Europe hundreds of thousands of troops and tanks had apparently gone home but where they had been for a month, strange Birnam Woods of hilly contours and wooded groves never before seen in aerial photographs seemed to have sprouted near a hundred local Dunsinanes. An outwardly ancient Soviet trawler was limping around off Nukualofa, the capital of Tonga; Koa reported that "some of my boys out fishin'" had approached it innocently in a canoe, only to be driven off without warning by a spatter of bullets all around them in the peaceful sea. What might simply be old warehouses but could be camouflaged missile storage depots seemed to have appeared overnight in many places. Satellite photos revealed at least a dozen new camouflaged landing strips in Central America, Siberia, the deserted wastes of the Canadian North and on two of the tiniest uninhabited islands of the Indonesian archipelago. And the British and Japanese reported many other instances of suspicious developments, things that weren't there a month ago, minute changes in the face of the land and the depths of the seas that were almost unnoticeable but just sufficiently different so that sharp-eyed analysts had noticed them, and were beginning to wonder and to come to frightening conclusions.

And so, he thought with a vast and weary sigh that seemed to echo through the air-conditioned quiet of the Oval Office—now what should he do?

The world apparently was unanimously opposed to further strong action to stop this. His own people by now were so relieved and relaxed, so busy looking ahead to their last long holiday of the summer, so unwilling to gear themselves up again to the pitch of tensions at which they had lived for the better part of two months, that he doubted they would listen to him if he once again sounded warning. Even though the British, Japanese and other allies right down to far-off Koa were dutifully and with anxious, renewed concern, notifying him of their suspicions, their own peoples were no more desirous of being disturbed again than his own . . . and in Moscow, his antagonist was basking in a thousand spotlights, savoring the glowing media support of most lands including Ham Delbacher's own—formally greeting hundreds of congratulatory "peace thanksgiving" delegations from all over the world—and calling upon the President of the United States, it seemed almost hourly, to join him anew in summits, conferences, "meetings for all mankind, new sincere efforts to bring lasting peace to all the peace-loving peoples of the earth . . ."

He did not at that moment know how he should respond to what was very evidently a carefully planned, skillfully carried out, well-camouflaged deception designed to leave the Soviets in position to strike wherever it pleased them around the globe.

He knew even less when, shortly after 6 A.M. next morning, Saturday, Chauncey Baron awoke him with apologies and a grim-voiced recital of the latest news to shake the world.

He just knew one thing, in that blindingly angry and frustrated moment: he would be damned if he would ever surrender to Yuri Pavlovich, no matter how cleverly, or with what cold-blooded ruthlessness, he might plan the climactic stages of his "final battle to decide the fate of all mankind."

Not, of course, that it was entirely planning, the President of the Soviet Union thought with a satisfaction so great he could hardly contain it, as he sat once again in his Kremlin office studying the familiar map with its little red dots and bright silver slivers and little blue lights, now all in place awaiting his imperial command. There had been some luck involved, too, in this latest piece of news whose arrival he had been awaiting with an almost unbearable anticipation for nearly a week: although it did seem now, in retrospect, that like nearly everything else in his dazzlingly successful career, it had all been pre-ordained by history and his own amazing and all-conquering destiny.

Step by step, event by event, the hated Americans and their stupid President had taken the bait and fallen into his traps; and though they did not know it yet, the biggest and most decisive of all was about to open before them now.

He had calculated his effects from the beginning. Inch by inch through these past two months the United States and the world had followed him exactly where he wanted them to go.

He had blustered at H. Delbacher so the incompetent fool would become alarmed and give him some pretext for ordering the start of the long-planned worldwide maneuvers; and so it had happened. He had thrown an extra force of submarines into the Caribbean so the incompetent fool would become alarmed and attempt to get them out, thus alienating, the "Third World" by his apparent move to threaten the sovereignty of Cuba, one of its own (despite Cuba's many actions as Soviet cat's-paw in helping to conquer many of them)—and so it had happened. He had used his alleged response to a Cuban "appeal for help" to further enlist the "Third World's" sympathies and support; and so it had happened. He had withdrawn six subs and had appealed to the United Nations in order to divert world attention from the maneuvers and focus it upon himself; and so it had happened.

When H. Delbacher warned against sneak attacks and potential closing of the world's waterways, he had switched tactics, encouraged by the unexpected telephone call that had come to him, and had decided to create deliberately a different crisis that would test the President's courage and willingness to respond. And when H. Delbacher did respond, much more severely than Yuri anticipated, and when Yuri found that the event had turned United Nations sentiment against him, he had gambled, ruthlessly and correctly, that the world was so fearful of the whole confrontation that he could bring it even more firmly to his side by apparently bowing to its will and announcing termination of the maneuvers entirely; and so it had happened. And in the process he had neatly eliminated any UN Observers or UN Force to keep an eye on him. And then, with the fervent acquiescence of the Politburo, its members overwhelmed and overawed by his many brilliant tactical successes, he had achieved what he had intended the maneuvers to achieve all along—the camouflage and shield behind which a still large and fully adequate force could be secretly left in place around the globe.

Only twice in all this had he felt that he was far out on the edge of things—that he was really in danger of going too far, that he really might precipitate the open conflict that he desired no more than H. Delbacher. The first time was when he had miscalculated the President's reaction to the subs in Cuba and had provoked the ultimatum; and again when the incident off Diego Garcia had resulted in the President's shoot-on-sight order. But each time, with the cold ruthlessness that had taken him to the top in the merciless world of the Kremlin, he had turned the event to his own advantage—in the first instance by seeming to capitulate and moving six subs from Cuba, thereby enlisting worldwide support; and in the second by seeming again to capitulate, thereby receiving the world's worshipful gratitude while using the shield of withdrawal to leave behind a quite sufficient killer-force.

In all of this, only one element had not been carefully planned and foreseen by Yuri Pavlovich Serapin, quite the most brilliant man, he told himself, who had ever occupied the triple offices of President and Commander-in-Chief of the Soviet Union, Chairman of the Council of Ministers and General Secretary of the Communist Party of the U.S.S.R. That was the element symbolized by the telephone call, and ever since it had come to him so unexpectedly, almost a month ago, he had made the most of it.

He had ordered that it be followed up to produce just the result it was now, he hoped, about to produce. (He was not yet quite sure—the tantalization was apparently going to continue to the final moment—but he was almost sure.) Secret messages had been exchanged, secret meetings had been held, secret delegations had gone back and forth for intensive negotiations a dozen times in the past two weeks. Long-standing suspicions had been papered over, bitter antagonisms had been forced beneath the surface, internal arguments and struggles had finally been resolved in his favor, practical realities of power had created at last a cold-blooded meeting of minds.

The inevitability of history had produced its inevitable result.

He had always known that it would, for logic said that nothing else, in the long run, was possible.

And he, Yuri, had been chosen to be in power when it did; to take advantage of it with all his shrewdness, brilliance, socialist realism and foresight; to lead, now, the final battle, proud, glorious, invincible, triumphant over all mankind, *forever;* to say to history, at last, the great *YES* that history demanded.

He, Yuri Pavlovich Serapin! Fate, destiny, what you will—he realized with a humble awe at himself that history from now on was his. *His!* It belonged to *him,* and nothing any fool of an underarmed, outsmarted racist capitalist imperialist could do would be able to wrest it from his iron, invincible, unshakable grasp.

When the knock came at last on his door, and his secretary entered with hushed respect and a quivering excitement to announce his visitor he was not surprised nor was he agitated. An icy calm descended: all was as it should be. The moment, like all history, was inevitable.

"Vice Premier," he said, going forward slowly, extending his hand.

"Excellency," said Ju Xing-dao, taking it between his two leaf-thin old ones. "I have brought it, from Beijing."

SINO-SOVIET PACT! RUSS, CHINESE SIGN FIVE-YEAR ACCORD "TO RESTORE SOCIALIST HARMONY AND REPEL IMPERIALIST AGGRESSORS." U.S. ISOLATED. WORLD STUNNED BY AGREEMENT BETWEEN COMMUNIST GIANTS, ONCE BITTER ENEMIES. MANY LEADERS BELIEVE "IT MEANS WAR."

So began the Labor Day weekend.
So began the end of summer.
And perhaps—the next few weeks, possibly days, would tell—all else.

November 1979–July 1980

ALLEN DRURY was a Washington correspondent for twenty years for UPI, the Washington *Star* and the New York *Times,* covering principally the Senate with occasional assignments to the House of Representatives, the Supreme Court, the UN and twelve Presidential conventions and campaigns. He won the Pulitzer Prize for Fiction for ADVISE AND CONSENT, his first book. This is his eighteenth.